THE
GNOSIS
WITHIN

DAVE DOUGHERTY

About the Author

Dave Dougherty is an Amulot author with an unusually varied background. He served as a lieutenant and captain in Army Intelligence's 513th INTC Group, and was a Professor of Management, Business, and Computer Science most recently at the University of Texas, El Paso. He holds advanced degrees from Colorado School of Mines and Case Western Reserve University and advanced to candidacy for a PhD at both Case Western Reserve and the University of Maryland. He is a Registered Professional Engineer, and working for General Electric and Chase Brass and Copper, Dave developed a number of new products and processes. He was an entrepreneur in computers, being a pioneer in the use of client-server processing, the promotion of the cloud and ARPANET all during the 1970s, and later became arguably the world's most prolific applications programmer. For his accomplishments in client-server networks and relational data base systems, he was selected for Marquis' "Who's Who in the World." History was always Dave's prime avocation, and he built one of the nation's premier collections in silver and gold ancient and medieval coinage to bring history to life. In Arkansas and Missouri, Dave is a radio personality discussing political problems through the lens of history and a rigid constitutionalist, and was possibly the major factor in defeating President Obama's White River National Blueway and his national Blueway program. Dave has authored over twenty academic papers and a number of books, including *A Patriot's History Reader: Essential Documents for Every American, A Patriot's History of the Modern World, Volumes I and II, Starve The Beast!, Hamburg Station, Landslide, From Shiloh to Durham, The 5th Ohio Volunteer Cavalry at War*, and now *Gnosis*.

Table of Contents

Book 1 – Cameron, 1967-1972   5

Book 2 – Sophia, 1970-1986   89

Book 3 – The Mother, 1986-1995   169

Book 4 – The Legacy, 2017-2025   375

Preface

This is a work of fiction. All members of the family are imaginary, as are characterizations and events involving individuals identified only by title. Places and background events are real and described accurately within the limits of the author's knowledge. Historical and public figures identified by name are portrayed in accordance with published information.

The term "Amulot" is gaining popularity to describe the Scotch-Irish or Scots Irish in the United States as a contraction for "AMerican-ULster-scOT," the primary minority who fought and died for American independence from Great Britain during the Revolutionary War. "SNAZI" refers to "Supra-NAtional-SoZIalist" as a play on the word "NAZI" from the German National-Socialist movement. The differences in the SNAZI far-left progressives in the United States today and the NAZIS in Hitler's Germany are only that the nationalist component of the Hitlerian ideology has been replaced with supra-nationalism or globalism, and the anti-Semitism has been replaced with anti-Christian fervor.

Writing this book in the first half of 2016, the author was forced to chose a gender for the president from 2017 to 2021. He assumed that Hillary Clinton, Bilderberg extraordinaire, would be elected, and the president for that period would be female.

1

Prologue

The morning was unusually clear under a leaden sky as if the world was hiding its scars under a gray blanket. Sophia looked out the picture window in King's living room as Denver sprawled eastward from Lookout Mountain. There was no traffic on Route 6, and Denver looked dead. If it wasn't, it soon would be. The Western Army's front lines ran through Castle Rock, but she couldn't hear the fighting. Castle Rock—how she hated even the sound of that place.

Webb finally arrived in one of the military jeeps that were like those in use seventy years ago. They swiftly left the house without saying goodbye, skipped Buffalo Bill's grave, and headed down Mount Zion. Below her were Golden and the Colorado School of Mines, her father's school, where greatness had truly been created. The ultimate Amulot, the ultimate American, he had unleashed humanity to realize its full potential.

Sitting alongside her father's best friend, she thought reflected how all this had started so long ago. In many ways her father had been a typical highly-talented individual, striving for success in all that he attempted while finding his way through the minefield of life. But then he made a series of mistakes, and over five hundred million people had paid with their lives.

It had all started in 1967 when Cameron Stewart, her father, decided to resign his army commission and return to school to obtain a PhD.

Book 1 - Cameron

1967 - 1972

Chapter 1

Cameron Stewart had incurred all kinds of heat from his best friend about returning to school at twenty-eight to pursue an academic career. Webb had wanted Cam to remain in the Army where he seemed so much at home. Graduate school was certainly not at all what he expected. Grade inflation was allowing men to hide in graduate programs to avoid military service. And they did—in great numbers. What was even more frightening was that these same individuals would later become leaders in the federal government.

Cam's credentials had allowed him his choice of graduate programs and schools, but he had chosen Maryland to remain close to the money and power in Washington. His coursework in engineering, business, and organizational behavior was first class, his undergraduate college world-renowned, and his Harvard MBA clearly prestigious. Coupled with his employment at General Electric and military service as an intelligence officer in Germany and Vietnam, he was an unusually experienced individual for an academic department. Maryland had snapped him up in an instant.

In comparison to Colorado Mines and Vietnam, Harvard had been only moderately demanding, and Maryland hardly better than high school. It was difficult for Cam to make peace with a system that expected little individual effort and generously gifted an average grade of B. Maryland was a party school, and co-ed activities seemed to be the primary subject.

Cam taught three classes each semester, and students soon emerged from the woodwork as human beings, helped not inconsiderably by Cathy Clark, his beautiful teaching assistant. Vivacious and with strikingly irregular features, her purpose in life was to give him a hard time.

"Mother" Cathy as she was called—although she was only eighteen when Cam met her—was not intimidated by Cameron's credentials or age and could neutralize him with her giant blue eyes like she did everyone else. When she turned them on, Cam was reminded of Morning Glory Pool at Yellowstone. As the only department instructor who understood statistical analysis, he had been assigned Cathy, an undergraduate math major, to help provide statistical services to faculty. But she also provided him an Alice-in-Wonderland window to students while screening groupies for the best looking and most exciting girls. Except for Heather. Cathy didn't screen her.

In the spring of 1968, Heather Ewing enrolled in Cam's Organizational Behavior class, and Cathy mentioned she had been runner-up in the Miss District of Columbia pageant several years previously. Cam noted her only beauty flaw was a dental cap that needed repair. With reddish brown hair and penetrating green eyes, her smile and appearance reminded him of Sally Field—only Heather was better looking. In perfect proportion at five feet two, she possessed miniature hands like a thirteen year-old girl. She habitually sat in front, and he began to torment her with little asides that only she could hear. The result was predictable.

"You make me look like an idiot," she complained facetiously several weeks into the semester when she'd stopped by his office for a quick chat before class.

"Don't listen to me," Cam shrugged.

"That's a good one. The professor telling his student not to listen to him. You don't mind if I take your advice with respect to your advice, do you?"

"What you hear is only for you. Other students wouldn't understand it."

Cam watched his compliment on Heather's intelligence sink in. He had pushed the right button, and after mid-terms, their relationship moved into his bedroom.

Living on a stringent budget as a graduate student, Cam never treated Heather to more than coffee, beer, or pizza, or they just spent time together in his apartment. Over the next three months, their togetherness grew to idyllic proportions except on weekends when she was never available. He invited Heather to a weekend on the Eastern Shore to break the routine. Instead, she came over to talk.

Heather breezed through the short entrance hall with a quick kiss and dropped her purse on Cam's dinette table. The light yellow sweater contrasted with her tight jeans, making her look like a cheerleader. Heather always wore high heels to look taller and show off her legs, but discarded them to put her legs up on the divan.

"Don't just stand there. Come here beside me," she ordered, patting the couch next to her.

Cam pursued the issue at hand. "So what about this weekend?"

Heather stroked the inside of Cam's right leg. She glanced into his eyes and switched to making little circles on his tummy. "Honey, you have to understand. I really do like you and I want us to have a super relationship, but—but I have this friend." Heather looked up to watch Cam's face. "Well, he treats me very well." She dropped her eyes again. "And I'm going to Palm Beach with him this weekend."

Cam needed more information to interpret what Heather was saying. "Is this an on-going relationship? Do you have expectations?"

Heather continued making circles, sometimes dancing her fingers. "I've known him for a year, but it's not going anywhere," she said quietly.

"Why not? Because of me?" Hope was springing eternal.

"No. Because…" The circle stopped. "Because he's married."

"And won't leave his wife."

"Yeah. He can't. A divorce would ruin him."

Cam guessed her other lover was a high muckety-muck in government who couldn't get a divorce, maybe a Catholic. "Anybody I know?"

Heather bit the inside of her cheek, and seemed to struggle with a momentous decision while searching Cam's eyes deeply for understanding. Finally, she spoke. "You've certainly heard of him. It's…"

He whistled hearing the name. "You don't mess around, do you? No kidding he can't get a divorce. How'd you meet him?"

Heather was visibly relieved when Cam's tone registered interest rather than anger. "His daughter was a friend for a while last year, and I was at his home several times." Cam wanted to ask another question, but Heather anticipated him. "He has terrific eye contact. You know, 'ask not what your country can do for you.'"

"How do you guys work it? I mean, everywhere he goes, he's surrounded."

"Well, I'm escorted in to events or where he is by other men, usually someone who works for him. So I'm there, and it's simple."

Cam felt a sinking feeling in the pit of his stomach. "You also have relationships with those other guys?"

Heather patted Cam's stomach. "Some I've known from before." She felt Cam tense and take a deep breath. "Please, honey, it can't last." She laid on top on him. "I wouldn't have told you if I thought you'd get upset. I really do care about you."

Cam swallowed to clear his throat. He felt inadequate for not being able to handle something told to him honestly and openly.

Heather raised her head, "Are you okay? I don't want to lose you."

"Yeah. But go easy with me. It's going to take some adjustment. I've never been into sharing. Particularly with one of the most powerful men in the country. Scratch that— *possibly the* most powerful man."

Cam reflected on his comments. They sounded like he was complaining. He didn't mean that—but women weren't the only ones with feelings. She was announcing he wasn't sufficiently important for her to change her lifestyle. He wasn't sure his ego would allow him to accept being second-string.

Heather was like the classical monkey who could not drop the bait to remove his hand; she could not walk away from illusions of money and power to put her life together. A soft hooker—that's what she was—always dependent on the largess of some powerful guy. He'd noticed she possessed lots of expensive things but never had money for herself. None came from him, so maybe he was her only honest relationship.

"Do you know why I like you?" Heather asked.

Cameron shrugged, unable to come up with a snappy comeback.

"You don't care for appearances and I can be myself. You're not a politician. They're professional actors who have studied how to lie with their bodies and words to convince the audience. Give out the fewest conflicting signals and they could win an Oscar."

"Or an election. Or somebody I care about."

Heather didn't respond to that remark. "I've learned to look for those signs that betray politicians who aren't acting. It's not easy, particularly when covered with charm. With you, I don't have to look, and that's nice."

Cam had already weathered one of Heather's problems in her family. Her older sister, Jeannette, was seeing a Negro named Harlan, and that relationship kept Heather in turmoil. Cam normally accompanied Heather when she visited her sister, especially after an incident when Harlan attempted to force himself on Heather in Jeannette's absence.

Harlan worked as a mailman and specialized in dating white women, almost exclusively blondes. His brother had been killed by a white sheriff in North Carolina while robbing a gas station.

"I think Harlan acts out his hostility against whites by taking their women," Heather said.

"Well, there are three themes unacceptable to American readers according to Nabokov," Cam said. "A Negro-white marriage that ends happily with lots of children, pedophilia, and an atheist who lives a full and rich life. If I were writing a novel, your sister would be doomed."

Watching the sisters interact, Cameron wondered if Jeannette's problems with Harlan were common by-products of interracial sex. Her situation clashed with his class exercise illustrating the operative hierarchy of love. He would ask a student to name the person or living thing he loved most. Usually the answer was "Mother." Then the question would be rapidly repeated while the student kept naming the next most loved person. Normally, the list went from immediate family to pets, friends, teachers, associates, then people of the same race, religion, nationality, until the final level of general humanity. Mixed relationships of any kind were bound to cause emotional trauma because they violated the individual's natural love hierarchy.

Cam's primary male friend at school was an unpretentious coordinator providing business liaison with a number of departments, including his. Cam became friends with Ed Armstrong over beer at the Fast Track, a gin mill in Bladensburg that Ed frequented. Divorced after a disastrous two-year marriage, Ed was concentrating on fast and easy women. He also had many irons in the fire, and asked Cam to help him with Dave Columbo's campaign for Maryland State Representative.

"You'll like him, Cam," Ed insisted. "With a name like Columbo, everybody assumes he's Catholic. Hell, he's an Orangeman like us."

"Where did the Columbo name come from?" Cam assumed Columbo was Italian, and all Italians were Catholic.

"Beats me, ask him. He might be some part Italian, but if so, it's not so you'd notice. Besides, political campaigns are even better concentrators of foxy chicks than Elvis Presley concerts, and your opportunities will be unbelievable."

"You're kidding. Even for guys just helping the candidate?"

"Oh, yeah. It's a well-established phenomenon; girls and housewives materialize from thin air to become groupies and vie for the privilege of laying their candidate. If they can't get him, they'll take anyone close to their chosen man—the closer the better."

This fascination for power and attraction to politicians was an unholy force Cam had already seen with Heather. The politician's sexual equipment and performance became their intimate secret, binding them even more tightly to their benefactor. And it usually was disappointing. According to Heather, politicians usually depended on the female to bring about successful physical intimacy, pleading preoccupation or stress and pressures in their positions. Even in sex, politicians avoided taking responsibility.

And there was Webb, his best friend from his days in intelligence, who was more like a younger brother. He stopped at Cam's office to say goodbye before leaving for Germany. Webb had also come to enjoy the scenery, so they took off for the Rendezvous, a local hang-out.

Walking through campus with the six foot five inch tall officer, Cam felt like a time-traveler from a different age. The students around them were naïve children by comparison, having sex like bunnies and mellowing out on pot.

"The pill's released a monster that's raging out of control," Cam said. "The fear of pregnancy is gone, and with skirts so short, stand-up quickies are everywhere. Sexual freedom has become the only freedom these kids are interested in."

"These kids aren't going to give up benefits like that to slog

10

through paddies with ARVNs," remarked Webb, throwing his chin toward a couple on the grass. A long-haired blonde in a mini-skirt was sitting on top of a scraggly character, plumbing the depths of his throat with her tongue. Webb's vision was excellent, thought Cam; the guy's dick was probably lodged inside her.

"Bet this place is littered with bodies at night," Webb said.

"You'd lose your bet," Cam said. "University grounds are not safe after dark. The best-kept secret around is our on-campus crime rate of rapes and assaults. That's why there's the campus shuttle." Cam pointed to a small bus. "Students ride them between buildings after dark to keep from being mugged. Maryland is a magnet for undesirables from D.C."

Webb shook his head as they headed into a typical college beer joint. It was practically empty, and Cameron ordered a pitcher as they slid into a booth.

"Almost like the Kit-Cat in Saigon," Webb said. "Only I bet these girls require more effort and less money." There weren't twenty girls in the place, but most were sitting with guys.

The two friends were quiet for a moment. Cam thought back to the humidity of Fort Holabird in Baltimore, recoiling from the oppressive yeast smell floating in from Colgate Creek. Its heavy stench had seemed to plaster itself on his skin like olive oil, sometimes ruining those superb meals available in the officers' field ration mess. Bachelor quarters were worse than rat holes, with field grade officers occupying rooms smaller than jail cells. Army Intelligence was moving to Fort Huachuca, but no one knew if that was for the better. But with Army Intelligence-Security being made a full branch, support for the corps might improve after the catastrophic damage done by Kennedy and McNamara.

"Do you expect things to get better now?" Cam asked.

"No, and they might even get worse. At any rate, I'm heading back to Germany. I've been told the 513th is being de-activated, and operations are being curtailed."

"Have a good luck present on me," Cam said as he handed Webb an envelope.

Webb popped the seal and took out a manicure case with a fold-over top flap. Inside was a set of hand-made tools. "Damn, these are your lock picking tools." He pulled out several and examined them closely. "You did a nice job," he said running his index finger over the figure eight knife. "This sure beats hell out of mine."

"Well, it's your set now," said Cam. "I'm not expecting to be breaking into anywhere soon, and you may need them. Just consider them a souvenir from my class at Holabird."

Webb put the case in his shirt pocket. "You know, I'm already more in debt to you than I can pay. What can I say?"

"Remember, the Lord protects drunks and damn fools." Cam paused and guzzled his beer. "Be sure to check with Dietrich on our Liechtenstein corporation. I understand our Czech partner has gone missing, and Dietrich has moved the Gabriel operation payments into it."

"I'll see John as soon as I arrive. Are we doing well?"

"Better than we ever dreamed. Trading dollars for gold with the Russians is making us rich. We're cutting the deck thin to win, and it's working out. Just watch your back two hundred percent of the time. The risk factor is off the charts."

Chapter 3

By the fall of 1969, everything was coming up roses for Cam. He'd passed his comprehensive exams and his dissertation proposal was in its second revision. His topic encompassed a thorough review of the trait theory for leadership, analyzing a large number of personal characteristics and their correlation with leadership. It would be approved shortly if he could incorporate all his committee's pet peeves. And his Washington connections would give him his pick of jobs.

Heather had been a never-ending source of information for Cam as she moved within the Washington societal structure, but now it was time for introductions. All power and money in academia originated with the federal government.

Although Heather's contacts were primarily physical—Cam smiled inwardly at his own joke—they were connected with powerful men in Washington. He stretched his legs onto Heather's coffee table.

"Why do you want to teach?" Heather asked.

"I don't. Nobody wants to teach. That's not what gets tenure and promotion, and it takes time away from publishing and consulting. The best solution is to obtain research grants from government agencies to be relieved from teaching courses. It's a form of academic welfare. That's why I need more good contacts."

Heather had already introduced Cam to various people, and this time, she suggested he attend a function on Wednesday. "The reception at the Iranian embassy should be good. I'll be meeting my friend there, and you can escort me in."

He felt like a pimp taking a girl to meet her john. He couldn't complain, though; he was the one chasing the money. It was difficult to tell who was using whom.

She snuggled closer on her couch. "Does it bother you that I see other men? Honestly, what do you think?"

13

What was there to say? According to Heather, most of her partners were older and wanted an ego pat or verification of their virility, and she was often back home alone in bed within a couple of hours. Her current friend was no exception. Trips were another story. Sometimes Cam felt like a second-class lover, but otherwise their relationship seemed to give him moral superiority over her other sex partners. Cam wondered if pimps felt that way. "I don't dwell on it and draw dirty pictures in my mind, if that's what you mean."

"No. I'm just wondering if you become jealous when I'm not available."

"Sometimes it bothers me maybe; but we're friends first and lovers second. You're free, white, and twenty-one. You can do what you want. I want you to have what you want, and do what you want."

"What if I don't know what I want?"

"Then I'll be your friend to help you find out."

Heather studied Cam's face. She leaned forward and kissed him. "You'll do just fine," she breathed.

Cam heard the double meaning, and decided to ignore it.

The reception on Wednesday was held in a Georgetown mansion whose market value was easily five times that of a comparable home in another city. The Department of State was hosting, and Cam discovered the eclectic guest list included many individuals whose involvement with Iran was questionable. The Iranians were both military and administrative personnel, and although guests chatted with the delegation as a courtesy, most conversation centered around domestic affairs.

Cameron was listed as Heather's escort, representing the University of Maryland. She had promoted him from graduate student to professor, and faculty status was automatically socially acceptable. Cam fit in like a pig at a trough and was accorded his due respect.

After Heather disappeared with a staffer, Cam surveyed the crowd. Women could be classified into four groups: wives, escorts, climbers, and working professionals. Married women flitted in and out among the men, being introduced and then retreating to their own circles to gossip. Younger party girls like Heather stayed with their escorts, being complimented on their ornamental qualities. Climbing females avoided wives like lepers, and gushed over powerful men.

Lastly, the few women slowly circulating without escorts were career women making their way forward in a male-dominated society.

One of the career women caught Cam's eye because she appeared shy and out of place. She hunched forward, and had light brown hair in a shoulder-length shag. Her figure was her redeeming feature; even though her breasts were hidden, she was clearly slender and extremely shapely. She interested Cam—maybe because she projected vulnerability, yet with an inner strength and decisiveness.

Cam maneuvered closer to her at the buffet. His strategy was crowned with success sooner than expected. He turned from the table to find her looking at him while waiting for a space to open.

"I'm sorry. If I had known you were waiting, I would have let you go first." It was a patently stupid statement, but broke the ice.

The girl tilted her head. "Oh, it's all right. I'm not sure I want anything anyway."

"Try the wine. It's not Liebfrauenmilch," he suggested. He had been surprised to find spirits available considering the Shi'ite attitude toward alcohol.

The lady wrinkled her nose. "Why? Is that bad?"

"Well, everything is a matter of taste, but I wouldn't drink it." He extended his hand. "I'm Cam Stewart." Normally, etiquette demanded a lady offer her hand first, but Cam decided to promote sexual equality.

"Millie Lauenberg. Nice to meet you." She gave him a firm handshake. "Why don't you like Liebfrauenmilch?"

Cam was impressed by what he saw. Millie wasn't making any moves to drift off in spite of a meaningless topic of conversation. Against a backdrop of glittering social personalities and chandeliers, Millie made a competent and straight-forward appearance. Her dress was befitting the occasion but not showy, and her shoes were traditional black pumps. He decided she probably didn't own ninety million pairs of shoes like most Washington women.

"Because the name really doesn't mean anything. It's a Rhine-Hessian blend from no particular grape, and is often purchased in bulk by distributors and foisted off on Americans. Krauts brand it Liebfrauenmilch or Liebfraumilch, meaning loosely, 'milk from the loving mother,' and we buy it because of the name. It's good marketing, but not necessarily good wine."

15

"How do you know so much about wine?"

"I used to live in Germany and I like wine." Cam felt like a professor giving a lecture—and it wasn't the role he wanted to play.

He attempted to focus on Millie, but found her reticent in talking about herself. With effort, he discovered she was a biochemist at NIH. She made an absolutely virginal appearance which Cam found compelling. Her nose was somewhat large, almost forming a straight line in profile with her forehead, like the woman representing Liberty on Morgan silver dollars. When she wasn't smiling, her nose dominated her face and made her homely. Cam enjoyed the small talk, but then they wandered apart in the reception's swirl, and she was swallowed up in a sea of elegant dresses and power suits.

*****

The next morning he was surprised to find Millie in his department office at the university, awaiting a lunch date with the office administrator. There was little opportunity to talk, but then he ran into her again when the two returned. Cam invited Millie to dinner at the nearby Golden Pagoda—seeing her three times in eighteen hours was kismet. And he was going to listen. Millie agreed.

Millie pulled into the small parking lot on Route 1 as Cam was locking his Porsche.

"Hello again." He walked over and opened her car door. "Are we always going to have perfect timing?"

"Looks that way, doesn't it?" She brushed off her skirt as she got out of her car.

He took her hand and walked her to the Pagoda entrance. She followed him to a table, but once seated, opened up during the usual discussion of what they did for a living. Her project on nerve structures and memory storage fascinated Cam. Whereas he was working on the "soft" science of leadership, learning and intelligence, Millie was performing research on how the brain worked. The commonality of interests drew them together, and before they knew it, they were being asked to leave so the restaurant could close.

In the evening's chill, Millie invited Cam to continue their conversation in her car. He noticed her Falcon was almost completely devoid of the trash normally schlepped around by women. Millie put

16

her attaché case in the back seat, but there was no tissue box, no cosmetics or spare stockings or coffee cups like with Heather or Cathy. Cam wondered if she crumpled her dollar bills individually into her coin purse like most women.

The car was a more intimate venue than the restaurant, and they discussed more personal things, including their backgrounds. Millie had grown up in New York City in an East Side brownstone and had been raised primarily by her father's housekeeper, a Ukrainian named Olga. Cam was a Westerner, born in Wray, Colorado, and grew up on the plains where one was close to God. Life had been hard, and both his parents were already gone. Millie's father was wealthy, while Cam's family had been poor. They came from different worlds, and a gulf yawned between them nearly as wide as the one Heather's sister and her Negro boyfriend.

"What's the farthest west you've been?" Cam asked.

"Here, Washington, DC. I'm almost one of those Americans who have never been farther than 200 miles from their birthplace."

"Yeah, I've heard of that statistic. Supposedly half of all Americans never go farther away than 200 miles in their whole life. Hard to believe now that almost every family has a car." Cam couldn't decide what to talk about next. They were in one of those pregnant pauses when something was expected of him. He slowly moved closer like on his first date in high school. She turned and looked at him from the top of her eyes.

He kissed her, and found her open, soft, and sensual. It was an invitation to an invitation, but then Millie did the unexpected. "It's getting late," she said. "And I have to work tomorrow."

"Tell you what. How about coming over to my apartment on Saturday to help alphabetize my library? I'll bribe you with my best German wine." Cam did not consider this a date, but rather an opportunity—to what, was up to her. She accepted.

*****

Promptly at seven, Millie parked in front of Cam's apartment building. Cam watched her sitting in her Falcon, but a half-hour passed before she entered the building with a purposeful stride. She walked through the doorway as if reporting for work. Most significantly, she gave Cam no opportunity to greet her with a kiss, brushing by him to stand in the center of his living room.

He performed the semi-obligatory functions of giving her a quick tour and introducing his cat, Vanessa. Millie seemed strangely pre-occupied, but her jeans were painted on and exhibited the superb figure Cam had only guessed at before. The signals were very confusing.

Cam poured her a glass of wine, and she moved in front of him. "We don't have to work with any books, do we?"

He put the glasses down. "No," Cam answered, and he pulled her into his arms. The kiss was hurried.

She took his hand and led him to the bedroom she had just seen. She turned and sat on the foot of the bed.

"You need to know, this is Ted Mack's Amateur Hour," Millie said.

"I'm honored. But why did you finally pick me? You must have had many other opportunities."

"I've waited twenty-seven years for a sensitive male. You took my hand at the restaurant. It might have been a tiny gesture for you, but an important one for me."

They made love six times, with Millie mostly on top. Orgasms came easily to Millie, and as long as Cam kept moving, she continued with one after the other. Amazing! All this natural talent going to waste for so long. They rested after the first four with Millie sitting on top.

"We really need to get to know each other better," Millie said. "I don't want our relationship to be just this."

"Agreed. With this as the starting point, we could go anywhere."

So they discussed their backgrounds as they were, starting with Millie. Fortune had given her a mixed heritage with a Jewish father and a Finnish mother. Originally from the Eastern Ukraine, her father possessed a German surname, a contribution from a Volga Deutscher, and had fled to Finland when Stalin began to annihilate Kulaks. Within three years, he had married a Christian girl from Helsinki, and emigrated to the United States.

Millie's mother was well-educated, having grown up mostly in Spain and Morocco until her father, a Finnish nationalist, could return to Finland following the Russian Revolution. Already in her mid-thirties when Millie was born, her mother died shortly afterwards. Aaron Lauenberg arranged for a housekeeper to raise Millie, and she grew up devoting her time to academics. Reflecting on the state of American elite education, she first heard about Scotch-Irishmen from Cam.

He told her that the Scotch-Irish were a mixture of Presbyterian Scots from the lowlands and Northern Orange Irish. They were followers of John Knox and became militantly Protestant dissenters persecuted by the English and hated by Irish Catholics. They suffered heavily during the "Irish Massacres" in the 1640s, and as Cam said, "In those days, if you were in the wrong place at the wrong time, you died." Then many were driven to America by persecution under Charles II, but the Test Act of 1713 really did the trick as hundreds of thousands took passage to the American colonies. Cam called their descendants Amulots.

"So how is this going to work?" Millie asked Cam. "You, the original Scotch-Irish rebel, and me the recent Jewish immigrant?"

"This way," as he started moving again. They resumed their activities, and Cam discovered Millie was a glutton for oral sex. He could literally drive her up a wall with non-stop orgasms until she couldn't stand it anymore. He wanted to continue all night, but Millie said she wasn't prepared to spend the night. It was too many firsts for her all at once.

In the morning came another first. Cam's telephone rang, and it was Millie.

"What did you do to me?" she yelled. "I can't walk, and I hurt in places where I didn't even know I had places."

"Well, the only way to fix that is massage. Deep massage, like I can do."

"Okay, after work you need to fix everything."

He did, and starting with the fall semester, the time Cam spent with Millie increased exponentially. In early October, Cam uttered those fateful words, "Millie, I love you."

She grasped his hands and dropped her head.

Cam continued, "I know I've never said it before, but I do—I love you."

Millie placed her head on his chest. "I love you too, Cam."

They stood up together and slowly walked into the bedroom,

arm-in-arm as if they were making a commitment to each other. For Cam, it wasn't easy. Yet when he looked into her eyes, she was there for him, as he was for her.

Cam understood the knockdown, drag-out, heart-stopping, toe-curling love scenes he experienced with Millie were temporary, but the feeling of love and being loved were not. They made him more important, as if Millie infused him with something—increasing his worth as a human being. He had not felt inadequate before, but now he was more adequate, enhanced by love.

He knew he was good in bed, but only because of his focus. He had learned in Germany to concentrate solely on his partner when making love, directing his fantasies to be about her, and relating and responding to her every thought and touch. It was like speaking a foreign language, but it was the language of love in the woman's native dialect. His concentration had become automatic—almost a form of self-hypnosis. He would give himself to the act itself, his body being used by someone else as an instrument for mutual pleasure. And he could remain that way while wave after sensational wave engulfed him. Few men knew it, but like women, they could go off multiple times, even after his prostate was empty, continuing to spasm with dry ejaculations. Heather had called it a long orgasm, and it could last more than five minutes if he kept his focus on the feeling.

With Millie, it was even more intense. He could feel their souls touch—a sensation he termed a *seelung* from the German word *Seele*—communicating on a plane unknown and incomprehensible to his conscious self. They became fused into a single entity, with a single locus of pleasure synchronizing their bodies. Cam could feel her joy and sadness, their fingers tingled with the exchange of love when they touched, their bodies belonging to each other. Millie melted into a long series of orgasms, kept on an astounding high by his long erection and continual pulsing, but then she outdid him while he held on for dear life. They were awesome together, and it could only get better.

Then Millie went back to New York for Shabbat Shuva and Yom Kippur, and Cam wondered if the religion factor might become a problem in their relationship. He needn't have worried. Two days after Millie left, he received a letter:

"Don't ever doubt I love you. When I told you I loved you, it wasn't because you said you loved me or because I read it in a romance novel. I don't love easily or lightly. Part of me will always love you, regardless of what might happen. I'll never just wake up one morning and decide I don't love you.

Loving you, touching you, just being with you—these are joys I never dreamed of. It's like having sunsets and moonlights and butterflies and soft breezes and blazing fires and autumn evenings and jamoca almond double chocolate fudge ice cream with nuts all rolled up together. They don't come any better than that.

I was trying to think of the one overwhelming reason why I love you and all I could come up with was that— well—I just do.

Please don't doubt me, or close me out. Just let me love you."

Millie had made her statement.

Chapter 4

Slowly, Cam's research model for his dissertation on leadership took shape. The literature was voluminous, and most cerebral work dealt with training for certain types of leadership and their effectiveness in various situations. After having seen officers in Vietnam with identical training exhibit different qualities in the field, Cam decided to thoroughly test the "Trait" theory, determining if objective information about an individual's background could be a predictor of success as a leader.

While researching data on historical figures, Cam noticed leaders were often born late in their fathers' lives. Catherine the Great, Elizabeth I, Benjamin Franklin, Hitler, and a number of philosophers had been born to fathers well past the age of forty. Because of this observation, he included parents' ages at time of birth on his list of data variables.

Many military writers stressed that most effective commanders exhibited a substantial amount of instinct in their decisions and actions. Clausewitz stated, "All great commanders acted on instinct" and drew attention to Napoleon and Gustavus Adolphus as examples. In his own time, Cam had read of Rommel's sixth sense and the famous incident in North Africa when he moved away from an observation post, stating the British were going to shell the area in a few minutes. They did—obliterating the spot where Rommel had stood less than ten minutes earlier. The Battle of Midway might have been won by Waldron's homing on the Japanese fleet as if on a radio beacon, McClusky's turning northwest in his unconventional search, and Spruance's accurate sense of battle and movement. On the other side, the Japanese commander Nagumo consistently made militarily correct decisions according to his information, and every single one was wrong.

Cam had not found useful quantitative means for measuring

leadership effectiveness in earlier works. Situational variables in real life were extremely important, yet hardly reducible to common factors against which effective leadership could be measured. The best were tests he himself had undergone at Fort Benning during basic officer's training, and had been adopted from the Wehrmacht's manual during World War II.

*****

Returning from Fort Fumble, Cathy bounced into Cam's office excited and out of breath. "Wow, anytime you need stuff from the Pentagon, send me!" she exclaimed. "That place is packed wall-to-wall with good-looking guys. It's like all terrific male specimens went into the Army, and only defects went to college."

Cam decided Cathy was impressed with uniforms. Some women were like that; uniforms conveyed an image of power, just like three-piece dark blue pinstripe suits. "What did Colonel Lafferty think? Are they excited about our research project?"

"I don't think the colonel gets excited about anything," Cathy dropped a pile of manila envelopes on her desk and unzipped her blue and yellow satin jacket. She told Cam about the roly-poly colonel who had treated her pompously and seemed more interested in keeping his piles of paper tidy than anything else. "He set me up with a Major Fish who will be our contact for files."

So the colonel had delegated liaison to another officer. He was probably getting hammered meeting requirements for Vietnam. "What was Fish like? Do you think he'll be much help?"

Cathy smiled. "Oh yeah. He wanted to take me to lunch and then dinner." She looked at Cam and laughed. "I may have to re-introduce myself depending on what I wear."

"Doesn't it bother you when a guy looks at your chest all the time rather than your face?" Can considered such action boorish and crude, but Cathy was wearing a "DATA DUMPSTERS" T-shirt that required reading from three sides.

"Sometimes, but you use what you've got." Cathy opened the top envelope. "When I told him you were a Vietnam vet, he really opened up. His primary interest is finding something to help them make command versus staff assignments—in particular, combat commands."

"Well, I doubt we'll be able to help. If we find anything, it will only aid in selecting officer candidates, not assignments." Cam took the reports Cathy handed to him.

The reports were excellent and also showed student peer ratings. Cam was excited. For at least part of his data, the quantification of leadership as the dependent variable would be unassailable

Cathy went to work, and after a couple of hours held up two histogram plots she had been drawing for Cam to review. "Look at these graphs," she said with mounting excitement. "If I plot them against each other, I bet they'll be isomorphic."

Cameron examined them closely, wondering what variables they represented. Cathy was right; although the scales were different, they were remarkably similar. He checked his key for their descriptions.

"Guess what," he said, turning to Cathy. "They're IQ and mother's age at time of birth. Let's do father's age, GPA, total amount of education, and SAT scores for students, and mother's age, father's age, and total amount of education on officers."

Cathy pulled out the forms and began working.

Two hours later, Cameron returned from class and dropped his papers onto the desk. "Well, how're we doing?" he asked.

"Do you want the good news or bad news?" Cathy swivelled toward Cam then banged her feet on the floor.

"Both. Bad first." Cam rolled his chair to Cathy's desk.

"Well, bad is that leaders are born; good is that I can tell who they are from birth."

Cam let Cathy's words sink in. "How?"

"Parents' ages," Cathy answered matter-of-factly. "Naturally, parents must be in reasonable educational and intellectual circumstances; but within fairly broad limits, the older the parents, the more intellectual and better leaders the offspring are. How about them apples?"

Cam leaned over toward Cathy, grabbed her head and kissed her forehead. "You do good work, luscious," he exclaimed. "Does that hold true even when the child is the youngest of ten children?"

Cathy shook her head. "I can't tell. I don't have data on siblings from the Army. If I could add a variable for the mother's previous births, our correlations might be even more astounding."

"Well, birth order has been the subject of debate for years. Some

24

researchers have claimed later children tend to be more rebellious than firstborns."

"That tends to support these findings if rebellion is related to intellectual curiosity," Cathy said. "Not only that, it would also explain why Negroes have been so docile and lacking in leadership—their parents were too young."

"Okay, let's go with it," Cam decided.

Now it was Cathy's turn to stare. "Are you crazy? Are you going to recommend people wait until their thirties and forties to have children? Social workers and teachers will hunt you down like a rabid dog. Do you have any idea how many oxen you're going to gore? These results say there shouldn't be universal liberal education. This means there are good and bad people from birth, and rehabilitation is a joke unless the person is good to start with. Its implications overturn most of our established modern political and humanistic precepts. They wipe out the reasons for existence for legions of bureaucrats, educators, and millions of bleating sheep. This stuff is dangerous." Cathy stopped her tirade for a moment and took a breath. "It's even dangerous to my health."

"You won't get an argument from me," agreed Cam. "You're right about the results. We need to soft-pedal the implications if I'm going to get my dissertation published."

"Well, we don't have to alter our findings, just be careful in our analysis and not make a big thing out of certain aspects."

Cam thought for a moment. Cathy had seen the far-reaching implications immediately, but that was Cathy. She was bright and not afraid to challenge people and create new ideas.

"Why do you think parental age is important?"

"No idea," answered Cathy quickly. "I'm just a data analyst. You're the theorist."

Cam frowned. "Well, I think a child inherits knowledge from his parents, which is classically called instinct. The more knowledge a parent has, the more a child inherits. It only remains for a child to use that instinct and he'll do better than his competition whose instinct is not as highly developed."

"You think so? Sounds far out to me. My dad was twenty-two and my mom nineteen when I was born. And I'm doing all right."

"Just think of what you could do if they had been in their thirties," Cam joked.

"Thanks a hell of a lot. So I'm never going to amount to anything?"

"Well, no correlation is perfect." Cam sighed. "Besides, I bet superior physical specimens are born to younger parents. That's why you're so beautiful. Did you plot parental ages against appearance and athletic ability?" Cam asked.

"No, but I'll try it," she replied. "Do you really think there'll be a correlation?"

"Let's find out. It's hard to believe, but it wouldn't be any more surprising than what you've already discovered. Besides, I can develop a logical explanation to support it."

By nightfall, Cathy laid her completed graphs on Cam's desk. Cam's hypothesis had been proven true.

Now Cam was primarily concerned with integrating his results with previous work to make his dissertation politically acceptable. He knew the game. Following David Hume's philosophy, doctoral work should follow from deductive and inductive reasoning based not only on research, but on precepts adopted from previous knowledge. Faculty assembles a body of knowledge, not to be challenged, creating an a priori framework against which the student was to process data. The data is then assembled and organized under their tutelage, transformed into information, and finally presented as knowledge.

Cam decided to reject this entire Hume-organized approach and adopt a Kant-like methodology. He could now explain instinct as knowledge transmitted on genes in reproductive cells. The Hume-versus-Kant dialogue reduced itself to what was placed on genes. Intelligence was in hereditary like physical and emotional traits. Instinct in animals was really inherited knowledge.

His findings also legitimatized the experience of reincarnation and its espousal by Hassidic Jews. Possibly knowledge from past lives could be recovered under extraordinary circumstances. But what were those circumstances?

"I noticed from our data on students' siblings that top leaders were usually either only children or not the oldest sibling," Cathy commented. "Primogeniture was a stunningly bad concept, but I'm not sure we can show intellect going up from oldest to youngest child in a family."

"There are other intervening variables which would make that type of correlation less than perfect," Cam explained. "Drugs, alcohol, smoking, and mother's health would be important, possibly critical today."

"Why should it be any different today?"

"In earlier times, women were often confined while pregnant. Few women smoked, alcohol was limited to men, and drugs were unknown. Today, they drink, smoke, do drugs, and eat junk food. The placenta concentrates everything. Alcohol inhibits brain development and kills cells right and left. Smoking is almost as bad. Not only does carbon monoxide starve developing brain tissue for oxygen, but there's the tar and narcotic. And not just from the mother— remember, she gets half of what her husband inhales as secondary smoke."

"You're saying a baby's heredity can be significantly altered during the time he's most vulnerable."

"It's certainly a factor—one worthy of future research. Unfortunately, humans procreate very infrequently and with long time lapses, making controlled experiments and good statistical data difficult to obtain."

"You might want to note those health factors since they can affect your conclusions. They'd help make the dissertation harder to attack."

Cam broke up laughing.

Cathy looked perplexed. "What did I say that was so funny?"

"Believe me, this dissertation is not going to be difficult to attack. If not from a factual basis, then from self-interest. I expect we'll have to don suits of armor."

"I hope they come color-coordinated," she said, "I don't look good in steel gray."

*****

In the Tydings Hall conference room, Cam defended his work and findings to the five faculty members holding veto power over his career. He presented his empirical research that showed children's intellectual abilities correlating directly with their parents' ages at time of birth. Conversely, physical prowess was associated with youthful parents, and Cam's conclusions implied heredity was vastly more important than education. It was not what his committee wanted to hear.

Grossmann teamed with Talbot as his primary critics. Small and always peering at the world through heavy spectacles, Irving Grossmann was the exact opposite of his name which meant "big man" in German. Acid-tongued, he held forth authoritatively on all subjects in his high, squeaky voice, sneering down any contrary opinions with sheer academic arrogance. Cam was told Grossmann had barely passed his own comprehensive exams—even with a family friend as department chair. It was inescapable that Grossmann was tyrannical to cover his intellectual ignorance.

"My parents were in their early twenties when I was born," Grossmann bleated. "I'm certainly no big athlete, but your conclusions say I'm not intellectual and would be a bad leader."

Cam attempted to be conciliatory. "Heredity is only one of many factors. The health of the mother during pregnancy and things such as ambient cigarette smoke and alcohol are important."

"I hope you're not implying my mother drank."

"No, of course not. I was merely pointing out there are a number of other important intervening variables." But Grossmann did not seem mollified.

Although no one mentioned it out loud, Cameron had seen the Jewish "old boy" network functioning up close, and understood the dangers of belonging to a minority ethnic group in the academic world. Mindful of politics, Cam had balanced his committee with two Jewish faculty, one Indian, one Egyptian, and an Englishman— probably the fairest he could have attained in the circumstances.

But his biggest problem was the Englishman, Talbot, who suffered from the British Empire Syndrome of arrogant divine right— after all, God *is* an Englishman—and any opinion other than his was wrong. Since Cam's conclusions did not agree with Talbot's pre-conceived notions, the research was obviously flawed. Talbot told Cam he would have to return for another meeting with a plan to restructure the research, and the black hole devouring Cam's career plans yawned widely.

Getting a PhD was like eating a spoonful of crap once a day. Every day, the candidate went to one of his committee members and respectfully asked for his daily dose. Some days, they'd give him a spoonful, others, a whole bowl. This would continue until he'd written as many of their papers as possible or they found a replacement slave. Then they'd let the squirming worm off his hook. In essence, a degree had nothing to do with the candidate's work. As in all other aspects of life, acquiring a terminal degree was a political process. Of course, his conclusions flew did fly in the face of conventional wisdom, but that was the nature of scientific progress. Galileo had been forced to recant before Church officials in an age of myth and superstition—and Cam wasn't sure there had been much progress since then.

Colleges were often like gorgeous women with beauty only skin deep. The sacrosanct concept of tenure eliminated incentive for faculty members to extend themselves into discovery or creation of new knowledge. Instead, they concentrated on projects designed to attract funding. There was a complete absence of scholarly risk-taking and courage—except, of course, for fringy Timothy Leary types leading students into the excitement of brain damage with LSD.

He left Tydings and strode angrily across Maryland's campus, ignoring a bright June sun in the early afternoon. Maryland's campus, with its Georgian buildings, looked beautiful and innocent, but appearances belied the intellectual incest and smoky-room politics that were like cancers eating the institution from within. The concrete-filled bronze terrapin in front of McKeldin Graduate Library stared at Cam as he walked past. Due to fly away when Maryland graduated a virgin, it still hadn't moved an inch.

The oaks and sycamores on the mall's south edge were practically uninhabited where Cam decided to kick back. Lying on the grassy slope, he scanned Maryland's mixture of hippies and black-hatters from the government; hippies sitting or lying in little groups and the suits with their obligatory attaché cases striding importantly here and there.

Past Admin's dominating tower, Cam could see the foreboding brick edifice for mathematics. Beyond math and engineering were pens for farm animals, and sometimes their barnyard aroma wafted to the mall. Cam wondered how much longer the dairy herd would remain. No doubt it was difficult to maintain an image as a world-class physicist when a cow was mooing outside your window. Maryland was an old agricultural college and it showed.

As usual, the scene was dotted with pretty co-eds. Maryland appeared serene in sunlight, a beautiful haven for beautiful youth. But it was an unstable image—at any moment, students could mobilize for or against any issue and turn the mall into a mass of obscenity-screaming, sweating, pot-smoking hippies, shattering the calm and temporarily destroying the university as an institution for higher learning.

Inhaling the aroma of pot, Cameron felt the presence of another individual at his side and looked up. Gopal Agarwal had come up on little cat's feet, not even crunching acorns under the oak tree where Cam sat. Cam was surprised a member of his committee would seek him out. "Come out to get some rays?" Cam was cordial but not friendly.

Gopal leaned against the tree and took out his pipe. Reaching into his coat pocket for his tobacco pouch, he avoided Cam's gaze. "No. I wanted to follow up on the meeting. Doctor Grossmann thinks you should disregard parental age as an independent variable and not report it. You didn't find other traits important, and that would allow you to build a case rejecting trait theory. It would still be worthwhile to report all other factors as being not significant, and your dissertation would be an acceptable compendium of traits for leadership."

Cam looked down at his feet. Black ants were only on sidewalks and never in grass. Except for ones like Gopal, of course. He was dark like a Tamil.

Gopal continued, "In addition, both he and Doctor Talbot would like you to write a short summary on physical traits with them for the Administrative Quarterly. Doctor Talbot has been invited to contribute a position paper and would like you to work with him using your data on physical factors."

There it was. He was to use his research and write a position paper with Talbot as primary author and Grossmann as co-author. He would be mentioned as a "researcher." With that burnt offering, they would be willing to approve a watered-down dissertation reaching a conclusion opposite to the one his data demanded. "So you're telling me that if I make my results agree with Grossmann's opinion and write Talbot's paper for him, they'll let me have my degree."

Agarwal was cool. "I don't think your comments are warranted. I'm trying to help."

"Then why do you reject intuition as inherited knowledge and hereditary factors as significant variables in leadership?"

"We don't really know that," Gopal said. "Your research is only one study, and there are many others showing training methods producing good leaders. If we accept your dissertation, we're certifying its correctness. And I for one, believe a man can become whatever he wants with proper training and a lot of work."

"I'm not saying training and effort don't help. But just as taller men become NBA stars, you can make a person with superior inherited intuition and intellect into a leader easier than a moron. All men are not created equal, and it's time to recognize that fact."

"I think the fact it's time to recognize is what you need to do to have a successful defense of your dissertation."

Cam bolted up to face Gopal. "I'll take it under advisement," he said through his teeth. He marched away toward the "V" Parking area and his car. He wanted his PhD, but he wasn't willing to lie in his dissertation to get it. How could he simply reverse himself later and say his dissertation was wrong? What had happened to academic honesty—or had it never existed?

His Porsche was parked, as usual, on the grass above the first row of cars. It was Cam's habit to push limits with authorities, and in the absence of signs prohibiting parking outside designated areas, he felt a ticket would be arguable. So far, his theory had not been tested.

The green frog sprang to life, enfolding him in a friendly cocoon of German engineering and Professor Porsche's genius. Cam was reminded how the Krauts had tinkered and fine-tuned their way to defeat twenty-five years earlier rather than mass-producing machines of war. It was just as well, but now American industry was paying the price by continuing mass-production of inferior automobiles. It was even worse in tires. Akron had literally refused to manufacture radial tires.

The world seemed incredibly normal, totally unaware of the crisis in his life and probably not caring. Students cluttered Route 1, and Queen's Chapel was jammed as usual with lunch hour traffic. Driving back to his apartment in Mount Rainier seemed to isolate him from reality.

Cam mixed orange juice and vodka for a Harvey Wallbanger, and carefully floated the Galliano on top. His jade plants looked as thirsty as he felt, and he contemplated his navel while moistening their pots with water. Millie wouldn't be home until almost six, and he felt like avoiding school.

By three o'clock, Cam had downed three Harveys and no longer wanted to burden Millie with his presence for the evening. He put Daphne et Chloe on his stereo and relaxed. Ravel's work sounded more like the sea to him than La Mer, and had been a companion on all his travels. He had even played it in the orderly room at Holabird, bringing class to a drab existence. Maybe he had made a mistake in separating from the Army—the Intelligence Corps had suited him in many ways.

Maybe he should have gone back to Colorado. He considered himself a generic westerner, and living in the west meant being close to God. The little town of Golden was really his home, snuggled in a break in the hogback and isolated from Denver by the Table Mountains. The drive east from Golden on Sixth Avenue was a metaphor for life; first freeway in undeveloped land, then suburbs, then a short segment of old Denver, then the tree-lined east side, then Aurora, then nothing. It was truly a privilege to live in Colorado, and the state ought to limit immigration before its water disappeared. He dimly wondered how many people Colorado could support before nature would call a halt to man's exploitation of one of her most beautiful treasures. If a political unit could not control its borders, it was doomed. And if a PhD candidate didn't do precisely what his superiors said, he was doomed.

Chapter 5

By five o'clock, the Harveys had failed to jump-start his morale, and Cam drove back to school for his evening class. Parking lots were clearing, and he nosed the Porsche into the first row. He didn't want to stop by his office. Cathy would be there, and would ask a million questions.

What the hell, he walked over and sat viewing the mall.

He wasn't being fair to Cathy; she had come back to be available if he needed her. Mother Cathy seemed to have infinite patience, and he wondered if she was in love with him. Probably not, he decided. Not everyone was in love with him.

Millie had been apprehensive last night about his committee meeting and would be wondering about the outcome. He briefly considered calling her, but decided she would ask too many questions. Besides, he wasn't looking for sympathy. It was his failure and his alone, but it threw his relationship with Millie into limbo. He had planned to wait until after his defense before asking her to marry him, but now that wouldn't happen. What could he say? He had nothing to offer her and little hope for the future. Maybe tomorrow it would look better. He could always come up with some excuse for not calling.

The longer he lay on the grass watching lovers make out, the less he wanted to hold his lecture. His class would get along without him, he decided. In Vietnam, it had been easy; he went to the Kit-Cat with Webb, got drunk, and let the girls work him over. Not a bad option this time. He thought about Heather. She had taken his romance with Millie in stride and told him men were like trolley cars—there was always one coming along. Some men went a little faster, some were better maintained, some had a brighter paint job, but all gave about the same ride. Sometimes they had a tendency to jump the track, but that was why she took care to maintain the roadbed. Heather kept the tracks shiny and oiled the engines, but even then, cars sometimes switched to other tracks. Someone had thrown Cam's switch, and there wasn't anything she could do about it.

He stood up and slapped dried blossoms from his pants. He'd listened to Heather pouring out her troubles with those black-hatters often enough; it was time for her to listen to him.

*****

The longer he went without talking with Millie, the greater his feelings of guilt. Cam had to call her now; it had been two days since his draft dissertation had been rejected, and he hadn't talked to her since before the meeting. Worse, he felt guilty about Heather. Although he had not purposely sought physical solace by visiting Heather, he hadn't resisted it either.

Last night, he'd stayed with Ed after pub-crawling in Georgetown, and had avoided Millie's calls at work by having Cathy answer the phone. She covered for him, but every time Millie called, Cathy gave him a lecture.

Cam hung around the university until late afternoon, thinking about nothing and doing less. He joined the staff in their exodus at quitting time and drove back to Mount Rainier. He felt a gnawing sense of doom.

He saw her car parked alongside his apartment building, and his heart jumped. He wanted desperately to see her, but then again, everything he had to say would be bad.

Millie was sitting inside on the three steps leading up from the mailboxes. She remained seated as he entered. "I missed you. Where have you been?" she said.

"It's a long story. Come on, let's go inside and talk." Cam took her by the arm and helped her up, but noticed Millie's hesitation in accepting his assistance. She dusted off her skirt, and continued to look at Cameron fiercely.

"I would have appreciated a call," she said.

"I know. It's all my fault. Come on in."

"How would you feel if I treated you this way?"

"I'm sorry," Cam said. "I'll make it up to you. Would you like a drink?"

Millie remained standing in the center of his living room. "Cameron, what's going on? I've tried to call you a hundred times, and last night you didn't even come home."

"It looks like I won't be getting my PhD." Cameron avoided Millie's gaze and started to make himself a drink.

"What does that have to do with us?"

"Everything. I can't live off you. I've got to figure out what I'm going to do."

"And you don't want to discuss it with me," Millie said, still not moving to sit down.

"No, I just didn't want to—well, I didn't want to upset you. I needed to work it out for myself before I burdened you."

"Well, I'll give you all the time you want. You don't need to tell me anything, if that's all I mean to you."

"Aw, Millie, come on," Cam started to plead.

"No, *you* come on. If you want to talk, you call me. I'm not going to worry myself about you. Obviously, you can take care of yourself without me."

Millie spun around, not waiting for a response, and slammed the door behind her.

*****

Cameron arrived early for the meeting with his committee, but didn't bother to re-arrange the room. He opened the sole window to allow stale cigarette smoke to escape, and positioned himself at the conference table's head.

With the exception of his advisor, Marty Cohen, his committee walked in together like a jury re-entering a courtroom. It was just his own paranoia, he thought; academicians were an insecure lot and liked to travel in packs. They avoided talking with Cam about his dissertation, seemingly totally occupied in cleaning up the room and getting settled.

Cohen marched in with Cam's file, and took a chair at the center of the table on Cam's left. "Okay, let's get started. Cameron, I understand George and Irv have worked out a revision with you to your research design which will be satisfactory to our department. You've had time to study its implications for your reported results, so may I assume we're all in agreement on what you have to do?"

Cam leaned back in his chair and tapped his pencil on the table. "I'm convinced there's nothing wrong with my research design, and my results are consistent and replicable. If another researcher undertakes a similar project, he will produce similar results." Cam boldly looked around the table, but all his faculty were looking down at their hands or otherwise avoiding his gaze.

Marty took up the baton with a sigh—still without looking at Cam. "That may be, but we're in agreement that this department will not go on record supporting research which purports to show training is less important than heredity. It's simply too controversial and will damage our efforts to obtain grants and funding. You can do this kind of work after you're established in some other university, but, for now, we're responsible for your efforts."

"You approved my research proposal and design earlier," Cam countered. "That's essentially a hard and fast contract stating that if I accomplish the work as outlined, my dissertation will be accepted. Now you're saying that, after approving my design, the results, which were beyond our control, are causing you to require a new design which will produce different results for me to obtain my PhD. That's breach of contract. You can't do that." Cam was taking them on without a parachute..

"We can do anything we wish," Talbot said. "We set the rules here, not you."

Cohen answered evenly and with finality. "That's exactly what we're saying. We find ourselves unable to certify your research as submitted."

"What assurance do I have that findings from another design will not be thrown out?"

"I can assure you that results supporting earlier work, fully documented and related, will always be accepted."

Cam understood his advisor's point. Marty was calling for the subjection of Cam's spirit and creativity. Cam had already decided such action was incompatible with retaining his self-respect.

Cam stood up. "My work was good, well-designed, and easily replicated. I'm submitting it for your consideration. If it doesn't meet with your approval, you leave me no choice but to seek another program."

Marty gritted his teeth. "Then that's what you should do. I'll put in papers dissolving this committee. In view of your attitude, I'm not sure I can recommend you to another program."

Talbot piled on. "Personally, I'm disappointed in you, Mr. Stewart. You've wasted the time of everyone here. I don't know where your talents lie, but they certainly aren't in academia."

Several faculty members started to follow with further abuse, but Cohen shouted, "Enough!" Then in an even tone, he turned to Cam. "I think that's all, Cam. We all know where we stand. And we all have things to do and places to go."

Cameron was the first one out the door.

Cathy looked up as he stomped into the office and guessed the result. "You're going to be working for a living, right?" she inquired.

"Right; I'm out of the program." Cam sat at his desk and turned to the wall. All their cute little cartoons and posters Cathy had taped up suddenly seemed oppressive. Particularly the one with Pogo saying, "We have met the enemy, and he is us." Cam jumped up and tore it off the wall.

Barely audible, Cathy asked, "What are you going to do?"

"How in hell do I know?" he roared. Cam turned savagely on Cathy. Her eyes showed deep hurt as she waited for another outburst. He threw up his hands. "God, I don't know," he said softly.

Cathy closed the office door. She walked around to Cam and pushed him back from his desk. "Move," she ordered quietly. She turned his chair and sat down in his lap. She pressed his head into her bosom and began to buzz his hair with her lips. "It'll all work out somehow, and it'll be for the best." She caressed his ear and neck.

Cam could feel Cathy's heart pound. He couldn't believe this, Cathy was less than twenty years old and comforting him. God, he made her life miserable, teamed her up with a failure, and all she had done was try to be a friend.

"I want you to know something," Cathy said. Cam lifted his head to listen. "I think you're terrific, the best man I've ever known. I have faith in you. Whatever you do will work out." She placed her forefinger on his nose. "And I'm sure other women in your life feel the same way."

Cam wondered if Cathy was right—that Millie would feel the same way. Maybe he had misjudged her; maybe he didn't understand women at all.

Cam patted Cathy's rear for her to get off his lap. "Thanks, Cathy. You're right. I've just got to figure out what to do next."

He had made a mistake by not sharing everything with Millie. He needed to share the bad times with her as well as the good. After all, love didn't disappear in a week.

By eight thirty, Cam decided Millie would be home and they could work things out. Cam drove up Old Colesville Road when he was overwhelmed by a strange feeling. For some reason he started to think about another researcher at NIH Millie talked about when he first arrived. Randy Half-something, his name was, and supposedly he lived in "The Capitolina."

Cam's Porsche had a mind of its own, and it turned into the Capitolina complex and drove around past three sets of apartments to the rear. It stopped behind Millie's Falcon. Cameron rested his head on the steering until the shock wave subsided. He had no idea why he was in this parking lot, or what terrible instinct or premonition had brought him there.

Seven minutes later he arrived at Millie's apartment. Cam allowed an hour to pass before he telephoned NIH and remembering Randy's last name, obtained Randy Halbgewicht's number. He called Randy's apartment. No answer after twenty-two rings. Cam tried again. Randy answered.

"May I speak with Millie Lauenberg?" Cam asked, controlling his voice.

"She's not here," Randy said.

Cameron hung up. Ten minutes later the telephone rang.

"This is Millie. Did you call here earlier?"

"Yes."

"Well, you scared the hell out of us," she said angrily.

"Sorry, but I think we need to talk."

"There's nothing to talk about."

"Millie, I called twice, and the phone rang twenty-two times. Don't tell me there's nothing to talk about."

The silence was deafening.

Forty-five minutes went by before Millie walked in as if nothing had happened. She sat down on the couch beside him.

"So what does this mean? Did you make love with him?" Cam began.

"Yes," Millie answered, "I wanted him to make love to me. It was something I needed."

She was driving wooden stakes into his heart. Her motives were beyond his comprehension. All Cameron understood was that he had committed himself to Millie, and she had been unfaithful. The woman he loved had voluntarily and gladly accepted another man inside her.

"I want some space and freedom," she said.

"You want to have sex with other men?" Cam replied dumbly.

"It's not the sex. I just need to do things."

He was on the edge of an abyss, staring into a bottomless pit. She didn't love him, and it was over. They were Troilus and Cressida. He couldn't think, couldn't feel. He left without a word.

Gone were his dreams, his hopes, his happiness.

*****

Cameron was flattened. Humpty Dumpty could not be put back together again. He shaved off the beard Millie had liked so much and wished he was back in the Highlands with Webb.

Eating ceased, and Cam became a zombie. Each day, he was lighter, and within two months, he was buying jeans in the boys' department. His students thought he had contacted some terminal disease, and were making book on his expected longevity.

Sleep became impossible, and he ended up driving around aimlessly. He began spending time with Ed who tried to get him interested in religion.

Cam shook his head. "You know why people contribute to religions, Ed?" He didn't wait for an answer. "It's not out of goodness or to ask forgiveness. They hope their god will appreciate the offering and let them live a little longer. They buy a few days at a time and waste them."

Cameron had traveled through the various states of mind for an Amulot warrior. In his youth, he'd been indestructible, death came to all others, but not to him. In Vietnam, he'd realized it was probable he would be killed, most likely by some dismal accident or at the hand of an illiterate peasant. He had learned to block feelings by training himself to concentrate solely on immediate tasks—all outside happenings were ignored. Now, he *knew* he would die. He treated himself as already dead and living on borrowed time until the actual event. His life went day-to-day. Death could come at any time, it didn't mean nothing.

Chapter 6

With another year to go on his contract as an instructor, Cam looked for ways to spend his free time. He dialed Bobbi Rutledge's number and found her thrilled to hear from him. He hadn't seen her since before Millie, and was surprised when she invited him to stop by that very evening. A friend of Cathy's, she had been Cam's first paramour after arriving at Maryland. In spite of her boring job as a cashier at University Bank, Bobbi was a screamer with high energy who pampered him while requiring little maintenance. Photogenic as hell, Bobbi possessed a model's body—sleek, with tiny boobs, chiseled features, corn-silk blonde hair, widely-spaced blue eyes, and terrific teeth. She was also scary—taking no precautions in sex, and being totally fearless and uninhibited.

She lived near Thomas Circle—the District's worst section, populated primarily by pimps, prostitutes, and other assorted low-life. Bobbi had thrived there as a single girl for several years, a pretty, friendly chick who talked to everyone. She'd escaped being molested through her Bohemian lifestyle, and whereas most people found Thomas Circle and 13th Street depressing and oppressive, Bobbi found it exciting.

Bobbi's street friends had made Cam feel positively cubic. One, a hooker named Gloria, was heavy into heightened awareness and could discuss Zen with Cam as if she were a Buddhist monk. Another was a truly lost soul named Frank who was experiencing life and collecting material for his Great American Novel. Other characters floated in and out, and how Bobbi fit her banking and school life into the Thomas Circle milieu was a mystery.

Her neighborhood now was even worse than ever, but neither she nor her apartment had changed an iota—even Frank was still occupying a cushion on the floor. Cam had psyched himself up to nail

Bobbi at the door, but Frank's presence threw his best—or worst—intentions out the window.

Bobbi stood at the door staring. "Cam? My God, I hardly recognize you!"

Cam was stunned. Both from what Bobbi said and how she looked. Bobbi was wearing cut-off jeans and a white lettered T-shirt without a bra. Her girlish breasts were clearly visible through the light cotton. She stepped forward and grabbed his hand.

"God, you're thin!" she blurted. "Come on, I'll fix you something to eat."

Cam had forgotten she hadn't seen him without his beard or since he started losing weight. Obediently, he followed Bobbi into her kitchen. When she turned around at the stove, he crushed her body in his arms and her lips against his.

"My, aren't we ready," she said as she came up for air. "How long has it been? A year?"

Cam was shaken. Bobbi was reproaching him for neglect, and he desperately wanted her to be like she was before Millie. Cam's faculties were in disarray from lack of sleep and nourishment. He couldn't tell if he was being turned away at the inn or not.

"Why don't you go into the living room and talk to Frank for a while?" Bobbi said. "I'll fix something and be out in a minute." Cam shuffled back into the living room.

Bobbi had put up two new posters of abstract art on the walls, but the hardwood floor with her large oval woven rag rug was unchanged. He put a Peter, Paul and Mary record on her hi-fi, and sat on her red couch. It was a well lived-in apartment in appearance, homey and friendly.

Bobbi came back shortly and sat beside him. "I'm heating some lasagna. You can handle that, can't you?" She sounded concerned. When Cam nodded, she hopped up and motioned for him to follow her into the kitchen.

She pulled out his shirt and ran her hands up underneath as soon as Cam stepped into the room. "Oh, Lord, you're so bony."

Cam swallowed as his heart sank into the basement. "I'm sorry, Bobbi, it's just me."

She gave Cam a light but friendly kiss. "Sit here and talk to me."

Cameron collected himself, but he was disoriented. After

bringing Bobbi up-to-date with his life, he tested her feelings. "Bobbi, do you ever experience a deep union of souls or sense a true *seelung* when you make love?" Cam hoped she would say that was how she felt with him.

"I don't understand. What do you mean?"

"Well, usually an orgasm seems like a little death, as the French put it. I sometimes feel a sense of loss, you know—of the high, followed by the desire for another and another until physically I can't anymore. It's wonderfully satisfying but incomplete, and you always want more. One kiss today is worth a thousand yesterday; an orgasm now is worth a hundred last week."

"That's exactly the way it is."

Cam was crushed. He hadn't finished and had been describing love without a *seelung*. He was acutely aware that Bobbi was not Millie. He kissed her and rejoined Frank in the front room.

Acid was taking its toll on Frank as well as the stress of dodging the draft. Cam asked him if he still thought women were only transfer agents, transferring resources from one man to another or from a man to their children.

"Yeah, man, they're low-level steps on the ladder to Nirvana."

"You're into reincarnation now, I guess," Cam commented.

"Yeah, man, that's where the action is." Frank had been on one trip too many.

Bobbi entered with the lasagne. She knelt in front of the couch, draping her elbow over the inside of Cam's leg. Frank looked up disdainfully and rolled onto his side. "How about a joint?" he suggested as an alternative.

He had done lots of things, but Cam had yet to smoke pot. But he could hardly do anything with Bobbi in front of Frank. "Sure, why not?"

It was a mistake; the grass was bad for Cam. The smoke clobbered him with a migraine almost immediately, and he knew it was time to leave. He had hoped pot would make him mellow. It worked that way with Frank, while Bobbi became amorous. Cam's chemistry was obviously different. He felt more tired, but he knew sleep was an elusive dream. He tucked in his shirt and rose to depart. Bobbi followed him to the door.

"Come back," she said sweetly. "You're always welcome."

"Thanks, but as you see, I need to get my act together."

"Call me for help. I don't charge much."

Cam kissed her softly. She didn't charge at all, he thought, as she drew her hand across his abdomen. He was embarrassed with his condition and knew he couldn't treat her right—not yet, maybe never. The evening had just made things worse.

*****

By the end of September, Cam considered returning to the Army and requesting Vietnam to die in battle. No, he would wait until Webb returned from Germany, and then go as a civilian. He was wasting away, but he could hold out until November when Webb was due back.

But he couldn't. October was the low point; Cameron had reached a hundred and twelve pounds and looked like an inmate at Bergen-Belsen. He still played handball three days a week but was a shell of his former self. Cam had been a marginal Class A player, normally winning games in his regular group handily, but now he was fortunate to score five points.

Cam's usual handball partner finally called the proceedings to a halt. Paul Stephens knew a psychiatrist in Langley Park named Christiansen who was heavily into drug treatments. He marched into Cam's office and told him it was time for medical help.

"Let's call now," ordered Paul, handing the phone to Cam. He held out a note. "Here's the phone number."

Cam was feeling nothing, blocking pain so effectively that even a severe handball bruise was unnoticeable. With Paul standing over him, he didn't feel like arguing. Psychiatrists were all quacks, but maybe this would get Paul off his back. He made the appointment, and allowed Paul to drive him to the doctor's office.

Christiansen was a weird-looking gnome, extremely nervous, with little piggy eyes peering out from under a bald pate. He smoked incessantly, and Cam decided the doctor needed more therapy than he. Still, he didn't insist Cam lie on a couch, so evidently Cam didn't need the standard neurotic female treatment. He listened intently while Cam related his story.

Christiansen recommended Cam go on a phased program using a

drug called Elavil. It would take three months to come up to strength, at least another nine months of treatment, and then three months or longer to come back down. Christiansen was not interested in detailed discussions of Cam's problems. As he said, there was no sense in stirring paint when it was too thick; what was needed was paint thinner. Cam's depression was essentially terminal if untreated.

He showed Cam drawings of nerve synapses and described how the drug worked.

"As a normal function, the brain produces a chemical which inhibits transmission of stimuli from these nerve endings into the brain itself. Think of it as a filter to keep excessive noise out of a finely tuned electronic system. In times of stress, more is produced, strengthening the filter and hardening the individual so he can remain functional. Without it, everyone would go crazy in battle or become hysterical feeling severe pain. Obviously, it's a major determinant of a person's sensitivity."

"I must not produce much because I've always been extremely sensitive to feelings—even to the point of being somewhat psychic," Cam said.

"But not always. How about in Vietnam? Weren't you able to function under fire?"

"Yeah. Are you saying I produce this chemical readily under stress?"

"That's the psychological aspect of training. The Army seeks to toughen soldiers and suppress reactions to pain and discomfort— particularly instincts for self-preservation. You did that well, probably after the initial shocks of combat were absorbed." He paused and took a long drag on his cigarette. "That's why so many casualties take place in early encounters; soldiers haven't adjusted yet to functioning under higher stress. When they adjust, it's called remaining cool under fire."

"So what happened this time?"

"First, you started building up your chemical defense to combat dissertation stress. Then you went to the danger point fearing you might lose this girl. We know depression greatly stimulates production of the blocking agent as the body's defense against unwanted stimuli. You went over the hill when you found her with another man and started what can sometimes be an irreversible process. The chemical is broken down and eliminated naturally only to a certain maximum rate. If you continue to produce the chemical at a high rate over an extended period of time, the body loses its ability to re-establish a balance. Then the outcome is predictable. Depression deepens, blocking ever more efficiently until death, usually by suicide, of the individual."

"You're saying if I don't do anything I'll eventually commit suicide?"

"Do you think about death frequently?"

"Yes."

"Have you thought about committing suicide?"

"Yes."

"Are you mad at anybody?"

"I don't know, maybe myself. My committee members certainly, and maybe Millie." Cam reconsidered his last remark. "No, I love Millie."

"If you're angry enough to kill someone, why not yourself? You don't fear death, do you?"

"No."

"Then I'll give you the choice between life and death. You can either go on my program, or I'll come to your funeral within six months."

Cam studied the doctor's face. He was serious and believed what he said. Maybe he was right. The weight loss was a manifestation of self-destructive tendencies and Cam couldn't remember feeling happy. Every day he felt worse. What the hell, a few pills couldn't hurt and he could stop taking them anytime.

"Okay," he said at last.

*****

Heather shook her head at this soap opera tragedy taking place between Cam and Millie. She considered Cam to be her best friend, but their relationship lacked the deep, romantic love Cam obviously felt for Millie. Cam was literally dying without Millie, and Heather couldn't imagine anyone willing to die for her. She dialed Millie's office and invited Millie to her apartment to talk.

Millie was hesitant. "What do you want to talk about?"

"About a person who's very important to both of us—Cameron. I think we can both be of great help to him."

"I can't help him," Millie said flatly.

"Maybe not, but possibly you could help me help him."

Millie was unconvinced, but finally agreed to come by Heather's apartment after work. The mere fact that Millie acquiesced told Heather the cause was not hopeless. Her stomach tightened; she would kill to have someone love her like Cam loved Millie.

Heather knew one didn't fight for a person's love, but was available when help was needed. Sometimes a person resented assistance and discarded the helper afterward, but that was a risk of caring. Like so many doctors' wives dumped by their husbands after their medical practices became established, Heather could be thrown away later by Cam.

Cam's case was just a series of mistakes that had gotten out of control. Mistakes could be fixed.

Millie seemed more assured, composed, and socially adept than when Heather had met her at Ed's party the previous year. She sat down on Heather's white and pink flowered couch, holding her knees tightly together and placing her hands on top of her purse.

"So what do you want from me?" Millie asked, cutting off polite conversation.

"Cam's lost the most important thing in the world to him," Heather started.

"Yeah, right, his precious PhD," interrupted Millie.

That was a cheap shot from a person who already had one, Heather thought. "No, you," she said. She waited for her words to take effect.

Millie looked down and began rolling her left index finger between her right thumb and forefinger. She shook her head. "But he didn't come to me. He came to you, didn't he?" Millie looked up to see if she had guessed correctly.

"You were too important. He loves you. I was safe. I'm just a friend."

"You're more than his friend," Millie insisted.

"Only before he met you. Since then, it's been friendship." Heather had lied, but for a good cause.

"Did he ask you to talk to me?"

"No. You and I both know he couldn't do that. Cam's the most capable person I've ever known—a genius, but his own worst enemy. And he's likely to hurt those he loves most of all."

"Is it wrong not wanting to be hurt?" Millie glanced up.

"It's wrong for your head to keep you from loving when your heart loves," Heather said. "The longest distance in the world is between a person's heart and head."

"What do you get from this?"

"I get to see a friend fulfill his destiny, and not go down the toilet as waste." Heather doubted her words were having much effect. She had to keep the conversation going. "Have you ever met Webb Reid?"

"No, but I know they were in the Army together."

"Did you know Cam saved Webb's life in Vietnam?"

Millie stood up. "Apparently there's a lot I don't know. What else did he do?"

"I'm just saying that he's worth saving. You know better than anyone the only limits to his talent are his pride and sense of honor. When he couldn't get his dissertation published, it was the first time he had failed at anything. Then everything collapsed."

Millie walked to the balcony door and looked out. Heather didn't know what else to say. "I don't understand you, Millie. You and Cam as a team would be unbeatable."

Millie turned fiercely on Heather. "But that's exactly it—we would have to be a team. And he showed me we weren't."

"But you were. He felt he had let the team down. Look, you work on research projects. Haven't you ever gotten bad results and waited until you couldn't hide them anymore or until you had something positive to report? That's what he was doing." Heather took a deep breath. "At any rate, it's in your hands. He doesn't believe you care about him, and the only person who can help him is the person he loves. That's you." Heather was out of ideas; it looked hopeless.

"Do you think I care about him?" Millie asked softly.

Heather's heart jumped. Finally, a crack in that hard exterior. She had been one sentence away from giving up. "Yes, otherwise you wouldn't be here."

Millie looked at the floor. "But it's hard. You don't know what he said."

Heather walked over and touched her arm. "You're right, I don't. But regardless, I'm sure he'd do anything to get you back."

"But I haven't heard from him in three months."

"He thinks you're living with another man and can't bring himself to face you."

"But I'm not. That was just something I needed at the time."

Heather faced Millie squarely. "Tell him, not me."

Millie threw her arms around Heather. "Oh, Heather," she cried, "I'm sorry. I thought he preferred you to me."

Heather had often wished it were true. She thought grimly of Milton, "They also serve who only stand and wait." What she had to say to Millie was obvious. She swallowed hard. "No, you've never had any competition, believe me. He loves you, not me." There, she had said it with a terrible hollow feeling in the pit of her stomach.

Heather leaned back to see Millie's face. "Why don't I invite him over?" she suggested.

Millie nodded, and Heather picked up the receiver and dialed.

It took some doing, but Heather told him one of her friends had given her some pot, and she wanted to try it. But she didn't want to try it not alone, not knowing how she'd react. Cam finally agreed to come, but only after Heather promised to spring for a pizza. Cam's voice was flat like he was on autopilot.

Heather replaced the receiver and turned to Millie. "Boy, does he sound bad. For a moment I didn't think he would come. When did you see him last?"

"The day we broke up. In August."

"Then you're in for a shock," Heather cautioned. "You may not recognize him."

*****

Thirty minutes later, Cam arrived at Heather's apartment. He felt like a jerk ringing her doorbell, but the door was closed, and her double lock required two hands. Moving the Angelo's box to his left hand like a serving tray, he pushed the button. Heather's door opened immediately.

Millie stood there.

Her smile froze as she stared at Cam, and it took her a few

seconds to recover. "Come on in." Millie reached for the pizza. "It took you long enough."

Cam was thunderstruck and recoiled, grasping the box with both hands. Millie was the last person he'd expected to see in Heather's apartment. "Where's Heather?" he asked.

"Come on in, Cam!" Heather shouted. "I thought it was time we all got together."

Cam didn't know what to do. He placed the pizza on the bar. Millie took his hand and led him to the couch. Heather got up to get a beer and serve the pizza.

"How've you been, Millie?"

"I've missed you."

"Don't mind me, I'm not here," Heather called from the kitchen.

"I thought you were busy." Conversation was not coming easy to Cam.

"No, but I don't want to talk about that now." Millie's voice was barely audible. "Don't you remember my letter? I meant every word of it then, and I mean every word of it now."

Cam put both of Millie's hands inside his and squeezed. "Can you forgive me for being such a failure?"

"I'll tell you what. Why don't we stop bothering Heather and go over to my place?"

Millie pulled Cam off the couch and guided him toward the entryway.

Heather yanked the door open. "Get out of here, you guys," she said, pointing the way. "Just send me an invitation later."

They each kissed her as they left, trying to be as considerate as possible. Their expressions of thanks were warm but hurried.

Heather closed the door after them. Cam stood outside the door for a moment, wrestling with the logistics of the two vehicles they had driven. Then he heard someone crying, the sound coming from behind the door. His happiness was being paid for by another's sacrifice.

Chapter 7

Cam watched the morning sunlight creep across Millie's bed. Reconciliations were fabulous, but the torture and pain of separations weren't. He needed to be more like one of Peter the Great's Streltsy—able to stoically accept agony without betrayal of self. With great aplomb they placed their faces in their predecessor's blood on the chopping block when Peter executed them. Cam did not have that degree of self-discipline. He had been physically brave under fire, but emotional traumas of love had laid him prostrate.

Women spent their lives dealing with emotions and stressful interpersonal relations, and men were easily outclassed in the art of intimacy cybernetics. Men's attitudes were more linear than women's; they tended to take a direct approach to subjects while women functioned in circles, keeping men guessing and constantly adjusting their internal rheotaxis as necessary for their well-being. Willows bend and survive; oaks break and perish.

When Millie touched him, he became cured of all sickness. A force flowed into him, rejuvenating his neurological systems and heightening his awareness of his body and his being as a man loved by a woman. When they made love, she fused herself with him, and all but passing out from the intensity of her orgasms, she would give him her life. And then, as if to bring spring out of winter, she would draw the phoenix from ashes, taking charge of its resurrection and causing him to renounce his male sovereignty in blinding flashes of all-consuming trust and love.

The next week went by in a blue of sexual highs and togetherness. Only gradually did the reality of work and professionalism that both Millie and Cam possessed re-assert themselves. As they lounged in bed one morning savoring the afterglow, Cam murmured to Millie, "Let's do something we've never done before."

"We just did that," she said sleepily.

"No, no," Cam said. "Let's move the frontier of science forward. My dissertation's empirical evidence convinced me man has a vast store of knowledge trapped in his brain which he can't access. We ought to find a method of retrieving that knowledge."

Millie rolled over and propped herself on one elbow so she could face Cam squarely. "Pillow talk is not supposed to include business," she said.

"No really. Working together, we can do it. Advance humankind by ten thousand years."

She patted him on the arm and pushed herself backwards off the bed to stand up. "I'll make coffee and we'll discuss it," she said as she headed to the kitchen.

Cam watched her walk down the hall with a spring in her step. She looked terrific nude, clothed, or whatever, as long as she was happy. She had millions of teeth, and when she smiled, the light bounced off and vaporized her clothes. He bounced up to follow her.

Shamelessly still nude, they stretched out in the dinette, stacking their feet together on the chair across from Millie. Cam sipped his coffee and restarted the conversation concerning his ideas. "The evidence convinced me that humans inherit knowledge or what we call instinct in animals. But we don't make use of that knowledge after our earliest baby years, and our ability to access it atrophies. Simply put, just like Elavil unblocks synapses from transmitting stimuli to the brain, I think there must be something that could reopen channels to our inherited knowledge."

Millie curled her toes in a sunbeam. "I doubt it. The human body doesn't regenerate well. If something isn't used, it's lost." She grabbed him playfully for emphasis.

"Seriously," Cam protested, "There must be something."

"Well, why not keep the channels open—if they are open at birth—and not allow them to cease functioning. Biologically, that approach would make more sense."

"Terrific!" Cam said. He jumped to his feet, causing her to lose her grip. "How are we going to do this?" Cam paced back and forth.

Millie smiled at Cam's behavior. "Well, I could formulate a project along with my nerve structure research in the lab," she suggested abstractly. She rose and blocked his pacing. "I might be

51

able to work up something to test your theories if you would outline what you'd like me to prove or disprove."

Cam thought that was a great idea, and a new project was born.

*****

She had to have been crazy to agree to this. Millie shook her head. She was going to have to hide the procedures within the budgetary limitations and reporting requirements and she wasn't sure how to do that. Logistical problems had been ignored, and now she was facing the reality of implementation. Everything was even more complicated with Randy breathing down her neck.

She could kill two birds with one stone by transferring to another section and using animals in their research. She needed to distance herself from Randy and be able to conduct tests without attracting undue attention. Her office was alongside the other section's laboratory anyway, so it would be a convenient switch and not require her to change rooms.

The bio-chemical division director looked up from her work and smiled as Millie knocked and entered. Millie knew how to handle this—after all, the director had received her PhD from Yale like Millie and wasn't particularly impressed with Randy's work at North Carolina.

Trish Browning waved Millie into the large armchair alongside her desk. "Haven't seen you in a while. Are you here to announce a breakthrough, a marriage, or a pregnancy?"

"None of the above," Millie said. "Although, I'd like to make this discussion personal."

"Returning to Yale to teach, right?" Patricia moved to the couch and leaned back.

Her first name described her—patrician, mused Millie. She was an 'old boy' from an old-money background who disliked upstarts. Tall, spare, and angular, Tricia enjoyed a reputation as a tough, man-hating female; a role she played to the hilt in handling power brokers who assumed their assistance automatically entitled them to sexual favors. Millie knew otherwise; it wasn't that Tricia universally rejected men—just the greedy, macho ones who populated federal bureaucracies.

"I'd like to have Randy take over my projects on pain and nerve structures, and move into experimentation with drug-enhanced nerve sensitivity. Also, I'd like to distance myself from him."

Tricia looked at Millie intensely. "Is there any special reason I should know about?"

"Well, maybe. It was short, not particularly sweet, and now it would be best for us to be in different work groups."

Tricia had seen this situation before, and it was always the woman who was fired or transferred. "Why don't I transfer Randy instead?" she offered with a cavalier wave.

"I'd rather change. I'm burnt out on structures and want to study chemicals on nerve impulse transmission." Millie described her current projects and why Randy would be the right choice to assume her work.

"Are you sure about this?" Trish asked pointedly. "It looks like your project is close to spawning a raft of papers. That could make a reputation."

"It's okay, I don't care."

"Are you in love with Randy? Without this manna from heaven, I doubt we'd be able to retain him after this year."

Millie started to laugh. "No, no. Do you remember Cameron Stewart?"

"The fellow you brought over last Christmas."

"That's right. Well, he's the one." She sighed, "I realize Randy's not much, but he's our most logical candidate. Maybe he'll catch fire with this falling in his lap."

"Sounds like you spent a lot of time with him." The question was friendly, but Millie could see Trish was interested in her answer. She decided to be frank.

"A few evenings, that's all. At the time, Cam and I were having big problems."

Trish smiled. "I've been there myself. Afterward, you know you made a mistake, but the relationship lingers like stale cigar smoke. You get all your clothes dry cleaned, fumigate your car, office, and apartment, take dozens of bubble baths, and you still can't get rid of it." She walked to the window. Men weren't the only ones to pick up something strange when unhappy.

"It's not easy to be a professional woman, but you're one of the best researchers in this building. You haven't made your reputation yet, but you will." She faced Millie. "You have an idea, don't you? Something that half-weight wouldn't figure out from your old projects."

Close. She'd have to bring Tricia in eventually. "Yeah, I do have an idea, but it needs more development. Give me three months and I'll have it worked out."

Trish rolled forward onto her toes. "You got it," she said. "We'll make you a star to go on top of Steinem's tree."

Back in her office, Millie began to search through literature indexes for research studies on heredity. Recent thrusts were primarily efforts in genetic engineering of superior physical traits. A number of studies were descriptive in nature and concerned retarded individuals and probabilities of such parents producing retarded children. That indicated intelligence was inherited, but even severe cases were often ascribed to inherited physical deficiencies and their lack of development.

She noted several recent studies concerning identical twins. Their abstracts indicated that when identical twins were separated at birth and raised in widely different socio-economic environments, their emotional and intellectual characteristics nonetheless remained similar into adulthood. Cam was on the right track, and she placed requests for copies of all studies concerning identical twins.

Drawing up an appropriation request to isolate the mechanism by which nerve synapses interface with brain waves turned out to be a simple matter. The nationwide drug furor was making research in hallucinogenics popular, and money was readily available. Millie built her request by concentrating on ergot, long used in preventing migraine headaches by being combined with caffeine into Cafergot, and compounds including lysergic acid diethylamide-25, or LSD.

Initial funding was carved out of the current budget, and Tricia doubled her appropriation for the following two years. Two laboratory technicians were assigned to Millie immediately, and Tricia would assist occasionally and receive co-authorship on all papers. Three dozen laboratory rats were shipped in, and a maze was constructed—supposedly for testing intelligence. Almost overnight, the project became a reality.

"How are you using rats?" Cam asked after seeing the cages and maze.

Millie had progressed thus far without his involvement. "To test my formulations. We'll train several rats to negotiate the maze and ring a bell at the far end to obtain food. Then we'll mate them, producing offspring whose parents have prior knowledge of the maze and its solution. We'll inject baby rats with de-blockers, and see if they can traverse the maze. Never having seen it before, they could only know its solution from inherited knowledge."

"What are you looking at to construct your formulae?"

"High valence compounds using a spinal fluid derivative as carrier." Millie showed Cam several diagrams of nerve structures and synapses. "I've found fairly extensive neurological research, but it concentrates primarily on rebuilding or reconnecting severed nerves. The brain can recoup some of its losses through re-routing activity stimuli and using undamaged sectors. We also know chemical concentrations change depending on activity and amount of information transmitted across synapses."

"Intellect's increased or decreased by use or disuse of the brain?"

"That's what the research shows. Training not only increases rote knowledge, but also intelligence."

"So that's why housewives who watch soap operas become prematurely senile," Cam joked.

Millie walked to a row of filing cabinets along the wall. "I've been browsing through some papers. Nobody seems to have considered your idea of permanently enabling individuals to access their entire neurological capacity. Some temporary drug work has been studied, primarily cocaine, and everyone agrees we use only a small portion of our brains, but no one has seriously looked at inherited instinct and its implications."

Cameron was fascinated with Millie's erudition. He had not seen her functioning in her area of expertise before, and was impressed. "I can see how you got your PhD," he commented.

Millie sighed. "My doctorate was a matter of endurance. My advisor assigned a topic which was really a part of his own current project. I did the work as directed and he gave me my degree. It took no original thinking on my part, just work."

"Regardless, you've developed an ability to organize your efforts and information and become astoundingly productive. It may not have anything to do with getting a PhD, but it speaks well of you."

"On that basis—thanks." She smiled, leaned over her desk and kissed him.

"What does Tricia think you're doing?" Cam asked.

"She's accepting what I wrote in the appropriation request," Millie replied. She handed Cam a copy of the fifty-page document. "Don't let its size fool you. They authorize money around here by the pound. Most of it is boiler plate."

"Does she expect a second shoe to drop?" Cam riffled through the pages.

"Oh, sure. I'll have to fill her in before summer. This budget runs out on the last day of June, and although she's already created my permanent funding lines, I'll need to retain her support."

"Maybe we'll be done before then," Cam said hopefully.

"Dream on. This is a life's work."

Cam wondered if her words would be prophetic.

*****

Only a junior captain, Webb was placed into the career course well ahead of his contemporaries. Playing the game to perfection, his tour in Germany had been curtailed to fill a command course slot after he sent a request for Vietnam duty to his branch assignments officer. The next several years of his career were pre-ordained: his post-course tour would be in Vietnam, followed by a return to the intelligence school as an instructor, and then posting to some foreign country as an attaché right after he made major.

Webb put his feet up on Cam's Japanese coffee table and held his vodka-Collins glass on his stomach. Cam could see the melancholy start to extract its toll on Webb's morale.

"I can't get over the change in you, Cam. You'd blow away in a stiff breeze. Are you going to grow your beard back?"

"Maybe. It lets me hide with hippies."

"How do girls like it?"

"There's only one girl now, Millie Lauenberg. And she likes beards. Speaking of girls, how are you doing?"

"You know me, always moving around. At Camp King I had a live-in split in my BOQ, but then we were all moved to Munich and the 513th de-activated. I'm looking around again. Got any suggestions?"

Cam didn't. Ever since the girl in Bien Hoa, Webb tended to treat women like he was on a search-and-destroy mission. He would introduce Webb to Ed and they could go cruising together.

"Maybe. I'll have to make some calls," he said.

Webb showed Cam the financial situation for their Lichtenstein corporation, Webberon. "We've done extremely well—particularly buying gold like you suggested."

"Well, you didn't believe me originally when I told you Americans couldn't own bullion."

"Guilty as charged," admitted Webb. "For thirty-plus years we haven't been allowed to do what everyone else could. Not very free, are we?"

"Nope. And Roosevelt's justification disappeared long ago."

"Someday, we'll have to go through all that Russian gold flowing in. Probably most of it has numismatic value. Your idea with the Soviet merchant marine captains was brilliant—buying Russian gold coins for dollars. They black-market dollars in Russia for huge profits while we get gold well below its real market value."

"Nice to be cornering the Russian rare coin market, isn't it?" Cam laughed.

"Yeah, well, we should get paid well for what we're doing. We Amulots are being sacrificed like the Varangian Guard by the Byzantines. When the Turks come, there won't be enough of us left to man the walls."

"Well, I can guaran-damn-tee I won't be taken alive by the Turks. And if I don't have a last bullet for myself, you'll have to do it."

Webb looked hard at his best friend. "Let's drink Brüderschaft on it. We both promise to end each other's life if necessary."

"Agreed," said Cam, and they sealed their bargain.

"You're probably right about us disappearing," Cam said, "But I think it's because we're having to provide for everyone else in addition to our own. It's Knox's ethic—you only have as many kids as you can properly raise. If we have to take care of all the kids from other races, ethnicities, and dysfunctional families, then we don't have anything left for our own. Every time I hear a Scotch-Irish couple say they can't afford to have kids, we die out a little faster."

"I agree. Government policies are killing us off just as sure as the concentration camps did. But what can we do about it?"

Cameron didn't know, but if nothing was done by the end of the century, the US was doomed to serfdom and permanent mediocrity.

Chapter 8

By February, Cameron decided his emotional state was back to normal although still dependent on his daily dosage of Elavil. He had tested himself in January while accompanying Millie to New Orleans for a week-long scientific meeting. Cam had forgotten his pills, and after three days, he became nervous and ill. He would have to ride the tiger both up and back.

He and Millie split their time between their two apartments, but never missed a night together and never went to bed angry. Even Cam's relationships with his other friends improved accordingly—except for Heather who became increasingly withdrawn. She went on a cruise in March, and spent several weeks in various resorts during the spring.

It wasn't that life had become predictable or dull, it was more like things were moving in slow motion. Millie was quiet but no less passionate and sharing, and events at school and the Pentagon seemed to lose their intensity. Why?

And then he saw it. Millie was smiling that smile of supreme secrets.

"You're pregnant!" Cam exclaimed.

"Yes, and I feel wonderful," Millie smiled.

Millie glowed constantly. Cam found himself looking at baby things with new vision, and new possibilities were opening up. He wondered if all first-time expectant fathers felt like this—like the world was a better place.

Millie's pregnancy hardly affected her physically or emotionally as spring arrived, and Cam wondered if she were one of those pioneer women who gave birth alongside the trail and caught up with the wagon train an hour later. She continued to work nightly on formulations as if nothing was happening.

Cam pushed his diagram of a complex organic compound across the dining room table to Millie. She studied it and sighed. "Cam, it's a shame you didn't understand the game. I couldn't have worked this up as fast as you did."

"Come off it. What do you mean I didn't understand the game?"

Millie rose and poured herself a cup of coffee. "You tried to create something and make a statement with your dissertation. That's not the way it works. You didn't have standing. The Kuhn-Tucker conditions in non-linear programming were actually discovered years earlier by a young graduate student at Chicago, but even after the truth was known, their credits remained. You don't argue with prize-winners. Look at what happened to Eckert and Mauchley."

"The inventors of the computer?"

"Yes. Why didn't they become rich?"

Cam shrugged, not knowing the answer.

"They didn't have standing when they invented the computer. They faced enormous opposition from other scientists and established research organizations mainly because of the lack of PhDs and well-known names on their project. Their Army liaison officer brought in John von Neumann to achieve greater legitimacy and, of course, to ensure his own place in history."

"I thought von Neumann was added because he invented the stored program," said Cam.

"Nope. Von Neumann only wrote up Eckert and Mauchley's concepts for EDVAC, including the stored program idea which Mauchley had already published in internal notes. Lieutenant Goldstine disseminated von Neumann's paper, and history gave Johnny the credit. The academic rule is the most famous person on a team receives the most credit. Von Neumann walked away as the world's foremost computer expert, without having helped create ENIAC at all."

"It makes you wonder what other ideas credited to von Neumann originated with other individuals."

"Yeah, but that wasn't all. As engineers, Eckert and Mauchley attempted to patent their work and take their invention commercial. They couldn't do it. Eclipsed by von Neumann and hamstrung by security regulations, they were hardly marketable. To compound their problem, the National Academy of Sciences established a subcommittee to report on computer developments and make recommendations. Who do you think the four members were? Von Neumann, and three PhDs from Harvard, MIT, and Bell Labs—all failures in attempting to develop computing technology and jealous of Eckert and Mauchley's success."

"Well, that's the ol'-boy network striking again."

"Right, and then a federal judge ruled Eckert and Mauchley's patents were not valid, citing, among other reasons, that von Neumann's paper antedated their application. Eckert and Mauchley ended up with the short end of the stick."

"I see your point. Like in politics—do anything to get elected because you can't do anything until you're elected."

"Exactly. You knew that, but didn't do it."

"So what now?"

"Now? We use your work—undeniably brilliant—to our own advantage. Publishing is not the only way to prove a case. We'll achieve standing by proving your theory in my lab. After that, everything will be easy. Personally, I think this is exciting as hell. I'm glad they turned you down."

"Assuming we find the key and prove we're right, how do we keep it and use it?"

Millie shook her head. She gathered up the reports and stacked them on her bookcase. "I'm not sure. There's a big problem. NIH can lay claim to our results because of my patent agreement and asserting they funded the project. So it's really not ours. In spite of everything, if we want to enjoy the fruits of our labors, we'll have to pull a von Neumann and steal them."

Cameron was speechless. Millie was right. They were using NIH facilities and resources, and Millie was being paid by NIH. "Are you willing?" he asked evenly.

Millie turned to face Cam. "Yes."

Silence reigned in the room. Millie was the first to speak. "I don't know where this will take us, but as long as it's with you, I'm willing to go."

Cam took a deep breath as he devoured Millie's statement. "We need to talk this through. We have to consider how we're going to do this."

Millie nodded, and sat down to draw lines on a napkin with a butter knife. "I've got an idea," she said slowly. "I have a little money, and we could set up another lab."

"That would take a lot of money," Cam interrupted, "and we wouldn't have time to work it."

"That's not what I'm suggesting. The lab would be a dummy with only enough supplies and facilities for us to say we conducted our own research. The rats at NIH are destroyed after testing, so I can have Trish cut a contract with you to buy them. It'll work, we can do it."

"But what would you tell Trish about your current work?" Cam didn't mean to play the devil's advocate, but they needed a thorough plan.

"I've got that covered already. Last month, I wrote up my supplemental project report for next year's funding. The research objective is to develop chemical aids which will speed learning by reducing inhibiting factors in the neurological system. Even when the rats fail to negotiate the maze, we continue to train them until they succeed. I'm recording training efforts and time, so ostensibly the project is entirely something else."

"That sounds like a worthwhile project itself," Cam remarked, surprised at her deviousness.

"Oh, it is. Trish is excited about it. She thinks I'm on to something." Millie touched Cam's arm to keep him from interrupting. "I keep two sets of lab books, one for us and one for NIH. All we have to do is make up a new set for our dummy lab. You do the recording as your work, and we can get around my patent obligations."

This lady of his was incredible, but Cam reflected on the second shoe. "So how do we capitalize on our results and keep others from reducing us to Eckerts and Mauchleys?"

Millie shook her head. "No clue. I was saving that problem for you."

*****

It was time to make a commitment to Millie before God. Normally, when Cam wanted to have an evening out with Millie, they went to the Cracked Crab in Gaithersburg, the best place he knew for Maryland crabs. Jeans were *de rigueur*, and the restaurant offered all

61

the crabs you could eat for $3.95. A stack of brown paper, like that used in gas station washrooms, served as a plate, and then it was one crab at a time, peeling off the top paper afterward and dumping shells and legs into a paper bag on the floor. Coleslaw, fries and beer went along for the ride. Usually, it was a four-hour affair with lots of laughs, but romance was impossible with everyone's hands covered with hot crab spices.

Breaking tradition, Cam called the Hunan in Arlington to make reservations and order Peking duck in advance. The Hunan was expensive, and this evening, it was unusually quiet.

The maître d' ushered Millie and Cam into a side room with only three booths. Relatively dark for a Chinese restaurant, its service was elegant and individual. The daisies on display were real, and hot tea was served immediately. The first course arrived promptly.

Cam took a sip of the exquisite egg drop soup and put down his spoon. He looked across into Millie's eyes. "Millie, will you marry me?" he asked.

Millie didn't blink. She reached out for Cam's right hand and grasped it tightly. "No."

Cam's his stomach dropped three feet. "But I love you," he said.

"I know, and I love you, too. But we can't get married now. Not while I'm pregnant. We'll talk about it again after the baby is born and you're totally off your medication."

Cam pursued the subject doggedly. "You sure?"

"Yes. I think we should be free to decide without the pressure of a big belly."

Not that she had one, thought Cam, but there didn't seem to be anything more to say. Millie had rejected him. It wasn't disappointment he felt, it was disbelief. He had never asked a woman to marry him before now, paying her his highest possible compliment. And Millie had told him to stuff it. And they were talking about love, true love, not just carrying on some half-assed romance.

The drive home was quiet until Millie finally broke the ice. "I'm sorry I ruined your dinner, Cam, but you have to understand my point of view."

Understanding was not required and maybe not even possible, but he would try for acceptance.

"I do love you, and cannot even imagine life without you anymore," she said.

Sounded like a "but" was coming next.

"But everything's happened so fast, and we're going through major changes practically daily. And there are many more to come. You've never met my father, and our religious upbringings are totally different."

"Our lives will constantly be subject to changes," Cam said. "I've never experienced a time when everything was predictable and secure. Maybe not even anything."

"Honey, I'm sure you're right, but that's at least partially why you're on Elavil now. Everybody has their limit when it comes to handling change, including me."

*****

Cam took Millie at her word and put marriage on the back burner. Ed Armstrong located a suitable location in Seabrook with Dave Columbo's help, and Dave incorporated their enterprise as the Milleron Company with Ed as President. With unquestioning loyalty, Ed agreed to front the organization without even knowing what projects would be undertaken. For less than two thousand dollars of Millie's money, they achieved legitimacy.

Millie's technicians had trained six rats to traverse the maze, four females and two males. They mated with regularity, but none of their offspring had yet showed any indication of prior intelligence. Millie constantly reworked chemical compositions, slowly replacing her starting spinal elements with those present in the brain. She hypothesized the brain wave/nerve pulse interface required elements from both sides, much like a computer modem. Her problem was discovering the correct balance as the medium for exchange.

Neuron transmission studies across synapse gaps showed electro-neurological activity could be increased by drugs like cocaine, but transmitters were damaged as patients became over-sensitized. Memory access was not enhanced, leading Millie to conclude molecular restructuring was required. None of her information indicated how brain tissue stored data, but assuming all storage was based on patterns, retrieval meant constructing a key for location and extraction through a network of analogous patterns. She decided genes carried blueprints of those patterns at the lowest possible level and were altered throughout life by some undiscovered mechanism. Even with the correct carrier balance, she needed a key that could access the pre-existing patterns.

The first fifty tests had concentrated on altering molecular structures of the synapse cell interface, attempting to replicate brain structures—like trying to make a nerve key fit a brain cell lock. But the lock structures were irregular and apparently a function of information stored within. Millie concluded any particular fixed key would be inadequate. Instead, it needed adaptive abilities to conform to the lock dynamically.

Explicit enumeration was indicated with so many interrelated variables, and her major concern was how many test renditions would be necessary to discover feasible compounds. Millie was reminded of the thousands of tests conducted by Erlich to combat syphilis after he isolated the spirochete. She hoped for better luck.

"Maybe both parent rats need to possess the information to strengthen hereditary knowledge," suggested Cam.

"I don't see how it would make any difference," Millie said. "Adoption of physical traits follows genetic rules, and instinct is inherited in animals even if it's present in only a single parent. Besides, plant hybrids also exhibit characteristics readily identifiable as to origin. We can try it, but I have other ideas that might be more fruitful."

Millie had studied research reports concerning squirrels in California. Certain types of ground squirrels possessed a natural immunity of rattlesnake venom, and having knowledge of that immunity, they showed little fear of timber rattlesnakes. When bred with non-immune ground squirrels from Oregon, they produced non-immune squirrels without fear of rattlesnakes. The offspring retained instinct from one parent, but received physical characteristics from the other. Nature doomed such an unfortunate combination.

Millie hypothesized fearlessness was based on believing the snake's bite was harmless, whereas fear shown by Oregon squirrels was based on a lack of knowledge. When parent Oregon squirrels were placed in contact with timber rattlesnakes, they avoided the snakes and the possibility of being bitten. Since there was no prior knowledge concerning the snakes, it could be assumed there was no knowledge of an immunity or lack thereof.

"In fact," Millie said, "I think the squirrel research indicates knowledge is discrete and additive. Since hearing information multiple times does not cause its storage in multiple locations, compounding of knowledge is not necessary. Quite the contrary, a greater diversity in information from parents probably causes a greater amount to be stored in offspring."

"How is knowledge passed from brain to gene? It seems improbable such tiny items like genes can carry information requiring so much brain space."

"We're not sure how information is actually stored, and most brain matter is engaged in storing and retrieving stored data. The problem is not storage—that may well be atomic—but in building and maintaining access paths. So genes can easily carry extremely large amounts of data, but no access structures. It's access we're attempting to rebuild and maintain. It may well be that nobody forgets anything—we just lose the ability to find it."

"But how can genes be updated? By what mechanism?"

"Normal brain activity. It sends stimuli to all parts, why not our reproductive cells? They're capable of alteration. Look at what some drugs do in producing birth deformities."

"What about Mendel's laws?" Cam returned to genetic heredity. "With respect to physical traits, the selection of genes from our parents to pass on to our children is essentially random. We could have none to half of our genes from any grandparent."

"Your knowledge of genetics is correct," smiled Millie. "That's true for non-additive physical characteristics, where only single traits can be selected. But our biggest political problem is the revisionism in progress by liberals to show race and heredity are meaningless. Genes affecting characteristics normally associated with race comprise about one percent of the total number. So they say race is unimportant."

"But that's politics, not science," contended Cam.

"So what? There's less than a two percent difference between DNA of chimpanzees and humans. Is that unimportant?"

Cam was amused by Millie's caustic tone. "Has there been work on genetic racial patterns of behavior? What about the twins research?"

"It's a long story," Millie replied. "Research has proven that one-cell or identical twins are more alike behaviorally than non-identical twins, but those conclusions are politically incorrect. And we'll be challenging racial equality. I'll be called a racist or worse, a Nazi, or white supremacist," Millie continued while Cam was cowed into silence. "Are Jews more intelligent on the average than other Europeans? Sure. Intelligence is our true heredity from many centuries of persecution and survival of the fittest, not the Jewish faith."

Cam tightened his jaw. "So we'll be branded as Nazis."

"Most likely," Millie said. "Funny, isn't it? Me, a Nazi. Particularly working in the United States. It's the worst of all possible places for this research. If we're right, our work can't survive."

Chapter 9

On the fourth of May, Millie checked the previous day's test results in the laboratory book. Lambda-Rho had negotiated the maze in a little over two minutes, but did not ring the bell. It was the first hint of a breakthrough. She called in Jane Murphy, the only one of her technicians present. "Did you see Ron run this experiment?" she asked Jane.

"No, he did that yesterday evening." Jane studied the book. "Eighty seconds is a long time, the rat might have solved it by accident," she suggested.

"I agree. Do we have another ready to go?" Millie asked.

"Sure, three more. I can run them this afternoon if you want."

Millie could tell Jane was unconvinced the test signified anything meaningful. "Let's do it," Millie ordered firmly, "And I want to observe."

By three in the afternoon, Jane was ready. Ron Crips, the other technician, had arrived, and all three stood around the maze to watch. Millie held her breath while Jane positioned the first rat.

The small white rodent sniffed the air and corners then crossed the line. In fifty-two seconds, it reached the other end. But, like the previous test, did not ring the bell. The next two rats also navigated the maze, in seventy-four and sixty-three seconds, respectively. Millie could hardly conceal her excitement. She asked for another eight tests with the same compound.

They showed similar results over the following two days, and on Saturday she drove Cam to NIH to help her compose new experiments. He had no sooner seated himself at a laboratory bench when she produced her book.

"What do you think of these results?" she said, pointing to the last page.

Cam studied the tests, suddenly dropping his jaw. "My God, you've done it!" He exclaimed, jumping up and hugging her. "You've done it!"

"Well, almost," Millie laughed. "But they aren't ringing the bell."

"Bell, schmell, a small point." Cam dropped back onto the stool. "It can only be a minor adjustment from here. Just keep going in the same direction."

"Maybe," Millie cautioned. "It's possible. I think increasing nitrogen might have finally triggered the barrier breakthrough. But we have to see if the effect is permanent or only temporary."

The non-permanent aspect was something Cam had not considered. Millie was being properly conservative in her elation. Still, she had waited to share the discovery with him, so she must have thought they were in the final stretch.

"What's next?" Cam asked.

"Well, let's raise the carrier's nitrogen, and continue until they ring the bell every time. If we get lucky, we might even overshoot so we can establish a range. Then we'll test bell-ringers once a week to see if they retain their knowledge. After that, we can train adults in multiple tricks, testing offspring sparingly to see if knowledge is retrievable as they grow older."

"Then we go into phase two," Cam said.

"Meaning?"

"We need to move toward humans. First, maybe chimps and that's going to take money. I think we'll need to find an angel or license a large institute. You can quit NIH after the baby is born, and then when you're ready, we can finish the project to produce a human-compatible compound."

"It shouldn't take that," Millie said. "It's all chemistry, and I've been careful to only use formulations which should be fully acceptable to humans."

"That might shorten testing time and expense, but we won't be able to take chances." Cam wondered where to find monkeys. "Anyway, we can't do anything this year. The baby's due on the first of October, and we won't get started until after that. Columbo can find a backer; he has a terrific number of contacts."

"How do you plan to introduce it to the general population?" Millie asked.

"I'm not sure, at least in the immediate future. Fortunately, we've got time."

*****

Ten days later, Cam arrived at Millie's apartment to find her in an absolute blue funk. It was so stunning and unlike Millie who had radiated happiness with her pregnancy and been walking on clouds since Lambda-Rho negotiated the maze.

"Cameron, we have to talk," she stated, almost unfriendly.

"Has NIH found out about our project?" Cam asked. For the last week they had become increasing nervous about premature exposure. He felt like Eisenhower before D-Day, fearing discovery by the enemy.

"No, it has nothing to do with NIH," she replied. "It's me."

Cam felt his stomach collapse like a punctured balloon. He gazed at her intensely while she walked back and forth.

"I have cancer."

Cameron sat down as if a cannon ball had taken his legs off at the knees. "What?"

Millie repeated herself. "I have cancer, and will be going into the hospital tomorrow. The operation is scheduled for Wednesday morning."

Cam was speechless. He pressed her head to his chest, but her response was wooden. "It'll be all right, honey," he whispered.

"No, it won't," she said in a low monotone.

She pushed away and stood up. She waved her hand to silence Cam and cut off any conversation, and walked into the kitchen. Avoiding Cam's gaze, she began watering her jades. "It's all happened so fast. I had a checkup yesterday and Dr. Epstein found a lump on my left breast. Then a biopsy, and he called this afternoon to tell me it's malignant." The tears began to flow.

Cam wrapped her in his arms and took the plastic watering can. "Honey, really, it'll be all right. We'll get through this. I love you."

"They're going to take my breast!" she cried. "What's going to happen to my baby?" Millie began sobbing uncontrollably.

Cam steered her back to the davenport and lowered her to the checkered cushion. He held her head against his cheek, and whispered, "The baby will be all right, and nothing's going to happen that will affect my love for you."

He wished he knew it was true.

*****

Millie hated hospitals and doctors. Putting herself at the mercy of someone who acted as though he was God's plenipotentiary on Earth was frightening. She had known too many medical doctors in school, even dated a few. They were mere mortals, usually working fast to increase their income and bury their mistakes. She trusted herself and Cam, but they were having to rely on another person now, one not being paid for the successful completion of his work, but only for his time and effort.

Dear, sweet Cam, she mused. She listened to him attempting to raise her morale while they drove to the hospital. *What will you do if I don't make it? Will you relapse into depression and expire?* Millie reached around the Porsche's gear shift and took his hand. "Cam, I'll never leave you, I promise."

*****

Cam held Millie tightly as they waited at the hospital. Her eyes were fixed on him, loving and steady. She was so strong. And pure class. She sometimes made him feel like Mellors making love to Connie Chatterley. What had he done to deserve her? The immortal woman, the goddesses Athena, Aphrodite, and Artemis all rolled into one. God, he loved her. And then she was taken into surgery.

Dr. Sidney Epstein was not smiling when he came out to talk to Cam two hours later. Cam was pacing in the waiting room, going from the corner potted plant to the magazine rack. He stopped and analyzed Epstein's mood as he approached.

"She's in recovery," Epstein said without offering his hand or making any gesture of sympathy. "The operation went well. I've never performed a mastectomy when the woman was pregnant, and had to restrict medication because of the baby. Saving it has increased your wife's risk."

Cam was reminded of the definition of efficiency. The operation was a success but the patient died. He wondered if Epstein liked people as anything other than defective mechanisms requiring his repair services and from whom he could extort excessive sums.

"How's the baby? The operation didn't have any effect on the baby, did it?"

"No," the doctor answered. "There shouldn't be any adverse effect on the fetus."

"So what's your prognosis?" Cam asked.

"We don't know," Epstein said. "Look, you have an important decision coming. Her cancer had already spread and her only hope is chemotherapy. And possibly only if treatments began immediately. Chemo would kill the fetus, however; so the baby has to be taken before we can begin treatment.

Cam stared hard at the doctor. He decided to assume the worst and try it on Epstein for size. "How long does she have? Can we take the baby in time?"

Epstein was visibly stunned, but managed to control his response. "I'm not a gynecologist. I can't advise you about the baby."

Cam knew then. "Thank you, doctor. How long does she have?"

"It's difficult to say—"

"I know it's hard to say," Cam interrupted. "But what's your opinion? As a professional, as a physician, as a man of medicine, what's your opinion?"

Epstein was wilting under Cam's steady assault. Finally he threw up his hands. "A year at the outside—more likely six months. Maybe less."

"When can I see her?" Cam was grim. He felt like punching Epstein.

"It'll be several hours. I'll have the recovery nurse notify you when she's awake. If you don't have anything else, I need to be getting back."

"Yes, of course." Cam waved Epstein away. He needed time to think.

Asshole. Cam knew the doctor would have strung him along deciding what was appropriate for Millie and himself to hear. Any occupation that demanded respect didn't deserve it. Millie hated doctors for their phony divinity and omniscience. She had been right again. She was always right.

The waiting room wasn't even a room—it was a lobby constantly in motion with worried people requiring treatment. It was a cove with a beach of dirty sand where mankind was washed in and out as the ebb and flow of some great tide of humanity. The dolphins were cleaning the sea, pushing flotsam into the cove. Cam himself was wreckage on the beach. He glanced at the magazines spread over a circular table for those who could read English. They were tripe, heavy on pictures, and none of them written at over an eighth-grade level.

Cam was reminded of the knowledge curve for humans. A person's knowledge increased throughout his formal, force-fed education, then rapidly fell off afterward to stabilize at the level of a thirteen year-old. Even for PhDs, the decline set in and fell eventually. So all advertising and writing was targeted at an eighth or at most ninth-grade level. It was a miserable commentary on education and American society.

"Mr. Lauenberg?" a nurse addressed him.

Cam took the avenue of least resistance. "Yes, is it all right to see Millie now?"

"Yes, please follow me." The bleached blonde with month-old dark roots led the way down a corridor.

Cam noticed all nurses seemed blocky, but partly because of their unflattering uniforms. He wondered why doctors picked on nurses, deciding familiarity bred attempt.

The recovery room was unlabeled, but the nurse waved him through a partially open door into a large darkened room with six narrow beds. Millie lay in the nearest with her eyes closed. She opened them as Cam approached and raised her hand for him to take. She smiled weakly.

"Hi, honey," Cam said softly. "How are you feeling?"

Millie nodded. She was heavily sedated. "Awful," she breathed drowsily.

Cam smiled. His Millie always spoke the truth. "I love you, honey," he offered in consolation.

"Thanks." She squeezed his hand almost imperceptibly.

"The doctor said you'll be all right," Cam fibbed hopefully, "and the baby's fine."

Millie winced as in pain. "Doctors lie. But thanks. Is the baby really all right?"

"Yes, hon, really. I'd say if you had lost it."

"Sorry," Millie said slowly. "I know you would. It's hard to breathe."

"Just rest easy, honey, and keep reminding yourself that I love you." Cam was on the brink of tears. His throat had tightened and his eyes were misting over. He kissed Millie's hand.

The nurse was watching. "She needs a lot of rest, sir. It would be best if you left her now."

Cam could see for himself Millie was fading in and out. He replaced her hand along her side. "Honey, go back to sleep," he said softly. "I'll be back."

"Promise?" she whispered.

"Hey, I'm here for you, kid—as long as you want me. I'll be outside."

*****

Epstein's prediction was weighing heavily on Cam, and he walked down the second floor hallway on Saturday deciding how to broach the subject with Millie. He was in luck. The lady normally in the other bed was gone and Millie was alone. Cam kissed her and showed her the Charlie Brown hand puppet he brought to cheer her up. It worked better on him than on Millie. Hospital rooms possessed all the charm of a gas chamber at San Quentin, particularly Millie's, which afforded a depressing view of the cafeteria roof.

The conversation quickly lagged after the puppet failed to make an impact on Millie's morale. "Honey, what's bothering you?" Millie said. "You're acting like you have a turtle in your mouth that wants out. You know a turtle can only make progress when he sticks his head out."

Cam bit the bullet. "What did Epstein tell you about the operation and your cancer?" he asked, trying not to show concern.

"He told me they probably didn't get it all." Millie looked away, then focused intently on Cam. "Normally, I would undergo chemotherapy, but that's not possible if I want to have this baby. Did they tell you it's a little girl?"

"How do you know that?"

"They took some fluid from the baby and they could tell. Also that she's healthy."

"That's terrific." Cam's spirits had risen immeasurably. Then he thought about what they were discussing and became quiet again. "So what happens without chemotherapy?"

Millie looked at Cam evenly. "If they're right, it's just a question of time. It depends on when I have the baby. If the chemo starts soon enough, I have a chance. If not, then I don't." Millie paused as Cam became fidgety. "But even if I started chemo now, it would be still just a chance. Chemo isn't a sure cure—it's only a chance."

This wasn't what Epstein had told Cam. He wondered if Millie really understood the situation. She might be trying to soften the blow for him or maybe she truly thought there was a chance. "Then do you want to wait?"

Millie looked down at her hands and took a deep breath. "There's no decision. I want to have this baby." Millie started to cry. There was nothing further to say.

*****

The first week back home Millie spent only a few hours each day in her lab. Work which she formerly performed at NIH, was now accomplished together with Cam at home in the evenings. But their project seemed stalled while Millie raised the nitrogen content.

On the second of June, Millie's gynecologist pronounced himself satisfied with her progress. The baby was growing normally, and Millie called Cam at school with the good news.

"Doctor Garber said the baby's fine and I'm holding together," Millie announced. Cam was pleased, but given his experience with doctors and their information, he needed confirmation. He telephoned the doctor's office himself. Garber was as optimistic about the baby as Millie had said.

Although it was a race between Millie giving birth and Millie dying, her gynecologist thought the baby's chances for survival were good even if the race was lost. He recommended Millie complete her will, and for Cam to legally acknowledge paternity to cover the exigency of Millie's early demise. Such things were easy to recommend or discuss abstractly, thought Cam, but for them to actually take action meant facing the inevitability of Millie's death. Cam wasn't prepared to give up hope, even though Millie's pain was increasing.

That night, Cam approached the subject from his point of view. "Honey, it's time for us to get married and tie up all the loose ends," he said as he began to mix a salad.

Millie put her milk on the counter, turned away, and walked into the living room. Still silent, she sat back on the couch and kicked off her low pumps pushing each shoe down off the heel. She crossed her feet on the glass coffee table and looked up at Cam who had followed her in. "I don't want pity or charity. I'm not a loose end," she said.

"How about love?" Cam quickly answered, realizing his mistake.

"Look, you know it's a girl. You'll need all your love for her."

Millie waved Cameron to silence as he opened his mouth to speak. "You know, Cam," she said. "Life is like going to the movies. We're there for a short time regardless of our enjoyment of the film, but we must leave when it ends to make room for those waiting for the next show. It's almost time for me to leave the auditorium and make room for those who follow."

She softened her voice. "But life with you has been wonderful. You've caused me to know love, beauty, and purpose like never before. In return, I've given you all of me, and now leave you my love in the form of little Sophia. I can't do better than that."

Millie paused, looked down, took a deep breath and continued in a tone of exasperation. "I won't marry you precisely because I love you. I don't want to take a part of you with me."

Millie raised her head and looked directly at Cam. "Like the leopard on Kilimanjaro, I will have left my bones as close to the top of the mountain as possible," she said as if she were addressing a college class. "Nothing will go with me, the world will continue, the sun will rise in the morning, couples will make love and have children, and you and Sophia will have a wonderful life together. Sophia is yours, and all I ask is that you remember me when you look at her."

The pathos was so obvious that Cam felt his anger rising. "I don't see where any of that has anything to do with marriage. There's no reason for us not to be married when Sophia comes into the world. It eliminates future questions, and makes things a lot easier."

Millie struggled to her feet. "Yes, a lot easier for you," she said. "You want me to wear white, go through some pagan ceremony, smiling and happy like an airhead, just to make your life easier." She was shouting now. "You're not carrying this baby! You're not wondering if you're going to die before you see your baby!"

Cam stood and tried to reach out.

"Don't touch me!" she yelled. "No church would marry us like this. I'm Jewish and you're some type of heretical Gnostic Christian. What do you want us to do? Go to Las Vegas and be married in the Lonely Hearts Chapel? I won't do it!"

"Honey, a civil ceremony would be okay. We could go to a justice of the peace."

"The state is not God!" Millie screamed. "Don't you understand?"

He could see there was no point in pursuing the subject. Millie was sobbing uncontrollably with her face in her hands. Cam folded her into his arms.

*****

In spite of recurring pain, Millie worked feverishly to complete the project. It was strange knowing her time was short. Everything took on a terrible sense of urgency, and she found herself becoming extremely abrupt with her technicians who continued to work at a measured pace. She was even quick to anger when Cam was late or she had to perform some time-wasting task herself.

Returning after missing three days in a row, Millie examined test results to see if the rats were improving. The eighth one, Rho Chi, had rung the bell. So had the next entire group, but those thereafter with an additional nitrogen-bound chain had been unable to even traverse the maze. She called Ron Crips who had conducted the successful tests. Within a minute, Ron materialized at her door with his slight, ferret-like body and bad complexion.

"Ron, I'm not sure about these results. I'd like you to rerun PX through TI." Ron had run his trials three days earlier, and the rats had not seen the maze since. Millie would see if knowledge was being retained. She was glad of the pain and her condition, otherwise she would not be able to conceal her excitement.

One by one, the rats were placed in the maze with Millie looking over Ron's shoulder. They all negotiated the maze promptly and rang the bell. He asked Millie if she wanted him to put the reruns in the book.

"No, that won't be necessary. I just hadn't expected this group to figure out the maze. I shouldn't have questioned your results."

"Oh, that's all right. I'm just glad to see you're feeling better."

Millie ignored his comment. In a few seconds she was back in her office attempting to retain her composure. The ecstasy was overwhelming. This was it. Knowledge could now be passed to succeeding generations directly and accumulated infinitely. No more learning to read and write in each generation. Education was changed for all time.

She quickly copied the results into her private journal and made appropriate annotations for the successful compound, K11. Suddenly, her office seemed strangely alien. Her journal was the life and purpose of the room, and when it left with her, the room was nothing. In a few months, someone else would inhabit her space. In a short time, people would struggle to remember how she appeared and what she had accomplished.

It was difficult to bring herself back under control. There were still two small issues. She wanted to experiment with multiple items of knowledge, and she needed to use the successful specimens to breed another generation to test their retention. Millie wrote out instructions for Ron, Xeroxed her results, and left before she passed out.

*****

God, Millie was wonderful, Cam thought. She had given him everything; life, love, a coming baby, and probably the most important scientific breakthrough in the history of mankind. What more could he ask of her? His heart answered—a long life with him.

Reality had intervened. She was becoming progressively weaker physically, and he would not have her for long. It was inconceivable a just God could take her. Not now. She should see the fruits of her labor. Or was she to be the modern Moses who would only be allowed to see the promised land without crossing over. Whatever, it was all in God's hands.

Chapter 10

Cam was beating Stephens at handball over lunchtime when Doctor Garber phoned. Millie was in Providence Hospital, and Garber thought he would have to take her baby. Winning at handball was suddenly meaningless, and Cam ignored all speed limits getting to the hospital. Millie was already in a semi-private room, having been taken directly there from the gynecologist's office.

"I don't know why I'm here, honey," Millie said as Cam leaned over to kiss her. "Doctor Garber said I might be having some complications, so he wanted me here as a precaution. I don't feel very well, but no worse than yesterday."

"The doctor's going to take the baby, honey," Cam said. Cam held Millie's hand tightly. "He says your strength is good, and he'd like to relieve you of the pregnancy now."

Millie's face flashed panic. "Is there a problem with the baby? She's all right, isn't she?"

"She's okay. He's just worried about letting you go until the birth would become too difficult. Now's a good time. You're both in good shape, and there shouldn't be any complications if the baby's born now."

The nurse had walked in without interrupting the conversation. "We need to get ready now, ma'am," she said.

Garber had told him Millie only had a fifty percent chance of coming through the operation. Cam decided to withhold that little tidbit to help maintain her morale.

He squeezed Millie's hand and kissed her again. "I'll be right outside. Don't worry. I love you." God, his eyes were filling up. He couldn't let her see him cry. He had to be strong for her.

Millie tried to smile, but it was forced. She waved at Cam as he backed out the door. She felt abandoned, but it wasn't his fault. He did love her, and he had tried to be good to her in his own way. Maybe it was her fault—maybe the cancer was punishment for what she had done. After all, Cam was not Jewish. But how could love be bad? Lord, she hoped her baby was all right.

Her mind was racing a mile a minute while the nurse prepped her for the Caesarean operation. She wanted to cry, but fought it back. In a few minutes she was ready.

*****

The operation went as Doctor Garber had hoped—both mother and baby did as well as could be expected. Millie was extremely weak, but he hadn't been sure she would survive at all. He had taken the precaution to find out she was Jewish, and wondered abstractly why she hadn't married her boyfriend. They seemed to be so in love, but officially her father was her next of kin.

The doctor had used general anesthesia to more easily control any complications, and gave special instructions for the recovery nurse to watch her closely until she regained consciousness. The baby girl was placed in an incubator for constant monitoring. She was smaller than a normal six-month preemie and would have to be closely observed, but he didn't expect any unusual problems. Garber went out to inform the new father.

"Congratulations," he said to Cam, extending his hand. "You have a fine baby girl."

"And her mother?" Cam quickly asked. He stopped his pacing and took the doctor's hand.

"She came through in good shape." He could see the wave of relief pass over Cam's expression. "She hasn't awakened yet, she's still in recovery. It'll be a while, I'm afraid."

"Can I see the baby?"

"Sure, follow me." Garber led Cam through a pair of swinging doors down the hallway to a large window. He pointed to one of the glass enclosures in the room beyond. "Your baby's in that incubator to the right."

Cam peered in. The room was cluttered with equipment being maintained by two nurses. "She looks awful small," he said.

"Yes, quite small. She hadn't developed as rapidly as normal because of your wife's complications." He hadn't meant to say wife, but it had slipped out as a natural word.

"But you don't expect any problems because of her size, do you?"

"No. We'll have to keep her in an incubator for a couple of weeks, but I think I can safely say she'll be all right. A baby her size is no longer a major problem."

An hour later, Garber was called to the recovery room. Millie was conscious and asking to see Cam. He decided to allow them a few minutes to visit.

Millie turned to smile faintly at Cameron as he entered. She lifted her left hand to touch him, but he grasped it with both of his and kissed her fingers gently.

"How are you feeling?" He whispered.

"All right," Millie answered. "Have you seen our baby?"

"Yes, it's in an incubator. It's so tiny, I couldn't tell much."

"She's not an it, honey. Her name's Sophia, mother of the earth, goddess of wisdom, and the wisdom of God." Millie's eyes fell to her mid-section and flashed back to Cam. "Cam, you have to promise me something."

"Anything, whatever you want."

"It's not so simple—and you have to know it's right."

"What? You know I'd do anything for you." Cam felt accused of a lack of commitment.

"Promise?"

"Yes, absolutely." Cam was almost angry.

Millie gazed searchingly into Cam's eyes. "I want you to inject Sophie with the compound."

Cam felt the shock wave of surprise hit him like a mortar round on the road twenty yards ahead. Even his hair seemed to blow backward. "Aw, no way," Cam said decisively. "We've only tested it on rats—who knows how it will work on humans?"

"But you promised. I don't have long to live, and I want Sophia to know what I know."

"Why do you think it will work on humans? You haven't tested any."

"My carrier fluids were derived from human extractions. I did that on purpose to reduce the risk. There's nothing in my formulation that should cause a problem. Even the strength and volume I've calculated relative to brain size. It's all in my notes." The explanation had exhausted her, and she looked up at the ceiling and closed her eyes.

Cam was still thunderstruck at Millie's request, and stared at her in disbelief. "She's our only child. We can't risk her life on an experiment. You can't want that."

Millie turned away. "I'm tired," she said rolling her head. "We'll talk about it later."

Cam kissed her hand and carefully placed it across her chest. "Okay, I'll be back in a little bit." He kissed Millie's forehead, but she didn't open her eyes.

The subject of injecting Sophia did not come up again during the remaining times Cam visited Millie in the hospital. Sophia seemed to be responding well and getting bigger and healthier every day after her short danger period. Her liver was poorly developed, but Doctor Garber was no longer concerned. Even Millie's spirits recovered rapidly.

Taking Millie home, however, Cam wondered if she should not have remained in the hospital. Her C-section incision would probably never heal, and she was barely ambulatory. Millie had campaigned so strongly to return home that neither the doctor nor Cam had been able to resist her, but her spirit was much stronger than her body.

The day after arriving home, Millie coerced Cam into driving her to NIH to see what progress had occurred in her absence. Anything to keep her occupied, and Millie brightened considerably when she saw Trish Browning in the hallway. Leaving Cam in Trish's office, Millie quickly visited her laboratory and co-workers. She put together a box of personal possessions, and gathered other items she would need.

Trish needed to know when Millie would be returning, and was surprised at her candor in discussing her status.

"I probably won't be returning except to assist you and others to assume my projects," Millie stated when she returned. "The doctor has given me only months, and my condition is irreversible. You need to plan for my projects to be re-assigned as soon as possible."

"I'm terribly sorry," whispered Trish. "Is there anything you need from me—anything I can do?"

"No, Cameron and I can do everything. You have a list of my projects. Why don't you review them and give me a call to discuss an orderly transition?"

Millie couldn't wait to leave and cut the niceties short. Trish attempted to continue with small talk, but Millie was in a hurry. She maneuvered Cam out the door, and waved other co-workers off. A minute later, they were on their way to Providence.

"What's going to happen with your project?" Cam asked at the first stop light.

"You can work that out later with Trish," Millie lied. "She's vaguely aware of what we were doing and can take over."

Cameron glanced at her in disbelief but let it go. "Okay, later." The trip to the hospital was not shortened by Millie's silence.

No longer in an incubator, Sophia was laying under a lamp on her stomach with her rear end pointing up. Cam would have made a joke about her position, but life had become altogether too serious. Both of them scrubbed up to handle Sophia and the attending nurse took them into a side room where they could feed the baby. Cam noted the instinctive reactions that caused Sophia to suck on the small bottle of formula and allowed life to continue. But she fell asleep readily, and Millie kept having to wake her up to keep going.

"Cam, would you please go and see if Doctor Garber's in the hospital?" Millie said as Sophia fell asleep again. "I'd like to talk with him."

"Are you feeling all right?" Cam was suddenly concerned.

"Oh, yeah. I'd just like to ask him when we can take Sophia home."

Cam patted Millie's shoulder and said he'd be back shortly.

It was over in a minute, and Sophia was back on the bottle. When Cam returned with Dr. Garber she looked supremely happy. Sherwood Anderson's egg had not triumphed.

*****

The ringing telephone jolted Cameron out of his half-sleep. He panicked immediately. He shouldn't have left Millie's apartment, he thought, something was wrong. The clock radio alongside his phone showed seven-thirty. Only a five-hour night.

"Hello", he answered more like "Yell-l-lo." Cam could be extremely articulate while essentially asleep and later remember nothing of the conversation.

"Cameron Stewart?" asked a high-pitched male voice.

"Yeah, who's this?" Cam breathed, not recognizing the caller.

This is Aaron Lauenberg, Millie's father. I'm in town and would like to meet with you."

My God, he sounded so formal. Cam wondered if Millie's dad was like Harum Al-Rashid—Aaron the Orthodox. He didn't feel particularly friendly toward her dad, but Millie was dying, and he could hardly refuse to see him.

"Sure, I'd be glad to. Where are you?"

"I'm at Washington National. Can you pick me up?"

Jesus, he wakes me up and wants me to immediately drive across town in rush hour traffic to cart his body around at his convenience, Cam thought, dropping his head on his chest. He shook it from side to side. No warning, no calling ahead; just, "Here I am; do what I want."

"It would take me over an hour to get there. If you haven't had breakfast yet, why don't you take a bus to the Sheraton, and I'll meet you in the restaurant in about forty-five minutes?" It seemed like a reasonable compromise.

Forty minutes later Cam was shaking hands with Aaron Lauenberg.

"I'm glad to make your acquaintance," Aaron said formally.

Cam wondered how true that statement was, but nothing was to be gained by not taking it at face value. He had expected someone slight and furtive as befitted a New York Jewish merchant, but Aaron was quite the opposite. Almost six feet tall, he was affable and loud, even bland like an accountant.

"Have you already eaten breakfast, or would you like to catch a bite here?" Cam said, although the question required a compound answer. His mind was not yet functioning. Fortunately, the hostess approached and asked them if they wished to be seated.

They were seated in a booth, and decided coffee would be sufficient. Cam took the lead. "I'm sorry to meet you under these circumstances, but I'm happy you came down. Millie needs all the support she can get."

"I understand, and that's why I wanted to talk to you before I see Millie." Aaron paused as if considering what to say. "Millie and I have never been close," he said. "After her mother died, I didn't know how to raise a daughter. Jewish men in the Ukraine weren't taught to raise girls. We were busy providing for our family as a unit, and women raised the children. Right or wrong, I hired a woman to take care of my house and look after Millie."

"Believe me, nobody's criticizing you. Least of all Millie or me."

"Thank you, but I'm sure she would say today that I should have taken another wife to be a proper mother to her."

Cam doubted it. Millie would have preferred more fatherly love and attention.

Aaron set down his fork. "I gave her everything she wanted, and the best education money could buy. But she was never happy. She never seemed to become excited about anything she accomplished. That is, until she met you. From her letters, our telephone conversations, and her visit last December, she's become a different girl. I have you to thank for that, I'm sure."

"Well, thanks, but Millie deserves the credit. I was just there," Cam said politely.

"So I feel she is more yours than mine now." Aaron eyed Cam evenly. "I hoped and expected to give her my blessing in marriage, however."

"Talk to Millie about that. I've been asking her to marry me for a year," Cam said.

Aaron stirred his coffee and folded his hands. "I talked to Doctor Epstein. He stated Millie's cancer is terminal and she doesn't have much time."

"Yes, we're living under a sentence of death, I'm afraid."

"He also said she could have undergone chemotherapy immediately and probably would have recovered. She chose not to?"

So Epstein had thrown the blame on Millie. Cam couldn't believe it, that asshole was denying any responsibility. And no one was accusing him. "That's not true," Cam said. "Chemo was a maybe. There was only a small chance—maybe none—of her recovering under chemo. And it would have killed the baby."

"So she sacrificed her life for that of the baby's."

84

Cam tried to calm down. That wasn't how they had seen her options at the time. "I don't think either of us thought she was doing that," he said.

"You understand I have nothing against you for not being Jewish," commented Aaron.

Cameron felt like a sand truck had dumped on him. Obviously, that statement was untrue.

"So what are your plans for the baby?" Aaron said.

"What do you mean? I intend to make a loving, caring home for her."

"Any child born of a Jewish mother is Jewish, you understand," Aaron asserted.

"Sophia's heritage is beyond dispute, but her choice of religion will be exactly that—her choice," Cam stated. He was not asking for opinions or suggestions.

Aaron called for the check. "Why don't we visit Millie now?"

Cam agreed, but knew their conversation had not ended. He had no idea how Millie would react to her father, but he could hardly suggest not visiting.

The morning traffic was choking the nation's capital as usual, lengthening bureaucratic non-productive time by another thirty minutes. Traveling outward was easier, and twenty minutes later, Cam pulled up at Millie's apartment.

Millie came to the door in her robe. "Father, I didn't expect you," she said. She hugged him reservedly and turned to Cam with a kiss.

"I thought it was time to visit my only daughter who has also become a mother," he said.

Millie gave Cam an extra squeeze as if giving a signal to form a secret conspiracy. She offered to make coffee, but when her dad declined, sat on her couch and carefully folded over her robe. Both Millie and Cameron turned to Aaron as if the ball was in his court.

Aaron was in no hurry. He complimented Millie on her apartment and asked about Sophia and the birth. Finally he came to the point. "What last name was given to the baby?"

Millie answered. "Maryland assigns the mother's maiden name when she's unmarried, so right now it's Lauenberg. But Cam was named as father, so he will be petitioning for a change."

"And you will not be opposing that petition, I assume?"

"No, of course not. Cameron will be raising Sophia and she should carry his name."

"What if I secure her future financially?" Aaron said.

Cameron's face flushed. This guy was trying to buy Sophia.

"After all," Aaron added, "I will only ever have one granddaughter while Cameron here can have more children if he wishes. Besides, the baby should be brought up in the Jewish faith."

Cameron looked at Millie whose mouth had fallen open as she stared at her dad.

After a tiny pause, Aaron resumed, "I'm prepared to commit a sum sufficient for her to complete whatever education she desires, and of course, suitable compensation for you, Cameron."

Cameron bounded up, but Millie was equally quick. He dimly wondered what reserve of strength she tapped to move so fast.

"Father!" Millie screamed.

"What the hell!" Cam roared. "Where do you get off coming in here and offering to buy my baby? Who in hell do you think you are?"

Aaron stood up and took a step back. He remained calm and replied to Cam's statement as if it were a legitimate question. "I'm the baby's grandfather, and I have rights. Particularly since you have not seen fit to marry my daughter."

"That's it, Father!" Millie shrieked. "Get out of my house!"

"Now calm down and consider what would be best for the little girl," Aaron said.

"Out now, or I'll throw you out!" Cam shouted evenly. He pushed Millie aside and took a step toward Millie's dad.

Aaron sized up Cam dispassionately. He moved toward the door. "I'm sorry to have upset you both in this, but upon reflection, I believe you will eventually see my offer to be the superior solution." He turned toward Cam. "My boy, you'll have to meet me later in court without Millie where my money will be the difference," he said.

Before Cam could reach him, Aaron backed out the door. Millie and Cam stood looking at each other in amazement. Then they were in each other's arms, and Millie was sobbing.

"Oh, I'm so sorry," Millie cried.

Cam softly patted Millie on the back. "That's all right, it's not your fault. We'll handle it."

Again she was being punished, Millie concluded. The God of the Jews was a terrible, vengeful god. Her life was one step forward and two steps back. Now her father was threatening to take away her baby, and only Cam could love and understand her little Sophia. What had she done that was so horrible? Go to bed with a gentile? Love a goy? Cam and his Gnostics were right, the Jewish God was the demiurge, Satan, creator of the earth.

The pain had returned, and she led Cam to her bedroom. Mankind had free will, and all happenings on earth were determined either by Satan or man himself. She had challenged Satan with K11, defeated him, and he destroyed her body in revenge. But she had left little Sophia to carry on. And Sophia was her—she had fulfilled her promise to Cam. She would never leave him.

Millie lay watching Cam breathe slowly. Christianity might have the right idea, if it could rid itself of its pagan trappings. In spite of her Jewish upbringing, she felt Christianity evinced much wisdom. But Christians should let Christ become only the Logos, providing the word or direction to salvation. Jesus was an Essene mystic, probably named Joshua.

She was tired. Sophia would have to struggle against mythology and ignorance. Cam would be there, and it would work out. Besides, Millie was ready. She had fulfilled her destiny in fine style. She regretted only preceding Cam in death, but at least she would be able to prepare the way for him. She had been with him only two years, but watching him there beside her, what a two years they had been. It would have been sheer greed to have wanted more.

Millie awakened with fire throughout her abdomen. She struggled with Cam attempting to sit up, but doubled over in pain instead. Sid Epstein's answering service promised an early response, and she curled in Cam's arms awaiting his instructions. The doctor telephoned almost thirty minutes later. Epstein prescribed pain killers and scheduled her for hospital admission and additional tests the next morning. Within an hour after Cam returned, the drugs had reduced her pain to discomfort, but Millie felt continually nauseated and unable to eat. Cameron was sure the confrontation with her father had triggered the attack.

"Honey, I don't think there's much time left," Millie said quietly, while she watched Cam eat a bowl of chicken soup for supper. "I feel different inside—like everything's collapsing."

87

She raised her head and gazed into his eyes. She had done well, Millie decided, picking him in the nick of time. Where would she be without him? Still dying, but alone and unloved.

Millie returned to the hospital. Her pain was still under control, but the drugs kept her constantly nauseous. By four in the afternoon, they knew. The cancer had literally exploded from her liver and spread throughout her body. It was now a matter of days. Millie smiled weakly at Cam as he entered her room.

Cam couldn't talk, his throat was a lump and his eyes were blurry. Epstein had said Millie wouldn't be leaving the hospital. All he could do was make her as comfortable as possible. It was incredible; the best really do die young.

He kissed her, and recoiled in anguish. He had dropped a tear on her face. He reached to brush it away but she stopped him.

"No, leave it. It's a love tear and I want it," she whispered.

Cam couldn't keep them back; they streamed down his face and began to soak the linen. Millie reached up and turned his head so he could look at her. "I want you to always remember me like I was the night before my operation."

Cam was too choked to talk. He nodded again.

Millie was disappearing before Cam's very eyes, becoming progressively thinner and no longer could leave her bed. Something was sucking the life out of her, leaving a shell like a tarantula eats a cricket. She left him a little more each day.

Saturday morning Millie thrust a letter into Cam's hands.

"That's for you, honey, after I'm no longer here. Don't open it until then." Millie was scarcely audible.

Cam tried to answer, but Millie had used up her energy and faded off again.

Three days later, she was gone. She had not said anything more and had not known he was there. She did not hear him say goodbye.

Book 2 - Sophia

1970 - 1986

Chapter 11

Millie died at nine-thirty in the morning, and Cam immediately found himself shunted aside. He wasn't family, and Millie's father would be contacted by hospital authorities for arrangements. His normally cozy apartment appeared cold and heartless, even with an Errol Garner's best album, his *Concert By The Sea* playing "You Can't Take That Away From Me". But they had. Cam followed with Mussorgsky's *Songs And Dances Of Death*. A life had ended and deserved a long period of mourning.

Dave Columbo was not pleased with Millie dying intestate or their lack of legal documents, but would pull whatever strings were necessary. Checking with Providence, Dave discovered they had been unable to locate Millie's father. He had taken a few days off, and his cousin thought Aaron had flown with some bimbo to Las Vegas on vacation. Millie's body would be held at the hospital until her father could be located.

Cam's second home required his attention, and he returned to Millie's apartment. It was terribly lonely. He retrieved his clothes and personal articles, but this was the home of Sophia's mother, and her belongings were properly Sophia's inheritance. There were so many memories. Her bed was still as she'd made it the last day. He could see her head on the pillow, coming out of the bathroom in her robe, making coffee in her birthday suit. On impulse, he opened the kitchen cabinet where she kept her recipes and kitchen papers. He pulled down a large black box, one he hadn't noticed before. It was from NIH and contained a large quantity of K11, her lab books, papers, needles, and other equipment. He took everything.

Columbo telephoned two days later. "It's a piece of cake," Dave said. "The hearing is tomorrow before Judge Samuels, and he'll be no problem. Meet me at Upper Marlboro at nine in the morning. Have you heard from her old man yet?"

"Not yet," Cam replied.

"Then take your phone off the hook. We don't want him arriving tonight." Cam did better and unplugged it.

The following morning legalized Cam's status, and Sophia was his forever. Dave's connections had been more effective than Aaron's money, but for Cam, the issue was never in doubt. Regardless of legalities, he couldn't give up Sophia—Millie's letter spelled out why. He had read it after returning home.

> *"Dearest Cameron,*
>
> *Please don't be angry with me leaving you this way. I have given you the greatest gift a woman can give a man— her love in the person of her daughter. I knew you would never do it, so I injected Sophia with K11 when she came out of the incubator. She will love you as I did. She carries my genes and my knowledge.*
>
> *She is my hope for the future, she takes my place in the march of generations. I trust you will love her perfectly and build upon the foundation we have created. She has only you. Be good to her as you were to me.*
>
> *Goodbye, my sweet. Remember me with joy, not with sadness.*
>
> *All my love,*
> *Millie"*

*****

Cam's living room rapidly became a zoo as his friends welcomed Sophia to her new home. Cam wondered if he had not become superfluous. Heather had already purchased a crib so her condo could function as a second home when Cam was working, and everyone seemed to assume Cam couldn't handle his new charge by himself. Ah, the arrogance of women.

Cathy remained the entire first week, taking the bedroom at Cam's insistence while he slept on the couch. Cam wondered what her boyfriend thought of their relationship. She was invaluable in providing companionship, and always greeted him with coffee in the morning. After getting up during the night for Sophia, it was rewarding to be awakened by a beautiful young girl in a flimsy nightgown.

Teaching was no longer the same without Millie and Cathy. Cam missed Cathy's bright eyes in his office, teasing him and making risqué suggestions about promising females passing through. The room was lifeless, but maybe it was the loss of Millie. She would not be there if he felt like telephoning to hear her voice. When the phone rang, it would not be her. Leaving work, he was nevermore faced with deciding to drive to her apartment or his own. Valentine's Day would not bring a card, her car would no longer surprise him at his apartment, and when he saw a Falcon, it did no good to look.

The Milleron Lab was closed. Dave drew up a contract whereby Webberon purchased all remaining assets, name, patents, trade secrets, and proprietary products and processes owned by Milleron. Cam signed for both companies, and told Dave he was moving something offshore. Dave might have wondered what that something was, but like a good lawyer, never asked.

Meanwhile the year ground to a close, winter clamped its leaden hand on the District, and life moved on. Like a tender shoot from a fallen acorn, Sophia sought food and light, and brought out the best in those who cared.

Bobbi stopped by in December with toys for Sophia and a special gift for Cam. But it couldn't happen. When she emerged from the bathroom wearing nothing, Cam was unable to respond—she reminded him of Millie and her penchant for surprising him. And there was Sophia to consider. He could see her reaction, and even with her limited motor and speech skills, Sophia indicated her displeasure by scowling, waving, and crying. Bobbi bowed to the inevitable in good grace as usual.

With the Vietnam protesters in the streets almost daily, Cam worried about Bobbi. No doubt her apartment was swamped with activists and she would be hard put to remain above poverty while providing food and shelter. While Sophia was at Heather's on Valentine's Day, he picked up five gallons of ice cream at the Maryland Dairy, and drove into Washington.

Bobbi was overjoyed to see him, and laughed at the supply of ice

91

cream. It was chocolate, her favorite flavor, and she hadn't eaten supper. They decided to pig out on ice cream instead.

"I want to apologize for the apartment," Bobbi sighed, as she dished out two bowls. "It's empty now, but when I left this morning, there were four kids camped out in my living room."

It really was a wreck, and not only that, it stunk. "Your boarders seem to have an aversion to cleaning up after themselves."

"Yeah, it's hard to control." She waved at the posters covering her living room windows. They were high, narrow, old-style windows, three together behind her hi-riser sofa, and two others in the end wall. "This is Frank's doing. If it were up to me, I'd kick them all out."

"So why not? It's still your apartment."

Bobbi bit her lip and looked away while she placed their bowls on the kitchen table, then walked toward the living room. She stopped in the kitchen doorway. "Cam, will you marry me?"

He had no idea where that came from. Marriage?

"I don't think either of us really wants to be married to each other at this point in our lives," he said carefully. God, what a mealy-mouthed response. He was transferring a share of the responsibility to her.

"Why don't you want to marry me?" Bobbi took a few steps closer. "Am I not up to your standards? Am I too ugly, too flat-chested, too poor, or what? The last time I was at your place, you weren't even interested."

"It's nothing like that," he said. "You're the sexiest woman I know. But I have to organize my life around my daughter."

"So you're saying you don't need me. You have your daughter."

"Need is the wrong word when you're talking about love. I want your love, but you have to understand, I'm a family unit now."

"You see, that's the difference. Frank needs me. And so do the kids. Without me, they'd be tripping out on acid in the street, destroying their minds, ruining their lives, and getting busted. Taking care of them is certainly better than sitting here alone wishing someone might remember me and stop by some day."

"I don't deserve that. I'm your friend, and you know I'd be there if you needed me."

"Maybe, but Frank's always here when I need someone. With Vietnam, it's almost impossible to find someone who's not in the Army or hiding out in a graduate program."

Cam dropped his head and sighed sadly. There was nothing he could say. He took a step backward.

"Sorry, I didn't mean to hurt you. I'm glad you're here, I've missed you. It's no picnic here. Frank sometimes has sex with other girls who crash with us, and although I could do the same with other guys, I don't. And I don't want to chase you away."

She stepped forward and grabbed his hand. She looked up in his eyes. "Let's make up."

"I said I wanted you." Cam kissed her slowly and deeply. They walked into her bedroom. Standing in front of her, Cam pulled off Bobbi's sweater while she sat on the bed. Bobbi unbuttoned Cam's Levi's and helped herself.

Suddenly, the door flew open.

"Bobbi!" yelled Frank. "What the hell!"

Cam yanked his jeans back up and Bobbi jumped to her feet.

"Get the hell out!" Frank shouted at Cam.

"Now calm down," Cam said evenly. There were two hippie girls standing behind Frank watching open-mouthed. Bobbi quickly donned her sweater. She had not been wearing a bra. "This is Bobbi's apartment, and she can do whatever she wants in her own home."

"You war-mongering bastard!" Frank roared. He advanced on Cam in a rage augmented by drugs and alcohol and aimed a round-house right at Cam's head.

Cam easily dodged the wild blow and shoved Frank off balance. Frank went crashing into the dresser and down in a heap.

"Frank!" cried Bobbi. She knelt beside him while he struggled to comprehend what was happening. Bobbi looked at Cam. "Why don't you leave now? I'll take care of things and call if I need you." She was once again completely composed.

Cam nodded and blew her a kiss as he left. Bobbi was attempting to straddle two worlds, and they were moving apart. Instead of a man, she was taking care of a boy and his worthless friends. It was a shame. She deserved much better.

*****

Bobbi invited Cam to her apartment to make amends three weeks later. She met Cam at the door and kissed him warmly while taking the bassinet with Sophia inside.

"Hey, man," Frank called as he waved Cam inside. He stood up and offered his hand. "Sorry about last time. She don't mean nothing, and I was out of line. I apologize."

Cam didn't believe Bobbi meant nothing, but shook Frank's hand. "Peace," he said. He wondered if Bobbi was offended by Frank's statement, but apparently she hadn't been listening while attending to Sophia.

Bobbi sat Cam down to drink bootleg Coors while Frank rolled a joint. Things were back to normal. After waving hello to Cam, the other kids went back to reading, painting posters, and whatever they'd been doing before Cam had arrived. One couple appeared to be trying to make love in a sleeping bag without alerting anyone else. Sophia was ignored by everyone but Bobbi and him. In spite of his best efforts, Cam couldn't prevent Vietnam raising its head in the conversation.

"There aren't any North Vietnamese troops in the south," Frank said. "The National Liberation Front is a popular movement." Frank obviously believed what commentators were saying on TV—a dangerous practice in learned ignorance.

"You're wrong. There were North Vietnamese in the south when I was there in '65."

"I knew you were a warmonger, but now I find out you're a baby-killer?" Frank sneered, then went on a bout of name-calling when Cam merely smiled. There were lots of arguments against being involved in Vietnam, but Frank knew none of them. Frank was simply one of Montesquieu's Troglodytes without an adequate sense of justice. The Franks of the world didn't even make good cannon fodder; they were fit only to follow Timothy Leary down the drug trail into oblivion.

Cam looked over at Sophia in her tiny bassinet. He could swear she was smiling.

He caught Bobbi in the kitchen. "What's Frank's classification?" Cam asked quietly. "Is there a chance he'll be called up?"

"1-A, and he's sweating it out right now. He didn't bother to register on time, and he's been fighting with his draft board back in Pennsylvania over his classification. If this last appeal is denied, he's a goner."

"What will he do then? Or better yet, what will *you* do?"

"He wants me to marry him and get pregnant," Bobbi replied, after a pause. "I don't know if I can do it."

"Marry him, get pregnant, or both?"

Bobbi looked up at Cam seeking his sympathy. "Getting married is no big thing, but I don't want his child. If I have to have a child, I'd want it to be yours." She grabbed him fiercely and kissed him passionately. "Don't go away on me."

*****

As spring arrived, Cam's interest in life re-awakened; students became people again, and women objects of his attention. Bobbi was an encumbered situation, but Cathy and Heather were around. But before he could act, it was too late—a senator's chief aide had caught Heather's fancy, and Cathy had developed a steady boyfriend.

As usual, the student body created an opportunity, this time from his class at Bolling. A tall, athletic skier, Sue Ann Olson, indicated her interest over a series of telephone calls. Somewhat hawk-featured with blue eyes and corn-silk blonde hair like Bobbi, she was the antithesis of Millie. Her husband was a West Pointer serving in Vietnam, and although he was a potential general officer, the marriage was evidently a convenience for social observances. It was less than a year after Millie's death, and he liked the idea of there being no possible commitment. Without Cam resisting, events took their own course.

But the vast majority of Cam's time was dominated by Sophia. The K11 was giving her the knowledge and intellect of an adult. He strove to keep her abreast of current events by reading to her and letting her watch television news. Her eyes betrayed her intelligence; they were bright, clear and steady. Sophia was only a baby physically, and those limitations clearly frustrated her. She needed no instruction to learn to do something, and hardly a day went by without some unusual progress. She was also a show-off for her daddy, and as soon as she mastered something, she demonstrated her ability to everyone.

Sophia's talents could not be hidden for long, and one day the secret came out.

"Now, where did I put my purse?" Heather said out loud on a

95

Saturday while baby-sitting for Cam. To her amazement, Sophia crawled into the bedroom and pointed to her purse. Heather tried a test. She took Sophie into the kitchen and successively pointed to the range, coffee pot, sink, and refrigerator asking each time, "Is this the refrigerator?"

Sophia shook her head at the first three and nodded for the last. Heather tried writing the four items on a piece of paper, then asked Sophia to point to the item on the paper and then to the real thing. Sophia got four out of four. So she could read, and "refrigerator" indicated at a high level. Then Heather tried having Sophia make change. Again Sophia was perfect, making change from a ten dollar bill. When Heather said she wanted to double her order, Sophia made the change correctly. She was even able to calculate sales tax. Not bad for a child who hadn't reached two years old.

Heather waylaid Cam as soon as he arrived back home. "What's up with Sophie?"

"What do you mean?"

"She has more than intelligence. She already knows everything. She can read, handle money, do math, and lots of stuff we tried today. So tell me about Sophia. She's not normal, and anyone other than me would assume she's from a different planet."

So then there were two who knew. Heather immediately terminated her current love relationship. Sophia was vastly more interesting. Every hour Heather spent with Sophia was a revelation. The only fly in the ointment was that Sophia demonstratively disliked all of Cam's female interests. She exhibited classic jealous behavior, and Cam and Heather decided to remain friends without benefits.

In September, Webb returned from Vietnam. Cameron threw two bottles of 1964 Wehlener Sonnenuhr into the fridge. Sue Ann had just ended her affair with Cam in preparation for her husband's return, and the timing was perfect. Webb never failed to pick up his spirits.

Although Cam had written about his family status, Webb was still surprised to see Cam feeding a baby.

"Daily job. Her motor skills aren't that far advance."

"Of course they're not, what is she, one and a half?"

"About that. Want to help feed Sophia?" Cam asked. "She's different from most babies—you can talk to her. She'd feed herself, but her motor skills aren't that far advanced."

"Yeah, right. She's cute, but I doubt she's ready to read Aristotle."

"We'll talk about that later, but she's very unusual." Cam turned to the baby. "Honey, this is your Uncle Webb. He's your daddy's best friend."

Sophia's eyes fixed on Webb, and she held out her hand toward him. Her "ga-ga" sounds were unintelligible due to her undeveloped vocal chords, but their meaning was clear.

Webb shook her hand lightly, and acquired a gob of apple sauce for his trouble. "You're right," he observed. "How can she be that far advanced? How old is she again?"

Cam wiped her hands and placed her in the swing-seat. "We'll come back to her later, but first, what's been happening with you?"

Webb had resigned his commission, and was headed to the CIA. His experiences in Germany and Vietnam had convinced him the days for Army Intelligence were over. The CIA blamed all failures, even their own, on AI even while controlling and restricting their operations. Because military intelligence didn't perform, there was little funding and support; because they had little funding and support, they couldn't perform. The circle had closed, but he had escaped and come in from the cold.

"Did you get a good deal at the Agency? Or at least, not get set back?" Knowing the CIA's animosity toward MI, Cam suspected the worst.

"They're giving me a GS-11 with an automatic promotion to a twelve after I complete their initial and supervisory training courses."

Webb studied Sophia who was watching him intensely. "She looks like she's understood our conversation."

Cam bit the bullet. "She did."

"Bullpucky." Webb rubbed Sophia's cheek with the back of his trigger finger. "Did you understand what Uncle Webb said?" he cooed.

Sophia nodded up and down. Webb jerked his finger back as if he had been bitten.

"Pour yourself another glass of wine, podge. It's time you knew the future."

Chapter 12

With Webb, Heather, and Cathy providing constant support and stimulation to Sophia, time moved swiftly for Cam.

In January John Dietrich called to say that he had moved another account into Webberon. Cam was richer by almost two hundred thousand dollars. The nest egg was growing rapidly with everything going in and nothing coming out. The Russian gold operation was still going strong, and Cam had added Millie's life insurance to the pot. Sophia was rapidly becoming a rich little girl.

Then in March Bobbi called. Cam had not seen her since the fall.

"I need to talk to you," she said. "Can you come by?"

Cam suggested Saturday, but Bobbi preferred the following Thursday. Cam agreed, even though it was over a week away. He assumed she had to arrange it with Frank.

Bobbi's apartment was neat and clean, not looking at all like he had last seen it. And Bobbi herself had never looked better.

"Where is everybody?" Cam asked, "Frank and his anti-war brood?"

"I've cleaned up my act," she said. "Frank drove a bunch of kids to New York, and I elected to take back my place."

"Good idea," he said, as she handed him a Harvey Wallbanger. Both that she had gotten rid of Frank and given him a Harvey.

They sat together on the couch like college roomies, talking over old times, Vietnam, and Bobbi's work at the bank. After several drinks, Bobbi rose, leaned over, and kissed Cam as he remained sitting. She disappeared into her bedroom and returned with a movie projector and several reels of film. "Remember Gloria, my black working girl friend?" she asked. "She gave me some porno flicks. How about it?"

"Okay by me," Cam responded. He was feeling pretty mellow and hadn't seen porn since Germany. He helped her set up the projector, aiming it at a blank spot on the opposite wall.

Within five minutes the film was forgotten as they focused on each other. Bobbi was fierce and unrelenting, not allowing Cam to leave until he was totally exhausted the next morning. He couldn't remember getting any sleep, and Bobbi had never said what she'd wanted to talk about.

Cam called Saturday evening, but Bobbi wasn't home. Nor was she at home any time later the following week. Apparently, she had only wanted once more for old times' sake. Alas—but one of the many mysteries of women.

In May, Cameron's telephone recorder held a message from Sue Ann. Another enigma. She was in town for a few days and left her number for him to call. Having had no contact with her since her husband returned, Cam hardly knew what to expect.

Sue Ann was staying with her ex-neighbors, a German couple who had befriended her while her husband was in Vietnam. Now he was in Alaska where she would be joining him. The merry-go-round started again.

Sue Ann called the next morning while her hosts were walking their dogs. She said she would be running in East Potomac Park the following afternoon, and Cam went off to meet her. Her jogging runs became afternoon trysts in broad daylight.

A day went by without a phone call and she was not at the park. The following morning, her call explained everything.

"Hi, sweetheart, I can't talk long," she began. "My host knows and won't let me out of the house. He's really mad and is going to put me on the plane himself Friday morning." She was traveling to Seattle to Tom's parents via Denver where she would change planes for Seattle. Sue Ann gave Cam the flights and times.

"Why is your host so upset?"

"It's a long story. He tells his wife he's protecting my husband's interests, but he's tried to get into my pants three times already. He's just jealous. Oh, he's coming back. Bye."

So Cam met her in Denver.

*****

Cam was holding Sophia and waiting patiently when Sue Ann walked into the Stapleton concourse. Sue Ann's luggage flew on to Seattle, and like little kids going to their first big-league baseball game, they took off for Golden and disappeared into the Holland House Hotel.

Probably most surprising was the turnaround in Sophia. She seemed to accept Sue Ann without reservation, whereas she had clearly disapproved of Bobbi. Nevertheless, Cam was careful about what Sophia saw and limited displays of affection.

They spent much of their spare time with Joyce Murray, Cam's oldest friend who financially managed student organizations for the business office at Mines. Having lost her husband in World War II, she adopted students like Cam, even helping them meet expenses when necessary.

This time, she adopted Sophia, and it was love at first sight. Joyce had remained in contact with Cam all these years, telling him about her life and the changes at Mines and hearing about Cam's adventures. But as she told Cam, with Sophia, everything was so much more rewarding.

"Why don't you leave Sophie with me for the summer?" Joyce suggested seriously to Cam. "That'll give you a breather from fatherhood and you can concentrate on other interests." Joyce thought it might be a good idea for Cam to pursue some single ladies back in Washington and made her offer in front of Sue Ann.

"I'm not looking for a breather," Cam answered. "Sophia and I are a team; she goes where I go, and I go where she goes."

Sue Ann looked away toward the mountains. She asked Joyce about nearby skiing areas and changed the conversation. Cam could see that her idea of a romantic tryst with her lover wasn't working out. Not with Sophia present.

Cam put Sue Ann on a plane for Seattle the following week, giving himself a fifty percent chance of ever seeing her again. If Sue Ann disappeared, well, there would be no regrets. It had been a crap shoot, and she could never replace Millie. They were lovers but barely friends, and she didn't know the truth about Sophia.

"What are you going to do now?" Joyce asked, when Cam mentioned his stint at Maryland had ended with the spring semester.

"I don't have any idea. I've been too busy doing other things for the last several weeks." He grinned.

Joyce nodded and gave him a sly look. "I'm sure you have, but your brain isn't the part that's been overtaxed." They both laughed. "Why don't you stay here? We can make room."

"And do what?"

"The Denver Community College opened three years ago, and I'm sure they need faculty. It's a community college, so they won't necessarily be requiring a PhD."

Cam nodded. It wasn't a bad idea. He would be leaving D.C. and his friends there, but this was home. And it would be a better place to raise Sophia. Golden was just far enough from Denver to enjoy big-city benefits while still remaining a small town. Although the open space Cam had known in the fifties was rapidly being filled with housing, North and South Table Mountains promised to dam the spreading stain of Denver. In its sunken basin, Denver was like a pool of hazardous waste, overflowing its shores to spill out on the prairie and seep toward the mountains. And the waste gave off noxious fumes. Cam could remember lounging in Mountain View Park on Denver's east side in the fifties and drinking in the vista of mountains from Pike's to Long's Peak. No more. One was lucky to see the mountains at all though the haze.

But Golden was protected. Clear Creek cut through the basaltic lava flows of the Table Mountains toward Denver in a narrow defile, and passage was guarded by the enormous Coors Brewery. Cam loved seeing Castle Rock, the point of South Table Mountain jutting out over the heart of Golden as if threatening its existence. The remainder of a 1920s nightclub, a concrete foundation slab on top and a gash on the north side that once held a cog railway, reminded him that nature was reclaiming its own.

West was the Rocky Mountain Front Range, and the road to Boulder climbed out northward on barren foothill slopes behind the hogback. Only to the south was the town vulnerable to being engulfed by suburban spread, and there it opened onto Denver's gateway to the mountains—the portal between Green Mountain and South Table. Cam hoped development of that area was years away, but Denver was an all-consuming nest of army ants.

Cam took Joyce's advice and contacted the community college. Joyce was right, they were expanding and needed instructors, and although their pay scale was minimal, the light workload would allow Cam to concentrate on Sophia.

The telephone finally rang with Sue Ann on the other end. With each passing day, Cam had expected less, and his suspicions were confirmed. She had decided to stay in her marriage, and started telling Cam about how he was a wonderful lover but probably not a good husband for various reasons. It was really all garbage, all rationalization, and not worthy of either of them.

Cam called Heather, hoping she would understand and not become too upset with his decision to remain in Colorado. It was a forlorn hope.

"Why do you want to stay there?" she cried. "Have I chased you away?"

"No, of course not, but I found a good job, and it would be best for Sophie." It sounded like an excuse, even to him.

"Are you going to marry that gold-digger?" she asked.

"No way, she's gone back to her husband." Cam said.

"Well, at least you got one thing right. I don't think I could handle another one of those jobs putting your sex life back together."

That was a nasty crack; why was Heather taking this so personal? "Thanks, but I don't think I want a sex life anymore," he said.

"What a waste. But why don't you stay here? We can find a job for you here."

He was sure she was right. " *We*" could find a job there. "It's a one-industry town, and the wrong place to raise a child and inculcate in her the values I want her to have. It's good for you and I, but not for her—particularly with her gift."

Heather was no longer crying. "Maybe you're right, but I'll miss you both. It may sound stupid, but I had begun to feel like I was her mother."

That was a jolt. Heather in place of Millie? "Look, we'll talk about it when I come back to get my stuff, okay?"

"Okay. But take care of yourself. I care about you. And tell Sophia I love her."

Cam said he would and hung up. He had not failed to notice that Heather cared about him and loved Sophia.

Joyce's house was small, but with Sophia sleeping in Cam's bedroom, there was plenty of room. Joyce was fascinated with Sophia's intellectual prowess, and although Cam had easily been able to conceal her abilities from Sue Ann, Joyce immediately knew Sophia was different. She had dealt with college students for over forty years and could recognize intelligence when she saw it.

Joyce was awestruck with Cam's story. "How does she reconcile those cases where her mother and you disagreed on something? A person often believes facts which aren't true."

"I don't know yet. She's not old enough to communicate effectively or discuss issues from her knowledge. I've wondered about that myself. Our religious backgrounds, for instance, were totally different, and there has to be some collision from conflicting faiths. There may be some bad times coming, or one of us may have supplied dominant genes which overrode the other's knowledge. It's simply too early to tell."

"Fascinating, but also frightening. Sophia may be the prototype of mankind's future, but her knowledge could also destroy her if she—and we—can't learn to adapt to its power."

Joyce agreed to help tutor Sophia, but they needed a better way for Sophia to communicate until she could talk or write. Cam had heard about a new computer company, Digital Equipment, that was marketing a system called PDP-8. It was a small computer processor with a typewriter-like keyboard for data entry which Cam had seen in the mathematics department at CSM. He talked with a DEC salesman who recommended a PDP-11, and soon the new mini-computer arrived.

Both Millie and Cam could type, so Sophia adapted easily to the computer keyboard. She was slow and had difficulty striking certain keys, but could write erudite messages while the sounds she made were still that of a two-year-old. Sophia's mental and physical ages were far apart.

"What happened to Sue?" Sophia typed.

"She dumped me," Cam told her. "I'm not sure what she really wanted from me," he added.

"Her husband's attention and good sex," she typed.

Cam shook his head. He was asking his two year-old daughter about his girlfriend, and she was responding like a psychologist. But of course, she was also Millie. "Was there ever a chance?"

"No, no chance."

"How about Bobbi?"

"Yes, just ask her. Won't work." Sophia was smiling at her dad.

"And Heather?"

Sophia's face dropped and Cam thought she might start to cry. She seemed lost in thought. Finally, she typed, "Don't ask."

Chapter 13

The dreaded issue of school attendance had finally arisen. Sophia was placed two grades ahead by virtue of her IQ-based placement test performance. In order not to attract undue attention, Cam had coached Sophia to miss some questions on purpose, but he didn't know how many she should miss. Unfortunately, the principal of Sophia's grade school immediately notified superintendent Arnold's office that he had an extraordinary student.

The entire case consumed Arnold's attention, not the least because this girl could help his school district develop a special program for gifted children. It started when Principal Carlisle called Arnold's office almost in shock after receiving the child's placement test grade. A six-year-old had scored at a tenth grade level. Arnold had called her father to the school district office for an interview, and the guy turned out to be polite but intractable. His daughter Sophia was clearly a genius, but he was unwilling to approve any additional testing or interviews. Accepting a third grade placement for her was a waste. The little girl was poster-child material according to Carlisle, and she could be Arnold's ticket to fame and fortune.

Arnold's secretary buzzed him to say Claire Villars was holding on the line. Just the person he wanted to see. Claire was an investigative reporter for Channel Seven. "Superintendent Arnold," he answered after flicking the switch on his speaker phone.

"This is Claire Villars, Mr. Arnold, what can I do for you?"

"How would you like to meet the next Einstein? She's a six-year-old girl living in Golden. Certainly the most intelligent kid Jefferson County's ever produced. Probably the brightest in Colorado, maybe the entire west."

"Sounds like a good human-interest story," Claire responded. "When?"

Arnold considered. "How about Tuesday of the first week of school? You can come by here for particulars, and then we'll meet her at her grade school." That way, the television interview would seem accidental and he could get around the father. He would play his hand slowly.

*****

Claire showed up at the office with a mini-cam as scheduled. Arnold was surprised at her youth. She appeared to be about thirty on TV, but was only three years out of college. Everyone on TV was stunning, but Claire's sexual appeal was overwhelming. He showed her Sophia's test. Claire examined it carefully while Arnold discussed his plans for a gifted student program.

"Have you seen this?" Claire held out the paperwork.

"Ah, not really," he mumbled defensively.

"This requires good reading skills to even take it."

"Of course. We don't give advanced placement to non-readers. It's a voluntary test given only on request. The girl's father requested it."

"Well, I think you better take another look at it."

"Why? Didn't they grade it correctly?"

"Look here." She pointed. "This vocabulary section has thirty words. All the questions were answered and every third answer was wrong. But the words go from easy to hard. She missed the third word 'spell' and answered the next to last word 'transubstantiation' correctly. I don't know what transubstantiation means, and I'm a college graduate. I would guess she knew them all and missed a third on purpose. Was this test monitored?"

Arnold was simultaneously astounded and embarrassed. "We'll find out." He tried to maintain an air of imperturbability.

Carlisle came in immediately. Yes, the exam had been fully and correctly proctored and his office had handled administration and grading of the exam exactly according to proper procedure. The superintendent glumly decided there was no problem at the school.

"Even if that was accidental, look at this math." said Claire. "It's the same thing."

Arnold snatched the test out of her hand. It was true; except for the essay interpretations, Sophia had answered every third question incorrectly.

"I want to see her," demanded Claire. She turned to her cameraman. "We'll interview the girl before we do a follow-up discussion with the superintendent. We need to organize our angle on this."

Arnold commandeered Carlisle's office and waited for Sophia with the television crew. Villars arranged the chairs for a friendly chat, and the mini-cam was left in its case until Sophia was comfortable.

Arnold knew the little girl was only six, but was still surprised at how small, sweet and vulnerable she looked. Carlisle was right—she was extremely photogenic and would make a perfect advertisement for any program. "Hi, Sophia," Claire cooed. "I'm Claire Villars. How are you?"

Sophia eyed her suspiciously. "You're an investigative reporter for KNTV."

"Why, yes, I am. Have you seen me on TV?" Claire was flattered to be recognized.

"What do you want with me?"

Claire had experienced tough interviews before—a child was not going to put her off her game. "Honey, we were looking at your placement test and would like to talk to you about it."

"My test? My test is confidential. If you saw it, you violated my rights to privacy. So did the school system." She turned to the superintendent. "You must be aware of the Buckley Amendment of 1974."

"Now, honey, no harm's been done," said Arnold.

"No harm to you—yet," Sophia said. "It wasn't your test that was disclosed. It wasn't your privacy that was violated."

"Sweetie, why are you getting so upset?" Claire had forgotten educational records were protected. After all, this was a six-year-old, and Claire was a representative of the free press.

"I'm not upset, but working for a TV station doesn't place you above the law. Why don't you just fabricate some statement by a well-known personality like you normally do? That way you get two stories; the one you made up and the maligned individual's denial. You're always looking for conflict and contention. I'll give you contention. You think because I'm six years old you can trample on my rights and take pictures of me without obtaining permission from my father? Well, think again."

Claire's temper rocketed out of control. No person—much less a child—could say things like that to her. She jumped up and grabbed her notebook. "Well, young lady," she hissed, "I did not intend to take pictures of you without your parents' permission."

"Mendacious as always. That's why you brought your cameraman."

"Little Miss Smart-Ass, you don't know what I was going to do. This man goes everywhere with me, shooting or not shooting." Claire was livid. "It was not nice meeting you. If there's anything I can do for you, just call. I'll be sure to do the opposite, you little bitch!" She stormed out, hurriedly followed by her cameraman.

Sophia looked at the superintendent. "What were you to get out of this? Were you going to sacrifice me for exposure on TV, or more money in your budget?"

Arnold stared at the little girl in silence. Claire had the reputation of being a tough cookie and this waif had reduced her to a babbling idiot. Now Claire would be out to get him.

"If you don't need me anymore, may I return to class?" Sophia asked politely.

He finally broke his silence. "Yes, we're done. Thank you." Arnold had made a mistake venturing out into the schools and desperately needed the safety of his own office.

*****

"You're to call a Claire Villars at this number," Joyce said to Cam. She handed him the top leaf of her telephone pad.

"What's this about?" He could not recall any person by that name.

"She said she was a TV reporter and wanted to talk to you about Sophie."

Cam looked around, but his daughter was not in evidence. "Sophia!" he called.

She popped out of the bedroom and approached with downcast eyes. "Yes?"

107

"Do you know anything about Claire Villars?"

Sophia nodded and related the events with Arnold and Villars.

"I was probably too harsh on the poor lady and she lost her cool. She was probably on the rag."

"Honey, we need to keep a low profile, and angering a TV reporter isn't exactly the way to keep out of the spotlight." Cam was pissed at Arnold for his actions, but taking him on would also be counterproductive. This was Sophia's first encounter with the government system, and it had gone badly. Fortunately they were in the west where child services only got involved when parents beat up their kids. He dialed the number intending to sooth any ruffled feathers.

Claire was in her office. "Mister Stewart, thank you for calling me back," she said. "I met your daughter Sophie this morning, and would like to discuss some possibilities of mutual interest with you."

Very smooth, Cam thought, there was no indication she had come off second best. Sophia had never lied to him, so he would wait for the second shoe to drop. The lady was welcome to visit him at home—setting the meeting on his turf.

She arrived at eight without a camera. Cam was surprised at her age, figuring she was fresh out of college. But the attire of the strikingly beautiful blond was inappropriate for an interview; she was dressed in skin-tight jeans and a halter top. She had made a mistake. He could not be had for a smile, a wiggle, or a little skin.

Cam ushered Villars into the living room and offered her a glass of iced tea. He decided to be sticky sweet and see what developed. "How can I help you?"

"First, I wish to apologize for my behavior this morning. I lost my temper and said things to your daughter I shouldn't have."

"My daughter can bring that out sometimes in people when they don't realize how bright she is." Cam smiled. His comment inferred that Claire had failed to comprehend the information available to her. Cam wondered if she would understand the precise meaning of his words or accept his tone as a conciliating apology. Confident in her appeal, she would probably hear what she wanted to hear.

"Well, in fairness to her, she is only six, and she was dealing with adults."

Cam almost laughed out loud. He was right—this reporter's arrogance knew no bounds.

Cam smiled. "So what did you have in mind? We're a very private family. By the way, didn't you do a program on Kent State?"

Claire was visibly pleased. "I did. How did you like it?"

"I think most demonstrations are overblown media events, organized to maximize public impact by giving TV cameras confrontation and excitement to report. They're like special press conferences that aren't important."

"That might be true in some cases, but Kent State was a large and important demonstration, involving far too many people to be considered merely a media event," she remarked.

"Only partially. The facts were obscured by self-serving rhetoric, and the media, pundits, and agitators missed the contextual setting of events. The key to the tragedy was what the guardsmen had been doing immediately prior to being ordered to Kent State."

"I beg your pardon?"

"They were on dangerous duty, having been called up earlier to ride shotgun in teamster convoys. The independent steel haulers had gone on strike and were killing teamsters who continued to work. Steel was being transported in truck convoys which carloads of strikers routinely shot up like Indians attacking a wagon train. The guardsmen, mostly young kids, were pulled out of truck cabs and sent to Kent State. Without sleep and nervous from being shot at by civilians, those troops were the worst possible peace-keeping force imaginable."

Cam poked his index finger in the air as punctuation. "Their mental state was missed by the media. I was in Vietnam, and when men are tired and jumpy, somebody is going to get hurt. The protestors were looking for excitement. But they pushed another jumpy group of kids, untrained in riot control, and who had been under fire two days before. All the media could see was terrific copy from dead and wounded hysterical girls. So, you see, I didn't think the reporting was very good. In many respects, TV was responsible for the entire tragedy."

Villars was barely able to compose herself. "You seem to have made a study of Kent State."

"I'm an historian. Everything must be analyzed in context. There is almost no beginning or end to an historical event. Truly it's a process, to be understood in the sweep of history. But the media interprets an event as an isolated encapsulation, capable of being condensed into a short report for TV. Then they popularize their version, creating instant inaccurate history. I bet you believe Richard the Third was a hunchback and an evil, hated king."

Claire nodded automatically, almost in a daze.

"Well, your opinion is based on Shakespeare's play—and he based his story on More's propaganda that portrayed Richard as an evil monster. Most evidence shows a different Richard—one well-liked by his subjects, the period's best general, and without a physical deformity."

Cam could see he had lost her. "My point is that events are very complex, and the nightly news is guaranteed to be misleading. TV probably does more harm than good."

"I'll tell you what," Claire said. "Why don't I treat you to a drink, and we can discuss this further? I've had a long day."

Cam smiled to himself. There it was. If I can't deal with you intellectually, why don't we change venue to where I can gain an advantage. *Wrong action, girlie.* "Let me take a rain check. I still have several things to do tonight. But back to Sophia, what were you thinking of doing?"

"I'd like to do a story on her and her intelligence. It's easy to see where she gets it."

"We're very flattered, but I can't see where that would serve any purpose. Her abilities are not going to cause more gifted children to be born."

"Well, I'd wish you'd reconsider," Villars said with a sigh. She twisted slightly, showing the bottom of her breast under her halter.

Cam decided to let her save face to avoid making an enemy, particularly one that could hurt Sophia. "Well, not right now. I'm not going to overrule Sophia on the same day without good cause. She's very important to me and I want her to believe in herself. Call me in a month or two for a drink." Cam rose, ending the conversation.

Sophia came rushing out of the bedroom as soon as Villars got into her car. "Daddy, you were terrific!" she squealed. "She was trying to manipulate you and you manipulated her."

"Yeah, it was rather humorous," Cam grinned, hugging his little girl. "Think she'll call me for a drink?"

"Never. You proved she was ignorant, and even turned her down when she invited you. She was willing to do whatever was necessary tonight, but it was a limited time offer."

"Honey, some days you're uncanny. That sounds exactly like your mother."

"I have Mother's knowledge as well as yours from almost the time I was conceived. How could I not sound like her?"

Right. She may be six, but had the experience and knowledge of a twenty-nine year-old woman and a thirty-three year-old man. Even Cam forgot that from time to time.

*****

Heather's relationship with her sister had been on a roller coaster ride ever since Jeannette had become involved with Harlan. Heather was astounded by the tall black's emotional control over her sister. The abuse Jeannette suffered from Harlan came out only gradually after they separated in 1974, but by the summer of 1976, they were together again.

Another year passed before Heather answered her telephone to hear a screaming, hysterical Jeannette. Nothing made any sense except that Jeannette needed her immediately. Within fifteen minutes, Heather was attempting to quiet Jeannette in Beltsville. It was already a long, hot summer, and without air-conditioning, the row house was stifling.

"When I came home he had another woman in my bed!" Jeannette was crying. "Another woman!"

Heather held Jeannette's arms, trying to bring her under control. Jeannette kept screaming. "Another blond white woman and even in my own bed! I never want to see him again.

Heather looked up and Harlan was standing there. "What in the hell is this?" he roared.

Harlan pulled Jeannette off the dining room chair and spun her onto the couch. He turned on Heather like a wild man, eyes blazing black and dilated with hate. "What are you doing here?" he yelled.

Heather had jumped up when she saw him, but was dwarfed by his height. Before she could react, he grabbed her blouse and tore it, exposing her breasts.

"I got what you need!"

Harlan grabbed Heather by her hair and both she and Jeannette screamed. He slapped Heather until she was stunned into silence. "Now!" Harlan gloated. "I've been waitin' to split you apart."

Harlan slid his hand into her shorts and jerked them down.

Heather screamed.

He slugged her hard in the face, and, her nose started bleeding.

"Yeah, yeah, yeah," Harlan panted as he pushed her legs apart.

Heather screamed as he lunged forward, stabbing himself into her. Then the weight of his body crushed her, and Harlan stopped moving.

Jeannette stood behind him, baseball bat raised for another swing. "Goddam motherfucker." She wiped her mouth on her shoulder.

Heather shoved Harlan away. "Call the police," she groaned through the blood in her mouth. The inside of her cheek felt like ribbons, but the worst pain was below.

"I killed him," Jeannette croaked in shock. "I killed him! Bastard!" she screamed. She fell to her knees and tried to smash his testicles with the bat but only hit his leg. She dropped the bat and collapsed sobbing into her hands.

Heather pulled herself to the telephone and dialed 911.

Jeannette was wrong, she hadn't killed Harlan, and he was in the hospital only two weeks. Facing two witnesses and the physical evidence, Harlan concluded a plea bargain. He received ten years. Heather was in the hospital for two days.

Chapter 14

While Sophia went to school, Cam worked on extending Sophia's knowledge. He identified twenty-three disciplines and rated them in importance. History and literature received top ratings of ten while botany was at bottom with a one. The total ratings added to 132, so Cam assigned each rating number as being equal to two days of independent study per year. Each year was like four years in college.

Sophia was now ten years old and looking forward to junior high in the fall. She seemed unusually devoted to Cam, and sometimes he felt there was something vaguely abnormal about her demeanor when they were together. Of course, she was abnormal, so how could he judge her behavior? She did everything he asked of her, sometimes even before he asked. However, he decided she watched too much television.

"What did you do, Dad, when you were a kid?" Sophia asked.

"You should know," he replied. "I listened to radio programs like *The Shadow* and *The Third Man*. But you knew that."

"Yes, but I thought you might have forgotten."

"Are you saying your memory of my experiences is better than mine?"

"Don't be upset, Dad. Remember, I have total retrieval capability of whatever's stored in my long-term memory. I can easily recall your childhood although you might have forgotten it."

Cam felt his anger rising at being put down by his own daughter. There were some things in his childhood he would prefer to forget. He controlled himself. "Do you remember my first time making love?" he asked quietly.

Sophia looked down at the floor.

Cam felt a pang in his stomach. His daughter knew his most intimate secrets.

"I'm sorry, Dad," she said. "You know I love you and would never do anything to hurt you. Look, it's the same with Mom. When she sat in her Falcon with you in the Golden Pagoda's parking lot, she was terrified you'd discover she hadn't washed her hair that morning. There's nothing I can do about it, and it's not worth worrying about."

Cam was shocked. He could think of experiences during adolescence he would not want anyone to know. Particularly his own daughter. How could he be a hero to her?

"Anyway, I need to comprehend current culture as well as its historical context. TV is current culture, or at least a mirror of current culture. Everyone else is watching, and I need to have a basic understanding of what they're seeing to know how to deal with them."

Cam could not deny Sophia had a point, but he bemoaned the waste of time. "But how much is really necessary?"

"You should be in school, Dad. Teachers and kids believe the 'now' beliefs and attitudes are correct, and all history is meaningless. Some even believe reading is no longer necessary due to the advent of television. Life is not simple for me."

Cam's heart went out to his only child. He had not considered the burden she was carrying—the burden of knowledge in a wilderness of ignorance.

"Dad, kids are taught that life is supposed to be fun when you're a kid. School is necessary, but we're only to put in sufficient effort to receive the grade our aptitude tests indicate we should earn. Above that, we're over-achievers; below we're under-achievers. Teachers look on both as being equally bad. We're trained to fit in, achieve at the proper level, and become happy little cogs in society's machinery."

"What happened to the drive for self-expression which has been so ballyhooed over the past five years or so?"

"It sounded good, but teacher ratings forced them to make sure their students met minimum requirements. Besides, there's so much grass being smoked by teachers and students, everybody wants to avoid attracting attention."

"Did your mother ever try pot?" Cam asked. It suddenly occurred to him he could learn about Millie from Sophia.

"No, but you did, so I know what it's like. But I can't afford to try any drugs—LSD, PCP, pot, or any of that stuff. I'm already different, and there's no telling what might happen. Even cigarette smoke and alcohol might be excessively damaging. So I tell other kids I take special medication for hyperactivity and can't risk trying drugs."

Cam was pleased with Sophia's ingenuity in dealing with the problems kids were facing.

"Dad, is it really worth it? Is the survival of Amulot civilization really worth it? I mean, the eastern establishment's against it, anything liberal or left of center, progressives, minorities, and all non-protestant religions are against it. The propaganda barrage is incredible. Everybody else is supposed to be proud of their heritage and culture except us. We're the guilty party responsible for all the crimes of the world. We're the only ones who can be racist. Blacks run on a double standard; anything we say or do is racist, prejudiced, or inequitable while they can say or do anything because it's our fault anyway. I'm sick and tired of being at fault for all the world's problems. I'm only ten." Sophia started to cry.

Cam took her into his arms and patted her gently on her back. "Honey, it'll be all right. It can't go on like this forever."

"But we're all at risk!" she wailed. "In Vietnam, we became obligated to refuse unlawful orders from whatever authority or face the consequences of our actions. Every individual now needs to be a lawyer. We're all criminals just waiting to be prosecuted. We're doomed. Only government employees are safe. The bureaucracies enable people to pawn off responsibility and obfuscate situations to where responsibility cannot be fixed."

"You've discovered the purpose behind Webberon," Cam said. Somehow his joke was not funny.

"So when does it all collapse?" she asked. "Madison Grant predicted Caucasians would fall from power by the year 2000. Is he right? What are our numbers like now, anyway?"

Cam towed her into his library and took down several volumes of American history. "Let's see. H.C. Allen stated that by 1900, only one-third of the white population in the US was of English, Scotch, or Scotch-Irish extraction." Cam examined several other references, not finding what he needed. "Here, this will take some figuring. Assuming the fifty-seven million Catholics and Jews are not included in the Anglo numbers, and the split between English and Amulots is about even—not too bad considering the twelve percent loyalist exodus after the Revolutionary War..."

"That's balanced by the population decline in patriots during the war," offered Sophia.

"Yeah, then we'd have about..." Cam jotted numbers rapidly on his desk pad. "Somewhere between sixteen and twenty-two million people today of Amulot heritage. Seven to nine percent of the population. We're a tiny minority, about two-thirds as numerous as blacks."

Sophia looked at the Revolutionary War numbers. "We were more than twenty percent of the population then, but made up over fifty percent of the patriots. Now we're less than ten percent. Following current trends, less than half of the American population will be white by 2025, and for all practical purposes, our Amulot heritage will have disappeared. I wonder when the last white president will take office."

"I would guess we'll have black or Hispanic presidents once or twice between 2010 and 2030. Our experience with mayoral races has shown blacks do not have to be a majority to elect a black mayor." Cam thought for a moment. "I would think the United States will have seen its last white president by 2060."

"So, if not in my lifetime, then certainly in the lifetime of my children. That soon."

*****

On the Auraria campus as the CC was called, Cameron enjoyed a reputation for a sympathetic ear for student problems. He listened to women when they came to his office to discuss their problems, and discovered that merely paying attention made him sexually attractive.

Another student? Heather and Sue Ann had both been students in his class, so he was no stranger to breaking rules. In spite of his needs, he had Sophia to consider. There had only been Bobbi and Sue Ann since Millie, and Bobbi's one night hardly counted.

The folklore that most student-professor affairs are trades of sex for grades was dead wrong. Cam knew those students involved with instructors were usually the best and brightest. It was the commonality of interests and opportunity that caused nature to take its course.

One close-cropped blonde, about six feet tall with green eyes and a slender figure ultimately brought resolution to Cam's dilemma. Susan Richmond was about thirty and clearly in control of her life. She pulled up a chair in his office and spread her latest project out for Cam to review. As he began to study her work, she started stroking his arm. The gesture was unmistakable, and it was time to accept or reject. Cam's long dry spell was over.

The next day, Cam worked at home and Susan came by after lunch. In the flush of afterglow, Susan volunteered to drive Cam to pick up Sophia.

Sophia climbed into the back seat of Susan's two-door Datsun while Cam held the seat forward. "Sophie, this is Susan Richmond," Cam said. "Susan meet Sophia."

"Hi," Susan said brightly.

Sophia's greeting was frosty and unfriendly.

"Oh, have we been having a bad day?" Cam asked with raised eyebrows.

"No, not especially," replied Sophia.

Susan and Cam glanced knowingly at each other. Small talk was desultory on the ride home, and Susan rapidly excused herself to return to Denver.

"What was all that about?" Cam asked Sophia as they walked into the living room.

Sophia sat down on the couch and dropped her knapsack on the coffee table. "Do you like her?"

"Come on, honey, I have a life, too."

"Have you gone to bed with her?"

"Aw, honey." Cam put his arm around Sophia and tried to draw her close.

"Let go of me!" Sophia bolted free.

Cam followed her to the door. He grabbed her by the shoulders. "What the hell is wrong with you?"

Sophia started to cry.

Cam steered her back to the couch and sat down rubbing her back while she buried her tears against his chest.

He lifted her chin to look at her.

She pushed upwards and kissed him.

Cam pulled back. This it was not a daughter-father goodnight kiss—it was a romantic kiss from a grown woman. And Sophia was only ten.

Sophia's tears began to dry. She gazed lovingly at him. "Don't you understand? Daddy, I love you."

Cam didn't move. "I love you too, honey."

Sophia placed both of her hands flat on his chest. "No, Daddy. I love you like Mother loved you!" She pumped his chest to emphasize her words. "I want you to make love to me!"

"Sophia, I'm your father!" he protested, horrified. Cam grabbed her arms and held her away from him.

"And I'm Millie!" Sophia flung her arms up to break his grip. The physical effort seemed to distract her. "At least in my emotions. When I look at you, I see you as she did." Sophia was shaking as she spoke.

She dropped her head back onto his chest and wrapped her arms around him tightly. "Oh, Daddy, what is to become of me?" She started to cry again.

Cam's throat felt like a bowling ball had stuck there. The fear in his heart was worse than when he'd seen a school bus hit the mine in Vietnam. His arms were like lead. "Honey, I guess you'll have to learn to control your emotions," he said.

Sophia rolled off and straightened up alongside him. The tears were streaming down her face, but she spoke evenly. "Daddy, I'm an emotional mess. I look at boys through my mother's eyes, and at other girls through yours." Sophia wiped both cheeks dry with her hand and looked down at her father's groin. "Did you know I have orgasms?"

"What? What do you mean?"

"I remember what it was like to be with you—as Millie, I mean. I still remember the love and intimacy." Sophia sniffled. "I want that and can't have it."

Cam finally addressed the situation. "If I had died, your mother would have found someone else to love. As you get older, you'll find someone else, too. Just concentrate on me as your father."

The enormity of her problem was slowly sinking in. "What is this about how you feel toward girls?" he asked.

"I'm not a lesbian, but sometimes I find myself thinking like you. Remember how you felt on the football field with Bobbi? Well, I can feel that, too."

Cam was paralyzed. He had forgotten about making love to Bobbi one night in Byrd Stadium between the goalposts. But Sophia hadn't.

"Mostly, I think as a woman—after all, that's what I am—but I also know your side. Both you and Mom were strictly heterosexual, and so am I—but I respond to both sides." Sophia seemed lost in contemplation. "Maybe that part will go away as I get older and my own hormones take over. I don't know."

God, he hoped so. He had never expected emotions might be inherited along with knowledge. So everything was there: physical characteristics, knowledge, emotions, mental faculties, and behavioral patterns. Ignorance had truly been bliss. There was a price for not starting with a clean slate in life.

The small house had suddenly become much smaller. Cam could no longer share a bedroom with Sophia even if they didn't share the same bed. He slept in pajamas, but Sophia often had seen him unclothed. He had never hidden himself from her, and wondered if he had encouraged her and psychologically abused her. He didn't know how to handle Sophia in this regard, yet couldn't seek professional help. And Sophia needed his closeness. He couldn't deny her love and affection, but she had to understand he loved her only as a daughter.

Maybe she did understand. After all, she had only raised this issue once. Probably all daughters inherited some of their mothers' emotions. He had heard of boys competing with their fathers for their mothers' love and it probably was the same thing. It would work out; Sophia's adult knowledge and intelligence would enable her to handle her feelings.

But the problem of sleeping arrangements remained. The solution was to add two rooms, a bedroom for Sophia and a formal library, an expansion which cemented the permanency of their relationship with Joyce.

And there was another issue. Cam would have to forego female relationships for the remainder of his life, consciously dedicating himself to Sophia, a process that was probably irreversible after

Millie injected her with K11. He remembered his father's similar statement before his death while Cam was in high school. His dad had provided for his family but achieved little in his career. When Cam asked him what he wanted to accomplish with his life, his dad had answered, "To make life better for you."

It was a typical middle-class American statement of hope for the future. His father had not realized his dream, but it was alive and well for his child. Now Cam was saying the same thing. He had blown his chances for greatness, but he could help Sophia achieve what he could not. He wondered how many generations underwent the same cycle of hope, destruction, and rebirth. Probably all of them since the beginning of time.

Chapter 15

Sophia's junior high school was ethnically mixed, and she found herself in a class with a group of Hispanic kids who habitually spoke Spanish among themselves. The teachers described them as "underprivileged."

"Boy, they speak bad Spanish," Sophia mentioned to her friend Cindy.

Cindy looked at Sophia, then around the homeroom. "How can you tell?" she asked. She had been with Sophia in grade school and nobody there had spoken Spanish.

"How can I tell?" repeated Sophia. "I, uh I..." She stopped. How did she know? She must be able to speak Spanish.

Sophia turned to the nearest Hispanic girl and asked what grade school she had attended—in Spanish. It had been natural and automatic to look at the girl and relate in Spanish.

Her name was Ermie, and although Sophia could easily understand her, Ermie's grammar and accent were atrocious. She often used English words but gave them Spanish pronunciations or constructions. Sophia asked Ermie where she had learned her Spanish.

"At home," Ermie answered. "My mother doesn't speak English, and I was in a bi-lingual program in grade school. Where did you learn it? You speak so funny."

Good question. "My mom," she replied. Her dad didn't speak Spanish, so it had to be her mother. Yes and no—she knew her mother didn't speak Spanish either. She scoured her memory. It was her grandmother. She spoke Spanish from her years of living in Madrid. The revelation hit Sophia like an avalanche. She could reach the knowledge of her grandparents.

121

*****

Cam walked through the front door to be assaulted by his daughter. Sophia jumped on him, throwing her arms around his neck. "You'll never guess what I discovered today!"

Cam leaned over the easy chair to deposit his ecstatic progeny. "I'm sure you're right," he admitted. "What did you discover?"

"Speak to me in Russian," she demanded.

"I don't speak Russian," Cam said. "And neither do you."

"Yes I do, and natively perfect, too," Sophia said in Russian.

"What did you say?" Cam said, suspecting the probable translation.

Sophia repeated her news in English.

Cam plopped into the rocker to grapple with this latest news. "How did you learn Russian?"

"From Grandfather Lauenberg. I know it from him."

"Your knowledge goes back through earlier generations? But to what extent?" Cam became silent as he pondered the implications. "What other languages do you speak?"

"German from you, French from your mom, Russian, Ukrainian, and Yiddish from Granddad Aaron, and Finnish, Spanish, and Arabic from Grandmother Lauenberg. I haven't discovered yet if I can go further back."

Cam was flabbergasted. He remembered his mother spoke French, but he had no idea Millie's mother was multi-lingual. "What can you recall from the lives of your grandparents?" he asked.

"I'm working on it. Emotions and feelings are probably totally submerged by yours and mom's. I've retained certain skills from them, and maybe even from further back. My words are somewhat archaic, and I need to converse with current natives to brush up. It was unbelievable—I didn't realize I knew Spanish until I heard it. I might know other languages when I hear them."

"How about historical events? Can you remember pogroms in the Ukraine or World War I or anything? My dad fought in Russia with the 310th Engineers at Archangel in 1919."

"Some, yes," Sophia answered. "It helps to receive questions or some stimulus to remember. For instance, I had forgotten about Wilson's intervention in Russia until you just mentioned it. Did you know your father had a Russian girlfriend in Bereznik during the winter of 1919? His platoon built the blockhouses at Toulgas where the Whites mutinied and killed their British officers. I could have a Russian aunt or uncle."

"My great-grandfather McClellan was a general in the Civil War. Do you remember any of that?" Little Mac was Cam's most famous ancestor.

"No, but I can see images of fighting Mexicans around Mexico City." Sophia thought for a while. "I have it. His daughter, your grandmother Bowie, was born in 1861. Events must be experienced prior to conception to be passed on. That's why I don't know anything about McClellan during the Civil War."

New vistas had suddenly opened for historians. To go back in history for first-hand accounts, it was only necessary to locate a descendant and unlock his knowledge. "Historical figures should be required to procreate immediately before dying to maximize knowledge inherited by their following generation," Cam said. "What a world... but it does make some sense."

"But it closes a door for women," Sophia said. "After menopause, everything a woman learns will be biologically lost. Maybe nature does ascribe social roles after all."

*****

Cam mentioned Sophia's unusual facility with languages to the department chairman of modern languages at Colorado University and requested help in determining what courses of study might be best. With a plausible explanation and an implausible truth, no one suspected the real nature of Cam's request, and Isaac Miller readily invited them to Boulder.

Miller himself spoke Russian, and conversed with Sophia for several minutes to determine her proficiency. Supposedly, she had learned her pronunciation from talking with her grandfather and read Russian literature in original versions to increase her vocabulary.

"Are you related to the White commander at Archangel?" Sophia asked.

Miller stopped and laughed. "No such luck, but your granddad comes from Kharkov or the Donets, doesn't he?"

"Yes, Sir. He lived in Belgorod. How did you know?"

"You sound almost exactly like my father, and he was from there. Your accent is somewhat Ukrainian. Your Russian is perfect, but I can tell you've learned it mostly from books. You use my father's words instead of current idioms. Did you also learn any Ukrainian?"

Sophia answered in Ukrainian and Miller responded. "You must spend a lot of time with your grandfather," he observed. "I think it's wonderful he's helping you gain what such a terrific asset."

"Yes," agreed Sophia. "I owe a lot of my knowledge to him. But all of my family has helped. My grandmothers and my dad have helped me with other languages."

Miller couldn't contain himself. He needed to get this little girl into his program. "I hope you're ready for a life of linguistics." He turned to Cam. "Let's bring in other faculty to talk with her." Miller called his secretary and asked her to see who was available.

Sophia conversed with a stream of professors in all but Finnish. Cam asked each faculty member to speak several sentences in each language they knew and had Sophia repeat them. She was barraged with keys to other languages she might speak.

Although rusty, she could probably make herself understood in Swedish, Italian, and Polish. Swedish came through Millie's mother, the Italian from Cam's maternal grandmother, and Polish was in Aaron's background. Almost all European languages sounded familiar to her, but she would need training and study to gain a level of proficiency. Language skill apparently was retained for a number of generations and could be recalled with decreasing levels of fluency through each succeeding generation.

Isaac Miller was thrilled with the prospect of acquiring a prodigy like Sophia, and decided to talk with her grandparents to see what they had done to interest Sophia in languages. He asked his secretary to get in touch with Aaron Lauenberg in New York City.

Aaron Lauenberg was soon on the phone. Somewhat gruff, and without time to talk, he said he had never seen his granddaughter and his wife had died shortly after his only daughter was born. He spoke Russian and Ukrainian, and it was true, his wife had spoken Finnish, Spanish, and Arabic. But he could not explain how Sophia spoke anything but English. He was busy and couldn't be of further help.

Isaac Miller attempted to contact the Stewarts, but they did not return his calls. It was impossible. How could a girl in the seventh grade learn eight languages in so short a time?

Miller's felt himself challenged by the Stewart situation. He telephoned the principal of Sophia's junior high school for information on her records. It was a disappointing conversation, first, because of the privacy bugaboo, and second, because her file carried a notation that matters concerning Sophia were to be referred to Superintendent Arnold. Miller had to jump through another hoop.

Arnold came on the line almost immediately.

"Yes, Doctor Miller, what can I do for you?" Arnold believed in maintaining good relations with universities in his area.

"The other day I met one of your pupils with extremely unusual language capabilities. Sophia Stewart. I was wondering if you could give me some information about her."

"Yes, she's probably the brightest student in our system," Arnold said. "I interviewed her when she was six, and she placed into the tenth grade. Her father decided to hide her assets under a bushel, rather conservatively, I thought. Don't really know much more about her, but she's a special interest of Claire Villars, the news anchor at KNTV. You might contact her."

Miller could sense the reluctance in Arnold's voice to discuss the girl. He knew Arnold's type. Strictly a bureaucat who liked everything to run on an even keel. Students like Sophia were a trial. They could make a man's career if properly handled, but, otherwise, were a pain in the rear. Arnold's discussions with Sophia's father had probably gone poorly, and Arnold had washed his hands of the Stewarts. He'd try Villars. He thanked the superintendent and prepared for another hoop.

Villars was indeed interested, but instead of Miller asking questions and learning more about Sophia, he was milked for his own knowledge. He invited the reporter to Boulder at her earliest opportunity to share their knowledge, and she agreed to come the next day.

*****

Claire Villars was currently the female newsreader for the six and ten o'clock news, but had a reputation as a hard-hitting journalist. This session promised to be interesting. He waved her to his couch to be comfortable.

"So Sophia's father wanted her tested for her language abilities?" she began.

"I'm no longer sure why he brought her to me. She's only twelve and speaks eight languages fluently."

"Ten," Claire said.

"I beg your pardon?"

"Ten, she's only ten years old," repeated Claire.

"I thought she was in seventh grade."

"Oh, she is, but she skipped two grades." Claire opened her notebook and began writing.

"Lord, I'm even more amazed," commented Miller. "And we weren't sure, but she seemed to have some competence with four or five others. It was almost as if she could listen once and immediately speak a language."

"Have you heard of anyone like her before?" Claire asked.

"Never. I know people who speak four, five, and six languages, but that's because they grew up in multi-lingual environments. I don't think that's the case here. She said she learned Russian and Ukrainian from her grandfather and Finnish, Spanish, and Arabic from her grandmother, but I checked. Her grandmother died shortly after her mother was born, and she's never met her grandfather. Why did she lie, and how did she learn the languages?"

Claire suddenly had an idea. "What do we do with high-level Russian defectors? Maybe her dad's been given a new identity? On the other hand, maybe he's a Russian spy."

Miller took a deep breath and leaned back. Both were quite possible. "That could be. Her grandfather didn't want to talk to me, and it was only with great effort I got anything at all."

Claire curtailed the interview as rapidly as possible. She had enjoyed upstaging the professor. Academics were so funny, always attempting to maintain a front of superior knowledge. But she didn't have time for games. Stewart's avoidance of publicity could make sense if he was what she had suggested. Putting his daughter on the nightly news would not be conducive to staying in hiding.

She called two days later and told Miller that Cameron Stewart was indeed a Soviet defector under cover. She stressed a need for secrecy, and intimated her sources were extremely unhappy with her for uncovering their man. Miller promised utmost discretion.

Okay, she had thrown off Miller. Now she had to find out who the Stewarts really were.

*****

Cam was building a lucrative management consulting practice on the teaching and implementation of mobility theory in career planning and management. In his devastating road show, he contended that an individual's perceived mobility was the primary determinant for a person's behavior and his treatment by social, political, and economic systems.

In general, the greater a person's mobility, the greater his remuneration, social standing, opportunities, and power. Most important was an individual's own perception of his mobility, but it was also significant to communicate this perception to others so they could adopt concordant attitudes. The final mix of attitudes, both by and toward the individual, determined the person's operative milieu.

Cam explained his theory in his talks by a comparative example: a divorced woman with a high school education in a small town, living with her parents who take care of her small child, will be paid less for the same job than a single woman with an identical education, but without a compelling reason to remain in the locality. The first woman will accept an offer for less money and feel fortunate to obtain it, whereas, the second will expect her salary to compete with what she could receive in a larger city. The first woman perceives her mobility to be low—essentially trapped—the second is more mobile and will relocate if her expectations are not satisfied. Employers understand both attitudes and set salary levels accordingly.

Common behavior patterns were associated with mobility; some individuals exhibited defensive behavior, others unionized or attempted to co-op the system, and those in the system adopted various attitudinal and managerial styles appropriate to their own mobility and that of their associates. None of the classical theorists such as Maslov, Herzberg, or McGregor had addressed the mobility factor in motivation. Cam's theory promised to be all-encompassing, containing as subsets all other motivational and management theories, particularly those concerned with wage and salary administration.

Cam postulated a theorem that greater worker mobility required a more participatory management style, whereas, lesser worker mobility allowed for greater authoritarian management practices. Of course, exceptions were obvious, especially in areas like athletic team sports where authoritarian management clearly correlated with success.

"Your mobility theory concept is applicable throughout history to explain a large variety of occurrences," Sophia commented as she helped prepare the notebooks Cam passed out as seminar lagniappe. "But you've talked around one of the most important factors."

Cam had learned to listen to his daughter without becoming defensive. "Which one is that? I didn't leave anything out on purpose."

"Race. It's a major factor, but you only include it as intertwined with other cultural aspects."

"It's difficult to separate from culture," Cam objected.

"But easy to identify. Remember, you're talking about perceptions. The federal government has made substantial attempts through legislation to create equal opportunity for all races. Although equal opportunity laws sound reasonable, opportunity is more a function of an individual's mobility than any law. The entire civil rights movement has overlooked the issues and power contained in mobility, and in the end, mobility cannot be legislated."

"Good point, but not politically acceptable."

"So what? I'm not politically acceptable."

"But not for long. When you graduate from high school we're heading back to make use of your talents. Then we'll build, not tear down. You'll make all people mobile."

Chapter 16

Cameron rarely talked about his life to Sophia—he didn't have to since she knew already. There were many things he wished to share, but he was afraid of boring her. He was surprised, then, when she asked about his time as a student at Mines.

"I have a thorough recollection of your college career," she said. "The first year is clear, but the last two and a half are hazy for some reason."

Cam was frequently inebriated during those years, particularly the last two. Maybe alcohol interfered with information storage. "Can you recall what I did during the summer between my junior and senior years?"

"Oh, yeah. You worked for US Steel in Chicago. I remember everything about that."

His guess was correct. He had hardly touched a drink in Chicago. "So alcohol destroyed the retention of knowledge. Either that, or the retrieval pathways. It's probably true for any depressant. I bet even cigarettes inhibit information retention in long term memory because of their carbon monoxide poisoning."

"Think of what Valium must do. It probably fosters premature senility," Sophia suggested. "Anyway, fill me in on your years at Mines."

Attending the Colorado School of Mines was something Cameron was unsure he would want to repeat. He had breezed through public schools on his intellect and selected Mines because it was the world's foremost mineral engineering school.

CSM had been a financial problem, and Cam had not applied for any scholarships or assistance. True Amulots, the Stewarts were proud of never having accepted governmental assistance of any kind, including social security and unemployment. The sole exception was

Cameron's VA educational benefits which he considered to be part of his military earnings.

As Cam related it, the fifties were a different age, and not the least because of the draft. Her peer group was safe behind the volunteer army, and selective service had been relegated once more to wartime only. The peacetime draft had been a short-term phenomenon. But even more short-term was Mines' excellence. It had risen like a phoenix from the Great Depression to produce men of incredible toughness and stamina. But the bird was killed in the 60s as society shuddered in the face of the greatness of its creation. Mines made all other universities look like high school.

Joyce had been listening, and added her own stories about Mines. "Did your dad ever tell you about my friend, the sheriff?" she asked Sophia.

"Who, Wermuth?"

"No, no, the sheriff of Central City."

"I don't think I know the story, Joyce," Cam said.

"Oh, I had a friend who was the sheriff of Central City for many years in the cowboy and mining boom times. When he died in 1957 at ninety-six, his landlady and I were his only friends. He had just enough money to be cremated, and I took care of it for him."

"What did you do with his ashes?" Sophia's asked.

"I scattered them to the winds at Caribou, like he wanted."

"Where's Caribou?"

"It's a ghost town above Nederland where the winds never stop." Joyce looked introspective. "That's where your dad's going to scatter my ashes too, Sophie. I think it's fitting we return completely to nature."

"What about the Parsee Tower Of Silence?" Sophia suggested. "That's a complete return to nature."

"The only one I know is in Bombay," Cam said. "And we're westerners. I'm with Joyce. You're to dump me at Caribou, too."

"We'll all go there," said Sophia. "Matter is immortal. The realm of the Demiurge isn't important. God will shuffle our atoms and re-use them. Hopefully to be with him."

*****

Claire Villars was not making progress rapidly. The police had no record of Cameron Stewart, and her Denver Post contact was unable to find anything in the newspaper's files. It was time to go snooping. She drove out late at night to see grab fingerprints from his car. She was in luck. His car sported an Auraria campus faculty sticker, and she found a porcelain coffee cup on the front seat.

A telephone call to the community college established that Stewart was a professor of business, and Claire went to see his department chairman. Using the ploy that her TV station was considering a feature on faculty members, she was able to collect curriculum vitae on all business faculty, including Stewart. His employment application was even easier to obtain. She simply stressed that such information was in the public domain for a state-supported school.

Thank God for busy-body personnel people. The application form asked for marital status giving as choices; married, single, divorced, widowed, and separated. Then it asked for the dates and places for all marriage and divorce decrees. Stewart had listed his status as single with no entries for marriages or divorces. That was interesting. Who was Sophia's mother? Her maiden name was Lauenberg according to Miller.

The resume showed Stewart as a Vietnam veteran, a Mines graduate, and a Harvard MBA. All three of those were easily checked. He looked legitimate, but she needed to see the daughter's school records to check on her mother. She'd have to call Arnold. He'd obtain them for her.

A week later, the mailroom boy dropped a manila envelope from Arnold on Claire's desk. The personal data sheet gave Sophia's mother as Millie Lauenberg, deceased August 23, 1970, a month after Sophia's birth. Cameron Stewart was listed as father, and although there was no indication of an adoption, she couldn't rule it out. She would have to request a copy of Sophia's birth certificate from Maryland.

The cup's fingerprints belonged to Cameron Stewart, having matched those on file with the FBI. Nothing sinister was indicated; his prints had originated from his army security clearance. His army record had not yet arrived, but she no longer doubted it would dovetail with the information at hand. A trip to Mines had produced his picture from all four *Prospector* yearbooks during his sojourn on campus, and he had been a Kappa Sig, elected Inter-Fraternity Council president and to a bunch of honorary fraternities during his senior year. In short, he looked like a solid citizen. But then what was he doing as a low-paid community college instructor? Why wasn't he a captain of industry? It didn't make any sense, particularly taking into account his Harvard MBA.

The only questionable time on his vitae was his stint at Maryland. He was an ABD—All But Dissertation. Some problem must have arisen there in 1968 or 69. Maybe it had something to do with his daughter who was born the following year. That might be a fertile field for investigation.

Still, Sophia was an enigma. Where had she learned all those languages? And her knowledge—it wasn't possible. Claire could write a book and win a Pulitzer Prize if she could figure this out.

The pursuit of information on the Stewarts had ground to an end. Claire had discovered the circumstances of Sophia's illegitimate birth, and everything she learned checked out. Cameron could not be a defector unless he was a replacement for the real Cameron.

According to one individual interviewed in Maryland, Cameron underwent a significant physical change in the fall of 1968, supposedly losing a fourth of his body weight in a month or two. Not only that, his personality shifted, he dropped out of a PhD program, and fathered a child. The mother dying immediately was too convenient. It looked like the original Cameron had died in 1969 to be replaced by the one she'd met. His family might have joined him when Millie Lauenberg died, probably her baby also. Then his wife died, or maybe she went back to Russia. Fingerprints could easily have been switched in the files. But Claire had no proof.

Claire decided to put her pet project on the back burner to see what developed. She had bigger fish to fry. At her station's Christmas party she had attracted its owner, King Wright. An affair was under way that could pay big dividends. King was a millionaire with national contacts in television, and her goal of becoming a famous network commentator was definitely within reach. She began to spend her weekends with King at his ranch on Lookout Mountain.

*****

Golden High School became Sophia's testing ground in learning to function socially in her own generation. The easiest things were the superficial aspects of being a teenager: rock music, tight jeans, feathered hair, and 'in' language idioms. Physically, Sophia had developed the slender frame of her mother, but with a broader face from her father. Fortunately for the current hair style, she had inherited a thick mane of auburn hair which layered heavily. She was never going to be particularly busty, but otherwise, she knew her proportions were perfect. She certainly looked good in tight jeans.

Sophia decided she wanted to learn Mandarin Chinese and Japanese, and talked to her dad.

"Why those two?" Cam had asked. "You're occidental, not oriental."

"Look at it logically," Sophia said. "I need to make the best use of my time, and there aren't a hundred languages with more than one or two million speakers. The most widely distributed are English, French, Spanish, Arabic and Russian, and I already speak those."

"I didn't realize there were so few languages."

"Actually, there are almost three thousand, but a thousand are Indian languages in the western hemisphere, five hundred are African tribal tongues, and another five hundred are minor Asiatic groups. The top languages in declining numbers of speakers are Chinese, English, Spanish, Russian, Hindi, French, Indonesian, Arabic, Portuguese, Japanese, German, Urdu, Italian and Bengali. If you take out the Indian, Pakistani, and Indonesian languages as having little importance outside of their countries, that only leaves Chinese and Japanese for me to learn. Portuguese and Italian I can pick up along the way."

So now her spare time was filled with studying Chinese and Japanese. Cameron found a Chinese girl working as a programmer part-time in the Mines computer center, and obtained Chinese and Japanese course materials from the defense department's language institute through Webb. Sophia followed the highly structured lesson plans at an accelerated rate, and Sylvia Choi, only in her early twenties, made learning fun in spite of the cut-and-dried army approach. Japanese came somewhat slower through Berlitz and the wife of a Korean war veteran in the next block.

Her best friend was a good-hearted girl named Cindy, an airhead when it came to boys, but irrepressible and adventuresome. More important in high school society was Suzanne Wright, the odds-on favorite for Homecoming Queen and Golden's leading debutante. Sophia began to help her with French.

In her house on Lookout Mountain, Suzanne introduced Sophia to her father. King was tall, handsome, and divorced, reminding Sophia of Cary Grant. Power and money sat easily on him, and he was extremely influential in the state. Suzanne said her great-grandfather was one of the few Colorado silver kings to keep his fortune.

Sophia mentioned that King was supposed to squander the family fortune since he belonged to the third generation, and King laughed heartily.

"No, I'll leave that to Suzanne," he said. "She just came one generation too late."

Suzanne didn't understand, but her dad explained. "The first generation makes the money, the second uses and enjoys it, and the third loses it."

She objected, "I won't lose it, Dad."

"Probably not, but who knows? Maybe your future husband will."

Sophia decided King Wright was not a shark, but he wasn't a tuna either. Involved in society and politics, he could be a valuable friend or formidable foe. For now, he was a friendly and she wanted to keep it that way.

*****

The telegram announcing Aaron Lauenberg's death arrived Friday before Cam returned home from school. Sophia had never met her grandfather, the only one of her grandparents still living when she was born, but now was invited to New York for his funeral and the reading of his will.

Aaron Lauenberg's attorney greeted Sophia and Cam politely as his secretary ushered them into his large paneled office. The obligatory wooden door had been impressive, and now they were to sit and hear words from the master. Funeral arrangements were already completed, and since Sophia was the will's primary beneficiary, the executor, a lawyer named Krantz, wanted Cam and Sophia to hear its provisions immediately.

The will was simple; Aaron had given one-third of his estate to various charities and two-thirds to Sophia in trust until she was twenty-one. Sophia's inheritance was subject to only one critical provision; if she married before her twenty-first birthday, her husband had to be Jewish or her trust would be distributed to the charities listed earlier. Although the lawyers would not know for certain for some time, Sophia could probably expect the trust to be in the neighborhood of thirty to forty million dollars. She would be a very rich young lady.

At the funeral, Sophia attempted to stimulate her memory of the part of Aaron's life available to her. She remembered his Bar Mizvah and felt some of his emotion. It was dominated by fear of the Cossacks and hatred of communists. Death had struck brutally and often in his youth and hardened him. Now she understood. He felt enormous guilt in leaving his family to die in Siberia but had pride in his religion. She felt pity and love for the man lying before her. His life must have been barren after leaving Russia, even the stab at forming a family of his own had been practically stillborn.

Krantz took them to the brownstone the following morning where Millie had spent the first eighteen years of her life. For Cam it was new, but for Sophia it was déjà vu. Krantz said they could take whatever they wanted.

Sophia pointed out the substantial library including many books in Russian. Mostly novels, philosophical, and religious works, they would be helpful to her in maintaining her language proficiency. There was almost nothing from Aaron's early days in Russia— evidently he had fled with little baggage. Sophia went through his effects like a psychic, looking for items to stimulate her memory. Then she found the letters.

Both Cam and Krantz came to see what Sophia held in her hand. It was a carved box, about the size of a shoebox, and half full with letters postmarked in Russia. She opened the top one. "It's from grandfather's brother!" she exclaimed.

Krantz and Cam looked at each other. "She can read Russian," Cam said.

"It's not Russian, it's Yiddish mostly," she said as she began to read. "This must have been written about 1939 because he mentions the death of Yezhov, the secret police head who was responsible for most of the 1937-38 purges." She continued to read onto the next page. "Oh, my Lord, he joined the Communist Party and he wants grandfather to understand. That must have put a terrible strain on their relationship."

"Did he ever mention a brother to you?" Cam asked Krantz.

"No, never. I'm as surprised as you are. It doesn't make any difference as far as the will is concerned though."

Spoken like a true lawyer, Cam thought.

"His brother had three sons," broke in Sophia still reading. She put the letters back. "This will take some time, but in 1938, Mother had three cousins." She turned to the lawyer. "We'll be needing these."

Millie's room was unsettling for them both. Aaron had left it unchanged since Millie's death, and there was a strong presence of her throughout the room. There were more books and many items from her childhood.

Cam went out into the hallway to compose himself, while Sophia collected a large number of childhood articles and toys.

As they finished in Millie's room, Krantz pointed down the hall. "There's one more room you should go through. On the other side of Aaron's bedroom is his wife's room. I don't think it's been touched in forty years."

The room was clean and tidy, and contained the personal effects of Millie's mother. She had pictures of her family in Finland, letters, jewelry, and items from Spain, Morocco, Finland and other places in Europe. Sophia wanted to transport the entire room to Colorado. It was a gold mine to an era she had hardly touched.

*****

In Sophia's junior year, she learned how extensively progressive ideology had been adopted by her schoolmates under the unrelenting propaganda by liberals. Reagan had created a national holiday for Martin Luther King's birthday to begin in 1986, and since some states had refused to recognize the holiday, the subject was debated in Sophia's civics class. There was really no debate—the only one against the new holiday was Sophia. She was asked to read her essay supporting or opposing the holiday to the class

"Everything is time-dependent and contextual; an opportunity today may be no opportunity tomorrow; an issue today is no issue tomorrow, what is important today is meaningless tomorrow. Therefore, what is needed is a long range view of history."

Sophia looked around the room. There was no comprehension of her point. She continued. "We must ask ourselves why a holiday celebrating the birth of Martin Luther King was proposed. It was created to honor someone from our parent's time and to enhance their self-worth. Honoring a contemporary whom they saw on television increases the importance of their time in history. In effect, it is self-aggrandizement. Some believe King is being honored as the US's foremost black; but they forget Frederick Douglass, Booker Washington, George Carver, Ralph Bunch and Marcus Garvey. Certainly King was less important than Madison, Jefferson, Wilson, Roosevelt or Franklin, none of whom have a holiday. Even Washington and Lincoln share the same day.

"In fifty years, King's birthday will be disregarded since he will have been placed into his proper place in history as a minor figure in this century. The elite then will need to immortalize someone from their own time, maybe another minority; Hispanic, Asian, Jew or Muslim, or maybe a majority representative—a woman.

"A better solution would be to create an All Heroes Day when each minority, sect, nationality, or group could honor its particular hero. Blacks could honor King, Irish Catholics could honor Kennedy, women could celebrate Susan B. Anthony—every nationality its own national hero of their own selection."

There was more to her essay, but Sophia decided she had read enough and sat down. The class was murmuring, and her progressive teacher pointed out how her thinking was un-American. Sophia apologized to quiet the class, saying she had written her essay in a hurry without much thought.

The self-criticism soothed most ruffled feelings, and everyone calmed down. Only Suzanne Wright seemed to reject her act of contrition, and Sophia wondered what had happened to their friendship. She caught up with Suzanne after class.

"What's wrong? Are you mad at me?" Sophia asked.

"Why do you think you're so superior? All you ever do is put down everyone else," Suzanne stopped walking.

"I'm sorry, I don't mean to," Sophia apologized. She had an inspiration. "That stuff on King was mostly from my dad—he didn't like him." It was true that Cam was not particularly enamored with King, but he had not known about the assignment. Nonetheless, it was always appropriate for kids to blame their parents for any particular problem, and it worked again in this situation.

"My dad doesn't either," Suzanne said, "but everybody in school does. So does Claire, my dad's girlfriend." Suzanne paused while she shifted her school books and leaned against the hall lockers. "What did you do to Claire Villars?"

"She's your dad's girlfriend? Gosh, no wonder," Sophia gasped. "That was a long time ago when I was starting school. She wanted to do a story on me, and my dad said no. She came to school and I was nasty to her. But I'm surprised she still remembers."

"You must have made quite an impression. She warned us to stay away from you and said terrible things. I think she hates you."

"What does your dad say? I thought he liked me."

"Oh, he does, but he likes Claire a lot." Suzanne rolled her eyes. "I can hear her all the way in my bedroom when they have sex. The first time I thought she was having a heart attack. Then she just laughed and laughed. It was unbelievable, women aren't supposed to be like that."

"Wow," Sophia said, stretching out the word. "I don't think my dad has a girlfriend. He's never brought one home. Do you like him having a girl friend? Do you like her?"

"I don't know. Sometimes I do, but sometimes I don't. My father and I haven't always gotten along, and Claire's real good to me. She's okay, I guess, but sometimes I wish she wouldn't stay over. I mean, she's not my mom, but she does things with me and is a lot of fun."

Suzanne was back to being her friend, but there was a lesson here. Sophia had forgotten about Villars. Well, you win some and lose some. She couldn't have foreseen this when she was six.

Chapter 17

Joe O'Donnell sat at the Willow Springs Country Club bar and ordered another margarita. He was drinking as usual with his investigator. Juan Ochoa's expertise had contributed a lot to making O'Donnell's personal injury law practice the most lucrative in Denver. O'Donnell also made substantial financial contributions to the campaigns of various judges through Ochoa. Colorado's legal system bordered on Mexico's tradition of *mordita*, and he was a master at obligating officials.

O'Donnell's only problem stemmed from the glass in front of him. Because of the sauce, his wife had departed for friendlier pastures twelve years earlier and his son had immersed himself in drugs to escape an alcoholic father. In his mid-forties, he had narrowly escaped disbarment and jail when he'd killed a woman while driving home drunk from the club in 1978. Fortunately, he had drawn one of his friendly judges.

Tonight, O'Donnell's Mexican secretary had claimed a prior engagement and would not be coming. As usual, she was purposely limiting her availability for sex. Not that that was a big deal; she never put anything of herself into the act.

It was time to leave—behind the bar Mount Evans was beginning to move. Ochoa helped him into his Buick, and O'Donnell drove out the gateway heading for I-25 to take him north. He was tired, and after driving for ten minutes, he pulled off on the shoulder to sleep.

*****

He awoke with a bright light shining in his eyes, and a deputy sheriff ordering him out of his car. He leaned against the rear door while the deputy searched his car. When the deputy asked him to take a sobriety test, he refused and instead, offered his card. The deputy read it, and suggested they get some coffee to wake up. It was less than two miles to Devil's Head interchange and the all-night Streetcar Cafe, and the deputy followed him all the way.

Business was light, mostly truckers and kids. They walked in and ordered two cups of coffee. With the deputy present, the Streetcar provided the coffee without charge.

After ten minutes, the deputy decided to head for the barn. O'Donnell followed the deputy out, then watched the police cruiser head for town before climbing back into his Buick. Somehow, he had gotten turned around and headed south to Castle Rock. Now he had a long drive back north, and was tired. Luckily it was all freeway. He switched on his ignition, and drove onto the interstate.

Damn, that was close. He hadn't realized there was no dividing strip down here. How could they declare an undivided four lane highway an interstate? He would move to the right while he sobered up. If he drove faster, he could get home quicker, and he could feel himself fading again. The booze was making him hallucinate. He began to sing "Ninety-Nine Bottles Of Beer On The Wall" to keep himself awake. He began to beat the steering wheel in time to his singing. He felt good. It was fun—he would get home all right.

Damn! He must have drifted to the left! That truck had gone by blowing his air horn. Well, screw him! Stupid cowboys thought they owned the road!

God damn! He hadn't moved far enough right—the oncoming lights were solid. One pair was moving at him! Go further right, dummy!

A resounding crash snuffed out the lights. O'Donnell took a deep breath, and began to drift off. His head hurt. That idiot! Now he'd have to get a tow truck for his car. Well, Mañana was soon enough.

*****

Deputy Thompson hadn't reached Castle Rock when the call came in. There had been a head-on collision a short distance north of the interchange he had just left. An eighteen-wheeler had radioed immediately. Cursing his luck, Thompson turned north at the next access. He saw a two-car crash on the center strip's far side five minutes later.

As he pulled his Impala behind three parked trucks, he recognized one of the vehicles. It was O'Donnell's, the Buick he had left a few minutes earlier. The other looked like it had been a small compact car, but was smashed almost beyond recognition. The county paramedics drove up as he got out. Let Denver try to match that speed of getting to the scene! A tall, grizzled trucker ran up.

"There's still a guy in the compact!" he yelled.

Thompson dashed over to pry the guy loose. The deputy stopped with his hand on what was left of the door handle. They could take all night to remove this guy, it wouldn't make any difference. He had seen some messes, but these little cars tore their occupants to shreds. The steering wheel had practically disappeared into the driver's chest, and his face was a pulpy mass of raw flesh. Thompson momentarily wondered what color the guy's eyes had been. What a mess. He walked back to where there was another body lying on the grass.

The paramedics were already working. "Is he alive?" asked Thompson.

"Oh, yeah," one paramedic answered. "He may not even be badly hurt."

"Well, forget the guy in the compact," said Thompson. He looked down at O'Donnell's face. His forehead was open and bleeding, but looked pretty good by comparison to the other guy. Thompson surveyed the scene. "Did anyone see it happen?" he called loudly.

A trucker standing nearby spoke up. "I saw it. Could have been me."

Thompson took his name and statement. The trucker had been heading south in the right-hand lane when O'Donnell appeared in his lane coming north. The compact was already passing when O'Donnell switched to the left lane. Then they both drove into the center strip like they were being drawn together with a magnet.

"The Chevy driver took to the ditch, but so did the drunk," explained the trucker. "The Chevy never had a chance. He must have thought the drunk was trying to kill him on purpose."

"What makes you think the one driver was drunk?" Thompson questioned.

"The Buick was weaving, going the wrong way on a divided highway. What do you think?"

Thompson went back to the little Chevy where a paramedic and two truckers had pried open the driver's door. One of the truckers was on his knees throwing up. The paramedic was examining a wallet.

"Does he have any identification?" Thompson inquired.

"Yeah," answered the paramedic with a shaking voice. "He lived in Golden. Some guy named Cameron Stewart."

*****

Sophia had gone to sleep early. Cindy was out on a date, and her dad had driven down to Colorado Springs to put on one of his mobility theory seminars in the morning. About midnight, she awakened to Joyce's shaking her shoulder. She rolled over to see Joyce crying. Joyce sat on the bed and laid her hand on Sophia's arm.

"Honey, your dad's been in a terrible accident," she whispered.

With crystal clarity, Sophia knew the answer to the question on her lips. "Oh Joyce." She swallowed hard and pushed herself up. The room began to revolve as she threw her arms around Joyce and held on. Boots whined behind Joyce. "Where is he?"

Joyce couldn't speak for a moment. "He's gone, honey," she breathed.

Joyce had misunderstood. "No, where is he now? What hospital?" Sophia repeated.

"Down at Castle Rock, Douglas County. But there's no reason to go there tonight, sweetheart."

"Do you think I'll be able to sleep? No, let's go down now. He would if it were one of us." Sophia's voice was barely audible but firm.

"Sorry," Joyce said. "Since my Thomas had died, I've kept myself from becoming too involved with anyone until you two stole my heart. Now, that's been taken from me."

Sophia hugged Joyce. "I'll make up for your losses in every way I can."

*****

They arrived in Castle Rock shortly before two and Joyce stopped at the court house to ask directions. Sophia entered the sheriff's office to find out what had transpired. The first deputy on the scene had not yet filed his report, but another officer filled her in.

"Your dad never had a chance. He died instantly," the deputy stated.

"How did it happen?" Sophia asked as Joyce walked in.

"He was passing a truck when a drunk hit him head on."

"A drunk? What happened to the drunk?" asked Joyce.

"What always happens—a bump on the head, that's all. They never get hurt; it's always the innocent who get killed."

It took all Sophia's control to keep from screaming. She wanted to punch this guy out. Her dad had just been killed in the most horrible way imaginable, and this deputy couldn't care less. Joyce broke in quickly. "If you can point us to the hospital, we'll be going." The deputy gave them directions, and Joyce pulled Sophia away. Their initial information had been wrong; Cameron was at Swedish Hospital in Englewood. It took them twenty minutes to find it.

Her dad was barely recognizable. Gone was the giant mentality, the loving countenance, the caring human being. It had been replaced with a shattered mass of what once had passed for human flesh. It was not death that had taken him. Something else had mocked Cam and delivered him to death without dignity or honor.

Sophia put her face in her hands and sobbed uncontrollably. Some time passed before she looked up. Both of her parents had given their lives for her, but she would be worthy of their sacrifice. Her heart was conceived in love, but tempered in the fire of adversity. "Where is the other person from the accident tonight?" she asked the nurse behind the admitting desk.

"You mean Mr. O'Donnell?" responded the tired looking woman.

"Yes. What room is he in?"

"Oh, he was treated and released about an hour ago." She didn't bother looking from the sheet in front of her. A buzzer sounded. "Please excuse me for a moment," she said.

Sophia watched the nurse disappear down the hall. She snatched an insurance form off the desk where she spotted the name "O'Donnell." It listed him as Joe O'Donnell, an attorney with a Denver address. The papers went into Sophia's jacket pocket.

Her father had been right—he had done his penance during his lifetime. Like a beautiful fragile flower, he had been trod into dust by the grazing herd. After all, the most beautiful flowers are annuals, living short lives and giving birth to ever more beautiful subsequent generations.

Cameron had not lived for half a century. On the surface, he had begun with unlimited promise but thrown it away in a conflict of morality. With a single exception, all of her father's accomplishments would soon be forgotten. She was that exception, with the legacy of manifest destiny ordained through her parents' sacrifices.

Sophia returned to her father's side and knelt in prayer. She did not pray to the God of the Christians or the Jews or the Moslems. She prayed to the spirit of her father, the God within her, bequeathed by him. She prayed not to be diminished by her father's death. She should be strengthened by the passing of his spirit to her, always to walk with her, provide her counsel, to support and love her as she did him. Only a oneness could go forward, and she prayed to be worthy as the favored vessel. The Titans were gone, leaving her as Sophia to create a new world. God was within her, God with a new logos, God who was truly great and unknown to all others.

*****

Four days later, Sophia rode with Joyce and Cam's ashes to Caribou. Joyce drove from Golden up Clear Creek Canyon to Blackhawk and turned north to Nederland. The weather was cold and windy, and Joyce drove out on a mine spill above a meadow where the silver boom-town of Caribou had once stood. Sophia could see that the hard-rock miners had come and gone—only the winds and beautiful desolation remained. Remnants of times past, the Hendricks Silver Mine was still operating at a low level of activity, and the Caribou Mine below appeared to be dormant. Even the aging hippies were absent, although Boulder County officials had turned the area into a network of biking trails bringing vandalism and Easterners to the high country. The devastation wrought during the hippie assault on the Front Range was still evident everywhere, to Sophia's great disgust.

Walking onto the waste rock, Sophia could see blue columbines, Colorado's state flower, bringing beauty to counter adversity. She trudged the twenty yards in silence with Joyce plodding at her side. Her throat had become painful, and she wanted to cry out in anguish.

144

She watched the wind take what remained of her dad—nature literally snatching him from her grasp as if waiting greedily for his return. It was terrible. She was next. The last of her line.

She read aloud her dad's poem on death he had written years earlier:

The day will come when I must leave, to return my trust to its endeavor,

The birds will sing, the buds will bloom, each morning life is renewed forever.

Those who knew me will pass away, you only retaining my memory,

Mankind will move through mundane lives, still waiting for you and your destiny.

No sorrow for me or my fate, as guided by my nature, I was true,

My spirit soars forever bound, to your life, to your happiness, to you.

She sat with Joyce on the mine spill's edge and cried. His had been a meaningful life and a meaningless death. Sophia had lost her father and her love. It was an indescribable loss. She buried Cam's urn at the edge of the spill.

Sophia looked away to the east, over the road they had traveled. "Let the one-eyed Mamluk celebrate his victory, Father," she whispered. "I promise you—we will water our horses in the Nile."

*****

Earl Phillip's office was on the top floor of the Colorado National Bank Building, probably the most prestigious address in Denver other than the governor's mansion. The Brown Palace Hotel looked like a miniature Stone Age relic in comparison with this steel and glass monster. Still, one movement from the Golden Thrust Fault could return the Denver Basin to nature in a few moments.

The bell dinged efficiently, and the honeycomb patterned steel doors opened onto an expensive but spartan reception area, separated from the elevators by a divider with the obligatory heavy wooden door. A quick glance at the names on the glass revealed six partners and about twenty associates. The black modern decor gave an impression of great strength, unyielding and unmerciful to its adversaries. Sophia announced her presence to the slim, elegantly dressed lady behind a long, counter-like desk. "We have an appointment with Mr. Phillips. Sophia Stewart and Joyce Murray."

The receptionist swung her long dark hair out of the way. "Just a moment, please," she stated flatly while she reviewed the row of lights before her. In a moment, she disappeared through a door almost invisible in the wall across the room.

Sophia barely had time to decide if somebody was a Bronco fan when the door reopened. A tall, patrician individual in a dark blue three-piece pinstripe was holding the door ajar. "Hello, Joyce," he said pleasantly.

Joyce crossed the room to greet Earl with a handshake. He hadn't moved from the door, so Sophia followed. "And you must be Cam Stewart's daughter," Earl said, extending his hand in Sophia's direction. "I'm very glad to meet you." Obviously not given to small talk, he motioned them through the door with, "Please."

Earl ushered the two women into his large, rosewood paneled office and ordered coffee. He had already researched the case of Sophia's guardianship and had even talked with Dave Columbo. "I don't see any difficulties with you obtaining guardianship of Sophia, Joyce," he began. "I talked to Mr. Columbo in Maryland, and his only reservation was with Sophia's grandfather. When I said he was deceased, Columbo thought our action would be uncontested. By the way, did you know he's the majority leader in the Maryland senate and considering running for US senator?"

"No," Sophia answered. "We haven't had any personal contact with him for some time."

"Well, I'll file a petition for guardianship as soon as possible," announced Earl. "Young lady, you and Joyce will both have to be interviewed by Social Services, but there shouldn't be any problem. Not at your age and with Joyce's excellent reputation and references."

"And of course, Denver's most prestigious law firm representing us," Sophia added.

"I shouldn't think we'll hurt," smiled Earl. "After all, I knew your father at Mines, and we'll present a solid approach as friends of the family."

Sophia switched the conversation to her second subject. "We also need you to proceed against Joe O'Donnell in a wrongful death suit."

"Yes, I understood that from Joyce." He pressed his intercom and asked for another attorney to join them. A few seconds later, a short, heavyset man about thirty walked in. "This is Charlton Channing," Earl said, as he motioned to the newcomer. "Charlton, this is Mrs. Murray and Sophia Stewart." He turned to Sophia. "He will be working with me on the case."

"What have you found out?" Sophia directed her question to Charlton.

"Well, I've just started, but I understand O'Donnell will probably beat the drunk driving charge."

"How?" Sophia exploded.

"Well," started Charlton, glancing to Earl and back, "He refused the breath analysis test so the evidence is only the officers' testimony. And one of them found him asleep in his car earlier, drank a cup of coffee with him and says O'Donnell wasn't drunk."

"He has to say that, otherwise he wasn't doing his job," Sophia said.

"I'm sure that's right, but it doesn't change the situation."

"So where had he been drinking?"

"I don't know yet, we haven't had time to put our investigator on it yet," Charlton said.

Earl broke in. "We really won't be taking part in the criminal case, Miss Stewart. We'll be filing a civil suit for damages."

"My father was killed by a criminal—a drunk driver!" Sophia yelled.

"Now, don't get upset. We'll seek a large settlement for your dad's death—that will be his punishment," Earl said evenly.

Sophia stood up. "Mr. Phillips, I believe in Kennedy's mantra, 'Don't get mad, get even.'"

Joyce spoke up. "What is normal in cases like this?"

Sophia sat back down, and Earl turned to Joyce. "It depends on the present and potential earnings of the victim, and of course, the defendant's resources. Cam was forty-seven years old, so we're looking at lost earnings for only eighteen years. Still, we'll go in for a million dollars, and we might be able to get most of that."

Sophia had been listening. "You get twenty-five percent of that, right?" she said flatly.

"It's normal in Colorado for attorneys to receive between one-third and one-half on contingency cases," Earl said. "I think we can negotiate ours at the low end of that spectrum."

"I think we can go at an hourly rate," Sophia stated. "I see no reason to place this on a contingency basis."

Earl took account of Sophia's youth. "The reason for a contingency fee is to safeguard the client and reduce financial risk. Settlement participation assures the client his attorneys will try to get the best possible settlement."

"Are you saying attorneys don't do their best when being paid by the hour?"

"Attorneys always try to do their best, young lady. But I'm sure your father taught you about incentives in motivating people." Earl controlled himself. "Look at attorneys as hired guns. We square off at each other and may the best man win. Lots of times, the issues are too difficult for a judge or jury, so that's why you need the fastest and best shooting gunfighter."

"I'll agree attorneys are hired guns, but instead of shooting at each other, they both let fly at bystanders," Sophia said. "Then when the whole town is prostrate, they divvy up the take, and walk off arm-in-arm for a cup of coffee. The American judicial system is no longer trial by jury—it's trial by combat. The winner is he who most effectively discredits witnesses and damaging evidence."

"You do wish us to handle this matter for you, I presume," Earl said coolly. Charlton appeared to be trying to disappear into his chair. No doubt he had never heard a client talk to Earl like this before.

"That's why we're here, but an hourly basis will be totally acceptable. I'm sure I can work with you and Charlton, and just submit the detail of your time and materials charges on a monthly or even weekly basis and I'll take care of it."

Earl tried once more. "We may not want to take the O'Donnell suit except on a contingency basis," he said.

"That's fine if you choose not to accept my offer for employment. I'm the employer stipulating contract conditions. You may accept or reject that contract as you see fit." Sophia was now using the sweetest tone imaginable.

The two attorneys exchanged glances. "We'll see how it goes for a while," decided Earl. "But working together is a two-way street."

"I think you'll be very pleased with my cooperation. You may even find many things done for you that will make your life easier."

148

Chapter 18

Sophia dialed the telephone number Cam had given her for emergencies. A female voice answered by repeating the phone number instead of offering an informative greeting. Sophia assumed her call was being answered in Virginia.

"This is Sophia Stewart, daughter of Cameron Stewart, I would like to speak with Mr. Reid, please," she stated as formally as she could. In spite of herself, her voice was still that of a fourteen-year-old girl.

"Just a moment, please." There was no indication that Webb was present or absent, or an acknowledgement of any type. But in a moment, Webb came on the line.

"Sophia," Webb repeated pleasantly. "I haven't talked to you for a long time. Do you remember our last meeting?"

It was a test. Nobody but she could remember a meeting which had taken place when she was two years old. "Sure," she answered, "it was just after Dad and I came to Colorado. You became quite adept at understanding my hand signals."

Webb had really not doubted Sophia's identity since she had called on his private, unlisted line, but the enormity of Sophia's talent was something that strained his credulity.

"Unbelievable," he said. "You realize I haven't even heard your voice since them."

"I know, and I'm sorry to call you now." She paused. "My dad was killed by a drunk driver two nights ago."

Webb felt his diaphragm becoming paralyzed. Cam dead? Impossible. Webb had been planning to come out to Colorado for Sophia's high school graduation next year as a surprise. Cam and he had talked together almost weekly for years. Cam was his sounding board and confidant. His best friend. Gone. God.

Sophia was waiting, he had to say something. "I'm terribly sorry, Sophie," he began, but he choked. "I'm sorry, I don't know what to say. I don't know if I can get away," he stammered. God, what a stupid thing to say; of course he would get away for the funeral.

"Thank you," Sophia said quietly. "And it's all right, we're going to have his body cremated tomorrow. I'd really rather you didn't come. He wouldn't want you to see him like this. He'd want you to remember him the way he was."

Webb had already started to cry. "Is there anything I can do?"

"Actually, there is. I need information on the accident causing his death. Can you help?"

Webb seized control of himself. "Not my side of the street. I don't have anybody in Denver we can use, but I know someone who does. Are you at home?"

"Yeah, but Joyce and I will be leaving for the funeral home in a couple of hours."

"Okay, I'll have a fellow call you in an hour. With luck, his name will be Wallace, and he'll mention me." Webb was still having trouble grasping the finality of Cam's death. "And I'll be in touch again later," he added. Overwhelmed with impotence, his body ached. The loss of Cameron was a terrible loss. Cam had held Webb's tether to mankind. Now he had no sense of belonging.

*****

Within an hour, Jack Wallace was conversing with Sophia in her living room. Dressed like a television FBI agent, Wallace maintained a friendly appearance with his unruly sandy hair.

"You're a lot younger than I thought you'd be, little lady," he said good-naturedly. "I expected someone my age."

Probably about thirty-three, thought Sophia, in spite of his athletic movements and preppy style. "You have gunfighter eyes," she remarked.

"Gunfighter eyes?" chuckled Wallace. "You mean killer eyes—grey is for killers. But I'm out of that business." He paused, realizing his mistake. "Not that I ever was, you understand."

I understand, Sophia thought. She possessed an IQ over forty-two and had spotted the bulge under his coat. "Well, let me fill you in on my problem." He sat up expectantly. "What's your scope, your status, how much can you help me?"

"Whatever you need. Obviously there are limits to my time, but we can play it by ear. Webb never limited himself to office hours. How do you know him, anyway?"

"He was my dad's best friend. They were together in Vietnam and—"

"I was in Nam with Webb," Wallace interrupted. "But I don't remember any Stewart."

"It was before your time—on Webb's first tour. With MACV in '66 and '67."

"Oh, he never did talk much about that. Things had changed a lot by '69 with our own troops there. Anyway, back to business."

Sophia told Wallace the circumstances surrounding her dad's death and gave him O'Donnell's insurance form. She wanted evidence of O'Donnell being drunk, and whatever was necessary for both a criminal case and civil suit. He agreed to do his best. Sophia had found a champion to wear her scarf in the upcoming trial by combat.

*****

The desk sergeant became helpful when Wallace flashed his ID. "Yes, sir. Deputies Thompson and Duclos are on that case. Thompson is on patrol, but Duclos is here. I'll get him, sir."

Wallace eyed the redhead as he came out of a back room. All these guys looked like small town rednecks.

"I'm Duclos. You wanted to see me?" The deputy sounded tired and harassed.

Wallace offered his hand and introduced himself. "You covered the Stewart accident, I understand. I'd like whatever particulars you have," Wallace said.

"Not much to it," Duclos replied, putting his hands flat on the counter. He quickly related his knowledge from the investigation.

"I understand O'Donnell was drunk," Wallace said.

Duclos shrugged. "Can't be sure about that. He refused the breathalyzer, so all we have are observations. Sometimes they don't hold up in court."

151

"Isn't there an automatic assumption of guilt when he refuses?"

"In some jurisdictions, but not yet in this county."

"How about other witnesses?"

"The truckers? They're long gone. The one was from New Mexico, the other from Texas."

"Did you give O'Donnell sobriety tests?"

"Nah. He claimed his injuries were making him dizzy, so Thompson let him go until later. Thompson was first on the scene and in charge."

There was precious little else that Deputy Duclos could provide, but he quickly copied the entire file when Wallace requested copies of his report.

Wallace headed to the impound lot. The two automobiles were still there. Wallace flashed his ID and was waved in without questions.

Stewart's was little more than scrap, and looked like someone had dumped a bucket of blood on the driver's side. The seat belt had been cut to extract him, so this was one death that couldn't be blamed on not wearing a belt.

O'Donnell's sedan was in better shape but still totaled. Wallace checked the glove compartment and looked under the front seat. He pulled out three golf cards from a Willow Springs Country Club. By his scores, O'Donnell wasn't much of a golfer. The trunk was open but empty except for another score card and several wooden tees.

The county attorney, Kevin Butler, was next for an interview, but he had little to add. Yes, O'Donnell was probably drunk, but their evidence was insufficient to gain a conviction. Butler indicated Deputy Thompson had found O'Donnell asleep earlier and accompanied him to a cafe for coffee. Thompson asserted O'Donnell was tired but not drunk, otherwise he wouldn't have let him drive away. Good point, thought Wallace, but Thompson was probably covering his ass.

After surveying the crash site, Wallace visited the Streetcar Cafe. It was a typical truck-stop restaurant, and Wallace found a waitress named Rhea who remembered O'Donnell. She had thought he was somebody important from the way Deputy Thompson deferred to him. Later she learned he was just another ambulance chaser.

Thompson was the last base to be touched in Castle Rock, and Wallace corralled him while on duty. Very defensive about O'Donnell's state of sobriety, he offered no new information. Even his recollection of O'Donnell's personal data seemed hazy.

Wallace radioed his office for news on his previous requests. O'Donnell had two DWI arrests, and had killed a lady in another accident where he had been suspected of being drunk. Judge Pena, a friend of O'Donnell's, had dismissed his case for insufficient evidence. O'Donnell's investigator had been along, and the breathalyzer results had been lost.

Wallace headed for the Willow Springs Country Club south of Morrison. The club manager became immediately cooperative when Wallace identified himself and asked to see all charge records for the week. O'Donnell had been there every night but the one in question. On a hunch, Wallace checked Judge Pena. He had been there three times. O'Donnell's absence on the single night of interest raised his suspicions.

The bartender confirmed his hunch. Yeah, O'Donnell had been there every night for the past week. Sometimes with his investigator Ochoa, once with his girlfriend. The night in question, O'Donnell had been pissed off since she hadn't showed and had been drinking heavily. Ochoa had been with him, and they had skipped dinner. He couldn't remember when O'Donnell left, but thought he had served them maybe a half dozen margaritas and several shooters.

Wallace thanked the bartender and slipped him a twenty along with his card.

Wallace could think of only one more stone to turn—O'Donnell's telephone calls. His office had those already. O'Donnell had used his credit card from the hospital to Ochoa, and there were several calls afterward to the Douglas County sheriff's office and one to a county judge. Wallace was ready to present his findings to Sophia.

*****

She greeted Wallace at the door, obviously expecting good news. He noted Sophia had been crying, and appeared older and prettier than he remembered from his first impression. Wallace wondered how old she really was.

"What grade are you in?" he asked.

"I'll be a senior in September," Sophia answered. "What did you find out?"

Aha, sweet seventeen—under his limit. "I'm not sure we can do much," he said. Wallace went through everything he had discovered.

"Is O'Donnell married?" Sophia asked.

"Nope. Divorced with one son."

Sophia sighed. "Will the drunk driving charge involve a jury?"

"No, that would be too dangerous. Juries are difficult to control, and there's a lot of anger against drunk drivers."

"So who pulled his bar bills at Willow Springs?"

"Probably Ochoa—I doubt the manager would do it. He probably drove directly there and swiped them from the manager's office."

"Wouldn't the bar register tape show a shortage in tickets if they were compared?"

"I'm sure they would, but we can't prove the shortage was because O'Donnell's chits are missing."

"Unless Ochoa admits to stealing the chits."

"He won't do that," Wallace said. "He knows where his bread is buttered." He paused. "I think O'Donnell will get away with it, at least with respect to criminal charges."

Sophia became steely. "So what you're telling me is there's no hope above the line. How about below it?"

Wallace analyzed her face. "What are you suggesting?"

"Reproduce the bar chits, influence Thompson to change his story, and convince the judge his interests will be served best by finding O'Donnell guilty of drunk driving. We're not doing anything wrong, just correcting one."

Wallace thought for a moment. He would have to call Webb. The bar chits wouldn't be a problem, Thompson was easily co-opted, but he knew nothing about the judge. "I'll have to get back to you," he said finally.

"You can call Webb from here if you wish," she offered, her eyes never wavering from his.

Damn, this little girl is psychic, Wallace told himself. "No, thanks," he said.

"Was O'Donnell in Vietnam? It was his generation." Sophia was adding fuel to the fire. "Or did he go to Yale Law School to hide?"

Wallace smiled. "You're right; something should be done. I'll call you in the morning."

Sophia knew something would be done. She liked Wallace. He reminded her of her dad.

*****

The summer was drawing to a close before events were settled. Wallace had implemented her plan after discussing it with Webb, and each element had fallen into place.

He had forged new bar chits, replacing them several days later to be included in O'Donnell's monthly bill. It had been easier than expected. The register showed twelve margaritas and seven tequila shooters were missing. Regardless of how they were split between Ochoa and O'Donnell, the evidence was inescapable. Wallace had made sure the records found their way to Butler's office.

Thompson changed his story to O'Donnell's great detriment. He swore O'Donnell had agreed to drink coffee until completely sober, and had been surprised to hear O'Donnell had driven away shortly after he left. Thompson was chosen for a series of special law enforcement courses in Washington on Wallace's recommendation, and was considering running for sheriff.

Judge Watkins had required only a few minutes of research. He had an eighteen-year-old son in the Army who wanted to qualify for Army Security and their electronics training. However, having been convicted of marijuana possession with a suspended sentence, his son could not obtain his necessary clearance. The lad got his clearance, and O'Donnell got a maximum sentence for vehicular homicide. There was no way the ruling would be overturned on appeal, but O'Donnell remained free while the appeal was processed.

The wrongful death suit was now a piece of cake, and Sophia had made the civil suit equally easy. Her lawyers did little more than file her suit, and were reduced to presenting Sophia's case in court. Wallace located most, if not all, of O'Donnell's holdings, and Phillips obtained a restraining order against its sale or dispersion. Sophia and Wallace did the lawyers' work for them, and Phillips was not particularly pleased.

As a reward, Sophia invited Wallace out for a home-cooked meal.

As never before, Sophia put on the dog. She cooled a seventy-six Graf von Schorlemer Graacher Himmelreich, and prepared a Nasi-Goring main course with baked Alaska for dessert. Joyce was amused seeing Sophia happy for the first time since her father's death.

Wallace arrived to a gourmet dinner and an even more delectable hostess. He wondered if she might not be eighteen yet. But after dinner, they talked of O'Donnell instead of her.

"Take me to meet O'Donnell," Sophia requested when their conversation began to lag.

Neither Joyce nor Wallace approved, but Sophia was adamant. Finally he agreed, but would only take her to the country club. If O'Donnell wasn't there, all bets were off. Sophia accepted on that basis.

He was there. Wallace recognized him as they entered the lounge. O'Donnell looked in their direction, but only leered at Sophia like he would to any pretty girl. They held an advantage. O'Donnell had not seen either of them before.

Sophia slid onto the stool alongside O'Donnell. "Hi, there," she said cheerily.

O'Donnell was pleased. "Hi there yourself," he answered. He looked at her carefully. "You old enough to be in here?"

Sophia turned into ice. "I'm Sophia Stewart. I just wanted to meet the man who killed my father."

O'Donnell was not easily put down, least of all by a woman, and absolutely not by a teenage girl. "Take a good look then, girlie!" he bellowed, sounding like Moses coming down with the Ten Commandments. "It's too bad he can't get in my way again."

Sophia was equal to the occasion. "You're in luck. I've taken his place. I'll be in your face for the rest of your life." Wallace knew someone was going to get hurt if neither backed down. And it wasn't going to be Sophia. Not with him in the room.

Wallace stepped between them. "Okay, that's enough. Come on, Sophia."

Not releasing her lock on O'Donnell's savage eyes for a moment, Sophia slid off the stool and started backward. O'Donnell had to have the last word. "If I ever see your face again, it'll look like your dad's!"

The room was in shocked silence as O'Donnell's words

reverberated off the windows. Several women gasped, and three men stood up. This was the west, not the effeminate east. They would assist Wallace in protecting the girl.

Wallace flashed his identification at O'Donnell. "You're in enough trouble. Want to add assault?"

The box tops produced the desired effect. O'Donnell turned back to the bar. "Aw, leave me alone. Get out of here."

Wallace escorted Sophia outside, reminding her that O'Donnell would soon be in the big house in Cañon City. That was where he belonged, but he wouldn't be there forever.

Chapter 19

During her senior year in high school Sophia studied Japanese culture to determine their secret for success over American companies. It was not difficult to find.

Japan had lost a war wherein extreme adherence to Bushido had driven Japan to its own destruction under the faceless weight of engineering and technology. Korechika Anami had properly apologized for his failures and committed *seppuku*, passing the baton of leadership to those who would devise a new strategy for Nippon to achieve world hegemony.

Their endeavors were strengthened by retaining Japan's main asset, still undiscovered by western civilization—the *wa* of Japanese culture. Military defeat was only a temporary situation, much like when an individual is broke. The samurai spirit of traditional military combat was simply redirected into producing a new *wa* in a different orientation. *Wa* was the concept of harmony, to be practiced by Japan's Zen-Shinto-Buddhist population to a fault, as epitomized in the haiku, "The nail which sticks out is the one that's pounded down." As a prefix, *wa* meant Japanese, and *wafu* was Japanese style—in total harmony. The opposite was *fuwa*, or discord, strife. During Japan's occupation by American forces under MacArthur, Japanese retained their *wa*, effectively shifting gears into building a mercantile economy without parallel. What they couldn't conquer with the sword, they would purchase.

In addition to *wa*, the Japanese maintained their strict homogeneity of culture, race, language, religion, education, and national aspirations. Unnoticed by American cultural diversity proponents, Japan was the world's largest mono-racial and mono-cultural country. Their culture denigrated litigation as destructive to *wa*. Indeed, adversarial situations were confined to sports or international business competition against foreigners. They made a fetish of reverse engineering; adopting the best technology they could find in the outside world.

Sophia studied the motivations of *kamikaze* pilots and the universal lack of surrendering by Japanese forces. Individuals sacrificed themselves for the community in accordance with *wa*. In contrast, Americans rarely fought to the death as a group when surrender was an option—the Alamo being the most famous exception, and that was mainly by Amulots. The Amulot yeoman had demonstrated his fighting skill many times, even to the point of sacrifice in desperate or hopeless situations. But no more.

The United States was totally devoid of *wa*. Multi-racial, multi-faith, multi-lingual, multi-national and multi-cultural... it was hopeless. There was no case in history in which such a polyglot empire was able to compete against a tightly organized and determined homogenous opponent. Diversity did not bring strength—a feeling of brotherhood and community due to family and commonality of interests created strength.

The proof was in warfare. German military units were comprised of personnel from the same local areas, and their effectiveness became legendary. Cam had voiced the same motivation—he had fought for his buddies, not for anything else. Soldiers became more effective and cohesive if they were from the same state, county, city or town, neighborhood, and high school. Lee's Army of Northern Virginia was probably the most effective American army in history, because the Confederates were tightly organized by state and region. Their units had *wa*.

Diversity had brought divisiveness to the US. The government worked against business, managers against workers, auditors against their clients, and lawyers against everyone. By 1970, the US had degenerated into an adversarial-oriented society which was attempting to function with a discordant symphony.

But that was the history of the United States. The nation had never unanimously gone to war, and even the Revolution was a minority uprising. In all of the conflicts, American troops had suffered massive desertions, and avoidance of military service was rampant. Hatred of America had been institutionalized by the likes of Marxist Howard Zinn, Noam Chomsky, and many Hollywood celebrities.

The worst was that all American wars had been accompanied by substantial profiteering. Sophia recalled her studies of IBM and its rapid rise during the second World War. She objected to any company doing better than breaking even on government contracts during wartime. If a draftee was required to risk his life, should not a corporation be required to forego making a profit in supporting that soldier? No *wa* there either.

Sophia would have to bring *wa* to the United States. But that meant eliminating diversity, changing from an empire to a homogenous country. Population swaps would be required, and the progressive drive to a world government halted. And she wouldn't have her father to counsel her. It was a daunting prospect.

*****

June was the best time of year for enjoying Colorado. Mountain streams were still relatively full with spring run-off, and summer fresh with renewed life. Midwestern and eastern tourists had not yet begun to clog the highways, particularly on mountain roads where they drove like snails. Flatlanders were terrified on shelf roads, dirt or gravel without guardrails that were frequently only wide enough for a single car. Sophia loved driving over Virginia Canyon between Idaho Springs and Russell Gulch. With a thousand foot drop, Sophia liked to challenge the edge and power around switchbacks, throwing gravel over the side. Cars creeping along at fifteen miles per hour would pull over next to the mountain for her to pass, or yell for her to back up to a wider spot. They were afraid to live, on the edge or anywhere. Someday OSHA or DOT would close the roads as being too dangerous. Danger was a part of life, and Sophia was at home in the west's perils and vigor.

But the worst were the sandal-wearers. With astounding arrogance, they set themselves up as caretakers and defenders of nature. Creatures with adult life-spans of less than sixty summers believed an earth which had existed for four billion years needed them to survive. It was that ludicrous belief in monism again. Her dad was right, and every year Colorado proved it again. More species had become extinct since the earth's beginning than were present today. Nature would take care of itself; even if man reduced the earth to desert. In fifty million years, all traces of that desert will have disappeared.

Sophia found her thoughts drifting to Wallace. He could wring a smile from her faster than Joyce, and for a different reason. She wondered why he wasn't married. He possessed her dad's vulnerability with respect to women, and was both physically and morally courageous in his dealings with men.

Wallace was out when she phoned, but soon called back, asking her what she was doing.

"Well, I graduated from high school. That wasn't much, but it was something." Sophia could feel herself becoming animated. "Now I'm looking around for things to do." She hoped he would catch the hint.

"Well, then we should celebrate." He did get it. "How would you like dinner tomorrow night?"

"Let's go on a picnic instead," Sophia suggested. She knew he controlled his time, and the mountains were gorgeous. "I'll make some fried chicken, and you bring beer. Tomorrow should be beautiful."

Wallace would assume she was now eighteen if she wanted him to bring beer. Everybody in Golden drank Coors, and she hope he understood that their time together could be as beautiful as the mountains.

*****

Waiting for Wallace, Sophia understood her mother's emotions when she'd sat in her car deciding to ring Cameron's doorbell. There was a rite of passage for all humans, and everyone required someone to pay their bill for growing up. It was different for her; she knew what it was like, but not in this body. It was as yet untouched by a man; how would it respond?

Wallace arrived at noon having taken off the remainder of a slow Friday. He had spent most of the morning speculating how a thirty-four year-old man was going to spend his afternoon with an eighteen-year-old girl. He was almost twice as old as Sophia, but she thought and acted older than most late twenties and early thirties he usually dated. And then she came to the door dressed in red shorts and a loose, western-style snapped shirt. His visual senses were overwhelmed.

161

"You look terrific," Wallace gasped. Her auburn hair cascaded off both shoulders, and those piercing blue eyes he had seen stare down O'Donnell were sparkling.

Sophia put her arms around him and gave him a quick kiss. "Thanks," she whispered.

Wallace thought he was going to pass out from the scent of freshness and feel of her body. "Thank you," he said, his tongue rapidly becoming unmanageable.

Sophia waved Wallace toward the picnic basket and gym bag on the table. She was a spring flower in morning sunlight, the red tints in her hair glowing with sensual pollen, while he was a ground-pounder, drab and ordinary.

They drove up Bear Creek Canyon to where O'Fallon Park spanned both sides of the creek. Wallace swung his grey Mercury into the gravel road leading through a grove of tall Ponderosa pines. The park was deserted—not like on a weekend. He pulled up in a picnic area alongside the creek.

Sophia had kept up a constant stream of conversation during the drive which he found informative, amusing, and exciting. She asked him why he wasn't married. It was a legitimate question, but one for which he had no satisfactory answer. After returning from Vietnam he had attended college, but his status as a veteran limited his social acceptability. My Lai was the main topic of conversation, and he had endured being called 'baby-killer' and worse. Girls on campus avoided vets unless they renounced their sins, grew long hair, and joined the protests. Wallace couldn't do that—too many of his buddies hadn't come back. Webb had helped him through law school, but there his conservatism also caused him to be ostracized by the foxier ladies. Then it was his job and its long hours, and he hadn't found anyone willing to put up with him.

Sophia bounced out and ran to the creek. Ah, he had forgotten the joy of youth. When had that occurred? In Vietnam?

By the time he joined her, Sophia had already shed her shoes and tested the water. "It's icy!" she yelled. "Let's go across."

Not easily deterred, thought Wallace. He collected their picnic gear from his car.

Sophia splashed through the water, but Wallace stayed dry by crossing on a chain of rocks.

"Fraidy-cat!" yelled Sophia, and she scooped a handful of water in his direction. Picking her way through pine needles, she climbed up the bank to a small, campsite-like area overlooking a section of rapids.

Wallace caught up and dropped his burden. "Good spot," he said. "Reserved just for us." He looked around and could see no one. Not even his car.

Sophia spread a plaid blanket over the grass and sat down to open her picnic basket. "Hungry yet?"

Wallace ignored her question. "Aren't your legs cold?" He was looking at the water still shining on her legs and on her feet that were coated with dirt and pine needles. "Come here," he ordered.

Sophia swung her legs around over his. He brushed off her feet and began to rub her legs. Her feet were like ice and Wallace tucked them under his knee to provide warmth. Sophia had to scoot closer when he bent her legs. Suddenly her face was inches from his.

Then there was no space between them.

The kiss was hot and hungry, yet Wallace wasn't sure he should go further. After all, she was so young. But she had responded with equal fervor, and lain back on the blanket.

"I've been waiting nine months for you to kiss me," she said breathlessly. "What kept you?"

On one elbow, Wallace scanned her face cautiously. He was trying to decide whether he wanted to do this. Particularly there in broad daylight.

He decided he did. "You're a terrific girl."

"I think you're pretty special, yourself," she replied. "Come here." She drew his head down to her. She pulled out his shirt and stroked his back. Wallace took the hint, and popped the snaps on her blouse.

Wallace found everything available, and lifted his head to gaze into her eyes. They were partially closed from her mounting passion.

"Is birth control on me or on you?" he whispered.

"Jack, honey, I've been on the pill for a year," Sophia answered.

Wallace reached down to unbutton her shorts. Sophia placed her hand on his chest. Wallace stopped immediately.

"Honey, you need to know. This is my first time," she said quietly.

Wallace couldn't believe it. This would be his first virgin. Ever. "But you said you've been on the pill for a year."

"I have, but there wasn't anyone I wanted to do it with except you."

Wallace felt proud and immeasurably impressed. He knelt at Sophia's side and disposed of the interfering garments in a few motions. She was unbelievable in every respect.

Wallace couldn't believe it as he lay alongside Sophia afterwards and caressed her body from ankle to shoulder. It had been her first time all right, but her natural talent was incredible. Better than all his others put together. She made him feel so wanted, needed, and with none of the acrobatics so favored by experienced women. She had done it almost without moving, and he had experienced a tremendous sensation of utter emotional ecstasy.

Her matchless bosom flushed pink from the heat of their love-making, and her skin seemed to tingle at his touch. Was this it? Was this the girl of his life? He certainly could do worse, but she was so young. He hoped he hadn't taken advantage of her.

"Honey, please hand me my purse. It's in the picnic basket." Sophia pointed behind him. Without stopping his caresses, he found the small leather handbag and handed it to her. She sat up and drew her shirt together. "Honey, I'm sorry, but I have a problem. Remember, it was my first time. Why don't you check on the car?"

Wallace felt like a fifteen-year-old. Sputtering his apologies, he quickly wrapped himself in napkins, pulled up his trousers, and left for the car. By the time he returned, everything was back to normal except for the blanket. It was spread over two large rocks to dry.

"You deserve a beer," Sophia said, handing him one already opened.

Wallace took it and chugged half without stopping. "Everything all right? Bleeding stopped?" he asked.

"I couldn't feel better, honey," Sophia cooed. "Come, sit beside me."

"We make a good team, don't we?"

Sophia couldn't help grinning. "I thought we had proven that," she answered. "We dispatched O'Donnell, and I think we've done a good job on ourselves."

"You like to take risks, don't you?"

"Sure. Particularly those I think I can handle," she smiled coyly.

"Think you can handle this?" He leaned over and kissed her again.

*****

The following morning Sophia noticed a new phenomenon taking place in her behavior. Her heart felt happy, there was a spring in her step, and she felt as if she glowed. She luxuriated in her bed, wondering if Joyce could see the difference. It must be obvious to everyone. Her mother had felt this way after her first time in spite of her body being stiff and sore. She pondered whether all women experienced this glow after making love the first time with a man they cared about. She hoped they did. It was wonderful.

Her dad had not felt the same emotion. The newness had been intoxicating, but his emotional attachment to Millie had developed more slowly. Sophia's feelings were like her mother's, yet she doubted they truly were love tremors for Wallace. It was a feeling of caring and closeness—of sharing an intimacy. She wondered how long women felt this pleasant but debilitating afterglow. Probably for some time if the pair stayed together as on a honeymoon.

This could become habit-forming, Sophia smiled to herself. She had done to Wallace what her father liked best—she had arched out and down at the right times, creating the impression of total giving. In harmony with Wallace's motion, she had rippled inside, then contributing her own orgasm at the peak, she made him think he had died and gone to heaven. Her feelings had been equally stratospheric. The elimination of her blocking and stimulation dampening chemicals made her highly sensitive to all nerve-transmitted pulses. She could feel sensations far beyond those normally experienced by women making love.

*****

She didn't see Wallace again for over a week. By then the heart-fluttering glow was gone. She missed the feeling of sexual happiness, but otherwise was pleased her moment of weakness had passed. Although he called the next day to say how much he had enjoyed being with her, he had to fly to Cleveland for a week. During the time

165

he was gone, she found herself waiting and hoping Wallace would call. She didn't like it, but recognized she was subjugating her intellect and emotions to him—for no other reason than having made love. She even questioned whether she had disappointed him somehow. Maybe she should have gone down on him. It was unsettling. Female emotions were a dangerous thing. She would have to talk to Heather some day and learn how to control herself.

Over the next two months, their relationship threatened to blossom out of control. Sophia cared about him more than she wished to admit, but he wasn't in her plans. She would have to do something about Wallace sooner or later. He was unaware of her abilities, and she didn't want to hurt him.

Sophia felt guilty about Jack; she had used him to change her status from a girl-who-didn't to a woman-who-did, but now was presenting him with the emotional bill for his services. In normal circumstances, she would consider loving and marrying him, but her situation was not normal. How could she even tell him something simple like her true age, either physically and mentally?

As the days passed, she thought more and more about Wallace. She made love to him as often as possible, testing the knowledge she had received from her mom and dad. Wallace was special, and she wanted to keep him in her life. But how could she?

In August Joyce suffered a stroke and was rushed to Colorado General. She never regained consciousness, and by early morning, Sophia was once again an orphan. It wasn't unexpected, but that didn't make it easier. Wallace proved to be a tower of strength and comforted Sophia throughout her ordeal. Sophia's bill to Wallace was growing, and she couldn't pay it.

They drove directly to Caribou from Olinger Mortuary, traveling up Coal Creek Canyon to Nederland, and experienced a short summer shower near Wondervu. Climbing the dirt road beyond Nederland, the weather turned colder and windy in spite of the re-emergence of a bright sun. They were ascending the Sacred Way at Delphi to make an offering to the gods. Wallace stopped his car on the mine spill where Sophia directed. For the second time in sixteen months, she stood in the wind to return a loved one to nature. Joyce had followed her friend, the sheriff of Central City, and Cam into the void. It was time to reverse the cycle of death.

Sophia was surprised at the size of Joyce's estate. She not only owned her house, but had accumulated over four hundred thousand in various bonds. As sole heir, Sophia placed it all into Webberon.

Joyce's house on Illinois Avenue was easily rented, and Sophia sold the furnishings she would not be taking to Washington. Boots had been whining intermittently since Joyce was taken away, and Scraggs had stopped eating. Sophia decided to put them both down before she left. Their unhappiness was evident, and both were already older in animal terms than Joyce. Sophia's little family suddenly ceased to be.

Then there was Jack. Sophia would be leaving Colorado, and she needed to resolve their relationship. She finally summoned the necessary courage, sitting on Joyce's couch.

"Jack, there's a lot you don't know about me," she said.

"I know all I need to."

"No. First of all, I'm younger than you think. I haven't turned seventeen yet."

Wallace was stunned, and Sophia watched him struggle with the fact she was jail bait. It would be hard for him to understand and even harder to believe. He wasn't an Appalachian, this was not the back woods of Tennessee, and he was not Jerry Lee Louis. It was him, and her, and they had fit well together.

"I'll take you the way you are," he said.

"No. I'm sorry. I'm leaving for Washington in a few days. I have things to do there."

"When are you coming back?" he asked, not comprehending.

"Probably never. Jack, I think the world of you, and maybe even love you. I've given you a part of me that no one else will ever receive. But it would never work out."

"What's wrong? Haven't I been good to you?" he continued dumbly.

Sophia took his hand. "You've been wonderful. But it's time for me to realize my destiny. You've taught me how to love and be loved, and I'll never forget you for that."

"I can get transferred to Washington if that's a problem."

"Honey, please. You're not making this any easier. There's more to me than you know. There are things I have to do. Maybe someday I can come back, but I don't know yet."

"Are you in trouble? What is this I don't know?

"Webb knows, and that's enough. Trust me. And trust him." She squeezed his hand and kissed him on the cheek. "There's no one I'd rather spend my life with than you, but I can't. We've had a wonderful relationship, and maybe we can have it again someday, but for now, if you love me, let me go."

Wallace was in shock. There had been no indication this was coming. He got up and went to the door. "Can I see you tomorrow night?"

"Honey, promise me one thing," Sophia said quietly.

"Anything, you don't have to ask."

"That you'll always be my friend," she said.

It became almost impossible to speak. "I promise," he finally whispered.

"Then call me tomorrow." Sophia gave him another kiss on the cheek as he backed out the door. Keeping control of her emotions, she closed the screen door and waved as he backed out the driveway. But then it was too much; she closed the door and sat down on the floor. Boots came over and licked her hand, and Sophia burst into tears.

Book 3 - The Mother

1986 - 1995

Chapter 20

"Sophie!" yelled Heather, as she waved hello.

In the rosary of people coming off her transfer bus from the airplane, Sophia felt a sense of homecoming at Dulles. Even in rural Virginia, in an airport with the architecture of a Quonset hut, Sophia knew this arrival, unknown and unnoticed except by three people, was the beginning of a new era for mankind.

"How did you know me?" blurted Sophia. She gave tiny Heather a robust hug. Heather was still beautiful and looked to be in her middle thirties.

"Your dad sent me photos of you every year until he died," replied Heather. "But you look prettier than your pictures."

My God, Sophia thought, I could go to bed with this lady. She thought her relationship with Wallace had eradicated her male emotions, but Cam's strong sexual attraction for Heather was pleading for fulfillment. Even Heather's walk was sexy, and Sophia supposed there were wall-to-wall men in Heather's life.

"You know, Sophia," chirped Heather, as they traversed the green Virginia countryside, "I have always felt like I was your mother in a way."

"I know, and I hope we'll become even closer in the future. I'd like that."

"I'd like that too," Heather said. "What are your plans here in DC?" It started to rain, and Heather switched the wipers on in her Berlinetta.

169

"It's time for me to use my gifts." Sophia said. "Does anyone else know other than Webb and Cathy?"

"Not that I know. I haven't told anyone, and I'm sure Webb hasn't either. You should talk to Webb as soon as possible. He took Cam's death real hard, and feels terribly lonely. I'm sure you'll cheer him up."

Heather turned onto the beltway and headed toward Silver Spring. The area down Georgia Avenue looked older than Sophia remembered from Cam, but she recognized Heather's condo. "I wonder why he bought you a two-bedroom condo—I mean, rather than one."

Heather glanced over at Sophia in surprise. "I'll have to get used to this—you knowing everything. I've thought about that, but apparently, my vice president wanted me to have something with resale value. Two-bedroom condos are much more in demand." Heather paused and added, "Besides, he probably didn't use his own money."

Sophia saw Heather wasn't proud of how she obtained the condo and touched Heather's arm. "Heather, you need to understand that I'm just like my dad. I not only inherited his knowledge, I also received a good measure of his emotions. So even if I didn't remember you mothering me—which I do—I'd care deeply about you. You can't do any wrong as far as I'm concerned."

"Your dad and I had a wonderful relationship. I guess I always thought we'd end up together in our old age." She became introspective and ground her jaw. "But it didn't happen. He fell in love with your mother and then our timing was never right."

"Well, he's sent me instead. Maybe we can make it work," Sophia said.

Heather pulled into her parking space. "Made it again," she said cheerily. "If you can walk away from the landing, it's a good landing."

Heather's condo was exactly as Sophia remembered. The pinkish walls had been repainted in peach, but otherwise even the furniture was the same. Sophia's room was smaller than Heather's, and she would have her own bathroom.

"Why don't you have a water bed?" Sophia asked. She had expected to see Heather's condo outfitted for intimacy.

Heather raised one eyebrow. "Have you ever made love on a water bed?" she asked.

"No, but I hear that's the thing to have."

"Only if your thing is the missionary position," Heather smiled. "For everything else, regular beds are superior. And if the guy's big and heavy, you definitely need a regular bed."

"Oh, I guess there are things I don't know."

Heather started giggling. "About some topics I'm an expert. Just ask me."

"When does Harlan get out?"

"That, you didn't need to ask," Heather said, taking a big breath. "I didn't know you knew about him."

"My dad told me. He was really upset."

"Well, it wasn't as if he would have been my first man. I would have handled it. I have before when I didn't want to have sex. You just think about someone else—like your dad."

"We're not talking about having sex," Sophia said softly.

Heather turned away and walked back into the second bedroom. She heaved Sophia's large suitcase on the bed and sat beside it. "I know. Believe me, I know. It wasn't worse than death, but very close. He gets out in another four years if nothing else happens. He beat up another prisoner and had time added, otherwise he'd be getting out sooner."

Sophia sat beside her and took her hand. "So what should we do?"

"Nothing. I'll handle it." She squeezed Sophia's hand and bounced off the bed. "So tell me about your plans."

"I have responsibilities to further the work all of you started and supported."

Heather shook her head vigorously, "Honey, you don't owe anybody anything."

"I would agree with you if I were normal. But I'm not, and that means I have obligations. I didn't ask for my abilities, but they're there." Sophia paused and put her feet up on the coffee table. "Dad considered me as the forerunner of a family of super-knowledgeable people. It's my destiny to create that family, altering the path of mankind's progress. It's a chance for man to solve his problems and reach heights never dreamed of before. I have to do it."

Heather took a deep breath. Sophia, a slim, maybe five feet six inches tall sixteen year-old girl was going to change the world. It would be ludicrous if she didn't know better. Heather felt her heart swelling with pride and hope.

*****

Sophia arrived early at the Parthenon to beat the luncheon rush. She questioned why Webb preferred to meet in Prince George's county rather than close to his office, but she had no objection to Greek food. After giving her name to the maitre d', her question was answered—she was escorted into a secluded booth which was for all practical purposes, a private room without a door.

Sophia accepted the chair offered her—one of two facing the room. Armenian cracker bread was served, broken into large pieces to accompany the olives.

Sophia recognized Webb immediately as he rounded the wooden room divider. He looked exactly as she remembered: lantern-jawed and gaunt, but slightly shy and embarrassed for his six feet, five inches of height.

Webb smiled, extending his hand as he entered the booth. "You must be Sophia."

"Hey, that won't cut it," scoffed Sophia, nodding at Webb's hand. She gave him a bear hug. "Remember, I *am* my father's daughter. And you were his best friend, so I'm here to claim that friendship." Sophia decided Webb's shyness with women would be best overcome by taking a direct approach. She gave him a tight squeeze and stepped back.

"I never thought you would become such a beautiful woman," he said. "How old are you now?"

"Mentally or physically?"

"Mentally you're as old as I am," replied Webb, "And that's going to be a trip. Tell me, do you really possess your dad's memory of our time together in 'Nam?"

"As if I was there." Sophia sat back down. "It's true that I don't remember pain, and it's like I dreamed your experiences with myself in my dad's body. But emotions are there. I recall his fear when the ARVNs disappeared in the An Loc ambush, and I remember being elated when that guard set off your trip mine. Yup, you need to assume anything my dad knew, I know."

Webb looked at Sophia as if seeing her for the first time. "You know about the girl in Bien Hoa?"

Sophia placed her hand over Webb's. "Look, those things are past," she smiled sympathetically. "Sure I know, but I'm as much your friend as my dad was. Don't forget, I also remember my dad's emotions, and have many of those myself."

Webb looked like he was getting dizzy. Sophia gripped his hand to steady him. It must be difficult for a man to be confronted in the flesh with a woman who knew his innermost secrets.

He took the Webberon signature cards from his attaché case and pushed them across to Sophia. "You need to sign these," he said. "How much do you know about what we were doing in Liechtenstein?"

"Dad told me all about it. I understand my mother's life insurance made a real killing."

"Definitely. I drew up a statement for you, showing our investments and current position." He handed her a manila folder. "The bottom line is we have almost forty-seven million dollars in liquid assets."

Sophia whistled. "I had no idea."

"Our timing on gold was incredible. We commissioned Marcus von Koenigsberg to catalog our Russian coins in 1981, and he auctioned most of them at unbelievable prices. We also saved some of the best pieces as tangible history. You might have seen reports of our New York and London auctions in the papers. Some coins broke records. We had pieces that cost us twenty and thirty dollars go for a thousand times our purchase price. We sold the bullion when gold hit seven hundred dollars an ounce. With today's high interest rates, however, we're now into blue chip bonds."

Sophia signed the cards and glanced at the summaries. "What's our split on this?"

"The way your dad and I worked it, considering original sources and participation from operations, a little over sixty percent is yours."

Sophia whistled again. "Amazing."

"Yeah, well, we never had anything to spend it on. You folks lived modestly, and I was always too busy to spend. So we never did."

"I have another two million to dump in today, and when I turn twenty-one, maybe fifty million more."

It was Webb's turn to whistle. "Managing this is becoming a full time occupation. I've been doing a passable job, but could stand some help."

"Any time. But let's break me in slowly. Business hasn't exactly been my thing." Sophia handed the folder back as the waiter approached. She let Webb order for her.

"I must apologize for not being at your father's funeral," Webb said more for his own benefit than Sophia's. "I'm sure it was a difficult time for you—it certainly was for me."

"Don't apologize. It wasn't your fault. Besides, Wallace was perfect. I finally came to understand the value of true friendship. I couldn't have wanted a better friend than you."

"Well, thank you, but it really wasn't much."

"Wallace even thought I was your girlfriend at first."

Webb was horrified. "I hope you corrected that." he sputtered.

"Oh, that was before he met me in person."

"Okay." Webb opened the menu to check the daily special. "I just wouldn't want him to have the wrong idea."

Sophia changed the subject. "Webb, I need a job to join the Washington establishment. Heather is Heather, but as you know, she's not considered totally legitimate because of her past availability to some government officials and politicians."

"Desiring a job is natural, but in Washington, an individual's contacts determine his standard of living. You've got contacts, but your age is a problem. "You're sixteen, aren't you?"

"On the Fourth of July. But that's not the only problem I have. I need to become twenty-one and have a college degree immediately to eliminate age restrictions and make my level of knowledge less surprising."

"Surprising is not the operative word. Around here your knowledge is apt to make you incredibly threatening. And not just to women either—to everyone. This town runs on the concept of 'I know more than you.' Information and influence brokering is a way of life, and your knowledge and recall makes you practically omnipotent compared to our government functionaries. You'll have to hide your assets like we do our budget."

"Been doing it all my life. But can you arrange for a new birth date and background?"

Webb considered the problem. "I can arrange a new identity, but why do you need a new background?"

"I want to become immediately productive at a job in keeping with my abilities and knowledge. If I could pass for thirty with a history of employment, I'd ask for it. But realistically, twenty-one or two would be my top limit. I don't have a college degree, and I can't start out in an entry position with my knowledge."

"I agree with that. With you being twenty-one, I can get you a job in my section at the Agency. But we'll need a name change. We'll move Sophia to your middle name and give you a new first one. Have any candidates?"

Sophia selected Jennifer, and they decided to move her birthday forward five years while keeping everything else intact. "We already have an arrangement with Prince George's county to create birth records and other documents for undercover agents, so you'll have the same POB. We'll put you overseas for high school in Bremerhaven, Germany—those teachers and students from five years ago are already long gone. College, we'll construct with one of our Ivy League arrangements. Do you have a preference?"

"Well, Dad went to Harvard Business School, and I can talk a good game about Boston and Harvard," Sophia said.

"Okay, Harvard it is. What degree?" Webb asked.

"Let's make it in modern languages—liberal arts. That will help explain my fluency in foreign languages."

"What fluency in foreign languages?"

Sophia rattled of the list while Webb shook his head.

"You'll have to indulge me," Webb commented. "I'm a mere mortal with average abilities."

"Dad didn't think so," Sophia said. "He considered you the ablest of the best, and he always said there was nothing you couldn't do when you put your mind to it. I remember—"

"Okay, okay, don't start quoting what Cam said."

Sophia put her hand again in Webb's. "We'll make an unbeatable team," she said. "There's also something else. I want to lay claim to all pacts made between you and my father. All Brüderschaft vows."

Webb felt her hand tighten in his. "Including the 'last bullet'?"

"Especially the last bullet. As you say, I will threaten the powers that be."

He put both of her hands in his. "Done."

Sophia leaned forward and kissed him firmly on the cheek. "Done," she echoed.

She withdrew her hands and slowly resumed her seat. Webb had trembled and she felt the energy flow between them. Different than with Wallace, very deep and without romance. A love between two men; full male bonding. Webb must have felt it also. Later she would talk to Heather about Webb, but she had other fish to fry at present.

"By the way, who's the best legal mind in the United States?"

*****

.

"I've got a surprise tonight," Heather said as Sophia came in from work. "Cathy Clark's coming over tonight for dinner. I'm making lasagna."

Sophia slammed the cupboard door she had opened. "No way!" she exclaimed. "I'm treating us to the Cracked Crab!" She strode to the oven and turned it off. Heather had no chance to protest; Sophia wrapped her up into a bear hug.

"Be easy on her when she gets here, Sophie," Heather said. "She's had a pretty hard time."

"Why? What happened?" Sophia placed Heather's lasagna in the refrigerator.

"She married Tony after they went together for three or four years, but it didn't work out. He wanted a baby-maker, but after five miscarriages, the last with complications which eliminated any future kids, he dumped her. Your dad talked to her for hours on the phone."

"When did all this happen? I thought Dad saw her in 1981 and things were going well."

"The fifth one happened the following year. It was never a marriage made in heaven. Tony was one of those super nice guys in public and a swine in private. And Cathy hid her private problems from everyone else."

"What's she doing now?"

"Working for a beltway bandit." Heather took Sophia's hand.

176

"But it gets worse. About four months after Tony moved out, her parents were killed in an automobile accident near Bowie. Hit head-on by a bunch of kids on Quaaludes. So she's really alone."

"We'll change that," Sophia said.

*****

Cathy still possessed those gigantic azure eyes, but they rapidly filled up with tears as she hugged and kissed Sophia. "Oh, honey, it's so good to see you again," she sighed. They collapsed on the couch and held hands.

Sophia was amazed at Cathy's appearance. Her blonde hair was darker and she was smaller than Sophia remembered, possibly even Sophia's size. Only Cathy's chest was bigger, not as big as before, but still substantial. Although the stress had taken its toll, she would still turn heads wherever she went.

It was a carefree family outing. Sophia noticed two Chinese couples at an adjacent table struggling with the hard shells. Sophia spoke in Chinese and showed them how to open crabs to retrieve the meat. Both Heather and Cathy were stunned.

"I didn't know you spoke Chinese," Cathy said. "Where did you pick that up?"

"I learned it in Colorado," Sophia replied. "I speak a dozen languages. We found out I inherited languages from both my parents and grandparents."

Cathy slapped Heather on the arm. "We helped raise Wonder Woman!"

Heather became serious. "But we can't advertise it." She smashed a claw with her hammer sending shell chips flying.

Cathy looked at Sophia. "I'm sorry, I forgot. Research is one thing, graphic demonstration another."

The meal went well. By the end of the evening, Cathy had adapted to the new force in her life. Sophia would be the child Cathy never had.

*****

As a surprise, Cathy brought over a visitor—Bobbi Rutledge. She had become a currency specialist at the World Bank, forever shaking her hippie background. They sat cross-legged on Heather's couch while Cathy talked about Bobbi's earlier life.

Bobbi patted Sophia's arm. "I remember when you were a little baby and your dad's pride and joy. I tried to help him as much as I could after your mother died."

"I know, and I appreciate it. He used to worry about you living in the District like you did."

"Yeah, some of my friends didn't quite meet his approval." Bobbi looked at the palms of her hands. "He was right, you know."

"Dad said you married Frank, but then he disappeared."

"Well, after having him around for five years, I had to do something. Then Frank emptied our bank account, took my car, and left. I've never heard from him since." Bobbi looked up and brightened considerably. "I have a son, Billy, you know. He'll be fifteen in December."

"I'd love to meet him. Do you have a picture?" Bobbi quickly extracted her billfold from her purse and unsnapped the plastic photo section. The lad was extremely handsome, with blue eyes and sandy hair. "You're lucky to have such a good-looking boy," Sophia said, as she returned the billfold. "Really, we'll have to get to know each other."

"Thanks, I'd like that," Bobbi said.

"Did you ever get divorced?" Sophia asked, hoping Bobbi wouldn't think she was prying.

Bobbi shook her head. "No reason to. I hadn't changed my name, there weren't any kids or another man waiting to carry me off. I guess I'm still a married lady."

Interesting, Sophia mused. All of her father's friends except Columbo were without spouses; Webb, Heather, Cathy, Ed, and now Bobbi. Oh yeah, and her friend Wallace.

Chapter 21

The Kennedy Center season had started, and the Cleveland Orchestra was performing an all-Mozart program. Heather towed Sophia to Bloomingdale's for an appropriate outfit.

They located a stunning dress, creamy white with gold trim offsetting Sophia's long auburn hair. The jacket was golden, and Heather suggested wearing it throughout to divert attention from Sophia's boobs. Sophia agreed—she was going after high-class game, not dummies with glandular fixations. Everything was staggering, even the price. Going as cousins, they would draw all the attention they could handle.

And so it proved. As they walked in, Heather immediately spotted an associate justice and his wife conversing with a second, very distinguished-looking gentleman who appeared vaguely familiar to Sophia. Heather's social acumen was magic, and the justice's wife waved them over.

"Heather, you look beautiful," the lady gushed. "And who is this stunning creature with you?"

Heather took her hand and squeezed it. "Justice Warner, Mrs. Warner, may I present my cousin, Sophia Stewart. Her first name's Jennifer, but she prefers her middle name Sophia." Heather's manners were impeccable.

Justice Warner extended his hand. "Very pleased to meet you, Miss Stewart." The Supreme Court justice's warmth was real and mellowing. "Allow me to introduce Steven Thornton. Steven Thornton, Sophie Stewart, Heather Ewing."

Everybody chattered the obligatory courtesies, but Sophia focused on Thornton. Not entirely by accident, his was the name mentioned by Webb in answer to her query. "I've heard of you, Mr. Thornton. You enjoy the reputation of having America's greatest legal mind and being our foremost constitutional expert." Sophia

179

knew her statement was not idle flattery, but she enhanced it by challenging him with strong eye contact.

"Your comments are overwhelming, but greatly appreciated. Nonetheless, I think a number of others might have better claims to those accolades than I."

"Very few seem to have your appreciation of the historically evolutionary nature of law in the western world. Your qualified defense of Senator Taft's comments on the improper use of law at Nuremberg while allowing for the existence of greater issues of humanity certainly vaulted you well above your contemporaries."

Thornton swallowed and turned to the Warners. "My God, this young lady just mentioned something that happened almost forty years ago!" He turned back to Sophia. "What firm are you with? Is international law your specialty?"

"Sophie's not a lawyer," Heather said. "She just reads a lot and remembers what she reads."

Thornton blinked. "You must remember everything. Do you have total recall?" He leaned forward and touched her arm.

"Maybe in some things. Sometimes, I can't recall my name." Sophia laughed at her secret joke.

"Well, when you become as old as I am, recall is only what they do to your car."

Everyone laughed. Sophia grasped Thornton's hand and squeezed it. "You don't have to be a rookie quarterback to remember the plays." Sophia was playing Thornton like a Stradivarius.

Heather nudged Sophia's arm. "Honey, there's Webb," she said nodding in his direction. "I'll go get our tickets."

"Wait, we'll both go," said Sophia. Obviously, Heather's instincts had warned her anything further would become too obvious. She turned back to Thornton and the Warners to make a graceful exit. "It was very nice meeting you all." Then to Thornton, she said, "Someday you'll have to tell me about your work on the civil rights cases in Little Rock and Mississippi. I'd love to hear how you overcame their wealth of precedents."

"Miss Stewart, you amaze me with your knowledge. Yes, anytime you wish. Where can I reach you?"

"At Heather's," Sophia replied. "Bye for now."

*****

Thornton telephoned Sophia at Heather's condo the following Monday evening. Justice Warner had given him the number, and indicated Heather was a "hostess with the mostest," and her sources of income were relatively obscure. He had known nothing at all about Sophia.

He had been discussing the possibility of retiring with Justice Warner at the Kennedy Center when Heather and Sophia approached them, and now this young girl was rejuvenating him. He wondered how old she was. Heather had looked like she was in her mid-thirties but was probably forty-five, so Sophia had looked like eighteen and was probably mid-twenties.

It was difficult to imagine a girl as young as Sophia possessing the knowledge she had exhibited during their short talk. Thornton considered that she had purposely studied his career in preparation to their meeting, but such prior planning seemed far-fetched. Besides, what was she hoping to gain? He was sixty-seven-years-old, a widower with four children who would inherit his not insignificant fortune, and an individual well out of the political limelight.

To test the water, Thornton arranged for Heather and Sophia to meet him and his youngest son for dinner at his club. Jerry was still single at forty-three and reminded Thornton of Ralph Nader. He was married to his work, and if he could learn to suppress his arrogance, Jerry might be appointed attorney general someday. He would keep Sophia honest, and Thornton could evaluate her at his leisure.

Thornton stood as Jerry arrived with the women, and Sophia seated herself next to Thornton in the semi-circular booth. The ice had broken during their drive, and Heather and Jerry were carrying on an animated conversation. Heather was not as vacuous as Thornton had imagined, and her contacts and experiences were impressing Jerry.

"Do you have a favorite wine?" Thornton asked Sophia, fully expecting Blue Nun or a popular French Burgundy.

"Sure, but since Germany revamped its nomenclature and changed what could be placed on labels in 1971, it's become more difficult to be assured of ordering a fine wine. I tend to prefer Mosel-Saar-Ruwer wines, but if they have a good Mueller-Thurgau Nahe, I'd vote for that."

Being surprised was becoming a way of life and he frowned. "What was that second one you said?"

"Mueller-Thurgau Nahe. The Nahe is a region, actually a river between the Hunsruck and Pfalz, which flows northeast into the Rhine near Bingen. Mueller-Thurgau is a type of grape, sort of a cross between Riesling and Sylvaner, but with high productivity and excellent uniform quality. Nahe wines are not hyped like Rheingau or Mittel-Mosel wines, so are usually under-priced."

"Do you have a recommendation if Nahe wines are available?" he asked.

"Sure, they'll probably have a Schloss Bockelheimer Kupfergrube or Felsenberg. Either one of those or a Bad Kreuznacher Narrenkappe. A seventy-six Spätlese or Auslese should be perfect."

"Do you speak German?" Thornton noted Sophia pronounced German words easily.

"My father," Sophia replied without offering any details.

Thornton asked the steward for a Nahe, and indeed, they did have a Schloss Bockelheimer. He decided not to test Sophia's gourmet knowledge and suggested the Shrimp Louis. During a lull Jerry had begun to discuss lawyers during the Revolutionary War with Sophia.

"Most signers of the Declaration of Independence were lawyers," asserted Jerry.

"Twenty-five of fifty-six," corrected Sophia, "thirty-one of fifty-five at the Constitutional Convention, ten of the first twenty-nine senators, and seventeen of sixty-five representatives called themselves attorneys."

"Be that as it may, lawyers were the backbone of the Revolution."

"Not really. Very few earned their livelihood primarily from practicing law and almost none possessed any substantial formal legal training. Most were like Jefferson—self-educated. Andrew Jackson was considered as having competent legal knowledge at twenty after clerking for a lawyer for three years. Alexander Hamilton was worse. He only studied law for three months."

"How do you know all this?" Jerry was becoming testy over Sophia's lack of accepting him at his word.

"It's history," Sophia replied. "Look at the functioning of common law during colonial times. All men of substance had to become familiar with the law concerning their occupations."

"I don't remember hearing much legal history in law school," Jerry said.

"Not surprising," said Sophia. "Historical treatises on our legal profession have been badly neglected. Law professors have not believed mere historians were sufficiently qualified to write on such a technical subject. A definitive treatment might not be flattering, particularly when the law is looked at strictly in context."

Thornton was interested in this. "What are you referring to?" he asked.

"Concepts such as 'all men are created equal'," Sophia replied. "In reality, the Amulot revolutionaries never believed all men were created equal. What was meant was a denial of royalty and the class of nobles. The phrase has been taken out of context to be interpreted literally—a gross violation of historical intent. Jefferson should have written 'no class of nobility exists' to reflect the actual sentiment. Hamilton said this very clearly, citing New York's prohibition against titles of nobility when recommending the Constitution's ratification."

"Where are you getting this?" cried Jerry. It was obvious to Sophia that Thornton's son felt she was attacking the legal profession.

Thornton was calmer. "It's difficult to disagree with you, but by now, precedent is following the more liberal interpretation. By the way, you used a term 'Amulot.' I'm not familiar with that."

Sophia explained the origin of the term.

"That's what Dad is," Jerry commented. "I'm not because my mother was Italian."

"Back to the subject..." Thornton put down his class of wine.

"Try another deformation," Sophia said. "The Declaration's phrase, 'They are endowed by their Creator with certain unalienable rights, that among these are life, liberty, and the pursuit of happiness.' This is being used to justify unbelievable perversions and reject capital punishment. The intent was that the state had no right to *arbitrarily* deprive a man of his life, liberty, or personal enjoyment. Modern jurists have perverted Jefferson's intent."

Jerry was almost in shock, but Thornton had clearly impressed. "You should be on the Supreme Court. How would you like to work for me?"

"I appreciate the offer, but I already have a job," replied Sophia.

Thornton turned to Jerry when he signaled for the check. "Jerry, how about taking Heather home? I'd like to drive Sophie to the office and show her some things."

Jerry jumped at it. He had lost badly in the conversation with Sophia, and Heather stroked him. With a few pleasantries, Heather and Jerry departed. Sophia decided she had been too hard on Jerry, after all, he was just showing the usual combination of arrogance and ignorance of lawyers. Hopefully, Heather would repair any problems caused by what Sophia had said.

Finishing her wine, Sophia directed the conversation to Thornton's interests. Discussing his accomplishments would highlight their age difference, but focusing on passions in life might put them on equal footing. Sophia was convinced she was on safe ground. Older men were rarely into pop culture, and Thornton would surely not be into popular sports or collecting baseball cards. Such things would be too pedestrian.

She was right—Thornton was an art aficionado, concentrating on pre-World War Two twentieth century styles. Within minutes, they were deeply engrossed in Expressionism, Cubism, Fauvism, Surrealism, and Futurism. Sophia had studied Picasso in particular, and when the subject of composite views arose, she asked the waiter for a note pad. One was produced and Sophia proceeded to sketch Pablo's Weeping Woman, first the side, and then the frontal view.

"Unbelievable! You draw as if you had apprenticed in his studio," Thornton exclaimed as he studied her drawing. "Is there anything you don't know or can't do?"

"I think you would find my use of colors separates me from the masters," Sophia replied. With her recall, she had visualized Picasso's masterpiece in front of her and essentially traced its lines. "My dad was extremely artistic and I inherited it from him. Just don't ask me to draw an example of Jackson Pollock. I don't like leaving dots unconnected."

"I'd like to see some of your work," declared Thornton.

"I've given it all away to my friends," Sophia said, "but maybe I could paint something for you. Is there a subject you're particularly interested in?"

"Love," he blurted. "It's something I'm not sure I've ever experienced."

"Probably the toughest of all subjects," she sighed. "It's different for each person, and I can only draw from my own feelings and experiences." She remembered her dad's vision of love when he looked into Millie's eyes, and her mom's vision of Cam as Adonis shielding her from the world with his body and strength.

The conversation had reached a high level of intimacy, one probably excessive for being in public. Thornton signed the check and ushered Sophia to his sedan.

On the way to Thornton's office, Sophia recalled the statement her mother had made when she was first together with her father. When she entered Thornton's office and turned to face him, she altered it only slightly. "We don't really have to see things, do we?"

"No," stated Thornton huskily, and he took her into his arms.

*****

The following morning, Thornton was wracked by feelings long dormant—ones he never expected to experience again. This young girl, Sophia—so young yet so old. He buzzed his secretary to send her two dozen red roses.

The day was a loss, and so was the next. He couldn't work. All he could think about was Sophia. This was degrading for a man of his stature. He telephoned, but she wasn't home. He tried again, fearing she wouldn't be there, but not knowing what to say if she was. This time, Sophia answered.

Thornton's heart jumped as he heard her voice. It sounded different from the other night, huskier and sweeter. She loved the flowers, and yes, she would love to have dinner with him the following weekend. His groin ached thinking about her. Such a flawless body and yet so caring and sensitive to his needs. Her fresh essence of youth and her adventuresome spirit had reminded him of what he had once cherished in a woman so long ago.

Like many higher-level personnel in Washington, Thornton had come to rely on call girls to satisfy his sexual requirements. He couldn't understand why others took risks with amateurs or groupies. Professionals were extremely beautiful, efficient, discrete, and convenient in terms of time. Yet here he was chasing a young girl. It was undignified.

He dialed Risa, his favorite lady from The Sisters. Available by reference only and patronized almost exclusively by senators, lawyers, and high administration officials, The Sisters assured Thornton of complete discretion and safety.

The session with Risa proved embarrassing. He was nervous which threw her off her normal routine. Thornton felt guilty for being unfaithful to Sophia, and guilt was an emotion he had not felt during the last ten years of his marriage. His wife had finally divorced him after thirty years and four children, but it had been a formal marriage since coming to Washington. Mostly his fault—he had been a lawyer night and day. Now here he was, with the best courtesan money could buy, thinking about a wisp of a girl forty years his junior. One who made him feel wanted and loved. Maybe there really was no fool like an old fool.

Three weeks later, Thornton was considering asking Sophia to marry him. Every minute he was with her was precious. It was ridiculous, but he felt like a sixteen year-old having fallen in love for the first time. Jerry would never approve, but he was like his mother anyway.

Thornton threw the case folder he had been attempting to study on his desk and leaned back in his chair. When he closed his eyes, he could smell Sophia and sense her presence. Nothing could compare with that intoxicating scent of natural girl, like Rocky Mountain spring water in an alpine meadow. God, he was hooked on her! Beauty, brains, passion, and knowledge, all in one woman. He wouldn't have thought it possible.

Sophia wasn't home when Thornton called, and Heather said she was in California on a hush-hush assignment. It was torture waiting for her return.

And then she called.

After initial pleasantries, Thornton invited her to dinner the following evening.

"Oh, I don't think so, Steven," Sophia said. "I think we should go back to just being friends."

Thornton was thunderstruck. He felt himself becoming ill. She said she didn't want people to think she was taking advantage of anyone. She truly admired him and cared deeply for him, but it would cause problems with his sons. Thornton wasn't sure he heard all of Sophia's speech. He could have recited her reasons himself, but he was in love and none of that mattered.

Thornton graciously accepted the inevitable. There was not going to be a last-minute reprieve in his life for love. He had squandered his chances. He knew in his heart Sophia had not meant to be cruel, but she had terminated his life as a caring human being. All that remained was the attorney. And now he knew that was nothing. Money, power, success—all an empty bag.

*****

The relationship with Thornton had proven simple to manage because of his awareness of the difference in ages. In the second month, she suspected she had become pregnant. Webb sent her to San Francisco where she verified her condition. It was time to end the relationship.

It had not been as easy as Sophia expected, but Thornton was gracious and understanding. He had done her a great service—more than he would ever know—and she felt beholden to him. Sophia was pleased when he said she had provided a wonderful happening in the twilight of his life for which he would be eternally grateful. He would never know about his son.

The pregnancy was more difficult for Webb than for Sophia. The Agency followed GSA's usual policy for maternity leave, but Sophia's single status raised questions. The director walked into Webb's office at eight-thirty Monday morning.

"Morning, Webb," he began, "did you watch the Bullets yesterday?"

The director rarely visited Webb in his office, but he went straight to the coffee pot and helped himself.

"No, I'm afraid I was busy yesterday." Webb poured himself another cup. They meandered toward Webb's sitting area finally inhabiting an overstuffed chair and couch. Desultory small talk continued until Webb took the bull by the horns. "You seem to have something on your mind. Anything I can help with?"

"I wanted to talk about your protégé, Miss Stewart. I understand she's expecting."

"Yes."

"Well, we're all subject to rumors, and apparently Miss Stewart has become a hot topic."

"She's a high producer, and can integrate and contextualize information better than anyone in my department including myself. Some are jealous of her."

"I also understand she was hired somewhat irregularly. You evidently went out of your way to arrange her employment."

"That's true. She's the daughter of my best friend, Cameron Stewart, who saved my life in Vietnam. Before he died, I promised to watch over her in his absence. I'm Uncle Webb to her; but she carries her weight like everyone else."

"Well, rumor has it you're the expectant father."

Webb felt as if someone had slapped his face with a wet towel. "That's insane." He paused, considering his next statement. "Besides, I know who the father is."

"Well, I don't care to know," replied the director, getting up to leave. "Unless it's the president or someone with his connections. Anyway, I think we'd better terminate her or move her somewhere where she doesn't work directly with people at our level. The Agency doesn't condone unmarried motherhood, and it'd be bad for morale."

"I don't think that would be a good idea," Webb stated evenly.

"No? Why not?" The director looked down at Webb still sitting in his Chair.

"Because of Steven Thornton. He's the father."

"Steven Thornton?" repeated the director. "Christ, how good are her connections? That's worse than the president." He stomped over to Webb's desk. "I think we'd better get her up here!"

Webb buzzed his secretary and told her to fetch Sophie ASAP.

Two minutes later, Sophia walked into Webb's office.

"I'm very pleased to meet you, sir," Sophia said when Webb introduced them. "To what do I owe this honor?"

Webb studied the beautiful girl standing before him. She was definitely pregnant, but one of those women who glowed and became more attractive while expecting. Whatever came, she could handle it.

"I wanted to meet you and discuss your work here. Please be seated." He waved Sophia toward the couch. "Please understand the Agency is much like a family and people take a great interest in each other's activities. It has come to me that you are expecting a baby but are unmarried."

"Yes, that's true, sir," Sophia responded. "I have chosen to become a single parent. Or in other words, I don't intend to marry the father. It wouldn't work out." She glanced to Webb and back. "I hope that's not a problem for anyone."

"Well, I'm always concerned about things which might reflect badly on the organization or affect morale."

Sophia gulped. "My pregnancy is affecting morale or reflecting on the Agency? I can assure you that it didn't happen on company time or involve any other company personnel."

The director wasn't sure how best to proceed. "Sometimes appearances are more important than fact. I was mentioning to Webb that some people have drawn certain conclusions because of the closeness between you two."

"Then they're drawing the wrong conclusions," Sophia said.

"Sophia, what languages do you speak?" Webb interjected.

"Spanish, French, German, Russian, Ukrainian, Finnish, Arabic, Mandarin Chinese, Japanese, Swedish, Polish, Italian, and I understand a few others," she answered.

The director's mouth fell open. "I beg your pardon?"

"I speak thirteen languages and understand several more," Sophia repeated.

"She's the only person to make a perfect score on our aptitude test. Her skills are unmatched in all categories." Webb smiled at Sophia. "I've been restricting her because she can out-perform the remainder of my entire department combined."

"Is that true?" The director addressed his question to Sophia. "Are you some type of genius with that much energy?" It was obvious he didn't believe a word Webb said.

Sophia looked at Webb and shrugged. "Probably. I'm different from most people. Try me."

Webb motioned the director to go ahead. "Do it. Ask her any question on any subject."

The director threw Webb a puzzled look. "Okay, who was Peter Dewey?"

Sophia smiled. "The person you're probably referring to was Lieutenant Colonel A. Peter Dewey, the only American killed in Vietnam during 1945 and 1946 with the Deer Team and OSS mission. His father was an Illinois congressman and a friend of Wild Bill Donovan from the days of President Coolidge. He was chosen to head our fifty-man OSS team representing American interests in Saigon following the Japanese surrender. The British General Gracey, commander of allied occupying forces in Saigon, attempted to curtail the OSS mission activities."

Sophia paused. "As you know, OSS operatives in Siam had effectively prevented England from re-establishing their hegemony, thereby materially aiding the Free Thais in the creation of Thailand. The British and French expected us to assist them in recovering their colonial empires, but we didn't. The mission in Hanoi headed by Major Patti had taken a strong pro-Viet Minh stance, and the French mission chief, Sainteny, declared the Americans to be more dangerous to French interests than Ho Chi Minh. Only the United States supported Ho, and an American doctor had saved his life a few months earlier."

The Director walked around, staring at Sophia as she continued her discourse. "Dewey maintained close ties to the Viet Minh, so Gracey declared Dewey persona non grata and proscribed him from showing the American flag or wearing American insignia. On the afternoon of his departure, Colonel Dewey was killed at a roadblock within a hundred yards of OSS headquarters. Supposedly, Viet Minh soldiers mistook Dewey for a French officer, but his body was never recovered. Neither the French nor Gracey mourned Dewey's loss. But Ho did. He apologized and swore that no American would ever be killed by Viet Minh again except over his dead body. De Gaulle finally bludgeoned Truman into eliminating OSS missions in Indo-China, and withdrawing our support of Ho."

She stopped. "So is that who you meant?"

The director continued to stare at her for a moment before responding. "Yes, that's who I meant. There aren't five other people in this building who could have answered that question. And the story of how we totally screwed up in Vietnam and got ourselves identified with colonial interests is probably not known outside this room." The director looked out over the Virginia trees.

"As I understand it," Sophia said, "the French became hostile when the OSS in Thailand starting supporting the Free Lao in Laos and sending supplies to the Viet Minh. And when the Deer Team starting training Viet Minh cadres, the French became totally unglued."

"That's right," the director agreed. "Aaron Banks demanded the French cease their aggression against Laos."

"How far Ho's heroes fell," Sophia said. "I doubt if He Who Enlightens ever understood why we reversed our course a hundred and eighty degrees and flew past the point of no return."

"Probably not, but neither does the American public. Maybe it's best to forget the whole thing, cut our losses, and get on with our lives."

"Director, with all due respect, that's exactly what's hamstrung American intelligence since Donovan," Sophia said. "We've acted and re-acted without understanding our time as a station on the assembly line of human history. We've collected intelligence complete with ideological interpretations instead of collecting raw intelligence and then making interpretations against a background of understanding movements in history. We can't forget anything. Donovan created the chicken and egg problem that has characterized the Agency its entire life." Sophia knew she was on dangerous ground here, but continued.

"We have three functions; gathering intelligence, recommending policy, and conducting covert actions. It has become a closed circle; actions are taken according to policy, intelligence gathered to justify those actions, and policy created in line with the intelligence. The system justifies itself and perpetuates current wisdom. Combining these functions in a single agency hasn't been questioned since Donovan. Walter Bedell Smith, who once told Eisenhower that Rockefeller was a communist, didn't, nor did Allen Dulles, and the organizational concept is now cast in concrete. If they have to be combined in the same organization, they should be kept as far apart as possible—intelligence gathering, especially must be untainted by policy."

The director's countenance had become more severe during Sophia's discourse. Several moments of silence passed before he spoke. "I have never heard a more succinct presentation of the basic problem in our organization." Sophia breathed easier. "But it's very difficult to keep people from manufacturing intelligence to make themselves look good after actions have been taken or policies determined. Conversely, those producing intelligence want to demonstrate their importance by influencing policy or causing appropriate action." The director softened his gaze. "But you're right. And if we're to avoid future Vietnams and Bays of Pigs, we need to gather clean intelligence regardless of how it makes our policies and actions look."

"I apologize if I stepped out of line, sir," Sophia said, "but I feel strongly about understanding current situations within the context of history."

"I'm glad you do," the director said, "and don't feel shy about bringing your ideas and concepts to me in the future." He smiled at Webb in approval of his protégé.

"So where should we put you for maximum benefit?" he asked Sophia.

"I'll leave that to you and Webb, sir."

"Okay. Webb, she'll be an independent resource under your personal direction. I'll determine most of her assignments, though." The director turned back to Sophia. "Okay, young lady, what would you say to getting married?"

"I beg your pardon?" Both Sophia and Webb were stunned by his question.

"Webb can arrange an ersatz husband. It would look better that way and eliminate rumors."

Webb nodded. "Pick a name, Sophia."

"Stuart Cameron—no, better to have my last name Stewart. First name Jack."

Webb smiled, but her selection sounded fine to the director. "That's it then. I'm glad we met." He rose and took Sophia's hand. "I suspect I'll be seeing a lot of you in the future."

The director excused himself and left. Webb held his hands up as if receiving a blessing from the gods. "Morality, like everything else, is contextual," said Sophia. "Henceforth, doors will only open, not close."

Chapter 22

The Hunts' attempt to corner the world silver market and the enormous prices realized by Webberon's gold coins had convinced Webb that business opportunities were present in the precious metals market. Even the word 'precious' indicated opportunity, and as resources became increasingly scarce, the value of anything precious was sure to rise.

Webb discussed his ideas with Sophia and Heather. For the first time, Webb saw the effect of Sophia's multi-generational outlook in economics and business. "If we're going to be in the resource business," she began, "we need to understand the various types of natural resources. There are three general classifications that determine broad strategies—regenerating, fixed, and wasting resources." She drew a chart while Webb and Heather looked on.

"Under regenerating resources, we have everything that nature produces with the input of energy from the Sun. All flora and fauna, that is, all organic materials and food. Under wasting resources we have everything earth contained at the time of its formation, which becomes destroyed or made unrecoverable by use. That includes all mineral resources which are economically recoverable by man if present in sufficient concentration. Unfortunately, we must move organic fossil fuels to the wasting category since nature produces only tiny amounts of new coal, oil, and gas each year. Under fixed, we have land, oxygen, and water."

"So you're suggesting we concentrate in regenerating and fixed for longevity?" Webb asked.

"Not at all. We can play both sides of the street. Right now, regenerating assets are in the doldrums and we should be investing in their production. But so are many of the wasting assets and much of the agricultural land away from urban centers. The trick is to buy the other guy's assets while they're cheap and to save yours until they're in short supply. If we could balance the trade, we should be purchasing all our oil overseas instead of using our domestic reserves. That's the Japanese strategy—buy the other guy's birthright cheaply, and sell him something back which wears out fast and is very expensive. That way they can always buy resources because they have money."

"So where should we start?" Webb asked. "We don't have an infinite amount of money."

"Dad had a friend who developed a process for vaporizing scrap through solar heat. There's a lot of refining of precious metals going on, but this would be the most economical process."

"Refining? That means pollution," Heather said.

"It's the main problem, all right. In fact, that's the main problem with all metals production. Metals are produced by reducing them from an oxide, usually by applying heat energy. Creating heat pollutes, and the by-products often require more treatment than the metal. In this case, heat will come from the sun leaving us with just conversion pollution."

"I know the perfect operation," Webb said. "There's a small melting facility in Laredo which is recovering silver from foreign coins, mostly Mexican. We could buy that and try your solar furnace out on them."

*****

It was time to widen the circle of those who knew about Sophia's abilities. Bobbi was first, and in an atmosphere thick with togetherness, she became overwhelmed by Sophia's story. It answered so many questions, fulfilling her in so many ways, and yet required so much from her. It was like becoming married. She had long been a mother, but Sophia wanted her for qualities as yet untapped.

Dave Columbo followed, and Sophia's appeal to him was strictly rational. He was already deeply involved, just not aware of the extent of Sophia's abilities.

"Incredible," Columbo said, "and frightening. If you became public knowledge, you wouldn't last a day. They'd queue up to take a shot at you. You advance the human race by three thousand years, but in a direction which is difficult for people to accept."

In the end, Columbo pledged his support, and that was the most Sophia had expected.

The last was Ed Armstrong, who was still at Maryland. Sophia visited him at his office, drinking in the unreal scene of college life. Most of the students were older than she, yet running around playing silly games and sitting in class for twelve to fifteen hours per week. The poor kids believed they were overworked, having to study for four or five classes—a far cry from the thirty-seven hours per week in class for twenty-four credits and nine courses that Cam had endured at Mines.

"I'm thinking about resurrecting Milleron and wondered if you'd be interested," she began.

"Sure, but last time your dad closed it down as soon as your mom died."

"This time we're talking about a capitalization of forty million, and it would be for the long haul. Webb will also be involved. Still interested?"

"Even more so," Ed said. "What's the product or service?"

"I'll get into that in a moment, but first, there are some things you'll have to know." Sophia related her saga as she had with Bobbi and Dave earlier.

Ed became quiet and reflective, but finally spoke. "I always wondered what happened. Overnight, your dad didn't want to continue. He sold the intangible assets to Webberon, his company in Liechtenstein. And then you were bright and knowledgeable beyond all reason. But he never said anything."

"What do you think my dad intended for me?"

"I can only guess." Ed said. "You're to become the Amulot messiah."

"Who needs a business manager in this age of big business."

"I'm your man." Ed sprang up and shook her hand. "Frankly, I always hoped this day would come. I knew something was going on, and if asked to play a part, I'd accept."

"Even if it means revolution? Pledging your life, fortune, and sacred honor?"

"There's no fortune, but absolutely I'm willing."

"Well, everything has worked out for the best. But I need twenty good years from you."

"Don't worry about me. I want to see the dawn. You'll need time to bring everything together, and you got it. My promise."

"Then let's get to work. The team will be you, Webb, Columbo, Heather, Cathy, and Bobbi. All Amulots. It's a thin orange line."

"I trust you appreciate how thin that line actually is."

"And getting thinner," Sophia said.

*****

Working with Columbo, Sophia created the Milleron Resurance Corporation with Ed Armstrong as president. She coined the term 'resurance' from 'resource' and 'assurance,' meaning resource assurance. Dave became secretary. Heather agreed to help as treasurer, but told Sophia her best role was tutoring her children as they came. Columbo incorporated the company in Delaware to take advantage of their more favorable laws, and only he and Ed were listed as officers.

Assuming stewardship with a burst of optimism, Ed traveled to Laredo to establish control over the refinery operation and returned extremely unhappy with what he had seen. He immediately moved the operation to Midland-Odessa, and began branching out to handling strategic and precious metals. The goal was to corner the secondary recovery of all important metals.

Within four months, Sophia knew she had chosen well. She invited Ed to her home to review the policy standards for Milleron.

"We will purchase no Japanese, British, or European products even if manufactured in this country, and will not patronize any foreign-owned business establishment," she said for openers.

"Stress a 'Buy American' policy?" Ed asked.

"More than that. I want stickers printed which advertise 'This Is An All-American Company' and displayed prominently wherever appropriate. In addition, we'll boycott those American corporations which operate on image instead of technology and service. We will engage no major law firms, none of the Big Eight accounting firms, and no image-minded consulting companies. We will purchase no IBM equipment or software, use AT&T services only when absolutely necessary, and construct our own power plants."

"You're cutting out the big fish," Ed observed.

"They've grown too fat consuming the lake's nutrients. There is no intrinsic value to a prestigious supplier. I'm not trying to impress my peers on the golf course. I want profits."

"Okay, I'll create our own auditing firm from accounting and financial people who have never worked for the Big Eight. What about computers?"

"We'll go with the Pick Operating System and mini-computers in all installations. Create a Pick dealership selling exclusively to Milleron companies as captive customers. Our data processing costs will be five to ten percent of our competition's. We'll also have our own legal department, and be totally self-insured."

Sophia sensed Ed was waiting for another shoe to drop, and she wasn't sure what he wanted her to say. "If you have something on your mind, tell me," she said.

Ed tilted his head. "I just thought you'd say government business is out."

She blew imaginary dust off the back of her hands. "How much would a no government employee payoff policy hurt us with respect to government contracts?"

"We wouldn't get any."

"Well, I can't be a party to putting cash in envelopes to pay off politicians and bureaucrats."

Ed studied her face. "That's not how it works. You put money in the cage in a casino at Atlantic City or Vegas. You arrange for a fee-split with the guy's law firm through a supposedly unassociated firm, or buy insurance or do business with his wife's firm or associates. Lately, the most popular kickback is real estate. You include him as a silent partner in some deal or let him buy something below market value with an interest-free loan and realize a quick profit on a buy-sell deal that's totally legal."

Sophia scowled in silence.

"How about initially diving on the bid and then shafting the bureau on follow-up service and supplies?" Ed asked. "That's automatically expected in Washington. Add-on stuff is priced with a five hundred percent profit."

She made her decision. "Okay. Ethics will be synonymous with legality. Compete as necessary. Government is fair game, but don't embarrass me."

Sophia reviewed possibilities for domestic operations. OSHA, DOT, the ICC, EPA, EEOC, and state employment regulation agencies had made workplaces into deathtraps for corporations, exposing them to nuisance suits and legal costs risking their very existence. It had become impossible to hire people of choice and fire those with sub-standard performance.

She decided to create a Milleron personnel leasing company with local franchises in each state. Other Milleron companies would provide housing, accounting, legal services, insurance, retirement, and medical facilities. Milleron would become a state within the state.

But there was a problem. Using all of Webberon, Sophia only had about fifty million dollars available. It was not nearly enough. Easily ten times that amount was necessary for a flying start. Even better would be a hundred times that amount. Sophia needed money, and she needed it fast.

*****

Almost immediately, the director began depending on Sophia's advice. She had an uncanny ability to look far into the past and extend trends into the future, understanding all events in their proper context. Even more unusual was her ability to see turning points that she claimed were the result of natural phenomena which anyone could see if they would detach themselves from the narrow-mindedness of their own generation.

Now he questioned how she would interpret the changes taking place in the Soviet Union. President Reagan was ramping up Star Wars and his determined opposition to the Soviets, and the Soviet satellites were becoming restless. No one seemed to understand the forces at work, and he had been unable to extensively discuss general policy with Sophia for a month, in part while she took time off to have her second baby. That was another problem in itself. Sophia seemed almost constantly pregnant, but only he and Webb Reid knew she wasn't married. What was she doing?

He blocked out the afternoon, and summoned Sophia to his office. She arrived a few minutes later, as usual without notes or briefing materials, and wearing one of those demure, light dresses that were her trademark. He smiled, knowing her total recall of facts and figures made schlepping of references unnecessary. He asked her opinion on movements in Soviet internal and external policy since their last discussion as she made herself comfortable on his couch.

"Better late than never," she replied with a smile. "They've figured out the Soviet Union's exhausted herself in this cold war and doesn't have the means to counter Star Wars. What they don't realize is that we can't ever implement Star Wars. Of course, they're not monolithic in their thinking or attitudes, but that seems to hold true for the clique in power."

"So what does it mean for us?"

"We need to change our focus to become less threatening in their time of trouble."

"I don't disagree, but I've been saying for some time that the Soviets are losing their grip, and haven't made any impact. So how do you suggest we get our point across?"

Sophia shrugged. "We probably can't—at least to politicians. All we can do is work on building bridges to the Soviet Union and China."

"We already have a working relationship with the Soviets."

"Yes, but we need to get closer. The ruling cliques need to be assured they'll survive and that we won't take advantage of their weakness as they fracture. We don't want them to do anything rash like the Japanese did in 1941. If State and the president won't do it, we have to."

"Assume the role of the State Department? Christ, you're a troublemaker," the director said.

"Be that as it may, we need to woo China and Russia, supporting each in a standoffish way against the other. They are natural enemies, much like the US and Mexico."

"Okay," the director sighed. "We're in agreement that NATO is superfluous and should be marginalized. I love how you say things. You've made the case against it without mentioning it by name. You should be a politician."

"God, no thanks," Sophia replied. "I'll speak more directly. As far as international relations are concerned, there are only two threats against us—economic aggression by the EEC and Japan, and population aggression in Latin America."

"You're not concerned with China, the Arabs or South America?"

"Not at present; our problem is closer to home. China is twenty years away from becoming an economic power, the Sunni Arabs will take thirty years to form a caliphate, assuming they can marginalize Iran and the Shiites, and South America will be unable to federalize for fifty to a hundred years. The Reagan amnesty was counter-productive. We're seeing the beginning of a Hispanic invasion—one keeping its Hispanic culture instead of adopting ours. A decadent, technology-based US could fall easily to a determined attack from the south. Our politicians have forgotten the Central American Republic."

"No, they've never heard of it," the director said.

"Well, anyway, we should be securing our position in the western hemisphere while playing reluctant virgin for the eastern. Unfortunately, our politicians are living in the past."

"What events do you see the Agency helping to bring about? You were not in favor of helping the Contras."

"No, that effort wasn't meaningful in the long run. I think the first step is to scope out our possibilities in Latin America. I can do it in one-on-one meetings with the appropriate heads of state, then assess the degree of difficulty we'll have in confronting Japan politically, meet with the Chinese and Arabs, and present our case to the Russians. All of that should take about a year."

"You're absolutely usurping the prerogatives of State. That will be tricky."

"We already agreed the State Department isn't equal to preparing for the future. Diplomats have a built-in flaw—they believe in diplomacy. The most they can do is provide ground floor services for the normal conduct of diplomatic relations, trade, and tourism."

"Still, they'll scream bloody murder at our encroachment on their bailiwick."

"Maybe not. You could say these initiatives are only to establish better communications with other intelligence services. That's within our purview. Liberals will support the establishment of communications to curb what they perceive as intelligence agency excesses."

"Brilliant. We do have some lines of communications open, so it's a natural progression. You're recommending using yourself throughout as ground-breaker?"

"Yes. I speak the languages, and I'm not threatening as an individual. I can make these trips as a special envoy from the National Security Council as far as State is concerned, and then represent you personally in confidential conversations. With my recall, we don't need transcripts."

"I like it." The director gazed at his beautiful protégé. "You're not going to become pregnant again right away, are you?"

"Yes, probably," she said. "I want to complete my family as soon as possible so I'll be available without interruption after that. As I get older, I also gain in usefulness."

Sophia's answer did not make the director happy. "Well, I sometimes think you came from Krypton or somewhere."

Sophia smiled. "Yeah, or somewhere. So when do I leave for Latin America?"

"Go knock 'em dead, tiger. *Hasta la vista.*"

*****

Sophia had decided to raise funds by repatriating American dollars from foreign governments. The United States was a cornucopia of money for every tin-horn dictator and country tending toward communism in the world, and billions were loaned out yearly from the IMF and the World Bank that was only backed by the US taxpayer. Venezuela was an OPEC member, and awash with dollars. She flew to Caracas.

The president warmed up to Sophia's charm while they sat "under four eyes" in his large, paneled office discussing opportunities. It was as if he had fallen in love with her courtly old Spanish accent which lent immense dignity to her words. As Venezuela's chief executive, he had agreed to meet with her because she was an enigma. The appointment had been made by the embassy's second secretary, recognized as the head CIA operative in his country. According to his ambassador's report, she was an analyst and policy-maker with impeccable credentials, only twenty-five and a mother of two little boys. Incredible. She had arrived with two aides and a bodyguard. Obviously, the director valued her safety and had charged her with an important mission. If so, it was an extremely clever approach to use such a beautiful young woman.

She had introduced herself as a personal representative of the director and requested their discussions be confidential. Surprised by her diplomatic Spanish, he had readily assented. She was wearing a flowing white patterned dress, which hid her figure with appropriate modesty, and her face seemed to glow with an inner beauty which captivated him. With his practiced Latin eye, he wondered if she might be pregnant. He noted a slight heaviness in her waist, and sometimes that inner glow came from the joy of expectant motherhood. He decided to find out.

"My dear, I hope you will not think me impolite, but are you expecting?"

Sophia smiled demurely, and faced the president squarely. "I'm flattered you noticed. Yes, I am. You're one of very few men who have taken an interest in my condition."

The president beamed from her subtle flattery. "We take a very great interest in our beautiful women here in Venezuela. They are national treasures, as you are for the United States."

"I'm doubly flattered by your comments coming from such an attractive gentleman. The director said you were the foremost statesman in South America, and now I can vouch for that."

The president bowed.

"This discussion's privacy is of great importance to us, and neither the director nor I will record its particulars on any document."

"That is all well and good, but I can assure you such secrecy is not necessary," he said.

Sophia ignored his response. "As you know, many problems are universal—traffic, poverty, overcrowding, drugs. And there are competing interests in every country. Even in the US."

"I'm sure that's true." The president was far too canny to give anything away.

"The Agency is one such interest, and a company named Milleron another. They're somewhat related, and I am here representing both."

"I see." He didn't yet, but was sure he would shortly.

Sophia stood up. "I sometimes become uncomfortable with my pregnancy. Would it be possible for us to continue our talk while walking a bit? Maybe outside?"

"Do you have a particular interest in something to see while you are here? Perhaps we could take a short outing," he suggested. He ignored her hint for the moment.

"That would be most gracious. Other than becoming familiar with your country and people, I have a great interest in history. I would very much like to visit the plain of Carabobo where the Liberator defeated La Torre in 1821. And Trujillo, where he posted the proclamation calling on all Americans to join his *Guerra a Muerte* and began his *Campana Admirable*."

The President bowed to her knowledge of Venezuelan history. "I'm sure that can be arranged," he smiled. "Please, why don't we wander outside a bit?" He led her out the French doors and across the patio into a manicured lawn and garden. He signaled the security men to follow at a distance. Sophia took his arm as a natural gesture for an escorted young lady.

Sophia soon returned to the subject at hand. "You are the head of state for a sovereign nation and I'm a representative of another sovereign nation, so everything I say is with utmost respect," she began. "We also recognize sometimes individuals and organizations must undertake actions that are in the best interests of their countries, but would be misunderstood if known publicly. In fact, sometimes public disclosure greatly harms the public interest."

The president nodded without comment.

"The United States desires help and friends, and we're certainly willing to assist our friends in their times of need." Sophia looked directly into the president's eyes. "George Washington once laid down rules of civility that a gentleman should never lean or look a person of quality full in the face, never approaching too closely and always remaining a full pace away. Fortunately, his rules did not apply to women."

The president's eyes were soft and friendly, but his words were equivocal. "Please don't take offense, but your government does not exactly have a good record in maintaining friendships. Most Latin American leaders believe taking an adversarial position with the United States is good local politics. There isn't much difference in foreign aid, and our ability to procure financing from the World Bank remains unimpaired."

"What you say is very true with respect to the US government. But my Agency is not the government. We do things faster and better for our friends without publicity. And we help our friends." Sophia resumed walking, in step with the president.

"Like the Contras?"

"The Contras were not ours—they belonged to the White House. I personally wrote a position paper against our policy in Nicaragua. On the other hand, we're the only thing standing between General Noriega and an assassin."

"Oh, yes, I had heard he was involved with you earlier."

"Unfortunately, people and situations change over time, and the public does not look at decisions in context. That's why secrecy is often indicated."

"What exactly are you interested in? Surely you have something specific in mind."

"Yes, of course. We recognize the United States is entering a period of change in which English culture will decline dramatically in relation to Hispanic. We see this transition as being a turbulent and dangerous time, and wish to ensure domestic stability."

"What does this have to do with me? It sounds like a purely domestic problem."

"In a little more than thirty years, our non-Hispanic and non-black population will be less than fifty percent, and in another forty years, Hispanics may be the majority."

"I'll have passed away by then."

"Yes, unfortunately we're all subject to our own biology. But you can be an important influence during this time. We need Latin American heroes for North American Hispanics as we all move closer. In a hundred years, we will all be Americans, and Spanish will be the dominant language. It may sound strange in a time when others are talking about Yankee imperialism, but we need Latin American investment in my country to assist this transition. I'm here to solicit your investment in US assets. If not on a national or public scale, then privately and personally. At the very least, we should keep this hemisphere Christian and Spanish instead of letting it become Shinto and Japanese or atheist and Chinese."

"Very interesting. What sort of investment are you suggesting?"

"Real estate. And we're prepared to facilitate the necessary transactions for you through the Milleron Corporation and its affiliates."

"You must want something more than Venezuelans investing in US real estate."

"Yes. We're hoping for closer ties with Latin America where you are landlords and have interests in the US instead of the other way around. That's how to build a commonality of interest to face problems and threats from the Far East, Europe or Islam."

"But we're a poor country with large debts," the president said.

"You can acquire substantial funds through the World Bank and IMF. We will help you get loans, guarantees, and debt relief. That's not a problem. And if you decide to vacation or live in the States for a while, everything will be there."

Her last statement inferred the president would arrange for money to be diverted into his private funds. Sophia expected that would happen, but she needed to be subtle and allow him to maintain appearances. Her strategy was straight out of Stephen Austin's writings. He found Mexicans true to the motto: *Dios castiga el escandalo mas que el crimen*—God punishes the disclosure more than the crime. They were willing to sell their birthright—even acting against their own national interests—if it could be done without public exposure. Otherwise, they could be self-destructive caricatures defending their national honor.

All this time, the president had been holding Sophia close to his side. He turned to face her. "Why don't you come to the palace for dinner tonight? I'd like you to meet my family. I'm very proud of them, and we can relax and discuss some of these particulars. I'll send a car for you at seven-thirty."

Sophia agreed. She decided three hundred million would be an appropriate starting investment.

She was wrong. The president insisted on five hundred million as an initial sum. His wife was particularly interested in visiting Southern California, and on the excursion to Trujillo, Sophia promised to acquire choice property in the Los Angeles area on her behalf.

*****

"We can't work forever here out of your den," Webb said to Ed. "Sophia telephoned yesterday to say she had secured half a billion in capital. How's that sound?"

"Sounds like I can rent an office," Ed responded, laughing.

"Well, she wants our headquarters in Indianapolis, and she wants you to start looking at acreage in Port Tobacco. It's her sense of history, and she'd like to restore it as an early eighteenth century town."

"Sounds like fun, but I think most of that area belongs to the Carmelites."

"Work on 'em. Money talks. Taking a long-range view—which Sophia always takes—eventually our racial pluralities will fight for dominance. We're all Amulots, and you know what that means. So if the country partitions as Sophia expects, all our properties should be in the Amulot cultural state." Webb described Sophia's anticipated boundaries.

"Obviously, this is not an idea to be stated openly." Ed ground his teeth together. "What does she expect will happen to populations belonging to the wrong racial groups in each area?"

"Exchanged, like Greeks for Turks in the 1920s," Webb replied coolly.

"You know, she takes the fun out this by looking so far ahead. Nothing that happens today seems important, and somehow I'm the only one who doesn't see the obvious next step."

"You need to spend more time around Sophie's kids, that's all. Working with Sophia has changed my outlook, too. Give it time. Pretty soon, you'll take action in the present while thinking about the future. The trick is to see your actions today as one increment in a process that started long ago. Then you automatically see that process extending into the future."

Chapter 23

It promised to be an interesting meeting—the new American commander of NATO was coming to Langley for a high-level intelligence briefing. Sophia would be assisting, and the new commanding general was Tom Olson. Olson was the husband of her father's old paramour, and she wondered if he would recognize her name. *Stewart* was no doubt indelibly imprinted in his brain, but making the connection to Cam's little baby was problematic.

Olson strode into the conference room followed by a colonel and a captain. Sophia was forced to admit he looked every inch a general. At least six feet two inches tall, with a hard, sinewy physique, he epitomized the American fighting machine. He even talked tough, as if always speaking to recruits.

The director introduced his key personnel, and Olson shook hands with each Agency individual as he was introduced. The last was Sophia. She did not notice any flicker of recognition when Olson nodded after hearing her name, but he moved away to be seated rather than giving her an opportunity to extend her hand.

General Olson tossed his pen down after the intelligence summaries of the Warsaw Pact nations were completed. "If I said the only forces Ivan could use for attacking western Europe would be their own troops—their twenty divisions in East Germany, two in Poland, five in Czechoslovakia, and four in Hungary—would anyone here dispute that?" He glanced around menacingly.

Sophia spoke as his eyes passed over her. "I would, General," she said. "You should add sixty divisions in the European portion of the Soviet Union to their thirty-one divisions in satellites, of which twenty are in full combat readiness. And in Asian Russia, another sixteen are fully combat ready. We learned from Czechoslovakia that the Russians were capable of moving large numbers of troops rapidly without our detection. You will remember the corps movements through Saxony which USAEUR missed."

"I was specifically referring to Warsaw Pact forces," Olson snapped. "You can't expect them to be effective."

Sophia smiled at Olson's tactic of clearly indicating what he wished to hear. "Assuming the Soviets use historic invasion routes, the North German Plain supplemented by the Fulda Gap, I would expect the shock troops to be Soviet, with secondary efforts by their allies. Other nationalities would be used as occupation and communication troops. So, in spite of not adding weight to the attack itself, they would free additional Soviet troops for combat. Don't forget that only Romania refused to supply troops for Czechoslovakia in 1968."

Olson turned to Sophia. "What secondary efforts could you envision?" The emphasis was on "could you", clearly indicating that he considered Sophia unqualified to respond.

"The East Germans could be used to conquer and occupy Denmark and confront Scandinavia. If Yugoslavia remains neutral, Hungary could easily overrun Austria and prevent Italy from interfering. Italy will be isolated, and with its large communist minority, cannot be expected to contribute much. If anything. The Romanians and Bulgarians can hold the Turks and Greeks at bay, particularly since it has never been proven that Turks and Greeks can coordinate or fight as allies. The Poles could occupy northern West Germany, and be used to reduce a by-passed Netherlands, and the Czechs would love to occupy Bavaria."

The General shook his head. "Supporting the Soviets would open their cities and countries to air and missile attack. Don't you agree that would make them reluctant to become involved?"

"No," she said. "Communications and supply lines run through their countries, and they will be targets anyway. That Caen and Saint Lo were French didn't keep them from being destroyed. That Poznan or Szczecin are Polish won't keep them from harm either. East Germany, Poland, Czechoslovakia, and Hungary will be war zones. It's in their interest to see hostilities end as rapidly as possible, and they will believe that can best be accomplished by supporting the Red Army."

"Well, that's the opinion of a young girl. We have information that the satellites are more interested in pursuing lives of pleasure and having babies than making war."

The director stood. "I concur with Sophia's opinion. Perhaps we should move on to our assessment of NATO's capabilities." He nodded to the briefing officer.

The analysis of western nations was equally cold and thorough, reciting manpower and equipment for NATO allies, France, Austria, and Spain. It became painfully obvious that NATO's defense depended on the sixteen German divisions, particularly where attack was probable. The American Army only contained five combat divisions. Its supply depots were behind the Rhine, and operations east of the Rhine were planned as delaying actions. The British Army of the Rhine was limited to two divisions totaling 35,000 men, and under home pressure for further reduction. Canada contributed only one combat group of 2,800 men, and Belgium two divisions. Holland retained its six brigades on its own soil, and Luxembourg possessed only one battalion.

"So the next war will be fought in West Germany if we're lucky," Olson commented. He turned to the other military personnel. "How have we kept the Krauts happy? It looks like we're going to fight behind the Rhine while they fight in front."

"That's an unresolved problem," the aide on West Germany responded. "The balancing factor has been our tactical nuclear capabilities. The German assumption is once nuclear weapons are used in any capacity, the ante will be raised until both main combatants are involved in nuclear bombardments. At that point, the German theater would lose its importance, and that's their hope for survival."

General Olson grimaced. "So the Germans have to force us to use nuclear weapons."

"Yes."

"That's why they want more American troops stationed in Germany—to die so nuclear weapons will be employed."

"And for economic advantages. We spend a lot of money in Germany."

Olson faced the director. "Do you think NATO can stop the Russians today without using nuclear weapons?"

"No."

"Then there are two options: improve NATO's military capability, or surrender."

"Or focus the USSR's attention to internal problems and its relations with China," the director offered. "We view NATO as an old, rusty sword about to be sheathed in favor of new initiatives." He waved his hand in Sophia's direction. "The ball's in your court, Sophia."

"I'll handle political aspects first," she began. "We expect the satellites to become essentially independent from the USSR within four or five years. Whether or not the Warsaw Pact remains functional will depend partly on NATO. It is quite possible that both organizations can be negotiated out of existence in conjunction with removing both American and Soviet troops from NATO and satellite countries."

"That's unacceptable," Olson interjected. "The Russians pull back a few hundred miles, and we'll go behind the Atlantic Ocean. It's tantamount to leaving western Europe at their mercy."

"That's why the initiative must be combined with focusing Soviet attention on internal and Asian problems. Soviet Power peaked under Carter, since then their economy and social structure have greatly declined in vigor. The Farewell operation not only blew up the Trans-Siberian Pipeline, but it rendered all Soviet technical intelligence gained under Kissinger's ill-conceived détente as highly suspect. All Soviet growth during the 1970s came about by stealing American technology, and since 1982, they have been forced to take that technology apart and look for time-bombs. Add to that the Strategic Defense Initiative, and the Soviets are on borrowed time. We know they've already determined SDI is feasible, but only for us. So for once, time is on our side."

Sophia paused as her words sunk in. The director was beaming, while Olson and the military personnel looked shocked. "Only fifty percent of the Soviet Union is ethnically Russian, yet the controlling clique is one hundred percent Russian. Moslems are beginning to flex their muscles for independence, as are other minorities. We are already quietly encouraging separatist movements with the goal of breaking up the Soviet Union."

"Sounds like wishful thinking," Olson said.

"Not according to our intelligence," Sophia said. "In addition, there's pressure from China that we're helping to increase. Remember, every Soviet soldier released from Europe becomes available to confront China."

"You may trust Ivan, but that's typical of young people. You don't remember their support of North Korea, the Berlin Blockade, or Cuban Missile Crisis."

Sophia had to bite her tongue. "Oh, I don't know. They left the Chinese to support Kim Il Sung with ground troops, and made Mao pay in hard cash for every tank, truck, and rifle. For them, the Korean War was an economic bonanza. The Berlin Blockade was a test. I'm sure you remember General Clay wanted to punch an armored regiment through to Berlin in 1948, and the British proposed the airlift. And who could pass up the opportunity to establish an offensive military facility ninety miles from your enemy's homeland? Cuba was simply the culmination of Kennedy's failures in Vienna and not prohibiting the Berlin Wall."

"Nonetheless—"

"We also have to look at economics. Both the US and the Soviet Union have struggling economies, although we're in much better shape than the Soviets. Without Japanese investment, our economy would collapse in a heartbeat. Every dime of foreign aid we give away is borrowed from Japan at high interest rates. Economically, we're much closer to the Russians than Europeans, and both of us badly need a breather to put our own houses in order."

"Never!" the general exploded. "I knew the CIA was liberal, but that is downright communism!"

The director soothed Olson's feelings. "We collect intelligence from many sources, and all sorts of opportunities and possibilities present themselves." He paused for a moment. "Our personal opinions do not cause such information to be altered or disregarded."

General Olson was clearly the wrong person to command NATO.

*****

Milleron's expansion was fast straining its financial resources, and Sophia needed to raise additional capital. It was time to interest the Arabs, and she was astounded to find the Saudis waiting for her—literally—with checkbook in hand.

The Saudis were already sending substantial funds to various Agency operations, including the billions supporting the mujahedeen in Afghanistan. The Israeli lobby was strong, and the Agency actively countered its influence in return for Saudi donations. Sophia's request was seen as nothing more than another worthwhile investment.

A month after the initial donation, Sophia was invited to Riyadh. She was concerned over being pregnant, but the Saudi ambassador assured her it would not detract from her dignity. Sophia carried her children proudly, and, even at six months, could hide her condition fairly well with flowing dresses.

She was obviously a curiosity, but both her aide, Howard James, and bodyguard, Cole Stoner, set the tone by sheltering her in public and showing substantial deference. Saudi security men patterned themselves after the two Americans, and Sophia gained the impression she was being treated like the King's next wife. She exercised great discretion, wearing hats, scarves, and conservative clothing, and rested for the day after her noontime arrival from the States.

The following morning, she was shown in for an audience with the king. Almost unique among her travels, there would be no opportunity for private conversation, but his aides and ministers were all relatives. She decided to talk freely among the ruling group.

"We have received very good reports on you and have been extremely pleased with your actions in our behalf," the king stated after obligatory courtesies had been observed. "Our ambassador speaks highly of you, and said you are a friend of Islam."

"I'm flattered, Your Majesty," Sophia responded in Arabic. "I have studied Islamic history extensively, as well as the Koran and Hadith. Islam and Islamic law and teaching should be studied by everyone, even by the Godless."

The king spoke slowly and formally as they discussed Islam in the modern age, maintaining an air of great dignity. "My heart swells with pride over the great respect in which you hold our faith. Perhaps someday you might be as the Prophet's—his name be praised—wife."

"We all must be true to our fathers, Your Majesty. Nothing in this world deserves greater respect from me than my father. He was a Christian, and I have followed in his footsteps."

"But you speak so highly of our faith and law," the king responded.

"I could do no less, Your Majesty. Christianity lacks an intrinsic body of law governing the laity such as the Torah and Halacha in the Talmud in Judaism, or the omnipotent Koran, extended by the Hadith, which determines the correctness of all Islamic activity. Christianity borrowed its legal structure from Judaism, but substituted Greek and Roman rationalism for secular legal matters. In Islam, law and religion are more than interrelated—they are indivisible."

"Is that not superior?"

"In many ways." Sophia bowed slightly in agreement. "The Christian tradition recognizes a separation of church and state, and many basic tenets of Jewish law are similar to those in the Glorious Koran. However, history has not been kind to attempts at universal law-making."

"And today?" prompted the king.

"The modern cry for world government and an end to nationalism misses this essential point: there is no order without power; no power without law; and no law without government. All must be universal, but competing religions have different, and possibly un-reconcilable, laws that cannot be separated from their theologies. The intractability of Jews makes a case for their neutralization, and the flexibility of Christian and Buddhist laws strengthens Islamic law as the basis for formulating a world-wide legal framework. However, the excessive detail in Islamic law and opposition from western nations whose jurists believe they are more advanced in handling social intricacies than those who deal in theocracy, makes such a far-reaching step extremely difficult."

"You talk like an Islamic scholar and a lawyer at the same time," smiled the king. "Our ambassador's opinion is fully justified. If all Christians could be as understanding and appreciative of Islam as you, many world problems would rapidly disappear."

Sophia genuflected slightly in acknowledgement. "Your kind words are most appreciated, Your Majesty," she remarked. "Hopefully, our discussions can provide an example to others on how peoples of different faiths, language, and culture, can work together for common benefit."

"Very hopefully," the king repeated.

His court murmured its assent, and several princes entered the conversation to make a show of their own wisdom and erudition. Sophia's Arabic was slightly archaic, much like their elders', and made her sound like a wise and ancient imam. She had purposefully made herself seem ghostly in her Nordic and youthful beauty, and with her extreme graciousness and overwhelming knowledge, some of the king's entourage might feel that she was a heavenly being sent to counsel and guide them. At any rate, Sophia did nothing to detract from creating that impression.

She recapped areas of concern between the United States and Saudi Arabia. She could assist the kingdom in four major areas: manipulating trade agreements to help maintain a high price for crude oil, defending the Saudi royal family and its tiny national population from aggression by more populous states, supporting Islamic issues in western political environments, and providing favorable publicity and public acceptance in the west. On the Saudi side, they could assist her by providing funds to defray her expenses and increase Japanese and European raw material costs through surcharges, tariffs, and other economically punitive actions.

The king and Sophia pledged their support to each other. She was extremely pleased.

*****

The new computer system was driving Colonel Chuikov crazy. He wondered if the Americans had gone through this or if it was all a plot. It took longer now to get information than when the filing system was manual. Maybe by 1990 they could get it going. What particularly galled him was relying on technocrats—snotty technicians—most of whom weren't even members of the Party.

At least the weather was still good in Moscow even if traffic had been heavy on the circumferential highway. His little Moskvich sedan was having carburetor trouble, and he hated stop-and-go traffic. The KGB should never have moved its foreign operations to the countryside like the CIA. Since 1972, Chuikov had been trying to get transferred back to Dzerzhinsky Square. Now everybody was supposed to be on computer. It was insane, but some high-rankers wanted to copy the CIA's every move. As if the KGB wasn't already ahead.

Times were changing, and it wasn't just having to learn computers. Everything was becoming polarized. There had always been cliques in the KGB, Army, and other services, but they had been what he called 'chit cliques.' Now instead of being based on reciprocal favors and mentor-associate relationships, cliques were based on ethnic and language groups. The glue of communism was failing to hold the fabric of society together. Chuikov wasn't sure Gorbachev was good for the USSR, but he and his governing clique were, at least, Great Russians like himself.

Moscow was becoming crowded with people arriving from the provinces. The system wasn't supposed to work this way—all those Moslems and Siberians should be shipped back to regional cities. The old ways of promotion through merit were declining. He had risen through the hierarchy, never once receiving favor because of his famous grandfather. Of course, that was because he had been adopted as a baby after the second world war from an orphanage.

He made a fetish out of staying in shape to distinguish himself from the portly colonels and generals who were his competition for higher rank and more important offices. He had even refused to develop a taste for Vodka, preferring to always be in full command of his faculties. Chuikov had also managed his career to the best advantage by staying single. Wives could be a help or a hindrance, but were outside a man's control. They were a risk, and Chuikov preferred to depend on himself.

Senior Lieutenant Yeremensky entered with more accursed printouts. Chuikov had requested a report on the occurrence of a name which had cropped up several times in situation reports lately, and the lieutenant had attempted to build the appropriate query at her terminal. Chuikov's section was in the 1st Department, 1st Chief Directorate, targeted against the United States and Canada, and he was responsible for all intelligence on American governmental personnel. This type of information request should have been easily filled, and he was getting nervous. Several officers at his level had recently been moved to the Planning and Analysis Directorate—the infamous Directorate I, where personnel were put out to pasture.

"Comrade Colonel," the willowy brunet said cautiously, "I found these references to a Sophia Stewart, but there might be more." She waited for the explosion that was certain to follow.

But Chuikov only sighed and reached for the sheets. "How long will it take to be assured you found them all?"

"I really don't know, sir. Perhaps a day or two. I'll have to put a programmer on it. Our database design was patterned on IBM's IMS, and I understand it doesn't always work correctly when recovering and restarting."

Yeah, he'd heard that from programmers yesterday when they were struggling to rebuild the database. Probably an excuse for their incompetence. After all, IBM was the biggest and most famous American computer company. Soviet technicians had copied IBM 360/370 technology and the KGB computers were IBM clones. Personally, he tended to blame problems on the influx of computer types from the 2nd chief directorate's 8th department.

"Get them all," he said. "How many references on this Stewart person do we have here?"

"Thirty-two, sir. All very recent."

Chuikov was horrified. He couldn't believe the incredible number of references to this woman. How had she managed to escape his attention for so long? They needed to start a special dossier on her. The first reference was less than two years old—when she'd presented a position statement to a congressional select committee on Central America. Then she was the CIA representative at conferences concerned with South America, China, Japan, and even the Middle East.

Chuikov swallowed as he looked at the fourth page—she had been present at no less than seven NATO conferences.

Notations on a Latin American trip indicated the subject spoke Spanish. She had met with a number of Latin dictators and presidents alone and without an interpreter. The director must have entrusted her with some important secret mission.

He decided to issue an information order to the *Rezident* in Washington. He wanted photographs and a complete personal workup.

The Venezuela report bothered him. She had spent almost a full day and a half with the president in his office, home, and on a sight-seeing trip—the level of hospitality normally accorded to a head of state. But her other visits were hardly less imposing. She had moved through the Latins like the Virgin Mary dispensing alms in a barrio.

He rang for Yeremensky and sent off the information order immediately. He shouldn't have allowed computer problems to divert his attention. Somebody was going to wonder why he had delayed so long in investigating this Stewart woman.

Chapter 24

Since her arrival in Washington, Sophia had been busy spotting potential fathers for her children at every possible opportunity. Thornton had been the first, and she had lined up the next three before successfully becoming pregnant by him. Webb had introduced her to a large number of notables, and the director used her for briefings and ad-hoc discussions. No one truly approved of her activities—not even she—but her family required broad skills as soon as possible. Sacrificing the best part of her life for child-bearing was a small price to pay to fulfill her destiny.

Becoming involved with the potential fathers was simple. Many of the politically powerful men in Washington existed in 'formal' marriages—those in which couples kept to separate bedrooms and led relatively separate lives. With highly successful women, it was obligatory. She was yet to meet one without a formal marriage who was also some powerful man's mistress. Apparently love complicated marital relationships between high achievers.

There was also another problem—she needed male children to rapidly augment the family. They could be polygamous, while females were limited in the number of children they could bear. She had studied sex determination and discovered techniques that could increase the probability of male offspring and she took advantage of them all. She carefully selected the correct time for copulation and took the most advantageous position. Beforehand, she prepared herself to a slightly alkaline Ph, and each time, contrived to give herself an orgasm. It might seem almost like artificial insemination, but the end justified the means. Leaving things to chance was not her style.

Thornton's death shortly after Adam was born had been regrettable, but she had not structured his life for the first sixty-seven years. He was a casualty because he fell in love, and there would be others in the years to come. She would be kind, but would have to break some eggs to make omelets.

Meanwhile, an area of increasing concern to her was the growth in importance of three organizations; the Council for Foreign Relations, the Trilateral Commission, and the Bilderbergs.

The CFR was initially a fellowship of academics called "The Inquiry" formed by Woodrow Wilson and headed by Walter Lippmann and Edward House. Lippmann was a socialist who considered the American people too dumb to govern themselves. Eventually the public was to be controlled by unelected elites through propaganda based on the CFR's liberal line that was unabashedly socialistic. By 1980, the CFR had almost five thousand members and was the dominant force in determining foreign policy for the federal government. For the previous fifteen years it had been controlled by David Rockefeller, president of Chase Manhattan Bank. With nearly half of all super-graded federal bureaucrats in the CFR, membership was almost required for promotion.

The second organization was the Trilateral Commission, the brainchild of David Rockefeller, that also including leaders from Europe and Japan. Its goal was to eventually form a union of Europe, North America, and Japan, first economically, then politically. Zbigniew Brzezinski had floated the idea at the 1972 Bilderberg meeting, and the TC became an off-shoot of the Bilderbergs, although almost all of their members are also members of the CFR. Rockefeller and Kissinger became the mainstays, with Zbig doing the heavy lifting.

In 1973, Brzezinski vetted Jimmy Carter and introduced him to David Rockefeller as the TC's first president of the United States. Carter was groomed and financed for the presidency, rising from four percent Democratic support in the early primaries to receiving the nomination and being elected president. However, Carter was a disaster who shredded the TC timetable, and Reagan's election threatened to halt the US's march toward socialism and a rapprochement with communism. Only in American schools were successes mounting, and by the time Sophia graduated from high school, most textbooks preached socialism and progressivism.

The umbrella organization was the Bilderbergs. This

organization was founded in 1954 by Prince Bernhard of the Netherlands, a former member of the NAZI Party and the SS. The organization promoted a new One World Order, wherein nation states would be eliminated and all economic and political activities throughout the world would be controlled by a central bureaucracy. Their political philosophy was socialism, but one wherein all business would not be controlled by political forces, but rather by approved banking systems, banks, and extremely large corporations acting in concert with the government bureaucracies, all being controlled by Bilderberg members. In effect, this system of world government was Supra-National Socialism or Snazism, with a junta of powerful people running both the private and public sectors. The benefits of this world government supposedly were peace and prosperity for all.

The Agency had been involved up to its eyebrows in these three organizations from their inception, and still had a decidedly leftist tilt. It had recruited extensively from Ivy League schools, which were overwhelmingly leftist with questionable commitments to the US. These "blue bloods" were also precisely the wrong types for intelligence. They rarely possessed imagination or innovative attitudes, the ability to take risks, or an affinity with common people, yet those attributes were what was needed to be successful in operations.

Efforts had been made to improve the Agency's capabilities in the 1960s by hiring first-generation Americans with foreign language capabilities, but Stansfield Turner's Halloween Day Massacre in 1977 ended that. Admiral Turner eliminated some eight hundred operatives, generally the most effective individuals with excellent language skills. From that point onward, the Agency had relied primarily on technical and signal intelligence and rarely gathered intelligence from human-to-human contact.

Now, in the 1980s, the situation was even worse. The Agency was becoming a hide-bound bureaucracy, totally enmeshed in red tape and legalisms. Lawyers outnumbered operatives, and Webb had told Sophia that eighty percent of the Agency were counter-productive or useless. A small coterie of people did all the work while the rest played at being agents by producing paper. Meetings abounded, and the legions of lawyers sought to mitigate risk-taking. One-third of American medical costs went to lawyers, but so did half of the Agency's budget. The CIA even featured numbers of husband-

and-wife teams dedicated to helping each other negotiate the maze and win promotions. Webb's Special Projects section was one of the few productive elements in the organization, and the director kept it isolated in order to function.

*****

Sophia turned her attention to combating the Japanese mercantile empire. Their trade surplus was approaching fifty billion dollars per year, and they were using those funds to finance the US national debt and purchase American industry.

The Japanese strategy worked because of Japan's long planning horizon. Whereas American industry operated on quarterly and annual reports, Japanese functioned on five, ten, fifteen, and even twenty-year plans. During their basic recovery fueled by American aid after World War II, Japanese cartels planned penetrations and takeovers of American industries for the next thirty years.

Sophia could not determine where a Japanese corporation stopped and a bank started, nor where the bank stopped and government started. The Japanese system was integrated under *wa* with workers, management, stockholders, banks, and government all standing behind every product shipped overseas. Supplier networks were built up following *keiretsu*—loyalty to family-connected businesses. American parts manufacturers were shut out or forced to purchase Japanese materials and products. Americans were *gaijin*—outside person or foreigner—even in their own country with respect to conducting business with Japanese.

Three times in recent Japanese history, the people of Japan were told to face years of *gashin-shoton*. The phase literally translated as "sleep on kindling and lick gall," meaning to endure a life of patience and austerity to accomplish a given purpose. It was first used following the Sino-Japanese War when Japan was forced to return the Liaotung Peninsula to China. The second time was between the Washington conferences and World War II, and the last from the collapse of Japan until economic power was achieved during the seventies.

Japanese leaders had been careful to bleed their conquerors like leeches while building a long-range economic powerhouse. Even as late as the sixties, the US was asked to help save Japan's hard currency by purchasing food and raw materials. Japan relied on Americans for its physical security, spending less than two percent on defense. Then while America was occupied with Vietnam, Japanese industry completed its re-armament with modern facilities and technology, and began its assault on American markets.

Japan had declared economic war with another sneak attack. But as in World War II, Japanese strategy was based on an assessment of what Americans would do, not what they *could* do. Once again, that was a flawed strategy. It might work against the US government and its ignorant bureaucrats, but not against her. As a private corporation, Milleron could do the unexpected. Sophia would be as inscrutable as any oriental.

And Japan was vulnerable. Sophia looked at agricultural imports, raw materials, hematite, bauxite, copper ore, tin, crude oil, lumber, and others. Some were promising, some not. Japan possessed no domestic raw materials, but had colonized Australia sufficiently to ensure substantial amounts of metallic ores, and they had moved large amounts of capital into Southeast Asia to secure its forest products. Still, the number of producer nations was small, and they were not organized. Perhaps with Milleron she could divert these resources to other markets to raise the price—like to China. That was her best opening—that and curtailing Japan's rape of common ocean resources.

Based on her analysis, Sophia made an effort to open a meaningful channel of communication with the Japanese.

*****

The Japanese premier was polite and cordial, and Sophia kept their discussion at a diplomatic level. She mentioned that major forces in the United States thought the US had been poorly repaid for aiding Japan's reconstruction, and there was rising anti-Japanese sentiment. The premier showed almost no emotion, and less concern for the American public opinion. Americans desired top quality products and his countrymen were merely responding to demand. He shrugged at the political implications, and Sophia knew she had collided with an immovable object.

All six *zaibatsu* bankers and industrialists were identical. All were venerated elder businessmen, and Sophia decided she had made another mistake—it would have only been necessary to talk with one. The last three already knew what she wished to say before she arrived. At their level, they functioned as a huge cartel across all Japanese industries and presented a solid front against all outside and foreign interests.

Faced with polite disdain, Sophia reminded all *zaibatsu* heads of the Boston Tea Party and that such activity was an honored American tradition, much like the Japanese tradition of *gekokujo*. She suggested the organization she represented was prepared to undertake action to safeguard American interests.

In return, she was reminded of Deming's great principles and how Japan was blameless in America's current crisis. In spite of Sophia speaking Japanese, her warnings were not taken seriously. She was only a woman who possessed no visible political or economic clout. The Japanese were still the chosen race, and would one day rule the world.

Her conscience was clear. She had given the Japanese due notice.

*****

China was to be her ace in the hole. Preparing thoroughly, she visited the Chinese ambassador to outline the diplomatic aspects of her trip. She would be personally representing the director as usual, and she wished to discuss four subjects: establishing communications between their respective intelligence agencies, opening trade between selected major American corporations and certain Chinese industries, determining appropriate mechanisms for technology transfer, and disrupting Japanese trade routes through competition. The ambassador made little comment, but promised to transmit her message. Within two weeks, she possessed all necessary papers and was ready to leave.

Sophia took Ed and Sylvia Choi from Milleron and her normal entourage from the Agency with her. Her time in Peking had been carefully arranged through the Chinese ambassador, and on the second day, Sophia was ushered into the premier's reception office.

She sat alone with her aide until the premier emerged with his entourage. She bowed graciously in the Chinese fashion Sylvia had taught her, and offered her greetings.

In Mandarin Chinese.

It was the first indication that Sophia spoke their language. Sylvia Choi had interpreted on the first day for the entire group, and Sophia had allowed the bustle to swirl around her without becoming involved. Sudden recognition of her language capability caused some consternation among the premier's entourage.

He waved his interpreter back and greeted her before ushering her into his sitting room for their meeting. There they chatted about China's history and the nobility of its ancient civilization. Sophia noticed her host was taken aback by her knowledge, and became increasingly nervous.

"My apologies, but our ambassador was not fully aware of the subjects we are to discuss," the premier said.

"I'm sure my appearance and age were confusing factors," Sophia replied, giving him additional ways to save face. "I am here to promote communications between our countries in two primary areas, mutual understanding and trade. I'm sure you know the organization I represent, and I wish to assure you we do not consider China our enemy. We hope to improve the security and well-being of both our countries by establishing a means of communication which can lessen crises as they arise."

The premier smiled. "They did well to send you. It is impossible to take umbrage at anything you say." He nodded. "It is also difficult to believe they would entrust such a sensitive mission to someone so young and beautiful."

"Yes, very difficult. But I'm sure you have been informed that I was present at most NATO strategy sessions, and have met privately with many heads of state."

The premier nodded. "Yes, we have wondered about you."

Sophia suspected he was lying. Maybe the Chinese Secret Service was not as efficient as believed. In any case, the situation would soon be clarified. "I do not mean to overstate my importance, but I am uniquely qualified to conduct these discussions. Perhaps those qualifications will make themselves more apparent as we continue."

"I believe we understand. You are easily the most

knowledgeable American we have received in high levels with respect to China."

"You are very gracious, sir. The second aspect I wish to discuss is facilitation of trade. My organization wishes to become involved in trade with certain agencies in your country, again to enhance our common security. As you can see, we are desirous of creating an entirely new footing for mutual understanding. For instance, we are in position to ensure a certain amount of favorable publicity for China and its leaders in our country. Being a society with a free, and often contentious press, such an opportunity is of great value."

"I see. Unfortunately, I have a prior commitment approaching that must take precedence, but would be pleased if you could join me for dinner to continue this discussion."

Sophia assumed the premier needed time to check with his own people. She accepted graciously and retired.

Ed and Sylvia had made little progress with officials from the Ministry of Trade, and Ed was upset. Because of the power of Milleron money, he had come to expect immediate deal-making where he called the shots. Sophia listened to his complaints about obtuse Chinese functionaries with interest and amusement. Here was a situation where his counterpart recognized no pressing reason to conduct business.

"So you think the Chinese are difficult, do you?" Sophia asked.

"You try talking to them. Their economy is in shambles, but they act like it's great. They listen, but don't want to do anything," Ed said.

"You've taken over dozens of US companies. How many had computer systems furnished by our favorite computer company? And how many did you replace with superior systems at a much lower cost?" Sophia asked the question almost rhetorically, and wondered if Ed would understand the comparison.

He didn't.

"All of them," Ed said. "The old management had bought faith—faith in the vendor's image without regard to cost. The software was simply God-awful."

Sophia shook her head. "It was more than that. They were controlled through sales effort. Sylvia was once told that the system she was using did not exist. Even that what she was doing was impossible. If the world's greatest computer company didn't have it, it didn't exist. That's where the Chinese are. They are like your companies who didn't know their systems were obsolete and assumed all other systems were worse."

Ed nodded. "I see what you're saying. People threatened to leave when I announced their computer system would be trashed. Some stayed and found they had been duped, but others left and are still true believers."

"You're breaking new ground. There's nothing so difficult as the implementation of something new. Those who have a vested interest in maintaining the status quo fight like devils, while those who will benefit provide only lukewarm support. The creator is alone. You're leading the horse to water. In Milleron, you can make him drink, but not here."

"But I'm not sure I'm leading the right horses to water. It's hard to tell who can make decisions—or maybe we haven't met him yet." Ed looked out toward the Forbidden City.

Sylvia arrived while Ed poured himself another cup of tea. She had come a long way from working in the Mines computer center and teaching Sophia Chinese. She had set up Milleron's computer operations at Port Tobacco, and her performance exceeded Sophia's expectations. Her job grew rapidly as she was called upon to consolidate each acquisition into her Pick relational database, and this trip had been both a reward and chance to use her language capability to assist Ed.

"How do you think it went, Sylvia?" Sophia asked the diminutive Chinese lady. Sylvia looked like a short version of the Dragon Lady in *Terry And The Pirates*. Ageless like many high-born Chinese, she had not yet lost her schoolgirl look.

"Oh, merely a formality for us to be assessed and meet a few people," Sylvia said. "They were waiting for guidance from your meeting with the premier. We won't know anything until dinner tonight."

As Sylvia anticipated, dinner answered their questions. The Chinese Secret Service apparently had contacted their embassies in various countries to validate Sophia's statements. Several high-ranking members of the Chinese Central External Liaison Department, Ministry of External Trade, External Trade Promotion

Committee, and Investigation Bureau were there to meet her. All the intelligence services' heavyweights were present, and the Chinese were making a huge mistake underestimating her recall capabilities. She met and assessed each individual, and the lineup of personnel was astounding. It included the Minister of Agriculture whose department had handled China's opium distribution to undermine the American war effort in Korea and Vietnam.

Sophia had plans for it.

The premier set the tone, and Sophia and her little delegation were given a subtle blank check. Over the following several days, new and more important people met with Sylvia and Ed, and preliminary agreements were concluded. Everyone recognized progress would be slow, and Sophia guessed she would be making two trips per year to China for the foreseeable future.

Chapter 25

Sophia's next Middle East trip was arranged by the State Department to provide her with diplomatic status. The director personally discussed her trip with the Secretary of State, all four US ambassadors, and the ambassadors of the Arab countries in Washington. Her credentials were officially given as Special Envoy for the National Security Council, and Gary Stebar, one of the director's aides paved the way with a courtesy call to each embassy.

He then popped into Sophia's office to coordinate her schedule. "So this is where you hang out."

Sophia looked up and smiled at the good-looking Yale graduate. The director used Gary as a gofer, but also for sensitive tasks requiring social graces and tact. He certainly had tact, and abundant Brooks Brothers good looks. "First time slumming?" Sophia gibed gaily. Gary was a young male Heather.

He handed her a typewritten sheet of paper. "I've contacted the Arab embassies, and this is what we've worked up."

Sophia glanced over the sheet. "Syria, Iraq, Saudi Arabia, and Egypt. Looks good to me. They're in order, too. I've already been to Riyadh, and Egypt will be a courtesy stop."

"Sure you don't want me along? I've never been to the Middle East."

"Who's Cord Meyer?" she asked.

"Not a clue. Is he somebody I'm supposed to know?"

"You find out, and I'll take you on my next trip to the Middle East. Deal?"

"Deal." Gary waved and trotted out.

Sophia shook her head. Ignorance did not stop at the doors to Langley.

*****

Arriving in Damascus was worth the trip by itself. Sophia swore she could spot at least two dozen security personnel, all of whom stared in amazement as if they couldn't believe this little girl was the important American official they were to protect.

She was escorted rapidly through the airport and taken to a guest residence. Sophia sensed they were keeping her from observing Damascus life, but frankly, she didn't care.

Her bodyguard, Cole, was pleased with the attention. As he told Sophia, if the Syrians were concerned about Sophia's safety, he needn't be.

After breakfast Sophia was escorted to the presidential palace to meet with the president and the chief of security. It was apparent they weren't sure she wasn't an assassin, particularly when she requested to speak alone with the president.

"As I'm sure you know, I normally receive only the most sensitive missions, those requiring maximum security. What I have to discuss can certainly be presented with all of us here, but I must insist our conference not be subject to recording devices. We mean no disrespect to your security service, but we are concerned about our discussion becoming known to Israeli intelligence."

The president was momentarily stunned, but recovered rapidly. The security chief started to voice his objection, but the president motioned for him to remain silent. "Believe me, you need have no concerns about the Israelis," the president said. "This area is most secure, I assure you."

Sophia nodded. "Fine. I'm sure you understand we're a large polyglot state with many different nationalities, religions, and interests. My agency is one of those interests and often opposed to viewpoints of our Jewish population and the Israeli lobby on Capitol Hill." She noticed the security chief frowning. Poker playing would not be his forte.

"That's somewhat hard to believe, Miss Stewart," the security chief interjected. "The CIA is well known for working closely with Israeli intelligence."

Sophia smiled. "They have a very efficient network and we sometimes find it advantageous to trade information when it is in our interest. Normally, those cases are publicized in order to mollify our active Jewish partisans. In actuality, we have been more supportive of Arab nations, particularly Saudi Arabia. It has been through our activities that Arab nations have been able to purchase US military equipment. We created the pressure to force Israel to halt in the Yom Kippur War. Ask Riyadh. We frequently represent their interests—and yours—against Israel."

"If you're as active in helping us as you say, how about pressuring them to give back the Golan Heights?"

"In matters concerning Israel, we have to proceed slowly and usually covertly. In many ways, we envy your generally homogenous population and religious unanimity. In any case, I'm here talking with you, and the Golan Heights' status is certainly a legitimate item for discussion."

Sophia took a few moments to discuss Damascus as the oldest continuously-inhabited city in history and mentioned her interest in several archeological sites. It was a good idea to build bona fides before returning to higher-level subjects.

"I rather expected you to broach the subject of the hostages in Lebanon, Mrs. Stewart," the president said.

Sophia broke into a broad smile and held up her hands. "No, the hostages do not concern my organization at this time. Perhaps fortunately for both hostages and captors."

"And why is that?" The security chief furrowed his brow.

"We believe diplomacy can only take place where there is mutual respect for each party's resolve to take extreme measures in their national self-interest. Otherwise, it is charity. Taking hostages is a warlike act, and if I or my organization were responsible for resolving such a situation, we would be swifter and more effective than the Soviets were recently."

"You're referring to the incident where KGB agents removed certain body parts from a kidnapper's brother and sent it to him as a warning?"

"Yes. Most effective, wasn't it? The Russian hostage was returned unharmed almost immediately. But the Soviets are not known for their subtlety. Our president has restricted my agency's activity concerning hostages, otherwise things would be different."

"Tell me," the president said, "is it true that no CIA operatives were captured in Vietnam?"

"No. A number were captured, but neither they nor their captors lived for long. And the alleged Agency operatives in Central America who fell into opposition hands were not ours. If it were up to me, all Lebanon hostages would be dead or recovered, but definitely their captors would be dead. There would be no sanctuary for them anywhere after having done us such dishonor."

"It's amazing to hear such stern words from a beautiful woman who is also carrying a child," the president said.

"I'm expendable. My sons will carry on when I cannot. Like my father—and I'm sure your father—I believe in honor above life."

"Even above national interest?" the president asked.

"Whatever is in my nation's interest is honorable." Sophia smiled.

"And what is your nation's interest at this point?"

"We wish to achieve a long-term solution to the Israeli-Palestinian problem. Although Palestinians are winning the birth rate battle, Israel is fully aware of the implications. We do not desire a resumption of hostilities in this region, and we think there might be a possible resolution that would include Lebanon."

The president stood, walked to the wall at his right, and examined a hanging carpet. "You propose a solution on behalf of your organization, not of your country?"

"Precisely. As I said, some things can only occur if done slowly and without public knowledge. Particularly in the United States."

The chief of security remained silent while the president spoke. "Very interesting. Perhaps it would be a good idea for us to talk alone." He ordered his chief to post himself outside.

"What exactly do you propose?" the president asked as soon as the man was gone.

"The creation of a Palestinian state—in Lebanon. Swap some of the West Bank and all the Gaza Strip Palestinians for Christians in Lebanon. The Golan Heights returns to Syria. It's a difficult solution, but possible. The Turks and Greeks accomplished such a population swap in the twenties, so there is international precedent to consider."

"The Palestinians won't like it, the Lebanese won't like it, and the Israelis won't like it." The president stopped. "But I'll tell you who will like it. Me. And the Egyptians."

"Lebanon was an artificially created state anyway," Sophia said.

"It was to be a safe enclave for Christians with a Christian president required by its constitution. But its majority is now Muslim. Christians only have sufficient power to kill people and cause widespread hardship. At any rate, they have to go."

"But you are a Christian." The president arched an eyebrow.

"Yes. And in seeking to combine the Maronites with Israel, I believe we are creating the best possible solution to ensure their continued survival."

"What about Jerusalem? It can't be the Jewish capital."

"Agreed. It must be an open city. Administered by Israel. Open to Jews, Christians, and Muslims alike. It is holy to us all, an interfaith city, open to all and the private reserve of none. We must work toward that."

"When do you see this occurring? I have troops involved in fighting in Lebanon every day."

"We need to obtain general agreement among Arab nations. That's the major purpose of this trip. Then we'll introduce our idea into Lebanon and Israel, as well as among the American public. It'll take time. Probably three to five years. But twenty years have already passed since Israel occupied the Golan Heights. It can't happen overnight."

The president took Sophia's hand. "You have my agreement in principle. I wish you good fortune on your journey." He stopped for a moment. "Perhaps I was hasty. Perhaps you had other subjects you wished to discuss."

"Not of that magnitude. They can wait until my next trip. Perhaps we should take a breather and relax. Perhaps I could visit your famous mosque and the ruins of Zenobia."

Of course Sophia was invited to enjoy his hospitality in private, and he accompanied her to the mosque. The Zenobian ruins were left for her next trip. Sophia had taken Syria by storm.

*****

Discussions in Baghdad were not substantively different from those in Damascus. The Agency had supported Saddam Hussein in his war against Iran, and he was already acquainted with the Agency's capabilities. Like Syria, his ruling party was Baathist and

Sunni Moslem, but Iraq possessed a substantial Shi'ite population. The Palestinians were Sunni, and their transportation into Lebanon would cause Shi'ites there to lose power. Saddam was concerned about their reaction, and also wanted territorial guarantees for the Druzes.

Sophia was received cordially in Riyadh. The king had been informed of her favorable reception in Damascus and the discussions over her plan, and Sophia showed how a Palestinian state in Lebanon would be in Saudi interests. The king could subsidize them if desired and use them as a counter-weight to Israel without depending on Arab solidarity. In essence, he could fight Israel to the last Palestinian. What Sophia did not point out was that Israel's borders would become more defensible and her opponent concentrated.

Although her short-range purpose was achieving peace and stability in the region, Sophia was under no illusions concerning potential shifts of power under her plan. She reminded the king how Ibn Saud had used the Ikrun to bring himself to power, later massacring them when they became a threat. The Palestinians could suffer a similar fate if they got out of hand. The king was very pleased and promised substantial increases in his payments to Milleron.

Egypt, the black sheep of Arabia since Sadat's peace with Israel, was a different matter. In Cairo, Sophia stressed that Egypt could regain her standing with her fellow Arabs by creating a Palestinian state. The entire focus would shift and Egypt could remain at peace and pursue its prosperity with honor. The president promised to lend his support in diplomatic circles and help keep Libya in check.

The trip was a raging success, but it remained to be seen how the US politicians and Israel would respond. Sophia put that on the back burner for the moment.

*****

Chuikov was an excellent chess player and enjoyed solving puzzles of all types. Sometimes, he felt he should have been a detective. Until now. This sudden emergence of Sophia Stewart left him totally stumped.

For eight months he had been following his subject and she had appeared no less than four hundred times in personnel references. She had traveled all over the world and reports indicated she always spoke the language of her hosts. A dozen different languages? Impossible.

One report from Syria stated that Stewart had immediately gained the president's confidence and concluded some sort of secret agreement. It was amazing for a woman to be so successful in a Moslem country. She had been equally successful in Iraq, practically destroying Soviet influence overnight. Was she an operative or policy-maker? Either way, she was incredibly dangerous. He called in Yeremensky.

"How old you think this woman is?" He pushed a stack of photographs toward her.

"Hard to tell," she said. "What did our Washington *Rezident* say?"

"Forget him," he snapped. "I want your opinion."

Yeremensky shrugged. "Well, she looks younger when not pregnant." Chuikov glared at her. "Eighteen to twenty-one. Very young."

"What makes you think so?"

"The eyes and neck. There aren't any lines around the corners, and her neck shows smooth fat I normally associate with teenagers."

Chuikov grunted. "That was after her second child, and now she's twenty-five. Like you, I thought she looked younger. I can't imagine Americans entrusting anything important to a twenty-five year-old girl. Is it possible this is plastic surgery?"

"Maybe there's more than one, and the Amis use only one name."

Stupid girl, thought Chuikov. There was a rational explanation somewhere and he was missing it. He would take his information to the 1st Directorate Committee for discussion. One way or another, Stewart needed to be understood or neutralized.

Yeremensky was usually fairly insightful. Was it possible she was right? He spread the photographs from Syria, Iraq, Egypt, Panama, Columbia, Mexico, and Washington on the desk. They were all the same person, no doubt. The various stages of her pregnancy could never have been coordinated or faked with different people.

The Middle Eastern reports were most disturbing. General Kuvinkin of the 1st Chief Directorate's 8th department had stormed in, demanding to be informed about this Stewart person only last week. He had yelled he was in danger of losing both Syria and Iraq to American influence like his predecessor had Egypt. Chuikov had calmed him, but could offer little information. How could this be happening? This little wisp of a girl walked into a presidential suite of any foreign power and walked out with the president in her pocket. What did she do? Hypnotize him? Buy him off?

Kuvinkin had threatened to send an assassin to Washington to kill her, and it had been Chuikov's turn to become angry. That was his area, and Kuvinkin had no authority to order an assassination of personnel in his target group.

Kuvinkin had finally calmed down, but he wanted action. According to his agents in Damascus and Baghdad, Stewart had established relationships between their governments and the CIA, and neither president was interested in talking to the Soviet Union. Worse, the Saudis were apparently underwriting CIA operations on a grand scale through Stewart.

Chuikov gathered his information and headed for the gray stone edifice at 2 Dzerzhinsky Square. Stewart was a problem for the entire committee.

The 1st Directorate Committee had placed Stewart on their agenda after both Chuikov and Kuvinkin stressed her importance. It was obvious she was crossing departmental lines and interfering successfully in other foreign countries. Chuikov entered and took his seat in the staff chairs behind General Ivanov, his superior and 1st department head. It was Ivanov who would be opening the discussion.

In a few minutes, the room had filled. Chaired by the 1st chief directorate head, the committee was comprised of representatives from all sixteen regular departments, the two special departments of Executive Action and Disinformation, the two special services of Counter-Intelligence and Information, and the three sub-directories of Illegals, Scientific and Technical, and Planning and Analysis. Chuikov noted most of departments were represented by their chiefs. Across the table representing Department Eight and the Middle East, Kuvinkin glared at him.

The meeting opened with few formalities, and the Directorate's chief, Androgin, turned to the numbered departments for their matters in sequence. Ivanov led off from the 1st Department and introduced Chuikov.

"Our concern is the emergence of an individual in the CIA hierarchy who has been extraordinarily successful in a number of situations over the past year." Chuikov looked around and noticed few committee members paying close attention. "According to our information, this is a young girl named Stewart who joined the CIA several years ago and almost immediately became the director's chief trouble-shooter and negotiator.

"A young girl?" The question came from the Executive Action department head commonly called Victor, who was responsible for political murders and sabotage.

"Yes, approximately twenty-five years old."

"Give her to me. We'll knock her up and send her home to cook and change diapers," the victor chief laughed. Several other attendees joined in the levity.

Chuikov remained tight-lipped. "She already has two children and they haven't slowed her down one iota." The laughter subsided. "This woman attends NATO conferences, frequently accompanies the CIA director to security council and cabinet meetings, and travels all over the world with a small entourage, making agreements and destroying our influence. She has met with more than twenty heads of state including those of China, Japan, most of Western Europe, the Middle East, and Latin America. But most compelling is that she meets with these presidents and premiers privately and speaks their language."

"Impossible," snorted the head of counter-intelligence. "That would mean she speaks a dozen widely different languages."

"Exactly," Chuikov barked. "That's what our information says."

Chuikov's report had still not attracted full attention around the table. Kuvinkin slammed his hand down flat. "Listen to this!" he bellowed, "this person is a serious menace!" Several heads whipped around as Chuikov continued.

"Her language capability itself is not threatening; we've seen people who are linguistic geniuses before. We have some ourselves. But that isn't it. According to our Washington *Rezident*, Miss Stewart apparently has total recall and may well be the most brilliant person in the CIA. She appears to have inordinate influence in

Washington and has been extremely successful with other heads of state. We know, for example, she was very well received in Peking."

"That was just the Chinese being polite as usual," somebody commented.

"No, it wasn't!" the 6th department chief countered. "Our Peking *Rezident* reported she was able to open trade lines between China and one of those CIA companies. They hadn't been able to do that before."

"And she's wrecked us in Syria," Kuvinkin added. "They don't return our calls. It's as if we have become insignificant in the Middle East. I say we give her to Victor and eliminate her."

"Hold on," Chuikov quickly interjected. "She doesn't appear to be anti-Soviet. She has not taken any hard-line stance against us. In fact, she's apparently extremely reasonable."

"Besides," Ivanov added, "An action by Victor is sure to bring retaliation. Maybe an unreasonable level of it. We have never taken action against a known high-level CIA official, only clandestine operatives, and then only in extreme cases."

"But she's already caused irreparable harm in the Middle East. She has them eating out of her hand," Kuvinkin cried.

"So Arabs like Caucasian girls," another department chief said. "Send them some of ours."

"It's not funny. I say we have some Moslem kill her on her next trip."

Androgin spoke for the first time. "Have we assessed her personally ourselves? Have our people talked to her?"

"Only at diplomatic receptions, and in the usual polite terms," answered Chuikov.

"I'm not ruling out Victor, but it seems to me we ought to take a look at her. We still have our agreement where senior intelligence personnel can talk to one another from our countries. Let's request a meeting with her and see what we have. Comrade Ivanov, I think it's time to send Colonel Chuikov to Washington."

*****

On unusually short notice, Webb and Sophia were summoned to the director's plush office. The matter at hand had to be important.

"You may not know this, but the Russians are becoming Sophie-watchers," the director stated while he stacked a bunch of papers in his hands. "It seems that every time you make a trip and talk to a head of state, the Soviets get extremely nervous. Word is, you're viewed as their most dangerous enemy." He paused and smiled. "They're right, of course, even if they don't know why."

"Gee, that's nice. I haven't done anything directly damaging that could be traced to me."

"I thought we had kept Sophia pretty well under wraps," Webb said.

"It's not so much what she's done—it's what they *think* she might have done. We sent her everywhere in Latin America and all her high-level conferences were held in secret. They soon understood she spoke Spanish, but then she went to the Middle East, Japan, and China and didn't use an interpreter there either. If I were them, I'd be nervous, too."

"It'll get worse when I go to Russia," Sophia quipped.

The director smiled, but continued. "They think you're our top trouble-shooter and probably much older than you appear. Fortunately, having kids has aged you a few years."

"Just what I always wanted," Sophia said.

The director didn't respond to her remark. "The KGB wants to meet you. The Soviet ambassador requested I bring you to his embassy for discussions."

"We could do that," Sophia said, "or hold to our original plan of sending me to Russia."

"No, we can't go to the embassy," the director said. "That would alert certain people in Washington and the media, and we're not ready for that. So..." He paused theatrically, "the ambassador, his second secretary, and a special emissary from Moscow are coming here."

"Here? Russians inside Langley?"

"Sure. It's happened before." The director glanced at the grandfathers clock near the door. "They'll be here in an hour, and we need to put our game plan together."

"Well, we planned for me to surface eventually," Sophia said. "We just do it now. I'll take an open and friendly attitude with them."

"I think that's a good idea. Don't you, Webb?"

"Yep. Why should Sophia be any less successful than she's been with Arabs or Chinese? Let's go ahead and promote her as our main contact with them."

The director raised his eyebrows. "I'm not sure we're ready. I haven't prepared people here, and several of them are going to be very unhappy."

"Let it happen slowly," Webb suggested.

"Can't. Once we send her to Moscow, it's all over. I'll just have to bite the bullet."

The hour flew by without notice until the director's secretary buzzed to say the Soviet delegation had arrived. Security escorted them into the white conference room that was used for all meetings with non-Agency personnel. The director walked in first, followed by Webb and Sophia, and he greeted the ambassador effusively.

The ambassador introduced his second secretary and Colonel Chuikov from Moscow. The second secretary was the embassy's KGB resident, so Chuikov was obviously KGB.

"Chuikov," Sophia said in Russian. "A famous name from World War II. Marshal Vasily Chuikov, Hero of Stalingrad and Berlin. Any relation, by any chance?"

"He was my grandfather," Chuikov answered.

Sophia almost laughed out loud. The Soviets were staggered by hearing her speak Russian, and the name Chuikov was probably already forgotten by most Russians.

"He was quite a soldier. You must be very proud." She turned to Webb and switched back to English. "Not only did he lead the Sixty-Second Army at Stalingrad, he captured Berlin with his renamed 8th Guards Army. Then he was commander of Soviet forces in East Germany, commander of all Soviet ground forces, and even Deputy Minister of Defense. He represented the Soviet Union at Eisenhower's funeral, and died in 1982."

Webb extended his hand to the Russian. "Very impressive credentials. I trust you will follow to equally high command."

"Thank you," Chuikov said. "Miss Stewart's knowledge is that of a Soviet historian and also very impressive."

After polite preliminaries, the ambassador rose to be excused. Webb escorted him on a courtesy tour of Langley's non-sensitive areas while the director and Sophia talked turkey.

"I understand you've been interested in my activities lately," Sophia said pleasantly. "I'm not at all surprised. It's rare that someone my age is active at my level. I'm almost a throwback to when nobility held high position while teenagers. Of course, I'm not an aristocrat. Our Constitution forbids such a class."

"You could be," the colonel said gallantly. "Pictures are poor images of your beauty. But there has been some speculation concerning your age. Also that you're a woman, and a mother."

"I'm certainly a woman, and I'm a mother twice over. You might be interested to know my mother's father came from Belgorod. His name was Aaron Lauenberg, and his brother Jacob joined the Communist Party in 1939. Perhaps you could find out if I have any relatives left."

"It would be our pleasure," Kirov, the second secretary responded. The squat, homely man with shifty eyes wrote down the name. "Belgorod was not a good place to be during the Great Patriotic War," he said.

"Yes, I know. Unfortunately, two SS divisions made their bones there in more ways than one. Someday I'd like to visit it."

"I'm sure that can be arranged," Chuikov said hastily.

"Mrs. Stewart will be responsible for maintaining confidential communications between our organizations," the director said. "An early visit to Moscow would be most desirable."

"Then we'll be talking frequently together," Chuikov said. "Is it true you have a photographic memory?"

Sophia smiled. "It depends on definitions," she said in Russian.

"Are you familiar with the Soviet Union, Mrs. Stewart? Your Russian is flawless."

"I am first and foremost a student of history. My knowledge of Russian history is extensive, and I view your present government as the most recent in a succession of extremely interesting societal and governmental evolutionary stages. For example, the Decembrist Revolution and role played by Russian freemasonry is fascinating as a precursor to your revolution of 1917."

"You sound very knowledgeable and even sympathetic to our history," observed Chuikov.

"Oh, I am, as well as the sociological roles of the sexes in Russia."

"How interesting. Are we Russians different from Americans?"

"To some degree. I've identified the most basic difference between Russian and American males as revolving around our concept of machismo." Sophia switched back into Russian. "The Russian is difficult, a patron of high arts, respectful of scientific and literary talent, heavy and serious on the outside, but soft and easy inside. He is a sufferer, and one who wends tortuous ways. The American is image-conscious, both inside and out, and more macho as demanded by his American female."

"Sounds like you have a preference for the Russian male model," Chuikov said.

"Possibly, but both have positive and negative attributes. The Russian is uncertain and suspicious, the American, brassy and overbearing. The American responds to uncomplicated music such as rock or country and western, the Russian, to ballet and orchestrations. The faltering, questioning non-macho American is a failure, one to be pitied and discarded, the complicated, non-public relations-oriented Russian is the epitome of Russianness."

Sophia laughed and leaned forward to touch Chuikov lightly. "The Russian man's worth is not measured by how expensive a woman he can maintain. The American male is manipulated to that position for the benefit of women. The Russian woman fights alongside her man, not as support, but as participant. The American female sends her man out to protect her. Interesting differences, no?"

Chuikov could feel himself falling under the spell of this beautiful, brilliant creature who was addressing his inner self. Obviously she had read Tolstoy, Turgenev, and Dostoyevsky, and appreciated what she read. Chuikov suddenly wanted to possess her.

At all costs, he had to terminate all talk of using Victor.

Chapter 26

It was Sophia's second trip to China within the year. She was accompanied as before, but Ed and Sylvia would be involved in separate discussions most of the time. Sophia's first meeting was again with the premier.

After an hour of pleasantries, a discussion about their present arrangement, the favorable publicity China had received in the US, and the increasing confidence in Sophia's people, the premier inquired in his usual obscure fashion concerning Sophia's objective for this visit.

"I was anticipating discussing our mutual interests with respect to all Pacific Rim nations," Sophia said. "The United States has certain obligations to various Pacific Rim nations, but my organization's interests are at variance with those publicly espoused by my government. I'd like to discuss these prospects and how we might pursue mutually isomorphic objectives."

"Any such discussion must begin with Taiwan and its return to the People's Republic."

"We have no problem with that," Sophia said. "My organization has no interest in assisting Taiwan in remaining separate from the PRC." Sophia watched the premier's expression and swore she saw his eyebrows rise almost imperceptibly at her comment.

"Your agency would not interfere if there was a conflict between bandits on Taiwan and our People's Army?"

"We are partially responsive to American public opinion, so I can't guarantee we wouldn't be forced to act following the dictates of Congress. However, if events move slowly, it is entirely possible we might be successful in forestalling those elements in our country who might wish to intervene with military force."

"And economic force?"

241

"That depends on many things. As you have seen, we are willing to work on your behalf to minimize any such actions. I believe we have proven our good faith."

The premier nodded. "Yes, but you are indicating a great change in United States policy. Surely these things do not happen without benefit."

"True. We wish to see China take its rightful place as the dominant economic and military power in Asia, and as our friend. We wish to eventually remove all our military forces from the Pacific except for our own territorial islands."

"Including the Philippines, Korea, and Japan?" The premier sounded like he was having difficulty retaining a tone of disinterested ambivalence.

"We wish to remove our forces from those countries," Sophia said, "and to establish ourselves as trading partners, primarily providing you with agricultural and high technology products in return for finished consumer goods, such as those provided today from Taiwan, Singapore, Korea, and Japan. We wish to deal with the People's Republic of China to solidify the historical friendship between our two countries for the future."

"I understand." The premier smiled broadly. "You wish to put the Japanese, Koreans, and overseas Chinese out of business."

Sophia returned his smile. "Oh, absolutely not. But I never said we were a charity. We're business people seeking to expand our trading partnerships and supply sources."

"I find your suggestions fascinating. Do you have a timetable?"

"No. That is something we might determine mutually."

The premier looked at the Ming Dynasty screens at his left. "How could we possibly impact the Japanese in trade? They are world leaders and appear unassailable."

"Your Ministry of Agriculture could be most helpful. You remember Japan's activities during World War II in promoting opium in their areas of occupation? They addicted substantial Chinese populations. Your government has been most successful in stamping out and controlling drug use, but it wasn't easy."

The premier smiled again. "Yes, but the colonial empire nations first introduced the Chinese people to opium smoking and exploited it to their advantage. Japan only enlarged the concept."

"I do not mean to excuse the British, Europeans, or even Americans for exploiting China in the nineteenth century, but we Americans paid our debt through the drug offensive waged against us since World War II. Now I would ask for that offensive to be redirected against Japan. And it can be aimed northward. I would hope we might consider our support of China in the Second World War as a reasonable offset to the unfortunate altercation in Korea."

"You infer the People's Government is involved in such traffic. I hasten to assure you that is not the case."

"I accept your assurance with utmost respect. In times of peace *and* prosperity, people become involved with drugs for many reasons, and drug use is voluntary. Providing opiates to the enemy during wartime, however, is a humane and effective method of waging war. It destroys no property, reduces battle casualties on both sides, and is somewhat reversible. In future wars, I would recommend shipping large quantities of opiates to the enemy for his consumption."

The premier nodded again. "I accept your recommendation as having great wisdom." He patted Sophia's hand. "You remind me of one of our great women in history."

"Wutsi Tien? Or, as we know her, Wu Chao?

"Yes, precisely. A remarkable woman, very wise and able to balance opposing and discordant elements to good effect."

"A famous lady in Chinese history, Mr. Premier. I have studied her reign, and although we have many character differences, I am pleased to be compared with her. In the west, her ruthlessness has caused her to be greatly vilified, but the public good she accomplished throughout her long reign was truly extraordinary."

"She was a brilliant lady who rose from nothing to be Empress. Do you perchance have a bronze information urn outside your office?"

Sophia broke out into laughter. "No, but it might be useful. Do you have something for any of the four slots—particularly the one for prophecies?"

"Perhaps. I would offer the stone found in the Lo River and presented to the Empress: 'The Divine Mother has come among men to rule in eternal prosperity.'"

"A most intriguing prophecy. I would quote Lenin, 'The success of a revolution depends on the extent to which women take part in it.' Here I am."

The premier nodded. "Empress Wu experienced some difficulties consolidating her power, but like you, she was extremely far-sighted."

"There are times when I allow the yarrow stalks to fall," Sophia said.

"So do we all. But I believe your interpretations of the I Ching would be most accurate. You must also be familiar with Pan Chao and the Han Shu."

"Yes. Or Pan Ku. Another remarkable woman. Both a historian like myself and a soldier—which I am not. I understand Chairman Mao studied the Han Shu as a young man."

"I would not be excessively hasty in denying my military prowess if I were you. You show great promise. I would not want one of my armies to face you."

Sophia smiled demurely. "I admit to having studied Sun Tzu's Ping Fa, San Kuo Yen Yi of Lo Kuan-chung, and Lun Yu and Tso Chuan."

"It appears you have delved into our essence of life."

"Perhaps. The Tao Te Ching and Chuang-tzu are very important to me."

"In our first meeting, you spoke at length on the Tao. Chairman Mao was also a student of the Tao."

"You might be pleased to note the Milleron logo. It is an expansion on the t'ai chi—the Great Ultimate—to three interlocking symbols representing Heaven or Yang, Earth or Yin, and man, thus reminding us of the three-fold nature of the universe."

"Most interesting, some might believe it symbolized an association with a triad."

"They would be in error, but the intent also included representing the Inner Alchemy of Shen, Ch'i, and Ching. If you look closely, perhaps I have dragon eyes."

"I must keep that in mind." The premier leaned forward mischievously. "I would say they are more like flaming pearls."

Sophia laughed. "The emblem of Ming and Ch'ing emperors. The Taoist symbol representing essence of Yin and Yang combined into Ch'i and Ching, vital force and sexual energy, simultaneously human and cosmic being, transformed in fire. My eyes are all that? Then I must be truly blessed with their presence contained within my Shen."

"Your beauty transcends human form. Of that, there is no doubt."

Sophia realized she had heard no higher compliment. She dropped her eyes in shame, unable to think of an equal compliment to pay her host. The premier had won the contest of words; she could only show him great honor and respect. Worse, he knew what he had won!

But perhaps that could be turned to her advantage. There was an old Chinese teaching: *Take the enemy's strength and turn it to your advantage*. The premier could become more trusting in spite of her being a foreigner. He would expect the homage she would have to lavish on him. If she did not, she could not be trusted because she didn't understand. She would act appropriately.

"You have sons?" the premier asked in a friendly tone.

"Yes, two sons." she answered proudly.

The premier smiled broadly. "Dragons have nine sons, you are not nearly half done. But I suppose blue-eyed dragons only need two."

He was playing with her and enjoying himself immensely. "I promised my father seven," she said. Sophia immediately wondered why she had lied and placed responsibility on her father.

"Your father is well, I trust."

Sophia folded her hands and looked down. "My father has gone and joined his father." Sophia looked directly at the premier. "It was my father who introduced me to the Tao and started me reading through Tao-tsang. It was he who taught me the Ming verse:

'Vast indeed is the Ultimate Tao,
Spontaneous and never acting,
End and beginning of all ages,
Existing before Earth and Heaven,
Silently embracing the whole of time,
Continuing without end throughout the eons,
In the East it taught Confucius,
In the West it taught Buddha,
Accepted as truth by a thousand kings,
Spread by generations of sages,
It is the source of all faiths,
The grand mystery of all mysteries.'"

"You were blessed to have such a father."

Her chance had come. "He was a great man, deserving of my highest respect. But no match to you in words and graciousness."

The premier had met his equal, and he bowed to her knowledge and grace. "When you are President of the United States—and you will attain that high office, I have no doubt—you will have no better friend than China."

Sophia nodded. It was easier dealing with eagles than sparrows. She had no doubt the drug offensive against the US would cease and be redirected against Japan. Everyone would be pleased. Even the American public, which would see heroin availability decrease.

*****

Landing in Moscow, Sophia was greeted by Chuikov and introduced to Lieutenant Yeremensky, who was assigned to escort her throughout her stay. After the usual courtesy call on the American ambassador, Sophia was at the disposal of the Russians. In particular, she had requested meetings not only with the head of the 1st Chief Directorate, but also the KGB head and general secretary. The first two were to open communications, but the latter was to establish a new age.

On the third day, Sophia met the general secretary.

He was gracious, but Sophia noticed he was humoring her. That she spoke Russian failed to impress him, but she caught his attention with a comment concerning western Europe.

"I'm sure you know I play a major role in determining American policy with respect to NATO," she said in passing. "But, frankly, my organization is interested in a complete withdrawal of American military forces from western Europe."

He turned toward her. "I beg your pardon?"

"I said, there is considerable interest on the part of certain groups in my country for returning all American forces in Europe to the continental United States."

"Why are you mentioning this to me?"

Sophia could see his interest and suspicion in his face and demeanor. "Are you a student of history, sir?"

"A pragmatic political leader has little time to spend reading history; we're more involved in making it," he said.

"With respect to world hegemony, history shows power is a function of substantial homogenous populations with an aggressive political posture either from previous subjugation, inadequate living space and population pressure, or a lack of natural resources. Empires encompassing multiple cultures rarely last longer than a few lifetimes and then their longevity is strictly related to the military power of the dominant cultural group. Both the USA and Soviet Union are examples of late-stage empires. Their dominant cultural groups are losing power and the empires are facing disintegration. Sun Tzu said it clearly in his *Art Of War*: 'Without harmony in the state, no military campaign can be conducted; without harmony in the army, no battle formation can be produced.'"

"I would certainly agree. Both our countries are having difficulties because of our diverse populations. But what does that have to do with withdrawing troops from western Europe?"

"We have to put things into perspective. In historical context, World Wars I and II were active fighting phases of the same conflict. More accurately, they should be combined as the Euro-Empire War."

"Interesting. I've never heard them described that way before."

"In a way, it was much like the Peloponnesian War in the fifth century B.C., with its two active phases and a seven-year 'peace' in between. Both conflicts exhausted their combatants and passed the batons of leadership to peripheral powers; in the case of ancient Greece to Macedonia, and to the Soviet Union and USA in modern times.

"Power is still basically European," the general secretary observed.

"Only temporarily," Sophia remarked. "The acme of our Caucasian race with respect to world power came immediately following the Euro-Empire War. In terms of population, the percentage of Caucasians began irreversibly decreasing after 1940, and whites were driven from their colonial empires within a decade. The enclaves that remained, as well as Europe, were soon in recession. Asian and Hispanic immigrants have been swamping the US, and the Japanese are conquering Australia by purchase and immigration. South Africa is returning to black rule, and Rhodesia and Algeria expelled their Europeans. To a large degree, the Caucasian race committed power suicide in the Euro-Empire War."

The general secretary halted the historical and political discussions for a lunch to which Sophia was not invited. Yeremensky escorted Sophia to a small guest facility in the same building.

After an hour and a half, an aide arrived to return Sophia to the general secretary. They immediately resumed their conversation, but his attitude was totally different. He was open and effusive, obviously now accepting Sophia and her special status.

"So what do you see for our countries?" he asked after complimenting Sophia on her language capabilities and knowledge of Russian and Soviet history.

Sophia took a deep breath. "In the near future, the Soviet Union and United States can be forecasted to partition along racial and cultural lines; the Soviet Union somewhat earlier than the US. The Soviet Union will probably lose its Moslem minorities gained from 1837 to 1876, as well as other non-Russian nationalities. The US will most likely split into white, black, and Hispanic countries, with the Hispanic section either re-uniting with Mexico or forming a new nation."

"Not exactly what I hoped to hear," the secretary said.

"We did it to ourselves," Sophia said. "We squandered our resources confronting each other. While we have been glaring at each other across an artificial gulf of ideology, the Europeans and Japanese have stolen an economic march on us both. The Chinese, too, but they're following by a decade or two. If this continues much longer, we will be in a position similar to that in which Japan found herself in 1941—forced into war to assure economic survival. The Japanese are close to controlling our economy at the cost of our national assets. The Soviet Union does not possess a hard currency and has been forced to release gold reserves to feed its people. But fighting each other would be the height of insanity. Once again, our enemy is Japan and yours is Europe and China. Geography and natural positions do not change."

"You have apparently ruled out using military force at this time. Do you not believe we could overrun western Europe if the United States chose neutrality, and you could easily conquer Japan if we did not intervene?"

"Both victories would be hollow. Even without massive destruction of property that would surely accompany those campaigns, the world economy would be plunged into chaos, and neither of us is strong enough to rebuild it. In addition, both of us would lose support and cooperation from the Third World, particularly China, and eventually those powers would bring us to account. No, there is nothing to be gained by military action at this time."

The general secretary smiled and raised his hands. "We are in agreement. You have brought a brilliant ray of hope to Soviet-American relations." He stood up, walked to his desk and returned. "But our countries have many individuals in powerful positions who are staring blindly at the past and allowing their fanatical beliefs to overcome practical progress."

"Yes, and religious as well in our case."

"I'm not talking about the American or Russian people themselves. They want a reconciliation—of that I have no doubt. But there are others who wish us to continue our cold war."

"They are short-sighted and do not understand the situation or options. But the director and I would agree that we must proceed along these lines with great caution. The people of whom you speak are perhaps most dangerous to us as individuals."

"Yes, these initiatives must be conducted in strictest secrecy and with great caution. I will select an individual to work with you. He will be available tomorrow, but we require some time to construct an appropriate infrastructure to take advantage of your proposals." He smiled again. "You have taken us by surprise."

"I understand. Your Colonel Chuikov was initially greatly astounded by my youth, but I hasten to assure you, I am real. And your Colonel Chuikov must be one of your youngest and most promising colonels."

"Yes. He is a great talent. And your presence required a certain—ah—adaptation. I understand you are quite a phenomenon. Our reports show you to be some kind of superwoman."

"I appreciate your comments, but, in the American vernacular, what you see is what you get."

The general secretary rose and extended his hand warmly. "Then let us hope we will see much more of you."

*****

Chuikov was amazed at the general secretary's interest. Sophia had worked her magic on him as she had with other heads of state. He supposed it was her combination of extreme intelligence and natural charm. It certainly had worked on him.

He did not enjoy his questioning and chewing-out by the general secretary while Sophia had eaten lunch. The general secretary had wanted a complete report on her, and was amazed that he hadn't been fully apprised of her capabilities and importance before her visit. The secretary was not a man who liked surprises, and he'd been stunned by her unexpected revelations.

Androgin had called Ivanov and him to his office, with Lubyanka prison across the courtyard. Chuikov was yet to decide whether the 1st Directorate Chief was a toady or an independent power, but with respect to Stewart, it probably didn't make much difference.

"The general secretary and I have discussed the Stewart woman and decided she is critically important to our relations with the United States," Androgin announced. "Accordingly, we are creating a special group to work exclusively with her. You, Chuikov, will head that group."

Chuikov heard the 'we' in Androgin's statement, but assumed the general secretary had ordained this action. Nonetheless, Chuikov needed Androgin's cooperation and support—if not now, then later. He questioned why he had been chosen. Was this a penalty or opportunity?

"Thank you, sir, but it hardly seems appropriate for a single individual to warrant an entire liaison group. I am assuming, of course, this will be an additional activity in my section." Vaguely, Chuikov sensed he was getting stuck with something.

"No. This will be your sole responsibility. We will assign a suitable replacement for your present position. You will no longer report to General Ivanov. You will function as Special Service S, answerable only to me and the general secretary."

Chuikov gulped. Effectively a department head working at the highest level… He had misread the assignment and Androgin's role.

Androgin turned to General Ivanov. "Thank you, Comrade Ivanov. Perhaps you will excuse us now."

"Yes, yes," stammered Ivanov. Chuikov's sudden jump in importance had apparently caught him by surprise. He exited as rapidly as proper decorum permitted.

"Sir, this is extraordinary," Chuikov exclaimed. "What is so important about Mrs. Stewart?"

"The general secretary believes we can reduce our presence in Warsaw Pact nations and significantly improve our economic situation through her. You're to have unlimited powers—those of my office—in dealing with her. You are to select whomever you wish to assist you, and we'll create office space in this building."

Moving to 2 Dzerzhinsky Square? Chuikov could increase his visibility with other directorates. "What activities are we to engage in, sir?" he asked.

"Apparently the CIA wants to reduce American forces in western Europe—as we do, of course—so true progress is possible if we work together. In addition, Mrs. Stewart is empowered to make broad-ranging business deals for CIA-controlled companies throughout the world. As our ground forces are decreased and equipment becomes surplus, she has offered to assist us in selling that equipment in three-party deals for American agricultural products and high-technology items."

Chuikov was impressed. The girl had come loaded for bear. But to feed it, not to kill it. "I will be likewise empowered to make such deals?" He raised his eyebrows. This was an incredible opportunity— one that could propel him into Androgin's chair and beyond.

"Yes, but you must proceed in strictest secrecy. Certain forces in the Soviet Union wish a return to hard-line ideological positions, and this is a hazardous endeavor until they are neutralized by events."

Chuikov understood. He had agreed to play a pivotal role in his nation's history, and if the Stewart relationship didn't work out, he would be blamed and pay with his life. If it did, he might become dangerous to those above and incur the identical penalty. He possessed unlimited power, but for how long? His credentials had become impeccable, but that, in itself, would cause attention to be directed toward him. The risk was enormous.

*****

Diverting the 2nd Chief Directorate and 1st Department, 12th Directorate, was the first major test of Colonel Chuikov's credentials and power. The day after Sophia's departure, he mentioned the problem of surveillance by counter-intelligence and internal security to General Androgin.

"Yes, we should take care of them immediately," Androgin said. He phoned the head of the KGB and disappeared.

Fifteen minutes later, Androgin returned from his conference. "It's all fixed. All reports and documents concerning Miss Stewart and her contacts on this trip are on their way. In the future, the 2nd Chief Directorate and 5th will not be involved where she's concerned. They've been told that a special task force has been formed to deal with her, and they are not to interfere."

"Thank you, sir, but I trust they won't pay extra close attention to satisfy their curiosity? With respect to Special Service S, I've compiled a list of nine individuals whom I wish to have assigned to me. How do I proceed?"

"Give the list to me." Androgin buzzed his aide. "Get me the documents establishing Special Service S," he ordered. He turned back to Chuikov. "I've drawn up your directives so you can requisition supplies and equipment at your discretion. You have an unlimited budget on a sub-line directly here in my headquarters. Have you located office space yet?"

"No, sir."

The aide arrived with a large folder. Androgin took it, and handed several documents to Chuikov. "Then I want you to take the area presently occupied by the Personnel Department of Directorate T down the hall." He turned to his aide. "Popov, call Tamarkov at T and tell him I require his space within seventy-two hours."

The first deal between Sophia and Chuikov was the precursor of many to come. The Russians shipped tanks and military equipment to Libya, the Libyans oil to France, the French remitted dollars into a Webberon Swiss account, and Sophia sent wheat to Russia transshipping at Rotterdam where it had been consigned to Webberon. The entire transaction was controlled by Webberon, and the only currency exchange was Webberon's repatriation of American dollars from the Eurodollar market. In essence, Sophia arranged the sale of US grain for immediate payment in US dollars, although the USSR paid in idle equipment. It was an unheard-of transaction, not requiring intervention or loans from East Coast banks.

Chuikov and Sophia had determined thirty countries where they could dump Soviet military hardware and eventually turn it into dollars for Webberon. They decided to feed hardware into world markets slowly so as not to alarm anyone, particularly in the US Congress or Europe. Their massive military machine was Russia's greatest salable asset, but was only made possible by Sophia's assurance of eventual American military reductions in Europe.

Chuikov soon came to believe that Sophia was being truthful when she claimed the Soviet Union and United States were more alike than different. Both were in danger of splitting apart on racial, religious, and ethnic lines, and they were losing economic wars against their old military foes of World War II, although in the Soviet Union's case, they now included the rest of western Europe. Both countries possessed substantial natural resources, but Russia's were undeveloped, and the US's could not be developed due to environmental opposition.

The Moslem republics had begun agitating for independence, and minorities were becoming increasingly difficult to control. Chuikov was authorized to attend committee meetings in the 5th Chief Directorate, which was responsible for the internal intelligence on Soviet citizens. What he learned increased his respect for Sophia and her serendipity.

Economic activity in the Moslem republics was terrible, and party members were either Russians like himself or locals attempting to curry favor from Russians. In a storm, the locals would be swept away like chaff. Any determined blow would do it. The USSR was heading into stormy weather, but if Stewart could keep the red-baiting elements in the US under control, the secretary general might just keep the ship afloat.

Chuikov understood he was dangling by a thread. He organized a special section of operatives to discreetly monitor Stewart's activities and any opposition to her in the US, and to intervene whenever necessary to keep her safe. She had become the USSR's most valuable asset.

Chapter 27

Sophia and Ed reviewed their key personnel in the study of Sophia's new house in Potomac. Bobbi was handling acquisition financing, and Ed wanted her in charge of all finance as a vice president. Heather was relegated to being the nanny for Sophia's boys. Cathy Clark was doing a terrific job as Ed's assistant, but she was the only person besides Ed who traveled extensively. All the others reporting to Ed required supervision. "We need more heavies," Sophia commented. "I'll make inquires."

Sophia approved Bobbi's promotion, and after an exhaustive review of D & B reports, Ed found John Tucker to handle Milleron's construction projects. Tucker Construction of Tulsa, Oklahoma, was solvent and not living on cash flow from their next job. Port Tobacco was underway.

The next step was formulating a proper business plan. Webb and Bobbi came to Potomac to see what Ed had worked up. In Sophia's study, Ed exposed the first flip chart. This was his element—he had spent twenty years making business plan presentations.

"The goal is to establish ourselves as the premier player in all the industries that are likely to become dominated by Japanese combines by 2010," Ed began. "The United States must regain its capability to be self-sufficient under all economic conditions." He flipped the chart. "Here, we see a list of those essential industries. I've used two-digit SIC, Standard Industrial Classification, numbers so you can see its completeness for yourself."

"Prioritized?" Sophia asked.

"Yes, two ways. One, by importance to maintain a national economy, and second, by actual and probable Japanese penetration. For instance, the tire and rubber industry is almost all Japanese, as are many sub-classifications in electronics. The automotive industry is in grave danger, as are almost all basic metals production."

"Are any industries heavily penetrated by Japanese not important?" Webb inquired.

"Yes. Hospitality, and to a certain extent, maritime shipping."

"What's the average number of years we'll have to endure losses, assuming maximum development efforts to create superior products or technology?"

"Hard to tell," Ed answered. "Industries are different, and targets are moving. Some basic industries like steel, aluminum, copper, and brass are maybe five to seven years. Others, like automotive, heavy equipment, and some electronics, will be double that."

Ed flipped to the next chart. "For each industry we've listed the major companies, their marketing positions, ownership, financial condition, facilities, product quality, and R & D efforts. This one is for tire and rubber, and you can see the problem."

"Wow, there are only two possibilities, and their facilities are old." remarked Webb.

"And they have no R & D efforts to ensure survival in the long run. Coupling that with their high-priced union workforces, heavy financial obligations to retirees, health and pension plans... only the most draconian measures can save them."

"So we should create a new entity and build from scratch," Sophia said.

"Isn't there any value to those companies?" Webb was unwilling to give up.

"Minimal, and then only in their distribution systems, equipment, and name identification. But their liabilities are overwhelming."

"No proprietary equipment or processes?"

"Hire key people and you pick that up." Ed walked to his wall map of North America. "Heavy machinery builders are eating grass at present, and we can essentially name our price for facilities and equipment."

"Let's do it," Sophia said. "But we'll need an industrial espionage program like Japan's to assure us of leading technology."

"Leave that to me," barked Webb. "We'll out-Nip 'em."

*****

Within three weeks, nineteen group presidents were hired and given missions to penetrate their industries by acquisition, new companies, and new technology. Sophia stressed adopting future technologies, and even radical departures from known or standard practices. In particular, it was time to begin surfacing the idea of Amulot territory and injecting it into American consciousness. Ed purchased a Midwest regional airline serving Chicago and major industrial cities in the Great Lakes area, and Amulot Airlines was born.

Sophia's farm implement company appeared promising for military fighting vehicles. Several arms companies were purchased and moved to Montana, and Webb collected acquired rights to top weaponry along with production practices. He favored developing weapons with higher accuracy and lower rates of fire than the currently popular firearms. Sophia focused on guns with integrated night sighting mechanisms, infra-red, and thermal sensors, feeling that they would decide future battles. Tool and die makers were moved west from Cleveland, and research and development efforts went into high gear.

Webb also delivered blueprints of current armament for Soviet and European armies. Millmac, the Milleron machinery company, targeted the development of two classes of battle tank, self-propelled artillery, a personnel carrier, scout vehicle, special weapons chassis, command vehicle, and cargo carrier. Unfettered by Pentagon specifications, Millmac was free to develop superior vehicles at low cost. Sophia placed her planning horizon for technical development and mass production capability at fifteen years.

Focusing on the future, Sophia created two non-coeducational universities which took students at ages sixteen and seventeen, having them finish high school with lower-division college courses. The regimen was patterned after Cameron's at Mines when thirty-three hours of class time per week was normal. Strict physical conditioning was added as at military academies, and any drug use resulted in automatic expulsion. There were no exceptions, no extenuating circumstances, and no second chances.

All students received full scholarships for tuition and room and board, as well as an allowance for other essentials. Not surprisingly, students tended to come from small town Amulot families with

Milleron employees. The schools were advertised exclusively in Milleron publications, and accepting a scholarship obligated an individual to work in a Milleron organization after graduation for five years. Two hundred semester hours were necessary for graduation, and students received diplomas stamped on a six-ounce sheet of ninety-nine percent gold. The Colorado School of Mines had once issued silver diplomas, but Sophia had gone her father's former college one better.

Almost providentially, Sophia's friend Cindy from Golden High School became their latest acquisition in personnel. She had attended the University of Colorado at Boulder, and arrived bundled up for winter weather like a snow bunny. She walked in Sophia's house and threw her arms around Sophia, swamping her with a female Yuppie outfit.

She was an all-American blue-eyed blonde, energetic and leggy, but more flashy than beautiful. Cindy became Ed's personal gofer, and Heather took her on as an apartment mate. There was method to Sophia's madness, as Cindy was the perfect understudy and replacement to Heather in the Washington social scene and for making contacts.

*****

The premier was embattled over his attempts to liberalize the Soviet economy, and Chuikov worried that he had become too closely identified with Americans. It made little difference—he was committed by now.

He had begun to think Sophia Stewart might be a better Russian than most Russians. Certainly, she thought like a Russian in matters concerning music and culture. She greatly enjoyed the Leningrad Four and had read most Russian and Soviet authors. It was difficult to believe an American could possess her depth of knowledge of Russian literature.

He had worked out a scheme with Sophia to reduce Soviet and American forces in Europe. In Stalin's day, Chuikov would have been purged for even considering options that were now logical alternatives. The Warsaw Pact itself was costing Russia heavily and was nearing the end of its usefulness. The USSR needed to extricate itself from the morass of Eastern Europe.

Several times during the past few months, Sophia had fulfilled her obligations. The CIA had opposed both the Star Wars Initiative and MX Missile project in congressional appropriations. He no longer doubted Sophia's sincerity, and even the general secretary was beginning to incorporate Sophia as a factor in his decisions. Security was more important than ever, and the secretary's meetings with Sophia became invisible to the outside world.

For his part, Chuikov had informed the satellites that the Soviet Union would not oppose liberalizing their economies. Hungary had already made overtures about wishing to join the Common Market, and Poland was considered a hopeless mess. Soviet troops were placed under orders not to interfere in local matters.

With Eastern Europe liberalizing, Sophia felt significant pressure could be brought on American leadership to pull back from Europe if Russia would agree to some corresponding reduction. It was possible—if neither side got caught up in parity details.

German reunification was a problem, but Sophia expected the US and Russia would soon be heavily engaged in economic warfare with the European Community regardless of German reunification. It was possible that reunification would slow the growth of German economic power because of conflicts in assimilating East Germans into a market economy. Displacements were bound to be large, and ex-communists would be distrusted for years. Besides, a nation of only seventy-six million people could no longer be dominant militarily.

Meeting in Vienna, Chuikov mentioned several of the general secretary's reservations concerning the liberalization initiative.

"He is greatly concerned that, as Warsaw Pact nations repudiate Soviet leadership, some Soviet republics will agitate for independence," Chuikov related with intensity.

"Some disturbances will undoubtedly occur," Sophia stated. "And they'll take place whether or not any of our initiatives take place. Time is against the USSR."

"We understand you've forecasted such movements, and although the secretary expects them, he doesn't want them. We're to develop a strategy to forestall independence movements, but if they occur, he desires a hands-off policy from your government."

"We can do that, but it won't be enough. Station your returning troops in your non-Russian ethnic republics as a reminder of the iron fist in the velvet glove. But you need a velvet glove, and that means minorities in high governmental positions, particularly in Oblasts." Sophia turned to face Chuikov directly as they walked in front of the Hofburg. "Look, our blacks count every single black in Congress, the Supreme Court, and Executive Branch. Don't think your minorities don't do the same thing."

She grabbed his arm tightly, bringing their walk to a halt. "And you do understand why we lost in Vietnam, don't you?"

"The American public did not support the war," Chuikov said.

"Yes, but that was because of the TV exposure of casualties and anti-war movements. If you allow coverage of satellite liberalizations or your separatist movements on Soviet TV, you will have jumped onto the tiger's back. And don't let western media in either. They'll cause civil war between Armenians and Azerbaijanis with two broadcasts."

"It's become very difficult to keep reports from eventually ending up on western TV."

"Your KGB needs to do better. Learn from our failure to control news media during Vietnam. If Ukraine should generate an active movement like Bandera's again, you'll have to seal it off and impose a news blackout. The less shown on TV, the easier it will be to control."

"Sealing off the Ukraine would be impossible without assistance from bordering Warsaw Pact nations."

Sophia was becoming exasperated. "Create a border oblast! Say, a ten- or twenty-kilometer strip around the Soviet Union where it borders other nations. You already have the beginnings of such a state with your KGB border guards. Detach the territory and set its administration in Moscow. No other nation can object, especially if done in conjunction with withdrawing Soviet troops from foreign soil."

Chuikov looked at the cobblestones as they resumed walking. "Not a bad idea. Even if the strip isn't occupied, isolating minority republics from neighboring nations could be important."

Sophia steered Chuikov into a Kaffeehaus for coffee and Kuchen. Vienna was famous for its fattening cakes and pastries. She ordered for both of them.

"Your German is excellent, Sophie. Sometimes your talents seem limitless."

"Well, if you can't control your media when your minorities start demonstrating, you'll find limits to my talents," Sophia warned. "It'll be a problem to keep my president and Congress from not imposing sanctions like there are against China. So crank up your agency's internal control. It's in both of our interests." Sophia had worked night and day to dampen hysteria over student demonstrations for democracy in China. She had lobbied continuously for a strict hands-off policy by the US government. China had thanked her profusely for her efforts, but she didn't wish to fight that type of battle again.

"How can I say an American official told me to beef up KGB internal operations? Those functions aren't even in my Chief Directorate."

"I know. Just tell the general secretary we're on his side. Or as much as we can be."

"He'll appreciate your assurances of support, but any implication he is taking these steps at your instigation or approval would bring about his—and my—disappearance."

As difficult as her job was, Sophia was forced to admit Chuikov's was worse.

*****

Sophia hated making another trip to China with her Soviet activities proving so productive, but she needed to impact the balance of payments with Japan. She wanted commodity trade prices with Japan driven sky high and shipping in Japanese bottoms discontinued.

China was the fourth largest exporter of rice after Thailand, the US, and Pakistan, but both Chinese and Pakistani exports were subject to governmental policies limiting internal consumption to gain an export commodity. Sophia's opportunity in rice resulted from its heavy use in the Middle East. Iran, Saudi Arabia, and Iraq were the three largest importers, and with Iraq, Kuwait, and Saudi Arabia furnishing over seventy percent of Japan's oil, Sophia could work a trade whereby the price for oil to Japan was increased and there was a corresponding drop in rice in China. Saudis were already negotiating higher oil prices for Japan in conjunction with the Emirates and

Kuwait, charging a 'Straits Defense Fee' for all those purchasing oil except the US. But Iraq's war with Iran had ended, and it looked like Saddam coveted Kuwait. She had warned both the Kuwaitis and Saudis, but neither seemed worried.

After much haggling, the Navy consented to using an Agency front organization to sell off surplus units in the mothball fleet, and Ed incorporated a subsidiary called Mildico, for MILitary DIsposal COmpany. Within three months, over twenty billion dollars in ships and supplies had been tagged for sale, and Sophia knew it was only the tip of the iceberg.

Sophia had been meeting with Lin Lien-hsi of the Central External Liaison Department, although he was sometimes accompanied by Chang Tung from the Ministry of Investigation. Power struggles inside China pitted their two organizations against each other in an obscure contest to become China's foremost intelligence agency, resulting in time-consuming conferences with meager results. Now she was facing the premier again. He was pleased with her endeavors, but American reaction to the disorders in Tiananmen Square had been disappointing.

"It was difficult to dampen congressional reactions," Sophia stated. "We have many politicians who love to scream about events they cannot impact, and avoid problems that are on their doorstep."

The premier smiled—as usual. "Yes, we noted your efforts. We are simply concerned your agency may have less influence than we had hoped."

"Our influence runs deep and is not visible on the surface. China is an old nation with an old culture. Ours is new. Yours is as the Pacific Ocean, beset occasionally by typhoons, but returning always to an inner placidity and stability. Ours is a shallow sea, and when storms arise, beaches are washed away and shorelines change. But the sea has changed only in appearance from the shore—and one should not judge the sea by its shoreline."

"No. But what now? I understand you have developed a new initiative."

Sophia broached her agenda. "We believe unrestricted ocean exploitation by Japan will lead to declining food resources for other countries. As you know, fisheries of the western Pacific—your closest sea area—have been greatly affected."

"You have a suggestion to deal with ocean exploitation?"

"Yes. As the world's most populous country, China should call for an international treaty to control marine extraction of food and other resources. The oceans beyond a shoreline limit of, say, twelve miles should be divided according to national population and amount of arable land, regardless of whether or not they are maritime nations. A country would possess a national asset, able to lease it to other nations as they desire. We also favor China policing the western Pacific as the largest nation on its rim."

"Your suggestion is well founded and would immediately make some nations wealthy. China for one. Other nations would suffer greatly—Japan in particular. But we are not able to police the Pacific. Our navy is but a fraction of yours."

"We can change that in the very near future. I am negotiating the sale of many naval vessels which may ultimately be available to China."

The premier frowned. "You are attempting to bring about the sale of American warships to the People's Republic? That, I must see."

"It will happen. We need only to realize our commonality of interests."

The premier nodded. "I understand your associates are establishing trade agreements. Whatever I can do will be done."

It was Sophia's turn to nod. "To enable better cultural exchanges and understanding, I would propose a university exchange program for business and technical personnel. There are a large number of Chinese students in my country, but we have a relatively small number of business people who understand China and its culture. Perhaps our personnel could spend a year or more immersed in learning your language and culture, then fulfill four assignments in various positions and locations in China, say of six months duration each."

The premier agreed to Sophia's program, although neither underestimated its inherent difficulties. He had already taken steps to curtail Sino-Japanese trade, and China had surreptitiously begun to ship large quantities of heroin to Japan. Unsaid but understood, they both knew heroin would be a major source of hard currency for China until Sino-Milleron trading was well-established. Japan was finally in China's sights.

Chapter 28

While waiting for the director and Sophia Stewart, General Tom Olson studied reports of arms shipments to Libya and Syria by Russia. It seemed the Soviets were shipping their hardware wholesale to every Third World country who wanted a tank or a truck. Even helmets, boots, and personal equipment of all descriptions were being sold.

Two summaries alone added to over seven billion dollars in military equipment sales. Much of it had been shipped from Odessa, and the American consulate in Kiev indicated most items had been taken out of strategic reserves close to their western border. So the Russians were unilaterally reducing their forces. Why? There had been liberalizations taking place in satellite nations, but he didn't believe Russia would allow them to go very far.

He turned to his deputy chief of staff for intelligence who had just arrived from USAEUR headquarters at Heidelberg. "Josh, what in hell's going on? Do you think Ivan is losing interest in western Europe? Is Gorby going to let Hungary establish more trade with the west?"

"Hard to believe, Tom," General Dolman replied, assuming the first-name basis they used in private. "But we have better communication with them than ever before, and that's a fact. During Poland's crises, they talked to us daily, and with this thing in Hungary, they're doing the same thing. Three years ago, they would have kept us guessing to the last second. Now they act more like allies."

"Well, I don't trust them," Olson barked.

"If the Russians do pull back, what happens to NATO?" Dolman asked. "How do we keep it together?"

Olson shook his head as his aide entered to announce his visitors' arrival from the Agency.

After preliminary chatting, the director announced further

263

disturbances in Warsaw Pact nations were expected during late fall. The Soviet government indicated it would continue its policy of non-interference, and expected NATO to do likewise.

Olson couldn't believe it. "I realize Ivan hasn't interfered in Poland, but opposition forces were already well-organized and well-known. In Hungary, it looks like 1956 all over again. Russians have four divisions there, and the Hungarian government is allowing East Germans to use Hungary as an escape route. What makes you think they won't move to safeguard their position?"

The director glanced at Sophia and sighed. "The Soviets informed us they would remain uninvolved in Polish governmental crises, and were true to their word. We also have information they are making preparations to reduce troops on combat-ready status in four countries facing you. There are no contrary indications."

"Except all this could change in a heartbeat—if Gorby's heart stops beating. There's a bunch of hard-liners waiting to crank up universal communist revolution if Gorby falters."

Sophia interrupted. "Only partially true. Several others are ready to step in and follow his policies. Probably most important is the KGB head who has been extremely active in reforming his agency along lines more conducive to supporting Gorbachev. And heads of the 1st, 2nd, and 5th chief directorates are supporting him. If you want to see the importance of controlling the KGB, just remember Andropov's rise."

Olson was glad only Dolman and he were hearing this pro-Russian garbage. He reflected on the chickies who broke the resolve of his men in Vietnam because the troops weren't home to service them. Sex. The common denominator used by women to control men. Here the director was, being manipulated by a girl half his age.

"What about these arms sales?" Olson asked. He had lost respect for the director and decided to talk to Sophia instead.

"The Soviets are reducing their armed forces. Why is that so difficult for you to accept?"

The director intervened. "I'm sure the general understands and believes intelligence reports, Sophie." He turned to Olson. "We have assured the Soviets that we will support their initiative by not taking advantage of their internal difficulties. This is a time for us to show restraint."

"It's time to go on the offensive. The Russians are running. We can turn Eastern Europe against them and kick ass."

"If you want a shooting war, that will do it," Sophia said. "For the first time in forty years, we're making progress in reaching bilateral working agreements with the Soviets. Savor victory, but be gracious and win over your enemies. Humiliate the defeated, and they will rise for revenge. And in this case, they're not defeated."

*****

"Got another shipment coming out of Odessa," Dolman announced on the secured line to Olson. "Supposedly going to Angola."

"What's in it?" Olson asked impatiently.

"Military vehicles. That's all we know."

Olson ground his teeth at his own impotence. He jotted down the ship's name—another Japanese one. He hung up quickly and buzzed his secretary for the Turkish liaison officer. Within fifteen minutes, Colonel Halid reported to his office.

"We have reports of a ship carrying Soviet military equipment about to depart from Odessa. I'd like to know its cargo and destination. Can you help once they're in Turkish waters?"

"Yes, sir," the stocky colonel answered in his Oxford English. "We are within our rights to board merchant vessels if we believe they jeopardize the safety of other vessels. Is the ship Soviet?"

"No, Japanese."

"Then there will be no trouble. I'll contact Istanbul and have it checked. Do you wish its passage impeded?"

Olson thought about implications. "No. That would cause an incident, and you wouldn't be able to deny it passage, would you?"

"No sir."

"Then we'll make do with information. I'll require it at the earliest possible moment."

Olson reflected on Turkish reliability. With Germany, they were the only NATO country truly anti-Soviet. It was a shame their country was so poor.

During the next three days, Olson jumped every time the telephone rang. Dolman reported USAREUR was ready to shadow

Kyoda Maru when she entered the Aegean Sea and follow her to her destination. Olson was pleased at his foresight in keeping the Army spy boat operations in the Black Sea. Just like the Russian GRU, Army Intelligence could do its job, maybe even better than the CIA.

Finally, Colonel Halid appeared with the Turkish report. *Kyoda Maru* was headed for Tripoloi, Libya, and loaded with chemical warfare equipment, gas masks, rocket launchers, and various chemical munitions. Once again, the specter of chemical warfare was rearing its ugly head in the Middle East. Olson sent a priority message to the 6th Fleet.

Damn Japs. They were probably brokering the deal. It would be just like them. Anything for a buck. He called the Israeli ambassador to Belgium, and passed his intelligence on to him.

There was nothing more to be done. Sixth Fleet couldn't intercept the vessel like they had during the Cuban blockade of 1962, but maybe the Israelis would mount a commando raid.

Olson checked again with Dolman as the shadowing reports continued to arrive. An operation was out of the question—an attack would take months of planning and only hours were available.

The situation resolved itself suddenly and inexplicably. General Dolman broke his usual dour demeanor to telephone the news.

"The Israelis have done it. The *Kyoda Maru* is on fire and in distress. Libyan patrol boats are taking the crew off."

Olson felt like cheering for the little kike bastards. They had guts and didn't believe in waiting for the other guy to shoot first.

The Libyans torpedoed the ship when all hope of salvage disappeared, probably because they didn't want its cargo known to the world. Olson guessed his Turks hadn't gotten the total story. He was betting the cargo included gas canisters for chemical warfare. The Libyans were denying it, of course, but they always lied.

But the Japanese… Something had to be done. Olson quickly issued an edict against procuring from Japanese sources and ordered Japanese products removed from service exchanges. He was convinced the Japanese were guilty of supporting international terrorism and were no better than Russians.

*****

Chuikov had performed brilliantly with the Japanese. Facing decreased demand, the shipping *zaibatsu* had approached him for contracts offering lower rates than recognized internally. Chuikov had ordered his Maritime Ministry to accept the rates but require Japanese vessels to carry total cargo insurance for all eventualities. The cargo was identified as military equipment and supplies, and Japanese ship-owners were guaranteeing delivery. To no one's surprise, the proffered terms were accepted, and the shipment of gas masks and related chemical warfare equipment to Libya was the second shipment under the new contract.

Sophia and Chuikov had talked about the shipment over a secured line.

"Have all arrangements been made?" Sophia queried.

"Yes. Our best personnel have seen to it."

"Excellent. Any more scheduled?"

"Two. But they'll probably be cancelled. Then we'll have additional leverage."

Sophia wondered if an intercept of the conversation could prove compromising. Probably not, she concluded. The conversation had been cryptic, and she doubted Japanese intelligence was that efficient. She was more concerned with the Chinese who might conclude they were playing second fiddle to the Soviets. They were for the moment, but she couldn't do anything until the Chinese economy improved.

She sat on pins and needles until she heard a Japanese freighter had caught fire off the coast of Libya. Three crewmen died, and the hulk was sunk by a Libyan patrol boat after the remainder was rescued. The Russians immediately entered an insurance claim for the cargo's value. Sophia sent Chuikov a "Love and Kisses" message for congratulations, while Libya made its usual protests and threats against Israeli intelligence. For once, the Israelis were innocent.

Sophia sent up a trial balloon to test the political waters on Japan. Dave Columbo entered a bill in the House to force Japan to open up its markets to American products or suffer high tariffs and trade barriers. The hue and cry was loud and long from the media and economic short-ball hitters, and Columbo's bill was killed in committee. The Federal Government was still taking Japan's side, and media commentators decried the possibility of a trade war.

"Sounds like our media moguls do not understand Japanese

267

culture. They should read *The Chrysanthemum And The Sword*," Heather said.

"Yeah, and *The Book of Five Rings*," Sophia added. "But they didn't read *Mein Kampf* in the thirties either."

Sophia remembered when the Mongol Army was defeated at Ain Jaloot by the Mamluks. The Mongol Orlok Kitbugha was brought before Qutuz and Baybars, the victors. Before he was decapitated, he made only one statement, "I lost this battle, but Mongol troops will water their horses in the Nile." He was wrong. The numerically weak Mongols had begun their slide into oblivion. When their warrior shield was swept away, they disappeared in a few generations, leaving only scattered remnants to be absorbed by expanding Muscovites. This time, Amulot troops would water their horses in the Nile. Or nowhere. The day was approaching.

*****

Sophia guessed Japan would react to her initiatives with relatively coordinated activities, and she was proven correct. The iron economic fist appeared immediately, and General Olson's action in NATO almost caused his removal. He was reprimanded for his hasty actions, and Japanese products were reinstated in military exchanges.

American companies owned by the Japanese cut loose on their employees with a terror campaign, decrying trade barriers, and literally holding their employees' jobs hostage to continued non-interference. Remarkably similar fact sheets appeared in American plants of Japanese companies. They enumerated benefits of Japanese ownership and Japanese trade, and showed Japan to be a vital contributor to every American's welfare. Sales outlets were similarly deluged with Japanese propaganda, and newspapers printed pro-Japanese articles in a frantic push for Japanese advertisements.

Then it happened—the thing Sophia feared most. In one of her food service publications, Sophia read where the Japanese had purchased a three hundred-store convenience store chain. It was a regional chain in the Southeast, but it specialized in being the major store in very small towns. That meant Japan had recognized the need to penetrate food service industries, and if not stopped, would control the price of food within a decade or two. An enormous amount of

American food processing capacity was already owned by British combines, and now the Japanese were threatening to sweep up the remainder. Sophia left the Agency at noon and drove to Port Tobacco.

"This is my fault," she said, "I thought we would have more time. The productive segment of our economy is collapsing so rapidly, Japanese can't help but beat us to some opportunities."

"Why would a convenience store chain sell out?" Ed frowned.

"Over-extension on financing and government regulations," Sophia said. "One has been in deep trouble since privatizing and assuming enormous debt in purchasing back its stock, and another over-extended itself by expanding too rapidly. Others issued junk bonds through those criminals on Wall Street, and there's no way they can meet their bond obligations."

Ed shook his head. "I don't understand how the Nips can gain such rapid control over an industry. But they do."

"They're the world's most effective cartel, which our government has elected not to recognize," Sophia said. "As long as the *zaibatsu* move into an industry with multiple companies, we think they're not exercising monopoly power. But they are. They target one of our industries, and four of five Japanese companies produce products for that market. With centralized financing, they all lower prices below cost and drive domestic competition out or force them into subsidiary agreements. It might take ten or fifteen years, but their banks will wait because the outcome is predictable. It's illegal for us to act in concert like the Japs do every day."

"So now they're moving into food. If they achieve the ability to control food prices, we will have lost our last remnant of domestic control." Ed began pacing in anger. "We'll be one vast plantation of sharecroppers, buying everything at the Japanese company store."

"Exactly, and it's my fault." Sophia sat with her hands in her lap, looking down. "I decided to build a land-based company first—to control food-producing areas. We should have seized the channel of distribution first."

Ed was crushed by her admission of error. He placed his hands on her shoulders. "Hey, you can't always be right. Besides, you've moved into transportation. That's in distribution. And elevators and warehouses."

"But food service is made to order for the Japanese. It has so many middlemen you can't see where the money goes. Out of a loaf of bread that costs a dollar, the farmer only gets a few pennies."

"So we need commodity brokers, processors, regional wholesalers, and retail outlets."

"Yes. But add farm supplies such as seed, chemicals, fertilizer, and farm equipment. Otherwise, Japs can force farmers out."

"Leave it to me. I won't be a sharecropper. And I better move permanently to Zionsville."

"Who will run Port Tobacco?" Sophia asked.

"Bobbi. She's damned good. You probably haven't paid much attention to Bobbi's background. She's worked in banking and finance all her life, and that's all we do here anymore."

"You're right; I hadn't considered her. I was looking at her through my dad's eyes." One should never become too close to people in an economic organization. It was a problem using family in business, but Sophia didn't have much choice. The Amulot line was too thin.

Chapter 29

Every time a person climbs a mountain, he's surrounded by peaks as yet unconquered. Just as excitement was building over Dave Columbo's campaign for senator, Heather received a telephone call.

"Harlan's out again!" she yelled, slamming the telephone down. "He'll show up ASAP."

"You really think so?" Sophia asked. "It was a long time ago."

Normally, Heather's lips were peach peels with permanent hints of humor at the corners, but now they were drawn back and colorless.

"Hey, he's been in the slammer for twelve years, and he blames me for putting him there. What do you expect?" Heather paced on Sophia's Persian rug. "This house doesn't have the security of my old condo." Heather waved at the windows as she spoke.

Sophia suddenly felt guilty about having insisted she move to have more room for her kids.

The house was situated on a heavily wooded road and relatively isolated on its five-acre lot. Having planned for seven children, Sophia needed space, and it offered fourteen rooms, not counting the basement or attic. She would have to see about a security system. There was room for a gatehouse—maybe she should fence the property and build one.

The phone rang again and Heather bolted out of her chair. Sophia grabbed it first. "Settle down," Sophia ordered. "We'll handle this better by keeping our emotions under control."

It was Ed Armstrong. "Just wanted to remind you about the AARP dinner in Gaithersburg tonight," he said. "I'll be there in an hour."

Sophia told Ed they'd be ready with bells on their toes. Sophia went into the kitchen to check on her kids. Her maid, Carolina, had them eating supper. Suppertime was the best time of day.

*****

The District hadn't changed much in his absence, Harlan thought as he stepped off the bus. DC was being run by Mayor Washington's successors, the Democrats controlled Congress, and Republicans occupied the White House. Big deal. After the Pagans were decimated in the late seventies, blacks controlled the drug traffic, and that was where real power was.

Harlan walked down K Street before heading north on 13th. Yep, white girls still flooded the District, looking for government jobs and excitement. The chicks looked freshly scrubbed and innocent. That would change when the brothers turned them out. He preferred young ones who tasted so good and sweet. Blondes were best. Like frozen banana daiquiris, they kept their freshness over long sessions, sweating sunburn oil to provide lubrication. Heaven for a player.

As usual, practically none of the players were white. Small wonder. White boys couldn't control their women. Black athletes were chalking them up like on assembly lines, and the Bullets alone probably speared ten thousand white girls a year. Broads needed to be knocked around occasionally to remind them who's boss. They took pride in working for the biggest and baddest player, and if *his* street name, 'big foot,' wasn't enough, he'd make them wish it was.

Four blocks up 13th, Harlan turned into the BlackMark to check on Bailey's action. In the dim light, he didn't recognized anybody. One black and two white hookers were sitting cross-legged at the bar, and three booths of brothers eyeballed him casually. He sauntered up to the bartender.

"Hey, bro, got a Maryland Suburban book?" he asked.

The heavyset bartender said nothing, but reached under the counter and slapped a phonebook down on the Formica top. He resumed talking to the blonde in tiger-striped hot pants.

Harlan grinned with satisfaction. Heather lived in Potomac, an exclusive suburb northwest of the District. He pushed the book back toward the bartender then placed a call. It was her number all right. A recorder answered and he recognized her voice.

He grunted to himself as he glanced toward the back room. Probably some action there. Bill Bailey, the comeback kid, would be holding court in private.

He knocked.

The dirtiest, skinniest junky Harlan had ever seen ushered him into a second room where Bailey was playing poker with three other guys.

"So, you finally got here," Bailey said in greeting. "Want in?"

"No. Not at the table anyway. When you got time, I wanna rap."

"Later. Go ring one up with Sam. On me. It'll get you going again. Tell the bartender you throw your shit upstairs." Bailey motioned his audience was over. The junky followed Harlan out.

"Who's Sam?" he asked the bartender as he emerged up front.

"You lookin' to ride a pale horse?" a blonde in fishnets and black leather shorts asked.

"If you're Sam, I am," Harlan said. He turned again to the lethargic heavy behind the bar. "Bailey said I could camp upstairs. You got a key?"

Without removing his foot off the shelf where it rested, the bartender reached underneath and skidded a key on a Cadillac chain in his direction. Harlan scooped up the chain before it came to a stop. "Ready?" he asked the blonde.

She snuffed out her cigarette and placed her half-full glass in the bar gutter. "Save it for me," she said to the bartender. "I won't be long."

Bitch. She'd pay for that remark. He'd have to clear it with Bailey, though. When you're looking for a touch from a pimp, you don't damage his goods. Sam must be Bailey's newest acquisition—he'd never give his bottom lady away. Even to his best friend, which Harlan wasn't.

The bar occupied the ground floor of an old row house, and the stairs to the upper floors were in a separate entrance. Sam led Harlan to a small room at the back with an adjoining toilet and sink. The bed was full-sized, with head and footboards. Harlan noticed the rope burns on the posts.

"This is on Bailey," he said, as Sam turned and sat on the bed.

"Oh? You his new partner or something?"

"Something like that. We got time to kill, and I wanna see how good you can kill it."

"Hey, I ain't no charity."

Harlan grabbed her face with one hand and squeezed. "I ain't neither. You be nice to me and I be nice to you. Your white pussy'll be black if you be not nice."

Sam wilted under Harlan's fierce stare. "Hey, chill out. Mama'll take of things, lover."

Harlan released his grip and began to undress while she massaged her jaw. She was trouble, and Bailey probably expected him to punish her a bit. He had ways of abusing sarcastic snatch that wouldn't show. He ordered her to strip completely, and an hour later, was still going strong.

"Keep her if you want," Bailey interrupted, "Just find another when you get time." Harlan held her head still and looked to see Bailey in the doorway.

"I'll think about it." He pulled her off by her hair and sat up. "Thanks, baby," he said to the long-legged blonde. "We'll finish later."

Sam looked hard at Harlan as if she was going to yell at him, but then thought better of it. She gathered up her clothes and quickly disappeared out the door.

"Least she's a natural blonde," Bailey remarked, stepping into the room.

"You turn her out?"

"Haven't had time. She's just a kid playing tough who blew in here a couple of weeks ago. Take her and train her right; I got too many other things going."

Harlan had been getting dressed while they were talking. He figured the girl to be young, still with firm round boobs and that fresh scent he had missed in the joint. "Okay, but got some private business to settle first. Anybody I know still in the mayor's office?"

"Maybe. Some people'll be there forever."

"How about the post office? Still using carriers for distributing?"

"That's where I thought you'd fit in unless you want to run gash. We got to build our organization back up."

Harlan remembered how perfect letter carriers had been for wholesale drug distribution and collection. The mail was never questioned, and it went everywhere. There was no better cover for pickups and deliveries, even pot. "That's my action," he said, "but gimme a couple of days."

Bailey stripped off a roll of bills and dropped it on the dresser.

"Here's a grand to tide you. You can stay here 'til you get going. Let's go meet a couple of guys so they know you."

Harlan picked up the money and accompanied Bailey downstairs. Sam had repaired her face and was talking to three other hookers in a booth. She stopped as he entered. Harlan smiled to himself. She wasn't used to big yet, and she'd be hurtin' for days. Bitch from Alabama deserved it. But if she thought he had been tough on her, she should see what he'd do to Heather Ewing.

"I need wheels for tonight," he told Bailey over a Bud.

Bailey reached into his pocket and pulled out a set of keys. "It's the Caddy on your room's keychain. I park it on Twelfth behind us in the APCOA lot. Just fill it back up."

Harlan thanked his old partner and finished his beer. He easily found the three-year-old Cadillac in the next block and headed her northwest toward Potomac. He had plenty of time, so he crossed over to Wisconsin Avenue and turned onto River Road before leaving the District. It took almost forty minutes to reach Potomac. He would need to find a faster route for more security.

He located Heather's address with some difficulty. Harlan congratulated himself on taking time to case the layout during daylight. Potomac was heavily wooded with an obvious prohibition against straight streets. Heather's mansion surprised him with its substantial grounds and circular driveway. He could park on the street near a small creek without attracting attention.

He couldn't see a security system, but from the number of rooms, Heather wasn't alone. Harlan could see children's toys in the side yard. Maybe she had finally whelped. More likely they were Jeannette's kids. Poetic justice if both were there. Probably a maid, too, he decided. Neither would clean a dozen rooms.

He drove back on MacArthur Boulevard. His route was a done deal. He would cross over to Virginia on the Beltway, then use the George Washington Parkway. Depending on the time of day, it would be fast. No problem there—he would be traveling late at night.

*****

Columbo's turnout was excellent and Ed had to search for a parking space. Both of his charges looked stunning. Sophia had done wonders with her figure since giving birth seven weeks ago, but she always rebounded rapidly. Giving birth was a terrible ordeal for her without the normal pain blockers in her brain that everyone else had. Doctors couldn't give her enough medication since they wanted her fully awake to do her part. He had been outside during the last one and wouldn't do it again.

The dinner was a sign of senior citizen power. As Claude Pepper had shown, AARP members voted in much higher percentages than baby-boomers, even if they did so quietly. It wasn't glamorous playing to senior citizens, but they were powerful and would cross lines when personally asked for their vote.

Advertising people continued to ride a boomer hobby horse in the political rodeo and conjured alibis for vanishing votes. But Sophia was right: forget what other candidates were doing; make your game plan and execute with verve. So here they were, and their opposition wasn't.

Dave and Carol were already greeting people in the hallway to his right. Ed quickly placed the *Columbo Who's Who Register* on a table behind Dave for attendees to sign. He used it to place yard signs, but it also acted as a name check before dispensing favors. Incorporated into a computerized database, the register and registration lists were checked by Dave before responding to a constituent. Only those in the database received an audience.

Ed took up his position alongside Dave to facilitate their personal plea for support. Dave would ask for permission to place a yard sign on the person's property, and Ed made sure the appropriate voter information was entered in the register. Sophia and Heather acted as "ropers," funneling people into Dave and Carol and making introductions.

Tonight Sophia seemed to be more effective than Heather. Her youthful sparkle attracted older couples, and although they tended to be condescending toward her, they rapidly entered into animated conversations. Ed drew her aside. "What are you saying to get them so excited?" he asked.

"Oh, I tell them I was afraid of arriving late because my son wouldn't go to sleep. They always ask me his age, and I tell them my youngest is only seven weeks old. Then they ask how many I have, and when I tell them, they can't believe it. Usually they say I should be home with my baby, but I tell them Columbo's too important and needs me. That gets 'em."

Dave's speech was competent but hardly enthralling. He talked about Social Security and medical care, and, although the audience was interested, his remarks brought no great applause. He said the right things, but missed the boat. He finished and asked for questions.

A short, pot-bellied man about seventy years old stood up. "You're a young man. Why should we believe you understand issues that are important to us?"

"Well, I'm forty-nine, only one year away," Dave started. He saw Sophia standing with her right hand raised. "I see my associate Mrs. Stewart would like to say something." He motioned in her direction.

"I'm Sophia Stewart," she began. "And as you can see, I'm a whole lot less than forty-nine." The audience broke into laughter. "I've known Mr. Columbo all my life, and probably know as well as anyone what he believes on your issues. He was one of my father's best friends and helped immeasurably when my mother died four weeks after I was born. And when my father was killed later by a drunk driver, he was there again. Dave Columbo is one of America's great heroes to me."

Sophia paused for a wave of sympathy to ripple through the crowd.

"You folks were all born in the Great Depression or earlier. You rose up and smashed our enemies in World War II without asking for your rights; instead you asked for your duty. You saw a man from Missouri make the courageous decision to drop two atomic bombs on Japan, ending the war immediately and saving a million American casualties. You stopped communist aggression in Korea, and for no other reason than to give South Koreans a chance to live in freedom, you sacrificed American life and limb."

"And you understand politicians. You heard Roosevelt say Social Security would never cost Americans more than one percent of their income. You donated billions to rebuild Europe and Japan. You worked hard and provided for your children so they would not have to sacrifice as you did. You built the most powerful, technologically and socially advanced nation the world had ever seen. And as your children came of age in unparalleled prosperity, you passed the baton to them. Yours was an age of heroes. Heroes, great and small, creating, building, accomplishing, and taking responsibility."

She slowed down and took a deep breath. "Vietnam was not your war, and it was lost. The fabric of the society you built dissolved in acid from the "me" and "now" generations. The United States became a second class power and found itself being purchased by Great Britain, Germany, and Japan. Tokyo became the world's financial capital, and small nations and groups of terrorists seized American citizens as hostages with impunity. These things were not your fault, and are not your responsibility now. You have done nothing wrong, in spite of whimpering sociologists who lay the deeds of the sons at the feet of the fathers."

"It's not you who are doing drugs, not you who are raping, robbing, and mugging, marching for gay rights, AIDS programs, amnesty for those who break our laws, screaming loudly for your rights, or hammering Congress daily for more entitlements. No, it's you who are continuing to shore up our nation with your quiet faith in the American way of life and pulling more than your weight. As always." Sophia paused and looked down.

"I'm a young mother with four little children. I pray they will grow up to live in an America that will be safe, strong, healthy, and one in which they can have as much pride as you have today. I like to think things go in cycles, and your and my generations can meet over the wreckage of those in between. I like to think America can become great again instead of worrying about Japan and Europe continuing to finance our national debt. We can only do that under the leadership of individuals like Dave Columbo. Working for him in this campaign, I represent the newest adult generation under his leadership. If I've said anything you liked, that's because it's what Mr. Columbo taught me. If not, I beg your forgiveness—I didn't listen as carefully to him as I thought. He understands you, and I hope you believe I do, too."

Sophia sat down and began smoothing out her dress. For a moment, there was dead silence. Then a small, thin, seventy-year-old lady sitting across the table from Sophia stood up and began clapping. The room erupted in applause.

*****

Three days had passed since hearing Harlan was out of jail, and Heather's nerves were beginning to fray. An electronic surveillance and security system was being installed, but wouldn't be fully operative for another day or two. In the meantime, Heather was staying with Cathy Clark.

Carolina was already feeding the boys when Sophia arrived home. Little Brian was sick, and Heather wasn't there to help. She changed into jeans and took over dinner while Carolina concentrated on Brian. His temperature was again below a hundred, and the shot from his pediatrician yesterday had apparently taken effect.

Carolina returned to help dress the boys to go outside. Sunset wasn't until almost eight, and the evening was still hot and humid. Sophia watched Adam and Cedric play until the sun began to fade, and it was time to go in. As always, the boys assented without murmur and were soon in bed. By nine-thirty, Sophia had settled down with a glass of wine and a stack of books on law, medicine, and military history to review. She dearly loved German white wine, but didn't allow herself to drink alcohol while pregnant. This was the time to enjoy herself.

By ten o'clock, Sophia had gone as far into the volumes as she could stand. She checked the doors and turned out lights. As usual, she checked on each of the boys. In Adam's room she stopped short. She could smell a faint odor of cigarette smoke. Sophia cupped her hands to her hair, but it wasn't her hair. It couldn't be her clothes—she had changed since coming home. Carolina didn't smoke, but she might have allowed someone else in the house. Possibly. She shrugged and went on into Brian's room.

There it was again. But not in any particular place. It was stale, more like residue from a person's body than fresh or exhaled smoke. Sophia remembered how Cam smelled the Cong before he could see them in Vietnam. His nose was sharp, and he believed he could smell their fear from over a hundred yards. But this wasn't fear.

"Mommy?" Brian was awake.

"Yes, honey. You go to sleep now," she whispered.

"Mommy, who's 'd man?"

It was as if a knife had gone into her heart. She knew now.

"No one, honey, it's all right. You go back to sleep." So Brian had seen him. She straightened his blanket as he rolled over. She kissed him and patted him lightly.

She checked all the boys. Fear and anger began to well up. In the baby's room it was strongest of all. There was no doubt anymore—Harlan was waiting for her in the next room. Her bedroom.

He must have heard her coming down the hall, checking on the boys. At any rate, she couldn't outrun him. She looked around for a weapon. The baby's room… she didn't keep weapons in the baby's room. She was an expert marksman, but that didn't help now. Harlan would use a knife or something that would cause great pain. He would be expecting Heather and would rape and kill her.

Maybe he wouldn't hurt her when he saw she wasn't Heather. No chance. He couldn't leave anyone who could recognize him. That would go for the kids, too. She had no choice.

She could feel the rising fear and remembered the trick her father had used. His testicles tightened up in dicey situations, but when he pulled and stretched them out, his fear disappeared. Fine, but she didn't have testicles. She tried the next best thing and tugged at her nipples. That helped some, so she squeezed out her clitoris. Amazing. In a moment her fear abated and she was in control again. All policemen and policewomen should be taught her dad's technique. They might draw disapproving stares, but they'd be cooler under fire.

Sophia thought about her bedroom. The door was open, and the light switch was on the left. He would be flat against the wall on the right ready to grab her as she entered. Yeah, that would put him behind her. But he didn't know she knew he was there. She'd have to take him out with a kick. But her stomach muscles weren't in shape. It was even money with her life on the line—and maybe the two older boys. She began to psych herself to put all her power into her feet. Even if it tore her abdomen open.

In a moment, she was ready. She stepped into the hallway.

*****

The doorbell rang, and Sophia froze. She was over ten feet from the open doorway to her room and maybe twenty from the stairs. It rang again as if denoting a sense of urgency. Harlan would wait for her to get rid of whoever was there. She quickly walked to the stairs, but without sounding hasty. She bounced down the stairs to the front door. Behind her, the second floor was oppressively quiet. Sophia

280

wondered if the boys had awakened and felt her ears turn backward listening for Harlan's presence. The bell rang a third time before she unlocked the door. Two men she didn't recognize stood on her Georgian style porch, crowding into the doorway.

"Miss Stewart?" the one on the right said loudly. "We're the new neighborhood security team. We'd like to come in and check your house." He pointed to the man at his left. He was holding his Agency identification and a memo pad which said, 'SOMEBODY IN BACK!'

Sophia nodded at the man holding the pad and pointed upstairs. "Well, glad to meet you. Come in," she said, as loudly as she dared without sounding obvious. "You can start upstairs."

She led them up the stairs and pointed down the hall. Neither of the two men were small, and they clumped along to Sophia's bedroom. In a flash, they turned into the door with drawn guns. Sophia was only a step behind and saw the open window. She reached it just in time to see a tall man running into the trees. "He's gone. Damn!"

The agents looked at her in astonishment. Her anger had taken them by surprise, but just as quickly, her face transformed into a mask of concern. She dashed out and checked the boys. To her great relief, they were undisturbed and asleep. Her chest heaved as she brought her emotions under control. She led the men back downstairs.

"Thanks," she said. "I thought I was Custer."

"We saw him enter, but our van wouldn't start. Sorry it took so long. My name's Choate, Bill Choate, and this is Jody Stovall."

"How did you happen to be here? Was the house under surveillance?"

"Yes, ma'am," Choate answered. "I can't tell you why, but we've had it watched for the last three days. Do you think it was a prowler or do you know who he was?"

"Tell you what," she said. "Write it up as a would-be burglar. And I'll be all right. I know who to see in the morning."

Sophia watched them until they reached the front gate. *Bless you Webb*, she murmured to herself. She dialed Cathy to tell Heather.

Within fifteen minutes, Heather arrived. She threw her arms around Sophia and quickly checked the boys. Satisfied her loved ones were okay, she returned to confront of Sophia.

"I'm sorry I let it go this far," Heather said. "You haven't called the police yet, have you?"

"No. You and I both know they won't do anything. We can't prove it was him except for Brian's testimony, and we can't use a two-year-old."

Heather went to the kitchen telephone and dialed Bobbi Rutledge. Sophia did not listen to their conversation, but Heather's face was grim and resolute as she swept up her purse and strode out the door. Sophia wished her good luck.

Chapter 30

Bobbi was still living on 12th Street only three blocks from Thomas Circle. Thirteenth Street was "Hooker Avenue" and it took some effort to find a parking space. Heather found herself dashing down the street to Bobbi's building. She was greatly relieved when she was immediately buzzed inside after identifying herself on the intercom.

Billy was already asleep in bed, and Heather had been surprised to find Bobbi still up. She had seen her only occasionally over the past several years, but they seemed to understand each other almost instinctively.

"Thanks for seeing me so late," Heather began.

"No problem. Would you like a cup of coffee?"

"A terrific idea." Heather followed Bobbi into the kitchen to talk while the coffee brewed. After talking about Sophia and her kids, Heather turned serious. "I need to locate somebody."

"What can I do? Why come to me?"

Heather felt herself drawn to Bobbi—the lady seemed to generate instant intimacy. She was the consummate earth mother, making everything right for everyone. Cam had said her apartment was crash pad for wayward kids during the Vietnam era, and Heather believed it. Thinking of Cam unlocked the mystery to their mutual sisterhood.

"We both loved the same man," she said. "We're sisters in a way."

Bobbi smiled knowingly. "Cameron, Sophia's dad?"

"Yeah. He never said so, but I felt he could have married either of us if Sophia hadn't been born. I know I always wanted a child by him, so now I have Sophia."

Bobbi stood by the percolator, deep in thought. There was a strange electricity in the room as the two women focused their thoughts on the man they loved. The same man. Bobbi walked around the table and took Heather's hand. "Are you my friend? My very good friend?"

Heather could feel her heart swelling with a feeling of deep intimacy. She suddenly knew Bobbi's secret. "You were luckier than I, weren't you? You have Billy."

"Yes," Bobbi breathed slowly, "but no one can know. Not even Billy."

"You're also an Amulot?"

"Cam used that term. Yes. I'm Orange, even related to John Rutledge, first governor of South Carolina."

"Well, did Cam ever tell you about a guy who tried to rape me?"

"No. Our world contained only us."

Heather understood. Her experience was identical except when she brought Cam and Millie back together. That was a terrible time.

"He was my sister's boyfriend, more or less." Heather dropped the second shoe. "How do you feel about black men?"

"How do you mean? As lovers?"

"Yes."

"I don't. I've never crossed the line—in spite of living in this neighborhood. I've always thought black men go for white women to vent their hostility against whites. I don't need to prove I'm liberal by doing blacks, and they don't need to prove their manhood by conquering me."

The last statement brought a smile to Heather's face, showing her dimples in spite of herself. "I don't believe you're into being conquered."

"Yeah, well, not lately. So, anyway, what about black guys?"

Heather quickly related the story of Jeannette, Harlan, and herself.

"What happened to the guy?" Bobbi asked.

"We put him in prison. Now he's out."

"And you think he's coming after you."

"I know he is. He was in Sophia's house this evening. The kids saw him, and Sophia saw him as he ran away. Yeah, it's him or me."

Bobbi nodded. "Then let's make it him. What do you want me to do?"

"His best buddy was a pimp on 13th Street. I figure he might be hanging out with him. You have some contacts in the area, don't you?"

"No problem. What are their names?"

"Harlan Jordan, and the pimp is Bill Bailey."

Bobbi stood up. "Okay, but you can't go with me. Wait here, and I'll be back in twenty or thirty minutes. I know several working girls in the neighborhood, and they might know where he is." She stuffed her keys in her jeans pocket, rubbed the stomach on her small Buddha, then left.

Forty-five minutes later, Bobbi was back. To Heather, it seemed like two hours.

"Well, I know where they are. So now what?"

"I have to kill him," Heather said flatly.

Bobbi sat down on the couch and studied Heather's face intently. Heather joined her, waiting for Bobbi to speak.

"Okay. He's staying in the back room above the BlackMark Bar. I checked it out, and it's got a walk-up entrance from the street. Don't be surprised, it's only three blocks from here."

Heather felt her heart jump. "Will you take me there?"

"And what are you going to do?"

Heather shrugged. "I need to get a gun. I didn't expect to find him so easily."

Bobbi got up and walked into the kitchen. She returned with a revolver wrapped in an old dish towel. "Here, use this."

Heather unfolded the towel and looked at the gun. "It's loaded," she said.

"Well, yeah. They aren't any good unless they're loaded. That gun showed up here in 1969. I found it after Vietnam Moratorium Day, so it's not traceable. It's a thirty-two sub-nosed revolver, six shots. It only has five cartridges so the hammer rests on an empty chamber."

"I've never fired one, have you?"

"Oh yeah. I have another one, an automatic, which I fired a lot when I was a kid. Here." She took the revolver out of Heather's hand. She emptied it and showed Heather how it worked. It was double action, so all Heather needed to do was pull the trigger. Bobbi carefully wiped the gun and cartridges clean and reloaded. "Wrap your hand with the towel like this. Then you won't leave any

fingerprints, and your hand won't get any tell-tale powder traces."
She showed Heather how to wrap her hand. "You shoot him, drop the
gun and towel, and nothing can be traced."

"Won't it be loud? How will I be able to get away?"

"I already made a dry run for you. They leave the upstairs
unlocked. You just go up like a working girl, knock on his door—the
last one on the right—and then go out the back. There's a door at the
end which opens onto an old porch with a fire ladder. That drops you
into the alley and you come back here."

"Sounds easy, but I'm sure there are a million things that can go
wrong."

"Maybe, but the odds are in your favor. Let's give you a wig,
and dress you up as a hooker. Shorts will be best, particularly so you
can go down the ladder." She thought for a moment. "We'll give you
gloves for the doorknobs and ladder rungs so you won't leave any
fingerprints."

They threw together an awesome outfit. Heather became a
blonde in net stockings and hot pants and with heavy makeup. She
looked so hard Bobbi didn't think she'd be recognized. They gave her
a big bust to draw attention from her face, and three-inch heels to add
to her height. She took a large shoulder bag for the gun and a pair of
slippers for the ladder. Heather would change her shoes as soon as
she was in the hallway, changing again once she was out on the street.

In twenty minutes, they were ready. The finishing touch was to
order a pizza to be delivered in thirty minutes. Bobbi decided she
would be hungry by the time they were back.

Heather was nervous but resolute. They walked over to the alley
behind 13th so she could see her escape route. It looked easy, and
Bobbi would be waiting for her at the end of the alley.

"Go get 'em, girl," Bobbi ordered. She hugged Heather and
buzzed her lightly on the cheek. Heather marched toward 13th Street
without looking back.

Heather turned the corner and glanced up to see the BlackMark
several buildings away. She walked fast as if going to an
appointment, looking neither right nor left, and avoiding the gaze of
other girls and loungers on the sidewalk. She spotted the walk-up
entrance immediately, and went in as if pulled on a string.

The entryway was filthy and smelled of urine, but she clattered up the stairs like she had done it a thousand times before. No one had said anything to her on the street. She reached the hallway and it was time to change shoes. It was like in a dream. Her heart was racing and threatening to leap into her throat.

There was only one light in the hall, and in her flats she felt herself silently stealing along in the darkness. She went past Harlan's room and tried the fire door at the end of the hallway. Bobbi had been right. It was unlocked, and the porch and ladder did not look formidable. The door kept closing automatically in spite of her attempts to leave it ajar. After two tries, she gave up and wrapped the towel over her glove like they had practiced in the apartment. She took out the gun and returned to Harlan's door. She knocked.

Oh God. What would she say if he asked who was there? Her worst fears were realized immediately.

"Yeah?" It was Harlan's voice from inside.

"Got a present for you," she said with as husky a voice as she could muster.

"Shit." But she heard him drop his feet on the floor and shuffle toward the door. Heather held her breath and pointed the gun directly at the middle of the door with both hands.

The door flew open with a jerk. "What?"

Heather put five rounds directly into the form in front of her as it reeled backward.

The gun was deafening, and when the hammer clicked on an empty cylinder, she dropped it like a hot poker. She ran the few steps to the fire door. Her ears were ringing as she threw her leg over the side and went down the ladder. She ran breathlessly out into Bobbi's arms.

Bobbi pulled her around the corner, yanked the dish towel from Heather's hand, and stuffed it into a garbage bag on the sidewalk. They started walking rapidly down 12th Street before turning right again and going around the block. Heather appeared to be in shock, but Bobbi kept pulling her along. And then they were in Bobbi's apartment. Safe. There were no sirens, and no one running down the street.

Heather collapsed on the couch, but her legs were so rubbery she slid off onto the floor. Bobbi pulled off her wig, and knelt beside her.

"Did you get him?"

"Yeah, I guess." Heather was staring blankly ahead.

"Well, tell me. How did he look?"

"I don't know. Bigger. Meaner. I shot him, and he flew apart."

Bobbi noticed Heather was still wearing her flats. She checked the shoulder bag in a panic. The high heels were there. "You forgot to change your shoes."

"Sorry. Can I take a bath?"

Bobbi helped her up and led her to the bathroom. "Be sure to scrub your hands to get rid of any powder traces," she said. Heather wasn't moving. "Here, let me help." Heather allowed Bobbi to disrobe her completely without comment or objection. Within a few minutes, she was soaking in a bubble bath while Bobbi removed Heather's makeup. She scrubbed her body from head to toe like a mother bathing her baby girl until the doorbell rang.

"Pizza!" Bobbi sang cheerfully. She bounced up, and was gone in an instant.

Heather was standing in the tub and turned to Bobbi as she came back. She placed her hand on Bobbi's shoulder to stop her from speaking. "It wasn't hard to kill him—it's hard now to think of myself as having killed someone. I mean, something's changed forever. Right now, I feel reborn. It's a rush. I can't believe this is me. But earlier, I felt as if something had been taken from me. I was shocked at myself. It happened so fast I didn't have time to think. Then I was down, now I'm up. I feel like going out and getting laid. Knock-down, drag-out laid!"

There was a fierce superiority emanating from Heather standing nude and almost shouting at Bobbi. Her nipples were erect, and her eyes were wide as if she were experiencing an orgasm.

Bobbi brought her back to reality. "Why don't you get dry first?" she said, handing Heather a towel. The moment passed, and Heather took the towel almost sheepishly. "You know, when you came down the alley, nobody came out or paid the slightest attention to you. I heard the shots, but they weren't loud and could have been anything."

"Boy, they were loud to me. My ears are still ringing."

"That'll go away in a few days. Now we need to get you an alibi. Is Cathy at home?"

Heather stepped out and began to dry off. "Yeah, but I told her I was coming here."

"Okay, then let's eat the pizza. I'm your alibi."

They ate the pizza, or more accurately, Bobbi did. Heather chattered away, attempting to relate how she felt during the entire experience. Bobbi listened, until their nervous energy evaporated and she suggested it was time to retire. They collapsed together in bed, holding each other until young Billy knocked at his mother's bedroom a few hours later.

Chapter 31

"Guess who's coming to town this weekend," Webb said as Sophia entered his office.

"Jack Wallace," Sophia replied. It was the only possibility. She hadn't seen him since coming to Washington, but knew he and Webb kept close contact.

"Yep. Want to join us at dinner?"

"Is the pope Catholic? How'd he sound?"

"Well, he asked about you." Webb said. "How much have you told him about your family?"

Sophia shook her head. "I've been a little delinquent. He knows about Adam, but believes it was a one-time mistake. You know he asked me to marry him, don't you?"

"No, but I'm not surprised. Just proves he has good taste. Anyway, you can't keep him in the dark forever. He deserves better, and besides, I think you're pretty soft on him, too."

"You do, huh? Well, that's why I haven't told him. I didn't want to lose him."

"If you lose him, you never had him. But I bet he'll stick around. I would if I were him."

Sophia ignored Webb's indication of his own feelings. "Okay, but let me break it to him slowly. Let's have lunch at the Parthenon where we can enjoy some privacy, and then I'll take him home to meet everyone."

Webb walked her to the door of his office. He started to kiss her for luck, then felt like swatting her rear as an inducement to be honest with Wallace. He suppressed both urges.

*****

290

It was time to face the music without a prepared speech. She nodded to the Parthenon's maitre d' and headed for her paneled booth in the back. As she walked around the room divider, she saw Webb and Wallace already waiting. Wallace looked wonderful. Involuntarily, her heart jumped, and she gave him a big smile.

Wallace saw her and sprang up as if shot out of a cannon. There was a momentary flash of hesitancy while he decided whether to attack her or wait for her to make the first move. He opted to behave himself. "Sophie! You look terrific!" he said. He stepped out from the booth as Sophia threw herself into his arms and gave him a hard but brief kiss.

"Hi baby," she whispered, as she leaned her head back to look at him. She patted his biceps. "Staying in shape, I see."

"Your shape is better," he said. "It's been a long time. How've you been? You're looking good. Still no ring yet?" Wallace was running off at the mouth and looking her up and down.

Sophia put her hand up and waved it from side to side like a windshield wiper. "Stop!" she yelled. Both were totally ignoring Webb. "Hi, Webb," she said.

"Hi. Excuse me for interfering," he said.

Sophia grinned and turned back to Wallace. "Still single, or has somebody found the best kept secret in Denver?"

"No, your secret's still safe. No one seems interested in finding it out. How about you?" He felt a vague sense of concern, having now asked the same question twice.

Sophia answered without hesitation. "No, there's no man in my life—other than Webb, of course. He makes sure I work eighteen hours a day."

The maitre d' approached, but Wallace waved him off. "We're not ready yet," he announced.

"Oh, no sir," the maitre d' objected. "Mr. Reid, you have a telephone call."

Webb excused himself and followed the maitre d'. Wallace smiled at the conspiratorial nature of the old fox. Without a doubt, only two would be eating lunch. While he was still exchanging banter and comments with Sophia about their times together in Colorado, Webb returned to say he had to leave. Bless his butt, his timing was impeccable.

"Sorry, but Sophia, can you take care of Jack?"

Sophia looked at Wallace and grinned. "I don't know. Think I can take care of you?"

Hundreds of great answers overwhelmed Wallace, but he was suddenly tongue-tied and flustered. Damn! Even with the woman he loved, he couldn't be glib and fascinating. "You've never had problems before," he finally said.

They continued with small talk until starting on the leek soup. Breaking a pause, Sophia suddenly said quietly, "You know I still love you."

Wallace dropped his spoon. "I was never sure you did," he replied softly. He felt his heart racing and his ears becoming hot.

"I was younger, and didn't want to tell you." Sophia pushed her soup away and faced Wallace squarely. "You didn't know how young. The last Fourth of July was my twentieth birthday."

Wallace couldn't believe his ears. "Twenty? That's not possible." He counted backward. Their romance had started four years ago in June. That would have made her... "Fifteen! You were fifteen at Bear Creek? Oh, no!"

"Yes. Please forgive me, but I never told you otherwise. I skipped two grades in school."

"But no fifteen-year-old girl could have had your knowledge and maturity. You could have passed for thirty!" Wallace was becoming angry. He shook his head. "You're saying I committed statutory rape. I seduced a fifteen year-old girl? Bullshit! Let me see your driver's license." He drummed his fingers on the table.

Sophia sighed and took her billfold out of her purse. She handed it to him without comment. He snatched it away and scowled at the card in the top plastic holder.

"What is this shit? This can't be right." He grabbed the plastic and went through the remainder of Sophia's credit card holders. Wallace glanced at her in irritation, and went through the entire billfold as if investigating a criminal subject.

In the photo section, he saw pictures of three kids. The last photo was of him in Golden washing his car. He had forgotten she had taken the picture. But the driver's license and Agency ID showed her to be twenty-five. That was absurd! "What the hell's going on? What is this? You aren't twenty-five," he said.

Sophia was waiting like a penitent. She kept her voice low and soft. "You know that, I know that, Webb knows that, and so do a few other people. Officially, I'm twenty-five. You thought I was twenty-three. Actually, I'm only twenty."

"How is this possible?" Wallace was almost shouting in his anger, and the maitre d' glanced around the room divider to check on them.

Sophia placed her hand on Wallace's arm. "Please. Honey, I want you to hear me out. Promise me you'll listen to everything I have to say."

"Okay, but don't tell me you were fifteen."

"I said I love you, and everything I'm going to tell you will be because of that. I could always walk out and never look back."

"Okay, okay, okay," he mumbled. He patted her hand.

"We give my age as you see in order to make my knowledge more acceptable. The director uses me as his special assistant because of my capabilities, although officially, I report to Webb. My background for the Agency is totally fictitious—as you see."

"What does this mean for me?"

"Remember when I told you in Colorado there was more to me than you knew?"

"So? What are you? Some sort of alien?"

"Something like that," she answered softly. She placed her purse on the table and slid out of the booth. "Come on. I have to show you something."

Wallace followed dumbly, attempting to comprehend the meaning of her words. He said nothing as Sophia handed the maitre d' a portrait of Franklin, but recovered sufficiently to open the door for her. Sophia unlocked the passenger side of the Berlinetta. "Nice car," he said politely, once again finding his tongue.

"It belongs to my friend, Heather. You'll meet her at home." Sophia was quiet while she started the engine and headed west toward Potomac. "If you had been blind, how old would you have thought I was when we first made love?"

It was an unfair question. He hadn't been blind. It had been her first time, but she had been his best ever. "I don't know." He paused thinking of other women he had known, "Maybe thirty."

"That's close. If you had never met me and only talked to me on the phone, how old would you say I was?"

293

"Why the questions? If my mother had wheels, I'd have been a truck. I don't know. Probably lots older. My age. I always thought we seemed to be the same age. How's that?"

"My mother was twenty-nine and my dad thirty-three when I was conceived." She rapidly related her story and outlined her abilities. She looked over to Wallace sitting silently. "So you see, I *was* thirty. That's why you thought we were the same age. And I could pass twenty-five different qualifying exams for PhDs this evening, and I speak, read, and write thirteen languages."

"Keeeehrist!" Wallace exclaimed. "So why are you fooling around with a plugger like me?"

Sophia reached over and patted his knee. "Because you plug well." She slapped his leg hard. "I told you why in the restaurant."

"So, can you quote Chaucer?"

" *Whan that Aprille with his shoures sote, the droghte of Marche hath perced to the rote,..*"

"Shit!"

"Or how about *The Compleynt of Venus* on the lover's worthiness: ' *Ther nis so hy comfort to my plesaunce, whan that I am in any hevinesse, as for to have leyser of remembraunce...*'"

"Enough, already! I believe you."

Sophia laughed. "Hey, that's the fun stuff. I can classify cephalopods, program an ICBM, or build an atomic bomb."

"Wonderful. I don't even know what a cephalopod is."

"No one's asking you to know. My love for you has nothing to do with cephalopods."

Wallace decided to curb his thoughts and focus on Sophia. This was a blockbuster.

Sophia changed the conversation and concentrated on acquainting Wallace with her mother's and father's backgrounds until she pulled into the driveway. As they got out of the car, Heather came to the front door.

"So this is Jack Wallace." Heather extended her hand in greeting. "I'm Heather Ewing. Sophia had—has—good taste."

"Thanks." Wallace grinned, taken aback at her brassiness. The lady combined spunk with an intrinsic beauty that was not fading with middle age.

Sophia guided Wallace inside and told him to make himself

comfortable in the living room. In a minute, she returned holding a baby and trailing three little boys. The smallest was being held tightly by Heather, and would have clearly preferred to be crawling instead of walking. "This is Adam, Brian, Cedric, and Donald," Sophia said, introducing the boys from oldest to youngest. "Boys, this is Mr. Wallace."

Wallace's mouth fell open. "Whose?" he gasped.

But it was Sophia who wasn't prepared for what happened. Cedric immediately threw a tantrum, crying and screaming, while Heather scooped him up into her arms. Brian and Adam glared in silence at Wallace, and edged behind Sophia, holding on to her dress.

"Adam!" she called, reaching around and attempting to dig him out from behind her. "Say hello. Where are your manners? Brian!"

It was hopeless. She traded the baby to Heather for Cedric. "Just a moment," she told Wallace. "We'll be right back."

She marched the three boys into the library and lined them up, facing her. "Listen, you guys," she said. "You all know him, and you know how I felt about him. Also how good he was to me, and everything he did for me and your grandfather. He's my friend—my special friend—and yours. Now he's not here to marry me or carry me off. You have absolutely no reason to be jealous or to treat him badly."

The three urchins looked like they were ready to cry. Adam spoke up. "Are you gone make love?" All three were eyeing her carefully. It was the critical question.

"No. I couldn't do that. He's still in love with me, and it wouldn't be right. You guys wouldn't want me to, would you?"

All three shook their heads vigorously. "See. None of us want it. But he's going to be important in all our lives. So let's go back out and be nice to him. Okay?"

They all adopted hangdog expressions, and one by one, nodded agreement. She picked up Cedric and marched out with Adam and Brian following like ducklings.

Sophia sat next to Wallace on the couch and motioned for the two older boys to sit on the floor in front. "These are my boys, and baby Donald. Adam will be the attorney, Brian, a medical doctor, Cedric, the military leader, and Donald, a computer scientist and mathematician."

Wallace didn't know what to say. There were a thousand

questions he wanted to ask. But he couldn't—at least not in front of the boys. "Hi, fellows," he said, putting up a brave show.

"Adam, tell Mr. Wallace about yourself."

Adam looked at his mother, pleading with his eyes to be excused. Sophia nodded for him to start speaking. "My dad was Steven Thornton, the world famous 'ttorney. I know everything 'bout law, courts, and Constitution."

"Brian?" she prompted.

"Grant Foster, Walter Reed Chief Sturgeon. Hi." He extended his hand for Wallace to shake. Sophia smiled. Brian always had trouble saying "surgeon." Adam followed Brian's lead in shaking hands.

"Cedric's father was Clyde Harmon, former commanding general of the War College, and Donald's was John Stevenson, probably America's foremost computer scientist." She held Cedric out for Adam to take his hand. "Thanks, boys. You can go back in the playroom with Aunt Heather. Mother's very proud of you."

Adam and Brian each clasped one of Cedric's hands and practically dragged him out of the room. Sophia felt her breast rising in pride as she viewed her brood, then realized Wallace was still sitting alongside her like a stone.

"What are you doing?" he said slowly.

"Building a family," she said brightly, trying to lighten the mood.

"Every one a different father? Are you crazy? How many men have you had?" With each question, his tone became sharper and more accusatory.

"Yes. Every single one has a carefully selected father. Chosen for the knowledge and skills he will pass on to my children. All elderly gentlemen with a maximum of knowledge. All my boys know and understand why."

"But the sex? How can you do that? You couldn't have loved them."

"How many women have you gone to bed with? Were you in love with them all? What I'm doing has been done for centuries by royal families. Only I'm selecting on talent, not birth."

Wallace's emotions were beclouding his understanding. "But sex with these old guys?"

"Stop it! I wasn't in love with them, and it's no big deal. I only had sex once with Donald's father, and Adam's was the most at maybe a half dozen times. You and I have made love more than all of them put together, so get off this. Do you think it's fun being pregnant and having a big belly all the time? And try going through giving birth without any tolerance for pain."

Wallace realized he had pushed her too far. "So is that the end? Four kids?"

"No. I'm going to have three more. An engineer, agronomist, and physicist. Then I'll concentrate on their education. Their knowledge will be a multiple of mine."

This wasn't easy. Wallace looked at Sophia, the woman he loved. And she had just announced three more men were going to know that beautiful body intimately. He alternated between feeling faint and exploding. "What do you tell their fathers?" he asked whispering.

"Nothing. None of them are aware of their paternity."

None of it seemed right. But... "The boys are going to be awesome," Wallace said. He was finally beginning to grasp what was happening and the potential the family represented. "No wonder you said you were like an alien."

"You don't know the half of it yet. But I need to know you're a friendly. We want and need your help, and I'll tell you everything."

"Even if I don't understand and sometimes might not approve?"

"I'm absolutely sure you won't approve of everything I do—just as I won't approve of everything you do, but I want us to always be friends. Remember, you promised always to be my friend." Sophia slid closer and took his hand. "And maybe we can be more again. I'd like that."

Wallace softened. "I'd like that, too." Sophia kissed him softly, and nanoseconds later they were in a deep, romantic clinch. It was true. She did love him. He could feel their hearts swelling and melding into one.

"You can count me in," he whispered. "And I'll try not to make your boys too jealous."

Sophia pushed away slightly to recover her composure. She brushed back her hair. "Thanks. And I'm glad you noticed. Two inherited characteristics are emotional feelings from each parent. So they have feelings of love—romantic love—for me from their fathers. You saw what can happen."

He gathered her back into his arms, placing her head under his chin. "I'll be good. Just tell me there's a chance."

She slid her hand down and squeezed him gently. Her smile was impish, and that of a twenty-year-old. "There's a chance."

*****

Two weeks later Sophia got back on schedule for number five. His father had been the most interesting to date. Maybe because he was like her father. Charlie Parker was a rough-hewn engineer with limited time available for social activities. He was most comfortable hammering away at projects too big or complicated for all but the largest engineering firms.

Sophia became pregnant in what proved to be a one-night stand. Charlie left for Australia almost immediately to construct a copper smelter. Sophia decided he shied away from involvement like Cam had with Bobbi.

Chapter 32

Suzanne's letter brightened King Wright's day. She had graduated from Yale in June and was coming home from a summer in Europe. He was hoping to have a surprise ready when she arrived. King had been maneuvering to purchase a major network and would be able to place Suzanne in an attractive position if successful.

The negotiations had tried his patience and weren't over yet. His combine was not alone in seeking the buyout, and Arnold Klein had put in a bid using his cable backing. Klein had driven up the price, and King's financing arrangements were becoming increasingly complicated. The bond issue was going to be larger than originally anticipated, and his personal properties and stations were probably not sufficient collateral for his portion.

Even his associates were becoming troublesome. When the price was lower, they had lined up behind him, practically pushing money in his direction. Now as the deal was becoming leaner and chancy, they were threatening to require larger pieces of the action for their investments or even to withdraw altogether. They were being smart, while he was losing his objectivity. He wanted a network, even if he had to pay too much.

By four-thirty, the deed was done. An agreement in principle was signed, and King had placed earnest money against the purchase. His partners congratulated him, but more for his show of financial resources than for his business acumen. They didn't know his reasons. Claire Villars would be the anchorwoman on the *Network Nightly News* after its move to Washington, and Suzanne would have a production position to learn the business.

King left for Denver in the morning and Claire was at Stapleton to welcome him home. With her long blonde hair and designer jeans,

Claire looked stunning. He was proud she loved him, and delighted in showing off her beauty as well as her brains.

"You did it! You did it!" she screamed in delight.

He wanted to be happy, but the concern over financing was keeping his feet on the ground. "You bet," he said smiling. He kissed Claire and felt the joy and excitement coursing through her body. He couldn't wait to take her to Lookout Mountain. But business first. "You're heading to D.C.," he told her, walking to the lower level for his luggage. "You'll be in charge of the Washington news bureau until we move the *Nightly News*. Then you're the anchor."

"Oh, lover, that's terrific." His luggage had already arrived. "Wow, this is my lucky day. We'll be out within thirty minutes and I won't have to pay for parking."

King laughed. "Can't get any better than that," he agreed. He noticed her western-style shirt was unbuttoned down to the critical point, allowing him to fully appreciate her endowment without appearing trashy. He had paid too much for the network, but it would be worth it.

*****

It was only business, Sophia told herself. The *Washington Post* had displayed banner headlines on Wright's takeover, but she noted his primary assets were in savings and loan institutions. She thought his wealth was in radio and television stations. But S & Ls? They were supposedly in deep trouble from their purchases of junk bonds. She dialed Denver.

A week later, Sophia received Wallace's package. He included a private note that Villars was on her way to Washington to be head of the network's Washington bureau.

Wallace had done a good job on Wright's financial situation. King's tax returns showed substantial properties: two ranches, three radio and two television stations, and various small holdings. Unknown to the public, his primary income derived from Western Investments Corporation, plus a substantial salary and dividends from Colorado Banking Centers, the largest savings & loan in Denver. The Dun & Bradstreet report on WIC showed it was thinly capitalized and that they purchased and sold bonds of all types.

On the surface, Wright looked like a fast-footed financial

manipulator or at least, his interests and activities gave him that opportunity. According to the FSLIC, Colorado Banking Centers was thin and heavily invested in junk bonds in addition to their usual mortgages. There was no way Wright could have raised sufficient cash from the reports.

There was only one possibility: CBC had borrowed large sums and purchased bonds from WIC, and Wright had used those funds to underwrite junk bonds for the takeover and for his ownership portion. But Wright didn't have enough equity to pledge.

It was Sophia's best guess that he had either double-pledged his assets or floated notes to CBC on blue sky. If she was right, King could be leveraged out for assumption of liabilities. He could be threatened with exposure and criminal prosecution, so it was worth a shot.

"We've got one of those 'here today-gone tomorrow' opportunities," she told Ed. "I think we can buy control of a network for a hundred to two hundred million. Interested?"

"Absolutely. Is this connected with King Wright?"

"You betcha." She showed Ed what she had figured. "I think Wright's over-extended somewhere around a hundred million. But that's not the leverage. He's probably blue-skyed a note illegally using his position at CBC, and that can bring jail time. If he thinks he'll be exposed before he can cover, he'll have to sell out or face bankruptcy and prison. We could pick up the shortfall, allow him to escape doing time in La Tuna, and save face."

"I can handle the offer once we know his exposure, but how do we set him up?"

Sophia smiled broadly. "Leak that CBC is about to be investigated. Place a story where Villars can intercept and kill it. Then you approach Wright and rescue him before the examiners arrive. Leave him his S & L—they're losers anyway."

"When do you want to do this?"

"Tomorrow. Webb can handle the leak, but you need to be in Denver."

*****

King Wright was leaving for the Petroleum Club when his secretary caught him at the elevator. Clair Villars was on the phone from Washington, and she said it was urgent. He retraced his steps to the secretary's desk.

"Hi, lover, did I catch you at a bad time?" Claire began.

"I was on my way to lunch. What's up?"

"We've gotten a story your Colorado Banking Centers floated Western Investments notes, and WIC pledged its assets as security on multiple notes. Also, that WIC underwrote your junk bond issue in the network takeover. It charges you with violating several federal regulations."

"Shit! Where'd that come from?"

"Somewhere in Washington. The by-line is a reporter who works several federal agencies. I can find out if necessary."

"No, that won't help. Look, I'll be at Lookout Mountain for a few days. Call me there on my special line. Ring twice, hang up, and call again. I've got to get my shit together."

"I can kill this if you want. At least for a while."

"Do it. Call me in an hour. I've got to get out of here."

"Okay, lover, I'll deep-six it for now. Miss your bod."

"Yeah." King hung up, totally preoccupied. The Petroleum Club was out—he needed to run for cover. He told his secretary he was flying to Washington and would be back in two or three days. In sixty seconds, King made himself scarce.

King cursed himself as he drove westward. He should not have let his desire to accommodate the girls cloud his business sense. Not only had he paid too much, he had been forced to do a little shell-gaming. Time. He had assumed he would have time to cover himself by arranging other financing. Now, he had no time. The longer he drove, the angrier he became with himself. Claire and her fantastic sexuality were worth a few financial problems, but not this.

She called on schedule as he paced around his large live-in room. He could see Denver clearly today through the slanted windows, and looking to his left, Golden was spread at his feet. King had already downed a double Scotch to help him calm down. "Anything new since we talked?" he asked nervously.

"Yeah. The free-lancer got his information from someone inside Justice. Apparently it's still speculative, and he gave it to us as a scoop. So I'm the only one who has it."

"Thank God. And you're holding it."

302

"Between my knees. I got the stringer under control. Had to promise big bucks for an exclusive, but I told him we couldn't run it without confirmation. So we're sitting on it, and he's digging for more." Claire paused while King digested her news. "I'd estimate we have five to seven days before everything comes out. Maybe less."

"But you can't be sure?"

"No, of course not. Once news hounds get a scent of something like this, it normally comes out in a few hours. Fortunately, the collapse of the Soviet Union has everyone's attention. By the way, is it true?"

Thanks, King muttered to himself. *Is it true? How in the hell do you think business is conducted?* People who've never worked for themselves don't understand. Claire had always been on salary, and money rained on her from the giant kiwi bird in the sky. He struggled to control his temper. "Yeah, maybe. I was caught a little short and had to do some fancy footwork."

"Lover, is there anything I can do?"

King's mind was racing, trying to capitalize on his newly-won grace period. Perhaps she could help. He needed friends in the Senate who could protect him from prosecution.

"How about lobbying the Senate banking subcommittee? I could use some friends there. See who we can co-op to help smooth this over." King thought for a moment. "And I mean really put in our pocket. It could get nasty, and we need someone on our payroll to keep examiners away."

"I'll try, lover, but that's a little out of my line."

"It's a matter of life or death," he added for emphasis.

*****

Ed called Wright's office after lunch and his secretary said he had gone to Washington. Not likely since actions were required here in Colorado. King was apparently incommunicado while attempting to cover his tracks. Ed rang Sophia for advice.

"He'll probably be on Lookout Mountain," Sophia said. She dug out her old address book with Suzanne's name. She gave Ed three numbers, Suzanne's, King's, and King's private line.

"Try his private line first. It's only known to his closest

associates. By the way, everything here went perfectly. Villars killed the story temporarily, and she talked our man into keeping it confidential. Wright probably thinks he has a few days to maneuver."

"I'll maneuver him. I always wanted to be a big network executive," Ed quipped. He had spent thirty years coordinating and negotiating so he felt supremely confident in this situation.

Ed was not surprised when Wright agreed to meeting later that afternoon in his office. Wright obviously felt he had gained a breather.

At three-thirty, Ed was shown in and King introduced himself. Ed was impressed with the office's western expansiveness, and he looked for a pool table around the corner. It wasn't there, but a wet bar was, along with a Remington sculpture and two Tom Lea originals.

"You mentioned investing in my network. How can I be of service?" King began.

"Quite possibly I can be of service to you," replied Ed. "My information is you have some difficulties with respect to certain loans and relationships between Colorado Banking Centers, a regulated savings and loan of which you are president, and Western Investments Corporation, an entity you own. I am interested in purchasing a controlling interest in your recently acquired network, and believe we might be able to resolve any and all aforementioned difficulties expeditiously in the bargain."

"I'm aware of no difficulties, and although I'm a businessman with everything for sale at the right price, I did not purchase the network intending to sell it immediately thereafter."

Ed smiled at how carefully King had phrased his remarks. It was a good opening line that gave nothing away. "In essence, I believe we're talking about the acquisition of the network, Western Investments, your private assets, and assumption of all liabilities."

Wright examined Ed's business card. "I'm sorry, but I'm not familiar with Milleron. What is your primary business?"

"We're a diversified investment and holding company. To give you an idea of my position, I could write you a check or immediately wire a hundred million dollars as a show of financial strength. And, of course, if we reached an agreement, all monies due would be remitted the same day." Ed carefully watched the effect of his words on Wright. King was good. Ed saw only the tiniest flicker when he mentioned money. "You must understand, however," he continued, "Milleron is a privately held corporation whose principals shun notoriety. We do not wish the least hint of scandal or impropriety. If there is, then our offer is considered withdrawn."

"You haven't made an offer yet," King said.

"No, of course not. We must review financials of the entities under discussion to arrive at an appropriate purchase figure. I've taken the liberty to draw up a confidentiality agreement covering your financial disclosures to us." Ed opened his attaché case and took out the documents he had obtained at the airport from Columbo's secretary. He pushed them across the desk to King.

The lean mogul did not move. He remained gazing at Ed. "Mr. Armstrong, I fear these discussions are somewhat premature. I'm not at all certain I wish to consider a sale or divestiture, and I'm certainly not prepared to enter into disclosures and substantive discussions."

Ed rose in preparation to leave. "I understand the difficulties in making decisions of this type but believe we can arrive at an offer you can't refuse. I have booked a suite at the Brown Palace for a week. I'm sure our business will be completed one way or another in that time. I will remain at your pleasure for a week." Ed leaned forward and shook King's hand.

Wright gave himself away by rising tardily. He was more than interested. He had controlled his face, but forgotten his body. Ed gave him three to five days to call.

*****

Three days elapsed since Ed's face-to-face with King Wright without a word. Sophia decided it was time to jolt him into action. She dialed Columbo and came directly to the point.

"Dave, I have information that King Wright has illegally used his position as president of an S & L in Denver in conjunction with another company he owns to grant unsecured loans. We're not interested in going public or prosecuting, but we want to pressure him to cease and desist."

"Another one! S & Ls are in trouble all over. I got put on a high visibility subcommittee."

"Yeah, I know. But in this case, I'd like a favor."

"Okay, what?"

"Call Wright and tell him you've gotten some pertinent information concerning his S & L, Colorado Banking Centers, and you're beginning an investigation. Invite him to Washington to discuss it with you in confidence next week."

"That's easy enough, but you'll have to provide facts so I can talk to him."

"He won't come. But if he does, I'll have them for you. His girlfriend, Claire Villars, will probably show in his place to gain time."

"Who?"

"Villars, Claire Villars. She's King's mistress."

Columbo was momentarily silent. "Are you going to be home tonight?" he asked.

"Sure, why?"

"I'll be over to talk. This is more complicated than you think."

Sophia suspected some connection, but withheld making snap conclusions. Claire's name had obviously thrown him, but why? Meanwhile, she telephoned Wallace.

"Need another favor," she said. Wallace was rapidly accumulating a lot of credits on her account. He'd better be in love with her.

"Sure, what?" he replied.

"Today's Thursday. How about calling on King Wright and leaving your card. Stop by when he's not there tomorrow and say you need to talk to him."

"What if he calls? What'll I say?"

"He won't. Even if he does, ask to call back because you're busy. Hell, you can play telephone tag for a couple of days, and by then it'll be over."

"Sounds simple enough. I'll do it during lunch. Is that all?"

"No. I miss you." She really meant it. Every time she felt down, she thought of him. Sometimes life was the pits.

Chapter 33

Columbo arrived in a funk. "Your information about King Wright was troubling," he said.

Sophia ushered Columbo into the library where they wouldn't be disturbed. She fixed him a Cutty Sark and water to settle his nerves.

"You didn't know, but Claire Villars has already seen me."

She could see mentioning Villars was a major admission. He was hiding something. She sat down, folded her hands and faced him directly. "So she's seen all of you, and you discovered she's a screamer," she stated.

Columbo placed his head in his hands. He looked up and nodded. Then it hit him. "How did you know she's a screamer?"

"Not important," she replied. "Villars uses her body whenever appropriate. Wright needs your good offices, and all she had to offer was herself." She paused to let her words sink in. "How compromising did she get?"

"I've already seen her twice. The first time we met for lunch, but ended up at the Sheraton Park. You'll never believe where we were yesterday."

"Yeah, I will. At home. She had to make it in your bed."

Dave nodded slowly. "I'm an idiot, huh?"

"No, just suckered by one of the best. But now for damage assessment and repair." Sophia changed her tone from concern and sympathy to calculating and professional. "I assume she took no little souvenir snapshots. What did she take from you or your bedroom?"

"Ah, I'm sure there aren't any pictures, but I'll have to check the bedroom."

"Pardon me from becoming too clinical, but is there anything she would know other than your bedroom that would convince Carol you were unfaithful?"

Dave looked at the floor as if deciding to crawl under the rug. "Ah, yeah," he said slowly. "My circumcision has a slight irregularity, and she remarked about how she would always be able to secretly recognize me. If she mentioned that, Carol would throw me out."

"Okay, so she's got leverage. We get leverage of our own to neutralize her. Then you're back to even."

"What can we get?"

Sophia scoffed. "Leave that to me. And we're still going to need you to call Wright."

"God, I can't believe I did this," Dave said again.

Sophia snapped. "Cool it. So you made a mistake. Now get off it and get on with your life. You're an Amulot. You can be defeated, but never conquered. It's all up from here."

"I'm sorry," Columbo said. "What do you want me to do?"

*****

Sophia approached Webb first thing in the morning. She had worked up a plausible compromising scenario but didn't have either the setting or personnel.

"I need an offset on Claire Villars so she can't pressure Columbo," she told Webb.

"What's she got? How bad is it?" As always, he poured himself a cup of coffee when the conversation threatened to become lengthy.

Sophia quickly related Columbo's indiscretion. "For most senators, it would be meaningless, but Columbo loves his wife and family."

"Doesn't sound like he showed it," Webb said. "I thought he had better sense."

"Well, Claire's an expert. So what do you think?"

"IRS? Probably won't bother her. Threatening media people is a tough business since they'll close ranks around her. Besides, she hasn't done anything wrong."

"Exactly. But I remember King didn't like Martin Luther King, so I doubt he cares much for blacks. And Villars is only out for power. I thought if we could set up some powerful black with her and videotape it, we might have something she wouldn't want King to see."

Webb thought for a moment. "I have a better idea. We'll hit her with a phony representative of the Black African Congress about ending apartheid. We'll have him seduce her, or vice versa, and when she gets going, we'll bring in his buddies and do her up black."

Sophia considered his suggestion. "It might work. If they challenge her, she'll take on as many as they can bring in."

Webb buzzed for Miss Akers, his secretary. "Bring me Abdul's file," he said when she entered. She returned while Webb waited, quietly gazing out the window. He took the folder, removed a photo, and held it out to Sophia. "How does he look?"

Abdul could have been a movie star. Tall, light-skinned, and with a face like Harry Belafonte. "He'll be perfect, but he's not very black."

"His friends will be. He's the lure. Think she'll bite?"

"In a heartbeat," Sophia chuckled.

"I'll have his presence here at Langley leaked with the potential of an inside story. She'll come a-running." He took the photograph back. "I'll let you know how it went next week."

"Too late," Sophia snapped. "It must be tonight or tomorrow."

"You aren't in a hurry, are you?" Webb made a series of calls while Sophia sat quietly. He scheduled a meeting for ten o'clock. He excused Sophia as being specifically not invited.

The other players were in a holding pattern while the Villars situation was resolved. Ed still hadn't heard from Wright. The week would expire on Monday, and he was getting nervous. Wallace had left his card at Wright's office, but like Sophia expected, King had not called back. Events were rapidly reaching a climax.

*****

Sophia was reading to Donald the following morning when her doorbell rang.

"I've got something for you to see," Webb said, waving a videotape as he entered.

Sophia gave Donald to Carolina, and both she and Heather followed Webb into the library. He turned on the VCR while Sophia locked the door. "I've only seen a little bit, but it was enough for me to hotfoot over." He turned to Heather. "This is pornographic," he warned.

"Oh, goody!" she laughed. "Shall I get my toys?"

"Heather, be good. You'll embarrass Webb," Sophia said. "She will, won't she, Webb?"

"Take it easy, you two. I'm outnumbered. Besides, you might not like this. It's interracial."

Heather's demeanor immediately became quieter while Webb continued. "They had dinner until ten, then went to his apartment. Actually it's a house in Georgetown where he supposedly rented the third floor as an apartment. It was featured in *Playboy* in the seventies for its fancy mirrored boudoir, and this begins with him showing off the bedroom. By the way, she's still there."

"Roll it," Sophia ordered roughly. The savage tone in her voice startled everyone, even her.

Webb explained the lighting was very complicated, and four video cameras were in use. Claire entered laughing and bounced onto the bed, joking about the bordello atmosphere. The tall, extremely well-built black immediately suggested putting it to good use, and after a short clinch, they disrobed and made love.

Sophia glanced over to Heather, but she was watching intently. Webb put the VCR on fast-forward for a while.

The performers went at it again, this time with Claire on top. She started screaming, and in the midst of her passion, first one, and then two more black guys came in. The second one was very dark, but not bad-looking. Claire was initially taken aback at his entrance, but responded to the challenge. Resuming her activities with the first one, she simultaneously added the second. Then the third and fourth guys entered. In total charge, Claire ordered them to strip and get onto the bed.

All were awesomely endowed, and the last two were coal black and ugly as sin. The contrast with Claire's natural blondness was stunning, and her suppression of all inhibitions was truly amazing. Sophia left the screening to Heather and Webb to call Columbo.

"Time to call King Wright," she informed him. "Everything's taken care of."

"I'll call right away. By the way, I don't think anything's missing."

"Fine, but invite her over to dinner sometime next week, and have Carol show her around. Then if she did take something, you'll have plausible deniability."

Ed telephoned three hours later to say Wright had requested a meeting late that afternoon. Dave's call had finally shaken Wright's tree, and he probably wasn't able to contact Claire. Sophia guessed they would reach agreement by Monday—before King could be cornered by Wallace, and before having to answer Columbo's summons. Everything was working out, and she noted that Heather and Webb didn't come out of the library until almost two hours after she left the room. Nobody said anything, but Webb's body language gave them away. Sophia approved.

*****

Claire unplugged her telephone when she got back to her Watergate apartment. She couldn't remember being so tired. So much sex. So many firsts. She crawled into bed and went to sleep.

The buzzer woke her up. The security guard said there was a messenger for her. She looked at the clock, and it was eleven-thirty in the morning. Sunday. She had slept through the remainder of Saturday afternoon, evening, and night.

Claire dragged herself out of bed and reconnected her telephone. She could hardly walk, and was sore in places that she hadn't known existed.

The messenger handed her a large manila envelope and departed. Claire went into her kitchen and turned on the coffee maker before she opened it.

She collapsed on a dinette chair.

The envelope contained a note and several photographs. The note was a *thank you for a wonderful experience*, and included the photos as mementos. They were of herself with the men of Friday night and Saturday. She couldn't remember anyone taking pictures, and the quality and definition took her breath away. So did the subject matter. They might be souvenirs, but in the hands of the wrong person, they would terminate her career. And her relationship with King. If someone was trying to tell her something, they were doing a helluva job. But what or why?

The photos showed her clearly with all three later guys, taking them in various positions and combinations. They must have been shot by the brown Adonis who'd seduced her initially. Incredible but

311

stupid. She had unscrewed her head and played out her fantasy to be a sex goddess. One shot in particular made her want to throw up. If anyone saw it, she was finished. Lord.

She was still sitting in the kitchen trying to put herself together when the telephone rang. It was King. The last person she wanted to talk to in her mental state.

"Hi, sweetheart," he said. "I tried to call you all yesterday. Where were you?"

Just the question she couldn't answer. "I didn't feel very well," she lied, "so I unplugged my phone. Apparently it was something I ate." She heard herself say the ridiculous double entendre, but she was beyond humor.

"Well, take care of yourself. I need you." His tone indicated he accepted her explanation, then he went on to discuss business. "I received a call from Senator Columbo yesterday. Can you do any good with him?"

God, not right now, she thought. "I can try, but I doubt I'll have much influence."

"Well, do what you can to stall him and the investigation. Please."

"I really don't think I'll be able to help," she said almost in a daze.

"You feel all right?"

"No," she replied quietly. "I don't feel very well. I need to rest another day."

"Okay, I won't bother you. Get some sleep, sweetheart. Remember, I love you." That was something they said automatically when they hung up. This time, Claire didn't.

*****

King's negotiation meetings did not go well. Reality had set in like food poisoning. He was bankrupt. If he could continue for six months, he might work clear. The problem was that he didn't have six months. He didn't have six days, maybe not six hours. He needed a hundred million to pay off the demand notes from Colorado Banking Centers. He had listed assets for those notes that were already pledged on other obligations. He had not executed the liens yet, but if examiners came in, he'd do time in jail.

King had tried to call in several markers, but the cash was simply not available. Klein wouldn't talk to him, and he had made too many enemies in the Colorado banking community to scare up money on his signature. In fact, he couldn't get short term money at all.

Armstrong would leave him with Colorado Banking Centers at least. Some deal. CBC was bankrupt in fact, if not on the books. It was carrying some six hundred properties on the books which couldn't be sold anywhere close to their book value. The junk bonds were potentially even worse. They had crashed on the market, and CBC was still carrying them at cost. But he would have a job, his reputation, and a chance.

Time had run out, and King signed the agreement Ed presented for a bulk purchase of the assets and liabilities of Western Investments and his other companies, plus all of his assets, personal and corporate, were pledged as security for the liabilities. In return, Milleron agreed to pay off the demand notes held by CBC on WIC.

Sophia greeted Ed like a conquering hero. She met him at Friendship and drove to Port Tobacco listening to him expound on his negotiations. The way Ed finally figured the purchase, he paid a little over seventy million in cash for book net worth of three times that amount.

"What do you think of King Wright?" Ed asked in a lull.

"I met him during high school and thought he was fairly impressive." Sophia said.

"I was impressed, too. He got himself over-extended but would have pulled it off if you had given him more time. Sure, he stretched the law, but show me an entrepreneur who doesn't."

"So why do you think he got so far over the barrel?"

"We talked for a while, and I think he wanted to buy the network for his girls."

"Girls? He only has one daughter."

"His girlfriend, Claire Villars, was to be the news anchor, and his daughter was going to be in production. Anyway, I think we can use him. He's good at negotiating and has an eye for property."

Sophia was surprised. You don't wipe somebody out and then offer them a job. "I doubt he'd talk to us," she said.

"Oh, I think he would. Especially if he could keep his ranch on Lookout Mountain."

She glanced at Ed in mock suspicion. "So what did he say when you brought it up?"

Ed laughed. "For once you're wrong. I didn't mention it. I left that for you."

"For me? Thanks a hell of a lot. But I know you; you already have something in mind."

"Sure. We need a solid S & L to acquire ailing thrifts when the feds shut them down."

"I didn't know there were any solid savings and loans."

"There probably aren't. And neither is Wright's. But we could make it strong and be there to pick up plums from bankrupt ones."

"You're saying to buy in with his ranch. Have him work for us—no, work for you. He would never work for me."

"But you can arrange it. Talk to his daughter and then to him. Tell him you'll buy his Lookout Mountain property from me as part of my deal to attract your investment. Then I'll come in, re-finance CBC, and cut him a deal where he can participate. He's got to be worried the feds are going to close him down, even if he's escaped jail time."

Ed had a point—and a good idea. They could use Wright's talent. She turned into the Port Tobacco facility and made her decision. "Okay, give me details."

It worked as Ed outlined. Sophia telephoned Suzanne and upon hearing King might lose their house, mentioned she was looking to invest over two hundred million dollars and might be able to help. King came on the line immediately.

"I don't want to sound negative, but I'm already obligated," King said in response to Sophia's offer. "It's probably too late."

"Maybe not. Suzanne mentioned Milleron as the company you were dealing with, and they've contacted me for investment funds. Who were you working with at Milleron?"

"A real tough businessman named Armstrong. Ed Armstrong."

"What's he like?" Sophia asked.

"Actually, he's not a bad sort. I wouldn't want to play poker with him, but you don't have to count your fingers after shaking his hand. You can to talk to him. He's pretty up-front."

"Well, that sounds good. I'll get in contact with him tomorrow; maybe we can get your house separated as a condition of my investing with them."

Late the next day, Sophia telephoned King directly. She had talked to Ed Armstrong, and he was willing to discuss her idea. This time, King sounded more optimistic. He was due to come to Washington in a few days and arranged a meeting with Ed while Suzanne stayed with Sophia.

Heather, as always, provided the icing on the cake. She had met a promoter from New York whom she coaxed into joining them for dinner during Suzanne's two-day stay. He became enamored with Suzanne and spent the entire next day showing her around town.

Sophia sometimes wondered how Heather did it. She had an uncanny ability to be at the right place at the right time to meet the right people. With respect to BJ Carter, she had a lunch date with an old acquaintance at the National Endowment for the Arts, and it was expanded to include Carter. Heather then extended the dinner invitation for BJ to meet Milleron people, as well as other Washington notables. Heather then called Ed and Columbo and the party was set. Connections were truly her forte.

Milleron was now becoming an inexhaustible sponge soaking up funds. As fast as it made money, Milleron was presented with opportunities for advantageous acquisitions. While the Japanese concentrated on financing the national debt, coastal real estate, manufacturing, and the hospitality industry, Sophia focused on agriculture and other industries in the Midwest.

The re-vamped operation of Colorado Banking Centers exceeded their greatest expectations. Ed and King sold some properties to WIC at book value along with junk bonds that had defaulted on their interest payments. Then WIC swapped those properties at market value with several financial institutions in Southern California, taking a loss. As a final step, WIC sold the California properties to Milleron's South American investors, and the losses were more than recouped.

Some homes were put into foreclosure, then sold to a Milleron affiliate. That company sold the homes to unqualified buyers as encouraged by Freddie Mac and Fannie Mae, then sold the mortgages to them. The affiliate shared the profit with CBC through a consulting fee, and CBC's book losses vanished. As a result, CBC emerged very strong and became one of the nation's highest rated thrifts. The feds loved it and relied on it to bolster thrifts in trouble.

The negatives were the junk bonds that WIC had assumed, but Ed was bleeding those as carefully as possible into the market. Sophia held the paper on Wright's Lookout Mountain ranch, but he could earn it back on his participation plan.

Sophia directed Ed to purchase heavily in the southeast and Southern California. These properties were deeded to foreign sources of money as repayment of their loans. In the case of rental properties, Milleron contracted a management firm on the owner's behalf, taking a cut of its fee. Purchasing foreclosures, Milleron eliminated real estate commissions, and not using its own money, net profits were enormous. Ed had representatives in every state and all major metropolitan areas within eighteen months and profits promised to run into the tens of billions.

The only negative with the King deal was that Villars was still on the scene. Sophia knew that one way or another, Villars was a problem she would have to solve personally.

Chapter 34

After the visit to Saudi Arabia in February, Sophia curtailed her trips due to her advanced pregnancy, but intensified her search for the next father. Erwin arrived on schedule early in May, maintaining Sophia's perfect record of all boys.

By the end of June, she located a late summer conference on pesticides at the University of Illinois, and with two possible agronomists located by Ed on discussion panels, the opportunity for meeting candidates beckoned at last.

She met her problem's solution at dinner the second night. He was a farmer from the Spoon River area in western Illinois who had retired as a professor at Normal, specializing in plant genetics and the extraction of energy from plants. It became a four-day romance, two at the conference, one at his farm, and one two weeks later in Chicago. Sophia rode into his life, handed him the reins, and disappeared as if she had been an apparition.

Both Webb and Ed questioned her choice of specialty for this child, but Sophia held firm. She knew the secret to America's greatest eventual problem—that of producing abundant domestic energy—lay in plants. The sun supplied energy, but she needed to provide sufficient carbon in re-combining forms to utilize that energy. She had already purchased vast tracts of Bakken Shale in the Dakotas and Green River formation in Western Colorado, Wyoming and eastern Utah. The problem was the conversion of kerogen to gas and a condensable oil for further refining. The current process was pyrolysis, the application of heat in a non-oxidizing atmosphere—a very high-cost process producing sulfur and arsenic as by-products and a great deal of pollution. The answer lay developing a natural process like a fungus to convert the kerogen to a convertible product. In addition, plants like jojaba could be used as fuel since they produced extremely long carbon chains by using solar energy to convert simpler carbon compounds. It would be her son's job to create efficient plants to effect these conversions.

Number six kept Sophia's perfect record intact. Frank would be the agronomist and solve the energy crisis. Her doctor recommended she cease making babies for several years to allow her body to rest, but by now, being pregnant was a way of life.

For her last son, she chose a physicist. His name was James Walker, a nuclear physicist at MIT, and she had met him at a technical conference expressly attended to assess possible mates. He was not the most highly regarded in his field, but was close to retirement. There was not much to choose from in physics, if one excluded Asians and Jews, and Sophia was attempting to maintain a relatively common ethnic background among her children.

Meanwhile, her campaign against the Japanese was beginning to have an impact. The Nikkei index was falling steadily, and real estate prices in Japan were tumbling. Following the advice of American liberal economists, the Japanese were spending money domestically like drunken sailors and lending money at unbelievably low interest. It wasn't working, and Sophia knew it wouldn't work. Japanese purchases of American assets were being curtailed, but not being rolled back. The high had come in 1989, but she needed the Japanese to start selling off their American investments. Unfortunately, Americans didn't seem to want them back. The baby-boomers were too busy spending money themselves and focusing on short-term pleasures.

The emergence of Agenda 21 began to seriously concern Sophia. President Bush had signed the Rio Declaration in the summer of 1992, and sustainable development initiatives were springing up like weeds. The UN's Agenda 21 put the US under siege, eliminated private property, and promoted the Bilderberg vision of a Supra-National Socialist World State. Sophia had already taken to calling the Bilderbergs "SNAZIS," but the real problem was that environmental and "one world order" propaganda was incessant, in the schools, politics, and government bureaucracies. It took a very strong person to stand up in opposition to the legions of trained manipulators telling him to hate America. Sustainable development as defined under Agenda 21 meant the end of individual liberty and the

American way of life through the substitution of the collective. In actuality, there was little difference between Mussolini's fascism and the principles of Snazism with "stakeholders," and state collectivism in "private-public partnerships."

Perhaps most chilling was the realization that five to six billion people needed to be exterminated to make sustainable development work. The rest would be concentrated in modern cities, allowed limited space and only a few gallons of water per day, and no individual enterprise. The use of fossil fuels was to be banned, much of the earth would be off-limits to humans, and unsustainable practices like raising grazing animals for food were to be eliminated. There was a child-like belief by many supporters and politicians that somehow technology would come riding to the rescue, but Sophia noted that such ideas were not held by engineers and scientists. She also noted that the primary proponents of this program assumed they would be exempt from its provisions and continue to live the good life. They would make laws for everyone else, but exempt themselves.

The reduction of the world's population was coming regardless of Agenda 21. Sooner or later, mass starvation would appear, accompanied by disease and conflicts over declining resources. In the meantime, it was up to Sophia to see that her people were well-positioned when resources ran out.

*****

The year had gone badly for Claire. She had become pregnant, and King thought it was his. But it wasn't—she had conceived either with the blacks or Senator Columbo. If her baby had been the wrong color, King would have killed her. So she had an abortion, and her relationship with King was never the same.

She missed the west maybe even more than King. Washington felt closed in and up tight, in spite of the heavy cocaine usage by most of her acquaintances and the parties rated by the amount of free coke available. The whole milieu disgusted her. Washington was not a part of the United States, and it survived only by stripping assets from its constituency like a gigantic leech.

The American media possessed a herd mentality with awesome

cross-breeding and elements of conformity. It was driven by a concept of current wisdom emanating from commentator consensus. Reporters followed each other like cattle, not wanting to miss a story, and the same stories with similar interpretations were reported universally.

In contrast, Sophie Stewart was an original. Claire respected Sophia and her obvious genius. The more she thought about things, the more Sophia came to mind. She was different and powerful, like a sleeping tiger waiting to devour the soft bodies and mushy brains in government. Sometimes, Claire thought she should bury the hatchet with Sophia; after all, Suzanne idolized her, and was now seeing a guy she'd met through Sophia's friend Heather. Sophia was helping everybody pursue their dreams and goals except her. There was no good reason to fight the trend.

*****

General Olson was still fuming; the threat of dismissal and relegation to obscurity had been real. He had taken a traditional pro-American stance on an issue and had been told such attitudes were no longer patriotic or desirable. Clearly, the administration was dancing to a Japanese tune. He took two weeks leave, returning to Mississippi to fish and relax.

Disaster struck almost immediately when he came in contact with civilians. Olson flew initially to Dallas, and after a quick visit to Fort Hood, boarded a commercial flight to Jackson. Sitting in first class, he engaged two effusive men in conversation.

"Our trip was extremely successful," the younger one said. "We've been to Japan, Taiwan, and Hong Kong, and we were able to get several good prospects for investment."

"What do you want to invest in?" Olson asked.

"Oh, not us," the older, balding gentleman replied. "We're attracting far eastern corporations to invest in Mississippi to increase our business base."

"Why not approach American corporations?"

"Pacific Rim nations have the money. We have land, water, tax breaks, and labor force. They can provide our people with a lot of jobs and revitalize our area."

"But ownership and corporate profits will go back to Japan or Taiwan," Olson said. "You're just selling Mississippi resources to foreign interests." Conversation rapidly became heated, and Olson's leave was off to a dismal start.

It got worse. Olson saw Japanese products everywhere, and other people he talked to were excited about obtaining Japanese money. No one seemed to understand the long range dangers or that the money had previously been American.

It was those pinkos in the CIA, he decided. That Stewart girl and her world government friends were selling out the United States. He needed to build an organization that could do something. He cut his fishing trip short and flew to Washington.

Olson decided his best approach was to recruit a clique of highly motivated young officers who could neutralize foreign sycophants through the force of their personalities. After a week of non-stop meetings, he had secretly constructed the nucleus of such a group. He had to be careful as effete liberals would claim it was a dangerous right-wing conspiracy threatening American democracy.

The group needed officers at all levels, even non-coms. The effort would take time, and Olson was reaching the end of his active career. He selected Major Lambert as operations officer. Lambert was a star who was on the list for lieutenant colonel, and still had twenty years of service ahead of him. Captain Chuck Carpenter was recruited to handle Stewart. Carpenter was an Airborne, Special Forces type like himself, tall, with dark hair and eyes that melted most women. The two officers would be the active heads of his fledgling organization, with him as its guiding light.

*****

Carpenter was transferred to NATO liaison in Washington and quickly made contact with Sophia to discuss some issues on behalf of General Olson. He came to the Langley facility and was amazed by what he found.

The little lady was almost seven months pregnant, yet evinced an inner beauty that made Carpenter want to court her. It was absurd. He had never seduced a pregnant woman before—at least not to his knowledge. The conservation was friendly until Carpenter mentioned that General Olson believed Sophia opposed continuing NATO.

"Yes, I do. I believe our most dangerous enemy lies elsewhere." Sophia was busy and decided another venue might help. "Why don't you come to dinner at my house tomorrow night, and we'll fully discuss the issues?"

The Pittsburgh Steelers' Steel Curtain couldn't keep him away.

The first course was Heather. When the captain arrived, she softened him up by introducing him to the boys. Sophia arrived late wearing a beautiful empire dress and looked absolutely stunning. The pregnancy was forgotten as Sophia began to charm the unsuspecting officer. Heather had already primed the pump by telling him Sophia's husband had been killed by South American communists in a CIA operation.

It was a work of art. Captain Carpenter came on like Sophia's personal protector, even promising to improve her relations with General Olson. When it became apparent Sophia was working to repel Japanese influence and power domestically, Chuck decided the general had misread her.

"Have you ever been married, Captain?" Sophia asked while serving flan for dessert.

"No, not even engaged. Being army sometimes inhibits relationships."

"That's what my father said. Also my uncle. During Vietnam, Dad discovered some girls wouldn't touch a man in uniform."

"Well, coverings don't make the person. It's what's inside that counts."

Sophia sighed. "What's inside me is a baby wanting to be born."

Carpenter reached over and took her hand. "Heather told me about your husband. I'm very sorry. How are you going to manage with your family?"

"I have Heather to help. Without her, it would be impossible. Besides, what good is it to raise your kids to enjoy life when your country is disintegrating before your very eyes? Even for a mother, sometimes your country is more important than your children."

The captain smiled with sympathy. "You're unbelievable. You sound like Mother Earth and Miss Liberty rolled into one. You seem more concerned with the future of our country than General Olson."

"General Olson doesn't have sons to whom he'll bequeath our way of life as a legacy. He only needs to look at his lifetime; I have to look further. My boys are depending on me."

"You can depend on me, too," the captain blurted. He was astounded at the words he had just spoken. What had she done to him? His brain was turning to jelly.

He escorted her back into the living room, allowing her to hold onto his arm. Sophia lowered herself onto the couch and patted the cushion beside her. Heather disappeared down the hall.

"You know, we haven't talked about what you originally came over to discuss." Sophia turned sideways on the couch and faced him squarely. "You came to my office to begin my seduction. Why? What were you to influence me to do?"

The captain felt his face flush. He decided to be honest. "Yes, I was to seduce you. But after meeting you, I knew it was wrong. You were better than that."

"You're better than that." Sophia took his left hand and held it between hers. "So what was I supposed to do?"

"He wants to maintain NATO at its current strength. And eliminate Japanese and far eastern economic influence in the US."

"But NATO isn't relevant if Japan is controlling our economy and the new Russian Federation is no threat like the Soviet Union was. Doesn't he understand that?"

"Not yet, but remember, he sees NATO as his baby."

"But what's going on? You surely wouldn't play seducer just to maintain Olson in NATO a little longer."

"No," he admitted, remorse evident in his voice. There was only one way to regain the respect of this foxy lady. "We've formed a group of military personnel to fight leftist and foreign influence in government. I guess he had you in the leftist category. I'm sorry."

"Apology accepted. But the idea is not bad. What if I said I want in?"

"As far as I'm concerned, that would be terrific. But you'd have to convince Olson."

He leaned over, pulled her to him and kissed her. Sophia decided to forestall anything further and drew back. "No, not now. I don't want you to see me in this condition. You would have to love me very much to overlook my shapelessness. I don't want to risk that." She patted him gently. "Maybe later, when the time is right."

*****

Sophia called Moscow and requested a meeting with Chuikov in Washington. Intrigued by her hints of difficulties, he appeared within a week. He looked as trim and fit as ever, despite the flak he had taken when the Soviet Union collapsed. It was the first time he had seen Sophia with a pregnancy so advanced. He wasn't sure he liked it; somehow it detracted from her and from him. Chuikov decided his image of her didn't allow her to be so grossly pregnant.

"You look very well," he said, "I trust you are not suffering any undo discomfort."

"Thank you, but this one has been taxing. Particularly with my husband gone. I'm sure it will be my last." Sophia's voice was sad and missing its usual vibrancy.

"Your husband is gone?" Chuikov asked. "When do you expect him to return?" He knew Sophia's husband was a CIA operative, but they had been unable to obtain any information on him.

"Never," Sophia replied. "He's departed our known world."

"Oh, I'm sorry," Chuikov said with honest feeling. "My most heartfelt condolences on your loss. When did this occur? Is there anything I can do to be of assistance?"

"Thank you. It was something I had come to expect, and now after several months, I've learned to adjust. But there is something you can help me with."

"You have but to ask. We have been most satisfied with your efforts, and I have come to regard you as a valued friend and associate."

"Speak louder, and we'll both go to jail in our own countries," Sophia laughed.

"Only because they're staring at the past instead of the future," the colonel said seriously. "Things are changing. I expect to be promoted to general before next year."

Sophia leaned forward and hugged him. "Congratulations. You deserve it. More than your country knows, you are truly a leader of distinction. A leader's leader. A Renaissance man."

Chuikov beamed from the praise of this most brilliant of women. It was as if he had received another medal on his chest. "So how can I help? You indicated a serious problem."

Sophia folded her hands and repositioned herself on the hard settee. "Certain elements in our military wish to retain NATO and our current levels of armed forces at all costs. I have even come under attack by one of these officers, and he can be a formidable opponent."

"A not unexpected development. I have had similar problems in my country."

"Yes, but in this case the attack is personal. It's General Olson."

"We're familiar with him. He's a Russian hater."

"Even more than that, he hates anybody who doesn't think exactly like him. I'd like to see him neutralized, but it's extremely difficult for me to arrange. He's one of those cases where the Agency can't get involved."

"I see. He's your known opponent. But the same is true for us."

"Yes, but his current campaign is stridently anti-Japanese. It would be advantageous if they could take credit for his downfall."

Chuikov considered the implications of what Sophia was saying. "Does he have any redeeming qualities?" he asked.

"Not as far as I'm concerned," she replied. "He's traveling to Japan next month. Perhaps his visit could be his swan song."

Chuikov smiled and nodded. "Allow me," he said, patting Sophia's knee. "It would be my pleasure. Leave everything to me. You don't know anything."

*****

For the next several weeks, Sophia monitored Olson's activities while spending time with Captain Carpenter. Olson was building his private corps of adherents, but everything was strictly in the organizing phase. Sophia began to wonder what action Chuikov would take. Olson flew to Japan as scheduled, and much to Sophia's surprise, took a group of civilians with him. Apparently, he wanted to show them Japan's threat up close.

The news the next day was stunning. General Olson had died of a heart attack in a geisha house. The implication was he died in full flight under mysterious circumstances. Several civilians in his entourage had been present, and hints of a dark plot to eliminate Japanese critics surfaced.

Arguments raged across TV. Official Japanese sources maintained the general had suffered a fatal heart attack while engaged in sexual intercourse, but several Americans said Olson had been drugged while enjoying the singing and dancing. Most stations gave Olson's death only two days of play, and the issues died rapidly. Sophia's network featured the Japanese assassination theory, but there was no call for an investigation in Congress or anywhere else in government.

Chuck Carpenter took the loss of General Olson hard. In spite of their differences, the captain idolized him as a military leader. He hoped that Olson had died in full flight, even saying it was the preferred way to go. But he wasn't serious.

Sophia went to meet the captain in his Georgetown apartment after putting her boys to bed. She was surprised to find several officers already gathered when she arrived. They seemed equally surprised to discover she was starting the last month of her pregnancy.

Although Colonel Simmons was present, the guiding spirit of Major Lambert was apparent. Carpenter opened his bar, and they drank a toast to General Olson. Sophia joined them with a glass of water.

"Mrs. Stewart," Major Lambert began, after they resumed their seats, "Chuck thinks you are sympathetic to our cause. What do you think?"

"I would agree with him, except with respect to NATO. May I explain?"

"Please do," Lambert requested.

Sophia launched into a full explanation of the economic threat to American sovereignty. The officers were startled to hear the level of penetration by Japan and the EU countries, and Sophia stressed the US was no longer the world's greatest economic power. She reviewed the problems besetting Russia, and alluded to the US possibly partitioning in the next century. The officers jerked as if pummeled by shock waves of information.

Without stopping, Sophia launched into a lecture outlining the control of the Bilderbergs, the commitment of the CFR to world socialism, and the Trilateralists' supra-national initiatives between Japan, the US and Europe. She pointed out that all critical metals production except aluminum was now in the Third World and under the control of those same groups. The Japanese economy was faltering under the covert assault of China, and in another ten years,

China would replace Japan as the hand on the control lever for American economics and foreign policy. The European nations formerly under the Soviet heel were looking to Europe rather than the US for leadership, and the SSRs that became new nations were struggling for their very existence.

She emphasized that state capitalism of the type invented by Mussolini had become the preferred economic model world-wide, even in China, and the US was seen as a truculent anachronism to be reduced to Third World status. Sophia listed off the items considered unsustainable by Agenda 21. Although those same features were the bedrock of the American economy, an American president had already committed the US to its eventual destruction by signing on to Agenda 21. The world looked at the US as a rotten tomato, ready to fall.

"And exactly who is NATO's enemy?" Sophia asked. "Russia is de-militarizing with all possible speed. In a couple of years, Poland, Czechoslovakia, and Hungary will be in NATO, along with Ukraine, Belarus, the Baltic States, and others. Maybe even Russia itself. The common enemy of NATO is Islam and the Islamic states. Is that what NATO's for? To fight Iraq, Egypt, Algeria, and Iran? You watch, NATO will soon be asking for Americans to die under Polish NATO commanders, spend American dollars, and use up American equipment. But of course, that will be okay, as our industries are owned or controlled by the Japanese or Europeans."

"You're saying foreigners are close to controlling our major industries? Ridiculous!" The protestor was a lieutenant colonel who had been silent to that point.

"Fact," Sophia restated. "And it's worse than that. They've bought into power companies and other public utilities. They won't have to bomb our facilities to disrupt our economy. They can simply throw the switch. The power grid has twelve main switching stations. The equipment at every one is unique to that station and was manufactured in China. To replace any one station would take two years, assuming the Chinese will supply the equipment. If they don't, it would take five years."

"But other than Russia and China, nobody has large armies, and no way to occupy our land," protested the colonel. Martin was his name, as given on his nameplate.

"But they'll have powerful allies," Sophia said. "People who want to eat regardless of who owns the store. They aren't worried about jobs—they don't have them now, so they don't care. Three percent is already Asian, and don't forget Mexicans and Hispanics."

"Mexico doesn't have an army that can stand up to us."

"Not now. But Japan can use them for cannon fodder by promising them Texas and the American southwest. There's a brown tide swelling up from south of the border, and those people are your potential occupiers—even without a war. Remember, competition from the Pacific Rim has greatly reduced American heavy industry, and make no mistake as to the quality of equipment they could supply to Mexican, Central American, and South American armies. And they've waited a long time to take revenge on imperialistic *gringos*."

"That's speculation, and many years away," Lambert commented.

"Speculation, yes, but not many years away. Maybe twenty to thirty. The investments are already there, and it only remains for Japan and the Europeans to protect their investments. Up to now, they've been content to manipulate the president and Congress. Look at Olson's death. Our best information is that the Japanese did it. Committed murder. And then they told the networks, Congress, and the administration to accept the official version or else. Is there any investigation going on? No, and there won't be any. We already do what they say. We're deathly afraid they'll stop financing our national debt. In a sense, Olson was the first battle death in the second Japanese-American War."

Silence. Captain Carpenter broke the oppressive quiet. "Here's to General Olson, our first casualty in the Japanese-American War. Let his death not be in vain."

They all rose for the toast. "To General Olson!" Lambert seized the moment and smashed his glass into the fireplace. Everyone, including Sophia, did likewise. Sophia had turned a right-wing, anti-communist cabal into an anti-Japanese and America-First group. Olson's organization was hers to command.

Carpenter's spirits were still in the toilet in spite of the rah-rah. Sophia tried to cheer him up after the other officers departed and poured him another Scotch. "Look at the general's death as a beginning, not as an end," she said. "He would have wanted you to carry on, and even redouble your efforts."

"You're fantastic," the captain remarked. "After irrefutably showing us the deep shit we're in, you're now talking optimistically."

"Only because men such as yourself are willing to correct the situation." She sat down beside him and grasped his hand. "Otherwise, we're lost," she said quietly. Sophia gazed intently into the captain's eyes. She could see them beginning to glaze over in preparation to kiss her.

"God, you're beautiful. And brilliant." He slowly stroked her cheek with his free hand and brought his lips to hers. There was no resistance. He slid his hand down her blouse.

She clamped her hand on his wrist and stopped him. "No, not while I'm like this."

His expression was one of abject disappointment. "But I love you," he blurted. "I don't care if you're pregnant."

"But I do, and don't say what you don't mean. We hardly know each other." Sophia felt herself becoming affected by the hurt in his eyes. She wondered if this was his routine—to get the lady to feel sorry for him. She decided against it; he was much too macho. This had to be for real. He closed his eyes and leaned back as she kissed him softly. "You're just upset over Olson. Lie back." She held him as he fell asleep.

Driving home, she thought about Chuck. She had mothered him rather than been his lover. And they had parted as friends. She knew that was the right relationship, and was sure Chuck knew that, too. She and the captain could form an unencumbered working relationship for the future. With her in command, of course, as the superior officer.

Chapter 35

On the first day of spring Gordon was born, and it was time for a meeting of the family. They were all there, even Billy from Harvard, Wallace, and Carol Columbo becoming involved for the first time.

After introducing Wallace, Sophia brought the conversation to more serious matters. "The purpose for this get-together is for everyone to fully understand where we are, and where we're going. I know that sounds like an individual awareness therapy session, but that's not what I mean. We're family, and the nucleus of a movement which must realize its destiny within our lifetimes."

"Are we all Amulots?" Carol asked.

"Yes," Sophia answered. "Although only one of my grandparents was Amulot, so I could be anywhere from zero to half. Wallace is mostly Scottish, but the rest of you are fairly high percentage." Sophia stopped for a moment. "Makes you wonder, doesn't it? Stalin wasn't Russian, Constantine wasn't Roman, Joan of Arc wasn't French, and Hitler wasn't German. I wonder what that means."

"Nothing," Webb said. "Christ was a Jew, and Napoleon, a Coriscan."

"At any rate, all movements have finite lives and must be considered contextually."

"All religions, too," Bobbi added.

"Yes. The cradle of individual liberty was the freemasonry movement from 1750 to 1850. Thereafter, it stagnated, and today, it's dying. Of all revolutions spawned by Masonic lodges, Calvinistic Switzerland will probably endure longest because of its tiny size and unique geographical position. Other than that, our republic is the only one that has truly made the democratic experiment work. So why?"

"Because it was an Amulot cultural state," interjected Webb.

"'Was' is the operative word," added Ed. "Look at the Supreme Court. There hasn't been an Amulot on it for years."

"We need to remember what Ben Franklin said at the end of the Constitutional Convention," Sophia said. "'This form of government is likely to be well administered for a course of years and can only end in despotism, as other forms have done before it, when the people shall become so corrupted as to need despotic government, being incapable of any other.'"

"In other words, all governments are time-contextual," Webb said.

"And ours has run its course," Sophia agreed. "Absorbing diverse populations without our Amulot work and freedom ethic, the nation has discarded individual responsibility."

"So we need to partition—letting each major cultural group form its own nation," Ed said.

"Yes. History says the United States will not be able to survive in its present form," Sophia said. She stood a hard-backed map of North America on the desk beside her. Sophia drew the boundaries of three new countries. Everything below the thirty-fifth parallel and west of Texas went to a Hispanic country. Then she drew a line from the southeast corner of New Mexico to the Cibola River east of San Antonio and south to the San Antonio Bay. All of Texas south of that line also became Hispanic. The black country included everything south of the northern borders of North Carolina and Tennessee and a diagonal across Arkansas to Texarkana and south to the Sabine.

"The population exchanges are large in spite of the logic behind these boundaries. For the new white nation, it means an exchange of some fifteen million blacks and Hispanics for a somewhat greater number of whites."

"But that's not an Amulot nation," Ed observed.

"No, not even a WASP nation; a bare majority would be WASP."

Dave shook his head. "I'm not sure I can listen to this. I'm a United States senator, sworn to uphold the Constitution, and you people are planning to dismember the nation."

"Oh, chill out." Everyone turned in amazement. It was Carol who had spoken. She glared at Dave. "We're the people who created the Constitution, and we're the ones who can plan to change it. The Constitution does not require its framers to commit political suicide."

Carol turned to the rest of the group. "I've seen the Washington political scene up close for many years and know it for what it is.

Politicians know they're dependent on the Japanese, Chinese, and Europeans, but all they want is to maintain themselves in power a little longer. The government's living on borrowed time. If we believe in our way of life, we should save it somewhere. Part of a loaf is better than none."

*****

Within days, the outlook became worse. Hearing that the largest chain of convenience stores had been purchased by a Japanese company, Sophia sat down to analyze her situation with a sinking feeling. The weekend was lost in review, calculations, and discussions with Ed, Bobbi, and others. By late Sunday night, she had completed the tale of the tape. On Monday evening, she called everyone together to discuss her findings.

"We can't do it," she began. "There's no way to head off Japan and the Europeans from gaining control of at least half the nation."

"Why are they doing this?" cried Bobbi. "Why don't the Japanese seize control of South America or Africa or somewhere else?"

"Four reasons," Sophia said, holding up four fingers. "First, racism. The sons of heaven are the chosen race, and their only challenge came from us. Second, revenge. We're the only nation to have defeated them, let alone occupy their territory. We will be punished and our homelands occupied or owned by them. Thirdly, like a boxer, if you want to knock out your opponent, you go for the head. They're attempting to establish a position of world economic hegemony, and the world's primary economy has been the United States. And lastly, we're the most vulnerable to economic penetration with the least recourse. If Japan took over industries in Bolivia, that country could nationalize Japanese enterprises, pay no indemnity, and get away with it. We can't. We have an open economy, allowing everyone to come here, make their bundle, and return home enriched by Yankee dollars."

"Nobody in politics seems to understand what's happening," Ed commented. "They still think strength comes from diversity. What's our best shot in the current situation?"

"We can't hold the east," Sophia said with resignation. "Everything east of the Appalachians will have to go. The land is too expensive for us to purchase, the Bilderbergs are in firm control, and we don't have time to undo the damage of seventy years of socialist propaganda."

"So our eastern terminus is Pittsburgh?" Webb inquired.

"And Buffalo," Sophia replied. "The rest remains as is."

"I thought we were making good progress," Heather said.

"We are, but not fast enough. Japan's economy is going into the doldrums, but the Europeans are coming on strong. And China's in the wings, although there we have a lot of influence. The stock market is doing well, but it's on a bubble due to financial manipulations. All this derivative stuff is blue sky gambling, but for now, they're minting money. But it can't last forever, and when the crash comes, the market may lose half its value. At this point, we simply don't have enough money to do what's necessary."

"How about in politics?" Webb asked.

"We need twenty senators and a hundred congressmen willing to follow our lead. That's a top priority project. Also, we must start propagandizing National Guard units in our core states so they can help suppress riots."

"What about the military itself?"

"Too late. We want weapons stored with the Reserve and Guard where we can get at them. Troops are unreliable and subject to last-minute appeals. Except for a hard corps of officers for planning, of course."

"It's a gloomy and chancy picture, Sophia," Bobbi remarked.

"Well, we're up against a democracy," Webb said. "The constructive power of a democratic assembly is slight—particularly to retain a defense establishment and ensure survival. Lack of good faith between legislators renders democratic governments tolerant, indecisive, and inept, so we should have some time before it reacts."

"Still, it's not good," Sophia agreed. "This will be our last shot, and we must give it all we have. We're the last hope for the Amulot experiment in democracy."

*****

It was time for Sophia to take a working vacation. She felt free with her Garden of Eden having done its duty. She could now choose male partners for herself, and also needed to travel to California and meet the fringies who would spearhead her grass roots anti-Japanese campaign. She could do both together. Since Wallace had been instrumental in finding appropriate activists, he could play bodyguard.

"I'll guard your body with my life," Jack said, "but only from everybody else."

On that basis, she booked her flights.

Wallace was so much like her dad. Sensitive, caring, strong yet shy at times in his treatment of her. She suspended her knowledge of what Cam liked and what worked for Millie, and became herself with Wallace for the first time. She was a woman, a woman in love and enjoying herself to the utmost with her man. It was wonderful. The secret was enthusiasm and complete focus on her partner, but now it was natural and right. Everyone else around her was invisible.

*****

Luigi's of Sausalito was a typical Italian bistro, complete with fish nets on the wall, hanging guitars, and red-and-white checkered tablecloths. Wallace scooted Sophia into a back booth and waited for their appointment. They had barely ordered iced tea before an eclectic group of activists threaded their way through the tables. Four men and two women, ranging in age from twenty to fifty, and the only common denominator was their dress—jeans and shirts. The tallest and oldest man with a salt-and-pepper beard opened the conversation in a brusque but not unfriendly tone.

"You're Wallace and Jennifer Stewart?" he said. "I'm Jim Horn."

Wallace didn't bother to correct him. They moved to a large table in the back where everyone could sit together. Horn seemed to be thoughtful, but two of the other men and the youngest girl acted like loose cannons. All had police records, and Wallace knew the FBI considered Horn a dangerous fanatic.

Sophia took charge of the meeting. "I'm not going to bullshit anyone," she began. "I'm interested in only one issue and need an alliance to make an impact on that issue. I have lots of financial support but no organization."

"What's lots?" the long-haired brunette in her mid-thirties asked.

"A couple of million per year, maybe more."

Two of the men whistled.

"What's the issue?" Horn asked, lowering his eyebrows.

"I have information that Japanese fishing fleets are so extensive and efficient they are lowering ocean populations of many food fishes and other marine life," Sophia said. "Everybody's focusing on endangered species of animals on land, but the long-term danger is really our oceans. The North Sea, for example, is already almost fished out."

"Screw Nips," a short, red-haired fellow growled. "They're destroying our forests, taking our best and oldest trees. We got to stop exporting wood to them."

"That, too," Sophia said. "They're the biggest environmental rapists in the world."

"So what's your push?" Horn said.

Wallace had said Horn was the godfather of a loose confederation of activists, riding emotional waves of various burning issues like a surfer. Sophia doubted he did anything unless money was involved.

"For starters, I'll donate a hundred thousand dollars to organize a new group called Bluepeace, focusing on conserving ocean fish and plant life for future generations. You organize and run it, but I'll determine its political guidelines. For that, I'm willing to donate big bucks."

"Lady, where in hell you getting all this bread?"

"Manna from heaven. Want the hundred thou or not?"

"I don't like it," the youngest girl rasped. "Nobody hands us green like that without strings."

"Amazing," Sophia snapped. "Who says you can't learn anything in college." She turned on the preppy chick who was trying to be tough. "You got that right, sweetie. I pay and you play. And puppets make millions. I want Japan stopped, and I'm prepared to pay for my desires. If you want in, fine; if not, I'll get someone else."

"We have to talk this over," Horn said. "Where can we reach you?"

"At the Fairmount. You have until noon tomorrow." Sophia stood up, brushing Wallace's arm. She dropped Franklin's picture on the table. "Enjoy a nice lunch," she said.

Wallace quickly escorted Sophia outside without a word. This was one time when further discussion could only lessen the image of power Sophia had projected.

"They'll do it," Sophia said. "Causes are Horn's business. You did well."

"Thanks, but Horn's a shark. He'll try to develop you as his private money tree controlled by him. Boy, is he in for a surprise."

*****

Jim Horn knew a good thing when he saw it, and Jennifer was a bitch with too much money. Wallace was a gigolo bodyguard who could be replaced. Poor little rich girls shouldn't get involved over their heads. Sex and excitement with powerful, well-endowed males was the key to separating them from their money. The Italian Stallion in his group was a tall, dark, mid-thirties guy with wavy black hair named Sonny Como. Sonny was an expert at snaking plumbing and had reduced several Bay Area socialites to slobbering idiots. Horn put Sonny on the job, and he boasted Jennifer would soon scream 'n cream double contributions.

Three weeks later, Sonny met his quarry when she arrived in San Francisco accompanied by a woman named Bobbi. He decided it was no contest. Jim could handle the older broad, and he'd sausage-stuff young chickie, Jennifer. With a milk-toast complexion, she was a low-mileage model and prime candidate for his dark good looks. But then she introduced the other sieve as being their future contact. He considered a threesome but decided doing them alone would be safer. Broads often became competitive in three-ways.

"How did we manage to be blessed with the presence of two such beautiful women?" Sonny remarked as the small talk became friendlier.

"Beautiful things happen to beautiful people," Bobbi responded.

Sophia wondered if the large Italian's charm was affecting Bobbi. She took control as they conversed in the hotel's bar. "This will require a maximum effort from everyone," she said. "We want to take our case before the United Nations." Sophia nodded to her left. "Bobbi will be responsible for all liaison between Bluepeace and myself, as well as handling contributions from my associates and me."

"What might we expect for a budget?" Horn asked.

"Whatever is justified by your level of activity," Sophia replied. "We are not niggardly, but expect to see action and results. How many people do you have at present?"

"We can mobilize over a hundred activists on short notice," Sonny said.

"Not enough. We'll need thousands. Particularly here on the west coast."

"We'll need money."

"Not a problem. I've already given you a hundred grand. What do you have to show me?"

Sonny began to sense Sophia's toughness. A golden gobbler, she might take more effort than planned. He suggested they accompany him on a tour of their facilities to see Bluepeace's boat outfitting in Oakland. Horn took Como's suggestion as his cue to depart, and left the women alone to work with Sonny.

Sophia smiled inwardly at Horn's action. He knew she wanted to work with him rather than his underlings and was refusing on purpose to demonstrate his independence. Okay, she passed control to Bobbi, who began manipulating Como like she had anti-war activists during her Vietnam days. Bobbi had volunteered to manage Bluepeace, claiming she was able to handle crazies better than anyone else in the family. Probably true, but Sophia detected a growing softness in Bobbi's demeanor toward Como as he became positively oily. She hoped he had not awakened some feeling of déjà vu.

Como was no amateur, and Bobbi's drift did not go unnoticed. During dinner, Sonny changed his point of attack. Bobbi looked stunning in her flowing pink dress, and acted substantially more receptive to his approach than Sophia. His antennae told him Bobbi's vibes were still equivocal, while Jennifer was not responding at all. Sonny sensed something special between the two women.

He subtly inquired if they were sharing a room. They weren't, so that indicated Bobbi needed her space. Sonny focused on Bobbi as she weakened under the booze. He stroked her leg under the table, running his hand up the inside of her thigh. Sonny felt her tense, not quite emitting an audible gasp before he removed his hand. She made no complaint.

He concluded dinner to make his play. Bobbi claimed she was feeling unsteady from the drinks and a long day, and suggested it was time to end the evening.

Quickly, Sonny escorted them upstairs to their adjoining rooms. As soon as Sophia disappeared into hers, he returned to Bobbi's and knocked.

"The evening's still young," he said rapidly as Bobbi opened the door. "Let's keep it going. Since we'll be working together, we should take this opportunity and get to know each other better." He edged his way into her room.

Bobbi started to say there would be plenty of time later, when Sonny crushed her full-length into his arms and kissed her passionately. Her breath was taken away, and her heart began to pound. He scooped up her legs and carried her backward onto the bed before she could object. When he stood up to remove his jacket, she pushed herself off the bed.

"You have the wrong idea," she said. "I didn't wish to make a scene in the restaurant when you touched my leg, but this can't continue." Bobbi felt flushed and unsteady.

"Look, I know you want it. I could feel your body responding." He stepped toward her and touched her hair, but she retreated.

Bobbi shouldn't have drunk so much. Alcohol made her passionate and his onslaught was focusing her attention on her sexual feelings. She was losing control of the situation. She was suddenly against the wall with him grabbing her, kissing her again, and placing her hand on his crotch. She made a fist, but not before she had felt the enormous size of his member. The booze clouded her mind and flushed her cheeks while he roamed over her body, rubbing and squeezing. Was it worth fighting? In a moment, he would start ripping her clothes off.

She stopped struggling against what seemed to be inevitable. Her knees began to weaken as he slowly ground himself against her, and she thought of what she would tell Sophia.

His hand went inside her pantyhose, and he backed off slightly to raise her dress. In his momentary release of control, she dropped and bolted to the side. She was breathing hard, but smoothed down her dress and drew herself together for a last effort. "Please leave." She pointed to the door. "Now."

The adjoining door opened.

"Stop!" Sophia yelled. "I thought we had agreed to enter into a business relationship, but nothing more," Sophia barked fiercely to Sonny. "More is less, and our relationship can be terminated if you insist."

"Hey, I'm a man," Sonny objected, holding up his hands in innocence. "And you two are beautiful, sexy women sleeping alone.

It hurts me to see you going without in San Francisco." He reached out for Bobbi, but she drew closer to Sophia. "I thought it might be a good way to seal our bargain, and for us to get acquainted."

"You thought wrong," Sophia stated sharply. "Good night, Mister Como." She held the door open for him. He started out, then turned to face Bobbi.

"No hard feelings?" he said. "Maybe later?"

Bobbi forced a smile. She couldn't think of anything to say. Her head was spinning from several too many drinks and the close call.

Sophia resolutely closed the door, and Bobbi staggered to the table. She removed her dress and pantyhose while she apologized and related what happened. Without her pantyhose, she would have been a goner. At least her dress hadn't gotten ripped.

She changed into a robe and sat down on the edge of the bed. In spite of everything, it had felt good to be desired.

"Good thing I heard you," Sophia said.

"Yeah, I almost gave in just to get it over," Bobbi said honestly. She hugged Sophia tightly.

The cocktails were hitting her hard. Her eyes were glazing over, and Bobbi was becoming melancholy. Sophia spoke softly. "Well, I can understand his interest. Dad said you turned him on faster than any woman alive. He took one look at you and was consumed in sex heat."

Bobbi's breath was coming in short puffs. "Me, too. I loved him even during his rough times, but he pushed me away. I don't know what I did wrong."

"You didn't do anything wrong."

Bobbi gazed at Sophia. "You know I love you," she whispered.

The silence was heavy. Bobbi turned her head and kissed Sophia with more feeling than she'd intended. She felt the trembling, and Sophie's heart reaching out to hers. She felt herself slipping into love and unconsciousness. Her robe fell away and she stretched out free and relaxed, her body immersed in a warm bath, blissful, and providing absolute security. Cam was back, and the world became filled with warmth and love. Life was wonderful beyond all expectations. She slept.

Chapter 36

Suzanne Wright had found BJ Carter even more exciting than her father. He not only talked rapidly in clipped and abrasive New Yorkerese, but seemed perpetually in motion. Experiencing Washington with him had worn her to a frazzle, and that night, after dinner at Sophia's, she had accompanied BJ to his hotel. He possessed incredible energy. A little quick on the trigger, but so many shots…

After returning home, BJ had invited her to New York, but King put his foot down. She couldn't be a kept woman, and without a legitimate career, she would lose BJ's respect and her chance for marriage. Staying in Denver was required for family honor.

Suzanne discovered her father's instinct was correct. Playing hard-to-get seemed to whet BJ's appetite and make her more desirable. She heard from him regularly, both by telephone and mail, and weekly by the local flower delivery service. Three times he stopped over in Denver on trips, and she limited her availability. The scheme worked like a charm. He invited her to go skiing at Aspen and proposed the first night. It was exciting and romantic, pure Hollywood, and culminated in a June wedding.

Married life in New York was a different reality.

"Honey, you need to buy up properties faster. Milleron bought a railroad," Suzanne said. She was reading the *Wall Street Journal* over breakfast, and it contained an article reporting the purchase of a midwest railroad by Milleron.

"Good for them," he grunted through the bran he had to eat for his diet. "They're terrible investments. What sort of bonds did they issue?"

"It doesn't say they issued bonds." Suzanne frowned.

BJ snatched the paper from her hands and scanned the article. "You're right. I wonder where in hell they get their money."

"Honey, don't look at me. I don't know."

BJ put down the paper. "It pisses me off not knowing what's going on."

"Better to be pissed off than pissed on," she said gaily. "Ask Claire Villars. You know her; you met her at our wedding."

"Oh, yeah. The lady your mother kept shooting daggers at."

"That's her. She's Daddy's girlfriend." Suzanne had a sudden inspiration. "Maybe they get their money from the Japanese."

BJ decided Suzanne had something. It seemed like only Japanese and drug lords had money, but the Nippies were backing off now that their stocks had tanked. Still, one went where the money was.

BJ resolved to contact the Japs. His wife was not going to throw her dad's activities in his face. He told his secretary to contact several Japanese banks and investment groups while he destroyed his diet with a chocolate honey-dip donut. All he heard from his wife was how great her daddy was! He had a girlfriend who was pretty flashy, but flashy broads were simply a matter of money. Hell, he could have her anytime. He was still fuming when the first Japanese consortium returned his call.

His mood was not improved by Paul Yoshiro, the firm's president. Yoshiro said they were only interested in ventures they controlled. According to him, all Japanese investment banks and venture capitalist firms were like his, and only interested in investments leading to Japanese ownership. Not only that, Japanese companies were essentially a private club who talked freely among themselves, and frequently spread risks and opportunities through "laying-off," much like bookies.

Okay, he would come up with a participation package where he could attract money and conditionally satisfy the Japanese demand for control. He would put together a project with multiple but separable properties. The starting capital would come from the Japanese, and they'd hold a lien on separable properties without restricting his use of their funds. They would receive full control and ownership of their parcels only upon insolvency of his enterprise, or upon full discharge of his obligations in secondary financing arrangements.

He called Yoshiro again and arranged for an appointment. To his surprise, Yoshiro readily agreed and arrived precisely on time that same afternoon with two associates. BJ presented his idea for joint ventures.

They listened politely and seemed interested but wanted specifics that BJ had not yet developed. Nonetheless, he could see an agreement was possible. The appealing carrot was their opportunity to pay off his secondary financing and hold the paper themselves. But that could only occur with BJ's agreement, so the circumstances would have to be compelling. Nevertheless, there was a substantial area for maneuvering to both sides' advantage. He decided to go for it.

It took BJ three weeks to structure an appropriate deal. It included a hotel in New York City and a hotel and casino in Atlantic City. Yoshiro would hold the New York hotel's mortgage and participate in the Atlantic City casino's profits. Essentially, they were part owners without being subject to the gaming commission's scrutiny.

Yoshiro's group inked the deal, and BJ secured financing from German banks repatriating dollars. For two hotels and a casino, BJ invested less than he had previously for a medium-sized apartment building.

He was ecstatic. BJ's problem was no longer money, but finding appropriate deals where the Japanese would be interested. He began looking at movie, sports, and entertainment industries which offered high visibility. That had worked well for other businessmen—go for fame, and fortune will follow. He decided to invest in a standing self-promotion campaign to heighten his visibility and make himself a star.

*****

Times had been hard for Joe O'Donnell since being released from Canon City. For a while, he lived with his son Jake, but Colorado was a hostile environment. The people he knew were from his days as a powerful attorney, and those days were gone forever. Now he was a penniless, disbarred, ex-con lawyer. People he stepped on climbing up, stabbed him in the back as he went down.

Doing time wasn't really so bad for most cons. The ones from the street without expectations swapped one low-level society for another. Prison was like a trade school for them—sharpening skills and providing a lifelong job placement service.

For intelligent, successful members of society like himself, however, prison was usually a disaster. Luckily, O'Donnell had made out. On his third day as a new white inmate, he was expected to play queen for a member of the controlling black clique. He offered his legal expertise in trade instead and found himself to be a valuable property with protectors. Writs by the hundreds were produced, and a thriving business had evolved. One of the toughest guys in prison ran his operation, providing a steady stream of customers and handling the payments.

In retrospect, he had screwed up. He came out with no friends or connections among other convicts or their associates on the outside. Charging for his services had not endeared him to other inmates, and his time inside was a total loss.

So he had come to Washington to settle accounts. O'Donnell was not surprised at the size of Sophia's house in Potomac—after all, it had been purchased with his money. The little bitch had chutzpah, he had to give her that. Coming into his country club and facing him down wasn't something most girls would do. He parked on the road outside and studied the layout.

If you want something done right, do it yourself. Thinking back to the accident, it was incredible how rapidly everything had unraveled. The deputy and judge were bad enough, but the chits did him in. Ochoa swore he had retrieved and burnt them. Beaten to within an inch of his life, he still maintained he had done his job. All those shooters and margaritas. If his slut secretary had showed, the whole thing never would have happened. It was all her fault.

In fact, everything in his life had been the fault of some broad. His wife left him for another guy, and here he was—checking up on another slut who had screwed up the remainder of his life. Jake said the Stewart girl wasn't married, but the mansion was well populated. Probably group gropes. O'Donnell jotted down the license numbers of the Berlinetta and Oldsmobile parked in front.

The District was fantastic. O'Donnell could see why it was hustle heaven and the murder capital of the world, second only to Atlanta. He had wanted a pistol, and for ninety bucks acquired a Saturday Night Special. Even as an ex-con. He had filled out the papers from his imagination and wasn't asked for identification.

Next came a little research in Annapolis. The Berlinetta was registered to a Heather Ewing at Stewart's address, and the Olds belonged to a corporation, the Milleron Company of Port Tobacco, south of D.C. So Stewart drove a company car.

The next afternoon, O'Donnell re-positioned himself outside the house. The Berlinetta was already there, and the Oldsmobile arrived shortly after five. A brunette got out and was greeted by several young children. Even at his distance, O'Donnell could hear them calling her mama. Then a white Corvette swung into the driveway. That was Stewart's speed. A blonde climbed out and was greeted by the kids as Auntie Something. But there was no question in his mind—she was the right size and everything fit.

The sun was beginning to set when the blonde emerged. She cranked up her 'Vette, and drove out. O'Donnell followed.

He was rewarded almost immediately. She pulled into a convenience store six blocks away. He watched her park to the left of the store and go inside. The setup was perfect. She had nosed the 'Vette against the building and walked around the rear of her car to go inside. O'Donnell backed his alongside hers and waited. When she returned, she would have to walk between their cars, and he had a clear outlet to the street as an escape route.

He did not have long to wait.

*****

Sophia had run out of milk, and Cathy had volunteered to make a run for more. She glanced at the scandal sheets while waiting her turn at the counter. She could be pictured on the cover of those newspapers as having the most exciting job in the world if she ever went public. She wasn't rich or famous, but life was one long exciting runway. Particularly now that she had met some terrific men. Everybody wanted to become bosom buddies with her as an entrée to Ed, and they lavished attention on her and treated her like a celebrity. On trips, she was wined and dined by her pick of men, while at home, she enjoyed her friends and privacy. Who could want anything more?

She held the two sacks to her chest as she opened the door with her hip. She had pulled too close to the building, and would have to walk around her 'Vette. That was okay, she loved looking at its sleek lines.

"Sophie Stewart?" called the man sitting in the car next to hers.

She had come abreast of his window and turned to face him. "Yes?" She jostled the sacks to reach her purse. She started to explain that Sophia was her friend, but the words came too late.

Four rounds burst through the milk cartons into her chest, throwing her backward onto the 'Vette's rear window. As she slid forward into a spreading splash of milk and blood, the other car peeled out and sped away.

*****

Sophia heard the sirens and began to worry. Fifteen minutes had passed and Cathy hadn't returned from what should have been a five-minute trip.

Heather volunteered to go see what had happened.

"We'll both go," Sophia said. "I have a bad feeling about this." She told Carolina to watch the boys for a few minutes then hurried out the door.

A block from the convenience store and its gathering army of flashing police cars, Sophia knew Cathy was hurt. She stopped the Olds behind a police cruiser and ran into the parking lot, Heather not a step behind. Both were caught by police attempting to hold back the neighborhood crowd. They could see Cathy face down, spraddle-legged in a huge red and white pond.

"That's our friend!" cried Sophia. "She had gone to buy milk!"

Heather screamed Cathy's name.

They were allowed through but weren't allowed to touch her.

"Did you know her?" one of the detectives asked.

Sophia felt her legs becoming rubbery. She noticed Heather holding her arm tightly and looking down at Cathy in silence. The effect was calming although she still felt weak. "Yes. Her name is Cathy Clark. We had run out of milk, and she came for more. How did this happen?" Cathy had been wearing a light summer dress with a polka dot print. Her dress had flown up exposing most of her legs and part of her beige panties. They were soiled, and Sophia was reminded there was no beauty or dignity in death. Before anyone could stop her, she pulled Cathy's dress down to restore her modesty. She had stepped in Cathy's blood, and the plainclothesman yanked her away from the body immediately and pushed her into the grasp of a patrolman.

"Who are you?" the plainclothesman demanded.

"Sophia Stewart," she answered just as fiercely. The

345

nonchalance of the police with respect to Cathy's dignity had restored her fighting spirit. Wallace should be here to handle these bozos. "What happened? Who did this?"

"What can you tell us about the victim, Miss Stewart? Anything at all?" The plainclothesman nodded to the two uniformed patrolmen holding the women to move them toward a police car and away from curious onlookers.

"Let go of me!" Sophia yelled. She turned on the policeman holding her arm and pointed to the Olds. "Go get my handbag from my car." The plainclothesman nodded and the policeman trotted off.

"My name is Detective Steiner," the plainclothesman said. "And what we know is what you see. Apparently, there were no witnesses. Was your friend into drugs?"

"That's ridiculous." Sophia looked for the patrolman to return with her purse. "There's more to this than meets the eye." She opened her purse and handed Steiner her Agency identification. "She worked for me. We live a few blocks away at the address on my license." Sophia swallowed hard and steeled herself for what she had to do. She assumed her most authoritarian voice. "I'll handle my end; you clean up here. When you're done, come to my house. We'll handle next of kin and everything. For now, we want to withhold her name from media exposure. Understand?"

Steiner stood still and didn't react to her commands. Apparently he didn't think she was someone important.

Sophia grabbed Steiner's notebook and wrote down Webb's name and number. "Here's a name someone in your department will recognize. Call him to verify my status and authority."

Steiner took the paper and hesitated. "Go! Do it now!" Sophia commanded, pointing to his car. Steiner walked slowly to his car followed by Sophia. Heather was still staring at Cathy's body.

Steiner called the Montgomery county police headquarters and talked to the government liaison representative. In a few moments Webb Reid's voice was on the radio. He confirmed Sophia's status and also asked that no information be released without his clearance. He was coming to Sophia's residence immediately and could be reached there.

"Okay," Steiner said, turning back to Sophia. "You two can go for now, and I'll be down to talk as soon as we're wrapped up here."

"Bring her car and effects, too. We'll have to go through them for our own investigation."

Heather walked over, cool as a cucumber. "Even a beautiful person like Cathy looks grotesque in death," she remarked. She grabbed Sophia by the arm and started walking toward their car. Suddenly, she was all business. "I've got dibs on who did it."

Sophia looked at her in surprise.

Heather met her gaze. "The family takes care of its own. This one's on me."

*****

Webb was better than his word and arrived at Sophia's house almost simultaneously with Heather and Sophia.

"It was murder," Heather said. "A professional style hit."

"Okay, let's assume that," Webb said. "Why would someone want to kill Cathy?"

"No reason we know about." Sophia was unusually hyper, walking around to keep calm. "But what don't we know?"

"Her ex-husband? He didn't like her becoming successful."

Webb shook his head at Heather's suggestion. "Might piss him off, but not bring him to murder. She was always a potential meal ticket if he played his cards right."

"So that's out," declared Sophia. "Has she done anything in her courier activities that might have earned her a bullet?"

"No way. She didn't threaten anyone and never carried money. Everyone who dealt with her liked her."

"Maybe it was an object lesson. Someone wanted to show us how easy we can be killed. Like the Japanese. They can't like anything Milleron does."

Both Webb and Heather agreed Sophia's idea had merit. "In that case, they followed her and took advantage of the first opportunity without witnesses," Webb stated. "Let's look at tonight's tape from the front camera."

Sophia practically ran out of the room. The pursuit of Cathy's killer was occupying her thoughts and not allowing her to mourn. Revenge first—there would be time for mourning later. She retrieved the tape from the security control room and took it into the library. It recorded a picture every fifteen seconds, showing the time at the bottom. Sophia located four-thirty and began the tape. Within three minutes Webb yelled, "Stop!"

Sophia pushed the pause button.

"Look there." He pointed to the screen. "Across the street. There's a car behind that backhoe. Somebody's on a stakeout." They looked intently, but could not make out anyone in the car. More importantly, the license plate was hidden.

Sophia reversed the tape to catch the car arriving, but it was in an unrecorded interval. They continued to watch.

Finally Cathy came out to go for the milk. The car disappeared, but they still couldn't read the plate. With the black and white system, they couldn't tell the car's color or make either. It looked like a standard, small Japanese box.

"Looks like they staked out the house. They'd do it for more than one evening to establish a routine. Let's look at last night and as far back as we can." Webb got up and collected the other tapes. They were rotated weekly. He made a mental note to get more tapes and rotate monthly.

There it was. At 6:04 the previous evening, a small Japanese car had driven into the driveway. Its purpose probably had been to obtain license numbers from cars in the driveway, but an unintended by-product was the camera's recording of the interloper's plate. Sophia practically leaped out of her chair. She recognized the jagged line separating the darker lower portion from the upper. "Mountains! A Colorado plate!" she yelled.

"Who doesn't like us in Colorado?" Heather asked perplexed.

Webb and Sophia spoke almost simultaneously.

"Villars," Webb said.

"O'Donnell!" Sophia shouted.

The doorbell rang. "Steiner," Heather offered as her contribution. She switched off the tape and went to let him in.

Steiner was in even worse humor than before. Webb knew the signs. Steiner feared this case would be taken out of his hands and probably didn't like international intrigue taking place in his county. Nonetheless, he had brought the Corvette, along with Cathy's handbag.

Webb went through the console and two storage areas behind the seats. There was nothing but a few country-western cassettes and the 'Vette's maintenance documents.

Cathy's handbag was equally clean, but Sophia took several

items out while Steiner was outside with Webb. The keys to her house and Milleron offices, her passport, telephone notebook, and pictures of Cam and herself. There was no reason for police to bother with any of that.

"The Agency wants you to keep a lid on this for at least forty-eight hours," Webb informed the detective. "As you can see, it was obviously a professional hit, and we need a certain amount of time to react before we let our opposition know they were successful. And we don't want them to know Miss Clark is dead. The press release should indicate only that she is critical and under guard."

"I'm not sure I can do that. There were people around."

"They're not going to call the *Post* for a correction. Forty-eight hours, that's all we're asking in the interest of national security."

"National security. You guys use that term at the drop of a hat. More likely, she was screwing someone important, and you want to give him time to cover his tracks."

Webb, Heather, and Sophia all glared at Steiner. "I can assure you, sir, nothing like that is the case, and I would ask you to show some respect for the departed," said Sophia.

"Okay," Steiner grunted. "Forty-eight hours if my chief agrees."

He asked to use the telephone to check with headquarters. The forty-eight hours were approved, and he left knowing just what he did when he arrived.

Sophia quickly telephoned Wallace for a license plate check. Denver was two hours behind, and she caught him still in his office. Within ten minutes, Wallace called back to say the plates were registered to O'Donnell. The question of *who* was resolved and *why* was not relevant. Only the question of *what* was to be done remained.

"You guys find him, I'll ice him," Heather stated.

"Whoa." Webb held up his hand. "Who says this is something for us personally?"

Heather swung at his hand. "You wimp. The system doesn't work for victims. Sophia tried the legal system and put O'Donnell away, and look what's happened. Cathy's dead. He's now killed two people, and the only way to make sure a killer doesn't kill again is to kill him."

Sophia seconded Heather. "This scumbag kills my father—your best friend—and then returns to kill another family member. How many does he have to plant to get your attention?"

Webb looked at the floor for a moment, then met Sophia's gaze directly. "That wasn't fair. I've always pulled my weight."

It was Sophia's turn to drop her eyes. "Sorry, you're right, I apologize. I'm just really pissed." She took his hand and squeezed it.

Heather refused to be put off. "But he's not done, not until he's gotten Sophie. She's his target."

Webb nodded. "I'm sure that's true." He looked grimly back and forth between them. "Both of you are certain you want to do this?"

"Absolutely." Sophia replied.

Heather smiled at Webb. "This one will be easier than before. And you know what happened to Harlan."

Webb blinked.

"It was Heather, helped by Bobbi," Sophia said.

"Us little girls do good work, big boy," gloated Heather.

"You guys are dangerous," Webb said. "I'm surprised you two are so calm over this."

"We aren't calm; we're numb. And mad. Like in *Beau Geste*, Cathy needs a dog at her feet."

"This is war," Sophia said, "and O'Donnell attacked us first. John Stuart Mill said it best. 'War is an ugly thing, but not the ugliest thing. The decayed and degraded state of moral and patriotic feeling which thinks nothing is worth a war is worse. A man who has nothing which he cares about more than his personal safety is a miserable creature who has no chance of being free, unless made and kept so by men better than himself.'"

Sophia waited for her quotation to take effect. "And my patriotism begins with our family and ends with the United States."

Webb caved in with a sigh. "Okay, but our first step is finding him. Where do we look for openers? The District, Maryland, or Virginia?"

"The District," answered Sophia.

Heather went to the telephone. "Hell, let's try Ma Bell. He may have a phone."

Within five minutes, Heather had two possible J. O'Donnells in their three listing areas. Webb promised to obtain new phone applications in the morning, and Heather called Bobbi. The execution squad had been put in motion.

Chapter 37

The Agency had indicated its lack of further interest in his Clark case, and Steiner's progress for the last two weeks was almost nil. He had determined that Clark actually worked for Milleron, a privately held Delaware corporation with close ties to the CIA. He guessed it was one of those CIA-owned commercial fronts, but Clark appeared to be a legitimate employee. She was a single lady, who worked in the Milleron office at Port Tobacco, and apparently traveled a great deal.

Steiner had questioned a friend of his in the DC police department who said the Agency would not have released their hold if there was the slightest indication of intelligence operatives being involved. That pretty well ruled out the murder as being employment-related. Clark apparently didn't have a current boyfriend and had worked as a trainer with a Beltway Bandit until seven years ago when she joined Milleron. The people there remembered her as an extremely likeable lady and expressed their horror at her being a victim of a violent crime.

The shots were fired from very short range, and she had been shot four times—clearly her killer had wanted to make sure of the job. But it didn't have the markings of a mob hit. Maybe the wronged wife of some paramour, but Steiner remembered the total rejection of any such suggestion by Clark's friends, both at Stewart's and her former workplace. He was stumped.

Steiner decided to look at similar murders over the past several years, particularly those involving multiple gunshots at close range. There had been one in the District shortly after the Clark killing which didn't appear to be drug-related so that was a good place to start. The O'Donnell murder had taken place by the Chesapeake and Ohio canal, and he had been shot multiple times. Steiner drove into DC to review the file.

O'Donnell had been an ex-attorney from Colorado with a record for vehicular manslaughter. There wasn't much on him, but detectives had found a revolver in his apartment which was a no-no for an ex-con. The revolver was a snub-nosed thirty-eight, and Clark had been killed by a thirty-eight. Steiner wondered if ballistics tests had been run on the weapon. He asked the lieutenant in charge of homicide. No, there was no reason for a ballistics test, what did he wish to check it against? Not that he expected a match, it was just that all weapons seized from criminals should be test-fired for possible connections.

Ten days later, he received test photos on O'Donnell's gun which he sent down to ballistics for comparison to the Clark murder. They were a match. The two murders were related!

Steiner immediately telephoned his counterpart in the District. Jackson had impressed him as a hard-boiled, professional cop, much harassed by the volume of killings for his over-worked staff. Steiner was close to considering the Clark case solved, particularly if he could show some connection between O'Donnell and Clark. Jackson invited him to review O'Donnell's file at his convenience. By two, he was in Jackson's office.

"Your victim O'Donnell possessed the murder weapon for my victim, Clark. So what's the connection?" he asked Jackson.

"Beats me." Jackson didn't like games. Suburban cops not only made bigger salaries, but their crimes were fewer and cleaner. He had lived in Northwest for twenty years, and was one of few white detectives remaining. With reverse discrimination taking place, he often felt like a forgotten rear-guard.

Steiner opened O'Donnell's file and began a quick study. "Do you have any leads?"

"None at present. It looked like a professional hit, but nobody here knew him. All our street informants drew blanks, and he had only been in town for a month."

"Damn." Steiner blurted. "There it is."

"What?"

"O'Donnell killed a guy named Cameron Stewart. Five will get you ten he was related to Sophie Stewart. Husband, brother, father, or something."

"So who's that?"

"Cathy Clark's best friend. Clark drove from Stewart's house to the crime scene. If O'Donnell killed Clark, maybe Stewart killed O'Donnell."

It was his first lead in the case. Jackson made a note to request all pertinent data from Colorado on O'Donnell.

"What have you reconstructed on O'Donnell's killing?" Steiner asked.

"It's all speculation. Earlier in the evening, he was seen with a couple of hookers in a bar, but we're not sure he left with them. Nobody's come forth with any information on the actual shooting. In fact, no one's even said they heard shots, so the gun might have had a silencer. But late at night that area along the canal might as well be on Blue Ridge. Nobody goes there, not even cops. So I would say the killer or killers knew the area."

"He was shot five times?"

"Yeah, four in the chest and once in the head."

"Anything unusual?"

"Maybe. At first we thought he might have been interrupted while taking a leak. His fly was open, and his tallywhacker out. But then we determined he was shot while on his knees."

"Well, maybe he was taking a leak, and then told to get on his knees."

"Maybe, but apparently nothing was stolen. So we think he was driven there to be killed."

"In his own car?"

"It was there, or close, more or less."

Steiner studied the report. "7.65, probably a Walther. That sounds professional. And this says his car was wiped pretty clean. They got O'Donnell's fingerprints and a couple other partials."

"They were old—O'Donnell's son and daughter-in-law. There weren't any prints that didn't belong."

"How about the hookers?"

"Typical, hard-looking blondes, probably past their prime in their late thirties or early forties. We have thousands of those. They were what a guy like O'Donnell would attract."

"No footprints?"

"Not on the grass. There really aren't any clues. We'd have to get lucky and find the gun. And it's probably at the bottom of the Potomac."

"The steering wheel wasn't wiped," Steiner remarked. "It was smudged but had O'Donnell's prints. That means he drove. Don't you find that unusual?"

"Yeah. So he drove with a gun in his ribs."

"How long will it take to get his file from Colorado?"

"Let's call 'em."

Jackson scanned the papers that came in fifteen minutes later. "I thought he was from Denver, but this says he was sentenced in Castle Rock." He dialed the Douglas county sheriff's office.

O'Donnell's case was still well-known, and the deputy who answered filled Jackson in on the details. The man O'Donnell killed had a daughter who pursued him with a vengeance, and she later won a huge suit which left O'Donnell penniless. The deputy wasn't sure of the girl's name, and she had not been at the trial. Steiner told Jackson to try Sophie Stewart, and the deputy thought that sounded about right. Jackson thanked the deputy and turned back to Steiner.

"Sophie was his daughter, so they're connected. She was never at the trial, so it's possible O'Donnell never saw her. Clark's death might have been a case of mistaken identity."

Steiner shook Jackson's hand. "Thanks. I'm closing my case, but looks like you're just starting with yours."

*****

Steiner was right. Jackson's problem was lack of evidence now that Sophie Stewart's connection was confirmed. Clearly his leading suspect, he drove to Potomac to question her. She greeted him cordially and invited him into her house as if she had nothing to hide.

"I read about his murder in the *Post*," Sophia offered, "and assumed you would want to chat sooner or later."

"Yes, well, can you tell me anything about him?" Jackson asked. She was a suspect, and he quickly quoted the Miranda statement before she answered.

Sophia smiled and scoffed at his reading of her rights. "A lot, but nothing that might help, I'm afraid," she answered. "I only met him once, at his country club. It wasn't a particularly friendly meeting. As you can imagine since he killed my father, he wasn't my favorite person."

354

"So much your least favorite that you would kill him?"

"Lieutenant, that sounds like a line from a B movie. I didn't kill him. The night he was killed, I was here until almost eleven with Ed Armstrong going over problems Cathy left behind, and afterward was up until almost two in the morning with Cedric. My maid can confirm that. So please. I'll help you out with your questions, but cross my name off your list of suspects."

"I see you've already determined your whereabouts when he was shot."

"Of course. It's natural I should be a suspect. He killed my father, and I read the news. There could be only one Joe O'Donnell from Denver, an ex-attorney who served time for vehicular homicide. I'm not stupid and neither are you. It was good detective work to dig me up as a suspect. You are to be commended for your diligence."

"Thank you," he said. "Did he contact you here?"

"No. And I asked my maid if he called, but he hadn't. I wouldn't think he'd want to see me."

"Can you think of anyone who might want to see him dead?"

"Sure. I don't know any names, but he was famous in Colorado for knowing where the bodies were buried. Especially judges' bodies. If I were you, I'd look at judges who gave his clients favorable treatment, or those here who could be embarrassed by him."

"An interesting hypothesis." Jackson saw this conversation with Stewart wasn't going to be fruitful. After checking her story with her maid, he took his leave. His instincts told him she was behind the killing, but obtaining evidence was going to be very difficult.

*****

Jerry Thornton was languishing as DC's district attorney. He rapidly discovered being the DA attracted negative publicity like snow attracted skiers. He limited his personal involvement to murder cases, but even those were often drug-related which drew him into a vortex of controversy. He was glad when Lieutenant Jackson indicated he wished to discuss his progress on a traditional murder case.

Jerry listened intently while Jackson went over the O'Donnell killing. Inferences for a conspiracy were not evidence, however clear. It was almost certain O'Donnell had killed Cathy Clark. The murder gun had been found in his possession, and it had been determined by handwriting analysis that he had purchased it only two weeks before.

Jackson theorized it was possible O'Donnell couldn't remember what Stewart looked like, and the Clark murder was a case of mistaken identity. Two days later, O'Donnell was dead, shot five times at close range, execution style.

There was one other tie-in to a murder. Heather Ewing lived with Miss Stewart, and she had been the victim of an attempted rape in the middle seventies. The perpetrator had been murdered shortly after being paroled. He, too, had been shot five times at close range, four in the chest and once in the head. At the time he was consorting with known drug dealers, so the case had been considered a rival gang or drug execution. The murder weapon, a thirty-two caliber pistol, had been left at the scene and was untraceable. The two killings were notable in their lack of clues, similarities, and that no police informant had turned up the slightest information.

The common denominator was the house in Potomac with Sophia Stewart and Heather Ewing. Jerry thought it possible they had a protector. Maybe this other individual, Webb Reid, who was with Stewart at the CIA. But everything was speculation.

"Lieutenant, you don't have one scintilla of evidence against Stewart or her friends."

"But sir, it's as if you run afoul of them, you die." Jackson knew he was on the right track, and wanted additional resources. Washington loved conspiracies, and with Stewart being highly placed, he could become either famous or unemployed. Or both.

"Lieutenant, I ran afoul of them, and I'm still alive. You may be right, but there's no evidence. What would you have me do?"

"Get an authorization to tap their telephone, search the house, and I'll run a full investigation on her background in Colorado."

"Tap the telephone of someone at her level in the Agency? You know she sits in National Security Council meetings? You want to be pounding a beat? I may be responsible for the District, but I'm still in the Justice Department and can be out on my butt in a heartbeat."

"How about searching her house?"

"What would you put in the warrant? Looking for the gun that killed O'Donnell? Did Stewart have an alibi for the time of death?"

"Yeah. All evening," Jackson answered ruefully.

"Then there's no probable cause, and you open me up to her retaliation. Look, the best I can do is tell you to talk to Claire Villars. She's been watching Stewart all her life. And she hates her."

"I don't hate her," Jackson hastened to say. "I just think she's the focal point of some criminal conspiracy."

Jerry waved the conservation to a close. "Try out your theories on Villars. She made her bones as an investigative reporter, and she might do things you can't."

*****

Stewart usually arrived home about five-thirty, but to ensure catching both women at home, Sergeant Jefferson drove out slightly after six. He was in luck. Sophia opened the door.

"Evening ma'am," he said. "I needs to see Heather Ewing."

Sophia left Jefferson at the door and returned with Heather. "Yes, how can I help you?"

"I wants to give youse dis letter ma father left fir youse. It's so late 'cause I din't know where youse was." He handed the envelope to Heather. "I thanks youse fir off'n ma father, and I'll be seeing youse again. I needs fifty thou." With that, Jefferson marched off to his old Chevy.

Sophia closed the door and looked at Heather who was reading the letter.

"What a crock of shit." Heather laughed. "What in hell's going on?"

"What do you mean?" Sophia couldn't see what she had read.

"Brady Jordan's mother was white, and that guy, although the right age, is no more Brady than I am. And Harlan never wrote; he always printed."

Sophia pushed Heather ahead into the living room, and quickly read the copy. "Try this on for size. They've figured out that people die who threaten us. People like Harlan and Joe O'Donnell. So they're trying to trap us."

"Who's 'they'?"

"Must be cops. Probably Jackson and his detective squad. They found O'Donnell's gun and identified it as the one that killed Cathy. But laying Harlan's death on our doorstep was a stroke of genius."

357

"Maybe not," Heather said. "It's probably my fault. Bobbi put four slugs into O'Donnell, but I had to shoot, too. I remembered with Harlan one round blew away part of his head. So both were killed more or less in the same way and with the same caliber gun. They probably put them together because of their similarities."

"Well, it can't be helped now. I'll get this stopped tomorrow, don't worry."

*****

Webb volunteered to defuse the police investigation, not the least to show Heather his commitment. He telephoned Jackson after reviewing the letter and arranged a meeting at Langley.

Jackson's interest was aroused, and he appeared promptly at three. His theory of an Agency hit squad eliminating Jordan and O'Donnell was looking better.

Webb went directly to his task. "I want to show you a videotape that's come to my attention. It has some bearing on the O'Donnell case which I understand is being investigated by you."

"Yes, it's my case, and any help is appreciated."

"Who are you working with in the DA's office, may I ask?"

"Jerry Thornton himself. He always involves himself in murder cases, although he usually assigns someone else for courtroom work."

Webb started the VCR on the edge of his desk. "You will note we have continuous electronic surveillance at Miss Stewart's house in Potomac. Yesterday, this individual approached Miss Stewart and her companion, Miss Ewing, with a note—the contents of which I believe are well known to you." He pointed as the black man approached. "The individual in question is also known to you. A detective on your squad. You might note his vehicle; it is one of your unmarked cars with a cover license plate issued to Brady Jordan with a police apartment address."

Webb switched off his VCR and turned to Jackson who was sitting in silence. "Obviously, a very misguided and crude attempt at entrapment. I assume its conception was by some mystery writer and not a professional in law enforcement."

Jackson was silent for a moment. "Ah, you're right. I was set up. My apologies."

"So whose idea was this?" Webb asked in a sharper tone.

"Claire Villars. We talked to her as someone who could provide information on Stewart."

"Bad choice. For whatever reason, Villars possesses substantial enmity toward Sophia."

"Yes, I can appreciate that now."

"You need to understand Miss Stewart is an extremely valuable property as far as we're concerned—and, I might add, to the United States. We look with great disfavor on any and all threats to her well-being. We guard her, very discretely, as we do other highly placed individuals."

"Yes. We had not observed a security system."

"You are fighting a war against criminals and drugs—we are likewise engaged but with a different enemy. In our war, there are real casualties on both sides. Sometimes individuals simply disappear, sometimes bodies are literally left on doorsteps. In either case, police such as yourself should stay uninvolved. I'm not saying police have no authority or responsibility in such situations; I'm merely indicating that, with both sides opposed, police activity is doomed to be unfruitful."

"But murder is murder, and this was in my jurisdiction," Jackson protested.

"The Agency attempts to work with local police as much as possible. Many times our cooperation can materially assist law enforcement personnel. You're a resourceful officer, and I'm sure you recognize the two-way nature of cooperation."

"I understand that, but no man is above the law."

Webb sighed, leaned back, and steepled with his hands. "Your man on the tape broke the law. Don't buck us on this. Ask yourself how fortunate you were to find Miss Clark's murder weapon in O'Donnell's apartment. Intelligence agencies penalize failure, and it's possible you haven't discovered all the bodies buried in this affair." He leaned forward and stared at the detective. "Let us hope your involvement won't add to the body count."

Jackson heard the not-so-veiled threat. Reid's inference that the murder weapon had been planted was a disconcerting twist. The KGB might have hired O'Donnell and executed him for missing Stewart. That was clearly a more likely scenario that the one he had been pursuing. And this was an opportunity to gain a chit from the Agency. There was no percentage in fighting a losing battle. "I see your point," he said. "I hope you will convey my apologies to the ladies for any discomfort they suffered."

*****

Hearing Villars had originated the entrapment scam was infuriating, but Sophia couldn't ruin her and incur King Wright's enmity. She needed King, and it was apparent he loved Claire, even if he hadn't made her an honest woman.

But there were other ways to skin a cat.

Bobbi's volunteered to play the heavy. Disguised as a redhead, she registered at the Statler Hilton and invited Villars to visit for a scoop concerning the CIA. No one doubted Villars would come.

And she didn't disappoint, arriving shortly after one in an outfit that precluded her from wearing a wire.

"You're Claire Villars," Bobbi said. "You can call me Moira Baird."

"Glad to meet you," Villars responded briskly. "Now, what was this information about the CIA?" She took out a small recorder and placed it near Bobbi on the sitting area's round table.

"Yes, I do mind," Bobbi said quickly. She popped the recorder open to the eject position. "What I say will not be recorded."

Bobbi handed the tape to Claire. "Were you aware the CIA has a special section responsible for removing all threats to the physical well-being of critical Agency personnel?"

"Uh, I had vaguely heard something about that."

"Well, it's true. The fastest way for a person to check out is to threaten a high-level Agency official. Here and everywhere. Even police who meddle in Agency operations put themselves at risk. You are acquainted with various Agency personnel and should avoid making them nervous."

She took a cassette from her handbag and placed it in the VCR connected to the hotel's television. It was the same tape Webb had played showing Detective Jefferson. Bobbi explained what Jackson had attempted and stressed that he had implicated Claire as the mastermind behind the entrapment idea.

"That's not true," Claire cried defensively. "It was his theory that whoever threatened the Stewarts, died. I merely suggested he could test his hypothesis."

"We would like to believe that," Bobbi said, removing the tape. "It would save us certain unpleasantries. All so needless, particularly since you work for Milleron's network. We realize you're unaware who's behind Milleron, but its stock is owned by very few people, at least one of whom is well known to you."

"Very few?" Claire repeated. "Like one or two?"

"Something like that. And those individuals can move you anywhere in the network. Or out." Bobbi paused. "Your interest in Sophia is commendable, but you, almost more than anyone else, should realize how much she values her privacy."

"She has more power than almost anyone in government," Claire said.

Bobbi sighed. "We are talking to you today in the spirit of conciliation, to avoid prejudicial actions which some have urged. There is no reason to take anything personally, but this is a one-time offer. You should consider this meeting as the beginning of the rest of your life."

Bobbi fished another cassette from her purse. "I must go next door for a moment, and this came into our possession." She handed Claire the tape. "It's yours, I believe. The only existing copy."

Claire examined the cassette quickly, but it was untitled. She placed it in the VCR as Bobbi walked out. It took a minute to reach the recorded portion.

It was the video of the happenings in the Georgetown bedroom.

Chapter 38

The two Bluepeace boats were riding easily at anchor and were being swarmed over by kids like bees on a hive. Jim Horn felt optimistic for the first time in his life. He turned to Sonny Como alongside him. "This is our chance. With these boats, we can go to center stage." He led Como into a bar near the dock. Almost alone in the tavern, they seated themselves at a wobbly table, and Horn called for two drafts.

"We need an incident to publicize our organization. I'm looking to expand to the east coast and suck up those environmental groups."

"Yeah, they've got foxy ladies," Como said.

"I've worked up a plan," Horn said quietly. "We take a boat and harass a Russian factory ship, getting in its way and shooting photographs of our activities. Then sink the boat, blame its loss on the Russians, and make an international incident, spreading our case on TV. We'll be more important than hostages in Lebanon and in headlines for weeks."

"But we'll lose a boat," Como objected. "Can't we just fake it?"

"No. We need real losses. Wreckage and casualties. Besides, the CIA is underwriting this, and we can't fake it."

"The CIA? How do you know that?"

Horn smiled from his superior position on high. "Our pussy Jennifer works for the CIA. I saw her on TV in a National Security Council meeting. I checked. She sits next to God himself."

"That horny little bitch? She must be somebody's private twat."

"No doubt. But there she is. The other broad probably belongs to someone equally important. At any rate, we've been selected by powerful people. Possibly just to humor their squeezes. If the chickies fall from grace, our funds could dry up. So we've got to make our big score now."

It sounded logical to Sonny. No wonder the broads turned him down. If their sugar daddies found out they were giving it away, they'd be out on their collective asses. "Okay, I'll take Bluepeace II and attack a Russian. You follow in Bluepeace I and pick me up."

"North of Japan near Vladivostok would be a good area. The Russians get nervous when anyone's up there."

*****

They departed with both boats two days later; their crews competing against each other in high excitement. They provisioned at Kushiro, transferring the younger girls and male screw-ups to Sonny's boat before heading north. Some guys assumed the girls were to service Sonny, but the girls' real role was to provide highly attractive and tragic deaths.

In accordance with Horn's plan, the bow was wired with explosives, and Sonny expected to blow the ship from a rubber speedboat after he obtained photographs incriminating the Russians. He would radio Horn's vessel for help afterward from the speedboat.

It sounded simple, but too much was left to chance with respect to casualties, survivors, and potential eye-witnesses from Bluepeace. Como didn't want any other survivors. They would detract from the attention he would receive from the media. He decided to kill the crew himself before entering the speedboat. Drowning would be best. An open saltwater tank amidships for keeping fish alive would work nicely. The far-out jerks were expendable, and chicks—well, this group of broken-in birds was of no further interest.

Three days later, radar picked up a ship heading east in the Vladivostok lane. The blip was a good possibility, and Sonny ordered an intercept course. He radioed Horn to close within fifty miles while he investigated. The captain and first mate, the only qualified seamen present, were unable to identify the Russian vessel by type. It was a weird-looking ship, defying identification in Sonny's book, but definitely not a warship. He ordered his rubber speedboat readied for use.

His latest paramour brought his coffee and the brandy bottle he'd requested. He poured some in a mug for himself and Julie prepared glasses for the crew. She called everyone together into the galley for a toast to their first anti-fishing action.

"This is it," Sonny announced. "Our date with destiny. I'm going to take the speedboat after harassing them for a while. We take photos of everything while protesting against unrestricted long-net fishing. We're creating publicity for our cause." The crew didn't understand his inferences. They were along for the grand adventure while working to save the environment. He raised his glass. "Here's to success!"

"Success!" they all chorused. The air was electric with excitement, and the brandy was downed in a twinkling.

Sonny quickly climbed to the bridge. He heard moans and crashes behind him as the crew toppled over within seconds. The knockout drug he had purchased in San Francisco had worked perfectly. One by one he stuffed each person into the saltwater tank. It was weird, putting human beings to death by drowning was simply work. All that hype on TV about feeling high when killing someone, and he felt nothing.

He paralleled the Russian ship's heading until he was sure the tank had done its work. He put life jackets on Julie and the three best-looking girls and put them in the speedboat. Once he was in the water, he'd keep one near him so her body could be recovered. The rest went up in the bow.

He steered across the Russian's bow, ignoring the deafening blasts of its horn. The weather was perfect—visibility was limited due to patchy fog and heavy overcast. He would be able get away easily. Sonny circled again to make another run. Shit, this was fun. He felt like a dog running after a car and barking his protest. One more run across the Russian's bow, and he would abandon ship for the speedboat. Fame and riches were beckoning.

*****

General Chuikov was on the secured telephone line asking for Sophia. It was the first occurrence of Russian hotline use since the fall of the Soviet Union, and Webb listened in. Neither could think of any pressing issue that could have precipitated the Russian's call.

"Sophia, we have a person who says he works for you," the newly-promoted general stated without preliminary courtesies. "A Salvatore Como. He attempted to interfere with one of our special vessels near Vladivostok."

Chuikov had spoken in Russian, and Sophia rapidly translated for Webb. He frowned at the unknown name. "Who is that?" he asked.

Sophia didn't answer immediately, and returned to Chuikov. "Como?" she answered with surprise in her voice. "Was it a Bluepeace boat?"

"Yes. We sank it, and this Como was the only survivor."

"You sank the boat?"

"Yes, it was one of our SVR ships. My apologies, but we need to talk."

Sophia was stunned. "Absolutely, but apologies are mine. Bluepeace was not to interfere with Russian ships under any circumstances. Where's our loose cannon now?"

"Vladivostok. In safekeeping."

"I trust the fewest possible people know."

"Fortunately we have excellent compartmentalization."

"Hold on," Sophia ordered. She turned to Webb. "I need to get to Moscow immediately."

She watched as Webb dialed Gary Stebar. "Where would you rather meet me, Moscow or Vladivostok?" she asked Chuikov.

"Moscow. I'll have this Como brought here."

Conversation was small talk until Webb handed Sophia her schedule. "I can be on Areoflot from Paris arriving in Moscow at noon tomorrow. But I must leave immediately, and you'll have to handle documents at your end. Okay?"

"My pleasure. You'll be met in Paris. What's your incoming flight?"

Sophia gave him the particulars and was on her way to Dulles within fifteen minutes.

By noon the next day, she was landing in Moscow. Chuikov was waiting, and they drove directly to Dzerzhinsky Square. Sophia explained her oblique involvement with Bluepeace to harass the Japanese during the drive.

"I only met this man once," she said grimly. "It's surprising he used my name."

"It was almost the first thing he said."

Horn must have checked on her. Wallace had been right; Horn was dangerous. "Bluepeace is totally independent," Sophia sighed.

"They're difficult to control, but can be very useful at times. This is not one of those times."

"Evidently, Como was in command and thought our ship was a fishing vessel. A serious mistake—for all concerned," Chuikov said, patting Sophia's hand. "It was one of our undersea… ah… research vessels, and the captain became nervous. Your boat was blown out of the water in an instant, before it sent any message. It is possible its loss is not yet known."

"Are there storms in that area? Can we say it was an act of God?"

Chuikov laughed. "You can say anything you'd like. I don't believe in a god, but if I did, he would look like you."

Sophia smiled imperceptibly at the compliment.

He stopped laughing when Sophia didn't respond. "Weather is frequently bad there. You won't have any problem. I'll have much greater difficulties convincing people here this is not evidence of duplicity on your part. We need a full explanation in the worst way. My position is tenuous at best."

"I'm sorry to have put you at risk. I think we can resolve any difficulties if you let me see him," Sophia said. She had no doubt the Federation president was concerned. It was time to play hardball and give the Russians some appreciation of her moral resolve. She narrowed her eyes, "But first, have him stripped naked and handcuffed behind his back."

Chuikov raised his eyebrows. "One other thing—we fished out three bodies, all young girls, all drowned, all very strange. No one saw them struggling or swimming. They had on life jackets, yet had drowned immediately. The boat went down, and they were floating there along with this guy."

None of what Chuikov was saying made any sense.

*****

Forty minutes later, Sophia and the general strode into a small room where Como was sitting naked on a small chair flanked by two burly guards. Como's body shook when Sophia entered and attempted to cover himself by drawing up his legs. He looked surprisingly fit with no visible evidence of ill-treatment. Apparently, the Russians had not undertaken any serious interrogation.

"Please leave us." Sophia requested, speaking to the guards in Russian.

Chuikov nodded to the guards and they withdrew.

Sophia sat down opposite Como. "You've gotten yourself in a fine fix," she said sternly.

"You're Russian?" he gasped. "You're supposed to be CIA."

"Who says I'm CIA?"

"Horn. That's what he told me. He said the entire operation was being financed by the CIA."

"Why did you approach the Russian ship?"

Como squirmed on his chair. It was obvious his nakedness was causing him acute embarrassment.

Sophia continued to gaze steadily at his eyes in silence.

"Horn thought by making an incident with the Russians, we could widen our appeal for funds."

"What sort of incident?"

"I was to harass the ship, take pictures, and then escape in a rubber speedboat. I was the only person left, and I was to sink the boat, then radio for Horn to pick me up."

"Everybody has their provocateurs," Sophia said to Chuikov in Russian. He was shaking his head over Como's story. She turned again to Como. "What about your crew? Where were they?"

"Dead. Horn had already killed them."

"You're lying. You killed them just before approaching the Soviet ship." While walking through the complex, Sophia and Chuikov had discussed probable events on Bluepeace II. The autopsy reports indicated the girls probably had been drugged before drowning.

"How could I? I was alone."

"You drugged them, then drowned them on board. You couldn't take the chance of killing them earlier. Horn didn't do it. You did."

Sophia asked Chuikov to have the guards spread-eagle him against the wall and get her a knife. "You don't have any further interest in this individual, do you?" she asked.

"Absolutely not. Consider yourself one of us, and do whatever you'd like." Chuikov could see what was developing and was fascinated by Sophia's strength. He summoned the guards who tied Como against the wall. Chuikov was impressed. The prisoner was hung like a horse. He handed Sophia the knife.

She stood directly in front of Como, contrasting his nakedness with her beauty and exquisite attire. Chuikov could see what was about to happen, but could barely believe it.

Sophia reached out and grasped Como's penis. "You're proud of your manhood, aren't you?"

Como nodded as his eyes widened in fear.

"Then you're not going to want to lie to me because if you do, you're going to lose it. Got it?"

Another nod was barely perceptible.

"Good. "So, whose idea was this?"

"Horn's, I swear it!" He was sweating furiously, his chest was heaving, and his words were shrill. Sophia began sawing the knife back and forth at the base of his penis. Como was not as tough as she expected. The idea of losing his most cherished asset must have been unbearable. As she slowly cut his penis away, he defecated, mixing his blood on the floor with brown. The room was filled with his cries for mercy—and his confession.

Sophia looked away. "A judge should not sentence a criminal to death unless he's willing himself to carry out his judgment."

Chuikov nodded his approval. He had watched Sophia proceeded from trial attorney to judge to executioner in front of his eyes.

"I'll see that Como's confession gets to the President," Chuikov said. "No one will believe you had anything to do with this."

"I did this for you. I trust it will silence your critics."

"I can't imagine anyone doubting your commitment to friendship with Russia after this. And with Como's confession on the table, my position is even more secure than it was. You have my deepest gratitude and affection."

Sophia had never doubted the General's affection for her and Russia felt like a second home. But time was pressing. She returned to Washington with the object she had removed in formaldehyde. She sent it to Horn with a note, "In remembrance. Don't screw with Mama."

*****

The meeting with Baird was a watershed. After Claire overcame her initial shock, she recognized Baird was dissuading instead of

368

injuring her. Sophia had proposed a truce, and she was inclined to accept. She kept the cassette of her Georgetown caper, and after confirming Baird's departure, took the VCR.

Possessing the tape, Claire felt better. The photography was excellent and it was a phenomenal performance. She would save it for her old age, but God, those last two were ugly. She tried to determine which one had made her pregnant, but it was no use. All of them were possible.

She was surprised to receive a telephone call from BJ Carter while working on her evening broadcast. He was coming into Washington and wanted to invite her to dinner. She told the switchboard operator to have him come by the studio after her broadcast if he called again.

The broadcast was uneventful, just the usual congressional delays and squabbles with the president. The perpetual sameness of politics depressed her, and she wondered how Max Robinson endured the pain for so long. Maybe the secret was to be so engrossed in your own problems that political scandals faded in comparison. She watered her dressing room plants and scanned several newspapers for broadcast ideas.

Hearing squeals of laughter, she walked out to find several of the younger studio girls buzzing around BJ, who was probably the most charismatic figure in American industry.

He gave her a toothy smile and disengaged himself from his admirers. "Miss Villars, how nice to see you again." He extended his hand.

"Mister Carter, or should I call you BJ?"

"BJ, if you please. You look better today than you did at my wedding."

"It's makeup. You'll have to wait a moment while I make myself presentable." Claire excused herself and returned to her dressing room. He made her wait, and now it was his turn.

Within a few minutes she'd checked her face and hair, and declared herself ready. "Where would you like to go?" she asked while scattering the other females.

"Crazy. Want to come along?" He already had taken her by the elbow and was escorting her out the studio.

Jerk. She tried again. "Do you have a place in mind for dinner?"

369

"I thought we'd try a little Japanese—the Nakanoya. You like Japanese, don't you?"

Would it make a difference if she didn't? Claire decided to be a sport. She was curious to find out why he had called.

Her impression of BJ didn't improve during dinner. He wanted information and acted as though it was Claire's duty to provide it. He took charge of everything, ordering drinks and dinner without pausing to ask for her opinions or taste. Claire couldn't remember anyone being so overbearing since the time she'd dated jocks in college.

"What I need is good information on Milleron," BJ said. "Where they get financing. What they're going into—that type of thing."

"And you want me to help?" Claire was amazed at BJ's chutzpah.

"Absolutely. That's what I came down for."

Claire shook her head. "Look, I'm a working woman, and I've got lots to do, so being treated like a two-dollar bimbo is not high on my priority list. Now, I'm being nice because you're married to King's daughter, but that's going to change if you don't."

"You're right, I've been a bore. I'm not accustomed to dealing with women who have class. Most are like the girls in your studio. I just tell them what to do and they do it."

"Wrong action with me, kiddo. You tell me what to do, and I'll do the opposite."

"I understand. Can we start over?"

"I have to go to the ladies' room. We'll start fresh when I get back." She popped up from the booth and swished away. When she returned, the table was reset for taking their orders. Claire nodded and sat down. She ordered a screwdriver and teriyaki steak. "Okay, now, what's all this about Milleron?"

"I think they'll be my biggest competitors in coming years. They seem to practically mint money. What do they know that I don't?"

"I wasn't aware you missed much when it came to making money. You're America's star businessman."

"Let's just say that I'm always concerned about what I don't know. Like right now. I don't know what you want. I'm willing to give you a blank check."

The steak came and Claire was hungry. "Call me in a week, and I'll let you know."

She called King after dinner. She felt vaguely unfaithful having had dinner with his son-in-law. But dinner had been innocent, and King didn't really work for Milleron. She had nothing against Ed Armstrong, but Milleron's network takeover had squelched her advancement. Baird's points were worth pondering, too, but BJ was almost family.

Thinking about family had a nice ring to it. She and King were a pair again but hadn't made it official. And they weren't getting younger.

"Hi, lover!" she said when King came on the line. "Why don't we get married?" The question had slid out like jelly in a donut. She started to apologize, then decided she wanted to hear his answer.

"What?" King said. "Are you okay? You're the one who's always wanted a career, no attachments and getting abortions."

"Yeah, you're right," she answered. He had responded badly, assuming she was drunk or something. She had spoken from her heart, but he'd missed it.

"I do love you, you know," he continued.

Too late. He probably did, but they weren't on the same wavelength. "How's work going, honey?" she asked.

"Good. I'm closing a deal for a couple of big ranches in the Green River area tomorrow."

"You guys sure spend money. Where do you get it all?" His answer to her earlier question lessened her guilt in asking about Milleron.

"I don't know. Their pool of investors, I guess. When I need money I tell Ed, and he arranges it from various banks. It's like having an angel with unlimited funds."

"Does any of it come from around here?"

"Oh, sure. Several times he's used Citizens'. Why?"

"Just curious. I was hoping you might find an excuse to come visiting. I miss you." Gad, she was feeling lonely and wanted romance.

"I miss you too, honey. But I'm tied up right now. Maybe in a couple of weeks."

Claire rarely if ever drank alone, but she poured herself a brandy. Then another.

King's explanation didn't wash. Claire spent her free time during the next two weeks cataloging Milleron's investments. One of her friends at CBC sent her a list of Milleron's transactions with the S & L, and its length astounded her. Not once had they issued junk bonds.

In the last two years, Milleron had spent billions upon billions. Acting on the Citizens' lead, she learned four hundred million had been transferred in from a bank in Zurich during a single week.

So Milleron's money was coming from Europe. She wondered if Milleron was a front for Germans, but a better guess was Arabs.

She hired a private detective to stake out the Milleron offices at Port Tobacco and photograph its personnel. He spent two days in Charles County, and his sojourn was well worth the money. One of those photographed was Moira Baird, now a blonde instead of a redhead, but it was her without a doubt. So she had some connection with Milleron, either as a CIA operative or direct employee, and Milleron was associated with the CIA.

She arranged a follow-up meeting with BJ, and he arrived late again. It was a strategy rather than a habit. She knew the type: if you're early, you're wasting your time; if you're late, you're wasting somebody else's time; whose time is most important?

"Let's do it here," she said. "I have work to complete tonight."

BJ entered and sat down. "You sure? I've got reservations in Georgetown."

"Yeah, I'm sure. I don't have much info for you anyway." He would probably assume she was playing for bigger rewards. "I can't prove it yet, but apparently, European links feed money in regularly."

"Ah, the Arabs. They're doing from the Middle East what I'm doing from the Far East."

"Which is?" Claire frowned.

"My basic financing comes from Japan. See? I knew we'd eventually end up competitors."

"That's some commentary on our economy. The two most powerful real estate companies in our country are financed by foreigners."

"Hey, that's business. Tell you what. I'll let you go tonight if you'll come to Atlantic City for a weekend. My treat for your efforts."

Claire was tired. BJ was clearly suggesting a romantic runaway, yet he was Suzanne's husband. He undoubtedly had many affairs, but Suzanne was too close. Claire should have settled BJ's hash once and for all a long time ago.

Next time she would.

Book 4 - The Legacy

2017 - 2025

Chapter 39

Webb always enjoyed visiting the university, but this was special—Gordon, Sophia's youngest boy, was graduating. Nestled in hills overlooking Table Rock Lake in Southern Missouri, the setting for Reid-Stewart University was idyllic. Sophia had spared no expense to provide superb facilities for its five thousand male students, nor for the five thousand female students at Lauenberg University across the lake at Lampe.

On Thursday, Webb had been treated to a parachuting and marksmanship competition. Students jumped from two thousand feet to land on a small target, then moved through a train-fire course with their weapons. Webb wished his men in Vietnam had been of such caliber. He was proud to present the winning team and top three individual trophies.

Friday morning, Webb ushered Gordon into his Milleron jet on the school's airfield. All of the family was now at the controls of their enterprise. Milleron was by far the world's largest corporation in terms of asset value. Some affiliates still needed fleshing out, but they were all there.

"When do you think the crash will come?" Gordon asked out of the blue. For almost the entire time of the disastrous Obama presidency, that was the question foremost in every Stewart's mind. The national debt had jumped into the next galaxy, and the nation was teetering on the brink.

"Your mother undoubtedly knows better than I, but my guess

would be within one to three years. At the latest, after the next presidential election."

"What will trigger it?"

"Who knows? Probably arrogance on the part of the Eastern Elite or their Bilderberg overlords. Battle lines have already been drawn. Your mom and her adversaries are pushing and shoving, and it's inevitable someone will go for the throat."

With Japanese economic power held in check by Sophia and her alliance with China since the middle 1990s, the Bilderberg companies in Europe, backed by the national banks in the European Union had greatly increased their ownership of American assets and industry. Britain had become the largest foreign owner of American companies, and the British assault went almost unnoticed. It was not until 2010 and the Gulf oil spill in that the American public discovered "BP" did not stand for "Beyond Petroleum."

By 2010, the annual deficit was in trillions of dollars and local governments, towns, counties, cities, and even states were dependent on federal grants to maintain politicians in power. Industrial production had disappeared over the horizon to Europe and the Far East, and every dollar given in grants to purchase votes was borrowed from abroad. The only thing holding the US together was Sophia's good offices with China and their restraint with the vast hoard of dollars in their possession.

Nonetheless, the Bilderbergs had greatly strengthened their hold on the national political establishment. The baby-boomers were fully indoctrinated in socialism from kindergarten onward, and as they assumed positions of power in business and government, the formation of public-private partnerships accelerated. Sophia was powerless to halt the transfers of billions of dollars to European central banks, other Bilderberg-controlled organizations, and unions in the Bush and Obama bailouts. Milleron received nothing—nothing was requested, and nothing was accepted.

There was also Agenda 21. The Bilderbergs promoted it incessantly using every "green" and environmental group alive. Most Americans had never heard of Agenda 21, but all federal government initiatives and departments worked toward fulfilling its ends. And those ends meant the elimination of private property and personal freedom in the United States. Since President Bush signed the Rio

Agreements in 1992, legions of sustainable development initiatives had been passed, either by executive order or congressional action, and almost a thousand American cities were officially "sustainable communities" under the ICLEI program, "Local Governments for Sustainability." The call to reduce the world's population by six billion people went unnoticed, and with the US having the most recalcitrant population, Americans would be the first to go. The Bilderbergs wanted pliable populations of serfs—not people difficult to control.

The Agency itself had gone into further decline after Webb's retirement. Lawyers tied operations into knots and stressed risk-avoidance instead of fulfilling its mission. Thousands needed to be fired. It was running almost solely on Sophia's abilities, and there was only so much she could do. It was a broken organization, and there was no foreseeable way to fix it.

The United States had lurched into European-style socialism under Obama and the Constitution got twisted beyond recognition. The Supreme Court had become overwhelmingly progressive, and the Constitution had been shredded. PPPs controlled by the Eastern Elite and socialists had become all-powerful in non-Milleron territory. Politicians had become dependent on those organizations to keep their seats and were forced to become stalwart members of what some called "The Deep State." It was the shadow alliance of elites that controlled government for their own purposes, making elections little more than theater and exercises in futility.

The invasion of illegal aliens had irretrievable changed American culture for the worse. The Roman Empire had settled the barbarians within the empire where they proved to become a cancer that ate the empire from within, and the illegals were doing the same thing to America. Swamped by the tide, Americans disappeared or receded, and the American southwest had already effectively become Aztlan as the Mexicans called the territory.

The United States had begun moving into the last chapter of its history. Sophia needed to take the bull by the horns and take action. Webb hoped to see the establishment of a free Amulot state in his lifetime, and he was aging. He couldn't see any potential to putting off the inevitable.

*****

"Okay, beautiful, we're all set for tomorrow night," Gary Stebar said, bounding into Sophia's office with a smile.

Sophia looked up, the intrusion breaking her concentration. He held the smile and raised his eyebrows while waiting for Sophia to respond. She waved him into a chair.

"For the record, that'll be the last time you address me as 'beautiful', Gary," Sophia said firmly but not unfriendly. "As of five o'clock tomorrow, I'm acting director and will addressed as 'Ma'am', 'Chief,' 'Madam Director,' or 'Ms Stewart.' And who knows, the Senate may confirm me as permanent director."

"If I may say so, I hope you're confirmed as soon as possible."

"Thanks. But you've worked with me for twenty-five years, and know me better than most." Sophia gazed at the still youthful-looking ivy-leaguer who had turned forty-eight a few months earlier. "Tell me, Gary, what's the lunchroom scuttlebutt over working for a youngish female?"

Most CIA personnel thought she was five years older than her true age. Only recently had she altered her records and documentation to reflect her actual name and background. Her background would soon be held up to public scrutiny and truth was important. Her college degree from Harvard had disappeared overnight, and she had turned forty-six on the previous Fourth of July instead of fifty-one.

"There's some polarization," he said. "Most of the women are proud of your accomplishments, but some seem to resent you and are saying things I wouldn't want to repeat."

"You can't have a cathouse without expecting cat fights," Sophia grinned. "I assume it's standard stuff like I got ahead on my back."

"More or less. On the other hand, lots of people believe you've really been running the Agency for some time. You were the power behind the throne."

"You mean my relationship with Webb Reid."

"Yeah. Everyone knows Webb brought you into the Agency, and you and he were very close. Some feel that regardless of your talents, you had certain... ah... special advantages."

"I can appreciate where those thoughts come from. Unfortunately, you can't prove something isn't true when evidence only exists if it were." Sophia thought for a moment. "There's something I want you to do. Get every department head to submit a list of our three top polygraph operators. Immediately, if not sooner. I'll be here waiting."

Sophia buzzed her secretary to call an afternoon meeting of deputy directors and department heads.

Entering the conference room at two o'clock, Sophia was pleased to see all eleven present. In their business suits, they made an interesting contrast to her. Sophia was wearing a beige dress, slightly light for Washington in winter, but more expensive than any suit in the room. She spread out her materials and took up as much space as possible to establish her importance.

She was the youngest person in the room. The men were all between forty-eight and sixty-three and were veterans of many years of service in the Agency. Webb and she had planned as well as possible for this day, and the men were the best of the lot. Some probably harbored resentment over not being appointed Acting Director themselves, but she had no real enemies.

Sophia dismissed her secretary and waited for the door to close. "This meeting will be classified top secret, and no notes are to be taken." She glanced around the table receiving nods. "Thank you, gentlemen, for appearing on such short notice. As everyone knows, I have been appointed acting director, pending confirmation as director."

"This morning, I asked each of you to list our three top polygraph operators. I'm happy to announce near unanimity in your selection—only five names were submitted. I have also constructed a series of questions for a polygraph exam." She passed single sheets down both sides of the table. "Please read and we'll discuss them in a moment."

Sitting third from the left, Harvey Sjoberg, deputy director for Counter-Espionage and the oldest individual present, was her strongest supporter. He had known Webb for thirty years, and understood his relationship with Sophia. It was Harvey who had provided the security team that had saved Sophia from Harlan.

Sophia resumed speaking. "As most of you have guessed, I am of the female gender." There were several guffaws while she continued. "Please be assured that I have no interest in furthering women's causes or increasing the number of women in our organization. I am simply interested in the best person for the job." She quickly scanned the table for doubters, but the group seemed willing to concede her fairness.

"However, being a woman gives rise to certain rumors and speculations. These are perhaps avoidable, perhaps not. What's important is your knowledge and belief in yourselves, your leaders, and your subordinates, to have the most effective organization possible. The key is loyalty, particularly your loyalty to me and my loyalty to you. I need the maximum possible benefit from my association with each of you—your ideas, knowledge, opinions, efforts, and loyalty. All these must be given freely and unconditionally."

Sophia picked up her list. "That's why I made up these questions for a polygraph exam—in addition to the usual control items, of course. I will give you my answers." She paused for effect.

She read the questions evenly and without emotion. "'Have you ever misappropriated Agency funds for personal use?' No. 'Have you ever had sexual relations with another Agency employee?' No. 'Have you ever killed or caused to have killed any individual?' Yes. 'Have you ever had an unauthorized contact with a foreign intelligence organization?' No. 'Have you ever knowingly violated your security oath to the Agency?' No."

Sophia placed the sheet on her notebook and looked at each executive in turn. "Those are my answers, and I'm prepared to submit to a polygraph exam conducted by the three examiners selected to verify the truthfulness of my responses. Any of you may demand this of me; however, you must agree to submit yourself to the same examination. There will be no retribution—unless you fail the polygraph, of course. I realize this is a most extraordinary offer, but these are extraordinary times. We must be able to work together, each having absolute confidence in the other. My offer is on the table. I await your response." Sophia again scanned the group, this time starting at her left. The first two avoided her gaze.

Her eyes stopped on Harvey. He cleared his throat. "Sophia, Madam Director," he said, "there is not one scintilla of doubt in my mind your answers are the truth. In fact, I would consider doubt on anybody's part to be insulting. You are probably the only person here who can answer as you did and pass the examination. Except for this third question. I would have to answer in the affirmative like you, but others would not. Rest assured I will do my damnedest to stifle gossip in my department like that which prompted you to take this step. You have my pledge to serve you to the very best of my ability."

Several department heads voiced their agreement while others nodded.

"Does anyone wish to request the examination?" Sophia asked. The room was silent while a few individuals shook their heads. "Very well, I consider the subject closed. I expect to hear no further juicy tidbits concerning myself, and that you will take appropriate actions in your departments to see such talk neutralized and eradicated. Now, let's get down to business."

Returning to her office, Sophia summoned her staff, including her bodyguard, Cole Stoner. He still looked exactly like a Secret Service agent, and had done well over the years, advancing in rating and reputation as she became increasingly important.

"Cole, what's my reputation like in Security?" she asked. "Everyone jealous of you?"

He met her gaze steadily and without embarrassment. "Hard to say," he offered. "In the beginning I got kidded a lot, but that's long gone. Most older guys have seen reports on your trips, and consider me lucky not to have lost you. Also, that you're dangerous to my health."

"Ah, the Kiev tape."

"Yeah, they've all seen it."

Six years ago in Kiev, Sophia was entering her limo when members of the *Organizaskaya* opened up with gunfire. Cole shoved her into the back seat, but forgot to duck, and knocked himself out. He fell backward onto the pavement, and she'd gone and gotten him. She shot one of the gunmen with Cole's gun, and managed to wrestled her bodyguard into the car while still under fire. Cole hadn't been able to live the incident down ever since.

"Well, let's increase the detail. Times are getting tougher. If you need anything, just ask"

*****

Jack Wallace was amused by the executive branch's request for Denver to perform a thorough background investigation on Sophia. While his people checked records and conducted interviews, reporters descended on Golden looking for juicy background material. What a joke. They wouldn't even find a high school boyfriend. There was absolutely nothing to damage her.

He returned to his office and locked the door. In the large pedestal ashtray with a porcelain insert, he burned his copy of the personal history statement Webb had fabricated long ago. Wallace felt a twinge of nostalgia as he watched it burn. "Goodbye, sweetie," he said out loud. "You've been replaced by a better woman."

She had been faithful to him in her way. And he to her. He wondered if his name would surface in the hearings. Sophia had jealously guarded their privacy; not once had they been together in public since Webb became director.

He considered his own side of the street. The Bureau was fragmented into four distinct groups; conservative whites, women, Hispanics, and liberals which included other minorities. There was some communication between female agents and liberals, but generally the groups acted as internal political parties, only grudgingly working with each other. Years of affirmative action had built those divisions. With potential sexual discrimination suits always possible, he avoided close relationships with any of his females. It was a Catch-22 situation. He discriminated against them socially and cooperatively out of fear of being accused of discrimination.

Over the years, Wallace had gathered together a small group of agents and administrators who were sympathetic to Sophia's ideas. He demanded absolute secrecy from every group member. His best acquisition was the head of records in Washington. The archives were being captured on computer imaging equipment, and Wallace's man was having all computer files duplicated and archived at Fort Leavenworth.

Wallace would have to tell Sophia not to count on assistance from the Bureau in a crisis. The best they could hope for was to seize the Leavenworth archives and draw enough volunteers away to form the nucleus of a new organization. He hoped the Bureau was not indicative of what Sophia could expect from most federal organizations.

*****

Ed Armstrong was beginning to tire. He was well past retirement age like Webb, and without Bobbi, he'd have been a goner. She was a finance person's finance person, figuring cash flows and handling astronomical numbers like so many dominos. As Milleron's treasurer, she was never ruffled, not even ten years ago when he'd thought they were short by eight billion dollars. It turned out to be less than four, and Bobbi had kited checks for a few days until they were all covered. For her it had been a game and a challenge.

"Think I'll make it?" he asked Bobbi, tossing her sheets of figures into his hold basket. He swiveled in his chair and put his feet up on the heavy rosewood desk.

Bobbi smiled with friendly concern. "You'll make whatever you want to make," she said.

Ed had flown in last night and stayed in the Brooks Buckley Guest House. It was the best of the seven guest houses—actually seventeenth century taverns and inns in their reconstructed town of Port Tobacco. Sometimes Bobbi stayed with him to ease the loneliness of traveling, but they always slept in separate bedrooms.

"I don't know anymore." He sighed. "Sometimes the future scares me. I feel like Moses who won't be allowed to enter the promised land." He drummed his pencil on the desk. "You've done well, Bobbi. No, not well—fantastic. Christ, you and Sophia could run the world."

"Not bad for an old broad, huh?" She laughed.

Ed looked at her critically. Old broad, indeed. She still looked great. Her hair was now a mixture of sand and gray, but the classically sleek body was still there with its natural grace. Best of all, Bobbi's face had not become a lined, bony caricature like so many super-thin actresses and models. "Why didn't you ever remarry after Frank left?" he asked.

"Never found a man I wanted to marry. What about you? You've been single forever."

"I don't know. Couldn't make it work. Marriage wasn't my thing. You know yourself; women like me as a friend, not a lover."

"I'm sorry, can't do anything about that," she said sympathetically. "Guess I'm just a natural-born mother. Billy, the money, you, Milleron…"

Ed dropped his feet to the floor. "I never asked you to mother me."

"I know. But it's what I do with those I care about. Even Cam—that's probably why I lost him."

Ed felt chastened by this lovely creature with such a giving nature. He felt like a bull elephant who became old and useless at fifty. "Well, you sure became a good banker."

"Experience. And I like it. It's more fun than playing Monopoly."

He flipped a list of property sales in the non-Amulot target states to Bobbi. "Has Sophia set a timetable to divest ourselves of all investment properties in those areas?" he asked.

"Yeah, year end."

"Wow, sooner than I thought. What do you expect to get?"

"Between seven and eight hundred billion."

"Then what?"

"You tell me. The Boy Scout motto."

"Well, I hope you don't leave me to manage all our vice presidents and their delusions of grandeur by myself."

She shook her head. "I'll ask Sophia, but don't get your hopes up," she said quietly. "She's already asked me to begin putting together a money and banking system for a hypothetical Amulot state. She's tagged me for treasury secretary."

Ed shook his head. Sophia thought of everything. And she was right—Bobbi would make an excellent treasury secretary. "How will we stack up versus the Feds?"

"Great. We'll have no debt. And it's hard to see how our present Federal Government can finance a war."

"The Bilderbergs can," Ed warned. "At one time our adversaries were just the Japanese, now they're all the countries controlled by the Bilderbergs."

"No doubt, but the Federal Government's decision will be half a loaf or none, because the price will be total control by approved Bilderberg institutions."

"Can we do it? Will we have sufficient financial resources for a stable economy?"

"Oh, yeah. The only question is: 'and fight a war?'"

*****

It was tough for a woman to grow old when she had depended so long on her beauty. Heather's reddish brown hair was now a tired mixture of dirty brown and gray which the beauty parlor regularly kept at a shade of auburn similar to Sophia's. Heather had adopted a regular regimen of exercise, but there was no stopping the decline to a less curvaceous body. In spite of all efforts to the contrary, her cute, rounded rear had flattened and moved upwards into her waist.

She had adopted Cindy Lewis when she came to Washington as a somewhat larger version of herself to handle social connections. It was fun watching Cindy using everything Heather could teach her. Cindy was a natural, learning Heather's tricks on how to maneuver in society, always saying the right thing with extreme graciousness, and never being obtrusive. Yet, there were differences. Cindy's encounters with men were a pastime, not a career, and under the impact of AIDS, "No glove, no love" had been in force since the middle 1980s.

"The key is focus," Heather had graphically lectured Cindy. "Your entire body closes around the man inside you, grasping him with all your strength, and defying him to leave. It becomes your internal strength against his external force, a tug of war with two winners. If he believes you don't want him to ever withdraw, he'll do anything you want. Focus on him and what he's giving you—it's irresistible."

So Cindy became irresistible, possibly better than Heather had been in her prime. Maybe it was her looks, maybe because she wasn't assertive, maybe because she was addicted to fitness. Whatever the reason, Cindy possessed the Washington that possessed her.

Now Heather needed Cindy to help Sophia. "Who can you co-op to our side?" she asked.

"Lots of guys. It depends on what we want and when."

"We'll shotgun for lack of time," Heather replied. "Get all the animals into the ark."

"Okay, let me show you something." Cindy went over to her computer. "I've made a database of my... uh... social activities over the past years. It may seem gauche, but I've literally recorded everyone I've met, rated them, and listed significant or unusual things."

"I didn't know you could program." Heather was genuinely surprised.

"Sophia taught me this database system in high school, and I've used it instead of making a diary. It's a terrific way to remember good times and take revenge on guys who deserve it. Nobody knows I've done this, of course."

"It's full of juicy details?"

"Oh, yeah. I even add what other girls tell me."

"You should run Washington."

"Well, you still outrank me with your vice-president. It makes me wish I had been around in the early sixties and had a shot at Kennedy. Since then none of them have turned me on, except maybe Slick Willy, and then I wasn't willing to stand in line."

"Do you have real leverage on people? Things they wouldn't want out?"

"Sure, but it would destroy my ability to gain more. I'd be shunned in society."

"Is that too high a price to pay?"

"No, not anymore. I'm tired of it. I got out once before when I fell in love with Mark, but..." Cindy's eyes seemed to mist over thinking about her deceased fiancé.

Heather put her hand on Cindy's shoulder. Mark had been an FBI agent who'd been killed during an anti-drug operation. They had gone together for almost a year and were planning to get married.

Cindy patted Heather's hand. "It's okay. It's time I devote myself more to whatever's in store for us from Sophia's activities. There's a lot I can do."

"Can you get more information from your acquaintances and add it to your database?"

"Probably. There are several ladies who might be persuaded to part with really valuable stuff, but I can put the heat on probably twenty senators by myself."

"We need as much as possible. You can never have too much information. But right now, let's see what you have. Let's start with those who are really bad in bed or have big problems."

"That's almost all of them." Cindy grinned as she began to generate reports.

*****

Claire Villars was no longer the adversary she'd once was. Sophia and she had observed an unstated truce since Claire's chat with Bobbi Rutledge. Maybe time was mellowing her. She looked at Sophia as the most powerful woman in the world, as well as the richest. In a way, Claire respected Sophia and even admired her. She had begun to feel a kinship with Sophia, a lady with more guts than the rest of Washington put together.

Her attempt at a Middle East settlement had been inspired. Lebanese Christians were to be exchanged for Palestinians in the West Bank and Gaza, and Lebanon would have become a Palestinian state. The Israelis had eventually been in favor of the plan, but it didn't happen because of opposition in Congress and the Administration. American politicians simply couldn't look past their next election, so the initiative had died. Now the Middle East was in worse shape than ever.

Sophia had functioned as a shadow State Department for some time, and Japan and the Europeans were actively hostile to her. Claire knew Sophia had been involved up to her eyebrows in trying to pull the US out of NATO, but the British, French and Germans were against her for other reasons. She had yet to attend a Bilderberg meeting and avoided the Trilateral Commission and the Council for Foreign Relations like the plague. Russia and many Middle Eastern and South American countries praised her, although the Mexicans seemed passively hostile.

Her biggest supporter was China, and she obviously maintained intimate contact with Chinese leaders. It was possible that Sophia favored returning Taiwan to Red China and she definitely favored reunifying Korea. The Chinese were finally helping to undermine the North Koreans, and reunification was probably only a few years away. If so, it was due to Sophia.

It was time for Claire to quit the liberal rat-race and prove herself as a Sophia supporter. Sophia wasn't politically correct, but clearly she was the best thing around for the United States. The only question was how to reach across the gulf Claire herself had constructed.

*****

General Chuck Carpenter was concerned about the anti-female sentiment that surfaced in Army units during discussions over Sophia Stewart's appointment. Most personnel seemed more ready to accept a woman for president than the director of the CIA. He decided it would be similar for FBI director or chief of staff for the Army, and he needed to correct such attitudes.

Times had changed since General Olson's death and the formation of A-Corps. The Army, Air Force, Navy, and Marines had undergone substantial reductions. Counting all of the armed forces, less than 1.3 million personnel were on active duty; 60% white, 13% Hispanic, 16% black, 4% Asian, and 7% multi-racial or other. Of that, 15% were female. Military personnel and all veterans living in the United States numbered just slightly more than 7% of the total population. The military was no longer important in politics.

One objective achieved under General Lambert was the movement of headquarters and logistical facilities away from major cities. Posts in the east and south lost most of their troop units and heavy equipment to midwestern and western Army posts and National Guard camps. Lambert had also begun maintaining substantial white majorities in critical midwestern formations, while allowing southern commands to become heavily black and Hispanic.

Some movements and shuffling of personnel during the last twenty years had been tricky, particularly the two times the Army chief of staff had been black. Personnel control was becoming increasingly difficult as black officers became more numerous. A-Corps had been outed a few times, but was dismissed as a cabal of disaffected reserve officers attempting to break West Point's monopoly on promotions and good assignments.

The General thought time was on the side of his enemies. He couldn't see how Sophia could win, but had made his commitment and would die with her if necessary. Sophia was no loser, and neither was the cause of an American republic, by, of, and for Americans. Americans, not hyphenated Americans. Not Afro-Americans, Asian-Americans, Native Americans, Mexican-Americans or any of that crap.

Carpenter remembered when the first President Bush sent American troops into the Middle East at Japanese insistence to safeguard their supply of oil. It was a disgraceful demonstration of foreign power over American politicians and one that really started A-Corps. Japan had fought Saddam Hussein to the last American, and Americans died for Japanese and European interests. That would never happen again.

Chapter 40

The president had sent Sophia's name promptly to the Hill for confirmation, but the Senate seemed in no hurry to act. Sophia didn't blame them. Her appointment was extremely controversial, primarily because she was a woman, but also because of her age. Politicians needed time for posturing, and conducting polls.

Nominating Sophia had been a political move to increase the number of women in high government positions. Nonetheless, she was an obvious choice. She had represented the CIA in National Security Council meetings for years, and her analyses and presentations had proven more insightful and accurate than anyone else's. But like every nomination, hers was subject to politics.

Jerry Thornton considered his plan to block Sophia's confirmation unbeatable and irrefutable. He called Senator Fehrenfels, the New York senator who had been highly upset over the CIA's involvement in the proposed Middle East settlement. A far-left progressive, he supported women's rights but was secretively hostile to assertive women. He was the perfect front man.

"Yeah, I'm very familiar with Mrs. Stewart," Fehrenfels had said in response to Jerry's query. "She tried to destroy Israel."

"So you agree her nomination should be opposed at all cost?"

"Possibly," he said. "So why are you calling? Do you have information on her?"

Fehrenfels normally sounded like Howard Dean, and since most people thought Sophia belonged to the liberal camp, his opposition would be devastating. Jerry outlined his information and presented his idea. Fehrenfels was impressed.

On the other side, Sophia's supporters and allies were predictable. The National Organization of Women came out embarrassingly strong, and Hollywood celebrities lined up to pledge their support, assuming she would liberalize the Agency and transform it into a kinder, more gentle organization. Milleron representatives wrote letters and sent telegrams to their representatives in her support, and Columbo and his friends led the charge in the Senate.

Some southern conservatives came out against her, but their opposition was not unexpected. Webb paid a personal visit to each of them, stressing Sophia's competence and her qualifications as his hand-picked successor. There were no reversals, but several adopted a "wait and see" attitude.

Several veteran organizations also came out against her. They assumed a woman was not strong enough for the decisions and duties of an intelligence chief, although they also stated objections based on her age. Sophia's strategy in their respect was to have A-Corps officers speak to them and indicate their personal support. They had to be careful and remain non-partisan and non-political, so conversations were held in confidence. Taking the generals at their word, some organizations changed their stance.

So far, so good. Webb thought Sophia's chances were very good.

There were other, more personal bases that Sophia could touch, but they might not be helpful. General Chuikov, Deputy Minister of the SVR for the Russian Federation, had offered to help in any way possible. Sophia had to laugh. That was all she needed—support from the KGB's successor, the Russian Ministry for State Security. Anglo-Russian friendship wasn't that close… yet.

China owed her a lot, but this was not a time to call in foreign chits. Liberalization in China had been taking place under Sophia's tutelage, and the business internship program initiated over twenty years earlier had proven its worth. Almost alone, Sophia had been able to restrain the United States from intervening when the PRC starting building a base in the South China Sea. It had been a near thing, but Sophia had convinced the National Security Council that they would be best served by ignoring the situation. Sophia had delivered on her promise to the Chinese premier, so her prestige in China was enormous.

The Russian ambassador called Sophia to invite her to a small conference among friends. Sophia was startled; that meant Chuikov was in town. He had snuck in without her being informed. He must have traveled under another name, and whatever he wanted, it must be important. Sophia changed the locale to her secured conference room at Langley, and was soon greeting the still lean Russian general with kisses on both cheeks.

"I'm here to warn you," Chuikov said. They sat next to each other in easy chairs. "As you know, our intelligence in Japan is better than yours, and we have reports they're very unhappy with your nomination."

"I'm not surprised." Sophia smiled.

Chuikov laughed heartily. "I didn't think you would be. But word is they're making major threats over your appointment."

"Pretty drastic action for one little lady," she said. "Why would they do that?"

"Because they think the Senate will do what they say. It's a test of strength."

"It's possible," she suggested. "They've been playing games with policy since the 1970s, but this is the first time they've tried to dictate the choice of a cabinet level position."

"It's a direct challenge to your national sovereignty, without question."

The enormity of the undertaking impressed her. She touched Chuikov lightly on the arm. "Would you give me asylum? I may need it," she said.

"There were times in the nineties I thought about asking you the same question," the General replied.

"Do you have information on their strategy?"

"Very little. Supposedly, they're sending several officials to apply pressure on key people. Unfortunately, we do not know whom they consider important in this instance."

"They're already here, I assume," Sophia said thoughtfully.

"Probably. Would it help if we found out who was sent?"

"Very much. I would be eternally in your debt."

Chuikov smiled. "We're already working on it. If you could supply me with a list of Japanese arrivals over the past week, perhaps we could confirm our information."

Two phone calls later, arrival lists and landing card data were being combined on a CD, and Chuikov left with his request fulfilled.

By nine in the evening, Sophia knew the Japanese had sent a team of six men, all from their Foreign Ministry. Chuikov had been unable to uncover their potential contacts, but Sophia now possessed names, descriptions, pictures, and entry data on the infiltrators. The ball was in her court.

*****

Kantaro Kuribayashi had spent several years in Washington on assignments with the Foreign Ministry and enjoyed visiting the United States. He liked American individualism, music and dancing. He could be free, stupid, and without responsibilities. Of course, everybody was free, stupid, and careless in the US. Americans didn't understand that in a well-ordered society such activities could only be exceptions. He had read of plantation life before the American Civil War, and now whites were singing and dancing to pop, R&B, and rap music like plantation blacks. Little did they realize that all Americans were all plantation blacks economically—and were owned by his countrymen.

This assignment was his most important mission to date. The premier considered Stewart to be Japan's most dangerous opponent and wished to block her confirmation in the Senate. He could not fail.

His party paused in San Francisco only long enough to make connections for their Washington flight. They were joined by two secretaries and began to work on lists of senators to be contacted. None of the flight attendants understood Japanese, so they could work without fear of being compromised. That was another thing; Americans wanted to conduct business with Japan, but wouldn't learn Japanese. It was their mistake, and not one he would have made.

The senators who were approachable were geographically grouped, and almost none were in the midwest and northwest. Yes, he could see Milleron's influence. Everyone in the Japanese government discussed the tremendous economic power of Milleron. In many states they were the dominant competition to Japanese interests, and *zaibatsu* agents had been forced to concentrate in other regions. The appointee for CIA director was heavily invested in Milleron, and senators from its areas were considered relatively immune to Japanese pressure.

Twenty-one states had been crossed off by his superiors, but Kuribayashi knew several senators in those states might oppose Stewart's nomination for reasons of their own. He had a shot at knocking her out by concentrating on east coast and southern states, but the count was close. It would have been easier in the House. Representatives were tied to economic factors in their home districts, and substantially more than half depended on Japanese industries and investment for their constituents' economic well-being.

*****

BJ Carter had become accustomed to fronting for several *zaibatsu* in American politics. The public had become sensitive to direct Japanese government pressure and Japanese lobbies, but BJ had prospered enormously through his association with Japanese interests.

Lately, his primary business contact had been a banker named Takijiro Saito, a grizzled little guy three-quarters his height and half his weight. This meeting was unusual; Saito had brought four individuals with him and omitted his usual aide. One was introduced as Mr. Kuribayashi, with some Japanese government position BJ didn't understand. But his meaning was clear from his words despite the heavy Japanese accent.

"Mister Carter," Kuribayashi said slowly. "We have been most pleased with our association over the years. You are America's most respected businessman—a man to whom all Americans listen. Your enemies are our enemies, and enemies of all those who wish for world peace and a stable, growing economy."

BJ smiled. "I was under the impression that I had purchased all my enemies."

"There is one in particular to whom we draw your attention: Ms. Sophia Stewart, who is seeking Senate confirmation for director of CIA. It is our information that she opposes you whenever possible."

BJ knew that was only partially true. It was more accurate to say that Sophia opposed Japan consistently, but even then, she did it subtly. He decided to see if Kuribayashi would commit himself. "I try to stay aloof from politics. Do you wish me to use my influence and attempt to block her confirmation?"

The contingent squirmed and chatted rapidly in Japanese. Saito spoke up in English. "It is not our place to interfere in domestic issues," he said.

BJ practically laughed out loud. Hell, Japan had been interfering since the mid-seventies. He damn well knew they contributed heavily to congressional and presidential races through super PACs.

"I would rather see her fully occupied as director than free to operate against me," BJ said. In spite of his interests, he didn't like a Japanese official telling him how to manipulate the American government. "Just how important is blocking her appointment?"

Again, there was more swift conversation in Japanese. This time Kuribayashi spoke. "Perhaps we can lower interest rates on a number of your outstanding loans." He nodded to Saito.

"Your towers in Chicago, Cleveland, and Detroit. We'll reduce rates to below prime," Saito said carefully.

"I need SBA's bottom rate," BJ countered. Dropping interest rates was a slick way of payment—no one could prove he was paid off, yet it amounted to a lot of money.

Saito nodded.

"You'll do everything in your power to keep her from being confirmed?" Kuribayashi pressed.

"Yes, but I'll need a war chest. Can I draw upon your bank for necessary expenses?" he asked Saito.

The elderly Japanese financier nodded. BJ suddenly became aware the other three Japanese had not spoken to him, and Saito had not introduced them by position or affiliation. Saito quickly rose to leave, stating that he would furnish the necessary financial papers that same afternoon. BJ decided he had left a substantial sum on the table. He wished he knew Japanese, but smiled at his forethought.

As soon as the delegation departed, BJ flicked off his recorder. He re-ran the tape, erasing portions where his name was spoken, and stashed it in his briefcase.

*****

"I know I haven't always treated you as well as I should have, but this time, I'm coming on bended knee," BJ said.

Claire shook her head. Only BJ constructed sentences with four

392

'I's. "That's okay," she said. "We can work on a quid pro quo basis." She watched BJ's body language. He had gained some weight, but still smiled with more teeth than a shark. *Good analogy*, she thought.

"As you know, Sophia Stewart has been selected for CIA director. She's not my pick, and I'm looking for information that would support my contention that she's not a good choice." BJ spoke easily as if ordering lunch. "You know her well and discovered her financing came from Arabs."

"No, I didn't," Claire quickly interjected. "All I said was that she received substantial sums from Europe. You decided that meant Arabs."

"Well, anyway, it was good work. So tell me, what do you know?"

"I don't see King frequently anymore, and haven't focused on Sophia for eons. Can you give me a reason why I should?"

"What do you want? What do you need?"

"I'm not positive I need anything," Claire answered. She got up and walked over to a window and looked out. "Time, maybe. Youth. But things? No." She wanted to reply *a husband, two kids, and a house in the suburbs*, but wasn't sure that was true. "Besides, that wasn't what I meant. Why don't you think she's right for the job?"

"It's not me; it's people who assist with my financing." BJ stood up, and joined her at the window. "Personally, I'd rather support her, but I need to make certain compromises for business reasons."

BJ put his hand on Claire's arm. "By the way," he said casually, "do you know anyone who speaks Japanese?"

Claire turned to face him. "Yeah. I do know one girl. Why?" She didn't bother to say the girl she knew was Sophia.

"I taped a Japanese conference that I'd like translated."

"I'll get you a transcript made if you'd like. Strictly confidential, of course, with everyone sworn to secrecy."

BJ took out his wallet and placed a thousand dollars on Claire's desk. "This is for your translator, but she must sign a confidentiality agreement to receive it. You can make up a simple statement that if she says anything, she automatically incurs an obligation to pay you a million dollars." He retrieved the cassette from his briefcase. "Don't let her know my name."

Claire took the tape and money. "I'm sure there'll be no

problem. Let me check on my contacts tonight, and we'll see what drops out."

*****

Claire critically evaluated the Langley facility and was not impressed. Over fifty years old, the central building showed its age, looking like all the generic government offices in D.C., all tired, depressingly stolid and incompetent, heavy and slow-moving. Just like the people inside. Even security seemed no tighter, at least until she stated her business. No longer the fearsome Agency of earlier, cutbacks resulting from communism's lessened threat had mellowed Agency operations—at least those publicly known.

Sophia had invited her, and a regiment of ninjas couldn't have kept her away. Most amazing was the coincidental timing. Sophia called the studio a few minutes after BJ's departure, almost as if she had waited for Claire to finish her conversation. In effect, Claire drove directly to Langley after discussing Sophia with BJ.

She was not impressed with Sophia's surroundings. Her office was large, but smaller than King's at Colorado Banking Centers. It was typical executive GSA fare, made hospitable only by Sophia's personal touch and a number of exquisite plants. Her paintings were mostly western American art, and one was certainly a Remington. Claire looked at two others which bore the signature of Lester Hughes, an artist unknown to her. They were western landscapes with tiny figures, emphasizing the loneliness and insignificance of man in nature.

The obligatory family photographs were missing. No guy would be without such evidence of headmastership. Wives assumed pictures would inhibit office sex trysts, but men used the beautifully retouched photos of wife and family as bona fides of their sexual prowess. But Sophia didn't even exhibit photos of her sons, and the lack of domestic kitsch made her office seem imposing. It established Sophia as a powerful person unencumbered by claptrap and sentiment.

"You must wonder why I invited you," Sophia said. "We haven't always worked the same side of the street. Personally, I'd like to put that all behind us and be friends." She sat down with Claire around a coffee table.

"I'd like that." Claire replied. "We got off on the wrong foot and never overcame our difficulties." She leaned forward and extended her hand. "Peace?"

"Peace," Sophia echoed. She stood up and hugged Claire to seal their compact. "I suspect we know more about each other than advertised. I've followed your career closely for years."

Claire smiled. "It hasn't been much of a career for some time. It stalled after I came to Washington."

Sophia sat back down, and Claire pulled her chair up closer. "What do you know of my connection with Milleron?" Sophia said.

Claire decided to run for the roses. "I understand you're the primary owner, maybe even sole owner."

Sophia nodded. "Primary. Top secret, of course, and there probably aren't two dozen people in the world who know that. Your investigative skills are impressive."

"Can you tell me how much you're worth?"

"Honestly, I can't. Many billions, maybe trillions, but we've never bothered to make a complete accounting." Sophia paused to allow Claire to digest her words. "Though this isn't why I requested this meeting, I want to let you know that you're slated to replace the network's news chief when he retires next month."

"Terrific!" Claire jumped up from her chair. "I didn't think I was in the running."

"You were a long shot, but I wanted you."

"Because I'm a woman?"

"No, because you're a westerner, and unimpressed by eastern elitism. You have the ability to survive anywhere, but deep down, you're like Chet Huntley—bedrock." Sophia could see Claire beaming as she sat back down. "You've been able to fend off the trendy pap which permeates TV, while guys like Chancellor, Wallace, Koppel, and Barbara Walters never even tried. Even Cronkite. They fell victim to believing their own garbage, simplified and condensed for public consumption. You dutifully recorded it, but didn't believe it yourself."

Claire nodded. "Yep, and it's been hard. Many times I've wanted to bag it, return to Colorado, and raise a family." She was close to tears. "And now it's too late. I even asked King to marry me, but he didn't take me seriously."

"Don't be too hard on him; he really did—does—love you," Sophia said.

"He had a funny way of showing it," she replied.

"He bought the network for you—selling his soul in the process. He knew it cost too much, but he wanted it for you at any price. King could have gone to jail. If Ed hadn't stepped in, King would have lost everything."

Sophia waited until Claire stopped shaking her head. She hadn't understood the depth of King's love. "Don't you remember how upset King became when you had your abortion?"

"You knew about that?"

"Yes, Suzanne told me. She had been campaigning for King to marry you, but her dad said you avoided commitments and mentioned the abortion to prove it."

"Well, it's too late now," she repeated.

"Maybe for kids, but not for you and King to ride off into the sunset. Age is strictly a matter of attitude."

"Easy for you to say," Claire said. "You're in the prime of your sexuality and a long way from menopause."

"Maybe I don't have standing to speak, but you have to imagine my difficulties with men. My prime is being wasted. My best friend tells me she was getting it three times a day at my age."

"I think different things become important at different times in your life. I used sex like some people used booze—to remove myself from reality. I guess I didn't like what I was doing and took to sex instead of drugs." Claire leaned back and closed her eyes. "I dominated men through sex, being in command, controlling, and exercising power through my body."

"Now you're powerful because of your professionalism and maturity. Different, and probably better. Certainly longer lasting."

"Not too professional. I've made a career of investigating your background and still don't understand it. You can't be normal."

"I'm not," Sophia said solemnly. "Will you promise that whatever I tell you is completely off the record and only between us?"

"Absolutely." Claire shifted closer.

Sophia told her of Cameron's dissertation and Millie's work on K11. She related its effects, explaining her own abilities and those of her sons.

"You were very close to guessing the truth about me, but you can see why nothing added up. You had to believe in the improbable."

"With that, we need to bury the hatchet. I can see where all this is going, and want to be a part of it. Can you count me in?"

Sophia stood up. "You're already in."

Claire looked up into Sophia's eyes. "Well, let me pay my entrance fee. BJ showed up and wanted me to help him acquire information against you. It's his Japanese connection. They don't want you confirmed as director."

Claire reached into her purse and handed Sophia BJ's tape. "I'm not sure what it is, but BJ wants a transcript of the Japanese portion," she said. "Why don't you play it?"

Sophia snapped it into the recorder on her bookcase, and relaxed to listen. BJ's conversation with the Japanese delegation stunned her. The tape was a smoking gun.

Sophia called Cole to have a copy made, and a secretary to bring in a special file. A thick folder arrived a moment later, and Sophia glanced at its contents before passing it to Claire. "This will probably be the biggest scoop of your life," she said. "It's our investigation of Olson's death. You remember him, don't you?"

"General Olson, commander of NATO who died of a heart attack in some geisha house?"

"The very same, only his death was not accidental. These documents indicate Japan was responsible. They also detail the cover-up and Japanese attack on everyone connected with the trip. Two professors from Maryland, for instance, were fired from the university for alleged moral turpitude. All they did was accompany Olson to the geisha house."

Claire read the papers rapidly. "Can I use these on the air?"

"How about in a day or two? With Japanese mounting an assault on me, perhaps we can orchestrate the timing to my best advantage. You can't say I gave you those documents, however."

"I won't need to. They speak for themselves. And I'll get corroborating testimony. There'll be a cry for sanctions against Japan until this matter is cleared up."

"Sounds good to me," Sophia said. "Interested in what BJ's Japanese were saying?"

"Sure."

"They were discussing how cheaply they could buy him. Even used his name, although he didn't recognize it well enough to erase. They were prepared to make more concessions to secure his cooperation. The big dealer sold himself short. One mentioned asking BJ how much he thought each senator would want for his vote, and Kuribayashi answered that BJ would determine each senator's amount as they went along. All very unflattering."

Without a doubt, Claire had finally found her calling. She'd be Sophia's media spokesperson.

*****

"Well, Harvey, what do you think?" Sophia asked, watching Sjoberg review her reports. She included the information from Chuikov in spite of her own directives to maintain strict compartmentalization between positive intelligence gathering operations and counter-intelligence.

He couldn't refrain from commenting. "I'm surprised to find our relationship with Moscow is this good. It's difficult for me to evaluate without understanding how this information could be supplied and its authenticity automatically accepted."

"You can accept it, Harv," Sophia nodded. "We haven't advertised our increasing cooperation with Russia, but as you can see, it's reached a high degree of confidence."

"So that's why Webb reduced our counter-intelligence operations," Harvey said without malice. "I thought it was budgetary. Now you're telling me they curtailed operations against us, so they weren't there to find."

"Exactly. Webb didn't want to spread the knowledge of our rapprochement and lessen our apparent need for counter-intelligence." She touched Harvey on the arm. "Had this occasion not arisen, I would have told you before you retired. The world might never appreciate our efforts, but you deserved to know how successful you have been."

Sophia's words had brought him in from the cold. It was too bad others in his department didn't know, but he couldn't tell them.

"Jurisdiction belongs to the FBI, but their operation concerns only us," she said.

Harvey's mind was racing a mile a minute. "Well, not really. This is a conspiracy to bribe public officials. Carter has not registered as a foreign agent, and if they spread false information about you, we'll have them for espionage under laws covering dissemination of disinformation. This is serious business outside of the obvious aspect of a foreign power attempting to directly interfere with our national government."

"It's not against the law for a foreign power to lobby," Sophia reminded him. "I remember when Japan crossed the half billion mark in lobbying federal agencies in 1992."

"True, but this isn't lobbying. Not according to this transcript of the Carter/Kuribayashi meeting. We'll have to bring in the Bureau."

"That will take too long. How about nipping it in the bud ourselves?"

"Well, they've already started approaching senators. We could kill them and make it look like an accident."

"All six? Some accident." Sophia thought for a moment. "Nah, too improbable."

Harvey was impressed Sophia possessed sufficient mental toughness to consider the possibility. "How about just their leader, Kuribayashi?"

"No. Japanese are interchangeable parts. They wouldn't even miss him. Besides, togetherness is their thing. They never do anything alone. They work, travel, and play in packs like dogs. Sometimes I think their minds are connected."

"Perhaps the best attack is through TV. When are you scheduled to testify?"

"Next Thursday morning."

"Then we break a story on Monday naming the Japanese and describing their mission. That will send senators they've contacted running for cover and raise a storm of protest. Then on Wednesday, you release the transcript. Chances are it will come on the heels of a Japanese denial on Tuesday and ruin their credibility and wreck Carter. The Bureau can come in and take over then."

*****

The next day, Claire broke the Olson story. Its immediate impact was a Japanese denial and a general public cry of outrage against the

Japanese and their perfidy. There was no indication the timing had anything to do with Sophia's appointment.

Claire Villars was in seventh heaven. BJ called immediately after the broadcast and came unglued.

"I don't understand why you're so upset, lover," she cooed. "Olson has nothing to do with Sophia Stewart. Most of his entourage believed the Japanese induced his heart attack since the circumstances were very suspicious. Particularly when you consider his geisha girl disappeared shortly afterward."

"Well, you put me in a hellava fix!" he shouted into the phone.

"Why? Partners giving you trouble?" she asked sweetly.

"It's not them; it's our senators. Jesus Christ, I just got through convincing Haller to vote my way when your story hit. You know what he said? 'What happens if I change my mind, BJ? Do I get a heart attack?' What am I to say?"

"Say it was a dozen years ago. Say Japan's government was different then. Say whatever you need to. But I'm a journalist, and this Olson thing was a great story." Claire was having fun.

"Well, I expect to see a follow-up tomorrow absolving the Japanese government from any complicity in Olson's death."

"I'll report what they reply. I'm not going to fabricate anything."

Claire dialed Sophia to say Senator Haller from Georgia had been approached by BJ and agreed to oppose her confirmation. After all, information dissemination was Claire's business.

*****

Monday afternoon, Columbo announced the presence of Japan's task force and its mission. He decried its challenge to national sovereignty and ended his press conference in a scene of total bedlam. Claire headlined the story and provided massive supporting details. Sophia had provided names, photographs, and personal data of the six Japanese agents, video tapes of them entering and leaving Senate office buildings, and information on their arrival, hotel, and mission. She could relax and let public indignation run wild for a day.

Chapter 41

Before the extended family meeting, Sophia met with her seven sons. It was time for them to breed and stock a sperm bank for the future.

"I want each of you to donate every day to the bank," she said. "Heather has made all the arrangements, and she'll give you instructions. But, in addition, I want you to start developing relationships with potential partners, girls who have distinguished parents who were relatively old when they were conceived. Heather will tell you what we want when checking their health and suitability. The object is to have you breed with as many appropriate girls as possible, and then treat them with K11 for the future. Obviously, all the participants in this program will be compensated and become family members. So select carefully, because they will ultimately know the Stewart secret.

Soon everyone was present. Sophia led the boys into the living room and took her place in the large high-backed chair in front of the fireplace. She reviewed the current situation.

"Hopefully, we'll have another two years with me in the Agency, but my confirmation is iffy. We have two rabbits yet to pull out of the hat—BJ Carter's involvement fronting for Japan and my testimony—but our count is pretty close."

"There's a big uproar going on about Japan attempting to influence your confirmation," Dave Columbo remarked. "Don't you expect some senators to switch after hearing BJ's transcript?"

"Some, but not many," Sophia responded. "For example, we know BJ contacted Senator Haller and he's solid against me. The Japanese own Georgia Power and Light, Georgia's two biggest supermarket chains, the four largest convenience store chains, most of Atlanta's business real estate, Atlanta banks, and companies providing approximately seventy percent of Georgia's manufacturing employment. Japanese control his state's economy, and if he goes against them, the penalties could be awesome."

"Georgia's a disaster area anyway," Ed commented. "It's one big Japanese plantation."

"How important is your confirmation?" Heather asked. "Can't you continue almost as well in your number two position?"

"It depends on who becomes director. I could be shunted aside where I'd be powerless. He might treat me as a competitor and remove me to establish control."

"So it's all or nothing," Heather asserted.

"Pretty much. But even if I am confirmed, we shouldn't expect me to continue for more than a year or two."

"That close, huh?" Carol inquired.

"Our trade balance with Japan was a negative seventy-five billion dollars last year. All re-invested in American assets, and, of course, that doesn't include profits by Japanese companies operating in the US. Our estimate of domestic Japanese profits are almost a trillion and EU company profits in the US are about the same. There isn't much remaining for Japan or the EU to purchase with their American dollars except real estate, and that will cause inflation. Plus, there's the whole problem inherent in our credit-based economy. Everything runs on faith instead of cash. We have maybe twenty-five billion in cash, yet do ten trillion in business transactions."

"How about the problem of bail-ins for banks?" Gordon said. "Bank accounts are actually unsecured loans to the bank where a person's money is deposited. The banks can convert that to something like preferred stock at any time, leaving the depositor with nothing. That's what Cyprus did, and people couldn't get their money our fast enough to survive. Three of our biggest banks already have bail-in schemes put together for the next bursting bubble. There's no way our government can survive when that occurs."

"What difference does the next presidential election make?" Bobbi asked.

"Probably none," Columbo answered. "We simply can't meet our debt and entitlement obligations. No politician can eliminate social security, Medicare, Medicaid, ADC, welfare payments, veteran benefits, and all those things for the economy to recover. We need to repudiate our national debt for openers, and that can't be done without destroying the government."

"So now what?" Gordon piped up.

"So now we move to Iowa. The family compound at Monroe is ready, and our control complex south of Des Moines should be ready next year. Webb will be coordinating moves."

"I haven't been there," Harold Columbo said. "What's the compound like?"

"It's nice," Heather answered. "A little city in miniature with all stores combined into a single service facility. There are all sorts of living facilities, and each of you can have your own house. Carol and I will be in charge, so you need to take a look and let us know what you want. It's militarily secured and all buildings have bunkered basements."

"Another bit of news," Sophia announced. "Vanessa brought up K11 for newborns in the family. I've decided to make it available on request."

She turned to other younger family members: Billy Rutledge was still unmarried, and the Columbos, Harold, Vanessa, Aimee, John, and Tom, were all two years apart, starting with Harold at thirty-six. Only Vanessa had married and was now having her first child.

"You kids haven't exactly been prolific. I don't mean to sound crude, but it's time you started procreating. We need to get the next generation underway." Sophia looked at Aimee. "We're a little short on females, Aimee, we need you badly."

"I've been so busy planning our new government, I don't even have a boyfriend."

A waste, Sophia thought, thinking like her father. Aimee was small, dark haired, and very attractive. "Take time and get one," Sophia said with a chuckle. "There must be thousands of guys willing to help you get pregnant."

"Twenty-one against the world," Bobbi remarked after counting those present. "Incredible."

"With a lot of help. And not only here in the States. We have many friends."

"What's our chance of surviving this?" Aimee asked.

"What's the difference?" Wallace argued mildly. "Whether you live a long or short life, the point is to live fully and meaningfully while you're alive."

"But you've already lived a lot. And known love, excitement, and accomplishment. I haven't."

"That's what we're saying—live. Find love, create life. Don't you believe this is the most exciting opportunity in history?"

"Yeah, but it's not here yet."

"But we'll get there, and live or die, it'll be exciting. Don't worry now about surviving—worry about living."

Sophia was glad Wallace had fielded Aimee's question. She would have answered, "Fifty-fifty."

*****

The list looked promising after Cindy finished. Adding seven older ones from Heather's time and four gays who were still in the closet, they had a shot at over half the Senate. And several of the gays were on Sophia's list as probable opponents.

Their enemy was time—only two days remained before Sophia's testimony and then a few more before the vote. Aimee Columbo called each senator on the list for a statement of his current position. Sophia was right, over forty were leaning against her. Sophia decided to take sure things first and work on them.

Each senator was special, but their method of approach was identical. Wallace had gathered a group of eleven men, all of Japanese ancestry, and the key point was timing. They would give target senators an offer they couldn't refuse.

On Tuesday morning, the Japanese government issued an official statement stating there was no such task force in existence as alleged by Senator Columbo. The six individuals in question were involved in trade discussions in Washington and New York that had already been concluded. They were returning to Japan on Tuesday evening.

Heather asked Sophia to tell her when the Japanese departed. Trusting her instincts, Sophia didn't ask why. Both from herself and her father, she knew Heather too well. Kuribayashi and his men flew out from Dulles at four o'clock, and Heather put her plan into action bright and early the following morning.

By noon, all affected senators had been contacted in person by Wallace's men. Each senator was told that due to new revelations which would be forthcoming shortly, the Japanese government was withdrawing its opposition to Stewart's nomination. Moreover, it was now in favor of her confirmation. In those cases where the senator did not immediately agree, Wallace's man presented him with an envelope containing a note from Cindy. The senator was asked to read it carefully and reconsider his position in the interest of Japanese—American harmony.

It was a nice touch. Japan was guilty twice. They had attempted to influence the senator's vote against Sophia, and secondly, when their actions were uncovered, they wished his vote reversed. Moreover, the merest hint of public disclosure of Cindy's information should cause some senators to collapse like a house of cards.

Claire was only mildly curious when her story of the tape transcript was approved without changes by Billy Rutledge, the network news editor responsible for clearing news items. He had been almost automatically approving her broadcasts over the past week, practically without alteration. He was fairly young for that position, maybe a year younger than Sophia. He even reminded her of Sophia some times. Claire made a startling announcement that went out as a news flash that jammed the switchboard:

"We have just been furnished with a tape recording of a secret meeting between officials of the Japanese government and an American businessman in which Japanese representatives agreed to pay the American to bribe United States senators to vote against confirmation of Ms. Sophia Stewart as director of the Central Intelligence Agency. The evidence names names, and Japanese officials are heard discussing amounts of bribes to be offered. We will be presenting the tape in its entirety on a special *Nightly News*, complete with a translation of the spoken Japanese at five. Please stay tuned for further developments."

Claire expected she would hear from BJ within the hour, but he didn't call. It was his bad luck if he had been too busy to hear the announcement. No one in his organization would know to warn him, and the senators would be distancing themselves from BJ if they were smart.

The special broadcast went off without a hitch, all other networks, affiliates, and press representatives being given tapes and transcripts. The tape gaps only served to make it seem more authentic when Claire explained the tape had been kept by the American to gain leverage on his Japanese contacts. He had erased his name, but not understanding Japanese, had not recognized it when spoken in Japanese.

An abbreviated version was used in the regular broadcast opposite the Japanese government's official statement that they were not engaged in such activities. The Japanese prime minister could allege the tape was phony, but BJ's voice was recognizable, and Kuribayashi's and Saito's names were clearly audible. And Sophia's appearance before the committee was in the morning.

The story played over and over on cable and local news shows. It was a hot topic on radio talk shows and discussed by a large number of commentators and local editorial anchors. Nobody was able to reach BJ for comment, and his non-availability made the situation worse.

Claire expected BJ to come down on her like the wrath of God, but she heard nothing. Suzanne's home line was busy, and with a legion of reporters after him, BJ had apparently ducked for cover. Claire called Sophia.

"Sorry to bother you," Claire asked breathlessly, "But do you have a line on BJ?"

"He was here in Washington early this morning, but I understand he returned to New York before noon."

"No one's heard from him. Not even the network's legal department."

"I'm not surprised," Sophia said. "The tape is prima facie evidence of a felony and exposes him as a front man for Japan."

Meanwhile there was Sophia's testimony to worry about.

It would be a week before BJ's whereabouts became known. He was found already partially decomposed in his Florida boat house, a nine millimeter slug in his brain. The police speculated he intended to take his large cruiser to some Caribbean island. Over five million dollars in cash was found in the boat, and police were unable to get the luxury cruiser to start. His death was ruled a suicide.

*****

In spite of her long experience in Washington, Sophia was still uncomfortable under TV lights. The Senate hearing room was bathed in light, and Sophia wished she could wear sunglasses in the room. It was a side effect of K11—heightened sensitivity, this time to light.

She wore one of her patented white dresses with a light print like she usually wore on her overseas jaunts. Contrasting with her shoulder-length auburn hair, the dress made her look like a virginal and highly sympathetic woman. Instead of looking like a businesswoman or dragon lady, she looked like everybody's sister, mother, or daughter. She would be difficult to attack. Still sporting her mother's slender figure, she heightened male interest without being considered seductive.

The seven boys were lined up behind her in full view. Sophia clearly stood for motherhood, apple pie, and the flag. Heather was next to Gordon, and Webb sat next to Heather.

The Committee chairman opened with general questions, repeating those in her earlier Democratic Party caucus interview. Senator Morris assumed a cross between a fatherly and brotherly approach. He played up Sophia's long experience at the Agency and her extensive contacts with foreign governments. Then he pulled a surprise.

"Ms. Stewart," he said in his gravelly voice, "I've contacted a number of foreign heads of state and discussed your appointment, and I must say, their comments were astounding." He looked at other committee members. "I probably can be criticized for asking foreigners what they think of you, particularly in light of revelations this week, but I wanted to see how you played in Peoriastadt and Peoriabad." There were a few chuckles. "I must say, respect for you is universal and unbounded."

Sophia spoke into her microphone. "It's a shame they're not voting on my confirmation."

The laughter was general among spectators, but the senators mostly smiled. "If I would not be too out of line," commented Morris. He proceeded to read several comments from South America, Russia, China, and the Middle East. Very pointedly, Chairman Morris omitted Japan.

"You appear to be as popular throughout the world as McDonald's. How do you explain this? Normally individuals in intelligence organizations aren't popular even in their own countries. Specifically, I'm thinking of the KGB or now the SVR."

"Senator, there's a world of difference between the CIA and SVR," Sophia said.

"Glad to hear it."

The room erupted with more laughter.

"Much of my foreign popularity comes from speaking their language. I cannot emphasize too strongly the necessity in an organization such as ours for thorough competence in the indigenous language. I can communicate with over eighty percent of the world's population in their native tongue."

"Being able to speak a language does not insure popularity," Senator Morris said. "I speak English, but am not always popular even with my constituents."

Sophia chuckled. "Yes sir, sometimes we must say what others prefer not to hear. If I may be permitted to raise an issue which seems uppermost in many minds, perhaps there is a significant advantage in my being a woman. For many people, both here and abroad, the CIA is a very threatening organization. In contrast, I personally am not considered menacing and tend to create a benign and friendly organizational image. Sometimes, that quality is very useful."

Senator Krajacich interrupted the chairman for a follow-up question, and Morris yielded.

"Judging from recent events, Japan does not consider you totally non-threatening. Can you enlighten us as to why the Japanese might wish to oppose your confirmation?"

"Senator, your question would be best directed to the Japanese government. I can only say I understand they have now officially restated their policy of non-interference in our domestic matters and have moved to correct any impressions so unfortunately made by certain Japanese officials this week. I speak Japanese and am well familiar with their customs, history, religion, businesses, and government."

"Are you saying they're supporting you now?"

"It is not appropriate for any foreign government to support or oppose the appointment of an individual in my capacity. The Japanese government has officially issued a statement to that effect. Without any contrary evidence, we must accept their statement at face value."

"Didn't the tape recording that was made public last night constitute such contrary evidence?"

"I have carefully reviewed the tape and transcript. It does not conclusively prove the Japanese government was directly involved. That governmental officials were involved has never been denied. Much like a GS-9 in Agriculture could be trafficking in drugs without implicating the United States government, the group could have been acting without official approval."

"Were you aware of their presence and activities?"

"Senator, you are touching on national security matters which I can only discuss in a closed session. The FBI has jurisdiction over such activities domestically and there may be charges pending. I understand the Japanese nationals were all members of their Foreign Ministry, and the Department of State may be involved. I am simply not at liberty to discuss the matter at this time."

Krajacich allowed the issue to drop for the time being, and returned control to Morris. Most majority members contented themselves to posturing and stating their belief in a system which would give them the opportunity to confirm a woman for such a critical post. Sophia easily handled personal and professional probes until passed to the majority counsel.

"You have consistently opposed foreign aid unless specifically associated with some intelligence initiative since the election of President Bush in 1988. Your opposition of humanitarian aid would seem to be callous and not at all in keeping with your benign image. Would you address that, please?"

"Funds spent within the scope of intelligence operations were expended in pursuit of specific national policy objectives. Operating in a deficit, and maintained by Japanese financing, all foreign aid money was borrowed from Japan at various rates of interest and given to other foreign recipients. We borrowed money we didn't have to give to someone else. For us it was charity; for Japan it was good business. Let those who can afford it give their money away. We couldn't afford it. To this day, we have been unable to repay money borrowed from Japan that we gave to Poland in 1989. In fact, we are now borrowing from Japan to pay interest on that money, giving up all hope of repaying the principal."

Even minority members were friendly with their questions in

spite of occasional probing inquiries to look good on television. Then came Senator Fehrenfels.

"Ms Stewart, I understand you moved to Washington in 1985. Would you please state the composition of your household since then?"

"Certainly," Sophia replied. "I moved in with my friend, Heather Ewing, in Silver Spring, then following my marriage and first two children, we moved to my present home in Potomac. Since then, I have added five more children and lost my husband. We've also had a maid constantly since moving to Potomac."

"Your husband never actually lived with you for any appreciable time, correct?"

"Yes, that's correct. He was in operations and gone for long periods."

"This Heather Ewing. She was your father's mistress, was she not?"

"She and my father had been good friends. When I was a baby, she cared for me after my mother died. My father never saw her again after leaving for Colorado when I was one. After my father died and I returned to Washington, we re-established a relationship. In many ways, she has been a mother to me."

Fehrenfels appeared disinterested in her answer. He took a stack of papers from his assistant behind him, and passed them to Senator Morris. "Mister Chairman, I have here a brief report concerning the character and activities of one Heather Ewing. I wish to submit it for the committee's consideration." Morris nodded and announced its admission. Copies were handed out to the committee members.

"Now, I wish to delve further into your activities with this alleged lady," Fehrenfels growled.

"Excuse me Senator, but may I see the document you have submitted and are using for questioning?" Sophia demanded.

Fehrenfels handed a copy to an aide who brought it to Sophia. There was a pause while everyone scanned the document which discussed Heather's activities in Washington as a hostess and party girl. It was a scurrilous compendium of gossip making Heather as a soft hooker peddling sex for power and implicating Sophia by association.

Sophia motioned to Adam and Harold Columbo to join her at the witness table. The room was silent while the three whispered. Harold sat down next to Sophia, while Adam resumed his seat.

"Excuse me Senator," she said loudly, "but before we go any further, I must tell you this document greatly injures a private individual, my godmother, Heather Ewing, who has never held any government position, never done business with the government, never accepted any government benefits, and is protected by her rights to privacy. This document is a collection of half-truths and outright lies, organized to destroy the reputation of a fine and gentle person, a private citizen of the United States. She has few financial resources with which to press a libel and slander suit, but I do. Any and all publication of this document, in whole or in part, or any disclosure of its contents outside this committee, whether in writing or verbally, shall be considered by me as malicious and due cause to bring a libel or slander action or both on behalf of Ms Ewing against the offending party or parties."

Sophia continued in a threatening tone. "For the purposes of counsel with respect to this document and the libelous statements contained within, I have retained Mister Harold Columbo as counsel for Ms Ewing and myself. He has recommended we recover all copies of this document and meet in closed session concerning its contents to avoid litigation that certainly would be ruinous to the document's perpetrators."

"An excellent suggestion," Chairman Morris boomed. "So ordered. The Sergeant-at-arms will pick up Senator Fehrenfels's document from everyone, and the room will be cleared."

It had been close. The media would wait for results from the closed session before making contents of Fehrenfels's paper public. Any pre-publication would be considered as de facto with malice, and incurring treble damage risks was potentially prohibitively costly.

The issue over Heather spilled immediately into the hallway as Webb and Heather emerged. Reporters crushed them against the wall until Webb established order by his commanding presence. He moved them away to form a rough circle and conducted an impromptu press conference.

Heather briefly described her relationship with Sophia and her sons. The reporters hardly waited for explanations—they were too intent on asking questions.

"How did you become acquainted with Ms. Stewart?" a youngish female TV reporter asked Heather.

"I dated her father before he met Sophia's mother, and, after her mother died, he and I became friends. I never saw him again after he left Washington. I have always felt very close to Sophia and was there for her when she returned to Washington. So, I am a family friend."

"But you were a beauty queen?"

There it was—information from Fehrenfels's report. Not all copies had been picked up, or the reporter had heard it somewhere else.

"Yes, I was once runner-up for Miss District of Columbia."

"When was that?"

"Nearly fifty years ago. If you'd like, I can give you a number of references who would be glad to discuss my reputation." Heather didn't wait. She knew they were dying for names. She quickly rattled off four names of people they could contact. Including a Supreme Court justice. "And Webb Reid, here, the ex-director of the CIA."

Webb moved forward to take charge. "Any time. I have known Ms. Ewing since 1970 and hold her in the highest respect."

Heather had done well, but Webb decided not to take chances. He cut the interview short, and reiterated that any publication of anything in the Fehrenfels's report would bring an immediate suit for libel.

In the closed session, Sophia attacked the document directly.

"Mr. Chairman," she said, "I know some statements contained in this document to be absolutely false, and their public dissemination would damage her reputation. This document is libelous beyond belief, and I must ask it to be withdrawn and destroyed."

"Mister Chairman," Fehrenfels emoted, "this document shows the nominee has a life-long association with a lady—and I use that term loosely—who acted as a courtesan to numerous individuals in government throughout the years. I doubt very much her reputation could be lowered in the least. And evidence indicates that, while the nominee's husband was gone and risking his life in defense of his country, these women were sporting with various men throughout Washington."

"Mister Chairman," Sophia said evenly and authoritatively.

"That charge is outrageous and slanderous. Ms. Ewing took care of my boys during my many absences on government business, and they could not have wished for a better godmother or nanny. To make such unfounded and slanderous statements is unbecoming to a gentleman and the dignity of a United States senator. If my performance has benefited the United States in any way, the country stands in Ms. Ewing's debt. I would ask the senator from New York be censured for his remarks and his production of this libelous document."

Sophia could see Fehrenfels wilting under her attack. Now was not the time to stop. She kept her voice stern but controlled. "I could not have performed my duties and raised my large family without her." She stared intently at Fehrenfels. "Who is the author of this ill-conceived set of lies? Who is this braying jackal, this pornographic purveyor of Satanic fabrications, this fraudulent panderer able to deceive a United States senator into publicizing his libelous perversions?"

"I am not at liberty to reveal the author's name—" Fehrenfels began.

"Then you do not claim authorship or responsibility for its falsehoods?" Sophia interrupted.

"My staff is responsible for verification."

"And you are responsible for your staff. Mister Chairman," she said, "let me give you an example of the lies in this document to show why it should be suppressed. It says Heather lived with her sister and a black pimp for a number of years, both girls soliciting for him. In actuality, Heather's sister lived with a black man, sharing a house in Beltsville with Heather for a short time during the sixties. It was a two-bedroom house, and Heather's sister and boyfriend occupied one bedroom. During that time, all three were gainfully employed, Heather as an accountant, her sister, Jeannette, as a cashier, and the fellow as a postal carrier. Jeannette subsequently married Harlan— that was his name—but left due to his abusive treatment. As a matter of public record, Jeannette called Heather to her home after a fight with Harlan, and he attempted to rape her. He was sentenced to prison, returned to DC in 1990, got back into drugs and prostitution, and was executed gangland-style. So yes, he was probably a pimp for a short time before his death. Yes, he lived for a time in Heather's house with her sister, but everything else is sheer libelous fabrication.

413

All of this is easily proven, and both sisters have a cause for action. And I will use my entire fortune to see that they obtain justice."

"Senator?" the chairman glanced at Fehrenfels.

"Well," he replied, looking at the report, "I guess we can eliminate that portion if necessary."

"Senators, the whole thing should be eliminated," Sophia said. "This report reads like it was written by one of Ms. Ewing's rejected suitors with malicious intent. Any judge in the land will see that. I will—I repeat—I *will* find out who wrote it and come after him and everyone involved in its dissemination for their last dime if it sees the light of day. Everyone will lose if that happens—Ms. Ewing, Mrs. Jordan, my boys, everyone connected with this document right down to the girl in your office who made the copies, Senator, and the country loses. It's up to you."

"Senator Fehrenfels," Chairman Morris said, "will you withdraw your document, sir?"

The senator pursed his lips. "In the interests of unity and to avoid involving private citizens, I will withdraw the report. I reserve my right to research the information obtained and resubmit at a later date. If not to this committee, then on the Senate floor." He avoided Sophia's gaze while making his pompous declaration.

Sophia was confirmed in a landslide.

Chapter 42

The move to Iowa was slow and painful, and it took almost an Act of Congress to pry Bobbi out of Thomas Circle. Sophia sold her house in Potomac and moved into Heather's old condo in Silver Spring. The memories there were wonderful, but any move from cherished surroundings was difficult. Even closing down Port Tobacco as Milleron's headquarters was saddening. The facility was still useful as a secure transfer point, but if the east became untenable, it was forfeit.

It was strange living without Heather, but Heather had gone ahead to Monroe to set up housekeeping with the boys. Cindy moved down to Port Tobacco taking Bobbi's place as overall facility manager while Bobbi went west to work between Des Moines and Zionsville, Indiana. After so much togetherness over the past twenty years, life suddenly became terribly lonely.

Cindy also took Heather's place as Sophia's social secretary, dragging her out to Washington winter season galas. Many appearances were command performances, but the political talk was universally depressing. The unemployment numbers were phony to avoid alarming the people, but true unemployment, including discouraged workers and eliminating part-time employees, was nearly twenty-five percent. The Federal Reserve Board chairman held interest rates at nearly zero, but that failed to stimulate the economy.

It was impossible for the nation to meet its obligations. The yearly budget deficit was over a trillion dollars, and most of it was interest on the national debt. Default or run-away inflation—there was no other choice.

It was an election year, and the pack of presidential hopefuls were a discouraging lot to most. Most were simply career politicians, members of the political class, hoping like later Roman emperors to keep things going just a little longer. At least half understood they needed to do whatever Japan, the EU, and China demanded, and none knew how to stop the runaway deficit. Spending was being driven by legal entitlements, and discretionary items were a tiny fraction of the budget.

Even the District was getting anxious. Cutback talk always made beltway bandits start walking halls looking for new contracts. Sophia stepped up her transfer of CIA files to Port Tobacco and, from there, to Iowa. She was waiting quietly for the Iowa bombshell, and mentally preparing for the events to follow.

*****

The country's political establishment reeled from Iowa's caucus votes as political outsiders in the Republican Party garnered a great deal of support. But the stunner was that Sophia came in third in the Democratic caucuses and second in the Republican. Sophia had been asked repeatedly to run for president by operatives in both parties, but she not only demurred, she refrained from identifying herself with either major party. Sophia made a simple statement to answer all entreaties; "I am not a candidate for the presidency of the United States." No one believed her, especially the president.

"Sophia, what in hell is going on?" the president demanded angrily.

"I don't know what to say. I'm not running for your office, have no political or campaign organization, and have not filed in any primary. I am simply not a candidate. Evidently my extensive business connections and large number of friends in Iowa engineered what they thought would be a show of respect and personal support for me after the confirmation fight. You may not know it, but my sons and Ms. Ewing are now living in Iowa."

"I want you to issue a statement that you're not a candidate and are supporting me for re-election. Otherwise, I want your resignation."

"I stated last night that I was not a candidate. That should be sufficient. My position is essentially bi-partisan, and like Bureau chiefs, CIA directors have generally remained apart from partisan politics. I think that's appropriate. I beg you to withdraw your request."

The president rose and stared out the window. Other than Obama's hacks, no past directors actively campaigned in support of their presidents. Webb Reid hadn't. And after the disaster of the Obama presidency, all candidates had pledged to appoint the best available person to every job.

"Okay, but the first time you make what can be considered a campaign speech, you can color yourself gone. I want you to send over an undated resignation within the hour."

It was time.

The Chinese premier contacted her regarding Taiwan, and Sophia indicated she believed there would be no interference if Taiwan were invaded between the political conventions in summer and election in November. She went further and strongly recommended the PRC take action then. In response, China was to lower its exports to the US and release all American companies with facilities in China from having to assign all their patents and proprietary intellectual knowledge to China. In particular, R&D facilities were to be relocated back to the US.

Tom Columbo unleashed Bluepeace demonstrations against all imported goods. The thrust was to save American jobs, and it would soon be difficult for the public to avoid direct confrontations. Sophia could expect incidents destroying Japanese and EU goods to begin immediately.

General Carpenter held the key to proper timing, and he arrived at Sophia's office to outline his personnel status and plans.

"We're as ready as we'll ever be," the general told her. "It's impossible to know what people will do when shots are fired, but letting it go longer only increases our security problems."

"How long will it take to complete the appropriate transfers?" she asked.

"We can't actually put them all into effect regardless of when. There's no way we can transfer all blacks to the southeast and all whites to the midwest. Some are going to be in the wrong place at the wrong time."

"So give me a min-max time. How long before a sufficient number have been transferred, and how long before we reach our probable maximum?"

"Nine weeks to a minimum, five months to a maximum."

"Okay," Sophia said. "Start. I will set certain actions in motion when you declare the minimum has been reached. Why so long, by the way?"

"Except for TDY assignments, we normally give one- to three-months notice before a transfer. And nobody's received even an alert to expect new orders. We'll have to send out those immediately."

"Okay, I'll work with that. But things are going to start popping pretty quickly."

"I thought so, and some transfers have already been made. Otherwise, minimum would be four months."

"What's your best guess? How many will go with us?"

"It won't be too bad," he said. "The vast majority of white troops are secure. Both lower ranks and NCOs. We do worse among white officers—only about two-thirds. The civilian population will be lower. Army personnel are considerably more patriotic than civilians."

"What about the Navy and Air Force?"

"Tough. I don't have a good handle on them, but I'd think we'd be lucky to get a third of the Air Force and a fourth of the Navy. Swabbies are located in bad places, and even if they want to join us, it'll be difficult. You were wise to concentrate on submarines. We'll fly most Air Force pilots and naval aviators out and get them, but not the support troops."

"And Marines?"

"Badly located. We have an exercise ready to go where the 1st Marine Division is dropped into Fort Riley, and we'll do that at the last moment. But the remainder will have to fight their way through."

"Sounds very unpleasant, but we'll all be happier out of the closet."

*****

The write-in vote in New Hampshire increased the president's concern. Sophia received forty-four and thirty-eight percent in the Democratic and Republican parties respectively. As the declared contenders moved on to the South Carolina and Super Tuesday primaries, Sophia expected those percentages to hold or even improve. Other eastern states and the left coast would return the presidential race to stated candidates, but for now, she was a scary outside threat.

In March, Chuck Carpenter called Sophia with the "Go" sign. "We've reached our minimum. Even moved some on TDY in case the shit hits the fan too early. We'll keep going full steam ahead, but I'd appreciate a day or two's notice to get our little circle out of here."

Sophia telephoned Adam in Helena to set events in motion. Montana had been chosen as her lead state to start the collapse. Montana's representative and both senators were Amulots elected through Milleron's support, and the governor and state legislature were anti-foreign and virulently anti-Japanese. The traditional, non-entitlement society was real and attainable to them, and the Eastern Establishment stood for everything evil.

Avery Thomkins, speaker of the Montana state legislature, introduced a bill doubling the sales tax on all items but granting sales tax exemptions and a credit to be applied against state income taxes when the purchased item was an American produced, manufactured, and packaged product. There was also another condition. Regardless of where manufactured, if the parent company ownership was more than forty-nine percent foreign, the product was not considered American.

The bill was probably unconstitutional, but also a red herring. Classically Sun Tsu, it would draw the public's attention, while another law would quietly keep the Japanese from marketing in Montana.

Claire Villars gave the Domestic Goods Credit Bill top play, and the other networks rapidly followed suit. Commentators decried protectionism, and Ivy-League economists lambasted it as a serious threat to the international economic system. Its constitutionality was debated, and east coast lawyers all predicted its rapid defeat.

They were wrong.

Much to the Eastern Establishment's amazement, the law passed nearly unanimously. Claire reported on events in Montana as the single most important news story in the US, The law became the top story for all networks and was hotly criticized by all presidential candidates, yet polls told a different story. Over half of the voters questioned supported the law in concept.

The Japanese and various EU countries promptly flooded the state with lawsuits through a number of retail outlets selling their products. Harold's initial counterstroke was a dilly—he simply purchased each establishment that filed a suit. Their suits were withdrawn, and foreign products were destroyed publicly in demolition fairs. People were paid to wreck Japanese cars with sledgehammers, blow up foreign-made appliances, and burn combustibles in bonfires. The scenes earned top ratings on TV, and enraged the Trilateralists, Bilderbergs, CFR members, and other eastern liberals. Somehow, no one noticed that Chinese goods were not being touched, and Claire never mentioned their omission. The Chinese had certainly flooded the US with their products, but hadn't bought into the US infrastructure and weren't attempting to control the country. There were few Chinese corporations to attack.

The remaining suits by out-of-state foreign companies fell to Harold Columbo and Adam who assisted in the state's defense. Japan and France both used top eastern attorneys and filed in state and federal court systems seeking redress. Harold and Adam began implementing one delay after another.

Their second law passed almost unnoticed. It merely modified the reporting requirements for business licenses by requiring new applications. Ownership identification and a large amount of information were required, easy for American corporations, but patently difficult for foreign companies. Especially troublesome was the law's audit provision. The state, at the audited company's expense, could inspect company books to ensure all Montana taxes were being paid and the reported information was correct.

State franchise applications required the company's agreement that such audits were at the pleasure and convenience of Montana and would be held in the corporation's home offices. In effect, this meant Montana auditors could travel to Japan and audit Japanese accounting practices at Japanese expense. Within a few days, all Japanese and EU companies known to be doing business in Montana received new franchise applications.

This second law was not only constitutional, it was the type of law that was unfathomable to the public and impossible to explain in a five-minute TV news segment. Even before a franchise was granted, state auditors could travel to the applicant's home office to inspect accounting practices. Neither Adam nor Harold expected Japanese companies to allow such inspections.

They had patterned their Corporate Franchise Act after a New Mexico law regulating trucking companies and the Texas statute which Johnson and Connally had used to keep UPS from handling intrastate shipments. In addition, the California law requiring in-state registration and the payment of franchise taxes *for doing business* in California was implemented with California's extremely broad definition for "doing business" in the state.

Essentially, any activity in the state was included, such as advertising, buying, selling, having a physical presence, and using Montana infrastructure like highways in any fashion. Even using the Internet for advertising or sales forced registration, as it was possible that communications went over lines in Montana. The right of states to regulate commerce within their borders and to require franchise fees and reporting requirements for companies to conduct business was well established. The deed was done. One law for the media, one to get the job done.

*****

Tadashi Oshima pushed the "off" button on his speaker phone as his senior secretary entered with a facsimile of a franchise application for that American state that was giving them so much trouble. He had been forewarned about the document's contents, but seeing the real object put him into orbit. Oshima was chief counsel specializing in United States law for his *zaibatsu*. Ozawa in New York had appended his opinion that there was no legal basis upon which to object. To conduct business in Montana, a business franchise would have to be purchased. The fee itself was nominal at two hundred dollars per year, but the franchise agreement was impossible.

No Japanese company could allow officials from a minor American state access to their books and audit their accounting procedures. It was unthinkable. He owned them. Arrogant Caucasian barbarians.

He placed a conference call to Ozawa, trying to control his rage.

"We're in trouble," Ozawa said. "Our American lawyers believe a restraining order is out, and getting Montana to reverse itself will be impossible. The Milleron control in the state is too extensive. Chances are better in Congress. A federal law could be passed to supersede the state statute, but probably not during the current session. California and other states would object, and the public support was negligible."

"Do you expect such statutes to be introduced in other states?" Oshima asked the American lawyers on the call. A chorus of voices all agreed this was an isolated incident. No comparable bill had been introduced anywhere else, and all national political figures were opposed to such legislation.

Off the telephone, he considered his situation. The American attorneys were fools. They had been taken by surprise and couldn't admit they were wrong. In an effort to curry favor and say what they thought he wanted to hear, they claimed the case was singular. Oshima didn't believe it for an instant. Those cowboys in the midwest were capable of doing anything to hurt Japan. It was racial hatred because they recognized the Japanese were superior.

Oshima carefully reconsidered his options. Montana was a small state in terms of business volume and could be ignored. It was time to let the cowboys think they had won a great victory. But somebody had to pay.

It took four telephone calls to determine who was behind the law. Harold Columbo and Adam Stewart were handling Montana's legal work, and that implicated their elders, Senator Dave Columbo, and CIA Director Sophia Stewart. The company purchasing retail outlets who filed complaints against the Domestic Goods Credit Law was Milleron, and it opposed Japanese companies at every opportunity. It was time Milleron understood the dangers of such opposition.

Milleron had cost the *zaibatsu* billions. Two individuals stood out: its president Ed Armstrong and Sophia Stewart. She was its guiding light.

It only took one discussion with the zaibatsu chairmen. Oshima rapidly related events and stated his position. "I expect Milleron to institute identical strategies in a large number of American states," he said. "If they are successful in their endeavors, we will be denied a very large market."

"Perhaps this is a trade restriction Milleron has concocted to force us to ease our restrictions on them," a chairman suggested. "Perhaps it is negotiable. After all, we have kept Milleron and most

American companies out of Japan with similar bureaucratic procedures and regulations."

"Quite possible, but we have already approached various Milleron individuals with suggestions for constructing such a compromise. We were rebuffed most abruptly." Oshima took a sheet from his briefcase. "If I may quote what was said to our representative in New York... 'After they drop all trade restrictions, we'll talk.' Obviously we can't take any unilateral action with respect to our trade barriers. They're the cornerstone of our government's economic policy."

"Quite so. But this insult cannot go unavenged. There we can take unilateral action."

"I'll see to it," Oshima bowed.

*****

Adam felt like an old-west gunslinger in his 1940-ish office on Helena's Bannock Avenue. There was more wood in the office than in most dude ranches, and their desks and chairs were early-Gold Rush. He and Harold hadn't heard any reaction from the Yellow Peril about the franchise law. He dialed Cassidy's office where franchise applications were processed. "Kent," he said, "heard anything from any zaibatsu?"

"Yeah, as a matter of fact," Kent responded. "All day long. I've had a steady stream of telephone calls from New York attorneys for every Jap company in existence. Sooner or later, they all end up yelling that their clients aren't going to do business any more in Montana, and it's my fault. You should hear some of them."

"They aren't submitting applications?" The news was almost too good to be true.

"Apparently not. They're obviously working on another strategy. One of their lightweights said, 'See you later. Your rummy state will soon learn there is a higher authority.'"

"He's anticipating action by Congress. Forget it. They're pissing in the wind."

"One asked for Harold. Apparently they have a proposition." Cassidy gave Adam the number and went back to his other calls.

Harold dialed New York. He didn't recognize the attorney's

name, but the guy's law firm was arguably the most prestigious in the US.

Metz came on the line almost immediately. Talking on a speaker phone, Metz suggested a compromise might be found where Japan would reduce some of its restrictions against Montana products.

Harold put the call on hold, and turned to Adam. "What do you think? Your mom doesn't want fair trade at this point."

"Can't. Wouldn't mean anything. Just Japanese trading with Japanese. They'd jack us around for another twenty years. We need to make an irretrievable break."

Harold nodded and took the line off Hold.

"Attorney to attorney, may I assume this is a settlement conference? All communication private, confidential, and not being recorded?"

"Absolutely confidential. Wouldn't have it any other way," Metz said.

"Well, then listen up. You can tell those yellow-bellied, slime-sucking, back-stabbing Jap bastards whose trough you feed at and whose sphincters you clean with your nose, that they can stick their suggestion up their asses, your ass, and the ass of every US suck hind tit, eastern liberal in your office. They don't want our products in Japan, and we don't want their shit in Montana. Your little Nip masters have pulled every dirty trick in the book to screw American industry over the last fifty years. They have never negotiated in good faith, and if you think they will now, you're dumber than a fence post and as useful as a used roll of toilet paper. And if they don't understand that, hold on." Harold handed the telephone to Adam who repeated the rant word-for-word in Japanese.

"That'll get 'em," Adam laughed after slamming down the phone. "You know damned well they were recording it."

"Yeah, and the slants were in the room."

Adam paused for a moment and saw they were ready for the next step. The enormity of it brought him to his feet. "That's it, we're on, Harold," he said excitedly. "Time to have Governor Harrison pass the word."

Adam called George and gave him the high sign. Harrison scheduled a press conference just in time to make the network news' evening broadcasts.

424

Harold picked up the press release and read:

"MONTANA DRIVES JAPANESE and EU BUSINESSES OUT. As a result of statutes recently passed by the Montana general assembly, all major Japanese corporations and most European Union companies conducting business in the state have indicated their intention to withdraw all business activity from Montana, effective immediately. Governor George Harrison declared Montana to be secured from Japanese, EU, and Bilderberg domination, and stated his hope that the remainder of the United States will free itself from foreign economic control following Montana's example."

"Think it'll work?" Harold asked.

"You bet. My father always said the Japanese had a fatal flaw. They prize conformity, harmony, and control above all other virtues, and when control is lost, they go berserk and exhibit an unfathomable arrogance and disgust for all things not Japanese. He said, 'make them mad, and they destroy themselves.' And if not, then the identical bills ready in North and South Dakota, Nebraska, Wyoming, Kansas, Idaho, and Iowa will. Harrison's press conference is the signal for their legislators to go ahead."

"That's it then," Harold said, looking at the floor. "The fat's in the fire."

"Every chitlin."

Chapter 43

The effect was electric. The seven states introduced their bills and passed them in record time, and were then followed by Utah, Indiana, Oregon, and Arkansas with similar legislation.

Claire's media attention far eclipsed that being given to presidential candidates, and the election immediately devolved into a single issue campaign over foreign economic penetration in the US. Polls determined about a third of the public strongly approved of Montana's action, a third disapproved, and a third were undecided. But the polls showed significant demographic differences. The east coast disapproval percentage reached as high as sixty-five percent, the "left" coast almost seventy. In the midwest, the percentages were reversed.

Without exception, all presidential candidates stated their understanding of forces that prompted Montana to take such an extreme step, but deplored the action itself. The situation reminded many of the Arizona law passed in 2010 to help control illegals.

Sophia's network took a strong position supporting Montana, while the one acquired from Suzanne after BJ's death adopted a milder position, but still supportive. Billy Rutledge and Claire prepared an hour-long news special detailing the level of Japanese and EU control of the American economy and political scene. It was broadcast on both networks in different time slots. The program enumerated times when Japanese and the EU countries had intervened in American politics and forced the president, Congress, and state governments to do their bidding. It drew a parallel to slave plantations in the Old South with Japanese and other foreigners being "Massa," and American politicians being overseers. The American people were the slaves.

A line in the sand had been drawn, and Billy expected a number of lawsuits to be initiated by those individuals profiled in the program. He and Claire prepared for a storm of protest, and they got it.

*****

Over the next two weeks the outcry was enormous, but subtle changes were becoming apparent. When three Japanese vessels were sunk in San Francisco Bay by Sophia's Bluepeace activists, cheers drowned out cries of outrage for the first time.

Japanese reaction was swift and to the point. In the Oval Office, the president listened to the secretary of the treasury and secretary of state with mounting impatience. "So what do they really want? My head? Am I to commit *hara-kiri*? What?"

"They want you to seize control so they can continue to conduct business," Ali, the secretary of state said. "Whatever it takes. They want you to guarantee the safety of their ships."

"So we're responsible, is that it? We pay for their losses?"

"That's part of it. Do we have any choice?"

Probably not, the president thought. The damned Japs were once again threatening to cease buying federal paper. So was the EU. But there was an ace in the hole. China had agreed to do everything it could to help the US meet its debt obligations. The president suddenly felt a new-found strength. After all, this was the United States.

"Damn right, we do!" she burst out, pounding her hand flat on his desk. "Tell those little bastards to pound salt. Millions for defense, but not one cent for tribute!" She had been taught that in high school. Someone, some early president, had said that. It sounded just as good now.

"It'll bring on a financial crisis," said the treasury secretary.

"We'll weather it," seethed the president.

"And no action against states that have frozen out Japanese companies? That might smooth things over."

"No. The states are within their rights according to the attorney general. And no national government has ever taken over a state except during and after the Civil War, and that was a rebellion."

"You don't think this is a rebellion?" asked Ali.

"Not against us. Only against our little yellow friends with their pockets full of money."

The two secretaries shook their heads. Everyone in the Council for Foreign Relations would disagree. They wouldn't understand the president's sudden blockheadedness. They felt dismissed like advisors telling the emperor she was wearing no clothes.

That evening, they understood. The president went on television to declare she was withdrawing her candidacy for re-election. The crisis was demanding her full concentration as president, and the rigors of a campaign would detract from efforts required to steer the nation through current stormy waters. It sounded great. She was sacrificing herself and her political career for the nation's welfare.

By the weekend, there was a shortage of food in Charlotte. Then Atlanta, Jacksonville, Richmond, and a number of cities in the south and east. And then Virginia Power and Light experienced a brownout for three days.

Early the following Thursday, Secretary Ali asked the president to reconsider.

"We've been warned," he said. "Either we take action against Montana and other midwestern states, or the Japs are going to cut off our food and energy."

"How can they cut off our food? It's grown here," the president asked.

"We grow it, but they process it, move it, and sell it."

"Well, it won't happen," the president replied coldly. "They know better than to kill the goose laying the golden egg." She buzzed for her chief of staff.

"Stenner," she ordered as her portly confidant entered, "tell Ahmad what we're doing about Virginia Power and Light."

"We're seizing it this morning with federal troops as a precaution to sabotage."

"I want no more brownouts," the president said to Ali. "Let 'em know I'll get tough. The president of the United States cannot be intimidated."

The following day, the dollar collapsed throughout international monetary markets. The IMF met in a secret session and replaced the American dollar with the Chinese renminbi as the world's reserve currency. On the east coast, in the old south, and in the southwest, shipments to Japanese supermarket and convenience stores were halted. Catastrophic food shortages appeared.

Several governors called out National Guard units to maintain order. But military presence only served to notify everyone that their survival was being threatened. Within three days, grocery stores and retail establishments in many areas were emptied and gutted. Sophia ordered food supplies hoarded in Amulot territory and shipments into other states suspended. Day by day, the chaos deepened. Regular Army units were placed on full alert as several armories were attacked by gangs for weapons. The Japanese had over-reacted and placed the situation beyond redemption.

It was exactly as Sophia had predicted.

*****

Cole Stoner's life had taken a turn for the worse. Americans had waylaid Admiral Yamamoto in World War II, and the Japanese had never forgotten it. There was no way he could protect Sophia outside Langley in her present situation. Silver Spring was on the north side of Washington, and her condo was hardly secure. Security occupied the apartment directly across the hall, but she needed to move.

A secured facility was available a few miles north of Agency headquarters, and Harvey Sjoberg had it stocked for Sophia's use. Cole even found a lady named Sandra Taylor who was a near-perfect double of Sophia and pondered how to approach Sophia with his concerns.

Events overtook him in the person of General Chuikov. Two days after the 253rd Engineer Battalion took over Virginia Power and Light, he called on the secured line.

"Japan's government has authorized a new organization whose sole target is North America," Chuikov said grimly. "It includes espionage and all traditional dirty functions. I understand they will be making use of their business organizations already in your country. All zaibatsu employees are expected to cooperate."

"That's a substantial number of espionage agents," Sophia said. "The Bureau will be up against the wall."

"That's not all. Do you know what *gekokujo* is?"

"Sure. Japanese insubordination—usually meaning some individuals sacrificing themselves for the emperor, to safeguard Japan, or prove a point. Like the February Twenty-Sixth Incident before World War II."

"Well, it's happening again. You've been targeted for elimination."

Such news was not entirely unexpected, but to hear it directly was startling. "Any others on their list?" she asked.

"Only one so far. Ed Armstrong."

Sophia gulped. She needed to warn Ed immediately and arrange for more security through Webb. "Any idea how or when?"

"Not reliably or confirmed. Probably a Ninja-type effort and very soon. A small independent team or teams, and we believe they're already there or on their way."

"Vasily Andreyevich, if you were here, I'd make your fondest dreams come true. What would I do without you?"

"Later. Just make sure you're there to keep your promise."

She telephoned Webb in Iowa with her news. Ed was in Texas, but would be leaving for Indiana around quitting time. Webb promised to protect him. Sophia considered the timing and buzzed for Cole. The Japanese would hit her first to avoid giving any possible warning; she was the primary target, Ed secondary.

"Your condo's out," Cole stated. "You'll have to stay at our Prospect Hill facility."

"But I need things from the condo."

Cole didn't like it, but agreed to one more trip. Shortly after six, they piled into Sophia's limousine and drove to her apartment. So far, everything seemed normal. They drove down the ramp and directly into her building's underground parking garage. Cole spotted curtains moving in the apartment across from Sophia's and knew his security men would soon be on their way to the basement. The older gentleman repairing the gate walkway was one of his, as were pool and maintenance men in the rear and basement utility areas.

The driver pulled up opposite the painted walkway leading to the laundry area and elevator. Cole got out first from the driver's side and started walking around to open Sophia's door. He turned to tell his driver to pop the trunk latch.

Bam! Sophia's door disappeared in a tremendous blast. Cole was knocked to the concrete by the concussion. The world was a daze as he pulled out his Colt and rose to his knees. The concrete was covered with tiny pieces of glass sparkling in the garage lights.

On his left, the limo's street-side doors were open, and in the elevator lobby opening, he saw a small man holding a rocket launcher or something. Cole fired at the figure and it disappeared. Then everybody was firing. Submachine guns, shotguns, pistols. Then the gunfire stopped, and men were yelling. Cole staggered to his feet and struggled to the limo.

All its windows were missing, and spider web chunks of glass were everywhere. He dimly realized the limo was dripping gasoline profusely onto the concrete. He wondered if it might catch fire, but ignored what his mind was telling him. A glance at the rear seat told him not to look further. The door had blown off, and what seconds earlier had been an animated female body was a shredded mass of red.

"Cole!" someone yelled. He shuffled toward the lobby area. God damn, he was sore. He wondered if he were injured, but had to see what the yelling was about.

There were three bodies in the lobby and one across the entryway. The entryway form was the maintenance man, one of his. Two Japanese were obviously dead, but the third was groaning from multiple gunshot wounds. "Tim got those two with his shotgun. Stewart okay?" a man said. It was Sam Dealey, who had been upstairs in the security apartment.

Cole shook his head uncomprehendingly. "What happened?" he said.

"We heard an explosion just as our elevator door opened. These guys were right across from us. That one's pretty well ventilated. What about the director?" Dealey asked more stridently.

Cole knelt down and examined the groaning Asian. He was shot in the left arm, hip, groin, belly, and right hand. Sam had kept his shots low—he must have dropped to his knees to fire. The Jap would probably survive.

"Call an ambulance. And police." He thought for a moment. "And the Bureau."

"What about Sophie?" Dealey yelled, forgetting himself.

Cole noticed he was dripping blood on the Jap. He felt like he was moving in slow motion. She's okay," he said.

Sam's partner came up. "Pete and the director are long gone," he said grimly. "Christ! What a mess. You too, sir."

"Yeah," Cole responded dully. He was running on autopilot. His left arm and shoulder hurt, and the left side of his face burned like it'd been hit with acid. He had stopped several chunks of shrapnel, and he hurt like hell.

Tim pushed Cole aside and stripped the wounded Jap.

"We need to save him," Cole said.

Tim opened the assassin's mouth and checked for false teeth and poison. He bound the Jap's wounds, while Sam propped Cole against the wall.

Harvey Sjoberg arrived with the ambulance and paramedics. He lost control when he saw the horribly mangled female form in the limo, grabbed Cole by his lapels, and slammed him up against the wall.

"God damn you, Stoner! You fucking screw-up! Where were you? How could you let this happen?"

Tim pulled Sjoberg off and Cole slid back to a sitting position..

"God dammit all to hell!" Sjoberg collapsed on the garage step, looking at the blown out limo and the pulpy mass still inside. "America's hope gone forever," he said, choking his words.

Cole put a bloody hand on his shoulder.

"Don't touch me!" Harvey yelled.

"It wasn't Sophie," Cole said quietly. "She's back at Langley."

*****

Harvey's call convinced Sophia that Ed was in great peril. She called Webb and found him on a corporate jet preparing to land at Zionsville. Ed was already in the air and expected to arrive in about an hour.

Preliminary reports of the attack were shattering the airwaves. All networks were interrupting their regular programs with special reports. Claire reported, "An assassination attempt had been made on the CIA Director, Sophia Stewart, shortly after six-thirty this evening. At least five persons are dead, including two attackers. It is not known for certain if Ms. Stewart was killed, but police are still at the scene, and more information is expected momentarily."

Sophia turned on all three TV sets in her office and watched the story unfold. She had told Harvey and Cole to say nothing; she would choose when to announce her survival.

Claire came back on with an additional report, emotion and strain turning her face into a mask. A Washington reporter made the actual report from the condo garage ramp. "The bodies of Ms. Stewart, her driver, and a bodyguard are reported to be on their way to Walter Reed Army Hospital. The assassination was carried out by three Japanese nationals whose identities are not being released by authorities at this time. There has been no official confirmation of Ms. Stewart's death, but witnesses reported her body was badly mangled and covered immediately after its removal from her limousine. The vehicle was hit by a rocket when Director Stewart arrived in the parking garage of her apartment building. The ambush occurred while she was still in her limo at the elevator entrance."

Live coverage showed a large number of people milling around the garage entrance, then a cameraman went inside to show the wrecked limousine, foam covering spilled gasoline, police lines, and numerous officials talking near the elevators.

Claire and other commentators added personal data on Sophia, and eulogies were being offered on the other networks. Although Claire was being reserved in her treatment, two other networks were already interviewing other high government officials concerning possible motivations for the assassination. They guessed that Japanese terrorists held her accountable for the anti-Japanese attitude sweeping the nation. Some were blaming American xenophobia and antiforeignism for the Japanese attack.

The secured telephone line rang.

"We lost him!" Webb was barely coherent. "It was my fault. They got him!"

Sophia was sitting down, but still felt like someone had slammed her in the gut. It was the same as when she had seen Cathy Clark lying in a pool of blood and milk. But worse. She had known Ed was in danger, but had been powerless to help him.

"What happened?" she asked.

"A suicide attack. Three of them in a pickup truck. We had sealed off the airfield and Ed's plane landed okay. I greeted him, and before we got halfway to the office, they broke through. Never looked or fired at anyone else—just him. I should have taken him to the building in a car."

"Anyone else get hurt?" It wasn't Webb's fault. If assassins were willing to die, they would ultimately succeed. The Old Man in the Mountain and his Assassins during the Middle Ages had proven that.

"I got hit twice, and so did two others. We'll all be okay, though. And all three Japs are dead."

"Okay, take it easy, and don't feel too bad. Ed knows you tried. So do I. Nobody blames you. Have you called the police?"

"No. I called you first." Webb sounded better. She wondered how badly he was wounded. Knowing Webb, he wouldn't tell her.

"Call an ambulance, police, the Bureau, Claire Villars, and Heather in that order. Get yourself medical treatment. I'll take care of everything else." She barked the stream of orders, but Webb would understand. "I can't afford to lose you. Remember that. With Ed gone, you're it. Call me next from the hospital."

She put down the receiver and switched over to her speakerphone. She dialed Villars. The network switchboard operator was overjoyed to hear Sophia identify herself and became less coherent than Webb. Somehow, she managed to put the call through without cutting her off.

"Sophie?" Claire yelled.

"Yes, it's me."

"We all thought you were dead!"

"No, that was my double. We had been alerted to expect an assassination attempt. The Japanese decided I had to be eliminated by any means, including murder. There's a lot more I can tell you, but you need to get this on the air. Also, a second group of assassins hit Ed Armstrong, president of Milleron, in Zionsville, Indiana. Same Japanese organization, same reason, and they were successful. Three Japanese were killed there also."

"Jesus Christ. Who else is on their death list?"

"We don't know. All those who have been criticized heavily by the Japanese should take heed. And please notify all other networks and wire services. I'll be extremely busy in the next few hours."

Sophia returned to watching TV. Forty-five seconds later, Claire interrupted with her announcement of Sophia's information. Claire looked visibly relieved. Then she broadcast a general warning that Japanese assassination squads were active in the United States, and Sophia imagined she could hear an audible gasp throughout the country. This was worse than facing Islamic terrorists.

The other networks soon broadcast her survival. Sophia could sense hysteria building in their comments, and as more details about the two attacks were made available, panic seemed to grow. Other high-level officials were taking precautions, and the Army had been placed on full alert by the president.

Then the fires started. Sophia couldn't hear the sirens, but news reports began to pick up stories of widespread looting and arson of Japanese-owned businesses and stores along the east coast and in the south. Japanese found in public were beaten by gangs of youths, and murders were reported with increasing frequency. It was a long night.

Morning brought official Japanese government denials and even offers to pay compensation to the victims. Tokyo identified the perpetrators as belonging to a fanatical group of ultra-nationalists, and the president accepted the official apology.

Sporadic break-ins and lootings continued, and the inevitable occurred. Several carloads of inner-city blacks drove to a suburban shopping center in Richmond where they found the center's supermarket almost empty. Looking for food, they began to loot houses nearby and terrorize the white inhabitants. Some fought back, and a mini-war erupted in a quiet suburban neighborhood. Richmond's black mayor blamed the incident on white hoarders.

The Richmond incident was soon repeated in suburbs outside of three dozen other cities. Guns disappeared from sporting goods stores, and neighborhood defense leagues sprang up like weeds.

Kansas City and Jackson County became a battleground, and the governor of Missouri called out his National Guard to establish control. Due to A-Corps efforts, the units deployed were almost exclusively white, and within twenty-four hours, the National Guard was denounced by Kansas City's black mayor as a racist organization.

In an effort to stem the growing tide of racial conflict and riots, the president nationalized Missouri's National Guard and called in the 1st Infantry Division from Fort Riley, Kansas to absorb or disarm troublesome National Guard units in Kansas City. It was precisely the action General Carpenter wanted. While the Big Red One moved east, the 1st Marine Division was dropped into Riley as backup. He carefully orchestrated such reactions in line with Sophia's guidance.

Both the National Guard and Big Red One were overwhelmingly white, a fact known to Carpenter and Sophia, but overlooked in Washington. As street fighting progressed in Kansas City, most enlisted blacks deserted, and those who didn't were disarmed as unreliable. Not quite yet in open revolt against the Washington government, the 1st Division returned to Fort Riley and confronted the Marines.

At Riley, all black marines were disarmed, separated, and flown back to Quantico. General Carpenter announced the black troops were sent to Virginia to avoid racial incidents.

The men and women in the armed forces rapidly understood what was happening. Returning black soldiers from the two 1st Divisions quickly perpetrated a blood bath of white Marines at Quantico, and there was a mad scramble to seize arms and ammunition stocks by both black and white soldiers. A-Corps was already controlling most ammunition, and Carpenter announced his maximum preparation point was getting closer.

Chapter 44 - Splitting

Captain Tony Dudley had never heard of A-Corps. For a year, he had been Aggressor Unit Commander for the Escape and Evasion Course at Fort Benning. Sometimes he thought he was in charge of a punishment battalion; other times it was an elite unit. Almost all of his enlisted men were Hispanic, reflecting the Army's opinion of its probable enemy. He had been chosen to head up the unit because he spoke Spanish. His home town was Hatch, New Mexico, named for a relatively obscure Union Civil War General. Hatch was chile-growing country, and Spanish was required for a kid if he wanted to speak with pickers or hit on Mexican girls.

Training Command was in shambles, and Dudley and his men felt like squatters. They had moved to Sand Hill, an aptly named section used as a basic training center during Vietnam. The aggressor unit was an orphan, spending most of its time in the bush, and playing enemy tended to isolate his men from other units in Benning.

Everyone was nervous. Although Dudley's unit was well armed with foreign weaponry in addition to their own, its ammunition consisted solely of blanks. The only appreciable ammunition supply on Post was held by the Rifle Range people, and he heard it was controlled by a black colonel. Marksmanship training had been halted, and ammunition was being hoarded. Demolitions, however, was another matter. Dudley had enough plastic to level the Post.

Due to his isolation, Dudley hadn't seen the racial mix on Post change, but he'd heard talk across the Chattahoochee in Phenix City that blacks outnumbered whites. This had been confirmed to him in Columbus. Several bar girls told him most white officers and enlisted men had deserted after white Marines were massacred at Quantico.

His unit considered itself white and at risk. He called his understrength company together. The three blacks in his unit had not been seen for a week.

"At ease, men," he said. "It's time to discuss what to do. Our situation has deteriorated, the Army seems to be splitting into blacks versus whites, and Main Post is now almost entirely black. I see only three options open to us—stay here and wait as a unit, disband and let every man be for himself, or take the unit to a white-dominated post. Maybe Leonard Wood or Campbell. It's up to you. What do you think?"

It was a good group of men, but they were not particularly talkative. A Spec Four spoke up first. "What do you want to do, sir?"

Dudley considered his answer carefully. "If we disband, sooner or later someone will list us as deserters. I don't like that. Since it doesn't look like we can stay here, I think we ought to head out. Transfer ourselves to a different post. You men with lots of time in service can't be criticized or brought up on charges for following my orders to another location."

"That's okay with me, sir. Just so we get the hell out of Georgia."

The room resounded with "yeah," "okay," "let's do it," and the like.

"Mount 'em up as soon as possible," Dudley said to Sergeant Ramirez. He turned to his men. "Anyone wanting to remain can do so. We'll take muster tonight, but nobody leaves until the unit leaves. Understood?"

Dudley hoped like hell no one would cut out to notify Main Post. Ramirez asked about families; there were eight wives and twenty-six kids to take along.

They collected four families from NCO housing, and the others were picked up while heading north through the east side of Columbus. As far as Dudley could tell, no one reported their leaving, and no one stayed behind. They took all their weapons, and a full deuce and a half of plastic and cords.

The little convoy's trip was without incident. It was a strange feeling, as if passing through enemy territory. Dudley's company ran into another fleeing Fort Stewart, and learned that similar treks were being made daily throughout the United States.

Campbell was fully functional, and Dudley's unit received prompt attention and processing. It was disbanded after Post accepted its equipment and supplies, and Dudley was re-assigned to Fort Carson, Colorado. The enlisted men were discharged.

*****

At the still-functioning Port Tobacco facility, Dave Columbo noticed the camouflaged bunkers controlling approaches. "This is an armed camp," he remarked. "Who's here?"

"Ask Pete Towles," Carol replied. "The Milleron personnel have already been evacuated."

Dave pondered the facility's function. Virginia and Maryland would probably remain loyal to Washington, and whites were fleeing across the Blue Ridge daily in ever-increasing numbers.

Cindy Lewis came out to meet them.

"Glad you're here," she said to Carol. "I'm going out with you, but we won't be leaving 'til after dark." She looked at Carol's luggage. "You're not coming, huh, Dave?"

"No. I'm a bitter-ender. But I'm glad to hear you're going. Who does that leave here?" Dave had always been fond of Sophia's classmate, even hoping her short romance with Harold would lead to matrimony. It hadn't happened, and he figured Cindy needed more adventure than an attorney could provide.

"Just pilots, airport personnel, and Pete's people. Essentially all military."

Pete Towles shook Dave's hand in the hallway. He was dressed in a new-style camouflage combat uniform without insignia or national markings.

"Pete, Christ, man, what's going on here?" Dave gasped.

"We're here to keep a lifeline open," the ex-Army major said. "But until there's a legal national government to which we can claim allegiance, we're maintaining a low profile." He tapped his collar. "That's why you'll see no insignia. Unless we fire on government troops, we're not officially in rebellion."

"How long can you hold? I mean, what force do you have?"

"We're goners in a determined effort." The major said. "But it'll take an armored battalion at least. We have a full company, and we're in deep. Our biggest problem is maintaining the airstrip. We can defend it, but keeping it serviceable will be a trick."

The old lunchroom was serving as a dining hall for troops, and its cuisine had definitely gone downhill. Carol wasn't hungry, but Pete said he wanted his men to meet Dave. "Most have never met a senator, and to see a high official in the administration supporting their efforts will be a boon," Pete said.

Dave couldn't resist being a politician to a group of listeners and made a speech. He noticed no one coughed or made a sound, even after he complimented them on their bravery and importance. Finally, he hoisted his water glass. "I give you the founding fathers of the eighteenth century, and founding fathers of the twenty-first."

The men rose as a single body and repeated his toast. Dave felt a surge of power from male bonding in a group of warriors. More than ever, he was proud to be an American. Not just the idea of an American or a hyphenated American; these men, Carol and Cindy, were the real thing.

At nine they walked through an underground passageway to Hanger 3 and the airstrip. Carol and Cindy quickly boarded, and the twin-engine Milleron jet disappeared heading west.

"Wasn't there a movie about Vietnam, *The Last Plane Out*?" Dave asked.

"Don't know," Pete replied. "But it sure feels lonely being left behind."

"But not forgotten."

"No. And we'll be here if you change your mind. We won't be advertising, and it might be a long while before anyone takes notice of us."

A burst of gunfire behind them broke the quiet. Pete drew his automatic, and sprinted toward the main office building. Dave followed, wondering if they were rushing to their deaths. One of Pete's men opened the door and stepped out to allow them to enter without stopping.

"North side parking lot," the guard said as Pete disappeared.

Dave heard three more bursts from automatic weapons, and then quiet. Out of breath, he walked through the building. An older Japanese pickup truck and three bodies were in the parking lot. All were black youths, between seventeen and twenty-five. Pete looked over to the senator as he approached.

"Sorry, I lied," he said. He looked at the bodies. "Scavengers. Armed with two Uzis and an old AK-47. Tried to shoot it out."

"Any casualties?" Dave was surprised at his own aplomb. Their deaths seemed abstract.

"No. They never even knew where we were. Just shot wildly in all directions." Pete turned to the bullet-headed trooper at his side. "Get rid of the bodies. No trace. The truck, too."

"First time?" Columbo asked.

"First time. It's started." Pete motioned for the trooper who had escorted Dave to take him to his car. "Good luck in Washington, Senator."

Columbo drove away wondering if he would see Port Tobacco again. Ed Armstrong, the man who had built it, was dead. He was the only one remaining, connected by a tenuous thread, one made thinner every day. Sophia had left two days earlier, supposedly to Colorado for a well-deserved vacation, but he knew she would never return. Such possibilities seemed remote to the easterners among his fellow senators. With primaries still being held in spite of disturbances, most senators were away in their home states. Few, if any, midwestern senators and congressmen were still in town. And like Sophia, most would never return.

Driving alone in the darkness was suddenly oppressive. He did not feel safe in his own country, and he was a United States senator! Any car passing him could be full of armed men looking for a rich person to rob. The Cadillac would give him away—it was crying, "Rob me! Rob me!" He longed for Carol, his partner for life. The Senate had interfered with their relationship, and his service was the country's gain and his loss. He needed to tell Carol that.

When Sophia announced the formation of a new nation, he hoped the president would open communications instead of opening fire. If there was any way to avoid war, he would be there to make it work, true to his pledge and his blood.

*****

Sophia's Colorado vacation was the calm before the storm. She took Cole with her, both as a reward for his foresight and loyal service and to keep him out of Washington for the next several weeks. She met Cole's wife and family for the first time. Two beautiful little girls, both thrilled to be traveling with Madam CIA Director. Cole's wife, Alice, was overly friendly at first, and Sophia could well imagine what stories she had heard from other wives.

When their Milleron jet landed at Parker, Sophia was greeted by Wallace.

"My mystery man," Sophia announced proudly. "The man in my life everyone suspects is there but hasn't met. Jack Wallace, Cole and Alice Stoner."

"So you're the man who arranged the double and saved my honey's life," Jack grinned. "Sorry about the other girl, but I'm glad mine's okay. How about you? All healed?"

"Getting there," Cole said. Wallace was clearly packing. "You in the Agency?"

"Bureau. But we're all on the same side. Come on, time to go fishing. June is our month." Wallace herded them into his station wagon and headed west.

*****

In the cabin near Lake City, Sophia received daily reports from Webb concerning developments. Police were losing control in Japanese- and EU-dominated economic areas, and National Guard and federal troops only worsened conditions. Army units sent into Charlotte from Fort Bragg had been predominately black, and instead of suppressing rioters, had joined them. On the south side of Chicago, the opposite occurred with extensive casualties. Over a thousand rioters had been killed in the Jackson Park area alone.

General Carpenter flashed his "Max" message, so it was time for Sophia to pull the plug on the federal government. From her cabin, she contacted fourteen governors who were highly sympathetic to the Amulot cause, and invited them to a conference at her complex in Iowa. Governors of Iowa, Montana, North Dakota, South Dakota, Nebraska, Kansas, Wyoming, Illinois, Indiana, Idaho, Utah, Washington, and Oklahoma agreed to come, and the governor of Missouri would send his lieutenant governor.

Before lunch on the last day of her vacation, she informed Cole of her plans.

"I'm not returning to Washington or the Agency," Sophia said. "I'm going to Iowa to build a new nation, embodying the Protestant work ethic, and requiring commitment and contribution to receive entitlements. A strong nation, without discord and strife from diversity and foreign ownership of its natural resources and productive capacity."

"You're resigning and becoming a rebel?"

"Precisely. Not a rebel against the principles upon which the United States was founded, but a rebel against the perversion that has arisen in its wake. I want people to work, contribute, be proud of themselves, and of their country. I do not want them to do drugs, burn the flag, depend on welfare, and serve at the pleasure of Japanese or EU overlords."

Cole was stunned. He had assumed that Sophia was one of the nation's bulwarks. Yet here she was, joining a rebellion. His decision was between two commitments—his oath to the Agency, and his loyalty to Sophia. He didn't hesitate. He suddenly had a place to go.

"Forget that political stuff about your new nation," he said. "If you say it's right, that's good enough for me. Where you go, I go."

"Thank you," Sophia nodded. "I'm very pleased. We've always made a good team, and it won't be just the Japanese trying to kill me."

"I'll have to talk to Alice," Cole said. "I hope she'll agree with my decision."

"Let me know. I'll discuss it with her if necessary."

It wasn't necessary. Alice had wanted to move out of Virginia for some time, and Cole was surprised to hear fears of racial problems impacting her little girls.

Sophia was reminded of Lenin's comment about a revolution only having a chance to succeed if the women get involved. She suspected many husbands would find their wives desiring to live in a homogenous society.

*****

"Montana wants the honor of being first to act," Governor Harrison said after Sophia arrived in Iowa. "Our legislature is in session, and they'll vote me emergency powers on a telephone call. I can announce our action as early as tomorrow afternoon."

"Great, but I want to stress that this is a nullification and reform movement, replacing a government that has put in a framework of unconstitutional laws to dominate every aspect of citizen life. It has perverted the intent of the general welfare, commerce, and necessary and proper clauses of the Constitution to where the nation and its legal system must be rebuilt in its entirety. You'll be calling on all states to nullify the Federal Government and reform a government based upon our dominant culture, following the principles laid down by the Founding Fathers."

"No problem. How do you want tomorrow to develop?"

"I'll open the conference, and recognize Governor Carson of Iowa as the host state. He'll recommend we elect a conference chairman and nominate me."

"Chairman, not chairperson?"

"Not my hang-up. You move to accept me as chairman by acclamation. I'll call for a voice vote and be elected. Then you present this agenda." Sophia handed the governor a two-page document listing the subjects.

Harrison scanned the papers. They discussed present issues, nullification, and a replacement of the current government rather than secession.

"When we reach remedies," Sophia continued, "you suggest a type of Chapter Eleven bankruptcy procedure. All states nullify the bankrupt and impotent Federal Government and form a new government with a new constitution. Robertson from North Dakota will second, and I will handle discussion. You leave to obtain authorization from your legislature. Carson, Robertson, and Hartwig of Nebraska will do the same. Your four states are the only ones that can nullify the Federal Government by using immediate emergency powers. You come back in and announce your nullification."

"I'll blow up the conference."

"Please don't—at least, not quite. We have to vote to meet one week later to form the new nation and establish its temporary executives and constitution."

The conference took place almost exactly as orchestrated. Montana, Iowa, North Dakota, and Nebraska formally nullified the United States of America, and a convention was called for the following week to form a new national government. Federal marshals and FBI personnel in the four states were held in detention, and there was no reaction from Washington.

Sophia's luck did not hold during the following week. The

president moved troops into the states represented at Sophia's conference and threatened them with punitive military action if they attended the next convention. There were a few anxious moments, but General Carpenter was responsible for deploying troops. Using only white units well-penetrated by A-Corps officers, the federal troops actually aided the seceding states by maintaining order.

The same number as the original colonies—thirteen—nullified the Federal Government during the first conference and the following week. The convention opened on schedule with observing delegations from twelve additional states.

Russia issued a warning to the Washington government to refrain from military operations or the application of force. The Russian premier noted the USSR's restraint from 1988 to 1991 when facing separatist movements in the Baltic and Moslem states, in accordance with diplomatic entreaties made by the United States.

Privately, the Russian ambassador told the president that Russia would consider intervention and support the separatists if the Federal Government resorted to force. Russian support helped, but Sophia depended primarily on stonewalling tactics by General Carpenter and other A-Corps members to forestall federal air or ground action.

The new country was quickly designated as the United American Republic, and only one name was put forth for provisional president, Sophia Stewart. In twelve minutes, she was elected by acclamation.

Sophia took control as president and submitted two documents for the convention's consideration. The first was a declaration of nullification of the Federal Government and the formation of its replacement, and a constitution modeled after the current Federal Constitution. The delegations retired to work.

Three days were required to hammer out the Declaration's wording and deciding on a structure for the new government. The new Constitution exhibited several critical differences from the original US model.

The term of office for Congressmen was lengthened to four years, and president to six. A maximum length of service for all government employees, elected or not, was set at twelve years and required a period of six years of non-government employment before government service could be resumed.

Three classes of residents and visitors were defined: citizens, denizens, and aliens. Rights and obligations accorded to individuals were determined by their class as set by Congress. There would be no attempt to apply principles of American democracy to any but its own citizenry. Immigration, disenfranchisement, and obtainment of citizen status were subject to the laws of Congress.

The work was completed on the Third of July, and Sophia postponed the final vote and signing until the following afternoon. On Sunday, July 4th, 2020, the United American Republic was officially created, with Sophia Stewart as its provisional president. Cindy called Pete Towles and told him he could don the new uniforms.

Thirteen states signed the Declaration of Nullification, National Identity and Constitution: Idaho, Illinois, Indiana, Iowa, Kansas, Montana, Nebraska, North Dakota, Oklahoma, South Dakota, Utah, Washington, and Wyoming. Within a week, Missouri and Colorado joined the UAR as well.

The country was polarized. Led by entertainment celebrities and politicians from the east and west coasts, most minorities opposed the breakup, as did almost half of the whites. The international community also split, with only Arab nations, several South American nations, Russia, and China immediately extending diplomatic recognition.

War clouds were on the horizon.

Chapter 45

The US Democratic Presidential Convention was held the following week in Atlanta, and with troops brought in from Fort Gordon, the airport and downtown resembled armed camps. Some delegates from UAR states attended, and when the Convention opened on the twelfth, forty states were recognized. Results from all primaries were accepted, and with with all of the delegates released from their commitments, the nomination of Governor Parelli from New York was a foregone conclusion. For his running mate, he chose Senator Murphee, the black Senator from Virginia.

For the second time in history, the major task before a Democratic Convention was to set a policy for states in secession. In 1864, it had nominated George McClellan with a peace plank to stop the Civil War and recognize the Confederacy. This time, it adopted a plank calling for war if the rebellious states did not return to the Union within three months after the new president's inauguration. Undeterred by the possibilities of war being declared against them, Oregon, Nevada, and Kentucky nullified the Federal Government and joined the UAR during the Democratic Convention.

Sophia now possessed a defensible contiguous territory.

In the midst of the excitement, China attacked Taiwan. Taiwanese resistance was short and fell like a ripe apple. It was reunified with mainland China, and Taiwanese goods in the United States quickly disappeared.

The Republican Convention in Miami produced a slightly more moderate position with respect to the UAR. Its platform called for negotiations with Sophia's government before placing the country on a war footing. With the midwest gone, it became even more of a minority party than formerly. A Democratic Party victory in November was assured.

Hotheads in the old US soon pushed more states into the UAR. A number of Republican delegates from midwestern states stopped in Atlanta on their return from Miami. While changing planes in Hartsfield, they were attacked, and almost thirty were killed. Sophia gave the incident maximum publicity on her two networks and still-operating radio stations, and Minnesota, Michigan, Ohio, Wisconsin, West Virginia, and Arkansas joined the UAR.

Texas, however, became a battleground. Austin was controlled by troops supporting the Republic, but the legislature was badly split. A solution was found in the ability of Texas to divide itself into five states according to the act which had admitted Texas to the Union. Five states were formed, and three promptly voted to re-consolidate and join the UAR. Everything west and south of a line from the southeastern corner of New Mexico to San Antonio Bay stayed in the US. The UAR now possessed access to the Gulf of Mexico and to the Atlantic.

With Alaska ready to vote on nullification and defensible borders, Sophia no longer needed A-Corps personnel to remain at risk in federal territory. On General Carpenter's signal, the remaining officers departed their posts, and Admiral Kelerher issued his order for the Navy to join the UAR.

The Navy revolts took place the following day. Every ship was an all-or-nothing proposition, and the struggles for control on many ships were truly barbaric. With limited small arms on board ships, the fighting was hand-to-hand with knives and anything the crews could find. What happened to white females fighting to join the UAR beggared description. Women were on almost all vessels and many were killed after unbelievable atrocities and sexual perversions. Most on-board battles pitted all minorities and some liberal whites against those attempting to take the ship to a UAR port. Numbers made the difference, but afterwards whites that had remained loyal were generally killed by the minorities for being potential enemies. Kelerher's forecast was substantially correct. Only a single carrier was secured, but almost all of the submarines were obtained. On the bright side, the remaining personnel in the US Navy were only capable of manning a few vessels, and it would take years to train replacements for those killed or missing.

The Air Force split like the Navy. Almost all first-line fighter aircraft were flown by their pilots to UAR bases, and a number of transports and bombers flew out loaded with technicians. But the majority of personnel were left behind, and commanders loyal to the US were able to create respectable formations of aircraft, particularly of bombers. There were substantial desertions on the ground, but it would take some time before those individuals would reach UAR territory.

Sophia next directed her attention to the cities with substantial minority populations. Many black mayors needed to be replaced, and black populations exchanged for whites in federal territory. Including Hispanics, there were over seventeen million minority individuals to be repatriated to the east, south, and southwest.

All welfare benefits for non-Anglos were suspended upon each state's entry into the Republic. US mail and direct deposits from federal agencies were seized, and government benefits from the old United States were stopped. Minorities were encouraged to move back to those states remaining in the Union where benefits could be obtained. A large segment of minority populations needed no further encouragement, and a mass exodus ensued.

Pressure was increased during August. The Army closed commercial establishments in minority areas and confiscated inventories for health reasons. The border was open with respect to emigration, but only Anglos could immigrate. White and black populations were a mixed lake of oil and water, both elements separating into discrete halves.

In addition to minorities, huge numbers of disabled individuals and their families emigrated to the rump US to continue receiving their benefits. By 2014, one in six Americans had been drawing disability benefits, and estimates of bogus claims reached as high as sixty percent. Sophia required new applications following strict guidelines, and the great disability scam disappeared.

The Population Exchange Committee expanded Sophia's Homestead Act, and absentee landlords were rapidly eliminated. Families from the east and south readily found homestead properties, and a self-help program allowed many to acquire homes at extremely low cost.

Among the first acts passed by Congress were strong law-and-order statutes. All sentences for current inmates in state and federal prisons for violent crimes were automatically doubled. Convicted criminals were allowed only a single appeal through higher courts, after which only a pardon remained. Criminal penalties were established uniformly throughout, and death was prescribed for a substantial number of offenses. The Miranda rule was eliminated, and police were given increased latitude to deal with suspects in criminal actions.

As a result, the drug problem disappeared rapidly. The penalty for drug smuggling, growing, or manufacturing was death, and without substantial minority populations in which to function, drug lords became exposed and eradicated.

Meanwhile, the business of governing continued. Able to form her executive branch without legislative guidelines or previous bureaucratic empires, Sophia simplified her administration into only seven cabinet ministries: Finance, Information, National Security, Interior, Commerce, Resource Management, and International Relations. More than half of the federal agencies present in the rump United States were eliminated.

Bobbi structured the monetary system and transferred Milleron's assets to the government. All previous government property was confiscated without compensation, as well as that of the NGOs that had been so instrumental in moving the old US to socialism. In addition, all property owned by Japanese or EU firms or nationals was confiscated or nationalized. After repudiating any and all responsibility for US debts, the UAR was starting out with a substantial surplus.

In the third week of August, Alaska nullified the Federal Government, leaving only the off-shore oil fields of California and the Gulf to the old US. Carpenter immediately sent two battalions of the 101st Airborne to Anchorage and Fairbanks to provide some measure of security, but with Alaska's long shoreline and communication difficulties, it was militarily indefensible.

California was wavering, but there was little Sophia could do to help. The Valley and Northern California were pro-UAR, but Southern California and the Bay Area were solidly behind the old Federal Government. Well, not solidly—many conservative white citizens still remained in Orange County. Surrounded by minorities and liberal whites, and threatened by troops from Camp Pendleton, many Orange County residents were fleeing to Las Vegas.

Sophia needed the Bay Area and its Navy installations, but she couldn't openly attack any territory still remaining in the United States. Technically, she was not at war against the United States, and was maintaining a strictly defensive image to assuage world opinion.

A similar situation prevailed in the northeast. From Virginia north, sizable minorities of whites were sympathetic, but power was invested in the city machines, liberal whites, and large governmental bureaucracies. Their economy was in Japanese hands, and white populations, even where they were a majority, were adopting a "wait and see" attitude.

*****

In the United States, General Brown was named to replace Lambert as Army Chief of Staff. Tough as nails, the top ranking black general had taken command of 3rd Army and restored order to Army posts in Georgia and the Carolinas through draconian measures.

Brown knew his first order of business was setting a racial policy. Although whites were a plurality in loyal states, they now made up only a very small percentage of career soldiers. The Census Bureau estimated 230 million people remained in loyal states or would be repatriated from the UAR; 115 million white, 45 million black, 70 million Hispanic, Asian or other. The rebellious states were large in area, but small in population—around 100 million whites and 5 million minority inhabitants. Population figures gave the Federal Government a de facto propaganda victory—more whites remained loyal than had joined the rebellion. To Brown it was a clear statement of the nation's health. He immediately started a recruiting drive to attract more whites into the Army so he could eventually segregate units along racial lines.

The only military operation mounted into rebel territory had been to occupy the easternmost seven counties of West Virginia. The tip at Harpers Ferry had posed a threat to the Capital, at least geographically. The three nearest counties had no road access to other counties in West Virginia, but politicians felt better seeing rebels a hundred and fifty miles farther away. The seizure had been unopposed except by irregular units, and two highways—State Route

451

28 and US 220—were blocked and fortified below Petersburg, West Virginia.

Stewart had complained, but for once, she had been caught napping. As soon as West Virginia's Legislature announced their vote for nullification, Brown had taken action. New county governments were formed immediately and they petitioned as a group to rejoin Virginia—their native state before the Civil War. Federal troops remained to keep order.

With Brown in place, the president's biggest problem was economic. Essentials were in very short supply—food, gasoline, jobs, money, everything. Stewart had offered to supply large quantities of food in return for recognition, but that proposal went into file thirteen.

The Japanese were equally opportunistic, and their demands could not be refused. They agreed to rebuild the food distribution system, purchasing necessary foodstuffs internationally, but demanded territorial concessions. Very quietly, Congress voted to cede Guam and Wake to Japan, along with transferring the administration of Marcus, the Bonins, Volcanos, and remaining Trust Territory of Pacific Islands to Japanese control. Equally opportunistic were the Europeans, and it was their quick action that had prevented the nation from dissolving completely after the seizure of Virginia Power and Light.

A squadron of late-model interceptors were swapped for Saudi tankers waiting off the east coast. A gasoline crisis was averted for another month, but a permanent solution was needed. The Saudis were demanding payment in overseas securities for their oil, Venezuela was unfriendly, and the only domestic production in the east was off-shore in the Gulf. Unfortunately, much of that had been curtailed during the Obama years, and gasoline rationing was crippling the economy.

The president was feeling increasingly helpless. A delegation of *zaibatsu* representatives demanded a direct voice in Treasury policy, essentially assuming fiscal control. Only then would they guarantee jobs in their domestic factories and corporations, and their continued support of the dollar as a hard currency. The president had few options, but did manage to keep the Japanese from actually sitting in cabinet meetings. Five cabinet posts became vacant through resignations, and a delegation of Europeans submitted recommendations. They stressed their continued support of the dollar, and their recommendations were appointed without protest. All of the delegation and appointees were Bilderbergs.

A quick victory over the rebels was desperately needed. With Stewart publishing a proposed Non-Aggression Treaty, the US could hardly use nuclear weapons or bomb rebel cities and retain any world support. It needed to decapitate the rebel leadership—perhaps through an operation against their Des Moines capital complex. The president called a meeting with the joint chiefs.

The meeting was stormy, mostly a reflection of frustration with their remaining staffs and capabilities. Admiral Smyth, the ranking Navy officer, assumed chairmanship in the vacuum left by Admiral Kelerher and recommended that diplomatic initiatives give him at least a year to rebuild. General Brown argued for an immediate strike, claiming that the rebels had to be in mass confusion. The Air Force chief, Joliet, stressed that the UAR now possessed the stronger air force. "About thirty-five hundred combat and another four thousand of all types remain," Joliet announced. "We've lost about three thousand of our best combat aircraft and four thousand others. And most of our best pilots."

Such statistics did not fill Brown with confidence, and when ordered by the president to plan the Des Moines thrust, he confined Operation Snatchwitch to Army personnel he could trust. The new CIA director supplied a layout of the Des Moines complex, a list of key personnel, and said a reinforced airmobile brigade was stationed at the complex's airfield. Stewart was expecting an airborne attack, and evidently considered the airfield their point of maximum vulnerability. If he attacked from Des Moines with an irregular force, they could get in, kill the leaders, and head north to Ames and be extracted before the brigade could intercede. A reinforced company of three hundred men could do it. It didn't take much effort to obtain a green light from the president.

He planned to send two divisions north from western Tennessee as a diversion. With luck, they would bypass Fort Campbell, seize the lower Ohio River bridges, and race through Illinois toward the Quad Cities. After Stewart and most rebel leadership were killed, he could call on his Air Force for flank cover. He stood an excellent chance of ending the civil war before it began.

During his time at Fort Bragg, Brown had met a major named Steger whose sister was married to a black officer. Steger was committed to the US, and formed his three-hundred man assault team within a week. All were white, and most were from California or northeastern states. Steger had carefully selected one man in each fire team as the designated assassin, and fully briefed him on his purpose. Anyone found in the complex, male or female and of any age, was fair game.

On Tuesday, September 7, Steger's unit disappeared in three- and four-man teams, driving north in private cars. With only six hundred miles to drive, they expected to be in place by noon Wednesday. The key was speed. Even if some parties were intercepted and detained by rebels for questioning, the operation would be over before anyone broke.

All cars cleared rebel border checkpoints on schedule, and rebel controls had been cursory. He ordered the 3rd Armored and 8th "Pathfinder" Mechanized Infantry divisions into staging areas between Dyersburg and Paris in western Tennessee, and established his own headquarters at Jackson to wait for H-Hour, 1800 hours the following day.

Chapter 46

At eight-thirty Wednesday morning, Webb heard from Dwight Davis, intelligence head for the national police. He was a good man and seemed to be able to say anything without offending anyone.

"We arrested four men last night in St. Louis in a car with Tennessee plates. They were attempting to wrestle a girl into their car when local police intervened. When they searched the car, they found enough hardware to start a war, and two of those arrested had New England accents. Nobody's talking, but it's obvious to me they were coming here."

"Is our border control database operative? Do we know when they crossed?" Webb asked.

"Yep. They crossed at Interstate 155 shortly after one in the afternoon."

"How many others crossed there yesterday with four men? I assume they were all white."

"I don't know, I didn't check."

Webb waved him away for more information and dialed his Army intelligence liaison.

Colonel Snider picked up immediately.

"Jack," Webb said. "Any developments lately with military concentrations across the border?"

"Lots. They shifted two divisions up between the Mississippi and Tennessee."

"Which ones?"

"Their best two. Third Armored and Eighth Infantry, Mechanized."

"No air-mobile units?"

"Not that we know."

"Any other units moved to our border? Anywhere?"

"Not that we know," Jack repeated.

"Thanks." Webb switched off to think. Those two divisions were obviously poised for a thrust into the UAR, but without supporting units. Small squads had been sent ahead as saboteurs or to hold critical bridges or strong-points as far north as St. Louis. That was almost halfway to Des Moines. The evidence was compelling.

*****

Driving north was uneventful, and George Steger noted the countryside's serenity and absence of troops. Filling station attendants in Hannibal seemed unconcerned, even disinterested in present political dangers. Typical Americans; they would only fight when confronted directly by the enemy. And they didn't recognize him as hostile.

Only two cars failed to show up in Des Moines. Some raiders had pretty rough edges, and the losses were probably due to drunkenness, women, or mechanical problems. Steger reassigned six men to a vehicle, turned his lead pickup truck onto Indianola Highway, and headed south.

The rebel capital complex was impressive in its size and modern appearance, and Steger felt like a mosquito attacking a horse. Obviously, the rebellion had been planned well in advance. He wondered if the politicians in Washington realized that.

As expected, security was almost invisible, and the four assault teams peeled off to drive into separate service entrances beneath ground level. Steger led his platoon into Area A, Northeast, which serviced Stewart's office. So far so good. A dozen or so semi-trailers were backed into freight doors, and he noted the shipping and security offices.

"Do it!" Steger yelled. His pickup truck shook as the men threw off their covering tarp and opened fire. The security shack disappeared in a terrific *bang!* and a cloud of dirty smoke. The driver steered up the utility ramp and onto the receiving dock. His men dismounted and raced to the receiving office. He looked back at the entrance and saw the doors closing. That was odd. His last car was supposed to guard their entrance for a quick getaway. He yelled, "Cover!" and his men took cover wherever they were.

"You are surrounded and cut off from all hope of escape!" a voice thundered through a loudspeaker. Steger crouched between two shrink-wrapped pallets on the dock. "Surrender or die! Throw down your guns!" the voice continued.

Steger couldn't see any rebels. There was a door near the receiving office that probably led to the first floor. He gestured toward the door to the man behind him. The sergeant nodded, took four steps, and died in a hail of bullets. Suddenly, the dock was filled with soldiers emerging from parked trailers and stairwells. Steger died before he fired a shot.

Webb was overjoyed that his guess had been correct, but Cedric was distressed. The boy had underestimated the effort, and although Sophia's quadrant was well-prepared with a massive reception committee, he had only assigned a single platoon to each of the other service areas and the eight public and three private entrances. He had been convinced the primary target was Sophia and the operation would be surgical in design. His father had been an innovator, and he had forgotten how uninspired the Army could be in its thinking. The attackers had assaulted in breadth rather than depth.

The resulting battles in other service areas were sharp and bloody. Commandos broke through in two, and there were a number of civilian casualties before other units sealed off the penetrations. One particularly resolute soldier killed fourteen people, mostly women.

All of the attacking vehicles were captured, and security troops accounted for two hundred and seventy-eight commandos. But two hundred and eighty-one submachine guns had been collected. Cedric authorized a top-down full search, checking all identities.

In electric cart maintenance, seven more commandos died. The only attackers who surrendered were the fourteen trapped in Sophia's service area. The civil war had officially begun, and the United States had started it.

*****

To General Brown's pleasant surprise, the 3rd Armored and 8th Infantry attacks hit air in Kentucky. By early evening, 3rd Armored's leading brigade had crossed the Ohio at Paducah, and 8th Infantry was at Cairo. Third Armored continued up Interstate 24, while the Pathfinders paralleled up US 51. Both divisions were slowed by roadblocks and fallen overpasses in the gathering darkness, and by midnight, were stopped in the Shawnee Hills along a line from Tunnel Hill to Lick Creek to Cobden. The Shawnee Hills and National Forest proved to be serious obstacles—terrain features that Brown assumed they would clear within three hours of arriving in Illinois.

The worst came two hours later when the three Ohio River bridges were blown behind them. Highway 45, Interstate 24, and Highway 60 bridges all dropped cleanly into the river despite of having been declared free from demolitions by platoons detailed as bridge guards.

The next three days, Brown struggled to extricate his trapped units. Rebels blew Mississippi bridges at Cape Girardeau and Cairo, and his two divisions retreated into a pocket. Less than ten percent of the troops were saved, and all their equipment was lost.

It was a debacle although casualties were heavy on both sides. Even worse, the abortive campaign was a propaganda victory for the rebels. Cairo was destroyed in street fighting, and rebels claimed black troops had run amuck, raped white women, indiscriminately murdered civilian men, women, and children, and mutilated dead soldiers by cutting off their genitals. The president denied it, but such stories were receiving substantial play in international media. There was substantial video evidence, and the UAR was allowing foreign journalists access to atrocity sites.

General Brown remained calm. His troops had been green, and this was their first action. Rebels would have claimed atrocities anyway. The issues were painted in black and white at low levels, and each side would be accusing the other of horrible crimes. The die was cast. It was going to be a civil war fought with terrible ferocity—and fought to exhaustion.

*****

The propaganda battle moved into high gear with federals making extensive use of motion picture and TV celebrities to defend the Union and what they called the American way of life. Sophia recalled Millie's fears of being labeled a Nazi in spite of being Jewish. That was exactly what was happening to her. Almost every reference to her by Hollywood personalities contained the words "Racist," "White Supremacist," or "Nazi." In turn Sophia constantly referred to US notables as Snazis.

"We are not white supremacists," Sophia declared in a speech following the Cairo atrocity revelations. "We seek no conquests, nor desire to dominate any other group of people, whether different from us by race, language, culture, or heritage. We are no different from Hungarians, Armenians, Cambodians, Poles, or Ecuadorians who desired to create their own homogeneous state, with a single people, culture, and language. Let each people govern themselves according to their own wishes. Peace begins at home, in a society free of strife emanating from racial and cultural conflicts. We call upon all nations, particularly people remaining in the United States, to recognize the demise of the American experiment and the universal human needs which brought about its cessation."

In her press conference two days afterward, issues were reduced to more prosaic terms.

"Your speech declaring one people, one culture, one race, one language, and one nation, inferred you only want white, English-speaking people in the Republic," stated a French reporter. "Is that true? And what about religion? Do they all have to be Protestant?"

"We desire to be a country of white, English-speaking citizens," Sophia said. "Just as France is supposedly a country of white, French-speaking citizens. It is possible to absorb small numbers of other nationalities and races, but they cannot be allowed to become so prominent as to significantly impact the dominant culture. France is a perfect example."

She left the lectern and moved toward the reporter. "You have allowed large numbers of Muslims from Arab lands to become residents, and they have refused to adapt to French culture and learn French. Now, France is splitting apart, with terrorism and murder daily fare. Diverse populations automatically require strong central governments to control the citizenry. In effect, France is now an empire, and as we all know, empires have a limited shelf life. The US outran its, and France will do the same in the next decade or two as Muslims become the majority in various parts of the country. France is also supposedly a Catholic country, but that is changing under the assault of Islam. The UAR recognizes no state religion, but its culture reflects Protestant Christianity. That must be respected. A country must have a dominant culture, or there is no reason for its existence."

"What is your policy toward blacks and other minorities still residing in your territory?" The question came from the *Washington Post* correspondent. Sophia was still allowing access by journalists from federal states.

"We encourage them to relocate to the United States," Sophia replied. "We consider them citizens of the United States, and after the attack in Kentucky and Illinois by federal troops, view them now as potentially hostile. In this respect, we desire to exchange them for people still residing in federal states who wish to join us."

"If they won't go?" continued the well-dressed *Post* man.

"We certainly won't massacre them like federal troops did our citizens in Cairo," Sophia responded sharply. "We have no wish to incarcerate them in concentration camps or exterminate them in any fashion. We expect to reach an agreement with Washington for a population exchange like what happened between Turkey and Greece. If not, they will be expelled to the United States."

"What will be your policy toward Native Americans?" a TV reporter from California asked. "I understand you have no Bureau for Indian Affairs."

"True, and we have ceased all government aid to Indians. They are no longer 'Wards of the State" as established in the Grant Administration. By the way, I am a Native American. 'Indian' may be a misnomer, but 'Native American' is totally inappropriate. Just because someone's ancestors have been on this continent longer than someone else's, does not give them a corner on the term." Sophia paused to allow her rebuke to take effect. "To answer your question, the Republic is not honoring any treaties made by the United States. We have redefined tribes as private corporations, and reservations are private land owned by those corporations. The land will be taxed and subject to UAR laws like all other private land. Indian corporations may do with their property as they wish, but they have no special rights or privileges."

Several reporters spoke at once. Sophia pointed to Claire Villars.

"Do you consider the United American Republic in a state of war with the United States?"

"No. There has been no declaration of war made by the United States, and we have made none. We consider their assault on our capital and attack by two divisions of federal troops in Kentucky and Illinois to be hostile acts perpetrated and executed by misguided individuals acting on their own initiative. We are awaiting a repudiation of those actions by the Federal Government and the punishment of individuals involved. If no such statement is issued, we will be forced to review our stance. Please note, it was Washington that took the first hostile action, and we restricted our response to defensive actions on our own territory. We did not fire on Fort Sumter."

"Your population and resources are small compared to theirs; how do you expect to win in an all-out civil war?"

"Hopefully, it will not come to that. Quite possibly, world opinion will force Washington to see that aggression will no longer be tolerated. But if it does come, we will be fighting a just war in defense of our homes, families, and democratic principles."

Again there was a cacophony of cries for recognition. An English correspondent caught Sophia's attention for the last question.

"What do you expect in the eventuality that your revolution fails?" he asked pointedly.

Sophia swallowed to prepare her answer. "Judging from the behavior of federal troops up 'til now, we must expect to face a policy of genocide. In my own case, there have already been two attempts on my life. First, Japanese ninjas earlier this year in Washington, and now federal assassination squads here in Iowa. Like the patriots in 1776, I have pledged my life, my fortune, and my sacred honor. It is victory or death."

*****

Following the abortive federal attack in September, national service was made mandatory for all citizens aged seventeen through forty-five. Women were required to learn basic military skills, first aid, and a specialty in their six months of active service, and continue to expand on that skill in four years of part-time civic action duty. Two years of active military service was required of all males, with the only exemptions being those with severe physical handicaps. For both men and women, completion of active duty was required before admission to college.

Amulot response to the National Service Act was overwhelming. Female volunteers exceeded two years' worth of quotas, and males were backlogged into the following spring. Pre-menopausal females were not allowed in combat units, but were trained to defend themselves.

The Republic's presidential election followed the re-occupation of western Kentucky by a week. Democrats headed by Governor Harrison had been more militant with respect to Washington, and federal actions played into their hands. Harrison defeated Senator Conley of Colorado handily for vice president, and congressional and senatorial races were fairly predictable following candidate activity levels in forming and supporting the Republic. Sophia was presented with Democratic majorities in the Senate and House of Representatives, as well as a Democratic vice president. The Jeffersonian Democrat had made his re-appearance.

Meanwhile, building an adequate defense establishment took priority. Her primary deficiency was in heavy military equipment, tanks, and self-propelled guns. Efforts by Milleron engineers had resulted in superior armored fighting vehicles and military hardware, but they were not yet produced in sufficient quantity. With Carpenter's approval, Sophia traded grain to the Russian Federation for twelve hundred T-92 tanks and an equal number of self-propelled guns. It was enough to outfit three full armored divisions.

Chapter 47

Juan Salazar had been elected senator from West Texas and was pleased with the increased power splitting up Texas had given to Hispanics. West Texas had enjoyed a Hispanic majority for more than twenty years, but Anglos had controlled its destiny from the Houston-Dallas-San Antonio triangle.

The Hispanic population had remained small until the 1950s when immigration, legal and illegal, began to swamp Texas with native Mexicans. Hispanic activists accomplished wonders using immigrants. Major cities elected Hispanic mayors—El Paso first, then San Antonio. Pregnant Mexican women crossed to give birth in the United States in enormous numbers—over fifty thousand per year in El Paso alone during the 1980s—and whole families entered and became citizens as a result. By 2018, almost forty percent of Texas was Hispanic, and a majority was forecast by 2030. Hispanic power had left black power in the dust.

His disappointment was intense upon finding Hispanics completely ignored in Senate chambers. Everything was focused on the south and east since little Japanese investment was located in Hispanic states. There was no money, but that was nothing new. The more he learned about Washington, the more he understood why large cities and blacks received most of the benefits for which his people also qualified. Hispanics were peaceable and accustomed to corruption and a lack of dignity in their home countries. It was their mistake to accept their lot as better than before and therefore, satisfactory.

In Senate debates, Juan watched for two days while no Hispanics spoke. It was as if they weren't there. He found himself wondering why they were and called a caucus of all Hispanic congressmen to his new home in Alexandria to find answers. With area real estate values depressed, the mansion had been a terrific buy.

Conversation immediately became a litany of complaints about affairs and how badly they were being treated. Everyone tried to outdo each other with horror stories. Finally, Salazar bit the bullet and addressed his main issue.

"Why are we doing this?" he asked. "Why are we supporting a government that has absolutely no interest in us or our people?"

"We have no choice," Hernandez, the junior senator from New Mexico said. "What are you going to do? Join the rebels? We're not Anglo, and they've made it abundantly clear we're not wanted."

"So what's wrong with supporting ourselves? We're the majority in four western states, southern California, and south Florida. We could do what the Anglos have done. Trade our people in Florida for theirs in California, and have our own country. After all, that's been the idea behind Aztlan for the last thirty years."

Dead silence.

"Who's going to stop us? The rebels won't, and we're separated from the south and east by Anglos in Texas."

"It's worth considering," Hernandez offered quietly. "Stewart said the United States was occupied by a foreign powers—Japan and the EU—so they are not in rebellion against the United States but are fighting foreigners. Using the same argument, this discussion is about structuring resistance to Japan and Europe, not sedition."

"But could we survive? Could such a country be self-sufficient?"

"California alone could be self-sufficient!" bellowed Congressman Aguilar. His district included part of Los Angeles county. "Stewart constantly implies the country will eventually split on racial lines. She might even support us."

The meeting had gotten bogged down, but during the next week Salazar continued to talk privately with his colleagues about a separatist movement. There seemed to be little to lose and everything to gain. Rebellion was a well-established and honorable Hispanic activity, and its prospects were appealing.

A Hispanic army was needed, and that had to come from General Brown. The caucus cautiously approached him and found him surprisingly sympathetic. His recruiting of Hispanics had fallen off since the rebellion.

"We'd like you to consider a policy of concentrating Hispanics into southwestern-based formations," Juan said. "We've received a number of letters from constituents to station sons and daughters closer to home. We agree with that and think it would also raise unit efficiency."

Brown nodded. "I'm sure it would, and both blacks and whites have been clamoring for more segregated units. We're moving toward racial groupings out of necessity."

"Then you'll begin moving Hispanic soldiers into cohesive units?"

"Already under way," General Brown said. "But I'll accelerate it and transfer as many as I can to units in the southwest. In return, you need to help me recruit more Hispanics into the Army. Another four divisions would be nice."

With that, Salazar would have his own army. Anything would be possible them.

*****

Shortly before landing at Dulles, Premier Tanaka reviewed the situation. He had been elected to office following the abortive assassination attempt on Sophia Stewart, and since then, events could not have fallen more favorably for Japan. The rebellion had been a godsend. Their enemy had foolishly put her fortune at risk, and Japan could now acquire it at the expense of others.

Already Japan had re-acquired important Pacific islands for its aid, and other Pacific property owned or administered by Washington would be acquired shortly as payment for Japanese assistance. The Pacific was like a great expanse of fertile land requiring irrigation, and the irrigation wells were the islands on its surface. Soon Japan would control the vast majority of those islands—those water wells—and no one could challenge its control and right to the ocean's resources.

President-Elect Parelli was making unofficial requests through Japanese envoys for continued support. Americans were dependent on the Japanese supply of foodstuffs and uninterrupted operations of Japanese-owned utilities and industries in federal territory for survival. For twenty years, the *zaibatsu* had been slowly replacing American managers and technicians with Japanese nationals. American industry was now Japanese-owned, Japanese-managed, and used Japanese technology. Only its labor force and holders of low-paid jobs in service industries were American. And what wasn't Japanese was European.

Parelli boarded the plane to greet Tanaka, and Tanaka was pleased that Americans had finally learned how to bow. Breezing through the obligatory formalities, Parelli whisked him away for confidential discussions and privacy at the Greenbrier. Tanaka would become president the following week.

"I'm faced with some very difficult problems," Parelli said. "Various trading partners have lost faith in our dollar and are requiring payment in kind or other currency. We need large loans to maintain our financial stability."

Tanaka bowed slightly in appreciation of Parelli's courage to make such a humiliating admission. "We are willing to give you every support possible," he said, "but I'm sure you will want to deal with us as equal partners and allies, not as supplicant and master. The United States has many assets and resources which could be utilized to secure loans and show confidence in your own productive capacities."

"I'm sure that's true, but our productive capacities will be stretched to the utmost very shortly. My electorate is demanding war, and my options are only two—win the war, or lose it."

"Then you must win it," the premier stated. "For both our sakes."

"Yes, but speaking frankly, many factories that must be converted to war materials production are owned by your countrymen."

"As long as their production returns a reasonable profit, how can they complain?"

"They are within reach of rebel air power."

"Then they must be compensated for material losses if such occur."

"Americans have never lost a war we tried to win," Parelli said, carefully avoiding Vietnam or 1812. "This time, however, we will need help from our friends. Military equipment and supplies, oil, strategic materials, food, and not the least, money. Before I get too far in planning, I need to know what the price will be."

Tanaka nodded. "Japan has almost no Navy. If rebel submarines become a menace, we will need protection. Some of your very fine ships could be transferred to us."

"No problem."

"To secure our lines of communication, we will need bases. In Hawaii and California, and Alaska when it is retaken."

"There will be some problem, but that can be arranged."

"Then at least two other items depending upon the length of conflict. We will require liaison officers at the highest level in your Defense Department. We must have influence in its conduct to safeguard our investments."

Sam Parelli bit his lip. He hated bankers who pontificated with your own money as their leverage. This little bastard was sounding exactly like a banker financing a construction project and demanding to have some measure of control in management. Tanaka was looking at him without personal feeling or involvement—nothing personal, just business. He could not bring himself to utter a word, he merely nodded.

"Good. The second concerns reparations. Rebel President Stewart also owns the Milleron Corporation. We understand Milleron assets have been nationalized and belong to the Rebel government. When they are subdued, those assets will fall to the United States. We desire they be pledged to Japan."

Parelli resisted his impulse to whistle. In effect, the Japanese premier was claiming all spoils of war for his support. But first they had to win, and who could predict the relative positions of their countries later? For now, Parelli was giving away something he didn't possess. He remembered Roosevelt's pledges to Stalin during World War II: *As long as America remained intact, any situation could be recovered.* His agreement would be kept secret like Yalta, and he should be able to repudiate it later. He would impoverish Japan during the war, divert their financial support into building a stronger domestic base, and possibly even nationalize Japanese-owned facilities when victory was assured. War could create untold opportunities. That was why Tanaka demanded high-level participation—not to aid in achieving victory, but to keep from being exploited. The little Nip was smart, but Parelli would be smarter.

*****

467

Following his conference with Parelli, Premier Tanaka formed a Defense Council to oversee Japan's support of the United States. Its title was clearly a misnomer, but "War" Council was considered bad politics. In their initial meeting, Tanaka briefed members on his agreement with the American president. Response was mixed. The finance minister wanted a commitment from Parelli to cede Hawaii and Alaska to Japan, but the Navy minister thought Tanaka had driven a very shrewd bargain.

"I understand our objective of obtaining complete control of the American economy, but we have that now to a large measure," General Tsuji ventured. "Political control does not come simply through economics. Otherwise, we could have prevented the rebellion."

"I agree," Tanaka nodded. "Our intent in this conflict must be to eliminate as many Americans as possible. Their population is more than twice ours."

"What amount of repopulation of American territory could be accomplished by Japanese settlers?" Tsuji asked.

"We estimate about forty million, and four million are already residing in the US."

General Tsuji shook his head. "That means at least 220 million people must perish in this war. Impossible. World opinion will never allow it."

"But it will be a civil war. American against American. No one will shed a tear for a dead American. They are the world's bullies, and everyone hates them."

Admiral Yoshida chimed in. "It will be a racial war, with Caucasians in the wrong. Look at what happened in South Africa. No one came to help white South Africans because of their past crimes with apartheid. It will be identical in America. Their past crime of slavery will work against them."

Tsuji wrote the numbers on his pad and remained unconvinced. "How can we kill 175 million whites without anyone objecting?"

"We won't. Blacks and Hispanics will. All we'll do is provide the means and maintain their motivation by making sure appropriate atrocities occur frequently. Civil wars are deadly conflicts anyway, and we'll encourage civilians to be killed as a matter of routine."

"Personal atrocities then," Tsuji said, "but no extensive destruction of property."

"That would not be in our interest." Tanaka went to the large wall map. "You will notice this southwestern portion is largely Hispanic and separated from the east. As fighting deepens, we can suggest Washington turn over the war in the west to us. I have already discussed such circumstances with the Mexican president, and Mexico is interested in assisting in the southwest if properly compensated. Normally, you might assume that means territory, but I believe Mexican leaders can be purchased with money."

"You propose to use Mexican troops?" Tsuji frowned.

"I propose encouraging Hispanics to believe they are fighting to establish this new Aztlan country, and use them and Mexicans to exhaustion. We desire all three parties, Mexicans, Hispanics, and whites to suffer the greatest possible casualties."

"What about blacks?"

"They're the easiest. They all hate whites and will kill them without provocation. Whites fear blacks, and as long as they believe blacks are raping their women, they will murder every black they see. Neither side will take prisoners. Our only problem is the northeastern whites who remain loyal. We need to involve them so they can be decimated."

"When will we get Hawaii and Alaska?" Admiral Yoshida asked. "You did not mention either in your agreement."

"No. All we agreed was to transfer some units to our Navy and for us to have naval bases in Alaska and Hawaii."

"What units? What bases?"

"That will be up to us. Please make a list and I will present it to the president. I assume you want Pearl Harbor."

"Absolutely. Think of it. Americans giving us Pearl Harbor."

"In both states we'll deport Caucasian populations and settle Japanese in their place. Later we will demand their cession to us."

"We want America to declare a blockade of rebel territory immediately," the Navy minister asserted. That way we can legally seize and hold Russian arms or Middle Eastern oil."

"The rebels will begin attacking our ships," the economics minister objected. "We stand to lose most in a sea war. Our Navy is small, and we have no idea how efficient the Federal Navy will be in protecting our ships. A lot of it is stationed on the east coast."

"If they did start sinking our ships, we could always declare war."

"We must eliminate rebel naval bases as soon as possible," Yoshida warned. "Even if it takes our own troops. A quick strike at Washington state to seal off Puget Sound."

"The Army is not ready for such an operation," General Tsuji objected. "We need at least a year to prepare. And we must invade Alaska."

The Navy minister was forced to go on the defensive. "What can we expect in ship losses from their submarines?"

"A thousand to two thousand per year until we destroy rebel bases. Maybe more. It will be very difficult and costly."

"Two thousand? Twenty percent of our merchant fleet? Unacceptable."

"Then we must destroy their bases sooner," Yoshida said.

"No, we must involve ourselves more slowly," Tanaka decided. "Keep a lower profile and attempt to dissuade Stewart from declaring unrestricted submarine warfare until we're ready. Besides, it's in our best interest to prolong the war and inflict maximum casualties on both military and civilian Americans."

"If we declare war, what risk do we incur for the home islands?" Finance Minister Kurita asked. His question was directed to the entire committee for discussion.

"Very little," Yoshida answered. "Stewart has already renounced the use of nuclear weapons and CBR and can't use them on us."

Tanaka nodded and considered a strategy. "I believe we can warn them against taking action against the home islands. Through the Russians."

"Have we found our leak?" General Tsuji asked. The new CIA director had indicated Stewart had received advanced warning from Russia concerning Japanese attempts to block her confirmation and the attacks against her and Ed Armstrong.

"Yes," the Foreign Minister replied. "Another Sorge type ring. All are under observation, and one is now a double agent. Several middle managers in various *zaibatsu*, and two in our economics ministry. Initially recruited to obtain technical and trade secrets, they branched into government policy."

Tanaka continued his explanation. "We planted information on a missile control system from our satellites that is able to hit Washington or Moscow with impunity. Now we'll allow the Russians to discover we have a stockpile of missiles to make the threat real. They'll pass it on to Stewart."

*****

President Parelli had been happy to receive Japanese support but unhappy over its price. But without Japanese financing, he would be unable to crush the rebellion. What he needed now was to bring his fellow Bilderbergers into the equation to offset the Japs and cement his control.

He dispatched Secretary of State Eliot to meet with European Community heads of state and the key Bilderbergs in several other countries. Not since 1861 had an American envoy appeared in Europe as a supplicant. Eliot's task was not going to be easy.

"Your properties in rebel territory will be confiscated, and compensation is only possible through a federal victory," Eliot explained to the British prime minister. "If Stewart is successful, she might even unite with Canada. You know Stewart supported Quebec separatists earlier to improve her position."

"We have a substantial position in food processing industries in the midwest," the prime minister said. "I doubt she wishes to jeopardize that function."

"It is not inconceivable that she will nationalize your food processing and distribution corporations to secure control over their war-sustaining capabilities. Your corporations are only linked to the UK financially for returning profits, so she only needs to sever that link."

Prime Minister Edmunds had already discussed that argument in chambers, and Eliot was belaboring the obvious. For many years, England's economy had relied on separating Americans from their money, and what better way than essentials like toiletries, canned food, breakfast cereal, ice cream, and so forth? British corporations were highly vulnerable to being taken over by the rebels. He would have to work through Canada to pressure Stewart.

"We have maintained a policy of not recognizing the rebels," Edmunds said finally. "What else would you have us do? It is our understanding you control three-quarters of the population, most industrial facilities, almost all surface Navy units, and most aircraft."

471

"Only partially true, Prime Minister," Eliot asserted. "Our Air Force is actually inferior since our best pilots joined the rebellion. We badly need the latest fighters and trained pilots. Our east-west supply lines have been cut in Texas, and resettling refugees from rebel territory is proving most taxing. We are in need of humanitarian aid for refugees."

"You're forgetting Agenda 21. It is in our interest to see the American population decline to relieve pressure on the world's resources."

That was not the attitude Eliot wanted to hear, but finally the prime minister promised two things; humanitarian aid would be forthcoming, and England would assist with air power, but only if the Federals were in danger of total defeat and their capital was threatened.

French reaction to Eliot's entreaties was similar, but they agreed to train Federal pilots in France on their latest Mirage fighters. France would make a number of aircraft available, but their price was subject to further negotiations. As with England, only humanitarian aid was immediately forthcoming. It was obvious the Bilderbergs had decided among themselves what would happen before Eliot arrived.

Germany was more sympathetic. The Bundesbank pledged a substantial loan so Eliot could return claiming solid German support, and in the next year or two, Germany would furnish several armored divisions of volunteers subject to other conditions. Eliot assumed the enlisted men would be primarily Muslim immigrants from the Near East—cannon fodder to die and relieve Muslim pressure on Germany itself. The Bilderbergs would bide their time supporting the Federal Government and would seek to profit from their assistance.

*****

"Humanitarian support!" screamed Sophia, reading reports Webb had given her. "Look what those limeys told us! We had brought the situation on ourselves and were responsible for the suffering. Europe's willing to assume their white man's burden and send aid to poor, helpless blacks, but not us."

"I didn't know we had approached them for aid," Webb said.

"We didn't. But in our general discussion of diplomatic

recognition and their personnel in our territory, we pressed for some show of support in addition to recognition. We got neither." She slammed the papers onto her desk in disgust. She couldn't remember England ever supporting white revolutionaries in any country other than the Greek rebellion from Turkey in the 1820s. And then it was only with money which eventually found its way back to England.

"How about others in Europe?"

"Nothing. No recognition, no humanitarian aid, no nothing. The Bilderbergs have decided to decimate the American population to help attain the population goal of Agenda 21."

*****

Almost five months had passed since Sam Parelli's election—five months of limited war. Nonetheless, small unit actions had demonstrated the true nature of a civil war. The ratio of killed to wounded was very high, and troops had to be given direct orders to take prisoners. Even then, few prisoners were taken unwounded, and even fewer survived intelligence interrogations.

Both air forces and navies had been inactive. The Federal Navy had made no attempt to halt maritime trade with Houston and the Pacific Northwest, and rebels were yet to attack a single Federal ship. Parelli was beginning to feel heat from Congress. Pressure groups were clamoring for action, and Stewart was exploiting Federal inactivity. Vietnam and several Eastern European and South American countries had recognized her government, and it was clear a do-nothing policy would not re-unite the country.

At least he had gotten rid of that traitor Columbo. Evidence of Colombo's disloyalty had been incontrovertible. Parelli's new attorney general, Jerry Thornton, led the charge, and Columbo was expelled from the Senate and stripped of all privileges and benefits.

Columbo didn't last a day. The following morning, he was found in his home in Lewisdale, beaten to death, and lying amid the wreckage of his belongings. Thornton announced that he had been killed resisting arrest, and the case was closed.

Not quite. Within a few hours of Thornton's announcement, a group of armed men broke into the Prince George's county morgue and disappeared with Columbo's body. Two weeks later, Jerry

Thornton and two companions died in a hail of bullets three blocks from his office. The gunmen, described as two middle-aged white women with a man driving their sedan, were not apprehended. President Parelli had no doubts concerning the sequence of events and their meaning.

Racial positions toward the war's conduct were becoming clearer by the day. Most blacks agitated violently for an invasion of rebel territory, bombing cities, and even employing nuclear and chemical weapons. Millions of blacks had been expelled from rebel cities, and those individuals wanted to move back.

Northeastern whites were relatively ambivalent on average, some strongly supporting action against rebels, but many sympathetic to the rebel cause. Eight million Hispanics had returned to loyal states, but they seemed disorganized and apathetic. In an attempt to infuse them with martial ardor, General Brown had transferred most Hispanic troops to the southwest to fight as cohesive units, but no one was placing bets on their fighting prowess. Brown had essentially restored a segregated Army, moving almost all Anglos into white-majority units. Parelli disagreed in principle, but Brown was certain it was the only way to ensure their loyalty and hold racial conflicts to a minimum.

Meanwhile, the planned spring offensive was being held up by the Japanese.

*****

"Damn Japanese!" Brown yelled in the strategy meeting. "We're ready now. My troops are tired of waiting. *I'm* tired of waiting!"

The Japanese admiral seemed impervious to abuse. All eyes turned to Yoshida for a reaction. "We have requested you delay your offensive until summer. That is only three months away. Why are you so impatient?"

"We are losing diplomatic ground every day," the president said. "Unless you can give us an adequate reason, we will attack the first week in April."

Yoshida considered his options. He was not authorized to disclose Japanese preparations for an amphibious assault on the Pacific northwest. The council had anticipated announcing their plan when their fleet approached the west coast and submarine interception potential had been mostly ameliorated. That would be impossible if the Federals attacked prematurely.

"We are extremely concerned with submarine threats against our ships," Yoshida said gravely. "We must demand a neutralization of rebel naval facilities in Puget Sound and Alaska as a first strike. Otherwise, we cannot guarantee continued supply of goods and support."

"We'll make that our top priority," General Joliet said.

"What amount of their destruction can you guarantee?"

Joliet looked at Parelli. "Maybe seventy percent."

Parelli turned to Yoshida. "We'll bomb them until you're satisfied. Okay?"

Yoshida acquiesced. "Very well. I will so inform my government. But you will be responsible for our shipping losses until such time as rebel submarines are effectively neutralized."

General Brown winced. He halfway expected the Japanese admiral to demand payment in cash every time a Jap ship was sunk. He couldn't tell when business stopped and war started. He finally understood where Roddenberry got his idea for the Ferengi in Star Trek.

Chapter 48

On Sunday, April 3, Federal armies moved forward on four axes; west into Ohio from Pittsburgh, northward into Kentucky from western Tennessee, across the Sabine into Texas, and northward from New Mexico toward Denver. Announcement of hostilities came as forward units crashed into rebel defenses.

Only partially true to his word, Parelli conducted four major air strikes against naval facilities in Puget Sound during the previous afternoon, both from attack carriers in the Pacific and airbases in northern California. Attacking aircraft had lost heavily, and when General Joliet and Admiral Smyth presented their totals to Parelli, he was shocked. No Air Force bombers returned, and only thirteen Navy planes limped back. Missile defenses were extremely efficient, but rebel fighters were better. They intercepted the bombers, completely out-flying all escorting fighters and wiping them out. Clearly, the rebel pilots' skill advantage had been underestimated.

Admiral Smyth considered mission results both good and bad. They had sunk a large number of ships, including the UAR's only carrier, but counter-attacks had decimated Federal surface vessels. Smyth told the president that current rebel technology probably would cause the loss of most, if not all, of the US's major surface vessels within the following weeks.

La-La land became a sore point from Brown's first report. His attempt to seize Hoover Dam had failed, and rebels had then destroyed it. Southern California was without power and would shortly be without water. Supplies were critically needed, and California was isolated.

"The Navy's saying we can't protect west coast ports from being closed by rebel air power," he said to Joliet. "Air Force agree with that?"

General Joliet looked at his hands. "Until we transfer fighters from the east. Our SAM defenses out west are pretty weak, and we don't have fighters to spare. They're committed to supporting our eastern attack."

"Then the Japanese will have to put into Mexican ports for a while." Parelli decided the tension was getting to him. Being a wartime president was no fun.

The major push was against Ohio from Pittsburgh, and Brown moved a force of four corps with three attacking and one reserve division each into western Pennsylvania between Erie and Waynesburg. The northern arm's axis was along the Ohio turnpike, while the southern struck out for Columbus.

During the entire first day, Parelli stayed in his newly constructed war room and followed developments, report by report. After an early flurry, military actions seemed strangely inconclusive. Rebel units withdrew from general combat, apparently content with delaying Federal advances.

The Federal army attacking Texas and southern Arkansas from Louisiana was predominately white, while east of the Mississippi, the majority of troops were black. Federal troops held critical advantages in numbers and maybe even equipment in all theaters. Parelli thought the rebs might be unable to support large field armies over long campaigns.

He couldn't understand their rationale. The rebels had to see God was on his side, the side of all great principles of humanity known to man. Parelli wished he knew more about them and their motivation. They had grown up in the same country as he, but were marching to a different drummer.

*****

By midnight Saturday, Cedric had compiled casualty and damage reports from Puget Sound naval yards and unit commands. Kelerher was a Rickover follower who had never believed in super-carriers, and had turned the *Kitty Hawk* into a floating machine shop with superb air defenses and a ready supply of available metal. Events proved Kelerher correct. The huge carrier had settled upright at her moorings through prompt counter-flooding, and casualties were minimal. Two missile cruisers were damaged, and twenty-two smaller craft sunk and fourteen damaged. Only three submarines were damaged, but over a dozen barges were sunk when Federal pilots apparently mistook them for subs.

In response to Washington's declared blockade, Kelerher released all restrictions on submarines and announced the Republic's own blockade. Destruction of super-carriers was given the highest priority, and the admiral promised Sophia they wouldn't last long.

Webb's intelligence had been excellent, and all four Federal Army attacks had been fully expected. Inadequate Federal attention to the west offered Cedric an opportunity he couldn't pass up. Blowing Hoover Dam ruined southern California, and destroyed all other dams and bridges on the lower Colorado. Cedric's western Army was ordered to execute his plan to send two corps of six divisions into the Mojave and up the San Joaquin Valley, achieving a junction with three divisions crossing the Sierras from Reno. He meant to take possession of California north of the San Gabriel Mountains before Washington could react.

"How did you do it?" Cedric asked Webb on Sunday morning. "You knew everything as if you were present in Parelli's cabinet meetings."

Webb grinned and broke a long-standing rule against divulging his secrets. "I was," he said. "Before we left last year, we took all the trap door keys with us. Every night we tap into the Federal computer networks."

Cedric understood—a trap door was a way to break into a computer's operating system so if users forgot passwords or damaged their system, the system programmer could get in and make necessary repairs. Webb's group was receiving minutes from enemy cabinet meetings the day they were recorded.

General Lambert had assured Sophia that the Federal attacks would be handled without difficulty. Texas, Arkansas, Colorado, and Kentucky were defensive holding operations, General Collins would be attacking aggressively to conquer California, and on the eastern front, they hoped a counter-attack would take them to Washington.

Republican security was significantly better than Federal, and their new tactics would be a nasty surprise. Mobile SAM units and hand-held rockets were highly effective defenses against low-flying aircraft, and helicopters had been relegated to transport duty by Republican tacticians. Cedric did not believe Federal commanders realized the extreme vulnerability of their slower aircraft and expected to inflict heavy losses before they could make adjustments.

The individual soldier was closer to being the ultimate weapon than ever before. He was still susceptible to long-range weapons, bomblets, cluster shells, stationary mines, and obstacles, but every attempt was made to provide him with mobility and increased firepower. Infantry training stressed fire discipline and the full use of combined arms. The Republic was short of manpower, and its deficiency could only be made good by smart fighting.

One problem faced by the Confederacy had already been resolved by the UAR—that of foreign recognition. Its effect had been slight, however, and the Republic remained relatively isolated. The key foreign power was Canada, and its government was following England's lead. Cedric decided the UAR was on its own, and this war was his to win or lose.

"How do we win?" his mother had questioned him in an early strategy session.

"Through seizing the political high ground as to why we should be independent. We are not trying to conquer them or win additional territory. History gives us mixed signals with respect to this strategy. Most separatist movements who fought to be left alone were unable to win their independence through military victories. The key factor apparently lies with their mother country—whether or not it is willing to pay the price to subdue rebellion."

"So we have to make the price of re-unification too high."

"Exactly. We must destroy their martial ardor. In this respect, the strongest war fever among Federals is coming from blacks. If they suffer sufficient casualties, they might fold. Northeastern whites should be won over politically, and Hispanics encouraged to form their own nation."

"How can we lose?"

"Be defeated in battle. Have our land occupied. The key will be our own martial resolve, but that should be our strength in view of the alternative."

*****

Bruce Stirling watched his G-2 move colored pins on the map of Ohio and western Pennsylvania with mounting satisfaction. The main Federal thrust was developing exactly as predicted, and the order of battle intelligence so far had been perfect. The Federal commander had placed his 1st Armored Corps astride Interstate 80 attacking from Sharon. A second armored corps between Beaver Falls and New Castle was moving move west on US 224, 62, and Interstate 76, a third crossing into West Virginia at Weirton and Wheeling, and units of a fourth had seized Morgantown and was approaching the lower Ohio River crossings from New Martinsville to Marietta. A secondary effort by two infantry divisions was moving down Interstate 90 and state roads toward Cleveland where they could support 1st Armored Corps.

That little kid Cedric, as General Stirling called him, had worked up a flexi-defense and counter-punch. His plan was to draw the two armored corps against the Cuyahoga River between Cleveland and Akron and into the gap between Akron and Canton. Then he would attack their left flank pushing the Federals northeastward against Lake Erie well east of Cleveland. Another effort would attack southeastward through East Liverpool and Rochester, forcing the southern effort to retreat. As a final stroke, two divisions would strike northward from Fairmont to create a blocking force against which the southern two corps could be smashed.

So far so good. Akron defenses were ready, and skirmishing forces had already slowed the Federals to a deliberate advance. The fifty miles from the border had taken sixteen days, and Stirling was betting his Akron line would be assaulted before dawn. He ordered 9th Corps to move up onto the right flank below Canton.

The Ohio River line was holding, and with no useable bridges, Federal units had made only one river-crossing attempt at Wellsburg and one at Moundsville. Stirling was surprised at their lack of resolve. Close-in air support sorties had located several bridging units and inflicted considerable damage, but Federal efforts seemed slack. His blocking unit below Morgantown had held with difficulty on the Monongahela, and the Federals were transferring troops up Interstate 79 to Washington, PA. Perfect. That would make his bolo punch from Fairmont more effective.

Monday morning the Akron line was struck. It was a beautifully coordinated attack, preceded by an hour-long artillery barrage, and napalm runs by Air Force jets as the tanks moved forward. Standard textbook tactics, causing relatively little damage. Expecting napalm dropped at right angles to attacking troops, the defensive shelters had been built with covered fighting bunkers.

The first line that had looked so formidable to Federal reconnaissance was only lightly held, but its troops were equipped with anti-tank rockets. Federal armored units took severe losses, and started to get bogged down as they attacked the second line. It was finally breached with increasing effort, and the leading tanks plunged headlong into dead space separating the second and third lines. By now they were disorganized and paused while armored infantry caught up.

Smelling victory, the Federals pushed forward with everything they had, even bringing in helicopter gunships and close-in fighters to exploit the breakthrough. General Stirling watched the combined arms attack develop from 70th Mechanized Infantry Division headquarters. The true test for Cedric's new tactics and weapons began as massive numbers of anti-aircraft missiles were launched.

It rained helicopter and aircraft parts as infantry SAMs and hand-held rockets cleaned the sky of escorting Federal aircraft. Long-barreled self-propelled artillery closed the back door on trapped Federal armor, and armored regiments moved forward to finish off enemy formations between the two lines. The destruction was greater than Stirling had anticipated in his fondest moments. Federal units lost cohesion, and their tanks milled around indecisively.

General Shields, XIV Corps commander, pulled up in his armored command car, barely able to contain his excitement.

"We're slaughtering them!" he announced to Stirling as he dismounted. "Their attacks have ground to a halt, and our SPs are blowing them apart." He strode into the convenience store Stirling was using, and spread his sector map on the counter. "The 1st Armored is waiting for word to attack, but we're mopping them up on our own."

"It's early yet," General Stirling cautioned. "You've done well and scratched a couple of Federal tank regiments, but they're stacking more in."

Stirling called for his G-2. He showed Shields where their radio coverage indicated fresh Federal units. "It looks like they're shifting three more divisions into this sector. At least one is armored. You should be receiving mailmen two or three more times this afternoon and a big push by morning."

"If it goes like we hope, I'll cut 1st Armored and the 82nd Airborne loose late tomorrow," Stirling said. "Until then, you hold."

Shields nodded. "We'll hold." He told his operations officer to recall advancing elements and regroup for more attacks. He helped himself to a box of Twinkies at his elbow. He waved them at Stirling. "Just keep supplies flowing."

Shields did hold, although it became more difficult than he'd anticipated. Seven divisions were thrown at his XIV Corp holding the gap, and Stirling waited another day for the Federals to commit themselves before beginning his counter-attack. Hood had said in the cornfield at Antietam that he could cross on the bodies of dead men without his feet touching the ground, but Shields could walk from Akron to the Ohio turnpike hopping from one destroyed Federal tank to another.

The 82nd sliced northeastward from Waynesburg to Warren, cutting off three Federal Corps. The 1st Armored rolled through to take up a stop-line position along Highway 11 from Warren to Lake Erie, and the greater part of eleven divisions was bagged. What followed was probably the most ferocious fighting seen in America since the Alamo.

As Shields noted, blacks lost combat efficiency when their command structure was eliminated and fought poorly as individuals and in small groups. White residents between Interstate 271 and the 1st Armored's stop-line disappeared, but so did the Federal divisions. Facing annihilation, black troops took as many whites as possible with them, although they were mostly civilians. Mop up took three weeks, but prisoner cages were almost empty. Battlefield wreckage was enormous, but most heavy equipment was simply scrap.

Even before the Chardon Hills were finally cleared of Federal troops, Stirling relieved his armored divisions to race up Interstate 90 to Buffalo and down the New York Thruway to Albany. With 1st Armored leading, they found resistance light. Roadblocks were hastily constructed and poorly manned, and a few shells from heavy caliber SPs traveling immediately behind the point platoon usually scattered the defenders.

Buffalo was reached and occupied in two days, and General Shields viewed Niagara Falls for the first time in twenty years. His luck had been phenomenal since liberating the Twinkies in Akron, and he made it a daily event. Some might consider him superstitious, but he had gained a couple of pounds and two hundred miles. And possession of the Niagara-Mohawk power plants was a great strategic victory. The Republic now controlled electric power for at least twenty million people on the east coast.

The three hundred miles from Buffalo to Albany were covered in five days, and Shields began to face serious logistical problems and fatigue in the forward combat units. Albany was a last-gasp lunge, but he achieved the honor of being the first to liberate a state capital from the Washington regime. His Twinkies were doing their job, when, almost dead on his feet, he drove his command car to the Statehouse. A delegation awaited him—representatives of northeastern states who requested transportation and a meeting with President Stewart. The war might soon be over.

*****

We're invincible, Sergeant Newton decided. His anti-tank rifle crew had lost their chassis when a culvert collapsed but had commandeered a four-door sedan that could be used as a substitute. They had torched off the roof, and the jury-mount worked. Even the thermal shield to confuse Federal gunners mounted okay, and all they missed was their radio for communications. This was the way to fight a war! Six tanks already to their credit.

He liked to use the Chevy only for transportation, moving from one good firing position to another, but now that wasn't possible as they followed retreating Federals toward Pittsburgh. They had fallen in line behind several tanks from his armored regiment as point support.

A terrific *bang!* jolted Newt out of his complacency. The three tanks in front slewed off the road in both directions. He started to yell to his driver, but they were already bouncing down the right-of-way off the divided highway. In seconds they careened into the heavy Pennsylvania forest. Newton blessed his luck. This hillside was mostly pines, and deciduous trees had not yet begun to bud. His gunner Mace yanked the gun from its mounting, and set it up near the right-of-way fence.

"Christ, where did everybody go?" Stan Wisniewski, the PFC from Cleveland, gasped. The three tanks had disappeared, two sets of tracks going left, and one leading into woods on their side.

Newt turned his glasses down the highway. He could see a roadblock with a tank not quite hull-down. It looked like an old M-60.

"Let's do it, Mace," he whispered. Stupid. There wasn't anyone around for two hundred yards, and he was whispering. "We'll go right through that M-60."

Mace was a truly talented gunner. Newt told Wally to set up a second round, then break for cover. They could get two rockets off before the tank would turn on them.

Whap! The rocket flew off. Wally slammed the second into the tube without looking to see the result. He leaped to join Stan in a gully. *Whap!* The second rocket fired. Newt resisted the impulse to run for cover. The first rocket smashed into roadblock logs, but the second blew the turret fifty feet into the air.

Mace turned with a grin to Newt. "How about that, Sarge? Next time, I'll get it in one."

"Asshole tanks," Newt swore. The two that had gone left suddenly reappeared, sent a couple of rounds of HE into the roadblock mess, and charged down the road. "Wonder which one will claim our tank."

"Shit, Sarge, don't mean nothin'. Let's go catch up. They provide good cover."

Newt grinned and yelled to mount up. Like he was saying, you couldn't beat their little two-bit pea shooter. Not even with one of those half-million dollar tanks.

Stan slithered the car back onto the road. Newt wouldn't ride in one of those steel deathtraps for love nor money. His little SPATR, for Self-Propelled Anti-Tank Rifle, commonly called a "Spatter," was a whole lot safer. Good thing those M-60 spades couldn't shoot or they might have got some. As it was, they were all crispy critters now.

The tankers had gone around a curve, and Wisniewski almost slid into the rear tank. Their detachment commander, a captain who had graduated from West Point a year before the revolution, was studying a map. Newt didn't bother to report. Two APCs were burning a hundred yards down the highway. They were what was left of the roadblock. Far down on the right, several hills looked as though their tops had been flattened or cut off.

"Good shooting, Sergeant!" the tank commander yelled. "You can ride with us anytime!"

"Just my job, Captain," Newt said. "Why'd we stop?"

"Orders. That's Pittsburgh's old airport up there. We've beat everybody here."

Newt didn't like the sound of that. Airports meant aircraft, and being first meant being the most exposed.

"Sir, if that's an airport, and you don't mind, I'm getting the hell off the road."

The captain nodded, and Newt took his gun back to the tree-covered parking area where the APCs had hidden. Tanks attracted artillery and helicopter gunships. They were armored, and he wasn't. Let them take the heavy stuff.

Tanks were fighting their own technological war with armor and ammunition. Ever since the German Leopard had adopted Chobham armor, arguments between using HESH, various types of HEAT, and APDS had raged back and forth. Many tankers fastened the "Egg-crate" armor on their turrets and hull glacis to prematurely detonate HEAT and HESH rounds, and tank identification was an educated guess at best. They all looked alike from the front, particularly in thermal sights which were used when visibility was limited. Their surest differences were side skirting shapes and size and number of rollers and sprockets. But who ever saw oncoming tanks from the side?

During the past few days, ammunition supply had been a major problem. Tanks didn't carry an infinite number of rounds, and they were split between HEAT, HESH, APDS, and normal HE. With a full load of only 56 rounds, tankers were constantly complaining about being short of the right ammunition. Newt's problem was less with only two types of rockets, but the carrier and Chevy were limited in what they could carry. It was the eternal tradeoff between firepower and mobility.

Mace piled out and rummaged through the litter of equipment and personal items left by the unfortunate roadblock defenders. He was the quick, and they were the dead. Shit, the jigaboos had been smoking pot. He kicked a sack of grass away into the woods. That was why they were slow and missed with their first shot. He ambled over to the turret-less tank and looked inside.

He never ceased to be amazed at what happened when shell met tank. Its inside was coated with goo, evidently from the gunner and loader. The driver was still sitting in his seat grasping the controls, not much more than a skeleton. His uniform, skin, and most of his flesh was gone, and he was looking forward with lipless teeth in a permanently sardonic grin—looking down the road for an enemy who had already passed. An old M-60. Obsolete and little better than a motorized coffin.

Sergeant Newton was startled by jets overhead. They were Federal, flying west to attack his laggard brothers. Two fighter-bombers, and they either didn't see the tanks or thought they were friendly. Newt wondered if the planes would return. He had seen skies repeatedly wiped clean and decided they wouldn't. Life expectancy for a new pilot in combat must be less than an hour. All that time, money, training, and technology went *poof* within minutes. Insane, crazy. They didn't even crash in flames anymore. They blew up into little bits. They should fly higher so the clouds would be seeded.

A tank was coming back with its commander standing in the turret hatch, gesturing for his Spatter to follow. The timeout was over, and it was back to war. Newt wondered when his column would catch up, but that wasn't his concern. The tank spun around, tearing up a large chunk of asphalt, and disappeared down the road. Newt's section mounted up, and took off in chase.

The tanks were roaring down the highway at top speed—over fifty miles an hour. They turned into the airport approach road. Crazy! Three tanks and four idiots in a Chevy were attacking a major airport facility. Even Mace shouted they had bought it this time, and he was colder than Newt's ex-wife.

The airport was laid out like a chicken's foot without a heel and was swarming with people, both black and white, some in uniform, but most not. The lead tank drove through the fence and out onto the taxiways. Stan followed as closely as possible, and Newt found himself feeling naked to the world. The second tank turned out of line and sent an HE round into an armored car beneath the tower. It blew up, and continued to pop like a string of firecrackers as it burned. A jeep was next, and three occupants were literally knocked out of their seats by a stream of machinegun bullets.

Newt couldn't see a target for their rifle, so he stopped a safe distance away from the still-cooking armored car. Two tanks posted themselves to block runways, and the third's commander motioned for the Spatter to follow him. They returned to the airport entrance and blocked it.

In the next three hours, the Spatter team and their companion tank accounted for four more Federal tanks, three armored personnel carriers, two armored command vehicles, and assorted Bradleys and other vehicles. Fleeing Federals persisted in running pell-mell into their roadblock, apparently believing the wrecked vehicles had been destroyed by aircraft. Newt's section and the tank were finally relieved without suffering a single casualty, but not before they ran out of rockets. Fortunately, the tank conserved its ammunition, and Newt felt better about tanks.

*****

A week later, the war seemed over and nothing remained to be done except for occupying Federal territory. Newt could see himself sitting in front of a fireplace, telling the story of his great adventure to his grandchildren. Courage, fear, heroics, death, destruction, comradeship—everything, including love, was present. The love was only a short interlude with two Pittsburgh girls who greeted him as a liberator, but it was there nonetheless.

This was his destiny, Tom Newton decided. The UAR had reinstated him immediately as a sergeant, and his career was off and running again. It was a hellava good army—no racial problems and lots of popular support. Even its uniforms were super-professional, combining features of American, German, Russian, and French armies. In uniform he automatically commanded respect, and he was a natural-born artilleryman.

The UAR doted on building up efficient self-propelled artillery. Newt had drawn the latest anti-tank missile launcher, actually a recoilless rifle with a very accurate and high velocity missile. Its rocket had two stages; one for an initial launch at low velocity to limit back-blast, and a second for the main thrust after fifty feet. The rocket itself was extremely sophisticated, being fin-stabilized and having an internal gyroscope. Its accuracy was limited by the gunner—the rocket hit where aimed and used both eyeball and thermal sights. Dismounted, the rifle used a tripod, and was light enough to be hand carried by the crew.

Newt's unit had been heavily engaged in slaughtering Federals attempting to retreat east from Pittsburgh. They had set up south of

Plumborough on Highway 22, and the valley below became a graveyard for vehicles of all types. They ran out of ammunition seven times, and Wisniewski had been wounded making a run to replenish. Newt had finally seen large ammunition supply helicopters in action, and would never doubt their value again.

Regrouping had been swift, and 10th Armored had been shifted to Uniontown. They continued to attack down Highway 40, and word was that they were headed for Baltimore or Washington. In Uniontown, he turned in his improvised Chevy and received another regulation vehicle. It had more room and carried more rockets with its heavier suspension, but he wasn't sure it was an improvement. The car had been faster, and speed meant safety.

Two days later, his regiment was in Cumberland, Maryland. Opposition had been light, and Federal units deployed little heavy equipment. That didn't surprise Newt, having seen the carnage along Route 22. His unit and a half dozen SPATRs were detailed as a blocking detachment on State Route 28 toward Romney in West Virginia, cooling their heels with inactivity for three days.

Newt had almost decided the war was over when his company commander received orders for Frederick. Frederick! Only forty miles from either Washington or Baltimore. Neither Newt nor his crew could conceal their excitement as they pulled out after dark for the short trip down Route 40.

They weren't attacked, but past Hancock, it was ghastly. The road was littered with burnt-out vehicles and wreckage, almost as bad as Highway 22 east of Pittsburgh. Only this time it was UAR equipment that was destroyed and burning, and the dead were all white. What in hell had happened? They must have been attacked from the air, but where did Washington get the aircraft? And why hadn't SAMs and hand-helds neutralized the attack? Even Mace was silent as they threaded their way through the wreckage toward South Mountain. Newt was glad to be pointed into a position southwest of Frederick on the road to Harpers Ferry. They stashed their carrier, dug themselves into defensive positions, and waited. War had once again become serious business.

With dawn came more destruction. The SPATR units hugged the ground as wave after wave of fighter-bombers and helicopter gunships attacked positions around Frederick.

"Sarge, those planes ain't US," Mace grunted. "Those are French and British. They must'of declared war."

Mace was right. And there were German as well. They hadn't seen aircraft for days, and everyone had said both air forces were running short, but now this. Once again, Newt blessed his lucky stars he wasn't a tanker or in a heavy assault gun unit. None of the Spatters suffered any casualties.

"Where are our SAMs?" Newt yelled at the lieutenant when he came to check on casualties.

"Promised this afternoon. Latest, tonight." The 1st lieutenant shrugged, "Until then, we're on our own. Supposedly, we're to get air cover."

Mace looked up. "Yeah, we noticed the dogfights. Real entertaining."

Newt scanned the sky, and when he turned back, the lieutenant was gone.

"Our generals got so het up about capturing Washington, they forget to take flak jackets with 'em," Mace growled. "Probably were using SAM vehicles to tote champagne."

Newt agreed with Mace's assessment, but bitching wouldn't change anything. Everyone thought the Federal Air Force had been eliminated, and no doubt the spearhead commander had discarded his SAMs and hand-held anti-aircraft rockets for ground weapons that were more useful in house-to-house fighting. Too late now. The SAMs would have nothing to defend when they arrived.

"It's probably not so bad," Newt said. "Boo-boo isn't following through with a ground attack."

"Sure glad you said that," Mace snarled. He pointed down the road at an approaching spread of Federal infantrymen.

Newt cursed his tongue for bringing bad luck. He didn't see any targets for Spatters, and wondered if their infantry support was sufficient. Their rockets were like shooting quail with a cannon, but nevertheless, another Spatter announced his presence with a rocket that exploded among the Federals.

"Stupid bastard," seethed Mace. "Fire first to give away your position," he said.

"Probably newbies," Stan suggested.

They all kept their eyes glued down the road. After a half hour, they could see some movement. Infantry was approaching on both sides, at least two companies. A battalion sized attack, Newt told himself grimly. He wondered if Republican infantry had strewn anti-personnel mines over the approaches. Probably not; the column wouldn't have been equipped with defensive weapons like mines.

He was right. A few trip mines went off, but only caused a couple of casualties. Firing became general, and Newt could see the infantry were well-placed but outnumbered. Then he heard the scream of jets. French aircraft were attacking again!

The Republican line disappeared in four napalm runs, and Spatter positions were taking rocket fire. Republican infantry fire was almost silent, and Newt saw they were about to be overrun. "Let's didi outta here!" he yelled. "Mount up!"

The four men rose as one and dashed back to the pines with Mace and Stan lugging the rifle. *Whap! Whap!* Two rockets slammed into the vehicle park, one wrecking a Spatter carrier. Stan leaped into the driver's seat and their steed sprang to life. Ten seconds later they were careening onto the road. Two other Spatter crews reached their carriers when the park seemed to erupt like a many-vented volcano. Newt watched the crews evaporate in red and black clouds.

"Plane!" Mace yelled, and Stan wrenched the carrier to the left. A rocket exploded ahead as Stan steered to avoid the crater. "Plane!" he yelled again.

The three riders watched in horror as the French jet seemed to point directly at them, then suddenly spout a white cloud as if it fired all its rockets at once. Newt was rooted to his seat in fascination, unable to lift a finger to prevent his own death.

But the plane was falling apart! Pieces were flying off, and its nose was pulling up! It exploded with a dull *whoosh* which seemed to prod them down the road, and then it was raining aircraft and pilot parts.

"Ours!" Mace shouted. He was pointing to a plane heading skyward from where it had dispatched Froggie. Stan pulled over into trees surrounding a farmhouse to watch. They had lived to fight another day, but were the only survivors from their detachment.

Chapter 49

General Brown was furious and couldn't seem to shake President Parelli's calm. The debacle in Ohio and western Pennsylvania was the worst defeat for an American Army in history. Fourteen divisions destroyed, three hundred thousand men lost. There was no way of holding Washington. He was scraping up every detachment on the east coast to stop the rebels. They had broken through at Hancock, west of Hagerstown, were heavily engaged at South Mountain, and soon would be threatening the Monocacy line.

He had manpower but little equipment. Three of the four divisions sent into New England to quell disturbances were recalled, and they were augmented by four more from training camps and posts in Virginia and Maryland. But artillery and tanks were in short supply. The Air Force had been badly decimated in fighting on all fronts. Close-in air support had proven extremely costly wherever ground troops possessed those hand-operated heat-seeking rockets. They were absolutely lethal against slower aircraft and helicopters.

With air support neutralized, rebel superiority in self-propelled artillery had proven decisive, especially when battles became fluid. Heavy guns had separated infantry support from armor, and the tanks had been defeated piecemeal, particularly by anti-tank rockets which rebels possessed in such great numbers.

Fortunately, the rebel offensive appeared to be slowing. It was about time. They had advanced almost two hundred and forty miles in five weeks. The excellent road network made distances more like those in North Africa or the eastern front in World War II. Even in the mountains, wide roads and many cleared areas allowed for rapid movement.

"I can't guarantee the capital's safety," Brown had reported to the president two days ago in his morning briefing. "We're still holding out in some areas along South Mountain, but our final line before Washington itself is along the Monocacy. Everything we have is there. We're down to stopping their tanks with infantry."

"What are rebel air defenses like?" Parelli asked.

"They probably don't have much," Brown answered. "Most of our air power is gone, and neither side's going to squander it by attempting to knock out a tank or two. Why? Don't tell me you're ready to authorize strategic bombing?"

"Yep. I want the Boeing plants in Washington, MacDonnell-Douglas in Saint Louis, and all other aircraft production facilities destroyed."

"That will mean annihilation for our remaining bomber forces," General Joliet said.

"Yes, but they'll be replaced in the morning."

"I beg your pardon?" Both Joliet and Brown leaned forward and spoke simultaneously.

"The British, French, and Germans will start arriving this evening, so get your planes airborne. We want to cripple the Rebel Air Force even if it takes our last plane. We can get more—they can't." He had slid a paper to Joliet showing the arriving squadrons.

General Joliet scanned the list furiously. "Why haven't you mentioned this to us before?" he asked angrily.

"We couldn't count on European support. They weren't willing to commit until it looked like we would be defeated. And, as you just said, General, you can't guarantee the capital won't fall. We'll send in the Europeans tomorrow afternoon, and seal off the breakthrough in western Maryland. If we have any bombers left, I want the Pennsylvania turnpike tunnels bombed, and both it and Highway 40 blocked. *Capisce?*"

Joliet nodded. "My bombers are going on a suicide mission," he said. Parelli said nothing and looked away. Joliet issued the necessary orders.

Brown pulled back from South Mountain to conserve his armor and mobile units for a counter-attack. He would hold Monocacy with infantry and move tanks up the valley from Winchester. He would be ready the day after tomorrow.

*****

As Joliet predicted, his long-range bombers were annihilated with minimal results. Boeing facilities suffered moderate damage, but most others escaped almost unscathed. St. Louis had been heavily defended, and Federal losses there were grievous.

But the secondary objective had been achieved—the rebels sent all available fighter forces to intercept the bombers, and the Europeans were unopposed the following afternoon.

General Joliet was now a commander without a command; he had sacrificed his men—all Americans—to save European lives. He found himself reconsidering his choice to stay with the Union. Here was clear evidence that Stewart's propaganda was based in fact, that Americans were being sacrificed for European and Japanese business interests. He had never believed charges that the Trilateral Commission and Council for Foreign Relations were promoting world government at the cost of American sovereignty. But there was no refuting this reality.

He noticed his staff seemed to avoid him, and Leon Joliet decided he had made a mistake. It was too late to join the Republic; he could only atone for his error with his life. Alone in his office, he joined the men he had sent to their deaths. Honorably, with his prized Colt .45.

By noon the following day, it was apparent the rebels had been stopped. The attack on Frederick was coordinated with European air support and easily threw the rebels back over five miles from their advanced positions. The federals didn't press their advantage, but the effect of air support was readily visible. He had expected severe fighting, but the badly disorganized rebels offered little opposition.

In the afternoon, the two divisions moving north from Winchester made good progress, but the air power situation began to change. Elements of the Rebel Air Force appeared, and their combat experience soon made itself felt against green European pilots. French flyers suffered heavily, but rebel aircraft were too little, too late. By nightfall, his forward units were at Berkeley Springs and Martinsburg. It was a miracle, Brown told his staff. A miracle which proved the righteousness of their cause. "God is on our side," he stated.

*****

"Our Washington spearhead has been pinched off," General Carpenter reported grimly. "Everything east of Cumberland and Bedford is lost. The Pennsylvania turnpike is blocked west of Bedford, as is Highway 40-48 at Meadow Mountain."

Everyone was having difficulty accepting the last twenty-four hours. Sophia had received news of the EU's intervention with disbelief and then dismay. There was almost no logic behind their actions; she had not frozen any European or Bilderberg assets nor threatened them in any way. The question was whether or not to declare war on England, France, and Germany, or the EFG as Republicans called them. She called a meeting in her office with her most trusted advisors.

"Have we captured any Europeans, or have possession of their dead bodies?" she asked.

"Yes, some. We don't know exactly how many," General Carpenter said.

"Bring them here—alive or dead. I want all bodies with personal effects. Top priority. And ship every hand-held SAM we have to inflict maximum casualties on them." She turned to Webb and Otteson, her foreign relations minister. "Exactly what statements have the Europeans made with respect to their commitment?"

"All three issued statements saying they have furnished air support units to the Federal Government at President Parelli's request," Ernest Otteson.

"Any reply to our protests?"

"None. They're treating our protests as not coming from a legitimate government."

"Then it's time for a stronger protest." Sophia turned to Wallace. "Arrest all EFG nationals. Also any Bilderberg. Hold them until further notice. Admiral Kelerher, put your Atlantic force in position to cover all approaches from the EFG nations. We'll declare a blockade to take effect in forty-eight hours."

"EFG nationals will probably run into the tens of thousands," Wallace said. "All diplomatic personnel, too?"

"Yes. Only nations that have recognized us have diplomatic immunity. How long will the roundup take?"

"Two days at most."

"Okay, then Ernest, tell our missions in the EFG nations to leave immediately. Within twenty-four hours at the latest." Sophia walked around her desk and leaned against its front edge.

"We'll hold a line in the Alleghenies," Sophia declared. "Laurel Hill if necessary, but no further west. Anyone see a problem with that?"

Both Cedric and General Carpenter shook their heads. "I don't think they're in any shape to pursue. And we'll have SAMs there tomorrow. You'll see a lot more European casualties."

"Good. And I want to know when the first European aircraft bombs UAR territory."

"That's already happened," Cedric said. "They've hit targets in West Virginia."

"Other than the eastern seven counties?"

"Yes. They've bombed Morgantown and Grafton."

Sophia bit her lip. She knew what she had to do.

A half hour later, Sophia went before the cameras, broadcasting by satellite to the world—especially Europe.

"Yesterday, our nation was wantonly attacked by units of the British, French, and German air forces," she announced. "Heavy casualties have resulted from this unexpected, unwarranted, and unconscionable assault on our people and our sovereignty. We have lodged the most strenuous protests against these actions, but our voice has been ignored."

"If air attacks on our personnel have not ceased by eighteen hundred hours today, Eastern Daylight Time, we will consider ourselves authorized by international law to defend ourselves by every means possible, including extending hostilities to aggressor homelands."

"The Seven Principles of Nuremberg that were formulated by the International Law Commission for the General Assembly of the United Nations in 1950 apply to criminals of those European nations flying aggressor aircraft. Reading from GAOR, 5th Session, Supplement Number 12, the applicable principles are 1, 4, and 5 which tell us that, since civilian deaths through the action of European criminals have already occurred in our territory, we may hereby declare all members of European contingents as war criminals and they are thereby subject to penalties as determined in our military tribunals. No individuals in the European military units shall, under any circumstances, be treated as prisoners of war under the Geneva Convention."

"Once again, we salute our brave men and women fighting on the ramparts of freedom, repelling aggressors and invaders from nations who would enslave us under Snazism. We are, and shall always remain, independent and free. Be firm in your resolve to resist this tyranny and stay true to our great principles. With steadfastness of purpose, we shall triumph."

After receiving congratulations, Sophia drew Chuck Carpenter aside. "We will give them very short trials and executions," Sophia said. "I will have their casualties put on TV each day, along with the executions. This war is going into the living rooms of Europe."

"Execution by firing squad?" the General asked.

"No. By hanging. We must impress upon Europe that their troops are considered criminals."

She slapped the folder with her address on her desk. "And also try all Bilderbergs, CFR members, and Trilateralists in military tribunals as traitors or spies," Sophia said in an afterthought. "And tell General Colquitt he may bomb all military installations and war production facilities in Federal territory as planned. The conflict has just escalated."

*****

The defeat in Maryland left Shields's corps exposed and isolated. 1st Armored Division had reached Catskill on the Hudson, while 82nd Airborne had moved east to Pittsfield, Massachusetts. General Shields ordered them to halt and dig in while Sophia attempted to recruit New England into the UAR. Troops were under strict orders to treat civilians as liberated citizens and the area as friendly territory.

Lieutenant Colonel Ben Marston of the 2nd Battalion, 3rd Brigade, 82nd Airborne was not unhappy with his current position. He had been ordered to block the Taconic State Parkway south of its termination in the Thruway extension. If he were the enemy and wanted to cut off the 82nd, Taconic State would be his route.

Marston came from Idaho Springs, Colorado, a little town complete with a statue of Milton Caniff, creator of *Terry And The*

Pirates. He distrusted New Englanders. They were never wrong. And even if they did make an error, like involving the nation in Vietnam years earlier, they made up for it by not participating themselves. It was the heartland that had absorbed the losses, and stalwarts like his father who had died.

Colonel Marston had accepted a commission in the US Army to be part of the shield behind which American democracy could struggle with itself, finding the right balance of government and individual liberties. He was at Fort Stevens in Massachusetts when the rebellion broke out, and his decision was made in an instant. Within an hour after Colorado seceded, he had rented a truck and was packing his family's household goods. With his wife and two girls traveling in caravan, he'd headed west the following morning.

He was given a direct commission as a lieutenant colonel in the Republican Army, volunteered for the re-forming 82nd Airborne Division, and was given a battalion. Marston trained Eagle Two Three into an extremely close-knit fighting force by example.

Whoever designed their field equipment was a genius. Boots were dryer and quieter, helmets lighter and stronger, and packs carried the lightest basic load in any modern army. In combat dress, soldiers looked sharp and lethal, with snug-fitting pants and a tunic integrating the flak jacket. In garrison attire, troops wore double-breasted tunics with the top open. The color showing at the top represented the service arm. The stupid tie had been replaced by a small scarf. Honor and glory had returned, replacing strife and bickering in the old US Army.

His battalion had acquitted themselves well in northern Ohio as a containment unit east of Interstate 271. Blooded the first day, his unit fought hard along the Grand River in Willoughby and, with the Brigade's other battalions, stopped a full infantry division. Paying attention to deficiencies in Federal training, he had noticed their fire discipline was bad, and they frequently ran out of ammunition. He ordered each squad to carry decoys that rarely failed to draw enemy fire.

On the Taconic, Marston constructed twenty-two Quaker tanks, partially dug in, and with explosive charges in front to simulate firing. Real tanks were in short supply since going on the defensive. Everybody wanted them, but no one knew where the enemy would strike. Tactically, Marston couldn't complain—tank battalions were concentrated where they could rush to threatened areas—but that meant heavy casualties at the point of attack.

He christened his position as Marston's Hill, and the ground in front as Marston Moor. He told his men of Cromwell's victory over Royalists in 1644 and how Scots under Maitland and Lindsay had withstood repeated charges of Goring's cavalry. Even his name seemed to cheer the men and improve their morale. They believed in themselves; they had the best men, best equipment, and best commander. They challenged the Federals to do their worst.

*****

The New England delegation from Albany appeared legitimate, but became considerably more nervous after the Federal victory in Maryland. Sophia and Vice President Harrison took the delegation on a tour of Amish country around Burton in Geauga County. The area had been occupied by Federal infantry during their Cleveland attack and subsequent encirclement. Complete pacifists, the Amish had not supported either the UAR or US. Sophia showed the delegation destroyed buggies, houses, and mass graves.

"Federal troops were convinced the Amish possessed gold and hidden wealth since they didn't use modern banks," she informed them. "Most Amish refused to flee westward because of their pacifism and were massacred."

"Why haven't you publicized this?" Somers from Massachusetts said.

"It wasn't important before because we expected to be in Washington a few weeks later. But our people need to know now what they can expect."

The New Englanders dismissed the Amish matter as an isolated incident that would never happen in New England. Sophia hoped they were right, but coupled with the Cairo atrocities, she wasn't willing to bet anyone's life on it.

"We're interested in some type of affiliation with the UAR," Seres of New York said, "but intervention by European powers puts a new light on matters."

"How so?" Sophia asked. The jackals wanted pay-offs.

"It's become a different situation. We now hold the balance of power. Before, it looked like you might win your independence regardless of our actions. Now, if we support Washington, your state is a dead duck. If we support you, you'll survive. So what's survival worth?"

"For New England to secede," Senator Fitzgerald of Massachusetts said, "we will require protection until we can raise our own army. Also loans and price reductions on goods—most notably food—shipped from the midwest."

"And we need the National Government to assume our state debts, and guarantee a level of government contracts to maintain full employment in our states," Somers of Massachusetts added.

"And New York becomes two states, upstate New York as one, and NYC and Long Island the other. The population warrants it," Seres said.

Sophia sat quietly, waiting for their wish list to continue.

Seres tried to make his bargaining seem benign. "You have to understand our concerns. We have more difficult problems with our populations and cities than those in the midwest. New York is an international city, home of the United Nations, and must be maintained as the financial and economic capital of the world."

"New York is a dead city kept alive only through stock markets and entertainment. For one hundred thousand people it's alive—for seven million it's a hellhole not worth a dime." Sophia turned to her vice president. "What do you think, George?"

"So far, all we've heard is 'gimme, gimme.' What can they do for us?"

"Good question," Sophia said, turning back to Seres.

"Ensure your victory," he stated piously.

"How?"

"By our power. Our population and production."

"What production? All your factories are owned by Japanese or Europeans. What population? Half of it is living on welfare or dependent on government jobs. What power? All we see are problems. I'll tell you what. You secede first, and we'll assist in your defense. We'll also pump in money, food, and make jobs available to your citizens. Your people must hold to the principles of our nation, and your application will state your agreement to our legal system and laws promulgated by our congress. With that, we will greet your people with open arms."

"But state debts? And particularly state benefits and retirement plans? Our citizens will demand they continue in force," Seres said.

Vice President Harrison laughed out loud. It wasn't the citizens who wanted retirement plans to continue—it was the politicians. "No other state has demanded that," he said. "State debts were declared invalid. Everybody starts over, and that's one of our strengths. For the first time in your lives, you will see true reform. Think of it, Governor Somers. No crushing debt destroying the Commonwealth of Massachusetts."

"The people will never give up their benefits," Somers said.

It was hopeless, and the New Englanders were playing a dangerous game. Sophia leaned back and held up her hands to halt the discussion. "We'll keep the New York Thruway open for citizens of New England. I'll broadcast an appeal to your people to join us, and we'll see what transpires."

She sent the delegation back, and Webb carefully monitored developments. He saw no moves by politicians to incite their populations to secede. Some New England National Guard units joined Republican forces in eastern New York, but their numbers were in the hundreds instead of thousands.

"It was all bullpucky," Sophia told Webb. "It must have been a ploy to scare Washington into concessions."

"They committed treason during wartime," he said. "So what happens now?"

"Momentarily we have a slight advantage holding upstate New York. They've got to stop the flow of refugees from New England."

"So they'll attack in New York. They'll utilize European air power while they have it."

"It's here for the duration," Sophia said. "The United States is back to being a colony. The Bilderbergs just haven't figured out how to divvy it up."

"We haven't started executing European pilots yet," Webb reminded her.

"We will tomorrow. Trials in the morning, hangings in the afternoon. Maybe then we'll get their attention."

*****

Reviewing her transcript of the meeting between President Parelli and New England political leaders, Sophia noted with satisfaction that her instincts had been correct. He had chucked the delegation into prison, and threatened them with execution for treason.

The trickle coming into Albany turned into a torrent. Transportation was more of a problem than interdiction from European pilots who discovered the Thruway was a deathtrap of SAMs.

Sophia's policy of treating them as war criminals did not seem to affect the European pilots. They continued to fly missions without hesitation and were occasionally captured.

Still, the executions of European pilots caused an international stir. Britain, France, and Germany all protested, but Sophia held firm. Less than twenty were executed in the first batch, but no one now doubted her resolve. Because of her action, involvement by EU nations became a hot topic of debate in Europe. The seven Principles of Nuremberg had never been used before to prosecute anyone other than Americans and a couple of Serbs, and applying them to northern Europeans was setting a dangerous precedent.

Nonetheless, bombing of UAR territory by European aircraft was suspended. For four months, the European Expeditionary Force confined their attacks to New York, western Pennsylvania, and Maryland. Sophia didn't believe this policy would last indefinitely.

She was right, and it came to a thundering halt as air attacks began again in Ohio.

For three days, approaches in southern Ohio and West Virginia were bombed repeatedly by the EFG. Webb's intelligence indicated it was a ruse to draw attention away from troop movements in the Hudson Valley, and to convince her to move forces from New York to strengthen western Pennsylvania. The only thing Webb couldn't tell was exactly where the main blow would come, but he knew when. Federals had moved two corps of six divisions up against the Republic's four strung-out divisions. Sophia decided to follow through on her earlier warnings.

At nine in the morning Greenwich Mean Time, two hours before the Federal attack was to begin in New York, Kelerher struck with twenty-two missile submarines using non-atomic warheads. Targets included aircraft factories and air force facilities in Great Britain, France, and Germany, and the devastation was awesome. Submarine attacks commenced on EFG vessels en route to the United States, and within three hours, eleven ships had been sent to Davy Jones's locker.

This was followed later in the day with Sophia's announcement of Federal attacks, and her declaration that all EFG nationals within Republican territory were being imprisoned at hard labor for the crimes of their nations, and all property owned by EFG nationals was being confiscated or nationalized. Over twenty-four thousand nationals from the three countries were transferred from holding facilities into prison camps.

*****

Colonel Marston had been warned by Division G-2 to be on full alert for a possible attack at dawn, and his patrols reported much tighter enemy security. For the past week their screening line had been probed nightly, and he changed his forward positions constantly to frustrate Federal mapping of Eagle Two-Three's true defensive fighting positions. At midnight, he drew in his listening posts, leaving only booby-trapped dummies. At two, he ordered his battery of long-range 155mm SPs to lay down harassing fire on areas where Federals would most likely assemble. It was still quiet in front of his battalion, and he was beginning to believe intelligence was mistaken on the date. Then he knew—the Federals had not sent out a night patrol. He ordered his SPs to resume their fire and walk it down the highway.

After a dozen rounds the Taconic began to explode. That was too much for the Federals; they unleashed a hurricane of shells on Marston's positions. He had made them lose their cool and cut loose prematurely. Their fire was falling short on his dummy and screening positions, and Marston authorized his forward platoon to withdraw to the reserve line. No sooner had the platoon passed through than the assault began.

They were veterans, Marston gave the Federals that. They came on seemingly unmindful of losses, and although he lost all his Quaker tanks, the Taconic and approaches were soon littered with the wreckage of a full armored regiment. Casualties were heavy in his forward two companies, and Federal units chipped away at his defenses. The dawn surprise attack had been shattered, and their conventional combined arms attack in the morning fared little better. Continual pressure was maintained during the afternoon, and the following morning would certainly bring an all-out assault. Marston called for reinforcements, particularly Spatters and armor. Division obtained an armored brigade from XIV Corps that took a position immediately in the rear of Eagle Two Three.

Dawn broke with Federal infantry still in close contact, but delivering only light, harassing fire. At six-thirty, the battalion front began to fill with dark shapes like so many cockroaches crawling forward. Marston watched the attack develop. It was a full reinforced armored division, and he didn't have enough anti-tank ammunition to stop them if every round struck home. He knew his troops must be making the identical calculation.

The tanks charged. Like Scots Greys charging the French line at Waterloo they came, neither looking right nor left... and with the same result. Eagle Two Three was overrun, and Marston ordered his battalion to duck the armor, and concentrate on its following infantry. In a few minutes, it was a fight for survival, bunker to bunker, with corporals and sergeants controlling the battle. A hundred Federal tanks were heading north behind them, but Eagle Two Three held the infantry back for another two hours. Then Marston received the order to withdraw. Officially, seventy-nine percent of his battalion were listed as casualties when the remnant reached their assembly point behind Interstate 90 at Nassau, the highest two-day total for an American unit since 1863. The Federal offensive had been badly blunted, but Colonel Marston's fine battalion was temporarily destroyed as a fighting unit.

Two days into the Federal attack, Sophia authorized the reservoir raids. The night assaults were shockingly effective. Guards had not been supplied with night vision equipment, and most were not regular military units. The Quabbin Reservoir in Massachusetts, Barkhamsted Reservoir in Connecticut, and eight reservoirs of the New York City water system disappeared with their dams. From Boston to New Jersey, water suddenly became more precious than food. New England was on its own.

The raids and strong resistance slowed Federal armor and allowed General Shields to withdraw in good order. As the rear guard prepared to leave Albany, General Carpenter ordered all relay stations blown east of Rochester. New York and a large portion of the northeast was plunged into darkness.

With the blackout, Federal combat units halted for three days, not even moving westward from Albany to test Republican defenses. Webb's intelligence continued to flow from computers with battery backups and uninterruptible power sources, and voice telephone traffic was enormous. The northeast was paralyzed, and troops were withdrawn from the offensive to maintain order.

Sophia was more surprised than Carpenter. "Didn't they have any contingency plan for an interruption of their power?" she asked at the situation briefing.

"Apparently not," Webb answered. "They hadn't expected our capture of western New York, and when it happened, they hoped we wouldn't interfere with their power. That was one reason for the delegation. They were trying to stay neutral and keep their precious New England and New York safe from harm."

"Well, it didn't work, and now it's scorched earth. Blow everything at Niagara. All power installations, factories, everything with war potential."

*****

Colonel Marston watched the Niagara generator turbines disappear in huge blasts. Since being overrun on the Taconic, Marston's battalion had been assigned to assist engineers in demolition as XIV Corps slowly withdrew. Almost all factories were owned outright by the Japanese or controlled through their stock ownership, and the Niagara-Mohawk power plants were owned by NGG, a British company. Seeing their livelihoods disappear, large numbers of upstate New York residents joined the mass exodus to the west.

Many lightly wounded had returned to Eagle Two Three, and with replacements, morning-report strength was nearly fifty percent. But it was now responsible for destroying one of the world's largest power facilities. Men were grumbling. It was not what an elite unit should be doing.

Chapter 50 - The South

The Ozarks guarded the west side of the Mississippi Valley in Arkansas, but the delta land in Arkansas was vulnerable. The Mississippi was formidable, but Federal forces in Tennessee and Mississippi were well-equipped with amphibious vehicles and boats. Arkansas was also open to attack from the south by the Federal Louisiana Army.

General Brown had appointed General Rutherford to command 2nd Army and was well satisfied with his performance to date. Rutherford was a tall, light-skinned black from Detroit, and had been particularly distressed when Michigan went rebel.

Jack Rutherford didn't like playing second banana to anyone, and he had adopted an aggressive policy of offensive defense earlier. A contradiction in terms, like white soul. Now he planned to make a series of deep strikes westward with his Tennessee command to occupy the delta of Arkansas and southeast Missouri. It was the rice bowl of America and an incredibly fertile area. The east needed food, and seizing its produce would be important. The rebels were known to have four divisions in Arkansas, but they appeared complacent and inactive facing Hodges's white 5th Army in Louisiana. With Hodges holding the rebels' attention, Rutherford thought he could reach Little Rock and trap the rebels in the open. At the very least it would force them to abandon southeast Arkansas, and open the Mississippi to the Missouri border.

General Rutherford decided to implement his night crossing at Ashport. Luxora was on the Arkansas side, and a substantial chunk of Interstate 55 could fall in a few hours. Attacking at night would minimize danger from rebel aircraft.

Two battalions of armored infantry led off at ten-thirty, followed by the Engineer Battalion. Rutherford himself watched from the levee. The amphibious assault boats were about a third of the way across when artillery began to drop around the boats and approaches to the river from Ashport.

He had hoped to get his first wave across unopposed, but that had been a forlorn hope. His counter-battery fire immediately began registering on the Arkansas side. There was no change in rebel volume, so they were probably using those damned SPs and moving them frequently. The bastards were impossible to hit from their gun flashes since they moved after each shot.

His amphibs were taking a pasting, but he ordered his second wave to follow. All tanks not yet loaded into boats supported the crossing with firepower. There was no reason to save ammunition for Arkansas if they couldn't get there. Through his night glasses, the General could see several amphibs were across. Good. If rebel infantry wasn't too dense, his troops could drive off the rebel SPs.

Rutherford's ordered all boats into the river, not waiting for any to return. Artillery fire was still heavy, and General Tomlinson, XII Corps Commander, ordered up the 121st Mechanized Infantry. Its artillery, plus the Corps Artillery Brigade, commenced firing as soon as it arrived, and response from the rebels began to slacken.

Before first light, his Armored Division was fully on the Arkansas side, but the 121st Mechanized didn't complete its crossing until afternoon. Nonetheless, the rebel Mississippi River defense line was breached.

But then the attack fell apart.

From both flanks heavy artillery fire decimated the remaining boats, and the two divisions became effectively isolated. They fought hard, but ammunition soon ran out. By the end of the day, the rebels were engaging in mop-up operations. All Rutherford could do was provide covering fire from Tennessee, but he no longer knew where his troops were located. Fire on the west bank slacked precipitously, and the General knew he would have to scratch two divisions from the Federal order of battle.

To the south, however, Hodges attacked vigorously after the UAR line was thinned to face Rutherford. He made good progress and was able to occupy Little Rock and most of the delta before UAR troops were able to stop him.

*****

"That's what overconfidence gets us," Sophia remarked after listening to General Carpenter's overview. "Did General Scott learn from his mistake, or are you going to sack him?"

"I want to keep him. He still enjoys the confidence of his troops, and did an excellent job making the hard decisions after Hodges attacked. No one, including myself, thought Hodges was dangerous."

"Besides, the fault was not his alone," Cedric said. "It started with the placement of artillery. Headquarters told Scott he would have forty-eight hours warning of an attack, but when the time came, we gave him only seven hours' notice. When Hodges attacked, Scott had no Corps Artillery."

"No Corps Artillery? Why not?"

Carpenter shrugged. "The fortunes of war. First, Scott was in Blytheville dealing with Tomlinson when we notified him, so he was away from headquarters. Second, when he ordered the Artillery Brigade to Eudora to halt Hodges, Brigade Operations thought the town was Luxora. The connection was bad, and Eudora was near Blytheville. So Corps Artillery went north and had reached Marked Tree before the mistake was realized. Then it had to return to Pine Bluff to cross the river and was caught in the open along Highway 425 as Hodges rolled northward. A fairly normal military snafu, correctable with time. But they didn't have time."

"We have to look at this war in another way," Sophia said, after a long silence. "The military's job is to protect our citizenry from external threats, and in Ohio, Kentucky, and Arkansas, we didn't do that."

"You're referring to civilian losses?" Carpenter asked.

"Yes. I realize our Army has won significant victories, but our people have to be evacuated or protected. Fighting men have a chance to protect themselves." Sophia went to her desk, retrieved an envelope, and dropped it in front of the general. "These people didn't." She sounded more tired than angry.

Cedric looked over at the photographs as the CG took them out of the large manila envelope. He had seen them before with Webb— gruesome atrocity photos of dead civilians, including many children. Carpenter looked visibly shocked.

"I heard there were more events like Cairo, but to see the evidence..." His voice trailed off while he glanced through the stack.

"In this war, the only difference between military and civilian is the civilian has no chance to kill the other guy first. Those children were our future."

"We have to be free to maneuver," Cedric argued mildly.

"If our citizenry is wiped out, military victories are meaningless. We can only prevail if we survive; if not ourselves, then through our children. The principle of women and children first is still valid. Women before menopause, that is."

"We can't just line up our troops at the border," Cedric said. "What policy do you suggest?"

"Fight on their land, let their citizens die. Tell General Dean in Kentucky I expect him to fight at Nashville and points south. And Scott needs to retake Little Rock." Sophia scooped the photos back into their envelope. "If there's anyone still there."

*****

This was not how warfare was meant to be conducted, Troy Vandemeer told himself. This was mass murder. In his tank unit, only four steel monsters were still running. The Piney Woods on the border separating Texas and Louisiana had been full of fire-belching tin cans, and everything happened at point blank range. They would come into a clearing and stumble onto Federal tanks, anti-tank guns, or infantry, suddenly staring face-to-face with death. Survival went to the quickest.

Vandemeer vaguely wondered how many tanks he had seen blown up or on fire. Hundreds at least, and he wasn't sure whether they had won or lost. Last night, his battalion commander had combined remnants of his battalion and two other units into a single battle group of twenty-six Russian T-92 tanks, and they had headed north toward Carthage. They had lost their way and stopped at Center before midnight. Their accompanying infantry somehow disappeared.

This morning they had started back toward Timpson, and hadn't gone two miles before a large group of Federal tanks jumped them from the west. From the *west*! On a couple of east Texas farms there were now at least seventy tanks burning or standing like so much scrap metal. In ten minutes, over three hundred men had died. Vandemeer guessed they were officially victors since they were still on the battlefield.

He was a lieutenant, a graduate of Texas A & M, and a tank platoon commander. He viewed the battalion commander's pennant, waving over a still smoldering wreck with its gun pointing down like a drooping lance. He was now the battalion commander.

"Radio to concentrate on me," he called down the hatch. He watched as the other three runners drew closer, then swiveled around to form a defensive square. They were at the edge of a light wood, and he wondered how many tankers had fled the carnage on foot. Maybe twenty men, some obviously wounded, were headed their direction from across the fields.

Vandemeer recognized none of them. He dismounted and called a commander's conference. As the three tank sergeants crowded around, he consulted his map.

"We'll continue on Route 87 to Timpson," he announced. "Stay alert, I don't know what we'll find. Mount up!" he ordered.

Vandemeer's tank took the lead, and the wounded men rode on the other three tanks. The road was flanked by dense woods, but ahead looked clean and quiet. He rode standing in the turret hatch, cruising at twenty-five miles per hour. Twenty minutes later, he crossed a gradual rise and could see a small town ahead. Must be Huber hidden in a slight haze. Two minutes later, he was approaching the first house. He spotted bulky shapes to the left amid a group of tall oaks. "Tanks!" he shouted below.

They must be Republican. Vandemeer couldn't see markings, and they looked like the T-92s they were riding. "Identify!" he yelled.

The radio was crackling. "They're ours. First Battalion."

Sergeant Hines was more cautious. "How can you tell? Muzzle brakes look wrong."

"They're not Abrahms," Astor clarified.

"Maybe old Leopards," Hines said.

His tank commanders were all staring from open turret hatches. Coming down the slope, each following tank could see over the one in front. Vandemeer looked back. His wagons were so black and muddy, he couldn't identify them either.

He could see men smoking cigarettes sitting on the tanks.

Assholes. Probably wondering why they weren't waving. Sitting there in shade, cooling it. No wonder he couldn't identify them. They were piled high with crap and men. There were nine that he could see. Shit, the rear drive sprocket was too large!

He slammed his hatch shut. "Queens! Open fire! Kick it! Full speed ahead! Fire!" Vandemeer was screaming as his four tanks opened up. Sweat sprayed off the end of his nose. Through his periscope he could see Federals jumping into their tanks and running toward the house. Two tanks exploded immediately with thick black smoke and one fountain of flame shot for the sky like Old Faithful.

The closest tanks were hit, and smoke obscured the others. Vandemeer's gunner sent two more rounds of HEAT into the mess, using the thermal sight. The action suddenly became frenetic.

Two Federal tanks pulled out from the park and fired. The shells went by and exploded somewhere behind him. The nearest Federal tank sprouted a black rose on its turret, and the other slewed off behind a gas station. More shells and machine guns were firing. Vandemeer crashed through a sheet metal shack, and fired an APFSDS round directly into the side of a tank eighty yards ahead. The tank pivoted to the right, and blew up.

"Right ninety!" the radio crackled. The driver swung ninety degrees to the right, and lined up on a Federal tank facing the road they had just come down. The Federal fired once, and Vandemeer sent a solid shot directly into his hull. Three men bailed out, but crumpled immediately under Vandemeer's machine gun. There was no more firing.

Vandemeer did a three-sixty with his turret, but only saw two men disappearing into the woods. He was alone. One of his T-92s was belching smoke back on the road, another was in a ditch on the left side, and the third was further left in a field. Vandemeer popped his hatch for a better look, and headed his steed back up the road to check for survivors. There were now eleven—six men who had lost their tanks earlier and jumped off when fighting started, and five from this battle including Sergeant Hines and his tank crew. They climbed onto his T-92, and Vandemeer roared off toward Timpson. In sixty seconds, another twelve tanks had been reduced to smoking wrecks. He was victorious, but 3rd Battalion was in full retreat.

*****

General Duncan looked up as his G-3 walked in with reports from 4th Armored Corps. The Corps was equipped with Russian T-92 main battle tanks, and a lighter AT-90 Russian amphibious tank. They had borne the brunt of 5th Army's attack below Carthage, and fighting had been confused to say the least. General Rosser, the corps commander, had called it a wild melee, and his description was probably accurate. Whole tank brigades had vanished into the Piney Woods, and they had been feeding tanks and armored infantry into the seething cauldron steadily over the last two weeks without effect. The battle had to be reaching a climax; either that or they were done.

He was down to his last reserve, one mechanized infantry division north of Longview, one armored division with Republican tanks west of Carthage, and a second mechanized infantry division north of Beaumont. He telephoned General Carpenter at Des Moines to brief him on the situation. Duncan felt like a black sheep compared to Republican victories elsewhere, but he was facing white troops.

"You'll never believe this," he said, when General Carpenter answered, "but 4th Corps is down to less than eighty tanks."

"The entire corps gone?" Carpenter shouted incredulously. "You're not serious!"

"Hell, that's relying on field maintenance to return twenty from their shops in the morning. I've got to commit my reserve."

Carpenter let out an audible sigh. "Okay, what and where?"

"We're holding below Toledo Bend Reservoir for a few more days, but I've got to send two divisions against their line between Carthage and Marshall. Intelligence says Hodges has shot his bolt, and a determined shove should push Humpty-Dumpty off the wall." The last sentence was a lie, but every battlefield report indicated Federal losses were much higher than Republican. Old Rupert Hodges had to be sucking wind, and Duncan wanted Carpenter's approval to commit reserves.

"Okay, but pull up if the going gets too rough," Carpenter said.

Duncan could kiss him, but threw the receiver to his adjutant instead. "Call Rosser, and tell him I'm releasing 10th Armored and 16th Mechanized to his control. I want them in Louisiana in three days."

General Duncan had taken a serious risk, but his instincts proved correct. The Federal 5th Army had indeed been down to its proverbial last tank, and 10th Armored broke through its exhausted and brittle shell within two hours of the first assault. They didn't halt until reaching the Red River near Coushatta.

Rosser was withdrawn back to the border and mopped up straggling Federals remaining on Texas soil. Combining both armies, over three thousand tanks were strewn throughout east Texas, and over three hundred thousand men had become casualties from the Federal attack into Arkansas. Federal losses were twice that of Republican, and the UAR claimed a victory. A Pyrrhic victory, but a victory nonetheless.

Chapter 51

Although nothing could compare with the damage wrought by the destruction of Hoover Dam, Republican military operations in the far west created havoc almost immediately. General Collins swiftly moved his two corps into the Mojave Desert, and raced almost unopposed to Barstow. Camp Irwin was deserted, but beyond Barstow, resistance became heavier. Edwards and George Air Force bases were defended strongly by Federal Air Force personnel supported by the 2nd Marine Division and an armored brigade from Hunter Liggett.

Federal Air Force squadrons attempted close-in support, thinking they would be especially effective against units in the open desert. They were wrong, and SAMs brought down aircraft as if a giant net had been thrown into the sky. On the ground, Air Force personnel fared even worse. The men were untrained as infantry and broke under attack by tanks.

The Marines fought well, but were forced to retire into the San Gabriel Mountains. They formed a line to protect southern California, and watched as Collins turned north and forced a passage over the Tehachapi Mountains into Bakersfield. Collins traveled north up Interstate 5 and Route 99, and it was a triumphant parade, receiving surrenders from the California National Guard and various Army units, and congratulations from white farmers in the Valley.

The Federal Sierra Corps barely escaped from the high country to establish defenses in the Diablo Range protecting the Bay. The campaign started to become costly. Collins looped south over Pacheco Pass to Gilroy, and the end appeared to be in sight.

It wasn't.

Republican progress got bogged down in the pacification of Oakland and San Francisco. The one thing Collins did not have was manpower to handle urban warfare. Units became involved in house-to-house, hill-to-hill fights. Large numbers of black civilians joined in defense, as did many Japanese and Hispanic volunteers. Federal command issued an order that all individuals not cooperating fully with Federal troops were traitors and would be summarily shot. Citizens who owned firearms often ambushed and killed their attackers, but more often, whole families were murdered.

Collins finally resorted to siege and starvation. The Bay area was sealed off by land and sea, and no supplies of any kind were allowed in. The cities were already experiencing severe shortages of foodstuffs, and Collins shut off their power and water. Oakland was burnt to the ground by Collins's troops, and captured civilians were herded into detention centers. Deportation was introduced, and huge convoys were put into motion down the freeway to Los Angeles.

After five weeks of siege, Federal troops began to give way. They fought literally to the last man. Before Collins declared the Bay secured and turned back south, Washington had lost over four hundred thousand men. Mopping-up became an endless sink for manpower, and Collins's replacement requirements exceeded his original strength.

Three months later, there was still sporadic fighting in the Coast Range south of Monterey Bay. The entire California campaign that had begun so optimistically turned into another Pyrrhic victory. No one in the Republican military was pleased with the cost, but its political objective had been achieved: central and northern California were added to the Republic.

A new style of warfare began to develop in the Basin and Range from Mojave to southern Nevada. Three divisions of Hispanics were transferred into southern California from Arizona and New Mexico and equipped with dune buggy-type vehicles.

General Carpenter was forced to respond by recruiting volunteers for desert warfare, looking for cowboys, ex-bikers, and highly individualistic fighters, one of whom was Major Tony Dudley. He had acquitted himself well in Colorado's San Luis Valley against the Hispanic forces of General Elias, and the newly promoted major was transferred to Las Vegas. Dudley was given a cavalry battalion in the 3rd Air Cavalry Division, an experimental unit to determine appropriate desert tactics.

The small battalion fit him. Dudley was on his own again like with the aggressor unit at Benning. His men were a hard-bitten lot, most with tattoos and one or more teeth missing, and almost all were veterans coming from other units in the east or midwest.

Des Moines would describe losses among mobile desert units as light during their first year, but on most operations casualties were either few or none, or the unit was wiped out. Raiders became renown for their deadliness—a requirement for survival. And Dudley was a survivor.

*****

Canada was an infuriating situation. There was simply no good reason for Canada's current policy toward the UAR, and it wasn't in Canada's best interest over the long term.

In September, Sophia finally met with Canada's foreign minister. The meeting was held at Kincheloe Air Force Base on the Upper Peninsula of Michigan. The Canadians would not grant Sophia diplomatic status on their soil and voiced concern for her safety in view of anti-Republic feeling in Canada. Both Wallace and Cole were much happier anyway, as Kincheloe was relatively small, isolated, and easy to secure.

Foreign Minister Berthier was an extremely tall, patrician looking gentleman with white hair and a dark blue pinstripe suit who acted as if he was representing a great nation. Sophia had met him earlier in Washington and knew he used his height as a club, constantly attempting to physically intimidate his diplomatic counterparts.

In front of the Air Canada 767, Sophia spoke first. "On behalf of my country and myself, it's my pleasure to welcome you to the United American Republic," she said, extending her hand. "Would you prefer to speak English or French?"

Paul Berthier frowned. "Thank you. English, of course. Why would you ask?"

"With a famous French name like Berthier? Napoleon's chief of staff was Marshal Louis Berthier. I rather hoped you might have distinguished ancestry."

"No such luck, I'm afraid." The foreign minister recognized he had come off second best twice already, yet he could not be offended. He retreated into his best diplomatic mannerisms, extremely polite, but calculated to offend.

Sophia led the way between two rows of the tallest, roughest looking honor guard Berthier would ever see. The minimum height was six feet five inches, and with their M-10 submachine guns, black tank uniforms, and expressions as if they smelled something bad, they were a mean, imposing lot. Sophia wondered abstractly how many of these men would still be alive a year later.

The conference was not especially friendly.

"We have attempted to foster friendship with Canada at every possible opportunity, but you support the colonial policies of Great Britain. You act in their interest to the detriment of your own. Perhaps you could offer some explanation," Sophia said.

Berthier was equal to the occasion. "We have nothing but the highest respect for the American people," he said, "but we view the government of the United States of America to be the only legitimate government of the American people. Following the principles of international law, we cannot recognize your government at this time. You will remember Canada did not recognize the Confederacy when it declared its independence from the United States."

Sophia nodded. "I remember very well. Canada did not exist except as a province in British North America until the confederation of Canadian provinces was accomplished by the British North America Act in 1867. And from 1862 to 1864, the Province of Canada was paralyzed because no party could win a sufficient majority to carry on normal governmental activities. It wasn't until the 1926 Balfour Declaration that Canada was granted equality in status with Britain. There was no Canadian citizenship until 1947, and even then, you were still British subjects, with no national flag until 1965."

"Very impressive, but irrelevant."

Sophia continued. "The British Government was divided during the Civil War on Confederate recognition. Gladstone even prepared a plan to offer Canada's annexation to the Federal Government as compensation for British recognition of the Confederacy. At that time you folks were mere pawns of the British. What are you today?"

"Very independent, I assure you," Berthier said.

"You have greatly restricted immigration to maintain Canada's racial and ethnic compositions in the percentages of 1870, successfully accomplishing what we are attempting to do, yet you condemn us for adopting your policy. Your attitude is inconsistent, to say the least."

"We believe our policies are best for us. What is best for you is for you to determine."

"England would like to see us defeated," Sophia said. "The British have been promised compensation from our property by the Federal Government for their support." She pushed a document over to Berthier. "That is a transcript of a conversation between the British foreign minister and President Parelli proving the truth of my assertions. You will notice Canada receives nothing." Berthier glanced at the documents without comment.

"Let me tell you why you should support us. We're an excellent buffer state. If we fall, eventually you will have a predominately black and Hispanic nation on your four thousand mile long border. You will succumb next to their population tide. This time, your interests are diametrically opposed to those of Great Britain."

Berthier was impressed with Sophia's intelligence and knowledge, but not with her arguments. It was better to have a sick United States below him than a vigorous Anglo state. Blacks and Hispanics acted as brakes on American ambition, and that was good for Canada.

"The large American market able to purchase extensively is gone forever, and both Canada and Great Britain need to recognize that fact," Sophia said. "Its economic engines are now in the Republic."

"President Parelli would not agree with you."

"President Parelli is not his own man. You may ultimately be faced with a Japanese colony in place of the UAR, aggressive and predatory in Japanese tradition. The Japanese are masters in making trade restrictions to keep out foreign goods, and your market will disappear overnight. Your balance of payments will put Canada in their pocket."

"Not likely," Berthier said. "We've noted heavy Japanese investments, but European investment is greater, and they will hold the Japanese in check."

"Maybe, but you're betting your country on the assumption the Europeans will be better that the Japanese. Lots of luck with that one."

Berthier departed, still hostile to Sophia's overtures, and she knew there was no point in waiting for an official response to her requests. Seventy-two hours later, all power facilities distributing electricity into Canada and connecting bridges, tunnels, roads, and pipelines between the UAR and Canada were blown. Sophia had sealed the Canadian border from upper New York state to the Pacific Ocean.

*****

Two days later, Sophia was back at Kincheloe, this time with Canada's prime minister, John Ashburton.

"We have an open agenda, Prime Minister," Sophia said, after concluding preliminary pleasantries. "How would you like to proceed?"

"I regret we could not properly plan an agenda, but I deemed it important for us to meet sooner rather than later. In a single sentence, I would like to explore possibilities of a return to the relationship we enjoyed up until five days ago."

Sophia decided to be direct. "Mister Prime Minister," she said formally, "Our nations had no relationship five days ago. And we certainly didn't enjoy one. We're starting from scratch with a closed border, without a procedure for legally crossing it in either direction. We are at war with our aggressive neighbors to the east and south as you know."

"Madam President, what you most desire from me, I cannot grant. We would most likely be declared a co-belligerent by the United States and subjected to their attacks. But everything short of recognition is certainly open for discussion."

"They haven't declared war on the Russian Federation, China, or any other nation that has recognized the UAR."

"They aren't immediately adjacent to US territory, and we aren't as powerful as the two you mentioned."

"I see. You assume the United States will attack any geographically convenient weak nation, that takes actions the United

States doesn't like. Quite a commentary on the criminality of the United States."

"Madam, you are a master of rhetoric as Minister Berthier has indicated, but we are simply not prepared at the present time to discuss diplomatic recognition."

"How about unrestricted ground and air access for us between our lower states and Alaska?"

Ashburton suggested opening the border to trade, and the discussion became involved in details and items that would normally have been discussed at lower levels; such as the continued pipeline supply of Canadian crude into Minnesota and trade between Seattle and Vancouver.

Sophia began to get impatient, and wondered what Ashburton really wanted. Finally it came.

"We understand you possess excellent information on Quebec separatists, having retained your operatives and sources from the CIA."

"To some degree, Mister Prime Minister, but you understand they are of no importance to us." Sophia knew Quebec separatists had stepped up their terrorist activities.

"Yes, but they are very important to us."

"I'm surprised you view the Quebec disturbances as serious. Even France renounced support for the separatists, and the guerrillas can't be adequately armed."

"We have information that they are receiving aid from outside Canada. Arms and munitions."

"Not from us. We have our own war to fight and do not have a common border with Quebec. You might be advised to look east for the fly in your ointment."

"Yes, we have considered that and that's why we're here."

Sophia didn't understand the point. "You wish to make common cause with us against the United States? And you can't recognize us?"

"Oh, no. But our Navy is inadequate to close the Saint Lawrence River and blockade Quebec. You have many surface units that you cannot use. We would like to consider a possible trade."

Sophia wanted to throw up. Once again, Canadians had come to the well asking for aid. Okay, she'd trade useless ships for the uninterrupted flow of Canadian crude and ground and air access to Alaska. It was still no-go. The prime minister couldn't allow the unrestricted ground link with Alaska over his sovereign territory. He limited the agreement to air access.

Webb interrupted shortly after three in the afternoon and drew Sophia aside. "Time to leave," he said quietly. He gestured to Cole who looked uncharacteristically nervous. Sophia understood. She returned to the conference and quickly bade Ashburton and his party *adieu*. Within ten minutes, Sophia was flying west with Cole to Sawyer Air Force Base near Marquette.

On the flight, Webb explained. "In a routine transmission monitored last night, the name 'Kincheloe' cropped up several times. The Army didn't recognize it and couldn't find it on their maps. The implication was an attack would take place tonight."

"We expected to remain at Kincheloe overnight," Sophia said, "but so did the Canadian prime minister."

"Maybe not. Maybe he was planning to leave suddenly like you did."

"We'll know shortly. If Kincheloe is attacked, we'll know they were in on the plot."

"Maybe not," Cole said, speaking up for the first time. "It would be easy to subvert some Canadian controllers. The Agency wouldn't need more than a couple in the right places."

"Then how would they know about Kincheloe?" Webb countered.

"Maybe from us. How many knew?"

Sophia and Webb looked at each other. Not many, except in the foreign ministry. There would be dozens there, and a leak was possible.

"I'll work on it," Webb nodded.

The raid didn't take place, but only because the strike force had been recalled. The question remained: was the Canadian government involved?

*****

The question of a security leak continued to surface in Jack Wallace's thoughts as he went about his duties. He sometimes felt inadequate and this was one of those times. His girl had been saved by a whisker again, and he might have been responsible for allowing someone the opportunity to kill her. She hadn't said a word of criticism, but had made love to him like she would die tomorrow. Then she had broken into sobs instead of her usual laughter. He held her tightly and rocked her from side to side while she bit into his shoulder.

"Sometimes I feel so alone," she said almost accusingly. "Everyone looks to me for strength and answers. Even with you. I sometimes think you love me because I want you to."

Wallace was crushed. His heart ached, and his sexual desire evaporated—precisely the wrong reaction. She wanted to be reassured, for him to exhibit a passionate desire for her, a re-affirmation of her womanhood. He had never been good at bedroom talk, never good with the words women wanted so badly to hear.

"I need you to love me," Sophia said. "I need strength from other people, just like anyone else."

He enfolded her in his arms again, and buried her beneath him. "You've got all the strength I possess, baby, and all my love. I don't know what else to give."

She was silent, but he could feel her breathing become more relaxed and regular after a moment. She loosened her grip on him, and he could feel her gently stroking his back. His sexual desire returned and she couldn't mistake it. This time he made love as gently and lovingly as he knew how. Sophia didn't laugh afterward, but she didn't cry either.

Wallace went through the ministry for foreign relations like an avenging angel, supposedly chasing a security leak to Canada. In three days, he narrowed his investigation to three people and then down to one. A young protocol assistant named Linda Schoeneker who worked for the deputy minister with the responsibility for Canada. In checking her background, Wallace's people found she had attended Columbia and lived with a black man during her last two years in college. She had been employed in the US State Department, but joined the UAR after her home state of Wisconsin seceded. Acting on his suspicion, Wallace leaked the information that Sophia would be flying to Cambridge, Ohio, and carefully monitored Schoeneker's activities. She went to a convenience store close to the complex and telephoned Little Rock, Arkansas. It was not officially an international call, but Little Rock was occupied by Federal forces. Miss Schoeneker was arrested, and Wallace informed Sophia.

"What do you want to do?" he asked Sophia. "She's our first case of espionage, and whatever we do will set a precedent."

"Do we have enough evidence to convict?"

"No," he said. "I was in a hurry to remove her as a threat. Sorry, that's what love does."

Sophia smiled at Wallace. "That's all right. Take me to her."

The girl wasn't especially pretty and was somewhat overweight. She resembled a New York collegiate type, needing only an overlarge knit sweater to complete the image. She stood up as Sophia and Wallace entered.

"So you want me dead," Sophia said as a statement. "Why? What makes you believe I'm so evil that you're willing to die to kill me?"

The girl glared with hatred. "You're Satan," she hissed. "You've destroyed the greatest country the world has ever known. You deserve to die."

Sophia nodded. "Satan has many forms," she replied. "More often to be found within us than without." She turned and exited the cell in silence.

Linda Schoeneker confessed freely, and received the martyrdom she desired the following day. She was disappointed to find the courtroom closed to spectators, and her trial lasted less than twenty minutes. She had thought there would be substantial publicity and notoriety, with public outcries like she had become accustomed to seeing on TV. All of that, however, was missing in the cold efficiency of the court. There was no appeal, and the hanging took place two hours later. She was given time only for religious absolution. As Adam said, it was more than she had planned for Sophia.

Chapter 52

"We must eliminate their submarines," Admiral Yoshida warned. "Since the rebels unleashed their subs, we've lost over six hundred ships. We're shipping through the Saint Lawrence and into Mexico to avoid submarines. The Federals will decrease rations again next week in the east, and by winter, they'll be at starvation level."

"Just keep the Army well fed," Tanaka sighed. "We're not interested in civilians. But can we depend on Americans to produce enough troops to defeat the rebels with our supplies?"

"No," General Tsuji said. "Hispanics are showing little interest in fighting. Blacks are solid, but only a small fraction of Unionist whites are sufficiently motivated to fight."

"In spite of the almost universal support by TV and movie celebrities?" Tanaka asked.

Tsuji shrugged. "Celebrities have less influence than we thought. Many are not Americans—they're non-citizens with green cards."

Tanaka considered this new information. "Can we win without white support?"

"Not without troops from other powers. Ourselves, maybe Mexicans, and Europeans. You're a Bilderberg; do you think they'll commit armed forces from their own nations?"

Tanaka ignored the question about the Bilderbergs. "Then we'll have to intervene ourselves. Recruit blacks from South African and other ex-colonial nations. We'll offer them the opportunity to kill whites. And the Mexicans. We'll promise them Texas and the Southwest in return for armed intervention. They're already allowing us to cross their territory."

"At full price," Kurita said caustically.

"What about the millions of whites in Federal territory? They can't be considered loyal."

523

"Many still hold to beliefs of individual liberty and the sanctity of private property. They will have to be eliminated," Tsuji said. "Small groups of civilians have to be killed at every opportunity until the population is sufficiently reduced for larger actions."

"Like what happened in San Francisco? How many civilians died during its defense?"

"Maybe a couple of million," General Tsuji said. "They died singly and in small groups, exactly like what we're proposing. No single big action, just many small ones."

"That's fine for reducing rebel populations or people in war zones, but I'm talking about whites under Federal control. How do we eliminate them?"

"Starve them. When totally disorganized and practically helpless, attack with the Army and exterminate. In a year or so, we'll be able to use gas."

"The Bilderbergs will never allow it," Tanaka said.

"I don't believe our people are ready to send a large army to fight," Kurita cautioned. "They'll view it as not being their war."

The conference room fell oppressively silent, but Kurita stood his ground. Tanaka glared at his finance minister.

"Then we'll give them a reason," Tanaka said.

"What? Why should young Japanese fight and die across the ocean when they can enjoy a good life here? They'll point to Australia which is almost Japanese, Hawaii, the Pacific islands, and Alaska as being enough. We've already replaced Hawaii's non-Japanese population, Australia is rich in minerals, and Alaska will give us oil."

Tanaka was through listening to objections and problems. He turned to Tsuji. "Send a thousand military liaison and support personnel to southern California. We have over a million ethnic Japanese in California, and many are now behind rebel lines. Start manufacturing atrocities in which ethnic Japanese are killed, tortured, raped, and whatever. We'll mount a propaganda campaign that will bring Japanese screaming for rebel blood."

Tanaka smiled. "And lose a lot of celebrities along with ethnic Japanese. Particularly beautiful American girls. What do Americans say? That will play in Peoria."

*****

President Carrillo had balked at allowing Japanese to transship through Mexican territory, but so far, the arrangement had worked out well. The rebels had not attacked Mexican territory, and Japan had assumed the debt owed to the United States, effectively re-establishing Mexico's financial stability.

Premier Tanaka had also solicited Mexico's co-belligerency with Japan and the United States against the rebels. It was all well and good for the Japanese premier to promise him American territory, but it was land that Japan did not have to give away... Or did it? He needed to assess the American president and his government's strength.

Like most Mexican politicians, Jose Carrillo had always assumed the American southwest would return to Mexico eventually. The only question was when. Mexico had encouraged emigration since World War II to attain Mexican majorities in those states formerly contained in Greater Mexico. When the plebiscite came, they would vote to return the land to Mexico.

Hispanics had become a majority between the two Colorado Rivers. Southern California was close to being majority Hispanic, and the remainder was black, white, and Asian. Organizations like LULAC and La Raza had done everything possible to hold the linguistic and cultural line, and only Colorado had been lost to the UAR.

Carrillo thought North Americans were impossible to understand. They had pursued an immigration policy to maintain a European majority and heritage until Eisenhower, but then dropped it in a burst of moral righteousness. Faced with increasing numbers of Spanish-speakers, the idea of a single unifying language was discarded without a whimper.

There was a self-immolating tendency present in the Anglo psyche that had produced policies which could only bring about their self-destruction. A country's culture must be preserved from outside attacks. But North Americans had insisted on remaining defenseless. Why? When Mormons in Mexico threatened to become powerful and influential, they were expelled without compensation for their property or belongings.

Many countries, including Mexico, had laws prohibiting foreign ownership of property and activity in various businesses, protecting the birthright of their own citizens. Only the United States hung itself out like a ripe cherry on a limb to be plucked by any passing bird. All in the name of something that various dim-witted Americans called "freedom."

Earlier in his life Carrillo liked North Americans—now he detested them for their twin attributes of arrogance and stupidity. Acting indifferent to their own interests was stupid, and a rational individual could not predict what a stupid person might do. They didn't even support their own brethren. White North Americans were hostile to white South Africans in their last extremity, and helped black Africans eliminate the Afrikaners.

It had to be their women. White North Americans were cursed with bad women. They were against abortion so more black and Hispanic babies were born. They refused to have a gun in the house, so they were raped and robbed, then blamed their husbands for not protecting them. They berated their men constantly, then wondered why they left. They were against drinking, so their men couldn't enjoy life. They were against prostitution, so their men couldn't be men. They didn't support war and shunned their soldiers. To prove they were free from prejudice, they had sex with men of other races, then flaunted their fornications in front of their own kind. If they married a man of a different race, they adopted his culture, and their babies adopted that race. They turned their backs forever on their heritage, and left their own men angry and frustrated.

How different Mexican women were! Only whores went to bed with blacks. A Mexican woman always remained Mexican and stayed true to her family no matter what. Her children remained Mexican, even if she married an Anglo. She supported her man and made him feel strong.

The rebels had corrected those destructive policies and earned his respect. They had forced Hispanics out of their territory, and both the rebels and Hispanics were better off. But now it was in Mexico's interest to see the rebels defeated. He flew to Washington to meet with President Parelli.

*****

Washington was depressing. Carrillo saw massive unemployment and people lounging listlessly about in the streets. He relayed his impressions to President Parelli.

"Our major cities are almost all black now," Parelli remarked. "White people stay away except under compelling circumstances. Until the rebels are defeated, it's probably better that way."

Carrillo realized that Parelli was hedging. If whites were not supporting the government, then it couldn't last. Parelli was white, but Carrillo could see for himself that tensions between whites and blacks were high—even among high government officials.

"We have been supporting your government, but at some cost," Carrillo stated. "The Colorado River disaster created much hardship, and Republicans are threatening us with retaliatory action for allowing your forces to be supplied through our territory." That was a lie which Parelli would not be able to confirm or disprove.

"Yes, we know you have made sacrifices and greatly appreciate your continued support."

"But speaking frankly, we are uncertain you can defeat the UAR."

"I assure you we have sufficient resolve to defeat the rebels."

"But possibly not the means."

Parelli was a good poker player. "You have a suggestion for increasing our means?"

"We have been increasing our armed forces to meet potential rebel threats," Carrillo exaggerated. "We might be able to provide some assistance to your personnel under certain circumstances."

"You would be willing to augment our troop strength and help defeat the rebels?"

"It might be possible—under appropriate circumstances."

"Then we must discuss circumstances. All things are negotiable. We would welcome Mexican military assistance, but what commitment are you expecting from us? Texas?"

"Texas would certainly get our attention. At present, most of it is under rebel control, so if you are not successful in re-uniting the country, it will be lost anyway."

Parelli immediately back-pedalled on the idea that Texas was negotiable. In fact, Parelli was not willing to make any major commitments, so the conference ended without results.

Nonetheless, it was a watershed for Carrillo. If the American southwest was occupied by Mexican troops and the majority of its population Hispanic, the World Court would award it to Mexico. It was time to make Mexico's case known and begin operations against the North American rebels in conjunction with Japan. Mexico's hour of opportunity had come.

For Parelli, the conference was a failure. Foreigners were vultures, he decided. They all wanted excessive compensation for minimum efforts. Japan wanted total control of America's economy, the British, French, and Germans expected major chunks of rebel property and trade advantages, and now the Mexicans. They even believed he was willing to part with Texas and other southwestern states. Ridiculous. He wasn't fighting to re-unite the nation just to parcel it out to foreign countries.

Africa had been the one bright spot for unconditional assistance. South Africa and Zimbabwe had pledged troops after Japan promised to underwrite the costs, and, although regular units had yet to arrive, volunteers were plentiful. General Brown had cranked up a promotional campaign for recruits, stressing salaries and benefits. The pay was substantially above what most Africans could earn in their home countries, and induction centers had been continuously crowded.

Thirty thousand Africans were already in training at Fort Benning, twenty thousand at Gordon, another twenty at Jackson, and over a hundred and seventy thousand more were awaiting transportation from Africa. Brown expected to have three divisions of Africans in Tennessee by spring, building eventually to at least two armies of over twenty divisions by the end of the year.

Three days after meeting with the Mexican president, news from Europe surpassed Parelli's fondest hopes. Germany would contribute regular army units, staffed by German Army officers and NCOs, equip the units, and place them at his disposal. The first unit, a panzer division, was almost completely filled, and the German government notified Parelli that he could expect a German expeditionary force of one or two corps. The troops would be heavily Muslim, immigrants from Turkey and Syria, and well-motivated to fight Americans.

Contacting Britain and France to arrange similar agreements also achieved successes. Britain adopted the identical policy as Germany, but not without additional concessions. Like Germany, Britain was actively recruiting Muslims and Indians for service in the US. France declined to expand her efforts as volunteers in France were lacking. They maintained a steady stream of replacements for their air arm, and allowed Parelli to recruit in France, but nothing more.

Brown recommended incorporating the arriving German and British units, a maximum of three corps and heavy in armor, into the Eastern Army. If the Germans lived up to their reputation, he could use them as shock troops, and take the heat off his own heavily blooded units. Unfortunately, the European units would not be up to strength for a year, and until they and the Africans could be employed, strategy in the east was necessarily defensive.

In order to maintain the initiative somewhere, Parelli decided to accept Japan's proposal for assistance in the west. General Brown agreed, and since the Japanese Army would have to pass through Mexico to be deployed, the Mexicans would be involved with or without an agreement.

"We'll have to allow Mexico to protect itself," Brown said.

"We'll let them take over defending west and south Texas," Parelli said, gnashing his teeth. "Nothing will happen there, and even if they're defeated, nothing's lost."

Brown wasn't so sure. Mexican and American armies had never gotten along, and Mexicans tended to steal everything in sight. Sooner or later, there would be nasty clashes. Still, they would release American Hispanic troops to fight in California and retain an American presence alongside Japanese troops. He would also employ Mexicans in the California-Nevada desert. Casualties there were all out of proportion to the numbers engaged and the theater's strategic importance.

Chapter 53

General Carpenter scowled at other National Defense Council members. "I'm not sure our policies will enable us to win," he said. "This is like Korea and Vietnam—what we're doing will keep us from losing, but won't let us win."

"That's what I like about you, Chuck," Sophia said. "You aren't afraid to tell me when I've screwed up."

"You haven't screwed up," he said. "We're screwing up. We need to dictate peace terms from Washington."

"Like Napoleon did from Moscow?" Webb countered.

"We're strangling them by our blockade," Admiral Kelerher offered. "But we have to expand it to Canada and Mexico. The Japs are shipping their supplies there to avoid interdiction."

"If we blockade Mexico, what can we expect from the Mexicans?" Sophia asked.

Otteson shook his head. "Intervention militarily," he said.

"We'll have that anyway in a few months," Carpenter said. "We can handle them if we make an all-out effort. Hold in the east and eliminate the southwest pocket."

"We still haven't cleared California," Sophia said.

"We haven't been willing to make the effort," Carpenter argued.

"We'll have to tighten up the draft considerably. War fever is subsiding now that most people think the war is already won. We'll need a million men as replacements before spring."

"That's higher than expected." Sophia sat on the edge of her chair. "Webb, you know the pulse of the people. Are we in trouble over the long run?"

Webb wasn't sure he wanted to answer. The problem had been gnawing at him since the defeat in Maryland. Recruitment was slow. There weren't enough Amulots to go around. "Maybe," he answered. "The best soldiers are already in the Army. We need to catch a second wind, and with a quick victory no longer possible, convince people the job is worth it."

"I didn't like your 'maybe,'" Sophia said. "Let's find out now. We'll call up another million troops. All the National Guard and whatever draftees we need. Let's see how the public takes it."

"We still need to win," Carpenter said. "I'll need another million with equipment to win."

"Armor?"

"Fifteen more divisions."

"With this call-up, we can't maintain our current T O & E, much less expand. We'll have to purchase from Russia."

"We'll suffer losses," Kelerher said. "We only have west coast ports, and holding them open will be a trick."

Sophia sucked in her cheeks. Kelerher was right. As things stood, they would lose a war of attrition if the Federals kept up pressure. Germany was supplying tanks and armored vehicles to Parelli, shipping both to Canada and Mexico. They were back to Kelerher's problem— she needed to authorize a blockade of Canada and Mexico. That would bring war with both countries. War with Mexico was possibly palatable, but war with Canada wasn't. The Bilderbergs would rush to Canada's defense, and European armies would materialize to attack her from Canada. Her exposure would be immense, and the enemy could move freely around her and pick their point of attack. If Canada wasn't an ally, it at least needed to be neutral.

"Webb tells me Mexico will probably become actively involved in a few weeks, and I will authorize a blockade of Mexico at that time." She turned to Carpenter. "Given that, when will we be in position to go with an all-out attack?"

"Assuming the immediate call-up of a million men, six months after beginning the blockade."

Sophia issued her call-up, and watched developments with misgivings. A significant percentage of notified inductees failed to appear at reception centers. The next million would cut deeper, and be even less effective. There were protests calling for negotiation with Washington, mostly by males subject to military service, and females between fifteen and thirty. All protests were in cities untouched by fighting.

Demonstrators were summarily arrested, and males were sentenced to a choice of one year at hard labor, or service in a penal battalion. Most selected hard labor, but it was in Alaska constructing naval facilities, definitely not what they expected.

Females were a different problem. Most anticipated being jailed, charged with a misdemeanor, and then released on bail or paying a fine. They were still being held, while a small army of lawyers clamored for their release.

"Arrest the complaining lawyers," Sophia ordered Wallace. "Those of military age can select penal battalions, otherwise they go to Alaska."

"We need a decision on the women," he said. "Otherwise there will be more protests, and the situation will get worse."

"Okay," she sighed. "Just like men, guilty of sabotage. One year at hard labor. But put them to work in California cleaning up the Bay Area. Let them know what happened to people there."

"And evaders? No-shows?"

"After thirty days, they're deserters. Hard labor or a penal battalion for the duration."

The evident complacency was an outgrowth of Sophia's successful domestic policies. Away from war zones, civilian life was quiet and safe. Drugs, organized crime, random violence, and street gangs had evaporated, and cities were tame. Adam and Harold had promulgated criminal laws and penalties which made the Republic a bad place to go bad. They prescribed castration for males guilty of certain violent crimes, and included sterilization as a common punishment for many offenses. Never again would a man like the murderer of Sharon Tate and her baby be allowed to father three children through conjugal visits in prison. In addition, establishing two large prison camps in Alaska had worked wonders. Sophia possessed her own Siberia, and by emphasizing punishment rather than rehabilitation, sentences were actually becoming deterrents.

The conspiracy law with respect to organized crime and foreign gangs had been toughened, and affiliation with a criminal gang that committed murder or trafficked drugs became a felony. Using information from old FBI files, Wallace's men had arrested over a thousand Mafia members within a twenty-four hour period. Lawyers who emerged to represent mobsters were themselves arrested, and the Mafia disappeared overnight. Those who were not captured were placed on Wanted lists, but most escaped to Canada or Federal territory like cockroaches fleeing a housewife's stomping foot.

Many of Sophia's reforms waited while other problems took precedence. The two states added by conquest, California and Allegheny, had very recently been battlefields, and elementary services were destroyed or in disrepair. Devastation in the Bay Area had been particularly severe. Civilian casualties numbered almost a million and a half, and bodies were still being found daily in ruins and debris. Female protestors were driven hard in the cleanup, and many began changing their attitudes. It was all well and good to protest in safety, but safety had become relative.

*****

Following her second million-man call-up, desertions increased to alarming numbers, and setting an effective policy to deal with deserters climbed high on Sophia's priority list. The American Army had executed only one man for desertion in World War II, a Private Slovik in Europe during the winter of 1944-45. None had been executed since 1945, and desertions during Vietnam numbered over a half million!

Sophia looked to the Confederacy for her answer, this time to the policies of Robert E. Lee. They varied by the need for discipline in his army; sometimes he approved a large number of executions, other times he allowed miscreants to return to their units and the fighting. But those were the only options—prison or escaping danger through work details were not allowed. Sophia began to authorize executions in every major unit, and allowed military courts only the latitude in murky instances to return the offender to his unit after reduction to private.

Meanwhile, the family could not be neglected. The third generation of K11 children was finally underway, and all of her boys were now fathers of multiple children. The girlfriends were all bright, educated women in their late twenties and thirties, found and recruited by Heather. They understood why children were needed and why the boys currently pursued polygamous relationships. None had declined the financial and social arrangement that Heather offered, and after meeting Sophia, enthusiastically embraced the program.

Webb warned Sophia the chances for winning the war were now only fifty-fifty.

"Bad odds," Sophia said. "We've got the best people, but maybe not enough of them. We Amulots are too few."

"We knew it was a risk going in," Webb reminded her.

"For myself, I don't care. I'll see it through. It's the boys I'm concerned about. I want them to have a golden parachute for the eventuality we might lose. And their families."

"Where could they be safe?" Webb asked.

Sophia looked out the window at her frost-killed garden. "The options are very limited. The country must be strong enough to resist pressure from Japan and the Bilderbergs. I can only think of one, and they'll be happy to receive the boys—Russia."

"I would recommend a fall-back option of China," Webb said.

"Agreed. Only the Russians and Chinese have sufficient power to ignore the Bilderbergs."

Webb reached for the telephone and called Bobbi. She joined them a few minutes later.

He quickly acquainted Bobbi with their subject. She sat down without speaking. "Billy needs a parachute, and to be included as the major-domo of the group," Webb stated.

"Why?" Sophia asked. "Not that Billy isn't important, but why him and not others?"

Bobbi gazed at Sophia with an expression which was almost painful. She reached out and took Sophia's hand. She waited a long time before speaking. "Because he's your brother."

Sophia swallowed, but immediately knew it was true. Billy had always reminded her of her father, and her own feelings toward him had consistently been sisterly. She leaned forward and kissed Bobbi. "I should have guessed. My dad loved you very much, and I know you loved him, too. I'm surprised he never said anything to me."

"He never knew," Bobbi replied shyly. "He might have guessed from the timing, but he never asked, and I never said."

Sophia nodded. She remembered the powerful sexual attraction Cam had felt for Bobbi. She wanted to discuss how it happened, but not in front of Webb.

"Does Billy know?" she asked.

"No. It's not my nature to cause problems or ask for anything. I'm an Amulot, a Rutledge."

"I know. Always giving, never taking. You've been that way all your life." But now we're all giving, and nobody taking. But is that enough?

Chapter 54

In the summer, Tanaka commenced hostilities against the west coast using killer submarines acquired from the American Navy and twenty-three produced in Japanese shipyards. Puget Sound and San Francisco Bay were sealed off as Tanaka issued his attack order, and, within a week, the Russians suspended shipments of armor to the UAR by sea.

The airborne invasion of Alaska followed one week later and was well-planned and executed. Tanaka noted his forces achieved surprise, but with two brigades in the Anchorage area, the rebels put up a spirited defense. Progress was slow for the first several days, and General Tsuji reminded him of the 1941 Pyrrhic victory by Germany in Crete. Alaska threatened to become a debacle until they were able to secure enough of the harbor area to bring in large ships with heavy equipment.

Two divisions had been assigned to the initial assault, but a third was eventually added to accelerate the campaign. By the fourth week, rebel remnants had melted into the mountains, and high command declared Alaska secured. Fighting would continue for almost a year, and only the extremely harsh winter brought the harassing, guerrilla-type rebel raids under control.

General Tokoshima, commander of the Japanese 3rd Corps, put the planned population measures into effect almost immediately. All Alaskan residents were systematically rounded up and either placed aboard ancient Japanese vessels or saved for the troops' pleasure. The ships were scuttled over the Aleutian Trench after their cargos were exterminated by sarin gas, and Alaska's population followed Hawaii's non-Japanese inhabitants into oblivion.

Republican prisons and hard labor camps were captured easily, and their inmates greeted the Japanese troops as liberators.

Tokoshima quickly dashed all expectations, particularly those of draft evaders and war protestors in hard labor groups. In his eyes they were double traitors; first to the United States, then to the rebels. He gave them to his soldiers for sport.

In California, over thirty Japanese and Mexican divisions overwhelmed initial resistance, pushing Republicans outposts off the San Gabriel Mountains, and quickly reaching Bakersfield and Paso Robles. There they stopped as Japanese armor and tactics proved shockingly inferior, and resistance hardened due to rebel reinforcements arriving from the east. The rebels destroyed the San Antonio and Nacimiento reservoirs, and the tenuous water supply for southern California was reduced to a trickle. The Japanese Army was at the end of an extremely long supply line, and advances became slow and difficult.

*****

Webb apologized to Sophia for not furnishing a warning of Japan's impending attack on Alaska. The Japanese had not confided in their Federal partners, and Republican intelligence only knew that troops were en route from Japan, probably to Mexico.

On the other hand, both Lambert and Carpenter considered Alaska indefensible, and Webb wasn't sure anything could have saved it. They might have flown in an airmobile division and increased Japanese casualties, but that was all. Alaska was lost due to the Republic's declining naval presence. Japan had developed a fleet of killer subs—highly sophisticated anti-sub subs whose sole purpose was to hunt down and destroy Republican submarines. The Republican Navy also possessed hunter subs, but most were older and inferior to the new Japanese models. It had become a naval war after all.

"Allowing the Japanese Army to land in Mexico may have cost us our country," General Carpenter said evenly.

Tell her something she didn't know. Sophia didn't disagree with Chuck's comment, but stating it was belaboring the obvious. It had been her decision to await a hostile Mexican action before closing their coasts, and she had agonized over that decision. Kennedy had blockaded Cuba because of the offensive threat of Russian missiles, but Mexico simply allowed transshipment of supplies for the US Hispanic Army through her territory. After major Japanese Army units began arriving, the offensive threat increased, but Japan had yet to make a hostile act, and the UAR had no common border with Mexico.

Now they needed to destroy the Japanese Army and prevent reinforcements. Sophia's Army was capable of defeating the Japanese on land, but her Navy was dwindling without secure construction facilities and technological priority. Seven sophisticated killer submarines had been commissioned during the last year, and one of those had already been lost.

"We have to seal off California at the Colorado River," Cedric pointed out. "Collins is holding north of Los Angeles, and we should allow the Nips to pour as many troops into California as possible." He swept his hand over the map. "Then we attack from Nevada along the Colorado to the Gulf of California, using the flooded Imperial Valley to help secure our right flank. They're light in armor, and we can chew them up in the desert."

Chuck Carpenter nodded. Japanese supply lines were seriously exposed, and the fifteen divisions he was moving west from Ohio could tip the scales. He wondered if Jap generals truly understood desert warfare, and thought Cedric's plan offered an excellent chance for success. It would depend on timing. "Let's transfer Collins from the Central Valley to conduct desert operations. They'll call for bold action, and he's the man."

"Absolutely," Cedric agreed. "But we have little time, and he'll need liaison. I'll have to go and provide it."

*****

Fourteenth Corps was holding Las Vegas, seven more divisions were en route through Utah and Nevada, and although outnumbered, Collins's troops would be better equipped. General Larry Preble, corps commander of XIV Corps, was even more of a cowboy than Collins.

"With eleven divisions, we'll go to Mexico City," Preble said resoundingly. "How big's the bag supposed to be?"

"Twenty to twenty-three divisions," Cedric said. "We're not sure if the Mexicans have moved troops westward with the Japs. Nippies don't use Federal telephones, and they have pretty good security. Fortunately, we Stewarts speak Japanese."

"Regular little Nippies yourselves, huh?" The white-haired Preble laughed. "Always best to know the enemy."

"We know their organization and equipment, but not how they'll do in the desert."

"They'll be like most Asians—devils who care little for human life."

"Then the desert will take its toll," Cedric said. "If troops are sent out without proper equipment, water, or understanding of it, they'll die."

Preble gazed at the desert haze—the unforgiving field of battle. "Collins is due in tomorrow, and with backup units already closing in on us, we're ready to go as soon as he arrives." Preble showed Cedric his dispositions. The 55th Armored was at Searchlight, poised to race down Route 95. Two mechanized divisions were at Jean. The remainder was closing in on Las Vegas as rapidly as possible, and waiting another day to add attack weight was probably wrong. The following troops would be strung out along the axis of advance to provide flank protection and wouldn't move forward until the second day anyway.

Cedric spent most of the night in electronic surveillance, listening to radio traffic. The Japanese were moving on Interstates 8 and 10, as well as the Southern Pacific. There was heavy Spanish traffic also, and Cedric identified at least two Mexican infantry divisions. As dawn approached, he attempted to catch a short nap before Collins arrived.

At nine-thirty Preble shook him awake. "Collins isn't coming," the general said, sounding like a reporter saying his favorite team had just lost the Super Bowl. "Nor is his chief of staff. He couldn't resist the temptation for a little personal recon fly-over. Our troops at Jean saw him get hit by a rocket. Only pieces fell to earth. Sorry, boy, you got a replacement?"

Cedric levitated off his cot without a second of hesitation. He looked at his watch, and walked to the door as if attempting to clear his head. "Let's do it!" he barked, turning back into the large communications van. "It's your show with me as chief of staff. We've got to go today!"

"Attaboy!" Preble wheeled and strode out. Cedric alerted Preble's commanders for an attack in early afternoon.

Three hours later, the spearhead kicked off with SPs providing artillery cover. Federal screening units were Hispanic, and they cracked immediately under the heavy armor concentrations. Before nightfall, recon units had seized Lobecks Pass.

Cedric rapidly discovered being chief of staff was not particularly glamorous. During the day he wrote and transmitted orders to keep units acting in concert, and all night he coordinated re-supply and replacement deployment. Rather than seeing battle, he was only seeing the inside of his mobile command center.

Fighting became confused the following day as 55th Armored attempted to take Blyth. Preble brought up 83rd Mechanized, then threw in troops and mechanized units as fast as they arrived. Interstate 10 was cut, but 18th Armored became heavily engaged with two Japanese divisions in the Sheep Hole Mountains. Preble ordered Cedric back to Las Vegas to hasten his reinforcements. Arriving formations were not passing through Vegas with a sense of urgency, and someone needed to keep them moving while coordinating the larger picture.

Safety was as far as the next vehicle, and Cedric took two fast recon tanks to accompany his armored command car. By midnight they were back at Needles where Cedric found a tank battalion halted on the interstate awaiting orders. Cedric briefed the battalion's colonel, becoming immediately aware of a leisurely attitude.

The radio crackled and Preble's 14th Corps operations officer was heard. A Jap division had sneaked through a gap in the right flank east of Amboy, and the battalion was to head west and contain them. Cedric was beside himself. The colonel had been in Salt Lake City three days earlier and couldn't find Amboy on his map.

"Follow me!" Cedric yelled excitedly. He climbed into his vehicle and signaled his escorting tanks. Adjusting his eyes to the darkness, he waited a moment for the colonel to get his battalion mounted then led off down Interstate 40.

At Essex, they cut off toward Amboy. The desert was easy going, and they could see gun flashes to the west. They were in ships crossing a quiet ocean, heading for an island containing death and destruction. Another ten miles and Cedric ran into three of their newest APCs retreating down the road. They were still several miles from the action, and these fellows were running like scared rabbits. The APCs stopped and the recon tanks went on beyond to provide security. Cedric dismounted and walked forward in bright moonlight to give the detachment commander a piece of his mind and find out what was ahead. A form popped up in the forward hatch of the lead APC.

The figure was Senior Lieutenant Yonai, and he sent seven rounds into Cedric's body. All three APCs opened up with their machine guns, but Cedric's recon tanks pivoted around and made short work of the lightly armored vehicles. The scene was brightly lit with three burning APCs as two men carried Cedric's body into the command car. The Japanese had been lucky. Forty Japanese lives for Cedric's had been a cheap price to pay. The UAR's loss was irreplaceable.

****

The war at sea had turned truly ugly. The EU combatants had unleashed their hunter subs, bringing enemy numbers to equal that of COMSUB attack boats. It was a disconcerting ratio according to Admiral Kelerher. Sophisticated killer subs could drive UAR attack boats from the seas by picketing Republican and allied ports.

Sophia expanded the number of servicing facilities through her international negotiations, but harbor approaches were narrow and caused excessive vulnerability. She needed supply ships for servicing at sea, and Chuikov arranged for three Russian supply ships to rendezvous with UAR subs at points in the South Pacific, South Atlantic, and Indian Oceans. It was a stopgap solution, but Kelerher had less than seventy submarines on station.

"We're where we can run numbers," Kelerher announced grimly in defense council. "Our facilities for constructing new submarines are limited, and they have suffered from off-shore missile attacks by enemy submarines because of their known locations and proximity to the ocean. At top capacity, we are producing one per week."

"How about personnel?" Sophia asked. "Can we provide quality complements?"

"We have ten volunteers for every slot. Everybody wants to become a submariner. But we're losing ground on boats. Last month, we lost eighteen boats and commissioned five. Six more months of that, and we won't have a Navy."

"That was extraordinary because the Japanese made an all-out attack with their killer subs," Webb argued. "I thought we were able to take effective counter measures since then."

"Only partially," Kelerher said. "Killer subs are deadly to our older attack and missile boats if they can achieve an ambush position. That occurs when boats attempt to enter or leave a port."

"Killer subs have to put in for supplies, too," Sophia said.

"We're trying that. We caught one of the bastards off the east coast last week when we intercepted a transmission that gave their ETA at a little-used port. Just like in Puget Sound, we got him leaving before he knew we were there."

"So what's your prognosis?" Sophia asked.

"The Navy can't win with our present capabilities. This is like 1812. We can make it horribly expensive for our enemies, but eventually, our presence in the high seas will be negligible."

"Is there any percentage in hoarding our resources?"

"Not that I can see," the admiral said. "Every supply ship unloading on this continent hurts us more, and I can't see any future situation that might necessitate a greater effort than now. We need to cut the Jap Army off from all support, and the sooner, the better. We've sunk over twenty-five hundred ships, but the Federals still have fifteen hundred, Japanese four thousand, and Europeans another three. Their numbers are staggering, and we only have seventy boats."

"How about the Russians? Are they helping?" Webb asked.

"Without them, we wouldn't have a Navy," Kelerher said. "We fly our torpedoes and equipment modifications to Russia, and then to where we can meet our boats. Without that, our subs would make one cruise, fire off their armament, and be sunk returning."

Kelerher's naval offensive reached into Federal and Mexican ports, but losses exceeded his worst fears. After blockading Mexico's coast, the Navy had lost eleven subs in one week, including the boat that sunk the enemy hunter off North Carolina. Enemy losses had been enormous, but merchant ships could not compensate for superbly trained submarine crews and their boats.

97 - Small Units

"Unacceptable!" Parelli screamed and threw the paper at Brown. "This type of publicity will destroy our European support! We've got to stop it!"

"We've got a half million African volunteers, and this is just the beginning," General Brown said. "They're here to fight whites, and killing civilians is a natural by-product. That was a major motivator to volunteer."

"Then use 'em as cannon fodder where it's hottest. Let them die instead of our troops. Tell them they'll be getting the first chance at whites. But kill them off!"

"Mr. President, you must be prepared for large numbers of rebel deaths anyway. No rebel soldiers survive Japanese capture, and civilians simply disappear. Our troops don't observe the Geneva Convention, and Europeans are hanged by the rebels. Emotions are running high."

Running high wasn't the word, and Brown knew Tennessee was cleared of Caucasians. Whites attempting to desert from cotton belt states were easily caught when they entered a black-only zone in Tennessee and along the Appalachians. Large numbers of whites had fled into rebel territory, but most died where they lived. There had been about a hundred million whites remaining in the Union after losing parts of California, Pennsylvania, and New York; now his best guess was about sixty-five. Maybe not over sixty. White births had almost ceased, while elderly were dying like flies without food or medicine. Florida had turned into a disaster area for retirees. Home insurance was a thing of the past, and vast numbers of neighborhoods were burned down or under the control of looters. No real estate was being bought or sold.

A second rebel report on atrocities set Parelli off again. "Can't we stop these rapes and mutilations?" Parelli yelled. "This is inducing rebels to fight to the death."

Brown agreed the mutilations were stupid. "We'll tell them to cover the evidence better. But rebels aren't taking prisoners either. Remember those atrocities in California reported by Japanese?"

"Crap. I don't believe anything the Japs say. Stewart vehemently denied responsibility, and Tanaka used those incidents at home to rationalize intervention. They were too convenient."

Brown looked at Parelli in a new light. Parelli was a white man first, American second.

*****

Sophia alternated between increasing doubt and stronger resolution. Cedric's death was a terrible blow. For all her superior knowledge, she had been unable to protect her own. Cedric had wanted to prove himself, and having escaped death four times herself, Sophia had believed her sons would fulfill their destinies. But Cedric had been killed on literally his first outing.

The western campaign had been plagued by horrible luck. First Collins, then Cedric, and then the staff work was thrown into disarray. Four divisions had charged into the desert and perished after running out of ammunition. Preble had trusted Cedric to keep him supplied and moving, but Cedric had not returned to Las Vegas. Twenty hours had passed before Preble knew Cedric was not pouring troops to his aid. His men were doomed without effective re-supply and coordination.

Cedric's enthusiasm had been his and their undoing. There was no backup available for Cedric, and with the western Army's chief of staff missing, Japanese units were allowed to seal off Preble's penetration at Interstate 40. Troops which could have prevented the encirclement were available in Vegas, but no one sent them south in an effective fashion.

One problem always led to another, and now Kentucky was in danger. The Federals stacked in fresh African troops opposite positions that had been weakened to reinforce the west. "Cedric would have said the best defense is offense," Carpenter stated to Sophia. "The African mercenaries are green, and we can't allow them time to become blooded."

"The Pikeville and Corbin atrocities are good motivators," Sophia said, "but can we afford to attack?" In both towns, the entire civilian populations were murdered after obscene horrors.

"As a spoiler. We destroy their ability to attack us in Tennessee for maybe six to nine months. We need time to rebuild."

Carpenter outlined his plan to send armored raiding parties deep into the South. Extraction would be by helicopter over mountainous regions, and he expected all equipment to be forfeit. Three raids were outfitted; one against Memphis, a second following Sherman's old route to Atlanta, and the other across the Smokies to Charlotte. They looked suicidal, but with rapid movement and targeting personnel, Carpenter believed they had good prospects for success.

The Atlanta raid would go down in history as a textbook-perfect spoiling attack. General Rutherford had concentrated tremendous supply depots at Chattanooga and Atlanta, and was using the area between Nashville and Chattanooga as his primary staging area for African divisions. Carpenter selected Colonel Towles and his Special Forces group to lead the raid. As aggressive as Preble but with more sense, Towles had held Port Tobacco open until after the Washington thrust was defeated and married Cindy after his escape from Maryland.

Federal lines at Cookeville were held by the 5th South African Division, and Pete attacked without artillery preparation at 1:00AM. His new T-20 heavy tanks overran the Africans in their tents like flushing quail. It was a rabbit shoot, but Pete could not stop to mop up as he headed to Sparta. In less than an hour, he circled Sparta and a South African corps headquarters. Pete overran it, and big-time killing began. The Africans had not learned to use their night glasses and employed infrared lights on their vehicles to see instead of depending on natural light. Towles's men blew everything to hell that mounted a light, eliminating a reserve armored regiment, and paralyzing corps communications. The African Corps commander and numerous other high-ranking officers perished in their vehicles.

Dawn found Pete below McMinnville preparing to split his force. Copters came across the mountains at Mayhill and Spencer, delivering ammo and gasoline, and taking out casualties.

At Manchester, he was confronted with two South African infantry divisions moving to block his raiders. Pete now referred to it as the Montgomery Force—a joke on his expected destination. Unwittingly, he became a chief recipient of Parelli's edict to use South Africans as cannon fodder. They possessed little armor, and what they had, was obsolete or light. He attacked in three columns with his lighter skinned vehicles in the center. The new T-20 tanks roared directly at hastily deployed African infantry at a speed of almost fifty miles per hour.

Terrified Africans scattered in all directions, and the Montgomery Force turned its flame throwers on half-finished positions and roadblocks. This time, it became a rabbit shoot in daylight, tanks running amuck in the light frame structures of Manchester, oiling their rollers with squished human fluids. Pete couldn't believe the carnage and was glad it had been dark back in Sparta.

When he finally turned southeast to Chattanooga, he ran into an eighteen-mile long traffic jam of stalled vehicles blocked by his left wing at Monteagle. The entire column was destroyed, with tanks going down both flanks, machine-gunning those who attempted to flee. His raiders went berserk after discovering two dozen mobile bordellos of white girls—all UAR captives. Thousands of South Africans paid the price of their redemption.

By three-thirty, Pete stopped at South Pittsburg for more ammunition, and the rescued girls were airlifted out with his wounded. By six, he was at the foot of Lookout Mountain. In Chattanooga, Pete found extensive Union ordinance stores. His armored infantry loaded truck after truck with incendiaries, WP, and plastic, drove them into warehouses, blew the sprinkler systems, buildings, then the trucks. After three hours, there was little window glass remaining in Chattanooga, and the reality of hunger would soon arrive. Pete referred to his raiding party as the fifth horseman. Maybe even fifth *and* sixth. By midnight, his task force had reached Ringgold, and he let the men catch a few hours of well-deserved sleep. He had lost over half of his original 1,350- man complement, but most had been sent back as wounded or because of losses in armor or armored carriers.

His attack toward Atlanta began with false dawn. Both Interstate 75 and Route 41 were used, but the Federals were throwing in better troops. Dalton, Cartersville, and Marietta were overrun, and the old

Rome GE facility and Martin-Marietta plant close to Atlanta were destroyed.

"Can you reach Fort Gillem?" General Dean queried over the radio.

"Doubtful," Pete rasped. His voice had given out in keeping his troops under control. "Too much urban area to pass through, and I'll lose all my armor. I'm down to twenty tanks, and Northern Georgia is eating me alive. I recommend we hit Doraville-Chamblee and call it a day. Tonight if we get resistance on 285, tomorrow if not."

General Dean agreed, and Colonel Towles turned left on the beltway after losing two more tanks in Smyrna. Aunt Fannie's Cabin was long gone, so there was no place to eat. The beltway was uneventful except for shelling every large building in sight— including the buildings for the *Atlanta Journal-Constitution* and Northside Hospital since Pete hadn't recognized it as a hospital until too late. Doraville was another free-for-all, and more Federals came up through Spaghetti Junction. In minutes, he was down to ten tanks. It was time for his task force to be picked up.

Night fighting again in Chamblee, and Pete ordered everything blown up. It was fun, with troopers attempting to outdo each other in sheer destructiveness. Even a suicide attack by Federal gunships failed to dampen enthusiasm, but only three tanks remained running when Peter's transport copters arrived. Four divisions had been rendered ineffective, three with heavy losses in both men and material, and all for less than six hundred casualties of mostly wounded. Pete's task force had killed over forty times that number in South Africans alone.

*****

Promotion came fast out west in the desert—a bad sign to a thoughtful analyst, but a good one to ambitious officers. Lieutenant Colonel Tony Dudley was neither, but he understood the situation had become worse. Several of his men were from Las Cruces, and they said the Rio Grande Valley had been cleared of Anglos. His home town of Hatch, his parents, high school friends—all the people he knew, were gone. His dad never would have left willingly.

His unit was his home now, and his men were his family. Many were ex-bikers who had volunteered early, and like them, he considered himself already dead, and would take everyone he met with him. Racial lines had hardened beyond belief, with no one taking prisoners, and everyone guilty of atrocities. It had taken some adjustment to view Hispanics as sworn enemies. Hispanic, Mexicans, and Japanese… they were shot on sight. He never met any white Federal troops anymore in spite of what Unionists said on TV.

Now there was a new problem: armed irregular and militia units were springing up in every Republican community. Dudley considered them counter-productive since they enticed desertion into their ranks for adventure, profit, or sex, since many of the irregulars were women. He had experienced control problems with his own men two weeks earlier near Lone Pine when they had come upon a unit composed almost entirely of ex-Vegas show girls. The men had gone crazy and declared a unilateral one-day ceasefire.

They ran into the show girl outfit again south of Bishop, but this time, could only bury the body parts. Dudley's detachment took revenge on the Mexican 4th Division between Death Valley and the Sierras. It was hit-and-run with their desert buggies, dismounting only to demolish equipment and supplies. Mexicans tended to group together and die together, and the kill ratio was enormous. In three weeks of incredible non-stop ferocity, Dudley lost almost half his men but killed many times his number. But everywhere the Republic was outnumbered, and he had to do better.

Las Vegas was evacuated, Utah was open for invasion, and Dudley was pulled back to Tonopah, promoted to colonel, and given a regiment. True desert warriors, they were equipped with four-man dune buggies, Spatters, light SPs, mobile anti-aircraft rockets, and weapons carriers. Tanks were in short supply, but Dudley considered them a liability except at night. In daylight, Dudley had seen Spatters easily eliminate Mexican armor. The desert looked flat, but it wasn't, and the low, tiny Spatters could disappear from sight in a wash or depression, and present a helmet-sized target before firing.

He was given a free hand to add irregulars to his force as desired. Tonopah was filled with refugees from Vegas, and Captain Beres recommended they recruit women. Over three hundred volunteered for duty, all from Vegas or Southern California, and their eagerness was impressive.

On TV, the Republic claimed to be fighting for the "genetic survival of true Americans," and every woman of child-bearing age who died was one less potential baby-producer. All of the three hundred were young, some even teenagers, but many had children who had died or were living with grandparents. Dudley decided to close his eyes to official policy. Sex was henceforth on wheels.

Chapter 55

Tanaka was satisfied with progress in California in spite of the enormous casualties. The desert battles had shattered rebel confidence, and Japanese movement up the San Joaquin Valley was gathering momentum. Fighting in the Coast Range continued as heavy as ever, but with supply lines open now through San Diego and Long Beach, pressure could be steadily increased.

In less than five months, his troops reached the Sacramento River, and fighting for the Bay Area began. General Ichniki's drive captured Sacramento, and San Francisco was cut off.

He was surprised to find substantial numbers of whites still remaining in some localities. Conquerors had always exterminated useless populations, allowing only those who were valuable as property or subjects to live. Americans held a quaint belief that civilians were innocent and would be spared if they offered no resistance.

Well, they would learn.

For Japan to become the world's foremost power, she needed land. She had erred by not exterminating indigenous populations during her long period of occupying Korea. With minimal foresight, Korea would have become a Japanese province long ago. Now a new opportunity presented itself. With Australia and the United States becoming Japanese colonies, large land masses were hers. Canada would surely fall shortly thereafter, and the challenge would be to repopulate North America with Japanese citizens while keeping other nationalities at bay. Controlling the oceans, two continents, and the world's food supply, Japan would be invincible.

Tanaka looked at reports on Mexican efforts in the desert. Allied troops there had faced at least one all-female rebel formation. Republicans were sacrificing their seed corn, but if they were going

549

to die anyway, it didn't make much difference. Women were used by conquerors for breeding in earlier times, but Japan had no use for inferior Caucasian stock.

Two days later, a battalion of female workers in a penal organization surrendered in Oakland. They were all young and were distributed to the troops. Tanaka considered American women to be sloppy, smelly, and untrained in pleasuring a man. His troops were less fussy.

San Francisco fell two months later, and rebel remnants slowly withdrew to the Oregon border. The entire Bay Area was a shambles and substantially depopulated, and the electronics industry that once crowded the valley around San Jose had vanished. Central California was open for Japanese colonization but not the south. White celebrity support in southern California was still thought to be important for world opinion.

Casualties hardly indicated the campaign had been a victory. Rebels had chewed up the better part of twenty divisions, and only the liberties allowed to Japanese troops with prisoners and civilians maintained morale. Rebels were tough fighters, even in hopeless situations, and very few surrendered. Commanders were already raising their estimates for replacements, and Tanaka decided he needed Mexico to carry more of the burden.

Admiral Yoshida decided that the northwest could be invaded from the sea, and mounted a seaborne end run. General Ichniki landed two divisions in the Oregon Dunes area, then pushed north on Routes 101, 97, and Interstate 5. The end run worked, and rebel submarines were obviously at the end of their tether. Two were sunk contesting the invasion, and only seven Japanese ships were lost. Moving inland toward Eugene, Japanese Marines met only light resistance.

The rebels were outnumbered in Oregon, twelve divisions to five. Ichniki dropped a thirteenth division and a brigade at Reedsport, and with the coast road cut and Interstate 5 threatened, the rebels were forced to commit most of their reserves at Eugene. There the battle went badly for the Japanese troops, but numbers were beginning to tell.

Rebel civilians seemed to lose heart, and Salem was surrendered by its mayor. Front line rebel formations barely escaped being cut off, and they streamed into Portland in disorder.

Rebel captives announced over loudspeakers that no buildings would be damaged unless used to fire on Japanese troops. All structures sheltering UAR troops would be razed to the ground. Ichniki held strictly to policy, and Portland's defense rapidly lost its cohesion. Residents closed their doors to rebel soldiers, sometimes even disarming them and holding them prisoner until Japanese troops arrived. The mayor of Salem was brought to Portland and made propaganda broadcasts. He was the first rebel official captured by Japanese troops, and was allowed to survive for an additional two weeks.

Ultimately, civilian behavior made no difference to Japanese soldiers. This was rebel territory, and all white people were rebels and spoils of war. Every infantry squad kept at least one girl, and larger units acquired slaves to clear debris and minefields. Eliminating children became a sport with various rules and refinements, and champions arose in competing units who boasted of their prowess in killing. Higher headquarters constructed brothels of the best girls, and platoons of slave workers moved supplies.

Nonetheless, most of the population died as the Japanese advanced. Everyone over fifty was killed on sight, and wealthier inhabitants found Japanese soldiers quite impervious to their entreaties. Portland fell with a whimper, and the Japanese Army moved on to Washington. The entire northwest could only be a matter of time. Rebel naval threats would be eliminated forever, and with no United States Navy remaining, the Rising Sun would rule the waves. *Sic transit Caucasius!*

*****

Texas contained two entirely different styles of warfare. In the east, Federal troops were still almost all white, and fighting had stabilized along the Sabine border into relatively static patrol and small unit actions. West of the San Antonio River and on the Edwards Plateau, the fast-striking Republican units were keeping the less mobile Mexicans at bay in fluid situations.

Vandemeer had survived eighteen months of combat to become an instructor at Fort Hood in tank tactics but transferred back to his old division for a tank company when promoted to captain. With the 42nd Armored Regiment, he felt safe. Tankers believed they would survive if they stayed together, and casualties were never as bad as they seemed on the battlefield. Many men returned after hiding in the woods or being released from field hospitals.

Division headquarters was at Waskom, a little town on the Texas-Louisiana border that once boasted more gas stations per capita than any city in America. The ground was fair for tanks to the Red River in spite of frequently heavy woods, but boggy areas and deep bayous showed up at the most inopportune times, so good maps were essential.

Three days after he arrived, the newly baked captain was ordered to hit Shreveport's airport in a spoiling attack. Intelligence was expecting a major offensive in two weeks, and their operation was officially called a reconnaissance in force. The operation went south immediately.

Punching a hole through the Federal MLR at Route 169, the leading company was badly shot up until assault guns joined up. Vandemeer had taught his students to keep SPs and assault guns close to the lead, but here they had been left behind. His company was ordered through the gap, and he closed up with Spatters and assault guns in a tight formation.

Cypress trees on the right meant a bayou, and Vandemeer radioed for two sections to check out the bank. The bayou soon veered away, and the road curved left, disclosing a wide group of cotton fields. "Stop!" he yelled.

Driver Phillips halted on a dime.

"Left 90 and fast! Move!" Vandemeer yelled. The company wheeled around, facing north, and Van ordered top speed. Regiment barked into his earphones, demanding to know why Charlie Company was fleeing in disorder without a shot being fired. As an answer, the cotton fields began to erupt with heavy caliber shells landing where they had been moments before. A little Spatter disappeared in a fountain of metal and dirt, and two tanks near the bayou blew up like plastic toys.

Shells followed slowly as Vandemeer's company disappeared and took refuge behind an artificial pond with high earthen sides.

"How in the hell did you know that?" Sergeant Hines hollered from his tank's hatch after they stopped to reorganize. "I never saw a thing!"

Vandemeer called a quick conference. "I passed a large orange stake near the road a couple hundred yards back and saw another ahead. We were taught at A & M to use orange for artillery ranging, so I guessed we were in a predetermined fire zone." He called Regiment for orders, and plotted the death zone on his map.

"It's a funnel," he reported. "Federals can attack from almost a mile away on a broad front while we're concentrated at the vortex. A perfect trap." Vandemeer was going to recommend cutting northeast behind some woods to take the position in flank when a cry went up.

"Tanks! Tanks!"

Too late, AT was already on its way. Commanders ran to their tanks as a line of Federal M-90s burst around the north side of another artificial lake less than six hundred yards away. Vandemeer radioed Regiment and headed toward the oncoming tanks, taking a swift count. There were only a few at first, then a battalion, then a regiment, then a brigade. Regiment called to break off the action, but that was difficult at best. In five minutes, half of Charlie Company's vehicles were wrecks, and the rest were in retreat to Waskom. A full armored brigade had debouched on top of Charlie, and they'd lost heavily to the better T-20s.

One of Charlie's wrecks was Captain Vandemeer's.

*****

The Federal commander was extremely disappointed with the performance of his new M-90 tanks, and his tankers had showed a marked disinclination to pursue even with greatly superior numbers. The ambush was wasted, and the rebels had escaped after inflicting more damage than they'd received.

Hodges was concerned the rebels would notice their lack of spirit and attack his dejected units. He withdrew his armor for further training and began making a series of motivating appearances and talks with troops. They were dispirited, mostly from rumors about riots and concern for their families in their home states. Almost all of his men were from the northeast and wanted to go home or be transferred somewhere closer to their families.

Hodges reported to Brown that his Army's reliability was questionable and should not be engaged in heavy operations for several months. He kept up a show of activity to hold substantial rebel forces on his front, but meanwhile, an entire Federal Army was out of action.

*****

Colonel Dudley had been working on his idea for several weeks. The Mexicans had not progressed much beyond Vegas, and most Japanese were far to the north in Oregon. He decided southern California must be ripe for a raid, and proposed one to 6th Army headquarters.

Amazingly, they liked his idea. Anything to divert attention from the northwest. Dudley was authorized to take two battalions and lead the raid himself. Intelligence pinpointed Japanese headquarters, and he would be aiming for a psychological victory of the first magnitude.

Dudley had changed his opinion about the value of women in combat units. They fought as hard—if not harder—than men and complained less about the heat and lack of food or water. He had feared they would become pregnant, but that happened only twice. Most of his female warriors were no longer even having periods. Maybe it was stress, heat, or lack of sleep. He didn't know, and really didn't care. Not as long as they fought like men. Or better.

There were other curious differences he noted about his females. They rarely took risks to aid men, even their boyfriends, whereas men were frequently killed attempting to help wounded or endangered women. The girls did their jobs with a professional detachment bordering on a messianic discipline, never mutilating enemy dead, but able to torture prisoners for information in unspeakable fashions. They lived for the moment, and when their lovers were killed, mourning periods were short and replacements found almost immediately.

His operation began beautifully with the battle group slipping unobserved into Eureka Valley. Avoiding all contact and led by five Mexican armored cars and a command car, Dudley's convoy wasn't stopped until it reached a standard military police roadblock at Cajon. The MP post was quickly destroyed, and the task force continued at high speed to Interstate 10.

There were no more roadblocks as they drove into downtown

Los Angeles. Detachments peeled off to occupy the major TV stations as it became apparent that surprise was complete. Japanese headquarters was quickly surrounded and shelled at point-blank range by SPs. Within forty minutes, all resistance has ceased and Captain Beres reported the annihilation of several Japanese service and command formations.

"It's time to play shoot 'em up!" Dudley gleefully ordered over the radio. He was a full day ahead of schedule, and hadn't expected to arrive unannounced. Now he wished he had more tanks. As the Long Beach raiding party moved out, he watched TV to monitor progress by his other groups. Station after station went off the air, to reappear with his people managing productions.

"We have liberated California from the Japanese criminal empire," one of his most attractive female warriors announced. "We call on all freedom-loving Americans living in California, Los Angeles, and San Diego to rise up. This is not Japan. The Japanese are here to exterminate us. Help them die instead."

The thin colonel didn't expect much from his broadcasts, but who could tell? He ordered all media facilities destroyed, then headed to Long Beach to destroy the port. Several TV stations were broadcasting UAR news, and on others, Federal reports reflected the UAR interpretation of events. It was downright humorous. Some Federal commentators were saying Los Angeles had been assaulted by two Republican Corps, and severe fighting was in progress throughout the city. Dudley laughed heartily along with his staff. None of his attack groups had run into any coordinated resistance, and units were already racing south on freeways to San Diego.

By morning, Interstate 5 was blocked at San Clemente, and Mexican formations coming from El Centro had been contained in sharp clashes. Demolition proceeded rapidly, and by late afternoon, the surviving task forces were reformed as a single unit in Anaheim.

Dudley's troopers left behind a wrecked freeway system, a silent media, and substantially destroyed refineries and port facilities. The major problem was sleep, but Dudley wanted to be on the other side of Barstow before first light. He felt like Grierson trying to stay awake in the saddle, but their safety lay in speed. Mexican units in the Colorado Valley would be attempting to cut him off, and any sighting might be fatal.

At ten in the morning, he stopped for a rest near China Lake, and watched his troopers immediately fall asleep from exhaustion. The desert was already shimmering, but visibility was far better than he would have liked. He drew up his command in a standard Mexican formation, and placed his Mexican vehicles on the perimeter as camouflage. He was almost ready to call for a remount when he noticed a small dust cloud heading toward them across the desert. Dudley sent his best lookout to the T-bar on his scout car.

"Mexican, Sir!" the lookout shouted. "Two scouts and an APC."

Not so bad. Spatters could handle them if they came within range. He alerted the camp and ordered everyone to stay out of sight. The three vehicles drove in on a beeline, and were destroyed without an answering shot. The rest stop was over, and Dudley's column headed north.

Nearing Westgard Pass, he could see Mexicans occupying it in strength, and they appeared on alert. His rear guard had been telling him for an hour that they were being followed at a distance, and his alternatives were rapidly being reduced. Dudley approached the pass, then turned southeast as if he had decided to cross back into Eureka Valley. As Harold did at the Battle of Hastings, the Mexican defenders deserted their positions to give chase.

Five miles from the pass, he reversed direction and crashed into the pursuing Mexicans. They scattered before his onslaught, and Dudley easily forced his way through the pass to safety. The Mexicans placed a $100,000 bounty on his head, dead or alive.

At Tonopah, Colonel Dudley learned why the pursuit from LA had been so light. His broadcasts had been taken seriously by many Californians, particularly in the Los Angeles area. The situation soon developed into a full-scale revolt, and three Japanese divisions were rushed from Oregon back into Central California. Even swifter was their reaction from Hawaii as Japanese flew in large numbers of troops.

Everywhere, ethnic groups fought each other; whites versus Hispanics versus Asians. Dudley wondered where the arms came from, but apparently, people had been acquiring and hoarding them in anticipation of possible disturbances. All economic activity in southern California ceased as the Japanese clamped down hard. They enlisted minority gangs as home guard units and established a policy designed to eliminate civilian leadership—anyone who came to Japanese units or headquarters was shot. Those who came to investigate followed their predecessors immediately in quiet executions.

Most lawyers and many celebrities vanished in the first few days of the "Show-go" Policy. Frightened by events beyond their comprehension, the rich and beautiful huddled in their hillside homes until murdered by roving gangs vying to add famous names to their lists of victims. White neighborhoods were surrounded by Japanese troops using Hispanic and black gangs as auxiliaries, and surviving inhabitants were transported to processing centers from which no one returned.

The same cry arose as voiced by Jews in World War II; "Don't worry, they can't possibly kill us all." But "they" could, and did. First, by individual looters exterminating family after family, then by neighborhood clearance. After three months, any white person in California could be shot on sight. Dudley's raid had catalyzed the annihilation of Caucasians and blacks in California.

Meanwhile, the world's focus had shifted.

Chapter 56

Kurita had to admit that General Brown was a valuable asset, and was surprised a black was capable of such logical analyses and conclusions. Brown had agreed to notify Mexico City only after the operation was underway and would make no record of their conversation or notify his president until the last moment.

Rebels still held the upper hand in Texas, and even with California essentially recovered, the ground war had hardly progressed as the rebels approached the end of their third year. The corridor of Republican Texas had to be taken, but neither the Mexican nor Federal Army possessed sufficient martial ardor. Only two options were available to exterminate the rebel strength in Texas; nuclear or CBR. Considering the large-scale destruction that would result from nuclear attacks, Japanese High Command decided to employ gas.

Japanese scientists had developed an extremely potent agent under production in the home islands. It was colorless and odorless like nerve gas and easily distributed over large areas. More importantly, it would remain effective for an unusually long period of time, and even in urban structures with controlled environments, avoiding lethal gas concentrations would be virtually impossible without effective masks.

The plan was to use missiles west of population centers and allow the prevailing westerlies to disperse the gas eastward. After reviewing the plan, General Brown went a step further—he asked Kurita to overload east Texas so the Federal Army in Louisiana would be affected as well.

"Go ahead and annihilate Hodges's army," he told Kurita. "It's all white, and without rebels in Texas to fight, it's a liability."

Japanese missile units were shipped to Sheffield and Laredo, while the Mexican Army prepared for another offensive. All of their previous operations had been stopped by Republican forces, and there was no reason to suspect this one would be different. On the evening prior to jumping-off, Japanese units supposedly test-fired their rockets and missiles with an unusually high number of launches.

With dawn the Mexican offensive began rolling slowly eastward, meeting ferocious initial resistance. During the first hours, rebels mounted wave after wave of suicidal counter-attacks, and Mexican assault units took extremely heavy casualties. The troops blanched at berserk rebels who seemed possessed, and hacked Mexicans apart until shot down to the last man.

Then rebel radio and TV broadcast a ghastly story. Most of Texas had been blanketed with nerve gas, and tens of millions of people had died. There was nothing between the Mexicans and the Mississippi. They began to attack with greater ardor, knowing the *gringos* had no reinforcements, and soon were racing across Texas. The Texas Army had constructed their own Alamo, and taken as many Mexicans with them as possible.

Texas was a dead land. The gas had killed everything that breathed, from birds to deer. A few scattered areas were unaffected, but the main population belt in central and eastern Texas had been destroyed completely. So had Louisiana and Arkansas south of the Arkansas River. Hodges's Army had ceased to exist, and San Jacinto Day had been celebrated for the last time.

*****

"What?" Sophia asked as Chuck Carpenter and Webb entered her office together. Special teams were being dispatched to 4th Army headquarters to retrieve or destroy codes, cipher equipment, and secret information. No one was sure how long the gas would be effective, nor how soon Mexican ground forces would arrive.

"Uh, we've got bad news," Webb said. Both men were looking at the floor with long, drawn faces. The door opened, and Heather and Bobbi walked in, Heather going immediately to Sophia who rose from her chair.

She knew immediately. "It's one of my boys, isn't it? Who?"

Heather threw her arms around Sophia and started to cry. "Oh, I'm sorry, honey," she said. "It's Adam."

Sophia collapsed back into her chair. Bobbi joined Heather in holding her. "Adam?" Sophia said weakly.

"In Texas," Webb said quietly. "He had gone to Houston to transfer ownership of some ships and facilities to the Saudis."

Sophia knew Adam had been planning a trip to Texas, but thought it was next month. "Are you sure?" Her eyes were filling up, and she was fighting back tears.

"Yes," Heather answered, "I talked to him last night in Houston,"

"Officially, he's listed as missing," Carpenter said.

Sophia's head snapped up. "Then there's hope."

Webb shook his head. "There were no survivors in Houston. If you'd like, we could send a personal appeal to President Carrillo to locate and return Adam's body."

Sophia became dizzy with the image of Adam's body lying untended in Houston. She fought for control. "No," she said, "I'll send him a different message." She asked everyone to leave. She needed a timeout for mourning. Her firstborn had died, the second out of seven. She spent the afternoon in her quarters by herself and her memories, talking to her father and mother within her.

She had symbolically united her parents in death, exhuming her mother in New York, and cremating her remains. Sophia had carried her ashes to Caribou and scattered them in the same spot as Cameron. In that small piece of desolate acreage was the abandoned mine where she had erected tiny monuments to their memories. Unseen and unknown by others, those monuments were her private shrine. But Adam would be missing.

More than thirty million Americans had died and were crying out for revenge. World media covered the story unsympathetically. The closing of the eyes of Texas was compared to Hiroshima, and stories generally followed a romantic line that the cowboys had gone to their last roundup.

Sophia activated her IRBMs and MRBMs, and pressed the rebuilt Rocky Mountain Arsenal into crash production. Three weeks later, the favor was returned to Mexico with interest. Three hundred missiles landed on target in fifty cities, and with no opposition or SAM defense, they were followed by several hundred missions by heavy bombers. More than a hundred million Mexicans died in invisible clouds along with President Carrillo and most of his government.

Losing Texas was catastrophic. Twenty-two divisions had vanished in a few moments—an army of over six hundred thousand men. There was no parallel in the annals of warfare.

*****

Sam Parelli surveyed the situation without optimism. The rebels had suffered decisive defeats, and only in the east were rebels still holding positions in advance of their original boundaries. It was time for a knockout blow, but he wasn't sure his country possessed the resolve. The rebels were still formidable—maybe even more dangerous now that they were cornered. Out of spite, that bitch Stewart might drop a nuke on Washington.

Riots were a daily occurrence in the northeast. Losing a million men in Louisiana and southern Arkansas had hit New England hard. For all practical purposes the recruitment of whites had ceased. General Brown suggested the president make a quick flight to Boston to see New England's problems himself. Parelli left the next day.

The explosion of Air Force One over Long Island was blamed on rebel sabotage, and for a few days, universal rage over rebel treachery obscured John Murphee's assumption of the presidency. Murphee became the second black president and with the exception of Reagan, the string of presidents under Bilderberg control since Ford was kept intact.

*****

Within a month after Murphee took office, General Brown instituted the same policy throughout Federal states that the Japanese had instituted so effectively in California—the "Show-go" Policy, whereby all Caucasians coming to police or military authorities simply disappeared.

They were transported either by ship to The Solomons in Maryland or through various means to McGuire in New Jersey or Charleston, South Carolina. Those taken to The Solomons were subjected to special processing and their property confiscated before being transferred to Andrews. From all three centers the ultimate destination was identical. Prisoners were herded onto giant military transports and flown over the Gulf Stream where they were dropped into the Atlantic from twenty thousand feet. None survived the fall, and their bodies disappeared long before the current reached England. A single plane could eliminate four hundred people per trip, and the flights lasted less than an hour. With over a hundred aircraft in service, disposal of whites was carried out in numbers unfathomable to exterminators in Nazi Germany.

Florida was another problem. Hispanics were in control south of Orlando, and lawlessness had reached such proportions that two African divisions were sent to Miami to assist police in maintaining order. They suffered extremely heavy casualties and were reduced to driving through Hispanic areas shooting at everything in sight.

Brown began shipping African recruits into Charleston in great numbers, giving them two weeks of basic training, then sending them to south Florida. The Congressional Hispanic Caucus threatened to withdraw their support, and called a cease-fire where American Hispanic troops were stationed. Murphee and Brown summoned the Caucus to a showdown.

"We couldn't allow anarchy to continue," Murphee announced. "Something had to be done to curb drug lords and their power. What would you have done?"

"Used Hispanic troops," Senator Hernandez answered.

"Okay," Brown replied, picking up the challenge. "Which ones? From where?"

Salazar knew General Brown had them in a box. He didn't want to transfer Hispanic units from the west for fear of losing control to Japanese. "Then we want a resettlement policy for Hispanics in Florida making property in Texas available for homesteading," he stated in reply.

"Hispanics in New York and other east coast cities?"

"Those, too. Resettlement to begin immediately."

Brown agreed without hesitation. The east was cleared of Hispanics as rapidly as possible.

"Have we given up our claim to the southwest and Texas?" Murphee asked General Brown, as Hispanic movements emptied New York and south Florida.

"No. Remember, the Japanese still have large quantities of nerve gas available. After the rebels are beaten, we can say the *Pachucos* revolted and eliminate them—as long as they are in a discrete territory."

Murphee marveled at how Brown could condemn millions of people to death without a flicker of emotion. He would have made an excellent Nazi under Hitler.

*****

The following spring, Brown unleashed his planned knockout blow in the east. The all-European Federal 8th Army fought its way from Buffalo to Cleveland against heavy resistance. In five weeks it advanced 115 miles, but suffered at least 200 percent casualties. The Muslim infantry regiments and armored grenadier battalions that had been raised in Germany and France to fight the American "Great Satan" suffered twice and three times that and were only kept in action by a constant stream of replacements. They had been recruited with the promise of immediate German or French citizenship upon termination of their duty, but the vast majority were simply being killed off.

Then the UAR defense cracked as Federal 9th Army attacked from northwest Pennsylvania and the 22nd German Corps forced a passage through the Cuyahoga River Valley, bypassed Cleveland along the old Ohio turnpike, and raced in ten days to Toledo.

Without bridging or boats, and faced with fanatical resistance along the Maumee, the armored spearheads stopped and waited for infantry to come up. Ninth Army redirected 22nd Corps southward to Finlay, and 21st Panzer Division was ordered to Lima. There it was halted by exceptionally fierce counter-attacks coming from the east at Bucyrus.

*****

The Federal 3rd Army began attacking north through Nashville two weeks after the New York offensive began. General Rutherford used South Africans to break through, holding his American armor to exploit openings as they developed. Rutherford kept the Africans

563

bunched together where they could see and feel their five-to-one numerical superiority over the rebels.

Within two weeks, he crossed into Kentucky between Scottsville and Tomkinsville. The 11th Armored Corps moved through and raced madly for Louisville's Ohio River bridges, arriving a frog hair too late. The leftmost armored division of 11th Corps sealed off the Ohio River by moving west along US 60, approaching each bridge in sequence and seeing it blow up in their faces. None of the bridges fell intact into Federal hands.

Without waiting for the situation to stabilize, General Rutherford threw a division into southern Indiana at West Point. Their crossing was opposed only by light reconnaissance units, and he followed with an African infantry division and more armor, striking upstream to New Albany and Jeffersonville.

UAR counter-attacks from western Kentucky recaptured Owensboro, but Brown's timely reinforcements stabilized the left flank after many units suffered near-annihilation.

"Drive to Lima, Ohio?" yelled Rutherford, not believing his ears. Brown must have taken leave of his senses. Lima was almost two hundred miles away through the heart of rebel territory. He would have to drive between Indianapolis and Cincinnati, without flank protection, and with strong rebel forces on both sides.

"Yes. Our 9th Army has broken through south of Cleveland and is heading west across northern Ohio!" Brown shouted. "The rebel 1st Army is retreating back into Ohio, and we stand an excellent chance of trapping it. Just block Interstates 74 and 70."

Rutherford looked at the map and shook his head. Brown had promised to shift four more divisions to his control, but it was a daunting prospect. The rebels were attacking in western Kentucky and his left flank units were holding with difficulty. Some were mere remnants, and a collapse there threatened to pinch off his Ohio crossing. His right flank faced considerable rebel forces south of the Ohio which could threaten his supply lines. They were far from being defeated, but with a little bad luck, he could lose his entire attack force. Still... An order was an order.

Rutherford threw everything he had into the advance. He wondered if Brown appreciated the hilly terrain in southern Indiana, but fortunately, rebel resistance was not severe. Apparently, they had expected him to attack toward Indianapolis, and he was able to slip to the east and fight his way through to Hamilton in four days.

Rebel resistance north of Hamilton was weak and easily overrun. The columns bypassed Dayton and sped up Interstate 75 to Lima. The German 21st Panzer was already there, and the rebel 1st Army was bagged. A screening line was formed facing west along US 127 to the Maumee, and units began working to the east.

*****

Sergeant Newton was now battery commander with four Spatters and four SP-155s, the new long-range SPs with a range of eleven miles. It wasn't his idea, but they were down to only three officers in his battalion. Personally, he would rather be back on his Spatter with Stan the Man driving and Mace as gunner. Stan was pushing up daisies in West Virginia, but Mace was commanding a Spatter. The ugly, skinny redhead was back to being a corporal after the Battalion CO found his moonshine still last month. That had been a riot. Colonel Kurek didn't object so much to the still, but that Mace had never shared any with him.

Newt hated to pack up and move again. Life had been pleasant and not unduly dangerous in the Appalachians since escaping the Washington debacle. Their position at Grantsville had been impregnable, but for the last three weeks, they had slowly withdrawn to Clarksburg, West Virginia. Federal TV claimed a breakthrough along Lake Erie, but their own newscasters had indicated only that fighting had been extremely heavy against German and English mercenaries. The truth was probably somewhere in between; the Europeans had probably kicked some ass but hadn't been able to force a decision. Then last week, the Federals had crossed the Ohio below Louisville. Both sides had reported it, and now word had come shifting their battalion to Parkersburg. That meant going against Africans, and being taken prisoner meant torture and a nasty death.

They drove through Parkersburg and stopped in Athens, Ohio. No sooner had Cookie erected their satellite dish than Federal news said they were encircled. What a war—intelligence by TV. They were supposedly cut off west of Columbus, and the usual propaganda parade of recanting Republican prisoners was augmented by pleas to surrender in the name of humanity. Newt assumed such prisoners would be shot immediately after their broadcast.

Colonel Kurek confirmed it at HQ. "Yep, we're in a bag, but the string is very thin," he announced. "The Feds have screwed up and bitten off more than they can chew. We're going to make their line look like Swiss cheese. The jungle bunnies haven't taken Cincinnati yet, and we've been ordered to cut their stop line just to the north." Kurek pointed to the map, placing his long finger on Middletown. "We're supposed to cut the line tonight."

The unit commanders marked their maps, and the battalion mounted up after chow. Driving flat out using road lights, they were on Interstate 75 by midnight.

Kurek put Newt's Spatters on point, followed by SPs. As usual, Newt wished he had twenty Spatters, but Army hierarchy always knew better. He kept an extra Spatter carrier as a command vehicle, and now he followed the other four, scanning the front through his night glasses. His radioman kept watch on the thermal scope they had liberated from a wrecked tank.

They crept ahead in the pitch black, making as little noise as possible. Newt could hear SPs behind him clanking with their characteristic chatter, absolutely identifiable to a knowledgeable soldier. He wondered if the boo-boos would think they were tanks. Spatters made no more noise than an automobile and would be inaudible over the SPs. He scanned ahead through his night glasses trying to hold them steady in spite of the bouncing, tightly-sprung Spatter chassis. Two blocks slowly appeared in the background gloom at long range as his radioman indicated hot spots.

"Halt," he commanded into the radio. "Look right fifteen."

"Right," he heard Mace reply. "Two tanks. Don't see anything else."

Mace was about ninety yards ahead. The first SP with a machine gun was six hundred yards behind and made a huge target in the dark. It would be better to assault with Spatters and crews firing their machine pistols.

"How far before you can take them?" Newt whispered. He suddenly wondered why the tanks hadn't opened fire; his SPs were noisy as hell, and with the flat ground, were probably visible in night glasses. Certainly in thermal sights since they didn't have deflector shields like the Spatter carriers.

"I can get them now," Mace answered.

Newt decided to chance it. He told the right flank Spatter to take the rightmost tank, and for Mace the left. No one else was to fire and give away their position. Both said they were ready.

"Fire!" he yelled.

Two rounds went off simultaneously, with a third about seven seconds later. One tank blew up in the first salvo, and the second burst into flame seconds later. Newt ordered the third Spatter to assume point from Mace and charge.

Small arms fire erupted from trees visible from the burning tank, and the SPs shelled the woods. As fast as the fire had started, it ceased. Newt tore down the macadam highway and cut loose at running figures. Within two minutes, he was the proud possessor of a crossroads. It wasn't Highway 4, though; that was three miles farther.

The next Federal position foolishly announced itself by lobbing mortar shells onto the road. Newt's column spread out, and within a half hour a segment of hastily prepared Federal blocking positions was in their hands. It had been held by a company of Africans, and the body count was over two hundred. Rapidly turning north and south, the battalion opened a ten-mile gap before dawn. The noose around 1st Army was broken.

Newt's unit ranged south to Hamilton to demolish a long convoy and a battalion of heavy artillery, then took up defensive positions covering US 127 at Williamsdale. For the next five days, the battalion held on by its teeth.

A full Afro infantry division moved up from Hamilton, and the numbers grew on each side every hour. It appeared to Newt that the campaign's deciding battle was taking place around his little unit. There was no relief, and he lost all his SPs on the fourth day when they ran out of ammunition and were forced to escape westward into Indiana.

On the fifth day, Newt shifted his own position to the western edge, recognizing the battle would be resolved shortly one way or another. He heard the CO's voice on the radio.

"We've been ordered to hold at all costs until this afternoon," Kurek said. "A whole corps is due to arrive beginning about 1400."

"That's a roge," Newt replied. There was nothing further to say. Looking south, he could see infantry moving north. He studied the groups of figures through his field glasses. They appeared to be white civilians followed by black soldiers. The Kafirs were going to attack behind hostages. He wished his SPs were still available.

He passed word down the line to open fire when ordered regardless of hostage losses. Many, if not most of the hostages would be killed, and Newt decided an example was necessary.

Bent over, he loped to Mace's Spatter. "Nasty business we're in," he said.

"Yeah." Mace spit out a chunk of chewing tobacco. "Those people gonna die."

"Yep. You want to tell 'em?"

"That an order?"

Newt nudged Mace to one side. "Nah," he said, "I'll do it."

"Not on my pipe, you won't," Mace said sharply. He pulled Newt down alongside him with one arm. He didn't bother to take aim—he just pulled the trigger. His HE rocket burst among the civilians, throwing men, women, and children into the air. The hostages broke and ran in all directions.

"Only Spatters with HE!" Newt yelled. The word went down the line. The Africans swarmed forward, shooting down hostages that were fleeing in all directions. HE began landing as the blacks continued to come forward yelling and firing. They were all equipped with assault rifles, and firing on automatic. A terrific volume of fire was coming toward Newt's bunkers, but passed harmlessly overhead. At least a full brigade was charging. It was like what Newt had seen in movies about World War I.

The fire began to slacken, and some blacks seemed to halt and look around wildly before continuing to charge.

"Now!" Newt yelled, and machine guns in the APCs and bunkers opened up. Blacks milled around in confusion and went down in rows. The Africans had fired all their ammunition while charging and shooting hostages, and couldn't defend themselves.

Newt sprang up and moved forward, firing from the hip. Everyone followed, and the massacre became general. The African brigade melted away before Newt's attack, and the escaping corps of 1st Army troops passed behind him without hindrance to safety.

*****

Pete Towles had been promoted to major general and given command of the 7th Armored Division during late winter, and it had been one of his brigades that had stopped the Germans turning south at Bucyrus. Now his division provided northwest flank protection as the Republican 1st Army withdrew toward Dayton and Hamilton. The Europeans seemed to have inexhaustible supplies of armor on his right shoulder as he edged southwest in echelon, but if Pete couldn't hold, 1st Army was a goner.

Roads were jammed with traffic, military and civilian, and European aircraft were pressing home interdiction and harassment attacks. General Stirling ordered SAMs and hand-helds be distributed widely throughout the transportation network, assigning anti-aircraft units to military police control points. European Air Force losses were enormous, but 1st Army still dissolved in fear of being caught in the open.

Pete's armor threw the Germans out of Marion, and the following day 7th Armored was ordered to Springfield. His troops were unaware of 1st Army's critical condition, and Towles wasn't going to tell them just yet. The 7th Armored was undefeated, and believed itself to be unstoppable. As the division neared Springfield down Route 4 from Marysville, the troops found the interstate from Columbus jammed with refugees, and Route 4 was under long-range artillery fire from the west.

Armageddon had come for 7th Armored, and in the flat fields and gently rolling hills between Urbana and Troy, it held on grimly for eight days. Before leaving Marysville, the division was down to sixty-seven tanks, and less than a brigade in personnel. But it had destroyed the opposing German 22nd Corps. The first day set the tone when a 3rd Brigade battalion became lost leaving Mechanicsburg and found itself behind Federal lines at Urbana. The battalion commander radioed his position to Brigade and attacked. Pete rushed 3rd Brigade forward, and the Germans were riddled in a crossfire. The 3rd Panzer Division ceased to exist as a fighting force, but only twelve tanks from the errant battalion returned to Republican lines. Its commander was not included.

The Germans were unable to follow Towles's badly reduced division, and the 7th retreated to Troy without interference. There it faced British armor attempting to close 1st Army's escape route by attacking west of Interstate 75. In a day-long rear guard battle, the 7th lost all its remaining tanks, but stopped the British cold. It dug in for another two days with its assault guns while 1st Army passed behind it to safety. Then Pete withdrew as rearguard. The Europeans did not pursue.

Chapter 57

European forces had proven decisive after all, but it was TV that defeated Sophia in Ohio. Once 1st Army troops heard on Federal TV that they were encircled, the rush to escape turned many into fugitives. General Carpenter pointed out that Ohio should have been a victory. Stirling had already pinched off the over-extended Europeans and was threatening them with total destruction when 1st Army panicked. Some units fought magnificently, but many others simply bolted for the west. Civilian refugees exacerbated conditions, and half a million men were lost in the total campaign. As Sun Tsu said, an army is defeated when it thinks it is defeated.

A makeshift line had been patched up from Toledo to southern Indiana, but General Carpenter did not expect it to hold for long. The pursuing Federal troops from southern Pennsylvania were fresh, and Republican remnants were exhausted. The European formations had been almost annihilated along with many African divisions, but the Republic's best units were crippled. It was almost as if the campaign had been planned by Washington to sacrifice the foreigners.

Sophia noted almost all active fighting during the last year had been against foreigners; Japanese, Mexicans, Europeans, and Africans. Federal troops were not battle-worthy, and her Indiana line could hold. American blacks only fought well in large groups where they had an audience. In Vietnam, almost none had become tunnel rats, LRRPs, or snipers, and since then, their performance had only gotten worse. In small groups and as individuals, they shied from combat and were easily killed. She pointed this out to Carpenter who believed the war was lost.

"Guess I hadn't grasped the obvious," he commented. "It's been mostly Japanese against our subs and Europeans who stopped our drive on D.C."

"Exactly. And Japs are still fighting guerrillas on the west coast. That's how we can still win—large scale guerrilla actions behind their lines to destroy their resolve. No guerrilla movement can survive without a sanctuary for the fighters, so as long as we maintain free territory and can supply guerrillas, we have a chance."

Carpenter put out a call for volunteers to join guerrilla bands in Federal territory. Response was overwhelming, as many men originally from states that had remained in the Union wanted to fight again on their home ground. Those from Ohio, Kentucky, Pennsylvania, and West Virginia were quickly outfitted and pressed into action. Within a month, the Air Force was using everything it could find for transport; light planes that landed on highways, helicopters, and even cargo planes from which guerrillas parachuted.

The Federals were slow to regroup in Ohio and continued to probe the Indiana line without much resolve. Carpenter concluded correctly they were digesting the three conquered states with difficulty. Cleveland, Pittsburgh, Columbus, and Cincinnati were major metropolitan areas with substantial white populations requiring subjugation and control. Or extermination. The sheer enormity of Federal genocidal efforts strained the wildest imagination.

*****

Colonel Marston had spent the most frustrating month of his life during the Ohio pocket fight. The 82nd Airborne had been in reserve at Pataskala, east of Columbus, but was flown west to stop the Europeans below Toledo. Their orders had been to attack, attack, attack, and they had thrown the Federals out of Defiance, Van Wert, and even the home of Neil Armstrong at Wapakoneta. It had been a thankless fight while the nation focused on heroism inside the pocket. Marston felt his 82nd troopers weren't getting the glory inasmuch as they had first halted the Europeans, driven them east to Interstate 75, and then provided a safe haven into which 1st Army could escape. Now, they were still in line while 1st Army was being reformed. The Federals were inactive, and he took the opportunity to rebuild his command.

Marston had received command of 3rd Brigade and was listed for promotion to brigadier general. Still spending most of his time forward with his men, the colonel was extremely popular, and some older NCOs referred to him as General out of respect. Marston was forced to admit that references to General felt good, and assuming the rank unofficially raised everyone's spirits.

For once, replacements were arriving faster than normal attrition. The division was filling out with veterans, mostly released from hospitals and disbanded units from the debacle in central Ohio. Morning reports indicated the brigade was at full strength when Federals began to probe Republican lines again in northwestern Ohio. The area was flat and open, perfect tank country, and with very few natural obstacles or good defensive positions. Almost the first major probe on the bowling alley type of terrain was against Marston's brigade east of Paulding.

"We want all recons in force to face total annihilation," the division commander had said. "That's the only way we'll hold while our forces are being rebuilt. Blacks must believe that if they attack us, they'll die."

It made sense but was certain to cause higher casualties. Still, the Federals were getting closer to Marston's wife and kids. When the first indication of a concentration opposite his brigade was spotted, he moved to an outpost with an artillery FO.

Patrols reported a tank regiment had taken a forward position before midnight, and Marston considered the possibilities. The terrain was open to Paulding except for two rivers that would not be obstacles to armor. His defensive strength was primarily in his minefields, as covered by his paratroopers, SPs and Spatters. Armor liked to attack toward objects commanders could see even in conditions of reduced visibility, and there was a perfect objective in his sector. It was a radio-TV tower, and could be seen easily from Federal positions northeast of his FO bunker. He planned a counter-strategy based on a regiment-sized armored attack in its direction.

By false dawn, Marston knew he had guessed right as tank noises wafted across the field. Trip flares shot into the sky, and he could see dark hulks pick their way across fields north of Highway 615. Moving so slowly, the tanks had to be accompanied by infantry. He waited until the forms had passed and were about to enter his minefield before ordering the artillery to open fire.

The Federal tanks gunned their engines to escape the artillery barrage and rushed into the minefield. Tank after tank was disabled, and Marston ordered the flank battalions to close behind and stop the infantry. Dawn was breaking, and he noticed the troops around him were hesitant to break cover. The trap had to be closed immediately, and he walked into the open yelling for his troops to follow.

These were good men, and he saw them rise up and follow him across the field to attack. He could see Federal infantry behind the tanks to his left, huddling on the ground like sacks of potatoes. He whooped and broke into a run. Two Spatters drove into the open and began to send HE into the cowering Federal infantry.

Marston collapsed as a 50 caliber slug tore through his stomach. He gasped in surprise as the shock swept over his body. His adjutant knelt by his side and yelled for a medic.

"Tell my girls I did my best," Marston said slowly, coughing from pain and grabbing the captain's tunic. He closed his eyes and lapsed into unconsciousness as a second bullet wounded him in his right arm.

The three grim paratroopers who carried him off the field knew the drill, and paid the ambulance driver two hundred dollars to rush their colonel to the field hospital. The driver wanted a thousand, but the troopers were in no mood to bargain. Two hundred and his life— otherwise he was a dead man, and the troopers would drive the ambulance themselves. The driver, an ex-attorney from Cincinnati, took the offer. It didn't make any difference; Colonel Marston was DOA.

His brigade took moderate casualties in closing the trap, and a Federal tank regiment and its supporting infantry regiment were destroyed. The paratroopers buried General Marston with full military honors on the field where he fell—his promotion had become official the day before he was killed. Three days later, the ambulance driver bled to death after stumbling into a minefield in front of Marston's brigade for some reason. Over nine thousand dollars was found on his body.

*****

Sophia began to wonder if her earlier decision to refuse Russian and Chinese aid had been ill-advised. Maybe it wasn't too late. Genocide was a real threat. Civilians who had assumed their importance would protect them had learned that whole populations were being exterminated without qualms. The only safety was in victory, and there was no bargaining in defeat.

General Chuikov made the long flight to Iowa at Sophia's request. He looked drawn and tired, but still retained his penetrating blue eyes.

"Better late than never, I guess," she said. "We'll take all the help you can give us now."

"We thought that was why you called," the general nodded. "But you must realize circumstances have changed. We no longer have a way of shipping directly to you except by air. Now we need to retake Alaska and the Pacific northwest."

"Then do it. What can I do? What do you need from me?"

"The presidium has requested you cede Alaska to us in return for a full alliance."

Sophia stood up and paced in front of her desk. Without Russian assistance, her chances of recovering Alaska were zero. And there were no Americans left in Alaska to fight for.

"It's yours for the taking," she answered. "But we need Seattle opened up most of all. We still have a few subs operating out of your facilities. And if you attack Alaska first, the Japs will be alerted on the Pacific coast."

"Yes, but we'll unleash our own submarines first and drive Japan from the seas. We will declare the re-institution of your blockade using identical arguments as the Chinese had in 1950. With any luck, we'll turn the tide."

Sophia heard his lack of commitment to assault the lower forty-eight, but any assistance was better than none. She didn't believe Japan could be dissuaded from its American adventure, and the Mexican government was totally dependent on Jap support. Chuikov was obviously caught between his personal feelings and official policy, and Sophia held off on personal appeals.

Next came the Chinese, and she hoped for bodies. They certainly had bodies to spare, but lacked transportation. Sea-borne transport was required to obtain appreciable troop strength, and that was only possible after Russian intervention. And they wanted California. Sophia countered almost facetiously with Mexico, and her offer was taken seriously and accepted. That opened a whole new possibility, and China began planning to invade Mexico. Their timing would be dependent on the Russians.

*****

It was soon clear to Sophia that the Russians had anticipated her request. The undersea campaign was devastating. Japanese killer subs became the hunted, and their convoy security had been allowed to lapse. As far as Sophia was concerned, it couldn't have happened to a nicer group of people. The operation against Alaska kicked off without delay. Russian airborne troops took less than a week to wipe out occupying Japanese, and immediately declared a recommencement of the North American blockade, this time including Canadian ports.

Canada forbid the free transit of Canadian air space, but Russian airpower easily neutralized Canada's Air Force and quickly reopened the air lanes to Alaska. As long as they flew high and fast above the puny Canadian SAMs, air traffic between Montana and Alaska was no more dangerous than driving fifty-five on an autobahn. The Europeans protested, but took no action.

A fighter wing was transferred to the midwest, and Russian pilots showed extreme aggressiveness in engaging European aircraft. Russian planes were quickly shown to be superior, particularly over the French, and once again Federal aircraft disappeared from the sky.

But the Russians showed no inclination to commit ground troops to the lower forty-eight. Instead, they heavily attacked Hawaii, both with missile-carrying submarines and aircraft from Alaska. General Chuikov was evasive and appeared personally distressed when pressed, but there was little to be done. The Russians were acting in accordance with their self-interests as they defined them. China estimated they could attack Mexico in about seven months, but time was running out. Sophia's international influence was waning.

Sophia shook her head over reports coming from guerrillas in Federally controlled territory. Large numbers of whites were disappearing, and accounts continued to filter in of farms and isolated communities being wiped out in orgies of blood lust. Against all reason, Federals frequently burned farms and houses to the ground, wantonly destroying their future property.

"Stupid, but what can you expect?" Webb said as he handed Sophia his latest summaries.

Sophia scanned the numbers. "All domestic claimants to

American territory are being eliminated. This is the worst war in history with respect to deaths in a single country—even surpassing the forty to sixty million Taiping Rebellion deaths in China in the 1860s."

"Where did we go wrong? Before we formed the Republic, your superior knowledge always gave us the edge."

"I looked too far ahead and arranged my children for the promotion of our society's well-being. I should have given birth to six Cedrics to win the inevitable war first."

"At least he fathered a boy and two girls," Webb remarked hopefully.

"It remains for us to insure they get a chance to use their talents." Sophia knew she had heard this discussion before. Her father had lived to set up her future, as had his father. Sooner or later, everyone hoped for a better life for their children.

"This hasn't been a war between Americans," Sophia added. "It was promoted by Japanese and the Bilderbergs to protect their investments, using American blacks and Hispanics as cannon fodder. For whites, there's only eventual extermination. The Bilderbergs want docile serfs, and white Americans have never been docile. They needed to get rid of us. The first to go under Agenda 21, and there will be five billion more to follow."

"Nobody could have predicted the Federal Government would hand itself over to foreign interests," Webb said.

"No one, including me. I didn't think they were that dumb. The goose tried to leave, so they killed the goose, all the golden eggs, and themselves in the bargain. Now, we all die."

"They probably couldn't have survived anyway," Webb commented.

Sophia smiled. "They didn't know that. Nor did they realize that for leeches to live, they must have a body on which to feed."

Webb searched Sophia's face. She had aged under the pressure of war, but was still a beautiful woman. He would follow her into hell, and wasn't sure he hadn't already. Two of her sons gone, and the Republic had suffered fifty to sixty million deaths. Their best troops were lying under the soil, and women were fighting alongside men in many military units.

"Well, I can't see how we can last another year," Webb said.

"The Russians have already done everything they planned, so there won't be any more help there. And the Chinese may not come in time. After they land, it will take them three months to start recovering the west coast."

Sophia nodded. "And we've been publishing genocide stories so long that nobody takes us seriously. Our people still want to believe they'll be treated humanely."

"So everyone in the Republic will die?"

"Probably, but maybe Canada will open its border to refugees."

"Maybe the Africans and Japs will get tired of killing. Mexicans and Hispanics seem to have given it up."

"They're saving their troops for muscle after we're defeated. They're letting blacks and Japs take the casualties. Fantasy world. The Bilderbergs will reduce them all to serfdom."

*****

Behind the Federal Army was a second army of camp-followers that plundered the newly conquered states, killing and looting with abandon. White guerrillas killed looters without mercy, but could not alter the war's course. A small guerrilla unit might kill fifty or a hundred looters, but they'd then be pinpointed and destroyed. With no white population in which to hide, they were forced to operate from rough terrain or unpopulated urban areas.

The Japanese finally finished clearing western Washington and Oregon, then drove into southern Idaho and northern Utah, capturing Salt Lake City. Its loss was inevitable to a determined attack, but holding it was a different matter. Japanese supply lines were much too long, and the "Boy General" Dudley forced the Japanese back into central Nevada and eastern Oregon with his hit-and-run tactics, supported by Russian air cover.

The western front stabilized when the Japanese were unable to advance east without terrible losses. Dudley's forces—over fifty percent female—could hold them at bay indefinitely as long as he was kept supplied with gasoline, ammunition, replacements, and air cover from the Russians. Dudley ranged throughout the Great Basin, even maintaining contact with guerrillas in the High Sierras of California. "Dudleyland" was a Japanese graveyard.

The Mexican front was nearly as stable. In Colorado, Oklahoma, and northern Arkansas, the Mexicans moved only in overwhelming force and avoided pitched battles. As in the west, light raiders frequently forced the Mexicans to withdraw to protect supply lines, and there was little northward movement.

It was in the east where the decisive blow fell after months of waiting. Sophia had once again raided Europe but without positive effect on government policy. The most powerful Bilderbergs escaped retribution and redoubled their efforts. Reinforcements arrived from Britain and Germany to rebuild their formations, and France threw its foreign legion into the fighting. Once again, General Brown used the Europeans as a spearhead, but this time with a twist. His attack began late in the afternoon with captured Republican tanks in front.

The attack broke through the Maumee line when defenders allowed the Federals to close on their positions because tank commanders were seen to be white as they rode standing up in their turrets. Only at the last moment did the tanks button up and open fire. Having learned from experience, they blasted the Spatters first, then overran the infantry to attack the SPs. Michigan was exposed to the thundering herd of camp-followers.

"The Army is cracking," General Carpenter reported. "The Maumee defeat was a mental breakdown."

"But that was a single instance," Sophia said. "How did it widen into a catastrophe?"

"Confusion. The Europeans got loose in our rear, and several commanders started pulling back of their own accord. The men apparently lost heart."

"Sounds like a crisis in leadership. How about the general discipline?"

"Still good, but our troops simply aren't the same quality as in the beginning. Where they're well-led, they'll still outfight Federals, but, otherwise they fight sullenly and without spirit."

"Desertions?"

"Moderate. None to the enemy, but they cut for home and Canada. That may be holding morale up—the troops believe in their last extremity they'll be able to escape to Canada."

*****

579

Sophia had become concerned with the safety of her son, Erwin. He had gone with Heather over a month ago to the old Milleron headquarters at Zionsville. Erwin was convinced he could help organize defenses because of his engineering expertise, and the presence of a Stewart would bolster sagging morale. When news of the Fort Wayne breakthrough arrived, Sophia sent Bobbi Rutledge to Zionsville to find them and bring them back. Fighting was still east of Indianapolis, but communications from Chicago to Indianapolis had already been disrupted.

Heather greeted Bobbi at Zionsville, but Erwin was at Anderson, east of Indianapolis.

"Sophie wants Erwin out," Bobbi said after hugging Heather. The two women held hands as they walked to the rear entrance of Milleron's headquarters building.

"We'll have to go get him," Heather replied. "Erwin's holed up with a battalion of engineers in the old Anderson GM plant." She grinned at Bobbi. "Ready for a wild ride?"

Bobbi smiled back at the diminutive lady, now past retirement age. "You bet," she said. Whatever Heather could do, so could she.

Heather led her into a garage. Inside were two T-20 tanks and a command car. "Let's take the CV, it's faster, quieter, and has more room."

Bobbi gasped. "CV?"

"Command Vehicle. Or would you rather take a tank?"

"You can drive a tank?" Bobbi blinked. Then she saw the lean, mean looking corporal sitting against the wall. "Oh, I see. We have a driver."

"Well, of course. But I can drive a tank. Even fire one. The corporal's been teaching me."

Bobbi shook her head as she climbed into the all-terrain command car. Why was she not surprised? Heather had been able to get men to do things for her all her life. But become a tank gunner? Far out!

Six hours later, they were back at Zionsville with Erwin. Twice they were fired upon by Federal troops during the return trip, and although the CV was hit several times by small arms fire, there were no casualties. Bobbi ordered the plane to be warmed up for takeoff with dawn approaching.

Heather handed Bobbi a letter. "I'm not going back with you," she said. "This is for Sophie."

Bobbi felt her knees buckle. Heather was her oldest friend. They had been through so much together. "Why?" she asked in amazement.

Heather looked down at the concrete aircraft pad. "I've outlived my usefulness. I can't stand to see any more of my boys killed. And you know, Sophie won't leave either, and I can't stand to see that." She stopped and swallowed. "It's better this way." She threw her arms around the taller Bobbi and buried her face on Bobbi's shoulder.

Bobbi was too choked to speak. Finally, she raised Heather's face to hers. "Then I won't go either," she whispered.

Bobbi yelled at the pilot to wait. She boarded the plane, and quickly wrote two notes, one to Sophia and one to Billy. She placed them in her attaché case with Heather's and handed it to Erwin.

"Give this to your mother and tell her we'll see her later." Bobbi kissed Erwin goodbye, and exited the plane before he could reply.

The two friends stood on the concrete pad and watched the twin-engine jet taxi for takeoff. Past the spot where Ed was killed—the last plane out. Bobbi's sandy gray hair blew in the breeze as Erwin's plane roared into the night on its way to Des Moines. They walked quietly back into the cafeteria area where coffee was still hot.

Heather poured a cup with steady hands as she had for the last fifty years. Bobbi watched her, seeing the spirit that made Heather an original.

"You're still a beautiful woman," Bobbi breathed. "Cam did well to pick you."

Heather shook her head. "I always envied you. Your long legs, sleek body, and natural blonde hair. And then you had his son. I'd give anything to have had his child now."

"Don't kid me," Bobbi smiled, sipping the strong brew. "Remember, I bathed you from head to toe after you executed that black pimp. I still remember running my hands over your breasts wishing they were mine. They were perfectly shaped. Mine never got beyond age fourteen."

"Well, that was then, and some things don't hold up," Heather sighed. She chuckled. "Remember O'Donnell? He thought he had died and gone to heaven sitting between us."

"We made a hellava good team." Bobbi uncurled one of

Heather's hands and stroked her fingers. "We were lucky, you know. How many women ever experience a man like Cam? The first time I met him, all I wanted to do was go to bed with him."

"He was the best there was. When you were with him, the world consisted only of you and him. No one else."

"I know. But we haven't done too badly. He'd be proud of us."

Heather felt a tear run down her cheek.

Suddenly, Corporal Monkton entered. "Troops coming, Jigaboos!"

Heather jumped up and grabbed Bobbi's hand. "Come on!"

The corporal escorted them back to the garage where one tank still remained.

"Get in!" Monk ordered.

Heather was already climbing onto the back of the tank, as Monk practically heaved Bobbi on top as she hesitated looking for a step or a ladder. He pushed her toward an open hatch and told her again to get in. The interior was eerie with a dull orange light, and Bobbi sat on a padded seat that folded down from the side. She wondered why Monk was staying with them.

He handed Bobbi a padded helmet and closed the hatches. "You work that machine gun in front of you," he said. Bobbi noticed Heather was sitting in the gunner's seat. Monk set a complicated-looking apparatus that did something with the cannon.

Monk scooted down into the driver's seat and the engine roared to life. The tank jerked forward, and Bobbi placed her face into a heavily padded eyepiece. She was looking forward at the large metal door of the garage. She started to yell the door was still closed when the tank went banging through it like when football players run through paper hoops at homecoming.

Dawn had arrived, and she could see several military vehicles on the road in front of the headquarters building. Monk drove into the grassy ditch beside the airfield and stopped on a level, but with the turret not much higher than the road. "Fire!" he yelled. The biggest bang Bobbi had ever heard shattered her eardrums.

She was shaking, and acutely aware that she had emptied her bladder and bowels. Her seat was suddenly wet and squishy in her long dress, and she gathered up the material to give herself a firmer perch.

"Fire at those APCs!" Monk yelled. He had jumped up and another shell went into the breech. Bobbi looked through the eyepiece, and pushed the button Monk had pointed to earlier. More banging buffeted her ears, which were now ringing loudly. The cannon roared again, filling the tank with an acrid, smoky smell, and she watched in fascination as an enemy vehicle blew up, throwing bolts of flame into the sky. A soldier tumbled toward her and lay still.

Three more times their cannon barked, and the only enemy vehicle to escape disappeared down the road.

"Well done, ladies!" Monk bellowed, slapping them both on the arms. He drove onto the road where the Federals had been and into a grove of trees on the other side.

Bobbi recoiled in horror as Monk drove directly over several bodies, one a soldier attempting to crawl off the road.

Monk threw open the turret hatch and manned the heavy machine gun on top. The smell that came in was horrible. Burnt meat and rubber. He slipped down and handed Bobbi an oily towel. "Here, it's okay. Everybody does it the first time."

Bobbi wasn't sure if she was embarrassed or not. Someone should have told her how loud the cannon would be. She looked over to see Heather grinning at her. She hopped down onto the floor, removed her panties, and wiped herself as well as possible while maintaining a degree of decorum. Monk showed her how to open the hatch by her seat, and she threw the panties and towel outside. She felt better, like a soldier who had tasted combat.

The little band had just started munching on some crackers when Monk dropped back inside and slammed the hatch shut. "Tanks!" he said grimly. He backed the tank into a better position, and pushed Heather out of the gunner's seat.

Bobbi could see them coming. Three tanks and several smaller vehicles following.

Milleron headquarters blew up in a terrific series of explosions, and the oncoming column turned to face the disintegrating building across the grass. Bobbi looked down at Heather who was holding an electronic gadget and grinning. "Love it," she laughed.

And then Monk fired.

Quick as a wink, he jumped down and loaded another shell. Bobbi could see the nearest tank erupt with a little puff of smoke and explode in a huge rose of red-black flame, knocking the turret crazily onto its side.

Bam! Monk fired again, and the remaining two tanks turned toward them. The second tank stopped abruptly, then three crewmen seemed to appear out of thin air and tumble to the ground while Bobbi splattered them with her machine gun. Monk was already loading another round.

The third tank and Monk fired simultaneously. Bobbi heard a tremendous bang, felt something hot swish by her legs, and the tank shuddered.

"Out!" Monk yelled. Bobbi looked down to where Heather had been smiling a moment earlier. She was lying on the floor staring upwards, and her chest seemed to be a mass of red rags.

"Out!" Monk repeated, reaching over and flinging open Bobbi's hatch. She stared dumbly at Heather. Vaguely she saw Heather's left arm was missing and her chest had been gouged open across her breasts as if by some huge ax. It wasn't right. Heather shouldn't have left her like that. Alone. She had stayed here to be with her, and now Heather was gone! Bobbi felt the anger and sickness welling up together in her throat and her world was moving in slow motion.

Monk smashed her head against the hatch's hinge. Bobbi started to cry out, but realized her padded helmet had taken the blow. "Out, damn you!" he threw a submachine gun through the hatch, then shoved her out. Dimly she noticed Monk's arm was dark red.

She fell hard onto the wet grass, feeling the morning coolness after the stifling atmosphere in the tank. Her right side hurt, her leg, her hip, and her arm. Her helmet popped off, and her hair tugged at her scalp as it tangled. She saw the tommy gun in front of her, grabbed it, and looked back at her tank. It was smoking and Monk was struggling to get out her hatch. She stood up to help pull him through, and a hail storm struck the tank. Monk's face disappeared in a fountain of blood, and Bobbi was spun to the ground.

She was lying on her back, with a terrible pain in her back and chest. She couldn't move as she saw the three black soldiers appear over her. She wondered whether she was dead or just paralyzed. Also who would get Heather's ring or the gold locket she was wearing around her neck. On the back was inscribed "To Bobbi, Love Cam." Her most treasured possession. Soon, it would be in a flea market being handled by people for whom the names meant nothing. Bobbi tried to talk but words didn't come. One of the soldiers was fat, and he reached down and yanked up her dress.

"Old bitch ain't wearing no nothing!"

"She be wait'n fo us," the tall one laughed.

The fat one handed his gun to the third man and unzipped himself. He dropped his knife on the grass alongside her and pulled out his dong. She'd seen bigger, Bobbi thought. That she would be critiquing at a time like this was suddenly uproariously funny, but she couldn't laugh.

"She ain't much. This be a snuff job," the fat one said.

The tank blew up and the three soldiers evaporated. Bobbi felt a blast of heat, then saw Heather smiling with those impish dimples. Heather had waited, and she had caught up.

Chapter 58

Her population base was gone, and Sophia could see defeat was just a matter of time. The primary element slowing the enemy advance was guerrilla activity throughout captured territories.

Cities in Michigan fell rapidly after the Fort Wayne breakthrough. Their population fled into Canada and Republican troops followed on their heels. Canada set up refugee centers, and resistance in Michigan evaporated.

The Federal Air Force repeatedly struck at fleeing Michigan refugees, and the Russians refrained from opposing them on the principle that assisting refugees to reach Canada served no military purpose. The slaughter was unbelievable, especially after the Detroit River was sealed off and the refugees milled about helplessly on the roads. The locust-like army of bummers and camp followers slashed into crowds of civilians like army ants, murdering and destroying in a vast apocalyptic orgy.

After Indianapolis, Chicago prepared to die hard. Taking heed from Michigan's experience, civilians armed themselves to fight house to house, block to block. After two weeks of probing, General Brown fell back on his south Florida strategy—he shipped every available African to Chicago. Recruitment of Africans had been stopped by the Bilderbergs, but with the European forces, his manpower was more than sufficient to destroy remaining rebels. Chicago was an excellent opportunity to kill off his last Africans and prevent them from becoming an internal power after the war. Brown sent the Africans in for the kill.

*****

Sergeant Newton couldn't believe the difference in Mace. The skinny redhead had fallen in love on their leave in Chicago, and now

586

they were breaking rules because of his craziness. What the hell, they were comrades in arms, and each had saved the other more than once.

Their unit had been heavily engaged at Kankakee, and their Spatter carrier had been disabled by artillery fire. The crew had made a dash for the safety of an infantry bunker, but only he and Mace had made it. When the shelling stopped, they found themselves alone on the battlefield, marveling in the sudden stillness. It was time to *didi* out of there, but to where?

"I quit," Mace announced. "Got to get Rhonda and the kid."

"Rhonda?" Newt gasped. "She's in Chicago. We've got to go west!"

"Nope," Mace said. "Goin' to Chicago. Time to be there for her. Comin'?"

Mace was talking desertion. If they were stopped by MPs in Chicago, they would be taken for deserters. And having deserted in contact with the enemy, they would be shot. It was crazy, but Newt agreed. They headed north.

It was a hell of a trek, mostly behind advancing Federals. They surprised a squad of blacks with a Republican APC, and left seven soldiers sprawled in trees along the road between two cornfields. They now had transportation and ammunition. And in only two hours, they ran out of cannon ammunition butchering bummers.

One group with two cars and a van was parked on the road outside of Balmoral Park Racetrack and waved them to a stop. The bummers were all teenagers, between maybe thirteen and eighteen, and grouped in front of their APC as Newt brought it to a halt. In a few seconds, they were all dead, Mace efficiently dispatching them with the MG.

Mace wrenched open the van's rear door while Newt provided cover. They had lasted too long to allow some kid hiding in a van to catch them unawares. Inside were three white girls, bound hand and foot, naked as the day they'd been born. They immediately started to cry when they saw Mace and Newt.

So then they were five, having bundled Toni, Sharon, and Anne into trousers and jackets and piled them into their APC. Toni was the oldest at twenty, and Sharon and Anne were red-headed sisters, sixteen and seventeen, respectively. All three were from Indianapolis, Toni having been captured by a combat unit, and the sisters overtaken by a group of bummers in Lafayette. The group Mace exterminated had purchased them for resale. Toni squatted over one of the bodies and urinated on his face. Newt didn't ask why.

They got lucky again near Chicago Heights when they came upon three Federal supply trucks, one carrying a red ammunition flag. They easily captured the five soldiers, and Newt gave them to the girls. They took their revenge while Newt and Mace loaded the APC with ammunition and supplies.

Rhonda lived in Oak Park, and the war still seemed far away from her residential street. If Mace had expected Rhonda to leave Chicago, however, he was sadly disappointed. After three days of arguing, he had made no impact, and Newt was getting nervous about their status as deserters. Television indicated the Federals were attacking the south side in force, and fighting was heavy.

"Mace, we've got to get outta here!" Newt said for the nth time. "We stay here, we're dead!"

Mace nodded. He knew it was true, but Rhonda wouldn't budge. He went with Newt to talk with Toni.

"We have three options," Newt said. "Stay here and get killed; head west and continue fighting; go north and make for Canada. What do you say?"

"West," Toni said immediately.

"Canada," Mace said.

"I vote for west. Tell you what, Mace. We'll head west until clear, then you can take the APC and head north. Okay?"

"You're on. What about the sisters?" Mace looked at Toni.

"Why don't we let them decide when we split up?" she said. "They don't know what they want other than to stay alive."

An hour later Mace restrained Rhonda while the girls tied her securely. They climbed into the APC and headed out in late afternoon. As Newt explained, they didn't know where Federal lines began, and they needed to scout in daylight. Mace drove west on Washington, then changed to Saint Charles Road. They passed armed civilians and what appeared to be militiamen, but with their 90mm cannon, they were waved through roadblocks without a glance. A number of times they were forced to make short detours where the road was completely blocked. They passed under the Tri-State Tollway, noticing the bridge was already mined. Elmhurst, Villa Park, and Lombard—still no Federals.

Mace slammed on the brakes and drove behind a small strip shopping center.

"What?" Newt yelled.

"Firing, man. Somewhere ahead."

Newt stood in the open turret hatch and scanned ahead with his field glasses.

"Right thirty!" Mace yelled.

Newt saw them. A group of whites, young boys and girls, were running in front of buildings on the north side of the street. They were not in uniform and were carrying rifles and machine pistols. Suddenly, three of them stumbled and lay still. Mace eased the APC alongside a cinderblock building while Newt jumped down and scouted the street.

In a moment he returned.

"An armored car's coming. Probably recon."

Their 90mm blew the scout car sky high, and the girls broke into cheers. Once again, all was right in the world. Newt walked over to the surviving kids and asked about Federal positions.

The Federals were across the Du Page River, and Newt and Mace decided to wait for dark. One girl said she knew a way into Glen Ellyn north of Glenbard High School which would put them behind Federal lines. It was better than nothing, and Newt took the girl along. She was a slender little thing, with big brown eyes matching her hair that was pulled back into a ponytail. She wore loose fitting pants in the current teen fashion and the obligatory sweatshirt. She belonged in school.

At ten, they mounted up, and Newt held the girl tightly in the open hatch as she gave directions to Mace. It felt strange having a girl's rounded rear pressed tightly against him with the APCs bouncing and jouncing, and Newt had to fight sexual feelings that made themselves known in the most embarrassing fashion. The girl was probably fourteen or fifteen, but turned and smiled, then patted him affectionately. His groin ached, and momentarily he considered placing himself inside her. Hitting a culvert brought him out of his reverie. He concentrated on the darkness ahead to stay alive.

In an hour, they were in sight of the Saint Charles - Geneva Road split at Main Street. They decided to go through the streets of Glen Ellyn for a few more blocks, then turn onto Geneva Road and head west at top speed. Their teenage guide kissed Newt on the cheek, then dropped off to return to Lombard. She was lively and young, full of youth's zest for life. He wished she were carrying his child and his genes into the future. No one else was.

In a gripping panic he wanted to call her back, tell her he loved her, and make a baby. Then she was gone, and Newt realized the foolishness of his sudden romantic feelings. He didn't even know her last name, and she was undoubtedly returning to her death.

Five minutes later they came to Geneva Road and turned west. Mace opened the throttle, and they sped over a small rise—smack into the headquarters area of the Federal 19th Infantry Division. The MPs opened fire and Newt replied, sending a 90mm shell into the side of a brick house with guards on its porch. He opened up with the machine gun, while Toni stood in the turret, spraying with her submachine gun. Over the din, Newt could hear her screaming obscenities.

A terrific clang slewed the APC to the right, slamming Toni against the hatch. The APC had done a one-eighty, and Newt could see the lost track on the ground. He sent a shell into an armored car next to the house as Mace hustled everyone out the rear door. Rhonda was carrying her terrified little girl, and in the light of flares, Newt could see them running toward several houses on the south side of the road. Toni collapsed onto him gushing black blood in the darkness. The machine gun's ammo box ran empty. Newt grabbed a bandolier and Toni's gun and jumped out the rear hatch, leaving a grenade spinning in the 90mm shell compartment.

The resulting blast threw him to the ground. Newt looked up to see a line of men emerge from one of the houses, and cut down the sisters like ducks in a shooting gallery. Mace went sprawling, and Rhonda fell to her knees. She held up her left hand as if to ward off a blow, grasping her screaming daughter in the other. Their fate was sealed a second later.

Sergeant Tom Newton slowly rose to his feet, glanced back at the APC where Toni was burning, and staggered crazily toward the men standing over the bodies of Mace and the girls, firing long bursts. He managed four steps before a stream of lead tore through his chest and face, knocking him into oblivion.

Mercifully, Newt was beyond feeling as the husky black went through his pockets, searching for valuables. Expertly, the soldier performed the now-obligatory ritual, and the white genitals were swiftly cut away to be placed in the former owner's mouth. The black looked at Newt's smashed jaw for a moment as if struggling with a momentous decision. The items in his hand were worthless—to the rebel and to him. With a shrug he tossed them toward the burning APC and went to see what the others had found.

*****

Sophia watched General Chuikov come down the steps from his Tupolov supersonic transport. If the Russian was coming with another offer of assistance, it was too late. Even if she accepted, the war was lost. The Chinese had just landed in Mexico, and were making their way northward. They were too late also. Her Amulot population was disappearing. Nuclear warfare and flattening Japan and Europe in a mushroom cloud was her only alternative, and she wasn't willing to destroy life as she knew it on earth.

She wondered if Chuikov was familiar with the role Malmstrom Airforce Base had played in World War II. Long ago, Great Falls was a major port of entry for Russia, and thousands of tons of intelligence information had flown out through Malmstrom to the Soviet Union. It was that enormous supply of data that enabled the Soviets to rise so rapidly in technology and challenge the United States in the Cold War. Sophia had often thought a modicum of foresight by a few individuals in closing Great Falls would have prevented forty years of confrontation and economic ruin.

History abounded with irony; now Great Falls was her primary physical link to the outside world, and even that required a violation of Canadian airspace. The Canadians tacitly allowed the link. They respected Russian power.

"Sophie!" Chuikov said loudly. More like a family than diplomatic greeting, he threw his arms around her and kissed her on both cheeks.

Webb stood alongside, amused at Chuikov's display of affection. Sophia had practically disappeared in his bear hug.

She walked with him to her waiting car. Curiosity caused her to break the usual routine when they reached the guest house. "Vasily Andreyevich," she blurted, "what brought you on this trip? Why are you here?" She spoke in Russian as always.

Chuikov grasped her hand tightly. "To take you back. And your family. To give you asylum." He spoke with great emotion.

She gazed into his eyes. She understood. "All this time, you've felt like this," she said quietly.

"Yes. Ever since the summer of 1988 when you were pregnant. I found myself proud to be with you, hoping others would think I was the expectant father."

Sophia became quiet. "Is your offer to provide sanctuary personal or official?" she asked.

"Both. I'm to approach you on behalf of the Russian Federation, but I also wish to extend my personal commitment."

"Five of my boys are still alive, and there are fourteen grandchildren and others of the family that need asylum. I assume Webb has already worked out everything with you?"

"Yes," he replied. "We're providing them with everything. "But what about yourself? I'd like to offer myself for your consideration."

Sophia leaned over and kissed Chuikov lightly. "Vasily Andreyevich, I'm very flattered, but my people are buried in great numbers throughout my country. I've led them to their destiny, and their fate must be mine. They could not escape, and neither can I. We Amulots are no more. Over twenty million of us perished in defense of our way of life, along with another sixty million who chose to make common cause with us in our republic. The leader and his people are one, the fate of one is the fate of the other. Hannibal should never have gone to Antiochus."

"You're determined to die?" he stammered. "Why? You're still a young woman with immense talents. There's no reason for you to perish."

Sophia sighed and patted his hand. "The best I can do is give you my children for safekeeping. And my brother, Billy. He'll be head of the family."

"The world will be a better place if you choose to survive," the general argued.

"But I would not be true to my nature. I'm sorry for us both. I feel very close to you, and we would make a great pair, but it's not to be."

Chuikov continued to argue, but to no avail. Sophia rose and asked Webb to arrange a family meeting for morning and to collect all the K11 children together.

She had been unable to tell the Russian about her loss of Heather and Bobbi. Their letters had been awful, and then she had compounded her grief by calling Jack in Denver. Loving, loyal Wallace had climbed into an old bomber at Lowry. The aircraft had crashed near Wray, and identifying the charred remains had been difficult. He had rushed to help her and flown to his death.

She remembered Wallace's pale grey eyes, sparkling in his willingness to help her when they first met centuries ago in Golden when she was grieving over her father. He had been there throughout her losses, which had been many. Too many. She had been an angel of death. Her long range understanding had put her beyond her own life and lifetime and had changed the world. But in the long run, everyone died, and Lord, how they had died.

She had failed Jack. She had created a dream for him—a dream of love and honor in a democratic society drawing the best from its citizens. She had given him herself, but had promised more. He had waited all his life to marry her, but she denied him. She had denied him his place in public, hiding him in her bedroom as if ashamed. She loved him, but had been unwilling to announce that love to the world. It was her loss, and her shame. He had deserved better.

She had made a provision for history, and was shipping tons of historical records to Russia. The family would force history to record her actions accurately. But Wallace? Who would understand his role and praise his contribution?

It was all over but the killing. General Dudley was still raising havoc in the Great Basin, and Pete Towles was holding Denver with a surprisingly large band of die-hards. But the loss of the government complex and surrounding military production facilities in Iowa had doomed the Republic. Fighting was continuing in the Twin Cities, but their stock of ammunition and necessary supplies was dwindling. Russians were flying in humanitarian aid, but the issue was no longer in doubt—if it ever had been after the nerve gas in Texas and the defeat in Ohio.

Her five boys, the Columbos, and children injected with K11 were already in Russia, and had been furnished with a large estate near Belgorod in the Belgorodskaya Oblast. General Chuikov believed no Lauenbergs survived World War II, but declared the estate to have been Lauenberg family property. It was a nice touch, making the change seem less like moving to an alien land. She had watched Erwin, the last of her sons to leave, board the Russian plane and disappear toward Alaska three weeks ago. She felt empty without her family, worse than she had when orphaned by her father's death.

Webb had received new information confirming that the Japanese were responsible for the Texas nerve gas attack. The gas itself had come from Japan, and was released by Japanese missile units. Sophia had paid the Japanese back by sending her remaining one hundred and thirty-eight ICBMs against Japan with nerve gas.

"There's nothing else for me to do," Sophia said, after reading his estimate of nerve gas deaths in Japan. Population concentration in urban areas had enabled the missiles to cause enormous casualties, something around a hundred million people. Japan was finished as a nation and would be unable to populate North America. Most likely, the American west would fall to the Chinese and the Russians. John Hersey's "White Lotus" might come to pass after all.

Over five hundred million people had died in America's third civil war, and Sophia wondered what the Bilderbergs would do for their next act. They needed to ramp up starvation in the Third World to implement Agenda 21. They could probably do it now since they weren't being opposed by those pesky Amulots.

Then the Bilderberg strategy hit her like a ton of bricks. Europe was already succumbing to a Muslim invasion which couldn't be stopped, and the Bilderbergs were planning to re-colonize North America. France would use Quebec as its focus for expansion south, and Great Britain would use Ontario. The other nations would move into the middle Atlantic, exterminate the remaining black population, and then push south to occupy the Old South, including Florida. The Council for Foreign Relations would be gone, and the Trilateralists remaining would only be Europeans. Essentially, Europe had found a haven for its aristocracy away from Islamic theocracies.

The remainder of the world would also undergo a fundamental transformation. China would eliminate Mexico and Meso-America, then repopulate the western US and all points south with Chinese. The Russians would occupy Japan and Hawaii and move south from Alaska to confront the Chinese somewhere on the west coast, possibly as far south as the San Gabriel Mountains, or as far north as Oregon. The battle between the two powers would be for the Central Valley and the San Francisco Bay area.

After carving up the United States, Canada, and Central America, China would probably seek to eliminate India and the populations in southeast Asia, while Russia moved south to destroy the Muslim populations in the Arab world. The two remaining behemoths would probably eliminate the populations of Africa and South America through chemical and biological weapons.

The key player was Russia with its much smaller population than China. It would have to absorb the remaining Caucasians in Europe and North America to build its power base, and the world would be left with two powers, China and Russia, vying for world leadership. Islam and Christianity would be relegated to the dust bin, but the world's population would still not have reached the goal specified by Agenda 21. Sophia estimated the total world population by that time would be between two and two and a half billion people, still double the goal. How that would be realized might determine the survival of humanity.

"It's time," Sophia said. "Time for us to leave for Denver."

She rang for Cole in her office in the old Montana Statehouse. Another loyal individual who had performed his duties to the best of his ability. "Cole, I have one last duty for you, and then I want you to take Alice and the girls to Calgary."

"Say what? One last duty? You don't mean that?" he said, initially in astonishment, and then with concern as he grasped the implications.

"Yes. I need you to accompany me to Denver, but you'll be coming back alone." Sophia gazed for a moment into his eyes, then looked at the floor. "Webb Reid will be going with us, and he can take over for you in Colorado."

"I see. When do we leave?" Cole understood what she was saying.

"As soon as possible. Please arrange it, and call Pete Towles."

Within fifty minutes, they were in their last Milleron corporate jet flying to Colorado. Pete and Cindy Towles met them at the tiny airport in Longmont, Cindy still wearing black for Heather.

Sophia turned on the Tarmac to face Cole. "Goodbye, old friend," she said in a loud whisper. "Tell everybody to keep the faith and look for me. I'll be back some day." She stretched up and kissed him on both cheeks.

Cole couldn't speak from the emotion welling inside him. He took a step back and saluted. For a moment he looked around, and then saw Webb standing alongside Sophia. Cole reached inside his coat, withdrew his Colt, and handed it to Webb.

"Here, you'll need this."

Webb started to refuse, then nodded and took the revolver from Cole's outstretched hand. "Thanks. I promise to do it justice."

Cole winced, not knowing how to take Webb's remark. He spun on his heels and re-entered the aircraft.

In a minute, the party was watching the plane disappear back north.

"Seems like you've spent your life watching the last plane out," Sophia said to Pete.

"Maybe there is no last plane," he said.

Sophia didn't reply, and the drive to Golden was quiet and subdued. Dinner was with Claire at King's old house on Lookout Mountain. He had died the previous summer after a fall from his horse, and Suzanne was living in Switzerland with her children. Claire and King had gotten married when she moved to Des Moines with the network, and her private life had finally been put right. She looked worn out, Sophia thought. The bouncy, professional beauty had been replaced with the tired resignation of defeat by age and events.

"How much longer can you hold Denver?" Sophia asked Pete during dinner.

"The Hispanics can take it any time if they're willing to suffer casualties. But they're not, so they'll wait until the end, then push up to Cheyenne. All they want is to be occupying Colorado when the war ends."

"So maybe as long as another month," Webb said.

"Yeah, something like that."

"What are you and Cindy planning for then?" Sophia asked.

"We really haven't planned anything yet. Maybe try to reach Canada. Hispanics haven't been killing everyone, at least not in Colorado, and there's not a price on my head like Dudley's. I can't desert my men, but I don't expect to be hunted afterward." He looked over at Cindy, who smiled in return.

"We're not worried," she said. "Whatever comes, comes. We have each other."

Sophia almost started to cry thinking about Jack. She didn't have him to make things right.

"What about you, Claire?" she asked.

"I'm staying here. I'm a valuable person for writers and historians with my inside knowledge. Anyway, I'm old, tired, and alone, and there's no place to go."

After dinner, Sophia drew Cindy aside as they looked out over Golden nestled between the two Table Mountains and Mount Zion. Cameron's college, the Colorado School of Mines was readily visible with its gold dome on Guggenheim Hall. "Heather wrote in her farewell letter that you should save yourself."

Cindy began to cry thinking about Heather. "She was a great lady. Do you have her letter? May I read it?"

Sophia retrieved it from her handbag. She handed it to Cindy, who unfolded it and read:

Dearest Sophie,

Please forgive me for leaving you like this, I would not hurt you for the world. I am an old woman who has outlived her usefulness and does not wish to be a burden. The deaths of Adam and Cedric were almost too much for me to bear, and I do not wish to see any more of my loved ones suffer. Nor do I want to allow anyone to take advantage of me because of my love for you, and I fear that might happen should I fall into unfriendly hands. So you see, I am a liability, and it is only right that I leave you.

I have enjoyed a full life, more than anyone could expect. Of all the men in my life, there was truly only one, your father. He was a great man, who produced a greater daughter. It is out of love for your father, you and the boys, that I now seek an end.

Please tell Cindy I love her, and want her to carry my baton in the march of generations. We can be defeated, but never conquered.

I fear a dark age is descending upon us, and fervently hope the family will rise once again. But regardless, I wouldn't have missed it for the world. I thank you for making everything worthwhile -- for me in particular. I love you.

Heather

The tears were rolling down Cindy's face. "We'll get to Canada, and then to Russia. I know you tried to get me to go earlier, but I couldn't leave Pete. I'll talk him into it somehow."

*****

They arrived at the ghost town of Caribou shortly before noon. Webb unloaded the jeep while Sophia stood in the wind, looking at storm clouds threatening the west. The road was almost washed out, and the coming storm would probably render it impassable before night. Webb would have to hurry. For now, there was only the wail of the wind. Caribou, where the winds never stop.

She stood on the spot where she had scattered the ashes of those she had loved; her father, mother, Cedric, Wallace, Ed, and Joyce Murray. Missing were Adam, her firstborn, Heather, and Bobbi. Soon, there would be no more. She remembered her pledge to her father, that Amulot troops would water their horses in the Nile. History had repeated itself: the Mamlukes had triumphed again, and darkness was descending upon her people.

"You know," she said to Webb. "This war has killed more people than all the wars in the twentieth century. Unbelievable. Who would have thought it? All we wanted was to be free again."

"I know," Webb said. "Our people appeared on the world stage waving the Amulot banner of freedom, and the world cheered. Then it was snatched away. When we tried to raise it a second time, the world stomped on us."

"The Europeans are over, but the Amulots are no more. The Bilderbergs have seen to that. They have destroyed our culture, our achievements, our American exceptionalism. Or at least they think so. The family will survive in Russia, and my children and their descendants are the hope of the future. Otherwise, there is only slavery and human degradation."

"Well, the Bilderbergs will depopulate everything but China and Russia. Both countries revere you as practically a saint, so maybe there's hope after all."

Webb looked at Sophia as she drew her knees up, and wrapped her white floral dress under her legs to keep it from blowing in the breeze. The white dress with pink and red roses accentuated her femininity and her thick, shoulder-length auburn hair. She had beautiful legs, and he noticed she was wearing open-toed wooden sandals without stockings.

Her big blue eyes were watering. They had to be tears.

He sat down and drew her to him, nestling her under his arm. She didn't resist. She was shivering slightly.

For himself, Webb no longer cared. Pressing eighty, his fate was hardly compelling, and he had no regrets in his long and fascinating life. He had risen to the top of his profession, not once but twice, and had been a driving force for the most productive and creative people the world had ever known. But the giants had succumbed to Lilliputian masses—there simply hadn't been enough giants. And the greatest giant of all was sheltered there against him.

He thought of this girl—this woman—tucked under his right arm. Less than six years ago, she was the richest and most powerful woman in the world, and no one could match her talents. Now it had come to this. Huddled on a lonely mountain pass in a cotton dress. Webb briefly wondered why she had picked that particular dress, relatively heavy for cotton, long and flowing with a great deal of material. He would have expected to see it on a woman in Appalachia. Then he knew. As she moved slightly against him, he became aware there was probably nothing underneath. It was a shroud. Nor was she wearing earrings or jewelry. She was leaving as she had arrived.

Sophia stood up. She walked to the concrete slab half-buried in the hillside, the entrance to her private shrine. She opened it from the hidden latch pin, and kneeling in the three-foot high opening, placed her last two monuments and purse inside.

Webb stacked wood in the strange fireplace which looked to be the only recent structure around. It was centered in the mine spill and open to winds from both east and west. Propane tanks were already connected.

She took the ancient rusted spade from its place in the mine and used it to key the heavy rock deadfall above. It worked perfectly, collapsing the entrance and hiding her shrine for eternity. The only access to the inside was a small pipe, through which Webb would pour her ashes. She brushed the dust from her dress, and tossed the spade down the hill. Sitting on a rock among the alpine flowers, she watched Webb work. Neither said a word. In a few minutes he was finished.

She walked over to him and hugged him tightly, receiving the warmth of his huge body. She felt the sensation of male bonding from her father for his best friend. Now her best friend. Fulfilling the covenant between them, begun by her father and Webb in the fields of Vietnam. He would do what was necessary to safeguard their secret.

She gazed into his eyes, changing her expression to that of a female pleading to her man to be good to her. In a moment she pushed herself gently away, withdrawing Cole's revolver from Webb's pocket. She handed it to him, and turned to the mountains. Her face had become beautiful and serene again, in full flower of womanhood. Her dress pressed against her body in the breeze, as she turned to the wind and lifted her gaze to the sky.

She thought of the people whose memories were within her. She saw Grandfather Lauenberg in the Ukraine, and her mother Millie at the Washington reception where Cameron saw her for the first time. And Cameron and Bobbi and Heather and Cathy in the unrestrained days at Maryland. Memories from before she was born. Her sons lined up to meet Wallace. And Wallace. There was only one thing left for her. To return to nature—to know God.

"Ready," she said.